THE CRITICS RAVE ABOUT C.S. FRIEDMAN

"Friedman writes cogently on the nature of human desire for knowledge and the dangerous covenants necessary to attain it."
—*Publishers Weekly*

"Truly one of the great voices of speculative fiction . . . The sheer imaginative genius, not to mention incredible power, of Ms. Friedman's formidable storytelling gift is indescribable—you simply just have to experience it."
—*Romantic Times*

"Some of the best writing I have seen in quite a while. . . . Very highly recommended."
—*Science Fiction Review*

"An ambitious first novel. This is space opera with brains."
—*Locus* on *In Conquest Born*

"Space opera in the best sense: a combination of high-stakes adventure with a strong focus on ideas, and characters whose fate an intelligent reader can care about."
—*Newsday* on IN CONQUEST BORN

"A debut of extraordinary power and awesome beauty."
—*Rave Reviews* on IN CONQUEST BORN

"Exceptionally imaginative and compelling . . ."
—*Publishers Weekly* on THE MADNESS SEASON

". . . one of the most intriguingly conceived alien species to be come across in all SF."
—*Asimov* on THE MADNESS SEASON

THE CRITICS RAVE ABOUT C.S. FRIEDMAN

"For those who like to explore the caverns of the mind, the journey is rewarding.
—*Kliatt* on THE MADNESS SEASON

"Hauntingly memorable protagonists, high drama, and vivid world building mark what promise to be a magnum opus of the imagination."
—*Library Journal* on BLACK SUN RISING

"Friedman has always been notable for the complex quirky detail work that makes her worlds fascinatingly memorable places to visit, and this is no exception. The style is lyric and fanciful, with arresting imagery."
—*Locus* on BLACK SUN RISING

"a pretty good mystery wrapped in an adventure story and set against an original and often fascinating background."
—*Science Fiction Chronicle* on WHEN TRUE NIGHT FALLS

"Secures Friedman's reputation both as a gifted storyteller and an innovative creator."
—*Library Journal* on WHEN TRUE NIGHT FALLS

"Stunning . . . combines good historical world-building, vampires, religion, and transcendence in a tale that is both entertaining and cathartic. . . . a feast for those who like their fantasies dark, and as emotionally heady as a rich, red wine."
—*Locus* on CROWN OF SHADOWS

THE CRITICS RAVE ABOUT C.S. FRIEDMAN

"Here are Friedman's usual virtues: plenty of action, brisk pacing, and characters and settings painted with broad strokes and vivid colors."
—*Booklist* on CROWN OF SHADOWS

"Friedman keeps her tale moving at a vigorous pace that's boosted through an abundance of well-chosen details . . . it is likely to hold readers' interest tenaciously. The ending neither requires nor precludes a sequel, so readers are left with some hope of again encountering Jamisia and the duel between the Guild and Earth that backdrops her adventures."
—*Publishers Weekly* on THIS ALIEN SHORE

"Once again Ms. Friedman offers us great richness in both concept and detail, ingeniously weaving together two strong plotlines and piquant characters into a superior reading experience."
—*Romantic Times* on THIS ALIEN SHORE

"Breathlessly plotted, emotionally savvy."
—*The New York Times* on THIS ALIEN SHORE

Novels by
C. S. Friedman
available from DAW Books:

IN CONQUEST BORN
THE WILDING*

THE MADNESS SEASON

THIS ALIEN SHORE

The Coldfire Trilogy
BLACK SUN RISING
WHEN TRUE NIGHT FALLS
CROWN OF SHADOWS

*forthcoming in hardcover

IN CONQUEST BORN

C. S. FRIEDMAN

DAW BOOKS, INC.
DONALD A. WOLLHEIM, FOUNDER
375 Hudson Street, New York, NY 10014
ELIZABETH R. WOLLHEIM
SHEILA E. GILBERT
PUBLISHERS
http://www.dawbooks.com

Cover art by Michael Whelan.
www.michaelwhelan.com

DAW Book Collectors No. 707.
DAW Books are distributed by Penguin Putnam Inc.

First Printing, May 1987
First Printing, Anniversary Edition, November 2001
5 6 7 8 9

To my parents and my brother,
whose pride makes it all worth doing.

And to my new sister Kim,
who is just crazy enough to
love us all.

Once Upon a Time . . .

An Editor and an Author went out to a fancy French restaurant to discuss the Author's manuscript. It was the first time they had ever met, and both were somewhat uneasy.

The Editor thought: *What kind of person is this? How do I approach her? Will she take it well if I suggest a few changes to her manuscript, or is she going to run away to some swamp and threaten me with a shotgun each time I tell her the plot needs fixing? Is there another book in her, or is this a one-shot deal? How do I ask questions like that without tripping over some unseen obstacle of ego and ruining the relationship?*

The Author thought: *What kind of person is this? How do I talk to her? Should I just tell her outright that I don't have a problem rewriting part of the manuscript, or is that the kind of thing professionals don't blurt out? Is she going to trust me to do my own rewriting, or will I have to watch someone else alter my text? Do the fine points of professional etiquette really matter here, or can we both admit that I'm out of my element right now, and focus on the work itself?*

The single moment seemed to stretch into eternity. In the distance, down the corridor of time, the Editor could hear the songs of her ancestors, desert warriors who had broken bread with men and women of diverse cultures and never lost their focus. Knowledge stirred in her blood, of customs so primitive that they spoke to the human soul, not in words, but in instinct. Customs that could bring strangers together by focusing upon the rudiments of life, rather than the complexities of protocol.

The desert wind blew hot in her hair as she looked up at the Author and said, "I hope you don't mind if I pig out. I haven't eaten all morning."

She could see the words being taken in, considered. She knew the desert winds blew for this one as well. Would she understand?

The Author met the Editor's gaze head on. "I hope you don't mind if I pig out," she said. "I haven't eaten all morning."

And thus was a partnership born.

Introduction

I never intended to get published.

Honest.

The work you hold in your hands started out as a private project, something I wrote for myself, and at best a few special friends. It is the result of school days so boring that I had to write fiction during classes to keep my sanity. Work days so tense that I had to write when I got home, to relax. Other days so . . . well . . . any excuse would do. I *had* to write, you see. That's not a choice, for some, but a condition. A hunger as visceral, as demanding, as the need for food or sex. Words build up inside you, they have to be let out. They have to have the proper form, too. It doesn't matter if your master's thesis is due the next day; if a chapter of a science fiction novel is screaming inside your brain to be let out, that has to come first. Else the passageway will be all blocked up, and no other creative juices are going to flow.

(And yes, I really did write a chapter for this book the night before my master's thesis was due.)

Where does it come from, this terrible muse? Perhaps from the father who showed me that writing was an experience full of wonders, who taught me that there was no greater pleasure than the crafting of a perfect sentence. He was a technical writer, and therefore worked within mundane worlds, not the fantastic ones his daughter would soon explore. He would say of himself, if asked, that he was not a true artist, simply a craftsman. But what a craftsman! I remember the nights when he would come out of his office to read us some sentence—or maybe just a turn of phrase that he had crafted—in which rhythm and meaning were so finely tuned that it was like music to him . . . and it seemed, when he read it to us, that it was music to us as well.

For sharing that music, my father, I thank you.

So I wrote. I created worlds, and they grew as I grew, and the stories I set in them began to take on larger scope. Once or twice I showed them to friends. The friends were enthusiastic, and urged me to seek publication. But I wasn't ready. I wasn't good enough yet, not in my own eyes. Perhaps I wasn't *hungry* enough.

And then, one night, it happened. I had come home from a

stressful workday of fourteen hours and couldn't sleep. I sat down at my typewriter to let off some creative steam, and the words just began to flow. Long, long into the night, until time was forgotten. Miles past exhaustion, into the hours before dawn when creativity is at its sharpest and the muse at its most demanding.

Thirty pages.

When I was done I sat back and just stared at those pages. I could still hear the music of the language in my brain, I could still taste the imagery of the story. Even in first draft form, the chapter sang to me. And I knew, in that moment, that I had crossed some unnamed line. My writing was ready. If I ever wanted to publish, it was time to try.

(For those who are curious, that's chapter eleven of the book you now hold in your hand.)

Would that have been enough by itself? Maybe not. Fortunately I had a friend who had been watching my non-career for years, and who had served as my main cheerleader every time I toyed with the concept of publishing. I called him to tell him what I had discovered about my own work, and he said I was a damned fool for not figuring it out earlier, and that he knew someone at DAW Books and if I could get the book to him by the end of the summer he'd see to it himself that it got the attention it deserved. That was Rick Umbaugh, and without his steadfast friendship and ungentle persuasions this book might never have come into being.

One summer. How easy a thing it seems now, in this world of word processors! Far more daunting then, given the size of the manuscript. I barely scraped together enough money for a Radio Shack computer and cassette deck. There wasn't any kind of indexing, you had to listen to the bleeps on the tape until there was a pause and then start it up to see what section you were in. God help you if you lost track of what was where on the tape. Was that only eighteen years ago? Now I have a word processor that shows me dancing paper clips if it thinks I need help, and getting it to leave my sci-fi spelling alone is a task unto itself.

I worked hard, that summer. Harder than I have ever worked in my life. Taking the fictional output of a decade or more and trimming it, tightening it, giving it focus. No time for writer's block or any other excuse. When it was all done and I packed it up for Rick, I put a page on top of the cover page just for him, and scrawled across it in black magic marker, in a hand that shook from exhaustion, I AM NEVER DOING THIS AGAIN!

I meant it, too.

I didn't find out until years later that he left that first page on top of the manuscript when he delivered it to DAW—that the first words of mine Donald Wollheim ever saw were the scribbled vow that I would never write another novel.

He clearly knew it for the nonsense it was. So did his daughter, Betsy Wollheim, who loved words as much as I did, and who taught me that an editor's input could sometimes be the most powerful inspiration of all. Her first child was born the same time this book came out, and I've always felt as if we gave birth to our first kids together. (Wave hello to the readers, Zoe!)

That's the book you hold in your hands now. And it is my pleasure to add to it a few things which I wanted to include originally, but which lost out to publishing schedules and sheer authorial exhaustion. I hope the music of the text speaks to you as powerfully as it spoke to me back then.

—Celia S. Friedman
Sterling, Virginia
April 2001

For ease of comprehension in the English text, all Braxin words have been rendered in the Basic Mode regardless of context.

IN CONQUEST BORN

ONE

Beginning 1

He stands like a statue, perfect in arrogance. Because his people love bright colors he wears only gray and black; because they revere comfort, he is dressed uncomfortably. His people are flamboyant, and display their bodies with aggressive sexuality; he is entirely concealed by his costume. Tight-fitting gloves and boots cover his extremities and a high collar conceals his neck. His skin is as pale as human skin can be, but even that is not enough—cosmetics have been layered over his natural complexion until a mask of white conceals his skin from the prying eyes of commoners. Only his hair is uncovered, a rich mass of true black, as eloquent as a crown in proclaiming his right to power. It is moderate in length because another people, enemy to his own, wear their hair long; his beard and mustache are likewise traditional—the men of that other race do not have facial hair.

He is very tired. And he will not show it.

The tiny shuttle spirals downward, from the orbiting Citadel to the center of Braxi's largest continent. Inside there is only one compartment; Vinir shares it with his servant, who operates the vehicle. For the lesser man's benefit he maintains the image of racial superiority which is as much a part of him as the black and gray he always wears and the ancestral sword at his side. Let the servant observe that he is not tired—he is never tired—the situation does not exist which can tire him. Now and then he catches the man glancing at him, when he thinks he is not being observed. *What is he wondering now?* Vinir muses. *Is the man human after all?* Or perhaps: *Can it be true that we are members of the same race?* The answer to either question will, hopefully, be negative.

"If you desire to sit, Lord. . . ."

"I am content."

In truth, he is exhausted. His nation, embracing war at every opportunity, is less than efficient during peacetime, and in such periods the government is the most crippled of all. This day was bad enough, trying to sort out domestic problems without the excuse of military priority to use when it was convenient. Then, just as the Kaim'eri were about to leave, Miyar chose to introduce the current Peace for review. That meant at least a tenth of dreary emotional confrontations and a thorough rehashing of historic precedent before they could even begin to discuss the real issue: when—and how—the current treaty with Azea should be broken.

Fools! Vinir thinks. *Someday the moment will be* right, *so unexpected or so profitable that we will know, simply* know, *the time has come. That's how we've always functioned—why pretend that it's different?*

It is very late. Vinir is grateful when the shuttle slows to a perfect landing outside his house. He nods his approval to the pilot and steps with false vitality down from the shuttle. Not long now, and then he can rest.

The Mistress of his House is waiting, as is her custom, to greet him as he passes through the forehouse and into the great entrance foyer which separates public edifice from private domain. She has a cut-gold vial in one hand and a cord of rings in the other, and hands him the former without word. He removes the stopper from the vial and drinks its contents. Immediately the mild restorative begins to take effect; he feels the exhaustion of the day loosen its hold on him.

"Records?" she asks.

He nods. "I'll go over them."

She spills the handful of golden rings into his upturned palm. In the old days it was his custom to review the state of his household each night when he returned to its confines; now, with peace slowing his work to a painful crawl, there are nights when he lacks the energy to give it the attention it deserves.

It isn't necessary, really. Sen'ti is both loyal and capable and has proven her worth a thousand times over. But trust doesn't come easily to a Braxaná, not even between the sexes, and he feels more comfortable knowing he has confirmed her work. With everything in her hands, from the finances of his House to his most tenuous political ties, he cannot be overcautious.

He motions for her to follow him as he strides through the foyer, to the massive staircase which dominates the building's center. Made of the finest natural woods, adorned with works of polished stone, it is a monument to the more barbaric side of the Braxaná. Momentarily he regrets the law which forbids the presence of a lift or transport in any Braxaná house. A pointless complaint. That law and others like it guarantee physical activity and Vinir has often supported them; nevertheless, at times like this he would prefer that something else did the work of getting him to the top floor of his home, where the private rooms of the Master of the House are traditionally located.

They pass servants. These are common Braxins, brown-haired and light-skinned in limitless variety but without the harsh contrast of the Braxaná that sets that tribe apart from all others. They stand back in awe as Vinir passes, overwhelmed by the image he projects.

The Lord and Kaim'era is a beautiful man; all of his tribe are. They bred for strength and beauty once and the results are breathtaking. If common Braxins worshipped gods they might try to apply a supernatural label to Vinir and his kind, in the hope of understanding them. The Braxaná are flawless in beauty, unequaled in arrogance, tireless and without emotional weakness. What more could a nation ask of its rulers—or its gods?

"I'll be glad to reach my own rooms," he says softly, and the Mistress of his House nods her understanding.

Two large doors separate his private wing from the rest of the building. Uniformed guards open them at his approach and seal them securely behind him; in the privacy of his own wing he prefers the human anachronism to more efficient but unpleasantly modern portal mechanisms.

"Well, we are alone," he says, by which he means that only members of his tribe are permitted beyond this boundary. He feels more comfortable among them, and certainly is freer to relax. They must never see beneath his mask of competence to discover within him any human weakness, but as for the image of racial superiority they are as much dependent upon it as he is, and unlikely to betray him on that point.

"We debated the treaty for two tenths," he says with scorn. "And we'll debate it again tomorrow—and the day after, too, most likely." He slips into the Basic speech mode, which is the language of the lower classes and does not contain the tiring complexity of the Braxaná dialect. "Personally, I think it's time to accept that Azea anticipates our action and therefore we need to move not when it's most viable militarily, but when it would be most unexpected."

"You have something in mind, I gather."

He pulls a ringreader out from the wall and adjusts it. "There's a colony on Lees—Red'resh Three, if you will—which I believe could be ours for the asking. A fair bit of mineral wealth, a decent position for a Braxin outpost, but not so desirable in either category that Azea would anticipate a move there."

"You suggested this?"

He shrugged. "What's the point? We have to put in our time arguing the basics, first. We always do. There's more emotion than reason evident when a treaty first starts to wear thin . . . what's this?"

One by one he has been dropping the golden rings on the reader and surveying their information on a small screen. Now his gloved finger rests against that screen, pointing to a particular figure among the population statistics of his House.

"I don't have that many Braxaná," he tells her sternly. "Not purebred."

"You do now, Kaim'era." She is smiling. "K'siva gave birth today. You have a son, my Lord."

He is astonished. The Braxaná are nearly sterile—the price paid for that inbreeding which guaranteed their beauty. True, he had known that K'siva was pregnant; how could he fail to, when they had gone through an involved ritual of Seclusion to assure the child's paternity? But too many children conceived by his people are lost before or during childbirth, and so pregnancy is more a cruel deception than a hope or promise, never discussed, rarely acknowledged, and sometimes genuinely forgotten.

"Alive . . ." he whispers.

"And healthy. They're waiting for you."

The rings are forgotten as he nods for her to lead him. He never dared hope for this moment. The men of his bloodline more often sire daughters than sons, to which rule he has been no exception. But a *son*—his to raise, his to influence in that strange mixture of genetic tendency and parental conditioning which results in adulthood. Quite different, he thinks, from being informed third-person of the birth of a daughter, and long overdue.

His Mistress leads him into one of the many guest rooms of

the Braxaná wing and there leaves him. Awaiting him is a woman whose beauty once seduced him to repeat the mistake of his ancestors. But in this case, had not the old fears been proven unfounded? K'siva was Zarvati, like himself, yet the union had proven fruitful. If the child had shown any promise of the physical or mental handicaps that might come of such inbreeding it would have been put to death immediately, and Vinir would have been informed—if he was told anything at all—of its stillbirth. A pure Zarvati child! How magnificent it might be, how great it might become! And a man's only son *should* be outstanding.

"Lady," he says softly. Braxaná are rarely gentle; this is one of those times. "There aren't words, even in our language, which can express my joy—or my gratitude."

She smiles, parting the bundle in her arms until a tiny face is visible. "Perfect in all things," she promises. And then she holds the child out to him. "Your son, Kaim'era."

Awkwardly, he takes the tiny body from her. Then instinct takes over and he knows how to hold it, just so. He forces himself to look up from the tiny face for a moment. "Ask what you will," he offers. "My House will supply it. Ask even to be kept and it will be done."

"I have my own House," she answers, smiling, indicating by her refusal of the second offer that she will accept the first. But later, after thought. A promise made at a birthgiving will be kept.

With a nod that serves both to thank and dismiss her, Vinir carries the tiny bundle that is his son outdoors, to the wide terrace which marks the outer boundary of his private wing. There in the starlit night he tries to come to terms with the miracle that this birth represents. Overhead the stars shine brightly through the dark Void that Braxi has conquered. The moon, Zhene, has just risen, and it glows with the sun's reflected glory; a protective forcefield glistens about it and its airlocks are silver circles against the whiteness. Beyond it, beyond sight, lies the vastness of Braxi's territory. And directly overhead at this time of night is the greatest battleground known to humankind.

"I give you this," he whispers, overcome by new and strange emotions. "When you're old enough to demand it, it'll be yours. As much power as a single man can wield, in the greatest multistellar territory man has ever known. I can't give you more. . . ."

He is suddenly aware of the emptiness above him. Peace reigns in the darkness where there should be war. "I'm sorry you were born in peacetime," he says quietly. "A bad omen. If I had known you would be here . . ." What? Could he have convinced the Kaim'eri to break the treaty in celebration of a single birth? Among a people where war was so valued and children so priceless, anything was possible. "It wouldn't do to name you now," he muses. "Not in peacetime." What, then? Would the Kaim'eri agree to break a treaty so that his son might be named? His laughter rings out in the darkness. Why not? Many of them would welcome such an excuse. And the timing! Azea would never anticipate such a move. Yes. . . .

"I'll give you war for your birth-celebration and Azean blood to seal your two names—one for your Braxaná soul and one for the world, so that all will know in addressing you that they can never reach beyond the surface. Except for women, sometimes." A faint smile plays across his lips. "You'll learn that soon enough."

His barbaric ancestors had presented their newborn infants to the stars, offering their souls to the powers which lit the sky. He stands beneath those same stars and holds his son tightly in his arms. He is too civilized to make the ancient offering, but too primitive to ignore its call entirely. A moment of silence serves in place of invocation. But contemplation of the night makes him all too aware of the peace which reigns overhead—peace which insults the traditions of his people and casts gloom over even a purebred birthgiving. Peace which has to end. Soon.

With a last scornful glance at the overly tranquil sky, Vinir carries his newborn son indoors.

The Emperor is aghast.

"What did they say?"

Patiently, the messenger repeats himself. "Braxin forces have taken the Azean colony on Lees," he recites slowly. "This constitutes open defiance of the" (he consults his notes) "nine hundred and eighty-fifth Comprehensive Peace Treaty between Braxi and Azea."

"Yes, yes, I know all that. What were their grounds—tell me that again."

The messenger reads it verbatim. "Kaim'era Vinir, son of Lanat and Kir'la, wishes to give his son the public name of Zatar. Therefore the Kaim'erate considers the current peace treaty invalid and without binding force."

Slowly the Emperor leans back in his throne. "Yes. That's what I thought you said."

2

It is an undebated fact that the planet Azea is in all ways hostile to human life. Not openly forbidding, as are those planets lacking an atmosphere or having a surface temperature near absolute zero, but nonetheless hostile to that lifeform which fate has chosen to place upon its surface. The poisons which lace its air are subtle; they arrive with the swirling winds and depart with equal invisibility, leaving death as the only witness to their passing. The native vegetation is mildly toxic to the human system; the native fauna, weaned on uncertain air and parasite-laden water, cannot be tamed or (unless specially prepared) eaten.

The people living on this planet have learned to adapt. They have had to. They have mastered that science which determines the patterns of heredity and they have turned this mastery, not to the purposes of biological conflict, but upon themselves.

Envision them: a people marked forever by a desire to survive on their own terms. Another race would have stressed agriculture and reached to the stars for plants that would thrive in the hostile Azean soil. This race designed a digestive system capable of expelling the local toxins and programmed it into their descendants. Another people would have built domes and lived eternally under their protection, always fearful that some disaster would break open the life-giving shells and admit the native air. These people designed lungs that would not constrict in agony and introduced them into the anatomy of their descendants. The solution was long in coming, for Azean genetics was only in its birth-pangs when the planet made its first harsh demands. Many died while waiting. But as a statement of success or failure there is ultimately only this: Azea is inhabited.

They are a golden people, homogeneous and unified. They take their mates from their own race and enjoy moderate, monogamous pleasures. All this is programmed into them. Birth defects are a thing of the past, as are hereditary weaknesses and inherited disease tendencies. Azeans live longer than any other Scattered Race, an ironic compensation for the death which plagued their early ancestors.

As for genetics, that science must work hard to find unconquered horizons. The stellar reaches are spotted with government-financed Institutes whose goal is to speed up the process of evolution—as Azea defines it. Scientists sift through piles of data to isolate those genetic codes which determine telepathy, longevity—any desirable trait which might otherwise be lost in a sea of dominant normalcy. Once they have isolated the proper genetic sequence they can program it into each new member of the race, saving (they believe) millennia of otherwise slower development.

Darmel lyu Tukone and Suan lir Aseirin are typical of their kind. They have richly golden skin because some scientist once thought it would be an aesthetic ideal; they have white hair because dark hair marks their enemies, the Braxins. Their first child has been conceived and now, with the celebrating concluded, the pair obediently proceeds to the nearest Center for Analysis and Adjustment to have it tested. Whatever might be wrong with the child, this couple knows Azean science can easily remedy it long before it leaves the womb.

If Azea is willing.

In a science where almost nothing goes wrong, something has gone wrong. There is agitation in departments which have previously known only efficient calm; messages flash to and from the Capital Planet, and at last to the couple themselves.

The child is not Azean.

That is lay language: the child, of course, is predominantly Azean. But patterns of heredity have surfaced which do not fit the Azean mold—genetic sequences which indicate that the child's founding line has not been so purely golden as its parents would wish to believe.

The image of a young girl is flashed across analytic screens. Slight of build, she stands as a female of another race would—shorter than the male. Her mother, who like all Azean women is as tall as her man, shudders. The child's skin is white, colorlessly Braxin in appearance. Her father, a Security officer, turns away from the image. Hair like blood, deep red and shining, pours unnaturally down over her shoulders. Other subtle differences are recorded below the image, and they all add up to one thing: the race responsible for the child's appearance is unknown, found nowhere in Azean genetic files or even in the lore of Azea's part of the galaxy. Yet once in each line of descent it infiltrated perfect Azean stock, to leave its recessive mark for future generations to discover. And now that mark has surfaced.

Mother and father are investigated.

Darmel lyu Tukone is an Imperial Servant with the highest Security clearance. He is a transcultural scholar with a specialty in Braxin/Azean exchange; there are less than half a dozen in the Empire who have mastered such studies. Called the Grand Interrogator by a war-conscious public, he specializes in applying Braxin psychology to Braxin prisoners in order to drag forth information from a people stubborn enough to resist physical torture. He is also the last known descendent-through-firstbirth of the revered hopechild Hasha, in token of which he bears the subname lyu, or "birth" in the Oldtongue, as did his firstborn ancestors and as will his own first child. His line alone among Azean ancestries has a record of every pairbond since the Founding. And there is no alien within them.

Suan is high in Security as were her parents before her, and theirs again for many generations back. It is not impossible that one of them mated with a non-Azean in secret. Nothing is impossible. But it is very unlikely, given the prejudices of such people.

Be rid of the child, they are counseled, and start again.

They rebel.

Peace comes but once a decade to Azea and such a couple must procreate when they can. There isn't time in the midst of war to savor the mysteries of birth, or to share in the first moments of a child's life. They have waited years and they are not willing to do so again.

The child will not be Azean, they are warned.

She is ours, they respond. That is enough.

The Council of Justice meets on the matter. A people whose definition of citizenship is based on genetic conformity must have a way to judge issues arising from deviation; thus the case falls to the Council.

The child will not be, can never be a citizen of the Empire.

Her parents pale, but they persist.

The child can never have the most basic Security clearance.

This is a blow to those who have made War service their lives. But it is too late to back out now. Men and women who are weak of will may fall to the Braxins, and these two have proven their mettle by that standard. The child will be born, they insist.

Uncompromising decrees follow in rapid order: the child may never set foot on Azea. She may not receive the benefits of Azean genetic science. Her appearance may not be tampered with. She may never in any way become involved with the War effort.

These are scare tactics and are designed to pressure the parents into submission. But they fail in this purpose and become merely law, gloom to darken the child's birth.

The girl is born in peacetime. But war, as always, comes again, and the nine hundred and eight-sixth Comprehensive Peace Treaty between Braxi and Azea shatters in a splash of human blood between the stars.

The fact that it was inevitable does not negate its value as an omen.

Viton: We recognize that in man's nature there is a drive to oppress others, be they truly alien or his own women. Perhaps the true measure of his power is how openly he can indulge in this.

From The Birth of Braxi: excerpts from the later dialogues of Harkur the Great and Viton the Ruthless, (House of Makoth, Kurat/Braxi; CCS prime-file: Dialogues) Not available in the Azean Star Empire.

TWO

Dear my sister,

By now you must have discovered my absence. Yes, Ni'Ar, not only have I gone, but return is impossible—not only to our home, but to any part of Braxi.

I hope you'll forgive me. I kept so much from you, and for so long, but I think you'll see as you read this that I had little choice in the matter. And I should thank you for all the support you gave me, though you could hardly understand the torment that made it necessary.

But let me explain.

You remember, I'm certain, that cursed year when Jenar attached himself to me. His brutality, and my helplessness to escape it, came close to destroying me utterly. When he finally tired of the game and left, I cried in relief—and I was determined to find some method of avoiding men for a time, though law demands we submit to any who ask.

Surely, my sister, you remember those zhents. Each day I hurried from my job to our compartment, where I waited until long past midnight. Only then did I dare to walk the streets for a while, when few were about. It was calming. You used to warn me of the danger, but better at that point a brutal death than another man like Jenar.

One night, as I walked by the Tuel waters, I saw a figure ahead of me on the beach. His back was to me. I almost turned back and ran, but something in his posture held me still, something that marked him as different than any man I'd ever seen.

His broad houlders were draped in a dark gray cloak, his legs and feet encased in high black boots. Where one hand was visible I saw a glove of the same color. *What fool,* I thought, *wears such clothing in mid-summer?*

Then it struck me. For only those of Braxaná blood, the upper class, cover themselves so completely and in so little color. Fearful, I had just decided to run from the place when he turned to me.

Hair blacker than shadow framed his pale face. His features were magnificent, deeply chiseled like an ancient sculpture, his body fine and his bearing arrogant. There are no words, my sister, to capture the beauty of his face and body, nor its effect upon me. I tried to turn away, as law demanded, tried to drop my eyes from his, but it was impossible.

I wanted him.

The traitor's brand on my forehead burned shamefully as he came toward me. Who was I to desire this harshly beautiful youth, this man bred for beauty? Though he had the right to put me to death for it, I stared at him. Let my eyes, at least, drink of what the rest of me can never taste.

A slender sword swung at his side as he approached me—a Zhaor, I guessed, the traditional weapon of the Braxaná. He walked slowly, with the grace of born nobility, a motion so fluid and beautiful that it hurt to watch. And closing the collar of his cloak was the Seal of the Kaim'erate.

A Lord, I remembered, as he closed the distance between us, to fall to my knees, but I couldn't bear to take my eyes from him.

There was an eternity of silence as he regarded me. I saw anger in those dark eyes—not at me, but the fury which had driven him to this place—Sulos, the sector of poverty.

"Who was the traitor?" he asked, his voice devoid of all emotion.

"My mother," I answered. The words nearly caught in my throat.

"Her name."

"Shyerre, my Lord."

His brow furrowed in thought. "I don't recall the case. Refresh my memory, little one."

"She attempted to . . . leave Braxi for Aldous, to serve the Holding in space."

"There was enough alien blood in her that she could have passed for Aldousan?"

"She believed so, my Lord."

"With what name have they doomed your future, little traitor?"

"Ni'en, my Lord." Never had the name been so painful before.

"Conceived in treachery—yes, I see. Stand, woman. Why do you stare at me?"

I remained on my knees—my fear would be less obvious. "You're very beautiful, my Lord," I whispered.

He smiled slightly. "So I've been told. Yet the women of my Race can find no desire for me, little one, only duty. And I respond poorly to duty."

Duty? What duty to a Race but that of the Braxaná females to bear purebred children? By Taz'hein, not purebred. . . .

He looked at me and laughed. He must have known my thoughts, because he nodded to me in answer.

Braxaná. Pure.

I lowered my eyes.

I felt his hands on my shoulders, and he lifted me to my feet. When he drew me against him I trembled, not from fear of him, but from hunger.

"You want me," he observed, amused. "Do you know, I ran out on the Kaim'eri Yiril, Vinir, and Sechaveh today. They tried to feed me women. In refusing, I've insulted the image of three of the most powerful men in the Holding, my father among them. Because none of those women could desire more than the favor of a Lord, or the child of a Braxaná—one more duty completed, that much closer to freedom. What pleasure should I seek with them?" He laughed softly, but there was pain beneath it. "They believe me impotent. Good. That's synonymous with harmless to my people. Let them keep that delusion—it gives me freedom."

He kissed me, then—just that, and yet so much. I've been used and discarded in less time than he took to savor that kiss. Weakly, warmly, I wondered if the sensuality of the Braxaná was perhaps more than legend.

"Where can I taste you?" he asked.

The question surprised me—where did one have to go? Our wanderings had brought us to an isolated bit of Braxi, carpeted by fine natural grass and lit by the light of the Citadel shining across the Tuel waters. What more could he want? I looked at him, puzzled.

"Little fool!" He was smiling. "The Braxaná sleep with their women."

Involuntarily, I shuddered. To be at the mercy of a male in one's most vulnerable time, to have no escape from his demands . . . to *sleep* with a man!

Truly, I thought, the Braxaná are still barbarians.

We sought such a place.

And yet, when I awoke in the morning alone, I was surprised at how I could miss his warmth beside me, his arm confining and yet protecting me.

By my cheek were forty sinias in silver—the upper-class custom of a gift for pleasure. Spare change no doubt for him; more money than I would ordinarily see in a year. Handling the coins lent an aura of reality to an anonymous encounter that now seemed little more than a dream.

I would have given it all back to sleep with him again, my sister.

I stepped over the landlord's body on the way out; the fool had tried to sneak in to rob the Lord's cloak. He had met his end before he remembered that the Braxaná sleep with their Zhaori close at hand. And, smiling, I remembered discovering the truth in the legend, that no passion exceeds that of a Braxaná who has just killed.

Two—three zhents later, I think. You were on assignment that night, preparing to leave for work, when he arrived. Did you notice him? Could you fail to? He wore our clothes, he'd painted his hair, he had come without his sword, but could such beauty be disguised? You passed him in the hall that night as you went out; can I believe you didn't notice him?

Without words, without questions, I ran to his arms when he entered, and therein found a welcome.

In his embrace that night, by his will, I told him of my past. I'll not lead you to believe, my sister, that he dealt with me tenderly, or even kindly. When the Braxaná have such emotions they crush them. But he displayed curiosity, so I spoke. How sweet it was to have a man listen, regardless of his motives! He told me, in return, of the affairs of state, of battle and politics, and of his Race, living to hate, living for pleasure but not knowing any longer how to seek it. I understood little of it, or even why he told me such things. Perhaps it was to get across to me the loneliness I sensed beneath it all, an emotion no Braxaná would lower himself to admit to.

Dawn came at last and he gathered his clothes. I knew there would be emptiness when he had gone, and also knew that nothing I could say or do would keep him there, or cause him to come back. Such pain was new to me. Needing to speak, afraid to reveal my train of thought, I asked for his name.

"Zatar," he said. "They call me Zatar the Magnificent, an attempt at sarcasm. Someday they'll say it and mean it."

"Is it true you have another?" I had heard, of course, of the Braxaná True Name—in superstitious tradition, given only to trusted intimates. I knew that to ask for such a confidence invited death by the Zhaor. I had only meant to ask if such things really existed. But he misunderstood

Anger almost crossed his brow, but it was replaced by a look of weary pain. "I'm not very Braxaná, I suppose, after all," he whispered. "I've confided enough to you this night to set my plans back considerably. . . . What's power over my soul, compared to that?"

I had no time to protest or explain. To hold the Name of a Braxaná is the greatest responsibility a woman can know. But the giving of a Name between the sexes must be smothered in pleasure, and so I was silenced.

"I'm leaving," he said quietly. "Perhaps it's fitting that I should have shared my Name so, at least once, first. But why it should be *you* . . . no, don't answer. I'm thinking aloud."

He was silent, then, and seemed to wish the same of me but I couldn't oblige him. "Where will you go, my Lord?"

"To Azea, little one."

"Azea! But how—"

"Shh! Listen, and seal your lips against speech. Even my father doesn't know this. I've been studying the enemy for years now. I can speak their tongue without accent, think like them, move like them. My cosmeticists have dyes and drugs which will bleach my hair and keep my beard from growing. Skin dye will bronze my skin. It's not unplanned, you see."

"You'll go among them?"

He nodded. "I'll defeat them at their own game—assimilation, a fancy word for intrigue."

"To what end, my Lord?"

His eyes grew hard and cold, the way they were on the night I had met him. "Power, pretty one. An interstellar Holding at my beck and call. The game is theirs, now, but after this venture, Zatar the Magnificent will start writing his own rules."

I feared him then—his anger, his hatred of his own kind and his passionate need for them—feared his possible failure, and even more, his success.

He slipped a heavy gold ring from his left index finger, where it fit snugly over his glove. He toyed with it as he spoke. "I've stolen enough of my father's poison to commit an assassination, or die trying. What's life, without power? I'm Braxaná, born to rule. And I will—despite that whole pack of fools!"

He placed the ring in my hand and gently folded my fingers over it. "Little traitor, I cannot take ownership of you. We may never meet again. But a token of ownership is Just Cause for refusing a man, and I know what you've been through at the hands of my sex. The ring is Braxaná; men will wonder at it, but none will question its use. Will you wear it?"

I nodded, afraid of that last kiss because its end meant

he would leave me. "You'll come back," I whispered when he had done, "and I'll wait for you."

He pried himself loose from my arms. "You're Braxin, Ni'en, don't forget that," he said sternly. "Let's not err as our enemies do. Find some pride in your heritage. Life is meant for pleasure, not dead memories."

He left me then. Yes, dear Lord, but what if memories bring pleasure?

I knew I was being followed before I saw the guard. I had heard the footsteps pacing my own, I had seen the shadows staying an even distance behind me.

I fingered the spot where Zatar's ring lay on a gold chain, hidden beneath my shirt. I tried to remain steady, tried to keep walking. All the while I kept glancing back, trying to determine the nature of this threat without being obvious about it.

Then I saw, and I knew.

The sash of bright blue, embossed with the Seal of the Kaim'erate. Central Guard! I stopped, turned to face them, fell to my knees, lowered my eyes. What else could I do?

There were three in all and I trembled as they approached, fearing for my life—and worse. The pain of a stun twisted deep in my nervous system, driving me into darkness; his Name moved silently across my lips, almost as a prayer.

Darkness. Then intense hunger—pain—a point of light in the distance. Voices about me: male, Braxaná accents. Pain again, severe pain, and descent back into darkness.

I longed for death.

"Is she awake?"

Cold water hit my face and I awoke, shuddering. A dungeon? My hands in shackles, pinned to the wall, my body dripping wet in the dank, still air? What ancient nightmare was this. . . .

Before me stood three Kaim'eri. One was older than the others, with the same facial structure as Lord Zatar, but much crueler in expression. One was middle-aged, with a face not incapable of mercy. The third I recognized even from Zatar's sparse description, and I instinctively knew that he was the one responsible for the primitive barbarity of my surroundings.

"Sechaveh is a loner and a sadist," he'd told me. "His parents fled the Holding to escape the Plague which thinned the ranks of my Race. But they took it with them and Sechaveh was raised by aliens, ignorant of his heritage.

"The man revels in destruction—peoples, planets, women. When they send him to war he returns with slaves and riches, and leaves behind him the rubble which once was a world."

The older man paced as he spoke. "Woman, we will be plain. My son has disappeared. Where is he?"

My throat was dry. "Your . . . son, great one?"

"Zatar, you fool! Don't play games with me. I've had him followed for some time now; we know he was with you the night before he disappeared."

Listen, and seal your lips against speech. . . .

I lowered my eyes, fearful. "He used me, glorious Kaim'era. Nothing more."

He struck me. I reeled under the blow, but the metal cuffs held me upright. I felt blood running in my mouth, and didn't look at my wrists for fear of finding the same. This, then, was Vinir—and the third man would be Yiril, whom Zatar had described as "the only Braxaná capable of mercy."

I envied those peoples with an active god, to whom they might pray for death.

I won't pain you, my sister, with descriptions of the tortures I endured, modern pains that leave no scars. Yiril forbade the others from disfiguring me—if I refused to speak, he said, or genuinely didn't know anything useful, they would need me intact to act as bait for the wayward Lord.

Ni'Ar, it wasn't courage that sealed my lips. Ignorant though I was of the politics that moved these men, I could clearly read the tensions between them. Sechaveh was restless, irritated by Yiril's restrictions. If I spoke, if I ceased to have value to them, I would be turned over to him. And that I feared more than the pain.

When was it that they cast me where they had found me, in the streets of Sulos? The three guards set to watch me used me roughly before dropping out of sight, while my body still shivered in pain.

They would wait—wait for Zatar, son of Vinir and K'Siva, to return to the lower-class filth he so enjoyed. They would kill us both, then; such was Yiril's suggestion. But I suspected, against all logic, that he knew such a plan was doomed to failure. Why then did he offer it?

For two years, my sister, I suffered the attentions of my three captors. And you! You congratulated me for such regular attentions! Little did you know. . . .

At night Zatar's gift of gold slept by me, its chain about my neck. But no longer did I dare wear it during the day. For often, without warning, the arm of a guard would drag me into an alley, or a darkened doorway, there to sate whatever lust the moment had conjured, in a mockery of the privacy their masters preferred.

Some nights when the pain became too great, I took Zatar's ring to the Tuel, and there wept. It was conduct unbecoming a Braxin, but bless it all! A moment's betrayal, I knew, if carefully planned, might end all of this. But I would not—*could* not—betray the one man who had seen through my shameful brand, to the woman who suffered because of it.

And when I felt his hands lift me from the grass one night, when with tightly closed eyes I kissed him once more, I knew from the touch of him that he was still clean-shaven; and as I felt the soft weight of his hair fall upon my arm, I knew without looking that it was still white as snow.

"Fool," I whispered happily. "The first person that sees you will kill you."

"They tried, little one. Three Central Guards with stun. And Zatar with Zhaor. Hardly a challenge."

I laughed, and I cried, and I held him.

"They've hurt you," he said quietly.

"No. I have no bad memories—only pleasure."

He laughed, a lusty laugh that revived the most erotic

of those memories. "I've not had a woman in nearly two years," he told me. "Do you think you can handle that?"

I smiled. "I can try, my Lord."

And he is fresh from killing, I thought, as his embrace wiped all else from my mind. His hunger I could sense, frustrated, powerful, demanding. What else is there to do with such a man but yield?

"I'm afraid, my Lord."

"You fear me?"

I pressed closer to him. "No. Not you."

"My father—the Kaim'eri?"

"Not beside you, no."

"Kurat, then? Its dungeons?"

In answer, I shuddered.

"Then we'll crush them, my little one—them and their creators."

The autocarriage slowed as we approached his home, a second-eon mansion. He helped me out, holding me close as we came to the door.

"Your palm," he said. "The House knows my hand."

Obediently I put my hand on the doorplate. A second's hesitation—then the door opened, revealing a guard.

"Lord Zatar!"

"My father's in council now, is he not?" I was pulled past the bewildered guard.

"He is, but—my Lord!"

Zatar pored his confusion and drew me quickly through the forehouse. The enormity of the building was overwhelming; the power of the man who owned it was beyond my comprehension. Through the tightness of Zatar's grip I could feel his rising tension, his exhilaration as he strode toward a confrontation with his father. He had chosen this moment with care and it was with calculated forethought that he chose to kick open the doors to the last conference chamber, overriding the portal mechanism with simple primitive force. The heavy wooden panels fell aside with a bang and he entered, taking me with him, accompanied by indignant smoke and the sputter of damaged circuitry.

To say that they were surprised would be an understatement.

There were five of them, all Kaim'eri, three of whom I already knew and feared. Until a moment ago their Zhaori had been set aside in an opulent weapons-rack, but as the doors fell aside they claimed their swords with Braxaná-swift reflexes. Only when they saw the cause of the intrusion did they relax somewhat.

Vinir's face, however, was livid with fury. "So now you're back," he hissed.

Zatar bowed, the very master of arrogance. "My father. Glorious Kaim'eri! I return to you on the wings of triumph." His voice dripped hatred and hinted at sarcasm as only the complex speech modes of the Braxaná dialect can do. I tried to fade into the shadows; the looks my former captors were directing at me could have nailed me to the wall had they had substance. I trembled. In answer, his grip on me tightened.

Yiril was the first to collect himself. With a low chuckle of amusement he pulled his chair back into place and sat. "Well, Zatar. Is this the new fashion you intend for the Holding to adopt?"

His hair, of course, was still straight, although we had dyed its color back and made some attempt at styling it properly. And he was cleanshaven, although we had bleached the bronze from his skin. (How delicious it had been, with him playing Azean at the height of pleasure!)

His eyes sparkled as he chose not to answer. "Please sit, Kaim'eri."

"What do you want with us?" Vinir snapped. He alone remained standing, while the others, still armed, regained their seats.

"I bring you news—good news. The Azean Interrogation Officer Darmel lyu Tukone is dead. Of our poison. By my hands."

There was silence. Vinir sat, clearly stunned, trying not to show it.

"That would explain—" one of the other Kaim'eri began, astonished.

"Quiet," Yiril ordered. He looked at Zatar; his face was unreadable. "The Empire's been trying not to let that news out. We've heard rumors, though, which this would explain. If so . . ." he smiled carefully, ". . . you are welcome."

Zatar grinned. "Thank you."

"Very dramatic." Sechaveh shifted position, laying his sword on the table with a clatter. "Now what?"

Zatar took a step forward, drawing me with him. "My inheritance, father."

The hatred with which Vinir regarded him was, nonetheless, tempered with respect. "All right," he said finally. "Granted, you've earned some recognition. A House of your own, your own finances, adult legal status. All well and good."

And I? Servant, even slave, I knew, if he would have me.

But then Vinir's face darkened and he pointed at me. "And this common filth? Mistress of it all?"

"Your choice of words, my father, but they are—in essence—correct."

I? Mistress of a House of nobility? No, no, no! I am branded, Zatar, branded! Ar, the shame. . . .

Vinir's tone was deadly. "I forbid it!"

"You can't. I'll sue for it."

"You're not inherited yet," the older man reminded him.

They glared at each other, a test of determination and dominance. A long time passed in silence. With what Zatar had done, it would be shameful for both of them if Vinir tried to keep him bound up in youthful dependence. But once he freed him to his inheritance, the younger man's staff was his own business. Finally Vinir said slowly, carefully, "She will never set foot on Braxi again."

"You'll give me the estate on Zhene, then?"

"Do you think you can be satisfied with that?"

Zatar's dark eyes sparkled. "Quite."

"Subject to those terms, then, I inherit you. Kaim'eri: you witness—Computer, send a transcript to Braxin Central Files. There. Now will you please leave? We have business to conduct—and this isn't your House any more."

"But I have business also."

Vinir looked more weary than angry this time. "What is it?"

Zatar chose his words carefully. "Which one of you, most respected Kaim'era, will bring forth my name in nomination at the Citadel?"

Vinir exploded. "Unheard of!" Others among the five agreed, clearly enraged by the request. Only Yiril did not protest. Yiril, who Zatar had said might well bid for an informal alliance if the situation merited it. That was, he had explained, the difference between a true ruler and a mere Kaim'era. Yiril was Kaim'era. The others, Zatar had told me, were less.

For a long moment Yiril studied the young Lord, while on both sides of him expletives reigned. And he seemed to see something in Zatar that satisfied him, for at last he nodded. "I, Yiril, Dliniri, son of Kerest and Sienne"—the others grew quickly silent as they heard the ritual words—"I, Braxaná, Kaim'era of the Holding of B'salos under Braxi/Aldous, bring forth the person of Zatar, Zarvati, son of Vinir and K'siva, for the consideration of the Kaim'erate, that he might be elevated to its membership." His wry smile asked: *enough?* "Am I confirmed in this?"

He looked at the others, particularly at Sechaveh, who saw something in his expression that made him nod almost imperceptibly in agreement. "I confirm your choice," he said quietly.

It was a direct blow to Vinir that the two of them should act in concert and all present knew it; the nomination of Zatar had marked the end of their political trinity. Weary, exasperated, Vinir looked at his son. The mixed emotions in his face, I was startled to note, included a fair measure of respect. "Is that all, now?"

"Yes, Kaim'era." No longer 'my father,' I noticed. He bowed and, taking me with him, turned to leave.

"Lord Zatar!"

He turned back to face his father.

"You have one day and night to remove yourself, your possessions, and this woman from my property. Do you understand?"

Zatar bowed his head in obedience. In a matter of minutes his relationship with Vinir had entirely changed; now he was an intruder—an enemy—in the other man's House.

"And Zatar . . ."

He raised an eyebrow, waiting.

"I'll send your House a bill for the door." And then, grudgingly: "Well done. Now get out of here."

He did.

"They'll hate you," he said. "You don't have to go."

"I want to."

"The Households on Zhene are entirely Braxaná. Only the first class uses the moon, and few live there all the time. You'll be outcast."

I kissed him, long, as he had taught me. How good to know I could bring him pleasure! "I love you, Kaim'era Zatar." I had to use Aldousan for the thought—it doesn't translate into Braxin the way I wanted to say it. And before he could correct my premature use of his title I asked, "Does that shame you?"

"No," he said gently. "I've lived too long among the enemy to be quite as emphatic as tradition would have it."

"Are they happy, Lord?"

"Yes, happy—they also suffer more for it. When Tukone died, his wife destroyed herself. Terrible waste of people, that." He pulled a pad and styla from a drawer. "Love is the ultimate weakness and the Azeans will destroy themselves with it. But you shame me, little one? Hardly. Here; write your sister farewell."

So I try, Ni'Ar, but his breath in my hair and his hands on my body demand I focus my attention elsewhere. So be careful, dear sister, and wish me well.

I am his, now. And he has just begun.

Viton: These gentle emotions, what good are they? Love, compassion, amity; what purpose do they serve? To my mind they are socially invalid, obstacles to emotional efficiency. There is no more constructive emotion than hatred.

THREE

Ferian del Kanar was less than happy about entering the housing satellite of Security Base Five, but because he was a Braxaná— or at any rate, because he was training to become one—he tried not to let it show.

"Something wrong?" an Azean crewman asked.

Damn. "Nothing."

He caught a glimpse of himself in the gleaming surface of the dock's interior wall and checked his posture, movement, countenance . . . there. A far better deception. "Nothing at all." So what if he was entering one of the most carefully guarded domifices in the Empire? So what if he was half-Braxaná, and looked as if that part was dominant? He was also Ferian del Kanar, one of the Empire's few Probes—and if the average person couldn't tell a Probe from a telepath, they knew enough of both to be impressed.

He settled the red-and-gold cord of his rank more comfortably about his head, nodded to the transport crew which had accompanied him thus far, and withdrew his clearance chip for a guard of the orbiting domifice to inspect.

Brightway: a haven of refuge for the officers of StarControl, the one place besides their Base where they might relax, knowing that the best of the Empire's science had been devoted to their safety. Here Darmel lyu Tukone had lived, had laid aside his interrogative duties nightly to be, for a short time, merely a man. Here his mate had come when the day's work was finished, to cast off her authority like a discarded garment and lie beside him in the safety of their home. And here they had died, both of them, the victims of Braxin poison.

"Ferian del Kanar . . ." the guard muttered. The Probe's adult name was unusual; Ferian had chosen it for that reason, The presence of a subname declared that he was (despite appearances to the contrary) Azean. That was enough for strangers to know.

"Temporary Clearance, eh?" The guard was obviously suspicious. Frowning, he slipped the clear chip into a computer slot and waited for an analysis. At last the screen cleared, and words appeared. VALID. CURRENT. CONFIRMED.

Still frowning, he nodded. "You're clear. Li Nath'll take you in." *And Hasha help you if you make trouble,* he added silently. He handed the clearance chip back to Ferian and gestured to one of the other guards.

"Thirteen/twenty-three. Search him first."

Ferian allowed himself to smile. With his velvet-black hair and translucent white skin, the Probe looked Braxaná enough to disturb any Security officer. And if that hair was long and his face was cleanshaven—concessions he had grudgingly made to the fashions of the Empire—that did not obscure the fact that he really was, in body and spirit, part Braxaná.

"All right," li Nath said, after a thorough search with a handheld scanner. It was clear he wasn't happy about his orders. "Come with me."

Level thirteen, subsection twenty-three. The corridors were a labyrinth in three dimensions, punctuated by sensor-panels which—much to Ferian's annoyance—demanded confirmation of his clearance before they would let him pass. An impressive display, he thought, but only that. For after all, when it came right down to it, the system had failed. Darmel lyu Tukone and Suan lir Aseirin were dead—*assassinated*—and all the scanners in the world couldn't change that fact.

"This is it," the guard said sharply. Distaste radiated from him as he touched the portal, alerting the apartment's only occupant to their presence. A moment passed—the near-silent *whrrr* of a scanner reminded Ferian that he was still under the domifice's observation—and then the door opened, and Nabu li Pazua, Director of the Institute in charge of psychogenetic research, greeted them.

"Ferian! At last." He was an older man, well into his twelfth decade, impressive both in stature and in psychic ability. The red cord of telepathy was bright against his skin, and the semi-military dress which he affected lent him an additional air of authority.

"Thank you," he told the guard. He motioned Ferian into the apartment and reset the portal behind him.

"You had no problem getting here?"

"Oh, I had problems." He let the Director of the Institute share his memories: security checks, verifications of clearance, a fight with his escort guards while in Kiaun orbit. . . . ~*But I'm here,* he concluded telepathically, then added ~ *Where's the child?*

~ *This way.*

The apartment which had housed Darmel lyu Tukone was a richly textured place, with fine knotwork covering the walls and soft-surfaced furniture that seemed to grow right out of the floor. Not typically Azean at all; that culture tended toward clean-edged surfaces in bright, contrasting colors. Here the walls were muted blue fading into Rahnsea green, with a faint touch of lilac woven into the pattern at irregular intervals . . . more Lugastine than anything, Ferian thought, though the texturing was unmistakedly Braxin. An odd blend of styles for a Security officer to adopt.

"In here." Li Pazua indicated a doorway. ~ *Be careful.*

~ *I always am,* Ferian lied.

He stepped into the dimly lit room and came to the side of a forcebed, where a lone figure lay in a sleep akin to death.

And stopped.

And stared.

"Tell me what you see," li Pazua urged.

She was a human unlike any he had ever seen, slender and pale and so fragile that it seemed impossible she had ever lived. Her skin was colorless, her hair an inhuman hue which poured over her shoulders and across her throat like a thousand fresh incisions, blood-colored and gleaming. "*Their* child?" he whispered, incredulous. "She's not Azean."

"Recessive grouping," li Pazua explained. "Look closer."

Ferian touched her mind with his special talent, and he realized why the Director had brought him there. Inside the fragile body, where there should have been thought, there was nothing. *Nothing.* Not rudimentary consciousness, not the vestiges of recent memory, not a single hint that the body had ever been inhabited. Stunned, he searched the inside of the child's mind, with the kind of thoroughness that only a Probe could master. And still found not even the promise of consciousness.

Which could only mean . . . Hasha!

"Ferian?"

He found that he was trembling. "How old is she?"

"Six Standard Years. Four and some, Lugastine."

"Pre-pubescent, then."

"Without question."

The implications of that!

~ *Ferian?*

He forced himself to speak. "It's telepathy," he said hoarsely. He groped for a chair, found one, sat. ~ *To come into one's sensitivity this early. . . .* He shuddered.

~ *You're certain, then.*

~ *Yes.* He touched her mind—or lack of it—again. Not even a murmur from the backmind! ~ *She's put up a block—and a blessed good one, too.* There were trained telepaths who couldn't keep him out; how had a child managed to do it?

The Director was calm and rational, an island of reason in the storm of Ferian's thoughts. ~ *Current theory states that psychic awakening is linked to the hormonic changes associated with—*

"Theory be damned!—or blessed," he corrected, translating the oath into its Braxin equivalent. "The girl is telepathic—*actively* telepathic. Look, Director, you wouldn't bother to shut your eyes if you'd never seen. What would be the point? She's seen the light and rejected it, and her mental lids are shut so tight that not a glimmer can get through—in either direction. That's as sure a sign of telepathy as I've ever seen."

"Can you save her?"

He frowned. ~ *Be specific.*

~ *Make contact. Bring her out.*

~ *Difficult . . .*

~ *But possible?*

He considered the problem. ~ *Have you thought of the possible ramifications? My signature is markedly Braxin—*

~ *My other Probes have tried,* the Director told him. ~ *All of them. If you can't do it, we'll lose her.* He sighed, projecting his frustration. ~ *Your emotional makeup is . . . unique. Maybe it'll make a difference. I hope so.*

He lapsed into thoughtful silence; Ferian considered what he knew of the case and then asked aloud, "She saw her parents die?"

"She was found by the bodies." The Director projected an image, since the term "bodies" could not encompass the carnage. Stiff black residue in two mounds of human length were the only remains of Azea's most valued Security personnel.

Braxin poison. That terrible semi-living substance which could lurk unnoticed for days in the bloodstream of a victim, then erupt suddenly into a mass of churning black hell. It had devoured Darmel, its host. His mate had come in contact with it while trying to save him and it had claimed her as well. And the child. . . .

"She was reaching out to them," Li Pazua explained. "The poison must have gone inert before she got to it."

"She was in *contact* with it?" Ferian asked sharply.

The Director nodded.

"I didn't realize that."

He looked at the body—frail, so frail!—and touched her brain stem with his awareness. "The metabolic signals are erractic," he mused aloud. "Continued stress?"

"You think she's trapped in a nightmare?"

"Perhaps."

Ferian sat down on the edge of the bed. Slowly, with a grace that was half genetic heritage and half training, he moved an arm across her until his hand came to rest on her forehead.

"I'm ready."

And he ventured forward, into the child's mind.

Where there was only darkness.

He sought greater depth.

~ *(Resistance.)*

~ *(Insistence),* he offered.

~ *(Darkness. Fear.)*

~ *(Gentle entry.) The intrusion is not a source of harm. Let me be absorbed into you. There will be no damage.*

~ *(Resistance to any contact.)*

~ *You need not touch me at all. Stand aside. I pass through and beyond. There need be no direct contact.*

~ *(Weakened resistance. Psychic fatigue. Potential yielding.)*

~ *Image: An amoeba of light yielding to the approach of a foreign particle. It passes through the cell, distinct and separate, and out the other side. The light-amoeba glows, whole and unharmed.)*

~ *(Compliance. Darkness parting. Inner silence.)*

The Probe strained his senses to the utmost; there was nothing. He surfaced enough to send ~ *No output.*

~ *Nothing at all?*

~ *Psychic reflex. No thought behind it.*

~ *That's what the others reported.*

~ *I'm going to try direct emotional input.*

He didn't have to say what they both were thinking; his perception of emotion was so unique among telepaths that such a course might succeed for him alone.

He formed and purified a bolt of emotion. Guided by a single thought, a single thread of inner consciousness, a Probe might reach the deepest and most closed portions of a mind. But there must be something to guide him, and that was what the halfbreed sitting on the bed's edge hoped to inspire.

~ *(Grief!),* he offered.

~ *(Unfeeling darkness.)*

~ *(Hatred!)*

~ *(Darkness without response.)*

~ *(Anger!)*

~ *(Absolute silence.)*

~ *(Accusation!)*

A stirring of thought in the distance—too faint and too fast to catch hold of. He cursed himself for not being superhuman as well as telepathic. Trying the same stimulus again, he received no response.

"But not dead!" he said aloud, with satisfaction.

He prepared an image, gathering it to him for transmission. It would identify him to the child with an instantaneous awareness of who and what had invaded the privacy of her mind. He chose the image carefully, on the assumption that her background would have instilled in her certain vehement prejudices. Then he forced it into her awareness.

The image was Braxin, and it flashed suddenly inside her.

The child of Darmel lyu Tukone rebelled. Waves of aversion rose about him, pressing against him, an instinctive reaction designed to drive him out without really knowing how to do so.

She denied his reality.

He persisted.

She broke. ~ *There is no Braxin psychic!*

He grabbed at her reaction and held onto it. One coherent thought could serve as a lifeline to her inner mind, locked though it was in silence. She struggled to withdraw from him, to return to that inner world which promised (but did not fully deliver) a release from all pain and disturbance. He let her go there. And he followed.

~ *(Boiling guilt. Self hate. A swamp of moral ugliness—the image of self.)*

These were not new things to him, and he brushed them aside.

~ *(Terror! Pain!)*

He grasped it.

The thought withdrew, back, back through the ugliness to a central core of torment, to

* * *

Darmel is screaming.

She is startled out of halfsleep, into a world beyond her comprehension. The air throbs with terror and agony, where before it was only air. Unearthly pain assails her—where is it coming from? Dimly she perceives that her mother has run out to the hallway; frightened, the child follows.

The living poison administered days ago to her father has matured. Rooted in his chest it mutates, growing and feeding on his flesh until it emerges by his shoulder, a living black coagulation of parasitic tissue. Had it appeared within an extremity he might have been saved, by the unhesitating amputation for which Suan's dagger was designed. But already it has reached areas too precious to remove.

Darmel lyu Tukone writhes in mindless agony. Black foam trickles from his mouth and the horror consumes his lips and neck from inside and out. His convulsions cast bits of the blackness about him, to the feet of his horrified mate.

And the child, who moments ago was merely a child, suffers his pain as though it were her own, his mindscreaming agony the catalyst for her psychic awakening. She dies with him, knowing intimately the madness with which he tears at his own flesh. Scoring a shoulder, with tearing strokes; striving, like a terriificd animal, to remove the portions of his body that pain him.

A scrap of discarded death is flung unexpectedly across Suan and takes root there before action can dislodge it. The black malignance burns to fresh life, quickly eating through clothing and flesh to intrude itself deep within her body. Knowing the manner of the end that awaits her, having only a moment of coherent thought left before the pain claims her utterly, Suan turns the forcefield blade into herself, acting before fear can weaken resolve. The suicide resonates within the child's terrified mind, alongside the fear and pain which are Suan's last living moments.

Against death-wish and agony the child struggles in vain, finding at last the key to closedmindedness. Then sight is gone, and hearing follows. Peaceful, blissful darkness envelops the tortured mind, leaving only thought in the relatively painless void. Thought . . . and memory.

I saw him.

Terrible, terrible knowledge; what child could face it and remain sane?

I saw him. The assassin. Hasha, help me. . . .

She remembers him as he was on that day, an Azean like any other . . . only *different.* They are in the Hall of Music, awaiting the end of an intermission, and she stares at him as he speaks to her parents. His words are false. His clothes, even his golden skin is false, and his Azean eyes . . . they should be *black,* velvet black, a deep oblivion to house terrible secrets. He is deadly, fascinating, a predator in human guise, and when those eyes turn to gaze upon her and the full power of his person strikes her, she shivers. How could she explain to an adult what she sees? Who would believe her? What adult would credit such a fantasy—for fantasy it surely must be!—or realize that her latent psychic power, active now for the very first time, has pierced through this man's Azean facade to discover an intruder beneath?

He turns back to his prey, hungry for death, and hands her father a glass of lightwine. She senses the hunter's instinct, shares it for an instant, and is overwhelmed by its intensity. But she does not cry out. She does not warn her parents. They wouldn't believe her if she did, and for good reason. She *must* be wrong about this—she must!

The killer smiles, radiating triumph. As her father drinks his death.

I could have saved you! You could have been prepared. I should have said something—anything! I should have made you believe. You could have lived.

I killed you!

She crawls forward, feeling her way; guilt has smothered her senses until only touch remains to her. Struggling to move despite the darkness which strangles her, she reaches to where the Black Death still seethes, striving to embrace the fate of the ones she has killed with silence.

Take me! she begs.

But the poison is finished, inert. Dead. Powerless to claim another victim, no matter what the justice of that death might be.

In the distance, an infinity of hostile minds threaten to break into the newly sensitive awareness.

In desperation, she shuts them out forever.

"She knows she's vulnerable, and alone, and . . . hated. She blames herself for her parent's deaths. She recognizes the truth in what she saw but lacks the knowledge to interpret it. There's self-hate to be dealt with, guilt, possibly her mother's death-wish internalized, and then of course her own . . . an enormous undertaking.

The Director nodded, pouring more wine for him. The deadening sensation of the alcohol was slowly bringing the Probe back to verbal coherence even as it cut off his psychic senses.

It had taken five large glasses of the stuff just to get him talking.

"Can you do it?"

Ferian hesitated. Took another drink. "You don't know what you're asking."

"What you were trained to do."

"I was *trained* to telecommunicate. I was *trained* to act like a Braxaná." With a long swallow he drained the glass again. "A once-in-a-lifetime opportunity, remember? The Ultimate Weapon. Send him to Braxi, let him spy for the Empire. At least, that's what you told my mother when you convinced her to live with the memory of her rape long enough to bear me to term." He shuddered. "That child's mind is an inferno of self-destruction. Don't commit me to it unless you're ready to scrape up my ashes."

"Listen." The Director leaned forward, broadcasting a sense of urgency to accompany his words. "The state doesn't want her. They'll let the Institute take her away and then forget she ever existed. Do you realize what that would mean? There's *never* been a potential telepath like this one! Never an initial rating as high as hers, and certainly never full awakening without the usual pubescent triggers. *Damn* her parents!" he swore. "We tried over and over to tell them. Why wouldn't they respond? If we'd had her in training—"

"You wouldn't have started that early and you know it. As for her parents . . ." he sighed. "They've more than paid for any mistake they made regarding her. And yes, I think something of her mind can be salvaged." With an unsteady hand he refilled his glass. "Twist the guilt to anger, the inner-directed hatred to an outside focus . . . it could be done."

"What kind of focus?"

"Her father's assassin, I think." *A predator with eyes of velvet death.* He shivered. "Or his race, if that fails."

"Braxin?"

"I will assume so. She does." *Braxaná,* he thought, and his stomach tightened as he relived their shared memory. How much of that fear had been hers, and how much his own? Those golden eyes that should have been black had seemed to pierce through to his very soul, and though Ferian's emotional reaction was not clothed in confusion as the child's had been, his assessment of lyu Tukone's assassin was much the same as hers. *A man I hope never to meet,* he told himself. *A man who is infinitely dangerous.*

"Saturate her with hatred, then? Toward Braxi?"

He nodded, knowing as he did so that he was committing himself to the task.

"You're going to take quite a beating in this."

Ferian forced himself to laugh. "So what else is new?"

And again he drained the glass.

Harkur: Civilized man longs for the illusion of barbarism. Either his culture fulfills this need by adopting its outer trappings, or he will be seduced by his first contact with a culture that does.

FOUR

In the darkness between the stars, a Purpose stirs. Guided by thought, powered by telepathy, it reaches outward from its creator—the Director of the Institute—and seeks, in the psychosphere of Lugast, its first assigned receptor.

Who responds.

~ *This is Adran li Kasure, Lugastine telepath.*

~ *Director Nabu li Pazua, at the Institute. I assume you've been briefed?*

~ *Minimally. You want a relay to Braxi?*

~ *Under my dominance.*

~ *(Image: Adran li Kasure nods.) Of course.*

~ *Prepare for subsumption.*

The lesser mind relaxes, drifts . . . and is absorbed by that of its master, in power if not in personality. Again, the Director reaches Braxiward, strengthened by the support of his student.

And makes contact on Kiau, and establishes further relay.

And reaches for Ienda.

Suul.

Adrish.

Until he pierces at last, with a tendril of thought, the Holding itself.

And Braxi.

~ *Ferian?*

The response is faint, but it grows in intensity as the Braxaná Probe focuses on the relay and adds his strength to the effort.

~ *Yes, I'm receiving. Difficult, thought. Is this the best that can be done?*

~ *Regretfully.*

~ *It'll have to do, then. Here's the situation. They've bought my story entirely. I had to take a basic gene survey, but they were only interested in verifying my Braxaná half; I don't think they've even got Azean codes on file. They confirmed the Braxaná blood, although their science is so primitive they couldn't get it down to a specific bloodline. The end result of all this is that I've been passed on as wholesome and acceptable, race-wise.*

~ Good. Are you settled?

~ I liquidated my precious stores into local currency and took a place on Braxi proper, near Kurat, the upper-class sector. With my Braxaná appearance no one asks any questions here. I tell you, the assimilation has only two problems.

~ The language?

~ No, that's fine. It's too complicated and subtle to speak straight; I wouldn't know which of the forty-two speech modes to start with, much less be able to hold two conversations at once as some of them obviously do. But with a bit of receptive telepathy I usually manage to find the right mode—or cover it up I if I don't. It's the food, mostly. (Sensory image: breakfast.) So highly spiced that it's really getting to me.

~ Hasha, I see what you mean.

~ And that was first thing in the morning. I'll spare you a look at dinner. They serve wine with everything, and I'll tell you, Braxin vintage wine may taste delicious but it's strong enough to fuel starliners. Seems they blend in a bit of pharmacopoeia, too: a dose of hallucinogen, maybe, or a mild aphrodisiac. What you gave me in training was like water to this stuff! No wonder they die younger than we do.

~ What else?

~ (Evasiveness. Embarrassment.)

~ Ferian. . . .

~ All right, all right, the women. What am I doing wrong? They're practically begging for sex with me—it's a racist thing, you know—but I made the mistake of assuming one might want to spend the night and was rewarded with some curses that . . . well, I'll spare you those, too. Evidently, I had dealt her Braxin honor some hideous blow. I've made some valiant efforts at being more violent, too, but all I get for that are more scratch marks. I hurt, Director.

~ Pain is a valid feeling, Ferian, remember that.

~ . . . And now that you remind me, damn the Social Codes, too!

~ Any contacts yet?

~ A few householders of the Kaim'eri, and a young Braxaná

named Selek. I'm calling myself Feran, by the way, so please use that as a callsign, or I'll slip up sometime in the wrong company.

~ What's with this Selek?

~ He took me to the Museum of Erotic Art. (Involuntary image: a composed Braxaná running a gloved hand down the thigh of a near-naked waitress. Involuntary explanation: Museum restaurant. Selek.) We talked a bit. There's no concept of friendship here, you know, at least not between members of the same sex. So how do I judge my relationships? I mean, what kind of scale do you use? I'll tell you one thing, though. I can see why they're not worried about spies—and they aren't, believe me. The only thing getting me through this is my telepathy. I can't see a non-FT managing to stay afloat here for more than a day. . . . Hasha, what I wouldn't do for a simple plate of scrambled eggs. Unspiced.

~ It'll come, it'll come. Is that all?

~For now. I've gathered our supposition was correct. The Braxaná do have a passionate distrust of any non-material powers; hence the development of telepathy has not occurred. No one discusses it openly, but I gather an infant showing such talents is disposed of—the Braxaná are big on infanticide, by the way. Keeps the Race superior. Anyway, I think I'm relatively safe. I'll open for relay at regular intervals, as we arranged.

~ Be careful.

~ I will.

~ Ferian? How's it going?

~ Fairly well. Who's on relay? It feels stronger.

~ Er Vlas picked up the last rung. He's a Probe, so you're sending abstract until the transmission gets into the Empire. Any news?

~ No. Just strengthening the contacts. Sechaveh set a useful precedent a few decades back, coming in out of nowhere and working his way up to Kaim'era status. I think they're less suspicious of me than they might have been before that. Selek has shown me Kurat and I'm somewhat known at his House, but little politicking goes on while I'm there, and nothing useful. He lent me the Mistress of his House—saucy little wench.

~ Sex life going any easier?

~ You get used to it.

~ How about food?

~ That will take a bit longer. I met D'vra today.

~ Who?

~ Sorry, that's right, how could you know? She's purebred, Mistress of the House of Yiril . . . here. (Image: a broad-shouldered, shapely woman, white-skinned and black-haired, arrogant, powerful, aggressively sensual. The world is dirt to her. When she enters a room, men come to silence. She drives any man—even an Azean—to a desperate daydream of conquest, but has the legal right to kill any who touch her against her will.)

~ That's really something.

~ Yeah. She seems to be interested in me, but I don't think I'm up to that. Anyway, Yiril and two of the others have a kind of power triad that runs most of anything. Seems it's so rare for any of the Kaim'eri to unite on anything that a few of them sticking together can be very effective. I figure D'vra would be a good way to keep an eye on this trio, if I can work myself up to it.

~ Triad: Yiril, Vinir and Sechaveh?

~ No, they ousted Vinir a few years ago in favor of his son. There's a man I hope not to tangle with! (Image: Zatar. Undertone: nervousness.) He's controlled and deadly. The others indulge themselves in any violent or nasty emotion that strikes their fancy and thus overlook my irregularities. Somehow, I think he'd notice.

~ Do I sense fear?

~ (Evasively.) I'd rather not discuss it.

~ All right. I won't press you. Safety first, remember; you do us no good at all if these men come to suspect you.

~ (Dry laughter.) Don't worry, Director. Self-preservation is the number one Braxaná priority. I'm no exception.

~ Feran?

~ Honored to be your enemy, Director.

~ What's that?

~ Sorry, force of habit.

~ Damned curious habit.

~ Braxaná greeting. What's wrong?

~ You feel . . . different.

~ In what way?

~ (Uncertainty.) More like your red-headed protégée.

~ Who is very Braxin.

~ I know. That's what worries me. Be careful, Feran.

~ I am, Director.

~ How's business?

~ Very pleasant. I spent a night with D'vra—her initiative, of course.

~ Marvelous, Accomplish anything?

~ That depends on how you—

~ Feran! You know damned well what I mean.

~ Sorry. You get so into it over here, and then I have to turn it all off when the relay comes through. . . .

~ Well, have better control of yourself. Are you doing anything constructive?

~ I moved into Kurat. I knew enough people to be safe and it seemed a better place for observation. I am Braxaná, you know.

~ Only half—and both halves belong to the Institute.

~ I know, I know. All right, I'm in excellent spying position. I'm established, reasonably respected, and my telepathic contact with you is unsuspected. I'm waiting to get a grasp on local politics before I go any further. And I'm looking for a Mistress.

~ A what?

~ Someone to take care of the House. You can't expect a man to run his own household, can you? Say, who's in the relay today?

~ (Four voices respond, mentally.)

~ Good, all male. Taste this image, Director. . . .

~ Feran. . . .

~ Honored, Director.

~ Never mind that. Our elementary reception class picked up that last transmission. No more telepathic pornography, is that clear?

~ But it was relevant to—

~ Not relevant enough. Is that clear?

~ (Pause.) Yes, Director.

~ I've spoken to my aides, and we all agree. You're to take a vacation from Braxi proper at the first opportunity. I don't like what I sense happening to your psyche.

~ What happens to my psyche is my business, Director, let's make that very clear! You want information, and I'm trying to get it for you! But don't tell me how to live, or where, or whom to have sex with, or how often, or anything!

~ Calm down, Feran.

~ Right now I'm very busy trying to find out who fathered me. Your spying can wait.

~ You're not serious.

~ It matters to me. Do you know what it's like not to know your father?

~ No one cares. You have a cover story—

~ But it isn't true. It's a shameful thing, A Braxaná knowing only his mother. Your "mission" will just have to wait, Director. I'm sorry. I'll get to it, I promise.

~ (Pause.) As you wish, Ferian.

~ *That's* Feran.

~ Whatever.

Standard 2D transmission, augmented/superluminal, reaching to Base One/Azea, and

Stabilized/subluminal, retransmitted:

"Director Ebre ni Kahv, please."

The head of StarControl stirs, flicks on the visual. "Speaking."

"Nabu li Pazua, of the Institute."

"Li Pazua . . . yes, I remember." An aide supplies the proper shortfiles; he glances at them as they talk. "What can I do for you?"

"You said to check in regarding Ferian del Kanar. I'm doing so."

The files says *Ferian del Kanar, prod rape Lia ki Jannor by Braxin (Braxaná?) ID unknown, conquest Lees. Potential Telepathy rated 9.38 +, FT = 9.33. Security note: FULL EXTENT OF CONDITIONING UNKNOWN.* He frowns, thoughtful. "Is everything going as planned?"

"He's fitting in well—perhaps too well. I worry that we may have overstressed the Braxaná side of him."

"If what you tell me is accurate, I see no harm in that. Unless there are other factors to be considered—"

"I've told you everything relevant to the situation."

"Of course." He finds the place on li Pazua's shortfile where the phrase *CONFLICTING LOYALTIES?* appears, and underlines it again. "And if that's the case, there's no reason to worry. You conditioned him carefully, and he'll adapt accordingly. Am I correct?"

"That was our intent."

"Then trust your plans. Trust Ferian."

After a moment he added, somewhat untruthfully, "I do."

~ Ferian?

~ That's Feran, Director, and I'm here. I've been waiting.

~ You were hard to reach this time. The last link in our relay couldn't find you—

~ I haven't moved.

~ No. (Pause.) But you've changed.

~ Perhaps.

~ What's happened?

~ Not much. Lina's pregnant.

~ Who's Lina?

~ My Mistress.

~ Oh. Congratulations.

~ (Image: Ferian del Kanar shrugs.) The celebration begins when the child lives, Director, not before. The Race is weak in that regard—practically sterile, in fact. We don't acknowledge pregnancies, only successful births.

~ Ferian. . . .

~ Can it be Azean?

~ What?

~ I said, can the child be born with Azean characteristics.

~ I don't think so. I'll check the codes on your reproductive process. (Pause. Alarm.) Why? Surely you're not waiting out the year—

~ I want to see my son born.

~ Ferian—

~ I will *see my son born, Director! Is that too much for a Braxaná to ask?*

~ This is going a bit too far; I think you had better come home. . . .

~ I'm not coming home, Director. I have no place in the Empire, you know that. I'm staying here. I'll do the work you want, but I'm staying here. That's final.

~ Does your Mistress know how to make scrambled eggs?

~ What's that?

~ Never mind. Nothing. How's the food?

~ Fine. The cook's work is a bit bland, but that's all right—I can live with it. I'm hoping to import someone a bit more accustomed to Central flavoring. I had Zatar over for dinner the other night, and it was embarrassing to serve him food so Azean.

~ Any interesting information?

~ Some. I think Sechaveh may have fathered me. I've learned to respect his untrustworthiness, not to mention his influence; to share his bloodline would make me proud.

~ Is that all?

~ For now. Walk in danger, Director.

~ You, too.

~ Feran?

~ The relay must be weak, Director. I can barely feel you.

~ The relay's fine; it must be you.

~ Just as well.

~ I don't suppose you've been earning your keep over there at last.

~ Oh, but I have! Ketir and I went into a joint venture in the Belekor slave market—all very secretive, of course—miserable business for a Braxaná to be found dealing extensively in aliens. I've been able to add considerably to my estate from the profits.

~ Anything else?

~ You must bear with me, Director. I've been using my telepathy to enhance sex; that takes a good deal of effort after all you did to divorce the two within me.

~ It was all for your survival.

~ The need has passed. I find the power less and less obtrusive. Braxaná were not meant to be telepaths, I'm afraid.

~ You were. Distinctly so.

~ That was twenty of your years ago, Director. A lot has changed since then. Sechaveh and I had a long talk yesterday—

~ You told him who you were?!!

~ Not what I was, but who I was, yes. I'm half Braxaná, after all. It takes more than an alien upbringing to cause one of these men to deny his offspring. And Sechaveh isn't overly fond of women, at least in the conventional sense, which means he has even fewer sons than most . . . anyway, whatever his reasons, he's accepted me. He granted me official bloodline rights and gave me an ancestral Zhaor which I'm busy training with . . . did you know the Braxaná females fence also? Viciously, too! . . . I don't know if I can make the next relay, Director. There's a costumed gathering at the Museum Archives at that time and we're all having Braxaná barbaric tribal outfits constructed. . . . I'm afraid that once D'vra and the others come like that, I really won't have the time or interest to get in touch. Live in danger, Director. And thanks for saving my life.

~ You're welcome, Ferian.

~ That's Feran.

~ Whatever.

* * *

"Director ni Kahv?"

"Speaking."

"Director i Pazua. We have some results on Ferian del Kanar."

"I'm listening."

"He's defected. Oh, I don't think he knows it himself yet in so many words, but I'm sure we've lost contact for good. He's told them his background, and they've accepted the Braxaná blood in him as good enough to cancel out the Azean upbringing. He has a typical Braxaná household, which means he has computer access to all the information we could want and he won't give us a word of it."

"Excellent."

"Yes, I thought so."

"This does give me faith in your reasoning. I must say, I had my doubts when we first discussed this."

"If we had just sent him in to spy it would never had worked. We would have seen something happen just as it has—a little more slowly perhaps, without my prompting, but just the same in the end. He'd be Braxaná and we'd have nothing."

"But this way. . . ."

"As I promised. His rapid assimilation into Braxin life is proof of his conditioning, as are a number of other signs I programmed into him. As far as he's concerned, his telepathic talent has gone dormant—he'll have no reason to suspect otherwise. Eventually, the Braxaná will realize his value as a negotiator and set him against us because he knows us so well. I guarantee you, put one telepath in the room and you'll have all the information you want. He's an open book—we designed him that way. To the right mind he'll broadcast everything he knows. And neither he nor the Braxaná will ever suspect it."

"You guarantee that."

"There's a block put in every telepath, cutting them off from conscious acknowledgment of their conditioning He couldn't admit to suspicions of that kind if they hit him in the face. As for the rest of them, Ferian has confirmed my suspicions regarding the Braxin culture—it is wholly nonpsychic. They'll never suspect a thing."

"Good. Excellent, in fact. So now we have only to wait?"

Li Pazua nods, exultant. "We have only to wait."

Harkur: A man's most sacred possession is his privacy of mind. Examine him, torture him, break him; still his thoughts are his own until he chooses to express them. This concept is one of the foundations of Braxin philosophy. Psychic ability, by its very nature, guarantees violation of this privacy. Therefore, we should not and will not tolerate it.

FIVE

There was a Braxin spy on Dari.

The news was not made public, but it was known by those who had to know. A message had been intercepted at the other end of the Azean Empire and the giant mechanical brains had decided that Dari was its destination. That was enough. Already StarControl had been mobilized, and every available Security agent moved to the sector in question. Every port on the planet was monitored. Every communications frequency was recorded and analyzed. Now there was only waiting to be done, for Dari was a political time-bomb which the wrong move might detonate.

Slowly, those few whose power or anonymity allowed them freedom of movement came to Dari. One of them was a child.

1

To a human, Laun Set was alien; true aliens, however, would rank him with human stock, His silhouette was faithful to the blueprint of the Scattered Races—a head above a torso, upright posture, two arms, two legs, all in mathematical symmetry as befit the type. His dark brown skin glowed warmly in the sunlight, thickly textured, and his eyes were stained red in the manner of the Bloodletters. And although more joints adorned his four-fingered hands than a human would consider normal, the theory of the extremity was still the same and the musculature similar.

He was naked but for a metal mesh loincloth, protective rather than ornamental. Gashes ran darkly down the length of one arm, black stripes in three lengths, nearly two hundred of them. They were marks of conquest and therefore tickets to continued life.

His opponent was ready at last, Drago, an older man from Filque. His left arm, recently broken, was barely through healing—a weakness to exploit. The arm would be slower in response, Laun Set knew—and Drago would expect him to take advantage of it.

From the packed earth of the Circle there arose to Laun Set's keen sense of smell the delicate odor of blood. It was something no outsider could ever detect, and even a Bloodletter lacked the sensitivity until the Hyarke was near beginning. He preferred packed earth for that reason, although a synthetic surface offered surer footing. Here the Blood of all the Fallen—

"Laun Set!" Drago's voice was harsh, in the manner of Darian formal speech. "Come ye to face me?"

The ritual gripped his attention. "To face you, and to feed your blood to the worthy."

"I will pour your essence out upon the earth."

Laun Set gripped his weapon tightly. "Then let us begin," he whispered fiercely.

They began to circle. The excitement gripped him utterly now, and the audience faded from his awareness. Hypersensitive feet tested the ground—damp and firm; good. Drago swung—it was a blow not meant to hit. Laun Set stepped easily out of reach, noting his opponent's manner of movement even as he revealed his own.

His weapon was long, slim, and deadly. On one end of its smooth wooden shaft was fitted a scythe-shaped blade, sharpened on both edges and straightened at the tip. The flat blade on the ada's other end was adorned with curling barbs—for the killing thrust alone, if that.

Laun Set attacked. His opponent's neat parry brought a curved blade dangerously close to his face, then down past his arm. Laun Set let it cut him before he pushed it away. It didn't matter who drew First Blood, provided it was done quickly. Better a controlled cut, unthreatening in the mutual courtesy of the Hyarke, than a Bloodletter desperate for this red inspiration, therefore dangerous in his chaos.

Laun Set's nostrils flared as he breathed in the odor of his own blood. It was a drug to him and his kind, that almost imperceptible smell, and it would inspire his reflexes to their greatest capacity. From the earth a thousand voices seemed to ring, and from his soul, which had absorbed the strength of over a hundred men, reflexes came which were not his own, knowledge which he had never learned. He was one with the hundred, in the Circle, serving the Hyarke, and all were centered on the kill.

He waited until Drago's eyes glowed with the Change before he struck again. Less would dishonor the other man's experience. A half dozen clashing, gleaming exchanges taught him the man's basic reflexes while exhibiting his own.

There was nothing now but the Hyarke, the bloodsport which was the soul of Dari. The Circle pulsed about him, a physical boundary pounding in rhythm with his own heartbeat. He had moved beyond conscious thought, into that nether world where the body moves faster than reason and trained instinct must take over.

They traded blows; sometimes one or the other cut, more often each was parried. Blood mixed with sweat and dripped to the ground. Occasionally the clash of steel bespoke a blow which might have left a man alive to conquer but deprived him of the right to progeny. The blood gave them strength and the ritual gave them endurance and they fought under the hot sun forever.

Then there was an opening. Laun Set saw it, let the awareness flow through his limbs and become action; without thought, he struck. The shaft of his ada tangled in Drago's legs and the other's faulty balance failed to compensate. He fell, and death awaited him. The long curved blade of Laun Set's weapon was turned toward him, its back to the dirt, and as Drago fell he impaled himself upon its gleaming length. He cried once, gloriously, a song of dying to accompany the outpouring of his lifeblood, and with that cry, in pain and glory, expired.

Laun Set waited while the essence of Drago's strength flowed forth from his body. Energy pulsed inside the Circle, free of the dead man but not of that boundary. Then the victor stooped beside his kill. "Worthy one," he whispered, cupping his hands so that the wet redness flowed into them. Drago's life-essence danced in the red fluid and strengthened Lauri Set as the latter drank it.

Then he stood back from the Fallen. Two young Bloodletters had entered the Circle and were rubbing his body with drugged oils which would combat exhaustion and compensate for the overdrive state he had fought in. They were all coming now, the spectators who were Bloodletters, for the Sharing, while those who were not of that brotherhood hurried to vacate the stadium, reverent of the ritual.

The two young men who had brought the drug knelt next and tasted the blood of the Fallen. Others knelt after them, touching dark hands to the killing wound, tasting Drago's strength and skill from their fingertips. Somewhere outside the, Circle the audience was gone, leaving no visible witness to the Sharing but those who were entitled to indulge in its mysteries.

A horizontal cut was made on Laun Set's arm and dye powder was rubbed into it. It was a long mark, for Drago had killed over a hundred opponents. Already the life force in the Circle was ebbing, absorbed into the dozen men of the Sharing. And as it was drunk by the last of them the Circle fell, becoming once more only a line on the packed, blood-soaked earth.

The ritual was over.

In the shadows, well hidden, a human girl smiled.

2

No one could have mistaken Torzha er Litz for a civilian. Her crisp stride bristled with military overtones and her eyes took in the details of her surroundings with sharp efficiency. Because she was Azean she was tall, lean, and golden; because she was Torzha er Litz she was impressive.

"I've come to see the Governor."

The native receptionist looked up at her with infuriating slowness.

"You are who?"

"Starcommander Torzha er Litz, from the *Vengeance*." She spoke slowly, assuming from his accent that his Azean was poor. Nevertheless, he seemed to take an interminable amount of time to absorb that information, and longer to get the Governor's appointment schedule on the screen.

She tapped one booted foot impatiently and looked around her. In structure the offices looked like those in any Azean building—simple in design, relying more on color than three-dimensional detail for decoration. But the colors were out-of-date and Torzha found them unpleasantly garish.

"Starcommander Torzha Litz," the secretary read slowly. Torzha suspected he knew just how much insult he was doing her by denying her the subname. She decided she disliked him.

"No appointment," he concluded.

"I *know* I don't have an appointment. StarControl should have called. Here—" She pulled her orders out of her half-jacket "—this will explain."

It took him a century, it seemed, to go over the cellose sheets.

She wanted to tell him: *Damn it, man, you've got a translator in your desk, run it through that!* But Ebre had asked her to bend over backward to avoid offending the natives, and she would certainly try. At least for the first day.

Just as her patience was reaching its end, the door behind the secretary slid open. Governor li Dara smiled broadly as he saw her. "Starcommander! I thought I heard someone out here. Please come in."

Without a glance at the desk she swept up her orders and followed him. "Your staff—" she began.

"Shh. Not here." He led her down a long corridor, to an office at the end. When they were inside, he made sure the door was well sealed behind them. Only then would he speak.

"I'm really sorry about that. They're usually good, you know, but your rank must have been just too tempting. Kir Lao speaks perfect Azean and is outstandingly efficient—anything else, I'm afraid, was strictly for your benefit. Ver?"

"Please." The drink was standing ready and she accepted a steaming cupful from him. She looked over the office, a simple room decorated in what she thought was a poor mixture of Azean and Darian. A glance out the window revealed a public demonstration on the street below. "Azeans go home," read one sign, and others had longer slogans which included such descriptive passages as "imperialistic parasites" and "alien filthmongers."

"Nice place you have here," she commented.

He followed her gaze out of the window and grimaced. "They don't actually rebel, you know, and the Treaty of Conquest gives them the right to assemble . . . like that." He looked up at her. "It goes without saying we're not popular here."

"I gathered that."

He sighed. "Which, of course, is nine-tenths of the problem. The standard list of things to do when one suspects there is a spy amongst the natives is invalid in this case. One wrong move, one overtly imperialistic gesture, and we just might lose this planet as a passive base."

"We could simply obliterate it."

He laughed, on the assumption that she was kidding him, then stopped when he saw her face. *Surely,* he hoped, *she's not serious.* "I'd be out of a job," he offered.

She gave him a faint smile. "Then it's out of the question." She looked out over the horizon. "No, I'm well aware of what this planet is worth as a base of operations, and equally aware of how easily we could lose it. That's why I was sent. Do you know exactly what a transculturalist is, Governor?"

He nodded. "We have a few working for us here. Translators, mostly."

She shook her head. "It's far more complicated than that. Simple translation can be done by computer. But in each language there are words and concepts that don't have a direct counterpart in any other. A transculturalist is one who can take the abstract ideas contained in one language and express them effectively in another. Which requires, of course, a complete understanding of both cultures. The primary job of a transculturalist is obviously translation. But there are other skills."

She turned away from the window and faced him. "My specialty is Braxin-Azean exchange, which only a handful of people have mastered. StarControl sent me here in the hope that I could reason out where your spy is likely to be hiding." She smiled indulgently. "This in addition to your other efforts, of course."

"Yes, of course." He obviously had his doubts about the approach but wasn't going to admit it. "If you'll tell me what you need in the way of facilities. . . ."

"A private office, standard computer access, a staff of . . . say three people, preferably Azean, answerable only to me." She recalled her reception. "Make that *definitely* Azean. And for a start, a copy of the customs records for the past eight Standard Days. I want to see who's been coming and going here. Starcontrol never should have left the ports open—" She waved his objection to silence. "Yes, I know, we can't infuriate the locals. Did you say in your request that you had a copy of the transmission?"

"I do." It was on top of the desk and he gave it to her, a thin celchip recording and its printed translation. She ignored the written text and slid the clear chip into place in the desk's decoder. The clicks and whirs of an interstellar code came forth from the speaker.

"I see," she said thoughtfully. "It *is* the Eman code, which is very strange because Braxi hasn't used it for years. And the augmentation—" She leaned over the desk to read it.

"StarControl said something about that. I can't pretend to understand."

"Simply that for reasons involving the science of interstellar communication, it was very likely we'd pick this up. I can't believe they didn't know that." She sipped her ver. "Not like them at all. The Braxins are many things, but rarely are they careless." She shrugged. "But then, that's why I'm here. Have you translators?"

"Dari-Azean transculturalists."

"Even better! I'll need the services of one. And a guide."

"I'll get you one. For any place in particular?"

"Yes." She looked out the window, as if by studying the faces of the demonstrators she would unearth some clue. "I want to see this blood-ritual, this Hyarke. I have a feeling. . . ." She looked back at him and laughed, lightly. "But I won't bore you with that until I have some more to go by. I should warn you now, even in war I tend to operate on hunches."

"Your record speaks for itself."

"Sometimes I think it's the only way to second-guess them," she mused. "As if they act in response to primal instincts, rather than reason."

He took a last drink of his ver and collapsed the cup. "There's a Hyarke in Toul tonight, now that I think of it, and I might have someone here who could take you, if I catch him before he goes off duty. Will you excuse me for a moment?"

"Please," she responded, waving her assent. When he was gone she went over the problem in her mind, and she laughed softly.

"One Braxin somewhere on this very large planet," she reflected, "and no real clues. Well, it could be worse."

She thought about that for a few minutes and then admitted, "But I don't see how."

3

He was posing as a Bloodletter, a ritual killer. Thus far his natural Braxin arrogance had aided his disguise; in any other strata of society it would have focused suspicion upon him, but in the tight circle of the Hyarke his Braxin nature was quite at home.

These were men who talked of gutted bodies at the dinner table, and whose palates were best lubricated by human blood. They carried the weapon of their trade with them at all times, long and slim and sharp on all its metal edges. About their necks they wore medallions with the single legend, "As is the blood, so is the man." And they lived on top of society, needing only to ask for an item to receive it gratis, to mention a need and a dozen Darians would beg for the chance to fulfill it.

Varik was a capable man. The eight years he had devoted to learning Darian and to training in Hyarke combat had proven both successful and necessary. It was true that he lacked any insight into the blood-trance which allowed them access to their ultimate fighting capacity, but the ritual suited his violent nature and his superior Braxin musculature, despite the adaptive surgery which disguised it, gave him an edge which balanced the scales. And although the risk was high—one failure meant death—he found pleasure in the role he was playing.

Braxi was done with him, but he didn't know it. He had been a rebel and it was considered too dangerous to merely execute him, for those groups which rose against the Braxaná—those few which were not crushed in their birthgiving—knew how to manipulate a martyrdom and would not hesitate to do so. So they had trained him for a higher purpose, removing him from his cultural context to aid in the destruction of Azea, and thus had made it clear to his compatriots that all men have a price: even Varik would serve the Braxaná. The others lost heart or nerve and were quietly murdered. Varik, seduced by the dual promise of adventure and elitism, was sent to Dari as a spy, in which capacity he had been successful. But the planet was also his tomb. Braxi's intercepted message had been no accident; Varik had fulfilled his mission and was being discarded.

Azea would punish Braxi's upstart.

4

Evening had come by the time Laun Set left the tavern. His body ached pleasantly from the attention of women and wine still fogged his thoughts, but his step was firm and even as he walked the Darian streets.

Night had fallen and darkness enveloped the city. Dari's three moons were shrouded in cloud-cover and did little but cast long shadows across the street. From one of these, suddenly and silently, a human girl emerged.

"Out of my way, human!" He punctuated his command by spitting at her feet; nonetheless, she held her ground.

"Greetings of the Blood Night," she said in ritual Darian.

He tried to dodge around her, but she remained in his way. He had a momentary vision of sweeping his ada into aggressive position and forcing her from his path, and he smiled at the thought of that moonlit blade etching a white path through her alien insides. But reality did not allow for such things; the humans, damn them, were not to be killed.

"Do you want something of me?" he asked finally. "Or is this some new sport?"

"I would like to talk to you."

"I have nothing to say to your kind."

He tried to push by her and in doing so brushed against her shoulder. As they came in contact he stopped, uncertain. Where had he been going, and why in such a hurry?

She moved away from him and the memory returned.

"You touched my mind!"

She nodded.

Against his will he was intrigued. "A telepath?"

She nodded. Her eyes were dark and wide and watched him closely as he considered. He'd had very little contact with humans and none with psychics. She was slight of build and appeared almost malnourished—hardly a threat to him. And she was clearly not Azean, for she lacked the height and golden skin of that accursed race. What was a moment of conversation, anyway?

"Talk."

"Not here. In private."

He laughed, loudly. "You have nerve, human! Very well. Since you speak my language, I'll let you do it where you want. Follow me."

With the practiced eye of a Bloodletter he analyzed her walk. She kept up with him despite the disparity in their sizes. *No one has ever allowed her her natural pace, he observed. And that stiffness is not right for a child, human or no. And the look in her eyes—I have seen that in Bloodletters just before the Hyarke.*

He took her to a dark quarter of the city and into an inn. His ada proclaimed his status and the inn's owner jumped to serve him. Two women arose from their seats to offer themselves for his pleasure; one left a companion who nodded his understanding. Laun Set waved them away.

"Just a room," he ordered.

Keys and directions were delivered to him. The human child, he noticed, was staying discreetly in the shadows. But as she walked across the lighted floor to follow him, a wave of exclamation marked their progress.

The room was small and was meant to be rented by the hour. Not until they were both inside with the door safely closed did he face her again.

Her eyes were wide and bright, the dark gray of unpolished steel. Her hair, the color of fresh blood, hung braided down her back. Her skin was so pale he would have been surprised to learn that she had ever been out in the sunlight.

"Now that you've done such wonders for my reputation," he snapped, "what is it you want?"

She moved until she stood with her back against the door. "First things first, Bloodletter. All out in the open. I'm an Azean."

He looked her over, then laughed unpleasantly. "No. I may not be human, but I know what Azeans look like."

"Would you like to see my racial papers?"

He tightened. *"Get out of here."*

She stayed where she was, her body blocking the door. "No. I want to talk to you, Bloodletter—but not under false pretenses."

"If you're Azean, I have nothing to say to you. So if you don't leave, I will."

He moved toward the door, but she refused to get out of his way. For a moment he nearly lost control and struck out at her. But he was not that much of a fool; to strike out at a child of Dari's conquering race would be an invitation to political execution.

And something in her expression impressed him, more so when he realized what it was.

She would be doing the same thing even if the law didn't protect her, he realized.

"You'll listen to me," she said firmly. "And then I'll go. But by Hasha, you'll hear me out first!"

He glared. "I spit on your Firstborn."

"I know. That's irrelevant."

He studied the raw nerve in her eyes and knew he could respect that. "All right," he said finally. "I'm listening."

She smiled; there was cruelty in the expression. "I'm hunting a man, Bloodletter, and I want your help. A Braxin, here on Dari."

He laughed derisively. "I'm not interested in your Azean—"

"Posing as a Bloodletter."

A cold stillness settled over them.

"That's not possible."

"I'm afraid it is."

"No. An alien in the Circle . . . it couldn't happen."

She shrugged. "As you wish."

"He's fought?"

"At least once since I've been here. And he didn't feel inexperienced."

"You . . . sensed this?"

"Oh, yes. I focused on him days ago."

"Can't you find him the same way?"

She shook her head. "There's a difference between picking up a combination of Braxin psychology and active violence, and knowing exactly where it's coming from. I can only focus on him in the first place because of an . . . affinity . . . I have for his mind-set. Telepathy has its limitations, and my training is far from complete."

"So. The Azeans need our help."

"No, Bloodletter. Not the Azeans. Only myself." She took a deep breath, and he thought he could feel the intensity within her: his imagination, of course. "I'm hunting. And I need local assistance."

Laun Set considered. The thought of working with a human was repellent to him, but the alternatives were loathsome. A human fighting Darians in the Circle defiled the proud Hyarke tradition. And as vehemently as he detested Azea, Laun Set knew that under Braxin rule the Hyarke would be the first thing to go. No—better Azea than that.

"What do you want me to do?" he asked at last.

"Listen." She smiled her triumph, and in that moment looked nothing like a child. "I'll tell you."

5

"I have that information for you, Starcommander."

Torzha looked up from her lists. "Thank you—just leave it with me."

Two days. Two local, very long, useless days. She had seen a Hyarke and her most basic question had been answered—she was certain the Braxin would have some connection with that ritual. No other subculture on the planet offered what that one did to one raised among the enemy; of that she was certain. Then again (she thought for the hundredth time), Braxi could have been cunning enough to anticipate her and to do the unexpected. No. Cunning, yes—but also vain. A Braxin would never pose as a passive, downtrodden nonhuman. Everything about the Hyarke appealed to the Braxin mentality and it would be the first place a Braxin spy would choose to assimilate. But that still left the whole planet. . . .

Her office was busy tracking down the names of all Dari's Bloodletters, along with their vital statistics. It was not an easy job. There was no central register to which these men belonged, and, in addition, their population changed nightly as the Hyarke continued to take its toll. One man she had suspected had died while she considered his records. And for that matter, did they know for a fact that the Braxin wasn't already dead?

Unsurprisingly, the customs lists had been of no use whatsoever. She had asked for clarification on one entry, more out of curiosity than anything else.

"We couldn't get much on her," the secretary continued. "The Institute has her files locked up tight."

"That's all right. This will be fine. Thank you."

When he left, she glanced idly through the notes; then stopped, her eyes narrowing. She started to read more carefully. The child had come from the Institute with Medical Clearance—somehow Director li Pazua had convinced officials that a journey to Dari was required for her mental well-being. Yet she had come alone, a mere child on a hostile planet. Potential ratings high, intellectually and otherwise. Transcultural ratings in seven combinations—well, that was to be expected from a telepath-in-training. Parents high in Security . . . the great Darmel lyu Tukone, no less. They were poisoned by Braxins when she was six. (She remembered the incident, did not remember there being a child. Then again, hadn't there been some scandal with that pair? Yes, and over a child.) Then she had suffered from psychosomatic blindness, for five years, ending—

Torzha read the date again, startled. Twenty days ago? But the Institute on Llornu was ten days' travel from Dari—that would mean she had regained her sight and immediately begun traveling here.

And she had been seen at a number of Hyarke rituals.

With sudden determination Torzha closed the folder and called her assistant back in. "Find out the exact whereabouts of this . . ." she consulted the file ". . . Anzha lyu. And get me cosmetics, a wig, clothing, et cetera. Bad enough being human here, without being Azean also."

He bowed his respect and left to obey. She leaned her elbows on the desk and mused: unrelated? She doubted it.

6

Dawn cast long shadows across the Circle. The packed earth had been dampened the night before and now was ready for combat.

Safe behind her dark complexion and Suakkan clothing, Torzha surveyed the crowd.

Row after row of Darian flesh filled the stands, fidgeting in impatience. Here and there a human sat—Rahnese, on vacation; Ikna, doing sociological research. There were a few Azeans present who had been stationed on the planet long enough to know how to act—or at least, they thought they did. The seats next to them were left empty until there were no other seats left to fill.

And the child was there.

Unobserved from across the arena, Torzha studied her. She had put in magnifying lenses under her Suakkan irises and now tensed to bring them into focus. The girl was small and delicately boned, sickly if one assumed an Azean standard. But there was no reason to do that; genetic proportion to the contrary, her appearance was solidly alien. Perhaps she was also not as young as she looked—what standard was one to use in judging?

The Bloodletters had come into the Circle.

The girl's clothing was a nondescript mixture of Imperial and Darian—no doubt an attempt to fade into the background without antagonizing the locals. She wore nothing to indicate her power. Was this because she didn't want anyone to know or simply because she hadn't yet earned the symbolic red cord with an FT rating?

So many questions—and no easy answers.

It was a long Hyarke and Torzha endured it. She found the entire ritual distasteful to an extreme and its cultural glorification repelled her. She had no love of blood and had seen quite enough of it in forty years of military service to last her a lifetime. She feigned enthusiasm, though, to guarantee her safety—the Darians had no tolerance for objective observers and on a number of occasions had killed such in bloodfrenzy. The fact that Ebre might avenge her death by obliterating the entire planet was no substitute for continued life; she leaned forward as they did, shared their tension, and gasped in concert with the thousands about her when the spectacle merited such response.

She was not sorry when it ended.

The local fighter—she recalled his name as Laun Set—was victorious, and fellow Bloodletters came to rub drugged oils into his body. That interested her far more than the combat. Apparently they managed some mental state in which the body functioned in overdrive, being faster and more dexterous than normal and completely denying fatigue. When the ritual was over, the mental support collapsed and the body was simply overworked and abused; without drugs to ease the transition back, one could easily die of overexertion.

The child was not leaving. Torzha noticed with surprise that she had remained in the stands as the general populace filed obediently out. She had meant to catch her outside the stadium and talk to her there, but if the girl was staying through the Sharing then something unusual was up. Torzha backed into a waiting shadow to watch.

With seeming confidence, the girl descended from the stands to the outer edge of the Circle and waited.

Darian custom forbade any non-Bloodletter from observing the Sharing. Of course, some did—it wasn't hard to do. But no one would dare watch from out in the open, least of all descend to the actual arena.

Apparently some of the Bloodletters were arguing the same point. One of the oil-bearers pointed at her in fury and directed a scathing tirade at the victor, who merely shrugged. Another spoke more softly yet seemed to have a similar objection to her presence.

But with a wave of his reddened hand Laun Set silenced them all. What he said to them, Torzha could not hear and would not have understood. Yet when he gestured first toward the girl and then toward the fallen Bloodletter, his language was universal.

The Darians avoided her as she entered the Circle, some respectfully, some in fury. Even Torzha was stunned as the child knelt by the bleeding body, speaking the ritual words (she presumed) and cupping her hands to catch the alien blood. Laun Set stood over her like a guardian, challenging with his reddened eyes anyone who might interfere.

Then it was over and the girl withdrew, as the others had, to the side of the Circle. The Sharing continued despite the interruption. One by one the Bloodletters tasted the essence of the Fallen. Some spoke softly to Laun Set before or after and a few expressed their anger more openly, but all, save one, drank. That one had apparently been insulted beyond his capacity for tolerance by her participation and he left without touching the loser's body. He was wounded, Torzha deduced from the bandage on his hand, and perhaps his temporary inability to compete made his temper shorter than usual.

The girl left with the victor, a part of the informal court that surrounded him. It was not a good time for Torzha to approach her, so she set an aide on her trail to determine her business and some way of finding her again.

Which, Torzha thought, was just as well. She needed time to think this over.

7

The image of Director Ebre ni Kahv wavered briefly, then stablized as military relay was synchronized. That was one benefit of working for StarControl, Torzha thought; insync communication was next to impossible without such a relay.

"I have good news for you," he told her. "Our negotiators have managed a conditional Peace in your sector. So you can continue your work on Dari without feeling that you should be back at the Border."

Torzha was amused. "Were you going to withdraw me from service here just because of the War?"

"No—but now you don't have to worry about it." He waved her objection to silence. "I know you, Torzha. Don't tell me it hasn't bothered you to be planetbound while we fought for Oria."

"Just because I was senior officer in that sector is no reason to assume I wanted to be there."

"Sarcasm acknowledged. Now how do I get you to train someone else in that damnable Braxin culture so I don't have to beg for peace every time we need you somewhere else?"

"Send some free time my way."

"Out of my own stock of it?—are you ever going to sponsor, Torzha?"

She sighed. The question and its answer had become a ritual

with which she was too familiar. "Yes, Ebre. Someday soon. As soon as a suitable person turns up."

"Suitable people do not 'turn up'—they're found. Start looking. The system exists for a reason, you know. It'll give you something to do in Peacetime. Now, as for the present problem: we've picked up another transmission."

She leaned forward, alert. "Tell me you have the hemisphere of receipt."

"I'll do you one better. It was timed to hit surface when the smaller continent in the northern hemisphere came into the line of transmission. How's that?"

She exhaled dramatically. "Ebre, there can't be more than a hundred suspects in that area."

"If you can't handle it—"

"I wasn't being facetious. That's a workable number. It's the capital continent, Bit Nua-San—you do mean that one, don't you?"

"That's the name I've got."

"There aren't that many Circles here—not to mention my own base of operations is right there—Ebre, I owe you dinner on Ikn."

"You can't afford it."

"Since when?"

"Not at the restaurant I'm thinking of. But if you can clean up this matter without losing us Dari, I'll take you there myself. Now, on to this other matter. He frowned. "Is it really important?"

"Is it a problem?"

He sighed. "Yes and no. The Institute is always a problem. I've dealt with them before, remember. Quite frankly, if they disappeared tomorrow, I wouldn't waste more than a minute on regret. Fanatics, all of them—I don't trust them, Torzha, and I don't think you should either. The degree to which their current Director is blind and deaf to military procedure is exceeded only by his passion for secrecy. Sometimes I wish he would interfere with Security, so that I could get Imperial sanction to squeeze his damned secrets out of him.

"Now as for this girl: just how important is she? Does she have any real bearing on the matter at hand?"

"I believe she may be looking for our Braxin."

Said simply, it had the desired effect. "If that's the case . . . Hasha! The breach in security that implies—"

"Is alarming, I know. And just as threatening as the spy himself.

Tell me: is there anything to keep the Institute from . . . say, eavesdropping on military communication?"

"A dozen and a half things—and none of them certain. Custom and etiquette, mostly. Actually, now that you mention it, nothing we can rely on."

She sighed. "So we've no idea what she's after, or how much she knows, or who, if anyone, is backing her. She could interfere with my work—blow the whole thing wide open! Or she could help me; I simply don't know. I need information."

"You'll have it." Off the screen, out of sight, he was calling up the proper longfiles and coding them for transmission. "I'm sending you everything I have; it's a lot to wade through, I know, but I don't want to try to anticipate what will or won't be useful. As for my reference notes . . . do you want to hear them?"

"Please."

"The child comes from the Institute for the Acceleration of Human Psychic Evolution, one of the most prestigious and certainly the most powerful of the Genetic Centers. All doubletalk aside, it owns her. Founded by fanatic scientists in 10,027, based upon the assumption that telepathic fluency would be the next natural step in human evolution. Their goal was—and still is—a combination of psychic and genetic science, intended to isolate the codes which make telepathy possible and introduce them into the race as a whole, while at the same time developing a training program that would enable people to get through the transition period with minimum trauma. This is their one and only goal, and all other concerns—including, I believe, loyalty to the state—are subordinate to it. First Functional Telepath trained, 11,287; the title implies conscious control over a broad range of psychic skills. There currently exist, in descending order of ability: Six Probes, twenty-three Functional Telepaths, and seventy Communicants. The rest are glorified psychics who have been trained to make some practical use of their ability, usually in response to one of the 'actives.' Nine thousand and twenty-seven of those."

"Only that many?"

"Apparently the Institute will only certify someone as 'psychic' when he or she can respond to non-physical stimuli with one hundred percent reliability—not to mention accuracy. A tall order, I gather. Which is not to say that there aren't some hundred thousand hopefuls hovering about the Institute's homeworld, hoping their talent will suddenly come into focus. Or something like that."

He glanced at his notes. "Currently psychogenetics is focused on finding the so-called 'trigger sequences,' secondary genetic codes which cause the controlling sequences to become active."

"Anzha lyu," she prompted.

"Parents Azean—wait, you have all that, don't you?" She nodded. "Potential telepathy rated 9.99—meaning they expect her to come into as much power as they imagine possible. She's halfway through basic training for an FT rating and hasn't got Probe potential, whatever that means. At her present level, Director li Pazua informs me, she's more effective than all but three others. Trained by a man I sent to Braxi, by the way, so there's no hope of help from that end. Records on her training aren't available to 'outsiders.' Li Pazua sent me a standard psychefile; edited, I'm sure. Of note are an obsessive hatred of all things Braxin and potential zeymophobia. And of course, the period of hysterical blindness."

"Ended not thirty days ago. How is that possible?"

"I quote: 'Psychosomatic sensory distortion among telepaths may be seen as a symptom of deep psychological disturbance, but should not be equated with actual sensory disability. A telepath is quite capable of experiencing the world through the senses of his/her tutors, and in fact often does so.' Li Pazua's cover letter," he explained. "It goes on to explain why the situation existed, in what ways they fought to correct it, and why her sudden unexplained recovery ought to be encouraged."

"I see."

"Useful?"

"Could be. Anything else?"

"On the girl? Just a warning. All telepaths are impressed with a Higher Purpose of some kind; in plain Azean, they're conditioned to serve the cause of psychogenetics in some way that takes advantage of their individual strengths and weaknesses."

"What's hers?"

"The Institute doesn't reveal such things; it would undermine the confidentiality of their training, li Pazua claims. In the case of the man we sent to Braxi, they conditioned him to serve the Empire . . . but I'd be very surprised if they didn't throw in a command or two for their own benefit. Be careful, Torzha. There are a lot of variables here."

"I see that."

"If she *is* telling the Braxin . . . Hasha, I don't like it. Take the matter into your own hands, if you can."

She nodded. "I intend to."

"You've got a lot to think about, so I'll let you go. Call in regularly."

"I will." She always did.

It was time for some Braxin logic.

8

Morning light played over the city of Kaleysh. In the streets children fought with mock adas and played rhythmic games with balls and ropes, chanting rhymes which enumerated the most vulnerable parts of the body. Few adults walked abroad; there had been a Hyarke the night before and most had attended. Now, worn out by the frenzy of witnessing such exertion, they lay abed in half-sleep, listening to their children chant the names of blood-spilling arteries in all the innocence of youth.

The Bloodletter himself was awake, moving with certain footing which belied the previous night's exertion. He had whispered a time and address to the young human girl and was going himself to that rendezvous. If the chants of the children awoke any memories of his own youth it was not evident on his face, which showed only a growing hostility and—perhaps—fear.

There was indeed a Braxin in the Circle. Laun Set knew it. The magnitude of the sacrilege was beyond expression; the need to act was irrepressible.

He passed through the inn's common room with a gesture that drove back his would-be admirers and went to the room he had described to her. If others noted their meeting, it was of little concern to him. There were worse crimes on Dari than talking to human children—and one of them had been committed.

She saw his face when he entered and reached out tendrils of thought to read his surface emotions. In their preparations of the night before they had mind-shared; now it was easy for her to read him.

"You didn't really believe me," she said. "But now you do."

The rage which had been fermenting inside him boiled to the surface. "No Bloodletter would have denied the Sharing—no matter who or what participated!" He remembered with pain the ravaged Circle, torn where the alien had walked through it, pouring precious life through its gaping wound. "No Bloodletter would have left—no one could have—"

His voice broke and he stopped. There was no way to express what was inside him, and he could only hope that she could read it directly. "No Bloodletter could have walked through a living Circle," he whispered.

"The mind of the Braxin," she said softly, "adapts easily to bloodshed. But it can't comprehend an active spiritual reality. He lives among your people. He kills them. But he doesn't understand them."

Laun Set looked at her, his face set in hatred. "He's going to die."

"That's what I intend."

"We're behind you. I didn't talk to the others. I couldn't. But I don't have to. Kyar—" he used the Darian word for huntress in the place of her hated Azean name "—they knew, as I knew, what had been done. They won't question you."

She smiled. "More than I could have hoped for."

His tone was one of anguish. "How could he even *pretend* to be one of us and not know?" He shut his eyes tightly against the memory. "Kyar, if you could truly understand what happened. . . ."

"I *know.* I saw, through your eyes. Through the eyes of all of you." She touched him gently, let him feel the sincerity through the contact. "I will avenge you. I promise."

He forced himself to relax and looked about the small room. After a moment he found the new-made ada, gleaming still with the oils of its creation, leaning upright against the doorframe. Stiffly he walked over to it, laying his own aside and hefting its lesser weight. "Dir Salau was willing to make this for you."

"Given your recommendation. He said to tell you that the proportions were unusual but correct."

He looked at her, then again at the weapon. "A bit long for your height, but he probably meant that to give you more reach. Yes, it's good." He stroked the shaft with pleasure; for the first time in a day and a night he smiled. "Pride in workmanship exceeds the bounds of racial hostility, I gather. This is excellently crafted."

She walked over to where he stood and touched a finger to the glistening metal. "So I can keep my promise to you," she said quietly. "And to the Bloodletters."

Little killer, he thought. *I do not envy your prey.* "When can we begin?"

She looked up at him. "Now?"

He handed her the weapon.

9

It bothered Varik, that scene with the girl.

If his culture didn't condemn any psychic curiosity, he might have realized that what disturbed him was not what had actually, happened, but rather an inner reaction to the telepathic probing he had undergone while watching the ritual. Inside, he knew—but on the surface, no part of his Braxin self would admit that something psychic had touched him, marking him.

But that child . . . that god-blessed child! He knew what bad form it had been to leave the Sharing, but to continue once a woman (or girl, he reminded himself) had participated went against everything in his Braxin nature. Where did she come from, anyway, and what was she doing there? Had he mistaken the custom somehow? Only Bloodletters could come to the Sharing, and only male Darians could do the Hyarke.

More than that was wrong. As surely as something buried deep inside him knew that he had been touched and examined mentally, some part of him also knew the purpose of that examination. He was being hunted. (Why did he keep using that word, rather than sought, or chased, or uncovered? Why did "hunted" just seem *right*?) The source of the knowledge was, of course, hidden from him, but the hunch was so strong that he had decided to trust it.

Braxi had not responded to his plea for help. It had surprised him at first, but then he realized what a fool he'd been all along to trust the Braxaná. He'd figured that as long as he was serving their purpose he was safe—that *was* the way to deal with them, wasn't it?—but either he'd been wrong in the first place or had simply ceased to be useful.

He was not bitter. He was angry at himself, but not bitter. For perhaps the first time he saw with open eyes the game they'd been playing. He thought they'd been manipulating each other when in fact he had done exactly what they'd wanted and received nothing for it.

He wished that he were home again, to carry out his original plans. But they would never let him return. Or maybe they would, to see what scorn his new body would receive, to be amused while an "alien" tried to stir the ruling race to rebellion.

They had trapped him perfectly and now he knew it.

There was nowhere for him to go and nothing he could do. The transmissions from Braxi would come whether he was there to receive them or not, and someday sheer chance would favor Azea and he would be discovered. Fear ate at him now and he had no way of bettering it. For the first time ever he came to terms with the crippling folly that the Social Codes were. Fear was a Valid Emotion, a useful warning sign, a crucial limitating factor in the struggle for self-preservation, and he had never learned to suppress it. Now, when he had to, he didn't know how. The Braxin in him wanted to enjoy the last of his life—for he knew now that an end was coming soon, and an unpleasant one—but fear paralyzed him and in his depression he could seek no pleasure.

For the first time he noticed how many more humans there were at the Hyarke, and saw his first Azeans there. And that child . . . something was wrong inside when he thought of her, something that made him cold and afraid, but he couldn't bring it to the surface of his mind to analyze it. He kept tying to convince himself that it was paranoia, but he had never been paranoid. That more than anything told him how wrong things really were.

He tried to leave Dari under his own power. That was when he discovered that all ports were being monitored, and just short of surrendering his identification he turned and fled the transport center.

He was scared. And rather than live scared, he decided to act—even if nothing constructive could be done. It was the waiting, more than anything, that was killing him.

10

Torzha lay still upon the Darian bed, dressed in her white under-uniform, immobile in her concentration.

If I were a Braxin (she asked herself for the thousandth time), *where would I be now?*

I would be at the Hyarke, or in some place connected with it. I would view the rest of Darian society with scorn and avoid it entirely. I would convince myself that I respected the Bloodletters as true men, because their ritual reeks of barbarism and the Braxin venerate barbarism. But deep inside I would have a warrior's scorn for any system that regularly kills off half of its most skilled fighters.

I would fight in the Hyarke, obviously well. But no matter how well I fight, no matter how often I survive, the very nature of the Hyarke defies Braxin tradition.

I am not willing to die to serve my people. I am willing to die if the odds of doing so are the price of my amusement—they counted on that when they sent me. But the odds in the Hyarke are never better than fifty percent, and the system of challenges can force me to fight when I would rather not do so. I will fight. I will find pleasure in fighting. But I am not willing to fight continually, to risk constant involvement.

Something pulled at Torzha's awareness, crying for attention, but she couldn't grasp it. Determined, she continued her reasoning.

I must have an excuse for non-participation. A Bloodletter is expected to respond positively to any challenge. It would be awkward to have to explain my reason every time, hence my excuse must be an obvious one.

She paused.

If I were injured, I would not have to compete.

If the injury were obvious, no one would challenge me.

But—here's the catch. Say I feign a broken arm, dress it with cast and sling as is the local custom, since Dari won't have anything to do with extrastellar medicine. I'm here to pick up on the military frequencies; therefore I have the equipment to do so. It can be found. I have to hide it someplace, returning to it periodically. That might be noticed. I don't want to be immobilized by anything, in case I need to act to save myself. Thus a cast is undesirable. I would need something which would not actually hinder movement, yet which would imply inability to participate in the Hyarke. . . .

It came to her suddenly and she sat up, startled by the memory.

The Bloodletter who left the Sharing had been bandaged on his right hand.

She pictured the Circle as she had seen it. He stood in anger as he watched the child participate, his hand bandaged over finger-splints as if it had been broken. If it were his dominant hand, then he was badly handicapped. Any Darian—any human, for that matter, would immediately assume this to be the case—especially the Azeans, who had made right-handedness a genetic standard centuries ago. But if his left hand were dominant, as was the case with most Braxins, then the bandaging would be a mere nuisance. . . .

She reached for her half-jacket with one hand and the visiphone switch with the other.

"Get me the Governor," she ordered. "Quickly."

11

When morning came, he moved. He had dreamed of traps, their jaws set with gleaming teeth, and had awakened in a sweat of fear and desperation. Leaving his possessions behind, he had bolted forth from his apartment and out into the street. And not a moment too soon. His last view of the building, as he turned a corner out of sight, was the flash of a white uniform approaching its door.

They had come for him.

He ran the streets, turning where there was a concealing alleyway, trusting that they would think he had done the fastest thing and taken public transportation in his flight. He did not know where he was going until his pounding feet took him there. Yes, the Records office—his instincts had been good. There would be hostages there aplenty, and a building full of files the government would not want destroyed. He might yet make it through this. . . .

He was not challenged at the door, though there were guards, nor did anyone question his presence as he bolted up the staircase to the most important offices. He was a Bloodletter. They did not even question him as he forced them from their work, and although they gave him questioning glances as he herded them into an inner office and locked the doors about him, no one sought to stop him.

Savdi! he swore, thinking of the stupid, harmless herd animals of his homeland. They were all savdi, and worse—were there no men on this planet?

Fifty office workers were his hostages—common Darians who were of no particular use to anyone. Yet the Azeans, ruled by their self-righteous defense of all human life, would not dare to drag him forcibly from his chosen citadel lest he hurt them. And of course, the local political situation made things even more favorable for him than they would be otherwise.

Contrary to appearances, Varik had no illusions as to his fate. What he *did* intend was to chose the manner of his dying. Not for him a crawling surrender to the white-haired enemy, nor the pointless gesture of suicide. If he had to die, he would do so in a blaze of glory. All the better if in doing it he could shatter Azea's tenuous hold on this planet and drag its diplomacy down with him. That was a Braxin death!

He paced nervously, incessantly. Surely the news was out by now! He went on the local frequencies himself, transmitting a distress call no local would actually have made. Azean Security could put two and two together—couldn't they? They knew who and what he was, that was clear. Wouldn't they realize, when they heard of a Bloodletter barricading himself in this building, what had happened?

The noise of the Darian streets had been a regular background to his thoughts since early morning. Now, suddenly, he noticed a difference. The hum of native life had subsided into a whispering near-silence, in which only an occasional foreign voice was noticeable. The clattering movement of local vehicular activity had ceased and even the music which played from a store across the square was lowered, then silenced. Varik was reminded of the unnatural quiet of animals before disaster, an analogy all the more apt in light of his opinion of the Darian natives. He moved to the nearest window and adjusted it until he could see out.

A crowd was gathered about the building, a veritable sea of native life held at bay by white-clad Security personnel. Ripples of protest and anger passed from one side of the crowd to the other, but no one dared to raise his voice in the stillness which Azean authority had imposed.

Varik picked but recognizable figures at the crowd's periphery. Governor li Dara—that miserable excuse for an overlord!—was deep in conversation with someone from the military. Who he was Varik didn't know, but his blue and white uniform spoke of stellar service and command position and. . . .

Varik looked more closely.

Female, he swore softly.

The Azean in conversation with the Governor was indeed a woman—it was so hard to tell, with that race! Varik's contempt for li Dara doubled. Was there anything a woman could say that would change the situation?

He saw her reach to her side for a communicator and he turned his own receiver to the standard Azean frequency. He would hear what she had to say; he did not intend to answer.

"Varik, son of Leman" Unexpectedly, she spoke his language—

he hadn't heard his native tongue in over two years and had to force himself not to respond just for the pleasure of conversation. "This is Imperial Starcommander Torzha er Litz, speaking in the name of the Emperor." He said nothing, enjoying his view of the tension building in the streets. Darian natives had become aware of the attempt to communicate and were shouting their priorities in the hope of being heard. "Those are our people in there, Azean, not yours!" one cried, and another: "We will not die for your damned War!" Varik smiled. He couldn't have planned it better. A crowd this tense, would surge to action at the slightest provocation, overwhelming the local officials in its fury and sparking a nationwide, later planetwide, rebellion.

With fifty natives at his disposal Varik could afford time for amusement. "Shem'Ar shemit-Ar't!" he transmitted—*a woman who commands men is the servant of Chaos.* He saw her stiffen in recognition of the well-known saying and its implications. She muttered something under her breath, then handed the transmitting instrument over to the Governor; Varik smiled.

"Governor li Dara!" he taunted. "Yes, I can see you—but from where? Would you risk a shot based on guesswork, maybe? The price of failure is high."

"You have nothing to gain from this."

Varik laughed. "And you have everything to lose. My enemies . . . I'll watch you fall. And knowing I caused it, I'll find pleasure in it. Should I cast a native out from one of the upper windows, onto the streets? Will that be enough, do you think—or should he be mutilated first? Which will the crowd find more effective?"

He saw li Dara wince. "We want to negotiate."

"Yes, because I can give you what you want . . . but in exchange? You have *nothing,* Governor, *nothing!* You're a man ruled by women; it's beneath my dignity even to be talking to you . . . the thought of *bargaining* with you is at best a meager source of amusement. Pray to your gods in the name of your mother that heaven provide an answer; for nothing short of that will save you."

He watched as the Starcommander put her hand over the communicator and whispered something to li Dara, probably an explanation of just what his insult had meant. Oh, this was amusing. So much so that he could push the thought of death into a dark corner of his mind and there—almost—ignore it.

Two others had entered that tight circle now, a child and a

Bloodletter. Varik recognized the girl immediately as the one who had participated in Laun Set's Sharing. His desperately jubilant mood darkened and his face displayed the tension of a hunted animal. Here was the unknown, and once it was present even the best-laid plans—of which this enterprise was not one—could turn into humiliating failure. His hand tightened on the window's control board as he watched the child talk to them, wishing li Dara had forgotten to switch off the transmitter so that he might overhear. Who was she—*what* was she—and what part did she play in this business? The fact that he could not begin to imagine an answer disturbed him.

"Varik, son of Lemar, Gatenna Braxin." The voice was the child's; after a long argument they had given her the communicator. How did she know his tribal background? "Listen to me, and listen well," she ordered. It was forbidden in his language for a woman to command a man, yet she not only did so but compounded the insult by using the Braxin Dominant Mode, which no alien woman was allowed to speak. Dark fury arose within him.

"Shem'Ar!" he cursed. "I don't talk to your kind."

"I didn't ask you to. Listen. I have a personal stake in your destruction. The Bloodletters are behind me, Varik. We'll come in there and get you, whether or not you spoil local diplomacy. You can only kill so many. One of us will reach you. And your death won't be a pretty one, Braxin."

"I'm not afraid of you," he lied, realizing in that moment how very afraid of her he was.

"I don't believe you. But even if it's true, I have an offer which you might find appealing."

She stopped at that and he was forced to press, "Which is what?"

"A Hyarke, for your freedom."

The Azeans seemed as startled as he was; evidently they hadn't expected this from her. The military officer switched off the transmitter and exchanged hurried words with her, the Governor, and the Bloodletter. In their posture he saw anger and frustration; in their gestures, finally, agreement. Li Dara took the communicator.

"I confirm Anzha Lyu's offer," he said. "A Hyarke, for your freedom. If you win, you're at liberty. We'll take you to the Border and set you on a ship toward home. If you lose . . ." he shrugged. "Given the Hyarke, that will settle our problem."

"Your word?" His voice was scornful.

"My word—and it's good, you know that, whatever you may think of the custom. I can answer for the onplanet authorities. Star-commander er Litz can answer for the Imperial forces, if you'll let her."

"And who is my opponent?" he demanded. "No Darian can meet a human in the Circle—who'll join me in the Hyarke now that my identity is known? Have you thought of that, Governor?"

The child took the communicator and held it for a moment before speaking into it. She looked up at the building toward where he stood. Though he knew himself to be hidden by the window's one-way opacity, he felt strangely naked before her gaze.

"I'm your opponent," she said softly.

That was it, then—a child! They wanted him, Varik, to do the Hyarke with a *child!*

In a rage of injured pride he turned from the window and strode the length of the hall. His life they might take from him—his dignity, never! In anger he threw open the door before him and paced the length of the room behind it. Darians cringed before him. A nation of savdi, with the Bloodletters the only men. Was he to die among them, imprisoned in a Darian body, playing against a girl-child for the amusement of the Azean Empire?

He slammed his fist into an office door and it shattered before the force of the blow.

"Ikom Braxit!" he cried—*I am Braxin!* But his exclamation was lost on the huddled Darians, and the Dominant Mode echoed meaninglessly down the corridor, fading into silence.

He was afraid. In the chaos of his actions he'd thought he had foreseen all possibilities, but he had not thought of this one. What did they mean, to pit him against a blood-haired child? What did they know that he didn't? And what in the name of B'salos *was* she, anyway? In the distance Varik heard the Governor's voice again, but he had dropped the communicator and was too far away to make out the words. Nor did he care to.

Think, Varik, think. The rage has washed over you and is gone. The situation is clear. If the Bloodletters are supporting the Azeans, there's nothing you can do here to cause any real damage. All your choices lead to death—that's a given. It remains for you to choose the manner of your dying.

If they give their word they will hold to it—that is the definition of Azea. Yet you, Varik, are bound by nothing—that is the defini-

tion of Braxi. Make what promises you will, therefore, to get the assurances you want.

They want you to fight a child. They must know something about her you don't. Your advantages are obvious—reach, strength, reflex. No one who is still growing can match the coordination of trained maturity. But they wouldn't set this thing up if they didn't have something down their gloves. The problem is, you're not going to know what that something is until you get out in the Circle.

I am larger, taller, stronger, and I know the Hyarke. Whatever her secret is, can it stand against all that?

The Azeans think so.

The Azeans can err.

So can I.

A child. . . .

There is nothing in the Braxin Social Codes against hacking a child to pieces.

Suddenly Varik laughed. To live as he had lived, to do what he had done, and now suddenly to be cautiously reasoning out a situation which was sheer lunacy to begin with! Yes, he would fight, because there was no other real alternative. And the next night would see him dead or free—but he would never be Azea's prisoner. And if he won—*when* he won—he would bargain for more than freedom. They would make him Braxin again and send him home, and he would let the Braxaná taste his wrath. That for the indignity of pitting him against a child.

He took one last look at the roomful of prisoners and his face contorted with loathing. And he would never have to look at these miserable creatures again—that would be worth it all!

12

The harsh Darian sun was at its zenith when Varik stepped into the Circle.

With a quick and scornful glance he took in his audience. None of the common public had come—there was no room for them. Three of the four quadrants were filled with Bloodletters, coming from all over the planet to witness this unusual Hyarke. *Have you come for the fighting,* he wondered, *or because you know that this day you can watch a human die? Or both?*

The fourth section glowed with the bronze and white of Dari's conquering race. *You will never have me,* he thought defiantly. *You will send me home or I will die, but I will never be yours.*

His eyes traveled over their numbers. Azean, official, with three Directors in the seats of honor—StarControl, Security, and what? Some private enterprise, no doubt, whose only identifying mark was a red cord worn low about the forehead.

Varik laughed to himself.

He was Braxin now. There was no mistaking it. His skin might gleam darkly with the rough texture of Dari, but his stance, his kinetic arrogance, was Braxin. Surprisingly, Azea had agreed to all his conditions—why? No matter. Soon enough the enemy would give him back his native physique and he would go home again . . . how sweet revenge would taste after all this!

The child stepped out into the Circle from the opposite side and held herself still for the inevitable examination.

What is there about this girl, he wondered, *that makes them so certain of my death? For therein lies the danger—some unknown factor they're certain I can't logically determine, something StarControl considers an adequate balance to my strength and experience.*

He studied her carefully. Her pale skin would have done a Braxaná proud and her strange red hair, bound in thin braids which stretched down her back, gave the impression of scars, as if from a whip. Her body was lithe and cleanly muscled. He frowned slightly; she was more developed than a child would be. He had underestimated her age, evidently.

No matter.

"Kyar Anzha lyu," he began, using both names in the Darian ritual opening. "I am surprised you dare to begin this mockery of a combat." There, let the Bloodletters stir themselves over that!

Steel eyes, unblinking, were fixed on him. "I will pour your unworthy blood to the ground, Braxin. I will bring you down in front of your enemies. I will teach you fear as you have never known it."

"I will teach you the fate of a child who dreams of blood," he whispered fiercely.

"Then begin."

Anger was boiling inside him but he did not let it rule his actions. *Very nicely played,* he thought, biting back the rage. *Refusing my name in the Hyarke.* He circled her carefully, watching for the myriad tiny motions that would betray her style, trying not to reveal himself as he did so. *Master of insult—what good will that art do you when these aliens drink your blood?*

She attacked. It was a slow, curving stroke which offered little real threat to him; he merely stepped aside.

What is your secret, little one? What makes the Azean Empire think you can best me?

Her next attack almost nicked his ankle, perfectly timed to compliment his reflexive response. *Good,* he thought grimly, *but not good enough.* He parried it aside and returned the gesture. The tip of his ada scratched her arm and a thin stripe of blood welled forth in response.

Now, for once we can discard all this mystical nonsense—

He started as her eyes glazed over, her stance changing almost imperceptibly, her balance improved. *Is that it then, alien child? You know the Change? You smell the blood and it drugs you, speaks to you? Is that your secret? Do you think even that will be enough?*

He should have attacked her while it happened, and a moment later he swore to himself for having failed to do so. It had been so utterly unexpected that she should undergo the Change that it took an instant for his reflexes to unfreeze, for his timing to be right again. He forced himself to attack; he failed, driving downward toward a girl who was somehow . . . different. With faster reflexes and greater strength she turned him aside.

And he knew that it had ceased to be easy.

He was wary now, like a hunter who had finally acknowledged the teeth of his prey. The advantage was still his, of that he was certain, but it seemed that the difference between them was less. And who could say what adjustments the Change would work during the course of a Hyarke, given a human subject? His speed was greater than hers, but less than it had been; her ada met his with more strength than he had assumed possible.

He tried to stop thinking, to concentrate solely on the Hyarke. But the seeds of doubt were sown within him, and slowly they took root.

What is it? He demanded silently—of her, of himself. *What is it you have that has won the confidence of an Empire?*

He pressed the attack with a complex maneuver which she thwarted, turning it to her own ends and almost cutting him. Again he initiated contact, coming closer, but still he was turned aside in the end. She was good. He would have to deal with that; she knew how to fight. Even that, he realized, he had not truly expected.

Under the hot sun they traded blows. Time came to mean nothing, marked only by the lengthening shadows and a growing red burn which spread across the girl's shoulders. Try as he might he could not reach her. His most intimidating feints failed to draw her attention and his strongest blow could not force her to expend one bit too much energy in an overparry. Her guard seemed flawed, yet every unprotected spot he strove to reach was suddenly barred by the strength of her staff, or by the long curved scythe which threatened to trap his weapon.

He began to fear. It took time; fearing a female is not something that comes easily to a Braxin. But as the sun baked him and his blood began to flow, a little bit from the arm, a trickle from the leg there, and there . . . the small wounds were adding up, yet he could not reach her. She was always too fast, or too ready, or . . . something.

Fear, claimed the ancient Braxin warriors, was a potentially creative emotion—a positive force in combat that could be twisted to a useful purpose. Fear overwhelmed Varik, and fear gave him strength. With new and desperate purpose he struck out at her again and again, in a multiple attack that fed on his fear and used it as fuel, and he forced her back with the power of his terror-born strength. He had a moment to think, and in that time knew that he had to change his tactics. It was pointless to bleed to death from a dozen minor wounds while trying to breach such an efficient guard; he would come down hard and force a perpendicular block. He knew the making of these weapons and was certain that her slender ada could not stand up to the full impact of his own. Once it broke, or even weakened with a lengthwise fracture, the contest would be his once more.

He maneuvered her to where he wanted her, and for the first time noticed the thin line demarking the Circle's border, directly behind her. He almost laughed, hysterically, in the sudden flush of triumph. *She can't cross it!* he realized. *To one who's been Changed, the line is like a wall of psychic force—she can't back over it, and I have the advantage!*

He forced the battle closer and closer to the edge of the Circle, backing her up until she could no longer retreat. Then, feinting to draw the parry he wanted, he brought his ada down with all his strength—

And she dodged.

Before the blow.

A cold sweat broke out on his forehead; his muscles strained as he recovered his position. *No,* he thought. *No. I won't believe it.*

He tried a direct cut. Again, this time smiling, she moved easily out of its intended path. Again her movement began as he planned, before he was committed.

Nor did she attack as the fear began to cripple him.

It can't be! his mind insisted—he needed desperately to believe that. He attacked blindly; her movements revealed in a thousand minute ways that she knew exactly what he intended to do as soon as he himself was aware of it.

And now the word slowly rose through his mind and came to the surface, the label he had avoided since her hunt first began.

Telepathy.

To his horror, she nodded.

No! It can't be!

~ *It is.* And the thought, *her* thought, struck terror in him to the depths of his Braxin soul as it resounded silently inside his mind.

~ *I will teach you fear as you have never known it.*

No!

She smiled as she circled him, as if she no longer had anything to worry about. Did she, at that? Could he stand against such a terrible power?

He had to, he told himself. And grimly he set himself for her attack.

He was fortunate that his skills were strong, for just before his new stance was set, in that instant when a lesser man might have been caught off-balance, she struck. It took all his skill to muster an adequate defense and even that allowed a shallow cut along one leg, barely preventing a fatal one to the torso.

Inhuman creature! But he knew that Azea hardly considered such power unnatural, and he cursed his own culture, which in treating it as such had crippled his adaptability.

He was losing now, clearly and consistently. Where she had previously scratched him, now she gouged into tender, necessary muscle, and no parry he devised could keep her away. Worst of all was the growing awareness that she had been toying with him before, which cut his Braxin ego far more brutally than any blade could his body.

I will not fall to your kind! He thought it as loudly as he could and hoped she heard. He was aware of the Azeans about him, watching intently, wanting the spy for their tortures, their mental games. . . . *You will never have me!*

And he attacked. Not because he stood any chance of success but because he was a Braxin and was not going to die a child's toy. To his surprise she retreated before him, and red dripped from her shoulder where his ada-tip had scored.

Mindless fury! Was there indeed hope?

He gave himself over to his rage and tried not to think at all. The odds were still against him but they were not nearly so overwhelming; for each wound he sustained he was able to reach her once, where before he could not at all. The sight of her blood fed his frenzy. *Is this what they feel?* he wondered. *Will the Circle talk to me now?*

He had backed her up toward the Circle's boundary again and he pressed forward, willing to bleed if that was the cost. With her back against its curve she would be limited in movement. There was a chance. It was a slight one, true, but any hope was welcome at this point, and it helped take the edge off the crippling terror and give him back the best of his skill.

Now. . . .

He moved in. A low angled blow would pin her against the curve even if she saw it coming. The gleaming blade whipped forward—

And she dropped her weapon.

And grabbed his wrist.

And the world went dark.

~ Feel my hate, Braxin. Let it flow over and through you, a private thing between the two of us.

He was drowning in a sea of violence. Terror overwhelmed him. A hideous alien thing was in his mind and everything else was forgotten.

~ You have no secrets before me, no privacies. I will probe you, enter you, strip you bare. Taste my hate.

He cringed before the onslaught, feeling his humanity crumble. He struggled for the surface, but there was nothing. Her mind was opened to him; unwillingly he was drawn into it, seeing nothing there but a seething sea of violent emotion, directed toward him. Drowning, he struggled.

~ I will strip you of everything that makes you human, Braxin. Before me you have no privacy, no pride, no image. I will take the

terror they conditioned into you and use it to break you down until nothing is left.

He was trying to fight her but he had spent a lifetime learning not to be able to. His people had nothing like this, nothing but terrible legends of mutant power which frightened children and justified infanticide. He had been taught not to face it. And the teaching had been good.

~ *Look at me!*

Against his will he did. Her mind was not young, not in any sense of the word. She had lived a dozen lives through the minds and eyes of tutors and had endured greater emotional trauma than most adults could survive. She was a creature of hatred and violence, and nowhere in her was there room for any gentle emotion, nor the stuff to nourish its growth. Recipient of adult instabilities, she had absorbed lust and hatred and the need to kill but had lived in a body incapable of expressing those things—until now.

~ *I will have you,* she thought to him, and there was a sexual undertone to the threat that froze him with horror. Suddenly he understood.

"You are Braxaná," he whispered.

Through her eyes, through the eyes of the telepaths in their audience, he saw her wrench his own ada from his unfeeling hand and turn it against him. He struggled to back up from the depths, but not quickly enough. Pain exploded inside him and he observed the blow as his eyes closed in death, reflected in a thousand minds, twisting, tearing. . . .

Then there was darkness, and an ending.

Ten thousand pairs of eyes watched closely as Anzha lyu drew back from the fallen body of her opponent, trembling with exertion, and tore the barbed end of the Braxin's ada free from his torso with one swift jerk. But she seemed to lack strength now that the fighting was over; the long weapon fell from her hand even as she fired it.

No one moved as she knelt by the body of the Fallen; every spectator had, in some special way, the right to witness. Muttering ritual words she cupped her hands beneath the killing wound. Red blood poured into it—Braxin blood, she knew, for they wouldn't have bothered to adjust his biochemistry that much. Her nostrils flared as she drank in the sweet odor.

"There will be more," she whispered to no one. "I promise."

She drank deeply.

The Sharing would begin now. Two of the Bloodletters moved into the circle with the drugged oil that would sustain her life. Laun Set had demanded the right to be one of them, and now he was the first to reach out to her with a glistening hand—

—and pull back suddenly with a cry, as if touching her had burned him.

There was sadness and understanding in her eyes.

"I never said I mastered it all," she said softly.

The other man reached out to her and she did not back away; like Laun Set he was unable to endure the contact.

"No," she whispered. "Touch Discipline. I never. . . ."

Bleeding, she swayed.

"Kyar—" Laun Set began.

"Finish the ritual for me," she murmured. "Finish it properly. See that no insult is done."

"There can be no insult, Kyar." And he added: *"Bloodletter."*

She tried to speak again but the strength had left her. Her eyes shut and she fell; instinctively Laun Set reached for her, and because her consciousness flickered out as she dropped into his arms, he was able to catch and hold her.

"Finish it," he whispered to his companion, and with the concerned comprehension of a Bloodletter the other nodded.

With a brief condescension to necessary ritual Laun Set carried her out, quickly.

And the Sharing began.

13

"I don't care who you are," the Darian said, "and I don't care what your rank is. The answer's no."

"But—" Torzha began. Ebre put a hand on her shoulder.

"If they say no, then it's no. She's not technically a citizen of the Empire, Torzha—she doesn't come under our jurisdiction."

"But in a matter regarding military security—"

"StarControl can't override the prerogatives of a Darian medical facility unless the subject is an Azean citizen. Special amendment to the Treaty of Conquest." He paused for a moment and watched her; at last he urged, "Look, I could use a breath of fresh air. Didn't the guard say something about waiting on the terrace?"

After a moment she nodded, and led him there. The Darian night was cool and he breathed deeply as he stretched.

"Eight Standard Days in that damned transport," he muttered. "Not for anyone but you, Torzha. A man needs a planet to stand on."

She was amused. "What about the five years in space I keep hearing about? Heroic sacrifice of ground leave rights? Endless battle and bloodshed and not a moment's rest for the weary?"

"That was quite some time ago—and a desk job cures you of that kind of endurance. You'll learn that soon enough." He leaned on the primitive metal railing and shook his head, incredulous. "Halfway across the Empire to see some child prodigy for Hasha knows what purpose—Founding forbid you should tell me that—and the primitive natives won't let a crowned head of the Empire into their precious medical facility. What idiot came up with the idea of a constitutional empire, anyway? Hasha, it's times like this I realize just how much power we don't have."

"Nothing personal," she said dryly. "You're just outranked."

"By some primeval killer who forbade visitors." He had switched into Ikna, which they both spoke, just in case someone was listening. "How foolish of me—of course."

Footsteps sounded lightly on the rough stone floor behind them; they turned and found a native waiting for their attention.

"Laun Set," Torzha explained. "A Bloodletter, and the man who's been watching over Anzha lyu." She introduced Ebre: "Director ni Kahv, of StarControl."

The Darian ignored him. "I heard you were here. If you want to see her, I'm willing to allow it."

Torzha started forward and Ebre moved to follow, but the Bloodletter stepped between them, his eyes cold with authority. "Only that one."

Ebre hesitated, then shrugged and backed off. "Evidently you outrank me, Starcommander. Please go ahead—I'll wait here." Then, in Ikna: "And when you come back please don't forget to explain to me why I came here."

Laun Set ushered Torzha out and with a gesture indicated the direction she should travel. Before joining her he looked back at Ebre.

"She's not one of you," he said to him, quietly. "She's far more like my kind than yours. It would be better if Azea just left her alone while she healed. My people know what to do."

Do they? he wondered, but he said nothing.

The Bloodletter led Torzha down a heavily guarded corridor, to a private room at the end. While they walked, he explained the situation. "She'll live, I'm glad to say. These things happen sometimes: the drugs go bad, or there's a mistake made in mixing them. Usually that means death. In her case we were able to compensate. But full recovery will be long in coming. Here." he indicated a door. "She's asked after you. That's why you're here. But I have to remind you that her mind is as exhausted as her body. Mask your tension, if you can."

She looked sharply at him. "Is it so noticeable?"

He laughed, and seemed about to voice a mocking answer, but at last said merely, "Yes. Go in, please."

The child lay in a primitive hospital bed, barely breathing. Light from the corridor flooded the room as Torzha opened the door, driving back the shadows which had dominated prior to her arrival. When she shut the door behind her she was left in near-darkness; the window had been adjusted to an eighty-five percent screen and the little light that passed through it was barely sufficient for human vision.

"My eyes are over-sensitive," the child explained, as though Torzha had voiced her observations. "Laun Set says this is normal, under the circumstances."

Her voice was a whisper, yet physical weakness did not seem to be the cause. "Your hearing?" Torzha asked softly.

The child smiled. "Also." She stirred as if she meant to rise to a sitting position, but lack of strength forced her back again to the pillows. "This isn't what you've come to talk about, though."

"Do you know that?"

"You mean, am I reading your mind? Yes and no. I'm not . . . how should I say it? . . . reaching inside you for information. But your surface thoughts, your immediate emotional concerns, these are obvious to me—I'm trained to take note of them as casually as I breathe. Think of a book—one can grasp its purpose by observing the cover, without opening it." She paused. "I'm sorry if—"

"I'm familiar with books."

"Few are."

"But those who study the Braxins have to be."

She was intrigued. "Transculturalist?"

Torzha nodded.

"And that *does* have something to do with why you're here."

"In that it concerns Braxi, yes." Torzha pulled a chair close to the bed and sat beside her. The child's sun-scorched lids, she noticed, were nearly shut, but beneath them there was a hint of vibrant life in the movement of her eyes. *It would take a lot to kill this one,* Torzha thought. "I'll admit I was more than a little hesitant to let you negotiate with the Braxin as you did."

"Then I'll admit I was surprised you let me." Her lids flickered open briefly and dark eyes studied the Starcommander. "Why?"

"I'm not certain I can answer you. I trust my hunches—they're usually reliable. I'm a good judge of people, and you inspire my faith. Also," she admitted wryly, "there were few real alternatives." She leaned forward, then said softly, "Anzha lyu, do you know just what you accomplished?"

Again that bright, piercing look shot out from beneath the sunburned eyelids. "Tell me."

"You are a Bloodletter." She looked pointedly at the girl's left arm—a dark gash was permanently incised above the wrist. Anzha's hand flexed in unconscious response to the scrutiny. "A *human* Bloodletter. Not some spy who dishonored the Hyarke by competing against the natives, but one whom the Darians chose to raise to their status. The reasons are irrelevant—the fact remains. To the Darian mind, human life had risen immeasurably in status. Not only has the crisis passed, but the situation has noticeably improved. Two centuries of diplomacy and you put us all to shame in a single afternoon. Anzha lyu. . . ." Her voice was suddenly lower. "Why did you hunt the Braxin?"

"For my pleasure," she said sharply.

"That answer would do your enemies proud."

"'To hunt a Braxin, one must think like a Braxin.' Do you know who said that?"

"Darmel lyu Tukone."

"My father. My family had a long tradition of service to the Empire. If not for . . . the obvious . . . I would have joined them."

Now, Torzha thought. *Say it.*

"You still can."

The girl looked up, startled. "Do you know what you're saying?"

Torzha smiled, amused. "I think so."

"I can't even become a citizen of the Empire, much less serve in the military. I'm banned from obtaining the simplest Security clearance."

"I'm aware of all this."

"Then how—"

"Let me tell you some things about the rulers of the Empire. The Emperor himself is a practical man, with little tolerance for bureaucratic nonsense. If the military says it needs you, he'll back you. Ebre values my opinion and will act on it; StarControl will support you."

"That's two."

"You'll never win over the Council of Justice. They can't go back on their decisions regarding you or it throws much of their work into question, As for the Combined Council of Nations, the Director of StarControl has an honorary seat in the House of Humans, through which he can argue on your behalf and also observe the workings of the Council to time things properly regarding it."

"Is ni Kahv going to argue vehemently on my behalf?"

"I doubt it. But Ebre's chosen his successor."

The girl's eyes opened wide in understanding. "You."

Torzha inclined her head in affirmation. "The news isn't out yet. I'd prefer it remained that way."

"I understand. That would mean three of the Five would be female. . . ."

"Two females and a T-san Breeder, but the result is the same—a fifty/fifty balance is as abhorrent to the Braxins as a female majority. To us it's a simple matter, not a sexual issue at all—but to them it will mark the changeover from a male empire to a female one. The moment of formal announcement will bring on renewed military activity and symbolic brutality. Just as it always does, in such cases."

She leaned over toward the girl.

"I want to sponsor you into StarControl."

Anticipation flashed brightly in those dark, alien eyes.

"You're taking on a real battle, there."

"Does that mean you'll do it?"

"The Institute won't let me go."

"For two more years, until your basic training is completed. After that you can commute from the Academy."

"They won't take me in."

"Ebre can override their admissions office."

"Will he?"

Torzha smiled. "If approached properly."

"You seem to have all the answers."

"I've tried to anticipate all the questions. I have no illusions about this, Anzha lyu—it's not going to be easy. But I see a tremendous potential in you that's wasted anywhere but at the War Border. What do you say?"

The child drew in a deep, thoughtful breath. "What can I say? This is all I've dreamed of doing, all I've ever wanted. And I have nothing whatsoever to lose. Yes, Starcommander. *Yes.*"

"Then rest, now, and regain your strength. Ebre's on Dari and we can do the ceremony here. After that, the Council of Justice will have to deal with you through me."

And the Council of Nations, she thought, and the Emperor. Not to mention the Institute, which claimed actual possession of the girl . . . but that was the easy part.

How in the name of Hasha was she going to explain this to Ebre?

Harkur: The more complex a language, the greater its capacity to influence the thoughts of men.

SIX

149 And as the water receded (*anticipation to dread, culminating by the end of line 150*)
150 A form was left adrift (*to sorrow, with a hint of morbid fascination*)
151 Pale arm draped over cold stone (*finality*)
152 A last spray to clothe its hand in death.

I waited.

The assembled company was silent. Their faces, hidden behind masks of Braxaná image, revealed nothing.

Finally Kaim'era Zatar nodded. I permitted myself to breathe again.

"It was well done." He waved for a servant to pay me. "Although I am surprised there was no taste of secondary eroticism in the last image, given your audience."

Mentally I berated myself for the choice; verbally I rose to defend it. "Before such an audience, is not erotic content inherent in the image itself? To fall into an overtly sexual speech mode would seem, to me at least, to be both unnecessary and overbearing, and would sacrifice the subtlety of the image's implications."

"Oh, I fully agree with your choice—but it surprises me that a non-Braxaná could be so perceptive." Gold sinias were laid before me in quantity; I tried not to betray the extent of my surprise. "Take them, woman—the performance was worth it."

I bowed deeply. "I am grateful, Kaim'era."

"A good poet is hard to come by—and a female, even more so. How did you come to the Art?"

I used the speech mode of recall and subtly drew on my mother's inflection: "By abandoning all profitable pursuits and devoting myself to insubstantial folly."

He laughed, and a few others among my audience smiled. The

rest were doubtlessly confused by my use of irony without speaking in an ironic mode-complex. How limited are they who can only follow two lines of thought at once! *My teachers,* I thought, *were correct: the greater the poet, the harder it is to find the proper audience.*

"A true artist, then," he countered. "Is your compositional skill as ready as your wit?"

I nodded with appropriate humility.

"On the ninth day of this zhent I'm arranging entertainment for nine of the Kaim'eri and chosen members of their Houses—about forty in all. I would like an original piece, dutifully inoffensive, strictly apolitical. Something violent would be appropriate. Keep it generally appealing; some of my guests are not known for subtlety." He paused dramatically. "There'll be time enough for that later if you do this one well."

I ignored the promise in his voice as his discretionary undermode cautioned me to. "I'll need a guest list," I offered hesitantly. I had been uncertain as to whether or not this was a reasonable request, but his smile told me he was pleased.

"I'll have one sent. You are staying. . . ."

I looked at the gold before me and decided to move. "Kurat-Seret, at the Dekor'va."

"I know the house. It will be forwarded. Have you any further business with me?"

"No," I said, my speech mode indicating: yes.

"Good." His promised: later.

I almost danced home.

Five nights—nine Kaim'eri—by the gods who abandoned us, it was not possible!

Anything is possible, whispered my poet's soul (in the speech mode of doubt). *Let me tell you the tale of a poet who hanged himself with promises. . . .*

Zatar's list arrived promptly and it was as thorough a guide as one could ask for. Nine Kaim'eri with no tastes in common and Householders with less. What do you say to a Braxaná who expects insolence, yet will not tolerate it—who expects to be praised, yet sneers at sycophancy? And how did I get myself committed to finding a solution?

I chose and discarded enough themes to stock a library with literature-tapes. Most were too subtle—some were not subtle enough—a few were simply rotten ideas to start with. My rented floor was littered with a carpet of discarded thoughts. I would have been satisfied to have a theme and be incapable of finding the proper words to express it; that was a poet's lot in life. But to be entirely bereft of a theme: that was a fate I would not wish upon an Azean!

History I discarded early. Such images were fine for amateurs, but history was a subjective science at best and every recorded incident was seen in different ways by different people. There is no worse torture for a poet than to hear "Yes, it was a fair performance, but weren't there four hundred and thirty-six Azeans taken at the battle of Kos-Torr, as opposed to four hundred and thirty-*two*?"

Likewise I discarded all tales of sexual desire. The variance in taste among my audience-to-be was enough to give a poet nightmares, and it did. I couldn't even use the amateurish last resort of throwing in a bit of everything, for Kaim'era Retev's Mistress found sexual experimentation distasteful.

Taz'hein! I couldn't have designed a worse situation if someone had commissioned me to do so.

Then I considered, and I recalled my oath of frustration. Taz'hein—the unconcerned traitor-god—father of the Braxaná. Did I have the nerve to present a religious theme to a people who scorned nothing more than active religion?

Why not?

Far into the night I scribbled and dictated. Once I had to run out with my recorder to pick up a new charge; while on the streets I narrowly avoided a male figure on the prowl for satisfaction. Did my time count as work-time enough that I had Just Cause to refuse him? I was unwilling to test the point. True, it's not impossible to compose poetry while serving as a receptacle for some stranger's lust, but it's blessed difficult.

Dawn broke over my first outline. By mid-afternoon of the second day I began to see the promise of a masterpiece. What had begun as a tale of glory had become twisted with subtle brilliance into something of far greater scope, and I could feel it happening as I worked. Level after level of meaning was added: something for everybody. For the simple, on the surface, a bloody tale of the divine origin of the tribe of the Braxaná. For Zatar and his kind, who are the men a poet lives to serve, a thousand layers of meaning to uncover, a touch of macabre humor here and there which would tell a second, third, even a fourth tale simultaneously, as only a mistress of the Art could do it.

By the fourth day it was woven, a verbal mesh of war, lust, and—of course—The Ultimate Treachery. I will tell you of the death of the Creator, I chanted as I fell asleep on my desk, and my mind used the opportunity to dream the thousand subtleties which that one line could contain, given the speech modes of the Braxaná.

"The poet, Lanst'va."

I bowed deeply, my heart beating wildly. I knew two of these people were at least moderately hostile to my Art; them I must win over if I valued my life. The rest must be pleased, seduced . . . manipulated. That was the true art which such poetry as mine involved.

1 I will tell you of the death of the Creator
(*Triumph/satisfaction/finality*)
2 And you who choose to mourn gods will be moved
(*Superiority tinged with amusement*)
3 And all who would accord folly worship
(*Emphasized superiority*)
4 Fall down upon bended knee before the fate of the heavens
(*Mocking command*)
5 And raise not your unworthy eyes to the Void of the living gods.

By the thirtieth line I had captured them, and I edited my work as their almost imperceptible responses advised. That is one of the challenges of spoken poetry; the best preparation still cannot anticipate an audience, and many poets have failed to communicate through unwillingness to adapt a treasured text. I saw my script as a living, vital thing, and as it reached out to these Braxaná I helped it to grow into something greater than the pre-prepared word could ever be.

In strong words I drew a glorious picture of the Creator. My images came from the mythology of other peoples, to whom no god was greater than that responsible for the creation of All. This was as it should be, in order that the magnitude of his fall might be all the more dramatic. Beneath the story, and far beneath the underlayer of irony which was the prevalent mode for this potion, I laced the work with enough subtle implications to allow them to laugh at my expense—for Avra-Salos, creator of the universe and all that he placed in it, my creator, was not the father of the Braxaná.

I let my voice darken in foreboding as I spoke of the creation of Taz'hein as a suitable companion for the One. Delicately I shadowed my speech with chaos as Ar was born, the mate of the First and the mold for womankind, whose birth left no thought free in the heavens, thereafter known as the Void of Consciousness. They were mine, these Braxaná, and I knew it. I worked by instinct, reciting from memory in some parts and improvising in others. And as far as I could judge, I was choosing correctly.

Ar in her dire glory swept over my audience, a goddess of chaos whose freedom decreed the bondage of man to the will of woman. I knew that in that moment, as I spoke to them, as I *controlled* them, that they feared that goddess as they would never have rationally chosen to do, these men who played falsely at atheism. Though most of them could not understand every layer of meaning I presented to them, unconsciously they absorbed it all. I saw this clearly reflected in their eyes and mannerisms as I continued.

The war of the sister worlds enveloped them then, and my voice praised Taz'hein for betraying and destroying his Creator even as I lamented the betrayal in pseudo-religious grief. Worlds shook—human blood ran in rivers—is this enough violence for you, Kaim'era Zatar?

Then, switching to the modes which imply sexuality and power, I spoke of Taz'hein's manifestation on Braxi and the begetting of the Braxaná. It seemed to please them so I lingered on that point, improvising more detailed description that I had originally intended.

With a sudden adjustment in tone I moved to the conditional bondage of Ar. I kept the implication of threat to a minimum; the mythological promise of her freedom in the event of female dominance would be too strong, coming as it did from a woman, if not handled carefully. I sensed that these men who had once scorned even that myth were not quite as certain of their own atheism by the time I was done.

My closing encompassed a view of the Braxaná barbarian, in whose ruthlessness resided the promise of future power. More would be cheap sycophancy. The Braxaná mythology already supports both the Social Codes and the Braxaná right to power. It can be enough when the poet presents it, rendering each word in a different mode, giving each phrase a thousand meanings.

There was silence.

Then Zatar nodded slowly, a sign that I had succeeded and should leave without word. Bowing deeply, I obeyed.

Before I had reached the outer door, his Mistress caught up with me.

"He would have you wait," she said. I stopped walking. "In here." She indicated a small sitting room off the entrance hall. It was decorated lavishly in the Central Braxaná style. Not being accustomed to sitting on the floor, cushions or no, I perched on the edge of a lowtable.

Some short time later the Kaim'era himself entered. I stood, that I might bow.

"An excellent performance."

"I thank you, Magnificent One."

"And it was not an easy assignment."

I let amusement color my voice. "I am very aware of that, Kaim'era."

"It was intentional. You've earned your business time the hard way, poet. I'm listening."

My heart was pounding. This was already farther than any of my kind had ever gotten with him, I knew, and Zatar's verbal reputation had attracted many a skilled poet.

"Your House lacks my Art, Great One."

"My House has its Master," he responded dryly.

I indicated my deep respect for his verbal skill. "But has it a poet? Doubtless your politics are rendered with unequaled skill, but have you an artist to choose the words which will give maximum play to the beauty of our tongue?" He said nothing and I continued without pause, lest I lose courage. "I can provide pleasure—pain—instruction. I'm trained to make any audience feel whatever I wish. I lay that skill at your feet. I will bring you simple pleasure, Kaim'era, or I will build you legends. You have but to choose."

I had run out of words. In silence he regarded me, his emotions masked by a stone exterior I knew I would never penetrate.

"Let's review your motives."

I trembled but nodded.

"You are a woman. As such, you cannot support yourself in any field requiring authority over men. The arts entail a special risk, since being independent of authority you have no way of demanding payment if such is refused."

"This is true, Kaim'era." And hit home, painfully.

"As an artist you are apart from the Braxin class structure. In the eyes of common society you are the lowest of all. Becoming part of a purebred House would grant you legitimacy and a second class designation."

"True, Kaim'era, but—"

"*And* you are a rebel. Did you think I wouldn't research your past? You inspired a crowd nearly to rebellion on Vreski as an 'exercise in oratory manipulation.' Only when you renounced your class privileges to devote yourself to more harmless artistic pursuits was your life spared—and even that by a close vote."

I felt a chill rising in the depths of my soul. I had changed my name, my appearance, and all other personal essentials since then. I had never realized he would be so thorough.

"In addition, I find it clear by your presentation that you revel in the manipulation of men." He raised a hand to silence my protest. "Just as the mistress of our language can work on a subconscious level, so can its master read as deeply. So. You want class, money, security. And you, a Braxin woman, would play a manipulative game with the Master Race, hoping someday to understand that nature which we keep secret from your kind and to command it under the guise of poetry. Understand that under the best of circumstances you would have to abandon your freedom at my door. Your every move would be watched. Your every word would be recorded and sent to me. Your poetry would be censored. And if your poetic approach ever disturbed me, I would have you killed without a second thought—perhaps slowly." He regarded me with a steadiness which made me shudder, and in silence made me reconsider just what I wanted to get myself into. Ultimate folly! What had I known of Braxaná ways, I who had thought only of my Art, and my pleasure?

A strange satisfaction crossed his face, almost as if he were aware of the humility his speech had fostered within me. He turned to go—but merely to reject my service, or to punish me for past rebellion?

He glanced back once before leaving, and his expression was again unreadable.

"Come to this estate tomorrow evening." His deep voice was

shaded with amusement. "Your Mistress will see to rooms and wages. Ask for her when you arrive."

I could say nothing, for he was gone too quickly.

Taz'hein!

Thus I entered the House of Zatar—I, artist and instigator, poet and revolutionary.

Doubtless had I been born male my life would have been different. I can imagine myself dying in the front lines of a premature revolution, fighting for the excitement of commanding the actions of others while striving to throw off the yoke of the Pale Ones' rule. But instead I was born a woman, and so must fulfill my dreams in a mode suitable to that sex. It was a hard fate to bear. I didn't mind the forced accessibility which most women waste time condemning, nor the children whose unexpected arrival cost me time and health. But the soul of a manipulator was in me from my birth, and that is a cruel misalignment of interests among such a people as mine.

So I turned to language. It allowed me to combine my creative and commanding instincts so subtly that few men realized the manipulative power of my Art. And when the Braxaná, who are more sensitive than most on this point, arrested me for my audacity, they labeled me shem'Ar rather than revolutionary—a woman in command of men, a servant of the goddess of Chaos Incarnate: the ultimate Braxin taboo.

I think it was my Art that saved me. The Braxaná show little mercy toward those that defy them, but that which pleases them is often safe from their rage. I pleaded for my life in a glorious display of their language which brought me the right to survive, once they had stripped me of the right to do anything but speak.

And now the House of Zatar! The thrill of it overwhelmed me; at the same time, I was filled with dread. Zatar had claimed my life and willingly I gave it to him. But how long before the essence of the shem'Ar arose again to vibrant life and cast me into danger through his displeasure?

When I was not obsessed by such fears as this my life was one of challenge and pleasure. The young Kaim'era whom I served was indeed a master of his tongue and it took an my talent and training to please him. But oh, the rapture of performing for a Braxaná audience! No sexual contact could bring such pleasure, no wine such intoxication.

It was my duty to instruct Ni'en in the delicate nuances of our language, and because it was Zatar's will she tried to be a good pupil. But even as she learned a speech mode it betrayed her; for each instance in which she applied it constructively there were another five in which she unconsciously allowed it to flavor her language, revealing more of her inner self than any Mistress of a Braxaná House could afford. Fully half of our drills were designed to strip the obvious from her communication, to teach her to express herself not as her class does, to express its feelings, but as *his* class does, to support an image and communicate acceptable emotions.

And how she worked to please him! Was her devotion wholly inspired by those emotions which we strive to deny (but which, the poet knows, persist in the human heart nonetheless)? Or because she was an outsider in his upper-class world, who must serve him or know complete isolation? Braxaná society shunned us both—her for her brand, me for my past. Where else could we have found fulfillment but at his side?

Few men in the House showed any sexual interest in me and most of those who did were sterile; a fringe benefit of service to the Braxaná. Such a situation allowed me to express sensuality in my work as I had not dared before, and I know this development both pleased and amused my Master even as it pleased and confused me.

My work was censored, as he had warned me it would be. But this was merely necessity on his part, a careful control over what his House presented to the others of his Race. He himself had no fear of anything I had to say. Often he called me forth for private performances and in such situations I might choose any subject matter and experiment with any manner of treatment. Others found him harsh and intolerant: this was his public image. Toward me he was demanding, yes, but also indulgent. Providing I labored with his pleasure in mind, I might do so in unorthodox manners.

I grew more bold. His alert black eyes seemed always to reach into my soul and read my motives, yet he never voiced any displeasure regarding my newfound poetic audacity. I had been preparing a major work, a masterpiece of subtlety which ultimately questioned Braxi's devotion to the Endless War; its presentation would be dangerous in the most tolerant of company. I did not imagine I would ever have the courage—or foolhardiness—to actually perform it. But a true artisan never wholly discipline his need for creative expression; thus it was that one day I caught my Master up in a stirring tale of war and intrigue which had for its underlayer a disturbing new view of the Braxin-Azean conflict.

He regarded me for some time in silence when I had finished. "Interesting," he said finally.

I trembled. Had I gone too far? The long piece I had slaved over was a masterpiece of language, but I would not have dared to perform it for any other man. Had I misjudged him?

"You have quite a mind, woman." He was pensive. "Quite a mind, indeed. I watched your audience the last time, you know. I always do. You sway their minds as no man ever could. There is real power in you. Power to influence men."

I was very still.

"Come to me tonight," he ordered.

I knew him well enough to recognize that for the dismissal it was. I was grateful for the exit; it allowed me to camouflage my fear with movement.

Control of men—wasn't that, in essence, what he had ascribed to me? Absolutely forbidden by any Braxin standard, intolerable in a Braxaná Household: punishable, as all infractions of the Braxin social order were, with death.

If he acknowledged me as a shem'Ar I would die; no pleasure I had brought him could buy me out of that fate. The potential had always been within me, of course, and such a master of language could not have failed to notice it, but if he saw it fully manifesting itself he would have no choice but to pluck the errant weed up by its roots.

It was with a cold heart that I went to him that night.

I had never tasted a purebred Braxaná; it was unexpectedly sweet. I found so little relationship between that lingering pleasure and the desperate arousal and release of the lower classes that they seemed to be two entirely different acts. I must say that in the face of death I knew great pleasure, and though my nature had disturbed him I do not think my body did so. He had me sleep by him; this is a Braxaná custom in which I had not indulged before and I found it disturbing. Rather than sleep I observed him, his fine features relaxed in slumber, one naked hand rising and falling upon his chest with the slow rhythm of his breathing. Three delicate golden rings adorned his fingers so lightly that even under the tight gloves of his traditional costume I had never noticed them; now they drew my eye to his long-fingered, perfectly manicured hand, which I had never before seen revealed in such a manner. I would try to remember the image for future poetry. If there were to be any future poetry.

He awoke when dawn's first light poured through the windows; fearful and unrested, I prepared myself for the worst. Yet he said nothing as he dressed. I could not help but watch him as he applied the Braxaná layers to his lean form; gray over gray over gray, and on top of it all a black shortcloak, gloves, and boots. Not until the choking high collar was tight about his neck and his medallion of rank lay golden upon his chest did he speak to me, or even acknowledge my presence.

"So you would command the ways of men," he stated simply, smoothing his long black glove-cuffs over his forearms.

"I will not dispute your judgement, Kaim'era."

He looked at me sharply. "Then speak openly. You enjoy manipulation."

Weakly I nodded.

"Of men."

Again I affirmed it.

"Men in power."

The blood was rising in my cheeks. "Kaim'era—"

"Yes or no will suffice."

I looked away from him. "Yes," I whispered.

"Which might be labeled the service of Ar."

I flinched. He was dancing verbal circles around the term, but the implication was clear. The shem'Ar cannot be, permitted to endure. Would he simply kill me, or would it be more unpleasant than that?

He noted my discomfort and a faint smile adorned his flawless features. "Fortunately for us you're a member of my House and thus a servant of my will; therefore a formal recognition of the situation is not necessary."

I found that I was holding my breath.

"You have a peculiar power, Lanst'va—a real ability to control the emotions of your audience without their being aware of it. I've watched you work since you came here, and time and practice have only added to your skill. I wish to call upon that talent. You are willing?"

I exhaled carefully. "Your will is mine."

"Excellent." He smoothed his hair. "What this means in the immediate future is that I might lend you out to some of the upper-class Houses. They've requested your service, oblivious to your power." He laughed. "I couldn't have asked for better. Later on, I will need to leave Braxi periodically." He held up a hand to silence any possible protest. "My plans make it necessary. It pleases me therefore that Ni'en finds support in your company. And it would please me even more if I could allow you to practice your Art in the other Houses while I'm gone."

I barely managed speech. "What do you require?"

His dark eyes focused on me wiht sudden intensity. "Even I can't allow a shem'Ar to exist. Therefore you must never earn that designation."

I waited. Evidently he saw something in my expression that pleased him, for he smiled more broadly, "It's a very technical definition, isn't it? A woman only commands men in her own right when her orders are her own."

I was beginning to understand. "But if the orders came from a man—"

"Then the woman is merely an instrument—albeit an efficient one." He nodded his satisfaction. "I will lend you to the others, if you are willing."

"Your will is mine," I repeated. Fear was being replaced by wild excitement. Was he going to set me among the Braxaná and make it my duty to influence their thinking? Could a woman know such ecstacy in a single lifetime?

I tried to maintain a calm exterior, but although I spoke in the Basic Mode I knew he could hear my excitement as I answered, "I promised to build you legends."

"I know," he said. "I remember. And I'm taking you up on it."

Harkur: An uninspired ruler works to develop those relationships which will be most to his advantage. A great ruler determines the most desirable relationships and assumes them into being.

SEVEN

The Emperor of the Azean Star Empire was an impressive man. Even among the tallest human race in the explored galaxy he stood half a head above his fellows. Cream-colored hair poured over his shoulders and down his back, streaked with gold as was the current fashion, and matched by a cream-and-gold robe of state. His face was the color of polished bronze and in it the whites of his eyes were all the more dramatic for the contrast. On his left hand he wore four rings, symbolic of the four other heads of state who were at once his servants and his masters. On his right hand he wore a ring carved out of zeymorite—a reminder of the Founding—which was inscribed with the two hemispheres of Azea, the seal of his office.

With the majestic patience of royalty, Pezh il Seth waited. The greathall was filled with his subjects: human and alien, military and civilian, they were born to rank or had been raised to it . . . there was no place for commoners, here. The sheer mass of the Court's attendance was almost more than the greathall could accommodate as it was. Not for the first time, he thought, *we could have met on Lugast.* Not for the last time, he reminded himself that some things must be done on Azean soil—for the tradition which bound them into a working whole was based upon a message embodied by that planet.

A herald stirred. "From the Council of Nations," he announced. "Grand Councillor Asabin Telia, of the House of Humans."

The woman who entered was a Lugastine, short and pleasant looking. Lugastine formalclothes swept to the ground in a flowing train of purple and turquoise which disguised the features of her body, while on her head a golden crown supported the fine crystalline veil which covered her hair and shoulders.

They always did know how to dress, the Emperor reflected.

She bowed to the monarch and took her place by his side, her veil tinkling softly as she moved. "From the Council of Justice," the herald continued. "Grand Justice Lish zi Reis."

The Azean who entered was a haughty man of some hundred Standard Years. Age was just starting to make itself visible upon him, and the wrinkles which were beginning to set themselves in his forehead gave him, if possible, a harsher dignity that he had previously possessed. He had chosen a black and burgundy gown for the occasion; the uniform of the Council of Justice was entirely black, but zi Reis had decided some time ago that that was too somber for state appearances and had dictated the application of color, in dark and moderate doses.

The herald prepared himself for alien phonemes. "From the Council of Nations," he said carefully. "Grand Councillor Sst Fftf Shk-k, of the House of Non-Humans."

The T-san wore neither crown nor robes, for its lowlying carapace was suited to neither. It paused by the herald to make a suitable gesture of respect and appreciation, for the T-san speech apparatus was so unlike that of the Scattered Races that its people were accustomed to being referred to by human sounds. The herald had made an attempt at pronouncing its actual name, and, given the inferiority of the human palate, had come reasonably close.

The T-san Breeder dipped its respect to the Emperor and took its place beside Councillor Asabin. The swirls of gold which it had painted on its upper surface blended in nicely with the rest of the company's attire, and although the T-san didn't fully understand the purpose of such ornamenation—its own government functioned with less visual pomposity—it could tell that the application was both appropriate and appreciated.

As always, the presence of his non-human colleague inspired awe in Pezh: for what Azea had accomplished, and against what odds that had been done. There were over a hundred species represented in the T-san's House, some from environments so alien to Pezh's own that any hope of his understanding them was at best an exercise in futility. Between them and humanity there was little common ground, and sometimes good reason for hostility. Yet human and non-human stood united before this Court, bound together by a common dream, a common nation. And if the government they shared was less than perfect, that was only to be expected; in the face of such diversity, it was nothing short of amazing that the Empire functioned at all.

"From the Emperor's military forces," the herald continued, bringing Pezh's attention back to the present. "Director Ebre ni Kahv, of StarControl."

Ebre's full dress uniform fit snugly to his muscular figure, a strong contrast to the flowing robes of the other humans. A black half-jacket covered the right side of his white under-uniform, its diagonal edge embroidered in gold thread and fastened with gold buttons to the layer beneath it. Embroidered planets ran down the outside edge of his black sleeve, one for each world he had subjugated through force or treaty. Gold braid proclaimed by its placement on the jacket his involvement in peace treaties, non-Braxin diplomacy, and other efforts in the Empire's name. About his white arm a band of brightly colored squares proclaimed in code his training and present status; the gold band above it, the most coveted decoration of the Empire, indicated that he was bound by personal fealty to the Emperor and was permitted to speak in his name.

Ebre came before his liege and knelt. "Majesty. May I speak?"

"Your words are always welcome," Pezh responded formally.

"It is said that though a man brings great glory to his office, he dishonors it if in the end he seeks to hold it past the proper time. Nearly a century ago the crown of state was placed upon my head; I have tried to do it justice. The Crowns of the time entrusted me with a great office and I believe I have served it to the best of my ability."

"You have done it nothing but honor," Pezh assured him.

"I thank you. I fear, however, that I am no longer young. My health begins to fail me in ways that medicine cannot correct. I am forced to recognize that I have entered into the last stage of my life, in which death may take me at any time, perhaps without warning."

He paused. "It is in the tradition of StarControl to hand down the Directorship while one is still alive, in order that the fleets may never be without an active leader. I feel that the time has come to do this."

"We will all be sorry to see you go, Director. But we are also aware of the custom, and the reasoning behind it, and approve wholeheartedly of your decision. I know I speak for my colleagues when I say that we release you from your office willingly, but with great personal regret."

Ebre's voice tightened. "I can't pretend that I'm not sorry to do this."

The Emperor waited respectfully for Ebre to regain full control of himself. "Have you chosen a successor?" he asked at last.

"I have, your Majesty. Will you permit me to present her to this Court?"

Pezh nodded. He could almost hear the "her" in that sentence reverberating all the way to Braxi. He, of course, knew of Ebre's choice, and had already given his approval. But the information hadn't been released to the others, for fear that it would reach Braxi before the ceremony. This time, he mused, the Presentation would be more than mere ritual.

"I present to the illustrious company Starcommander Torzha er Litz." Ebre extended a hand toward her and she came down the central aisle, took her place by his side, and knelt. Gold decorations adorned her white half-jacket in a noteworthy quantity; even if they couldn't read the details, Pezh knew, the other Crowns of Azea would be impressed. "Her given name means 'fire,' in the sense of that which purifies through destruction—an appropriate appellation for one of the Empire's most accomplished Starcommanders. Her adult name, Litz, was chosen after the Braxin conquest of a colony by that name—a conquest that entailed the slaughter of over two and a half million men and women, thereby embodying the essence of Braxin brutality. She bears it as a constant reminder of her purpose. In service, her record is outstanding; she is of brilliant tactical mind and commands respect in all branches of the military. She is the one best suited to inherit my office, and although I regret the necessity of withdrawing her from active Border service for this purpose, I feel that all aspects of our military effort will benefit from her assignment to the Directorship."

"The Starcommander's reputation is well known to us," Pezh told him, and he favored her with a smile. She was nervous—well, that was to be expected—but she was hiding it well.

He looked toward his fellow Crowns for response. It would not be unreasonable for any of them to ask for time to consult their various Councils and vote on the matter; on the other hand, when news of Ebre's intended retirement had come they had probably started immediate discussion of the qualifications of the obvious candidates. Had Torzha been on that list? Apparently so, for Grand Councillor Asabin nodded a subtle gesture of approval, as did

Grand Justice zi Reis, somewhat more grudgingly, the Emperor thought. And Pezh had dealt with the T-san long enough to know its gentle hiss for the affirmation it was.

"We accept your retirement," he told Ebre. "And we welcome your chosen replacement."

One by one, Ebre ni Kahv removed his five rings of office, four from his left hand and one, bearing the seal of StarControl, from his right. One by one he handed them to the Emperor, and then gave over the simple circlet which had been his crown. There were tears coming to his eyes, but his sorrow did not interfere with the ritual grace of his actions.

Pezh turned to Torzha, who knelt directly before him.

"I give you my life and my loyalty," she said, "and swear to serve you, your Crown, and the Empire, setting these priorities above all other things. And I vow to protect the Empire, its territories and its peoples, from all outside threats, including but not limited to that of Braxin aggression, in accordance with the precepts of the Founding."

He offered her his right hand and she pressed the seal of Azea to her forehead. "Know that as you serve my office, so am I bound to serve and protect yours," he promised. And he placed the seal of Azea, set in the ring Ebre had worn, upon her left hand.

One by one she knelt before the other Crowns, who offered her ritual acceptance and words of mutual service, and gave to her the rings which tied her office to theirs. The T-san had brought a translator to handle the verbal requirements but with a nod she dismissed him, and she exchanged the ritual words with the Breeder in its own aspirated tongue. Ebre smiled slightly, warm with pride. Had she studied the language just for this occasion? Pezh wondered. If so, it was a promising gesture.

She returned to her place before the Emperor and knelt there.

Solemnly he raised the circlet over her head and held it there; now was the time, in this moment of silence, for any last objections to be raised. He looked out over the assembled multitude (uniformed, most of them, and glittering with decorations), and past them to the windows which made Azea visible. There deathwinds swirled savagely, and gray dust smote the glass with soundless fury. No one spoke. After a moment he nodded, satisfied, and lowered the golden ring to her hair, settling it around her head. With hands on her shoulders he raised her, then, and presented her to the populace.

"Know that the Empire supports this woman in her office, and that she is entitled to speak for its Throne." He turned her back to him and offered his hand, smiling, for her to clasp. "Congratulations, Director." He guided her through her ritual acceptance, nodding as she shared an embrace with the Lugastine, a bow with the T-san, and a somewhat colder handclasp with the Grand Justice. There was a look in his eyes that seemed to anticipate trouble; given the new Director's political leanings, Pezh was not surprised.

Solemnly the herald announced the termination of the court. There would be a reception later, in the heart of the Imperial Palace, and there a thousand and one dignitaries who had not been able to attend the ceremony itself would have their chance to ply the Throne with questions. Pezh sighed inwardly. It was frustrating to play these political games on his own home world, where the very questions he faced were dependent upon unnatural air, upon the illusion of comfort which they created for strangers. Out there, in the atmosphere that only his race could breathe, the Azean dream had been born; only there, surrounded by the acrid odor of Death, could the purpose of his people be truly understood.

Officers of the realm nodded their respect, bowed, or groveled, as befit their culture and station; Pezh acknowledged it all with a diplomatic smile as they left the greathall's confines. First the Councillors, the humans adopting the pace of their slower alien comrade, then the Emperor, flanked by the past and current Directors. They passed out of the greathall itself, under the towering archway that marked the termination of ceremony.

As they proceeded down the adjoining corridor Pezh dropped back a bit, letting the Councillors get ahead of him. When they turned the corner he nodded a command to one of his guards, who threw open the door to a side chamber. Ebre, expecting such action of him (how well they knew each other!) entered; Torzha, after a moment's hesitation, did likewise.

Closing the door, Pezh shut the guards—and the world—outside. And transformed himself into something that was no less an Emperor, but which was more informal, therefore more approachable. He was, after all, a simple and practical man. Ebre knew that. The new Director would realize it soon enough.

"Well?" he said, turning to Torzha. "Ebre said you wanted to talk to me. He *implied* you wanted to talk to me before the Grand Justice did. And since zi Reis would think nothing of dragging me away from the reception to discuss business, I thought I would make myself available before we got there. Director?"

She blushed slightly at the unaccustomed title, and seemed surprised to find herself doing so. But her voice was not without strength as she told him. "There is a . . . situation . . . of great personal importance to me. I hadn't intended to bring it up today—"

"But Ebre thought it would be best if you did. And I agree. Generally speaking, I prefer efficiency to protocol." She brightened at that; good, because he had chosen his words to encourage her. He knew what she was going to ask, and had already made his decision. "What is it, Torzha er?"

She took a deep breath, for courage.

"It's about a young woman I've sponsored. . . ."

Viton: It is in the nature of man that he is antagonistic toward the others of his sex. Each man sees in another a potential competitor for the limited rewards of male success, and the hostility which arises between them is a part of the natural balance of human life.

It is possible, as in the case of father and son, that a closeness will arise between two men which threatens the functional hostility of each. It is the duty of society to provide an artificial means of encouraging the proper degree of antagonism.

EIGHT

"Bless him!" Turak swore, and drowned the oath with the last of the wine.

He was young, handsome, and purebred. His cloak was askew on his shoulders and his hair was disheveled—but the latter had been managed by a woman, so he let it remain as a monument to her touch. The former he rearranged as he raised a gloved hand to attract the proper attention.

"Wine!" he cried in the mode of command. "Suitable for my Race."

The woman beside him smiled and pushed the pile of empty bottles to the far end of the table. Inside her was a nagging concern for him, but it would be improper—and with a Braxaná, possibly fatal—to let that show in such a place. She would have to assume he could handle what he had drunk, though it would take more than a man to do so.

"May he come to worship an active deity!" he muttered, and she shot him a warning glance which she hoped would communicate that even in this place such language couldn't be tolerated. The winemaster stumbled past crowded tables to them, humble and nervous. "Lord," he said meekly, "I have no more Braxaná wine. Perhaps some other—"

"Why not?" Turak demanded.

"Begging the Lord's pardon, my Lord, but you . . . that is to say, it has been finished—" and to illustrate he indicated the tableful of emptied containers.

Turak, son of Sechaveh, stood and let the stool fall behind him with a clatter, rising to his full height and with a practiced hand gripping the other by his hair. "You tell me this is all you stock?" The winemaster waved helplessly to indicate the poverty of his patrons, to point out wordlessly that there was no call in such a place as this for high-priced luxuries.

"For the chance that a Braxaná will come here, you should keep enough to satisfy one man." His voice, penetrating and obviously inebriated, drew attention from all corners of the room. She was afraid of him but more afraid for him, and when he reached for the Zhaor he had not worn that day she stood and pulled him back.

"Lord, some air perhaps. . . ." He was trembling beneath the mask of his rage, and seemed disoriented. "I'll pay—" she began, but the winemaster was more willing to lose this small fortune than to risk Turak's presence a moment longer than he had to. "Take him with you, make him forget this place, and that's payment enough. I have enough problems without an upper-class vendetta."

How strong he seemed, and how weak he was! The eyes which gleamed alertly saw, in reality, nothing; the walk which appeared powerful and arrogant only did so because she supported him. In the depths of drunkenness the need for image was such a driving force that, although nearly unconscious, supported by a woman, he frightened the lower class patrons as he walked by them.

How can they be so weak, she wondered, and still maintain this image of strength? She took him from the main room out into the dark street. She had met him there while the sun, B'Salos, was still high in the sky. Now the moon had taken its place. She called for a carriage, leaned him against a wall, and tried to soothe him.

"I took you to taste you," he murmured. There was sweat on his face. "I probably can't even do that now."

She shook her head, smiling sadly. "It doesn't matter, Lord—there'll be other nights, other women. As for myself, few women of my class can boast of witnessing a Braxaná Rage. If I've served you in the least—"

"Oh, you have, you have! We need women so desperately, my kind. We can't approach our own sex . . . it's not like that with the common blood, is it?"

She shook her head sadly. "No, it's not. But that doesn't matter, Lord. There'll be a carriage in a moment; it would do you good to rest, and wait."

Half delirious, he murmured, "I will *kill* him. I have to. There's no other way. . . ."

A public carriage approached their call station and slowed to a stop. She pulled him gently from the wall, aware that one of two men had come from the tavern to watch but feeling it better not to tell him. He stumbled once, but with her help he reached the door and fell inside. By the time she had fed the address to the steering mechanism he was sound asleep, so she programmed the alarm before she told the carriage to depart.

Which one of the men watching, she wondered, would wish to taste the woman a Lord chose? Hopefully none of them—but then, Braxin luck was rarely that good.

* * *

"And you made a fool of yourself in front of *whom*? Not he upper classes, no, who at least would know you for the racial exception you are! No. You act like an idiot in *Sulos,* and disgrace our image in front of men who have never seen its glory. Turak, you're going to work hard to outdo this one."

"Father—"

With an angry gesture Sechaveh cut him off. "Don't tell me about your hangover. I don't want to hear it. And don't try to convince me that all this never really happened, either, or that it did but perhaps I'm exaggerating the details, because I *know.* I set Karas to follow you; he witnessed the whole thing. So!" His eyes were burning with anger; Turak covered his own with a wet cloth. "You," the Kaim'era proclaimed, "are a shame to our Tribe. You are a living example of everything the Braxaná seek to deny. I regret the day I chose to let you live to adulthood!"

"I regret the days you keep me in this god-blessed House! Father, don't you understand?" He raised his face from the cool cloth and with bloodshot eyes pleaded to be heard. "I can't go on like this. I'm thirty years old. My time has come!"

"Thirty, you say! What's thirty years in the face of two hundred? By the Azean calendar you're barely six, and sometimes I think that's more accurate . . . Turak, you are a *child.* I see in you none of the attributes of manhood. Am I then to inherit you, to proclaim to the world that I consider you a mature independent, when in fact I consider you no such thing? Act like a Braxaná and you'll be inherited according to your birthright!"

"As my father was?" he snapped, using the speech mode of irony. It was dangerous to remind the Kaim'era of his own alien upbringing, even with mode-veiled references, and he knew it. But he could not help but be pleased as Sechaveh's face darkened, as his eyes filled with a cold and terrible loathing. Hatred, pure hatred: the honesty of it was strangely refreshing.

"I overcame my past," Sechaveh hissed. "Could you have done the same, I wonder? Or would you still be a slave of alien women on some festering backVoid planet?" He laughed, his composure returning. "Perhaps that would suit you, Turak." And he turned away, his unguarded back the ultimate insult. "Perhaps that's what you really want."

He stood still for a moment, driving home the lesson of Turak's impotence—great as the younger man's anger was, would he dare to strike?—then strode to the door and passed close enough that it opened automatically for him. Then he turned back to his son, smiling as he relished his parting blow.

"The woman—remember her?—is dead."

"And you enjoyed that, didn't you!"

The Kaim'era's eyes sparkled. "That is not the issue."

"You and your blessed—"

"The others will die also; all witnesses to the incident must be disposed of, and quickly. But she died first. Slowly, Turak, very slowly. Does that bother you?"

The dark eyes were fastened on him, seeking entrance to his soul. The woman, the woman . . . what did she matter, except that he had wanted her, had drunk with her, had abandoned her to the Sulosian night? Only that his pleasure had consigned her to a lingering death and had fueled the sadism of a man he despised. "I am *Braxaná,*" he answered defiantly.

"Are you?" Sechaveh seemed amused, and that, too, was a deliberate facade, intended to wound him. "Are you *really*?"

Turak flung the cloth at him in rage, but it caught in the closing doors and was held there, dripping in mid-air, as the Kaim'era exited. "I can't go on," he muttered. "Not like this. If he's going to force me to it. . . ."

The door opened. The cloth remained and Sil'ne, holding it, entered. "Lord?" she asked gently.

He waved her in.

She was a short woman, black-haired in tribute to her half-Braxaná heritage but rendered slim-hipped by the genetic pollution of some less comely race. *What makes her stay with him?* he wondered suddenly. *What makes her willing to serve such a man?*

She was carrying a small tray, which she offered to him; on it was a swept-glass vial filled with a small quantity of painkiller. It was a general remedy and would be of limited value to him; nevertheless, it was preferable to nothing. He drank it gratefully.

Power. She endured Sechaveh because his House offered her power. No matter how much he hated women, he must have one to run his private affairs; no matter how much he hated *her*, he must bow—albeit ill-naturedly—to her competence. Braxaná custom demanded it.

"Did he really. . . . To that woman?" He was unable to voice more specific words, as if by doing so he would make the nightmare real.

She smiled faintly. "A commoner, Lord? I doubt it was worth his time. Probably a guard took care of her, and that swiftly." He knew she was lying, but was grateful for it. "Does it matter so very much to you?"

"He does it to strike at me," he muttered resentfully.

"He wants you to be immune to such things," she pointed out.

"He hates me!"

"As is proper." She took the vial, now emptied, from his gloved hand, and replaced it on the tray. "Is it not, Lord Turak?"

"Yes." He shut his eyes and leaned his head back against the raw silk cushions. "Of course. Very proper. Always hatred . . . I want to kill him, Sil'ne!"

She was silent for a moment, "If you meant that," she said at last, "*really* meant it, you wouldn't tell me. You wouldn't tell anyone, not even in jest. Too dangerous. The death of a Braxaná . . . that's a serious thing, Lord. So may I assume that you're not in earnest?"

He looked at her and tried to read her, but either he was too unpracticed or she was too guarded. What manner of woman would choose to serve Sechaveh, and could do so successfully, without falling victim to his wrathful misogyny? "You may," he told her, wondering at her strength as she left him.

If you really meant that. . . .

He had said it a thousand times and meant it as the Braxaná always meant such things: not at all, and entirely. He had dreamt endless variations of his father's demise and in all of them it was his hand that held the knife, leveled the stun, cast the bomb . . . but had he ever thought he really might do it? With all the risks that it entailed?

Ah, but it would be sweet!

He fantasized again—a cliff's edge on Matinar—but the vision was foggy. For once his imaginings failed to win for him the cathartic release that he could usually elicit from them. For dreams, in the face of reality, paled in essence and lacked true emotion.

Would he really do it?

Years ago he might have said no and been done with the idea; zhents ago, even mere days ago, he would have discarded it nearly as swiftly, after a brief review of the consequences. Now . . . it was tempting. Sechaveh had driven him to the point of desperation, not only by withholding the status of manhood from him but by *toying* with him, by feeding on his suffering . . . he was willing to consider anything other than sitting back and taking it all, day after day and year after year, as his father apparently meant for him to do. Revenge would be sweet, after all this humiliation. But how. . .?

He did not drink that night. It was the first time in many zhents that he faced himself without the false support of alcohol, but he wanted his thoughts clear and so he pushed the chosen bottles aside. With sober awareness he considered the Kaim'era's actions, and hatred burned so strongly inside him that he was almost driven back to his wine in an effort to lessen the blow. But no; this was reality. For a decade now Turak had been trapped in this House and bound to a man who obviously hated him with all the fury that was appropriate between Braxaná adults, yet who refused to allow him to grow to adulthood. Now it was time for his son to harvest his resentment and turn it to action. And if the action was risky and illegal—well, then it would have to be managed carefully.

He considered the nature of the problem: the Braxaná, who controlled everything of consequence in the Holding, had long sought to armor themselves against possible assassination by careful application of law and custom. There was no more heinous crime than the murder of a purebred Braxaná, and none more readily punished. In the face of such an outrage all laws were expendable, and all peoples besides. If a known murderer—even a suspected murderer—were to claim refuge on a planet, and if that planet was foolish enough to have him, then it and its population were forfeit, its inhabitants' lives inconsequential things to be snuffed out in the name of Braxaná justice. And woe betide the murderer who was captured. For him were reserved tortures both ancient and modern, blood-bringing and neuro-implanted, delicately timed to strip a man of dignity and strength while never quite robbing him of life. It was a picture so grim that it had often soured Turak's dreams of vengeance and proven them to be no more than impotent imaginings. But not so now.

He began to plan.

How does a Braxaná murder a Braxaná? The swords of the Braxaná are distinctly of that tribe and leave a telling wound; the poison of that people is only available to members of the Master Race and marks the murderer as one of them. Besides all that, there would be the necessity of some kind of final confrontation, which complicated matters immensely. But Turak was typical of his kind and could not commit himself to vengeance without the ego gratification of forcing Sechaveh to recognize the architect of his downfall. In that lay the greatest danger of all.

There were too many variables; he tried to convince himself of that, but he failed. Long days passed, rank with the humiliation of not owning property or women in his own name, days in which he fought the impulse to drink himself into oblivion, as he had so often done in the past. Once he had dreamed of earning his inheritance, as Sechaveh seemed to want him to do. Now at last he knew that to be impossible. His father was tormenting him, deliberately and with the skill born of practice, holding out the promise of independence only to withdraw it time and time again. The Kaim'era had made an enemy of his purebred son; Turak was determined that he must now pay the price for it.

Step by step he considered the problem.

If he killed Sechaveh, it would be clear that the man was dead; that could not be avoided. Another Lord might disappear indefinitely, but not one of the Kaim'eri. His death, therefore, must appear to be an accident.

But it would be foolish for Turak to bet his life upon such a ruse. He knew all too well how easily the Central Computer could wade through a plethora of unrelated facts and draw from them a simple, clear conclusion which could unmask a man's hidden activities. He had seen it done, and had no desire to be at the receiving end of such action. So: if he killed Sechaveh, no matter how carefully he worked it, it was likely that investigation would reveal him.

Unless, he thought, *it revealed someone else.*

It was his introduction to Braxaná politics.

He started paying attention to Sechaveh's House, wanting to gain as much information as he could without having to call up the Computer's files—because there would be a record made of that, and any record of any part of this was something to be avoided. It would have been easier if he had been inherited, for he needed extra eyes to help with the watching, anonymous faces to surround and observe his prey. As it was, though, he had to work alone, and it was that much harder.

He compiled a list of Sechaveh's assets as he knew them. He consulted the House computer for general information and was able to add to his list from that. He never asked anything directly. Sometimes it took him tenths, even days to work out the exact wording of a request so that no one who reviewed it would be able to determine just what information he had really wanted. Ayyara, for instance—Turak suspected that his father had mining interests there and he was considering the possibility of using the underground labyrinths to entrap him. But he could not ask the computer directly. Instead he feigned an interest in such things in order to prepare a portfolio of investments for the time when his life would be his own. He reviewed the mineral wealth of a hundred planets and a thousand companies, and only slowly, by asking just the right questions at just the right times, did he work his way around to Ayyara. At last his efforts were rewarded, for the computer informed him of the extent of Sechaveh's interest in the planet, the companies he dealt with, and myriad other details concerning the Kaim'era. Most important, of course, the information was buried under an avalanche of misguiding queries to the point where anyone asking the computer if he had specifically investigated Sechaveh's holdings would receive a negative answer.

That was his first major success. He was exhilarated by it, but not so much so that he forgot to continue the line of questioning until more useless trivia had obscured its other end. It was just as dangerous to end with the true question as it was to begin with it.

Ayyara, alas, was unsuitable, a secure operation with aboveground machinery. He had overlooked that possibility. But it had been good practice and now he applied himself in a similar manner to the rest of Sechaveh's holdings.

Zhents passed. He noticed a change in himself. No longer did he drink to excess, and rarely did he explode in fury before those who should not witness it. His determination to commit patricide and survive the consequences was an obsessive passion that colored everything he did. He became quiet on the outside; inside, no one but himself could see, his mind seethed with plots and counterplots, and the organic computer that was his brain struggled to sort diverse and disorganized knowledge into useful categories, and to draw from those a single picture of action that fulfilled all his requirements.

Now, when his father threw his dependence in his face he held in the rage. Now he learned that the face does not have to reflect the heart but the reason, the will, and the intellect. He learned to move without guilt, practicing for the day when his life might depend on it. He learned guile. With one terrible objective burning continually in his mind, he came to perfect a mask of disinterest that disguised his all-consuming passion. It was not enough that he was capable of such deception when the time of his vengeance came at last, for then such a change in him would itself be an admission of guilt. No, he must manage the image now and maintain it before the act, during, and after, burying his intent with the same thoroughness that he had used while drawing forth information from the House files.

He noticed these changes and for a brief time wondered if they weren't enough. Wasn't this after all what Sechaveh had always wanted of him? But the Kaim'era still regarded him with scorn (although certainly with less anger) and his look still clearly said: you are not worthy of the Race, or of adulthood. And Turak's anger burned to new heights, in which any doubts he had entertained were fully consumed and a new man was born—one who would not be defeated by House or custom, or even by law, for the force of his vengeance was stronger than all those things combined and it alone ruled him.

He had gained a reasonable picture of Sechaveh's business dealings; now he needed to find a possible murderer. It couldn't be too obvious a choice, for a man who was known as Sechaveh's enemy would never dare to strike at him this way. Or wouldn't he? Might not such a man consider himself above suspicion because others would reason it exactly that way? Turak shook his head, discarding the thought. It was a sound idea but too complex for the moment; he was untried in such maneuverings and needed something simpler to work with. Perhaps later, though—when Sechaveh was gone and he had his own business liaisons to protect.

It was harder to research the others than it had been with his father; he was not in their Houses, and had no instinctive knowledge of where to start, such as comes from having lived around a man all of one's lifetime and having that knowledge seep in with or without one's awareness of the process. The other men were enigmas only. Should he chose a Kaim'era? No, that kind would not be so foolish. But a purebred Lord, and one raised in a Kaim'era's House—such would have the ruthlessness and knowledge required to commit murder among his own kind, as well as the requisite recklessness.

This was safer ground on which to tread. His investigations were done using the House computer, which meant that no records would exist in the House of his intended victim, Even so, he was cautious, and was as circuitous in his study of the various Lords of Braxi as he had been regarding his own father.

And at last he was rewarded.

He was not the man he had been. A year or two ago, when he had first conceived of this project, he might have celebrated this success with a night of drunken gaming and doused his death-passion in a woman's embrace. Now, when he saw the pieces fall into place there was barely a hint of triumph across his face; a smile, ever so subtle, said that he knew this for the beginning step it was and recognized that victory was still a long way off—and that he could never afford to celebrate openly. He no longer needed to.

On the planet T'sarak there were farms, raised high above the fertile surface, in which Sechaveh had an interest and which other Lords were also considering for investment purposes. The T'sarakene—colonists at first, later citizens of an independent nation under Braxi—had decided to take advantage of their regular climate and plant the delicate plii-ei, whose blossoms yielded the Holding's finest aphrodisiac and whose leaves were medicinally invaluable in treating skin disorders. The vines had never been grown successfully outside of a small fertile band on their native planet, but T'sarak had a similar biochemical base and a minimal change of seasons, and its people decided to try.

Not until their fifth crop of costly vines had withered on their supports did T'sarak realize that they required more than good weather; their native world was a place of high winds, whose velocity tore loose the youthblossoms when their grasp on the mothervine weakened, allowing the secondary flowers to grow at just the proper pace for the priceless nectar to develop its valuable properties. The plii-ei had never grown well in artificial environments, so a hothouse would be of limited value. Besides, the T'sarakene had a better solution. They built lattice-work vinefarms and raised them high above the ground, into the planet's stratosphere, where the crosswinds of T'sarak might stimulate the plants in their accustomed manner. So were the plii-ei grown and farmed, not to the same perfection that they knew in the wild but very similarly, and in an atmospheric density more similar to that of home than the surface of T'sarak had to offer.

The Braxaná mindset was attracted to drugs of pleasure and regarding the plii-ei it responded accordingly. Sechaveh had underwritten the cost of the original farm construction and was rewarded with a share of the profits. A number of other Braxaná had approached the T'sarakene, but they had been turned away; Sechaveh had no intention of giving up his advantage, and saw to it that the farmers acted accordingly. Doubtless, there were a number of Lords who would like to see Sechaveh . . . removed. And doubtless the T'sarakene resented that a Central power should have such control over a vital part of their economy.

Turak smiled. Then, with all the care of an experienced Kaim'era, he began to plot the details of his father's demise. *Soon,* he promised Sechaveh, *you will pay the price for your cruelty.*

* * *

Mashak Vinemaster was a lean, high-strung man. In all his mannerisms there was an underlying chord of tension. His voice was harsh and he gave orders sharply, in a tone of voice that implied they could not be obeyed quickly enough to please him. And in truth they could not. He was one of the few who had dreamed of bringing the vines of T'sarak, and one of the fewer who had held onto that dream when the first imports died without secondflower. Now he was caught in a web of foreign economic intrigue—for the Central Braxins were foreign to T'sarak, though they had supplied the human seed that settled there—from which he longed to extricate himself.

He nodded sharply at the guards of Vineshadow and passed into the city. They knew him by sight—they had better. He had little time to waste and had no intention of going through lengthy identification verification at his own border. Woe betide the guard—or anyone—who got in his way.

The city: refineries, packaging plants, distilleries, and dormitory facilities for the migrant harvesters. There was an agreement among the vinemasters of T'sarak by which the times of planting and harvest were staggered, so that the same men might work each farm in turn. The city was nearly empty now, but soon it would be filled with the heady fragrance of the precious flowers and the pungent odor of the laborers' presence. A few workers remained at the factories and guards were kept at the entrances and exits; other than that, however, Vineshadow was deserted.

Mashak passed quickly to the base of the city's Tower and nodded to the guards there. He saw them start—they seemed to be new—but then they recognized him, if only from pictorial memory, and without a word let him pass. Good. It was nice to see the new men pick up the way of things so quickly.

He entered the lift and slapped the control down.

The cage he occupied hesitated only briefly before beginning its long journey upward through the towershaft. On all four sides of him at regular intervals were the cogravitic anchors that kept the Tower standing upright through its miles of height, balancing the weight of the pseudometal structure at right angles to the planet's surface. Through three sides of the cage he could see his lands; the fourth was filled with tanks of gas-fertilizer, doubtless waiting for the proper hand to come and apply it. Across the valley he could see other vinefarms, three of them his. He was a rich man, despite the massive tithes the vinefarmers had to pay to their Braxaná patron, and he intended to stay that way.

The cage ascended slowly, so that he might get used to the changing pressure. There were oxygen masks all along the sides of the cage, but he left them where they were on their hanging clips; he wouldn't be going all the way to the top.

What could it be that the Kaim'era wanted? He fingered the flatrendering in his pocket and wondered, annoyed, at the summons. It was no secret that he hated the Kaim'era Sechaveh and would rather deal with him via third parties; to him the Braxaná represented everything that was wrong with the economic system of the Holding, in which a man who risked life and limb to get a project going had to spend the rest of time giving someone else the choicest fruits of his labors. But the message had been clear: *Come here, and come here now.*

Far be it for Sechaveh to imagine that he had other things to do and could ill afford the time for this little excursion!

The cage drew to a slow stop and Mashak pushed the door aside. Halfway between the surface and the vines themselves was a landing platform for small aircraft, a mode of transportation that most of the wealthy preferred. A simple forcefield acted as railing, and although its faint glow was not now visible in the low-angled sunlight Mashak was grateful as always to know that it was there. He did not mind treading the walkways which wound between his beloved vines, but there the view was not so empty, not nearly so threatening. The open space of the landing platform and its seemingly sudden drop into nothingness never failed to unnerve him, and it added now to his annoyance at having been called here with no explanation of why.

He tapped his foot impatiently on the pseudometal platform. Between the winds overhead and the noise of his own irritated movement he almost missed the whisper of movement behind him. A shadow moved out of the corner of his eye, out of keeping with what he expected from this place and therefore more confusing than frightening. He turned; that is, he started to. Then there was a flash of sun-on-silver and a tearing pain that burst through every nerve in his body, and in his last moment of consciousness he imagined it was the hated face of his master/enemy that grinned at him with something akin to triumph.

Turak left the cage and went over to the body.

Mashak was unharmed by the stun's discharge but in his fall he had struck his head against the pseudometal platform, and a thin river of blood was wending its way down one side of his face. Turak wiped it away with the edge of his sash and arranged the man's hair so that it would cover the wound. Then, carefully, he hefted the body upright and carried it back to the cage, where he propped it up against the fertilizer tanks in a fair semblance of conscious boredom. He crossed the arms and pinned the sleeves so they remained in place, tacked the man's lids open so they stayed that way, and in general toyed with the unconscious form until only the closest examination would show that anything was wrong with it.

Then he took his place again between the stacks of tanks and waited.

It was but a short time before Sechaveh's shuttle arrived, and seeing Mashak in the cage, the Kaim'era doubtless felt secure in landing. He would have no servants with him, for such was his way in business dealings—Turak knew that. Nor would he be suspicious of Mashak's presence within the cage instead of out on the platform, as the Vinemaster's distaste for the view was well known on T'sarak, and therefore to him.

His breath held, muscles taut in readiness, Tarak waited.

The small shuttle anchored itself and after a moment of internal adjustment its sides parted, and a ramp spilled forth from it. Shadowed by the small ship's bulk, Sechaveh descended.

It took him only a moment to realize something was wrong. But in that moment Turak moved free of the cage's confines and into the open, and with a steady hand directed his stun at his father's chest.

Sechaveh was careful not to move. There was no weapon he could reach faster than his son could shoot, although he was, as usual, armed. "Well," he said quietly, his voice unusually calm for a man about to die. "Not badly managed. Lord Dumar, if I don't mistake it?"

Turak nodded. With his beard clipped short and his hair curled tighter and his makeup designed accordingly, he was a fair duplicate for Dumar. His father, of course, recognized him, but it was doubtful that strangers would. "If anyone who's seen me speaks, the trail will lead back to him."

"Not badly planned." The Kaim'era's tone was frankly appreciative, although he was careful not to jar Turak into firing with any unexpected movements. "A little elementary, but you definitely have a grasp on the concept of the thing. Do share the rest of it," he urged.

He did so, proudly. "Mashak's hatred of you causes him to make an unfortunate decision, and he attempts to take your life on this platform. That attempt fails. There is a struggle, the bodies are tipped over the edge while moving. . . ." He shrugged, implying the rest with the coldness of the gesture. "Two bodies in Vineshadow, and I doubt they'll salvage enough to draw any useful conclusions from the remains."

"And if anyone remembers you being here, they'll have the wrong description. Not bad, Turak. Dumar isn't my worthiest rival, but he will do. You sent a note to Mashak?"

"Yes." He smiled, pleased at his workmanship. "I used Dumar's access code and sent it from a neighboring system where he is presently vacationing. Where a woman I hired will keep him occupied and alone during the time he was supposed to be here."

"And she?"

"The Black Death."

Sechaveh smiled, relishing the image. "Ah. I take back what I said, Turak—*excellently* done, down to the last aesthetic detail. A job to make me proud. And I am. Provided you yourself are covered—"

He smiled triumphantly. "Of course."

"Is that all, then?"

Turak raised his weapon higher, fingering the trigger with obvious relish. "Not quite. The forcefield surrounding this platform has been sabotaged, of course. The forceshears that did the work were discarded as the saboteur left the city."

"And can betraced to—"

"The city of a rival Vinemaster."

"Superb!" Sechaveh did not look at all like a man about to die, nor did he sound like one. "Well, Turak, I'm very impressed by all this. A good plan, well executed, a little bit raw about the edges perhaps, but it definitely shows promise. That bit about the local rivalry is particularly nice—it'll give the Kaim'eri someone to punish who isn't of their own Race."

Turak's face was set. "I'm glad you appreciate it." He aimed, and the arm that would fire tensed.

"One thing more."

"Get it over with!"

Sechaveh's expression was enigmatic, unnerving. "You've overlooked one important detail."

"You can't bluff me out of this," he warned.

"How Braxaná . . . I do believe you would kill me, Turak. How refreshing! Few of us dare to actually take the lives of our enemies, in this day and age." He paused. "I have something for you, before you fire."

"What is it?"

Slowly, careful not to alarm his son, Sechaveh moved one hand to the other and worked loose a wide gold band from his left forefinger. He made as if to throw it, then reconsidered—the cage was directly behind Turak—and, dropping it to the platform, pushed it with the tip of his boot until it slid to Turak's feet.

"What is it?" the young man repeated, less sure of himself.

"Your inheritance."

The stun wavered.

"I anticipated you, you see. You can't kill me, of course. I've made certain my colleagues know of our enmity. Yes, Turak, always remember that even *I* have allies, and I've kept track of your actions for the past few years. So shoot me, if you wish—but only if you don't value your own life."

His arm lowered somewhat; the motion was unconscious, neither planned nor noticed. "You're bluffing," he accused, clearly uncertain.

"Am I? Then kill me, Turak. I shall die with the pleasure of knowing you'll be punished for it—very probably on the equipment I designed for just such a purpose."

Bless you! the younger man cursed inwardly. His hatred surged to new heights, his anguish also, but he dared not shoot. "Why this, then?" he demanded. He pointed a jerky finger at the ring by his feet.

"Because you've earned it, Turak. You've proven yourself a man. A Braxaná should be willing to destroy anyone who stands between him and his pleasure—even if that someone is another of his Race. Even his own father." His expression darkened. "There are others who call themselves Braxaná, but they don't comprehend what that title means, much less are they deserving of it. But you, my son—you, whom I have trained . . . you *are* Braxaná. At last." And now his eyes sparkled, and a smile, both amused and sadistic, danced across his face. "It took you long enough."

Shaking with shame and rage, Turak lowered his weapon to his side.

"Very practical," the Kaim'era approved. "A fine mixture of the barbarian and the statesman. Eager to kill, but able to recognize the limitations of his political environment. You'll make a fine adult, Turak."

"I hate you," he answered venemously. "You've had the better of me this time, but I swear, Kaim'era—"

"Of course you do." He cut off the next sentence also; "And of course you really mean it. I have no doubts about that. You'll have to wait, of course, until you're sure I'm not still watching you. It could be a while. But a man grows wise from enmity." He bowed slightly, very slightly, more out of humor than respect, but not entirely lacking in the latter. "I've waited a long time for this, Turak.

Congratulations. Now, if you will excuse me, I'm on a tight schedule. . . ."

He would have fired—he *should* have fired—but reality bound his hand and he couldn't find the trigger that would commit not only Sechaveh but himself to death. Helplessly he watched as the shuttle lifted itself from the platform and rose slowly into the sheetwinds of the stratosphere, and beyond. Floating youthblossoms marked its wake.

Just wait, Turak thought. *Someday.*

He remembered to take the ring.

Viton: For the true warrior, friendship is disarming and security is deadly. Both weaken a man by giving him the illusion of might, when in fact they undermine the very foundations of his own power by causing him to rely upon others. Anything that distracts a man from his chosen course is abhorrent to one who values his own strength.

NINE

Darkness 1

Anzha was trapped in someone else's dream.

Such a thing didn't happen often, but it happened. Intensity of emotion meant intensity of contact; in the close confines of the Institute, where hundreds of psychics lived, worked, and trained together, it was to be expected that occasionally two dreamers would come insync (as the Institute termed it) and share the same sleep-bound fantasies.

The odds against it happening outside the Institute were of course phenomenal. Nevertheless, in this case all the odds had come together. The dreamer was mildly psychic, permitting him to contact her in the first place; chance had synchronized their sleep-cycles so that on this night they fell into dreaming in the same instant; their emotional states were similar enough that it was easy to become entangled in the wrong dream, a mistake that was difficult to correct once it happened. And of course, Anzha had not yet finished her training. Had she done so, she might have turned away the intrusive images with clear and precise telepathic skill. As it was, the best she could do was attempt to maintain a sense of her own distinct identity in a world controlled by another, and wait for the dream to come to its natural end.

They shared a body—his—and traversed the familiar halls of Azea's Academy of Martial Sciences. A webwork of interconnected biospheres orbiting between Luus' fourth and fifth planets, the Academy was a beehive of constant human activity. Here the Empire's diplomats studied their art, and negotiators of the Endless War studied the ways of the enemy. The Biosphere of Humankind contained one of the Empire's greatest humanocentric libraries, and scholars flocked to it. Mock wars were waged on and about the system's outer planets, while Luus Three, Four, and Five were used for terrain practice; the combatants were housed in the Academy's sprawling network of domiciles, and warships were docked along its periphery. And, of course, there were the students: individually sponsored, rigorously trained, prepared (it was hoped) to master any facet of the War That Could Not Be Ended—or any lesser conflict which might cross their professional paths. It was impossible to imagine the Academy without a constant undertone of human striving; impossible to imagine that those halls would ever be empty, that even a moment might go by in which its facilities were less than wholly utilized.

Yet today, in this moment—in this dream—they were empty.

The dreamer traveled numerous streamlined corridors, progressing from an easy walk to a nervous run as he grew more and more afraid. Something was wrong; the Academy had been abandoned—evacuated?—and he was the only human in it. Panic assailed him and he threw open door after door, searching desperately for some sign of life besides his own. There was nothing. Some disaster had overtaken the Academy and he alone had been left behind. Fear arose within him as he imagined possible disasters, yet not even the worst of them could explain his isolation.

He was *alone*—in the empty corridors, in the abandoned Academy, perhaps in the universe. He ceased running; his legs, weak with fright, could no longer support such movement. In despair he leaned against a gleaming white wall, shut his eyes, and prayed for strength. *Blessed Hasha lyu, Firstborn of Azea. . . .* But even in that there was no comfort. The heavens were as empty as the man-made halls; his isolation was total.

From the stillness, then, came a whisper of thought. He started, and tried to listen, but it was not a sound that had jarred his consciousness. Triggered by a precise combination of hormones, his minimal psychic talent had awakened for a split-second—and through it he had glimpsed another's despair.

He was not alone! Guided more by instinct than reason, the dreamer ran through a maze of empty corridors, threw himself into a transgrav tubeway that gave access to the dormitory modules, and pulled himself, hand over hand, down its length. Someone else was here! Someone else the Empire had forgotten, as lost and as afraid as he was—he was certain of it. He swung open one door after another, scouring rooms with an eager glance, meeting only emptiness. Until at last he came to the final room, whose door opened of its own accord as he approached, revealing the source of the psychic disturbance.

He stopped, stunned, and simply stared.

She was beautiful: a goddess in repose, a celestial spirit lightly clothed in human form, a glowing monument to all that womankind might become. He came to her, trembling, afraid to speak lest he shatter the silence that had brought them together, and thus lose her. Unfamiliar hormones coursed through his body, and unfamiliar heat settled in their wake. His hands ached to touch her, but he was afraid; might she evaporate into empty dream-stuff if he indicated, by his actions, that he desired her? *Did* he desire her? Was this what desire was, this aching heat that urged him forward, that made him act in ways beyond his understanding—

—reaching to touch her at last, and—

—lacking a frame of reference, the dream fading, and—

—don't leave me!—

Anzha awoke.

For a moment she just lay there, letting her own heartbeat settle back into its natural rhythm. She had been caught up in male dreams before, but never one so profoundly Azean. The dreamer's loneliness had entrapped her, had brought her insync with his fear, but that was a mere prelude to the dream's true substance. Unknown to him, he was in the process of bonding; as his body prepared to mate for life, his dreaming mind toyed with images to accustom him to the face of his intended, and to his own natural urges.

To share such an experience was the last thing Anzha needed.

~ What about pairbonding, Director?

~ What about it?

~ Will I experience it? Am I Azean enough?

~ Do you want to be?

~ Answer the question.

~ You have the proper genetic codes: one must assume the instinct is dormant. Whether it will be triggered into activity is something I can't tell you. . . .

It was not the dream that upset her. It was the stirring of desire it left in its wake, a purposeless heat unknown to her parents' race. Azeans did not hunger after strangers, or lie awake at night with unfocused longing coursing through their veins. She did. There was nothing she could do to satisfy it, either, for the Council of Justice would jump upon such an opportunity to prove that her nature was alien; and even more than pleasure, she longed for an Azean identity.

But though she dared not indulge it, the physical hunger was there—and that, more than anything else, proved how truly alien she was.

2

Introduction to Braxin Psychology

Would the daughter of Darmel lyu Tukone care to clarify this point?

Transculturalism: Beyond Diplomacy

It is true you've thoughtshared with one of *them?*

The Politics of Communication

. . . was instrumental in settling the Darian affair . . .

She is so cold, so aloof. So different.

She thinks she knows everything.

So intense!

She's not really one of us.

Why is she here?

3

More than any other place in the Academy, the Terrain Skills Biosphere/Primitive Combat Center was home to Anzha.

She had been raised to the sword. On Llornu, the Institute's world, fencing was a favored sport; it challenged physical and psychic skills simultaneously, something few pastimes could offer. On Llornu, swordplay was lightning-swift, hands striving to move faster than thought could follow, ever aware that a moment's hesitation gave one's opponent the opportunity to study one's intentions. Here it was different, and less challenging. She was rarely beaten. Even the Combatmasters could not compensate for her natural advantage; given a moment to concentrate, she could lift an opponent's plans from his mind and instantly design an attack or defense to complement it. She could feel his pain, pinpoint his exhaustion, play upon his weaknesses. But still the sport pleased her, if for no other reason than because it was so familiar. And if the aura of barbarism clinging to the sharpened steel appealed to her violent nature, that was one more reason to frequent the Center's facilities.

Taking a practice sword from out of the public rack, she set the drill machine to a simple parry/riposte combination and began to practice.

"Cadet Anzha lyu."

She completed her movement, recovered to standing position, and turned to discover the source of the voice. An older man, a Lugastine, was nodding his satisfaction at her response. Because Azeans were not fond of bladed weapons, aliens were often employed in this Biosphere; nevertheless, it was rare to see a non-Azean wandering about outside of class time. "Sir?"

"You are too tense. Relax the wrist." He had a slight accent, which confirmed his Lugastine background. "Again."

She stiffened. Her form was excellent and she knew it; nevertheless, experience and authority radiated from the stranger's surface mind in such quantity that she accepted the criticism. With a nod she returned to her opening position.

Attack, just so; the machine responded with admirable speed, demanding all her attention. Nevertheless, she kept a mental eye upon the stranger as she moved, watching herself reflected in his mind, altered by his criticism. There she was, and *there* was the source of his commentary . . . she relaxed the proper muscles exactly as his mind directed, and was somehow not surprised too find her attack improved by the change.

She turned back to him, a question in her eyes.

He bowed slightly, clearly amused. "Lithius Yumada, Master of Primitive Armaments."

She was stunned. "I didn't know."

"Of course not. I didn't mean you to know, or I would have told you."

Lithius Yumada: unequaled in the field of lowtech combat, if rumor was truth. Certainly he was the only non-Azean ever invited to oversee a portion of the Academy's military training program. A master among masters, he scoured the galaxy for able instructors and forced them to excellence; the Academy's teachers must be perfect and he was the man to make them so. The students, to whom he was legend, rarely saw him; certainly they never bouted with him.

All this ran through Anzha's mind as she watched him take a weapon from the public rack, along with two bodyfields. One of these he threw to her. "Setting five," he instructed, in a tone that brooked neither disobedience nor delay.

Hastily, she clasped the belt about her waist and turned its light forcefield on. Setting five would protect her from physical injury while synthesizing the pain she would have experienced had she been unarmored. It was a setting rarely used.

Stance. Salute. The ritual of a Lugastine duel, devised by a people who prided themselves on dignity even while they killed each other. She took her cues from his mind, reading his expectations. And saw him smile.

"It is as they said, then. Telepathy serves you well, but I suspect you rely too heavily upon it. Take your guard."

He was fast, unbelievably fast, with a speed that belied his age. Almost too fast for her to anticipate him. He began a three-part maneuver, controlled her response until the last movement; she only broke free when his point was coming toward open target, and then with difficulty. Hasha! He had mesmerized her as a psychic might, yet he gave no hint of such power. It was the beauty of his movement, the controlled and deadly grace of it, which acted like a drug upon her mind.

It took all her skill to ignore that beauty and focus on the intent of his movement. It was harder still to read purpose in his thoughts, and to gain her usual advantage; he seemed to think with his body, bypassing the centers of reason in favor of trained reflex. But there: a hint of planning. She analyzed it, drew him into a trap of his own devising, twisted into a combination guard/attack (with her wrist carefully relaxed, of course) and struck him on his outstretched arm.

The pain was intense; she could feel it. But Yumada did no more than wince. When the worst of it had passed, he raised his sword to her again and instructed, "Resume." A dull ache remained, hardly enough to affect his movement. But now she had him.

The thoughts that supported his movement were subtle, but they were there. Knowing where to look, she plucked his plans from his mind even as they became action, gaining a split-second advantage that proved to be enough. Again and again she turned him aside; she initiated attacks of her own, learning his thought processes even as she failed to reach him. It was only a matter of time. At last she had her opening, a discrepancy between intent and action which left the outermost point of his left shoulder open to her. She struck, striving for the utmost speed of which she was capable. And hit him.

A moment to breathe, then, while he recovered. Her muscles ached from the unaccustomed exertion, and a thin sheen of sweat had soaked through her clothing. He was not quite good enough to beat her—no mere physical could do that—but he was good enough to make her work for her victory. *A welcome change,* she thought.

"You are tense," he instructed. She tried to relax.

"Again."

This time it was easier. They were both beginning to tire, which slowed their motions and made the temporal gap between thought and action even wider than before. Now it was no challenge to pick up on his plans, and although she still had to work to keep up with him, it was easier and easier to complement his movements with the perfect defense, or an appropriate attack.

He was good, though, unbelievably good. He held her back as long as a physical could ever hope to do, and only when the strain of prolonged bouting began to compromise his perfection was she able to reach him again.

A touch to his inner arm; there was the expected pain, and then he nodded. Satisfaction? Understanding? She expected him to end the bout, but his upraised sword signaled her to continue the contest.

Why? she thought. There was no real challenge—not if she was careful. His thoughts were clear, now that she knew how to look for them. It was always the same with non-psychics; even a legend such as Yumada could not hope to negate her advantage without telepathy of his own to call upon.

With care she attacked, sliding toward his left flank, diverting to a lower target when he moved to block her. His blade whipped around, caught hers, twisted it aside to combine defense and attack in one. She saw it coming, defended herself accordingly. Easier and easier. An intention sparked within him, became action—which she moved to neutralize—then his slender steel inexplicably slipped past her guard and a bolt of pain skewered her through the chest, numbing all her senses.

Her blade fell to the floor; she heard it, stunned to discover that her hand had betrayed her. After a moment the worst of the pain passed, and with it the numbness. She looked at Yumada in amazement.

"Through the torso to sever the spine," he told her. "Very good, Anzha lyu, but you rely too heavily on your special talent. A true master can negate that advantage, with the proper preparation. Which I have had."

Her vision was clearing, and with it her mind. "You knew."

"It was obvious. Equally obvious that, having such an advantage, you would come to depend upon it. A dangerous weakness, cadet—in fencing, or in war. Remember that." He took off the bodyfield and put it away. Placing his weapon in the rack, he told her "You have excellent potential, if you are a bit overconfident. Be wary of the opponent who is comfortably predictable; it may be that he plans one thing and intends another." He turned back to her. "You could be a master. I propose to train you. What do you say?"

She was stunned. "But my studies—"

"Your program allows specialization in Terrain Skills; I suggest a concentration in lowtech armaments. Primitive societies are ruled by the sword; if not in fact, then in ritual. And I think it would benefit you in a tactical sense to experience a challenge. Victory should never be taken for granted. Besides," he added with awry smile, "You have much energy in need of discipline. Such training would help you focus it. What do you think?"

It would set her apart. It would encourage her violent side, her non-Azean side, and develop skills which that race abhorred. It would banish any hope she ever had of fitting into the Academy's social structure; a student favored by such attention—from Yumada himself—could never reenter the mainstream of student life. It would reaffirm just how alien she was, and guarantee that the whole student body knew it.

But it would challenge her as she had never been challenged before, in body or in mind. And already the warmth of exhaustion was relaxing muscles that had been tense for too long; the sexual tension which was a constant undercurrent to her life seemed less demanding, as though it had found partial fulfillment in the intensity of their combat. If she could redirect that energy, even partially, it would be worth it.

Which is what he's offering, she realized. *He's not Azean. He understands.*

"I'm honored," she told him, bowing. "And I accept."

For better and for worse.

4

In the office of Commander San li Eran, Director of the Academy, StarControl Liaison:

"Sit down, Anzha lyu. I want to talk to you."

An uncomfortable seat in an uncomfortable office. The Commander paced as he spoke. "We're all impressed with your performance here, I want you to understand that." *We were surprised you could handle it at all, much less excel.* "Your record is outstanding." *It has to be, or you're out.* "I believe we should have a talk about your plans for the future."

Anzha said nothing, merely nodded. His thoughts were so loud it was hard to distinguish them from spoken words. Was he really so vehement, or was her control slipping? She was as yet only a student of telepathy, not its master. Was the strain of this place taking its toll upon her discipline?

"You are entered," he said slowly, "in the command program." *Against my will and better judgment.* "May I ask why you choose that particular path?"

Her voice carefully neutral, she told him, "My sponsor, Director er Litz, advised it. For reasons I agree with."

Yes, and she overrode my authority. "Which are?"

In fifty words or less? "I have intimate knowledge of Braxin psychology. I believe I can turn it against them. To do this I must be in a position of tactical authority—"

"Or an advisory position." *Which would make life easier for all of us.*

Against her. will, her voice grew cold. "An advisor can be disregarded."

You want power, is that it? He hesitated, feigned sympathy. "Cadet Anzha lyu, I'll be frank with you. Your record is excellent. Despite the lack of historic precedent, I think it possible—not likely, mind you, but possible—that you may indeed manage to become involved in the War effort." *Only because your sponsor is who she is—remember that.* "But to continue in the command program is sheer folly. The Empire will never tolerate a non-Azean as commanding officer in the Great War. Or any war, for that matter. The simple truth is that you're not Azean, and that therefore there are limits. Accept them, and you can accomplish something. But to refuse, stubbornly, as you're doing. . . ." He shrugged. "You're setting yourself up for failure." *Which would please me greatly, and others. But we fear StarControl's displeasure.*

"What would you suggest?" she asked quietly.

"Your goal is to kill Braxins." *You are obsessed with killing Braxins.* "Train as a fighter. The odds are good that your sponsor could secure you a berth. Your size gives you a tremendous advantage, and would make you valuable enough—"

"I thank you for your concern, Commander, but no, that's not what I want."

He darkened, and his thoughts were a storm of accusation. "You're making a mistake, Cadet."

"I've made my decision, sir. Director er Litz approves."

Then you are a fool, and so is your sponsor! "Listen to me: you may excel in academics and you may have support in high places, but to gain a command post requires Imperial sanction—and that you will never have. *Never.* You're wasting your time—and ours—by your insistence upon a course of study that can't possibly benefit you." *Why did you come here in the first place? You don't belong, and never will.* "Do you understand me?"

More than you suspect. "Yes, Commander."

"Now: In the interests of reconciling your personal ambition with the reality of your environment, I'm going to recommend regular sessions with our Morale Counselor, li Darren. Beginning next firstday, seventh hour. Is that compatible with your schedule?"

She forced herself to sound apologetic. "I'm afraid not, Commander. I'm due on Llornu the day before that, and won't be back here until third session." Since he had apparently forgotten the conditions of her schooling, she added, "I'm scheduled to alternate between the Academy and the Institute until my training there has been completed. Unless you have objections, sir."

"No. Of course not." *Go home, where you belong.* "We'll discuss this further when you return." *Do us all a favor and don't come back.* He nodded a dismissal and turned away, but his surface thoughts, angry and frustrated, were still focused on her.

Go home.

Go home.
Home?

Light 1

Return to Llornu: however much she disliked the Institute, it was a relief to come back to it. As the distance between them closed she could pick out its special aura, and she savored its reassuring familiarity. Thousands of minds, striving to fulfill their psychic potential . . . most of them were unstable, but that didn't matter. She wasn't wholly stable herself.

As her transport dropped into subluminal space, the images became clearer. Now she could pick out specific minds, distinct concerns. Poli, the Kuathan adolescent, had had another wet dream—and had dreamshared it. Embarrassing but common; a dozen psychics stifled their amusement long enough to offer him sympathy. Sar'a Noe, the gifted Zula Communicant, was practicing the difficult Zi Vesh Configurations in the hope of earning the red cord of a Functional Telepath. And Yersek li Daramos, the product of Llornuan breeding, was torn between his mixed human heritage—which reveled in the unrestricted pleasures of Llornuan society—and his Azean half, which was hungering to pairbond. She touched them all, and with satisfaction thought: *Not much has changed.* To which she added, *Perhaps myself?*

She disembarked at Llornu's orbiting station, an environment she preferred to the dubious pleasures of the onplanet facilities. Natural surroundings made her uncomfortable; she would rather put her trust in the controlled solidity of an artificial satellite than risk the uncertain surface below. Just days ago a minor earthquake had struck Llornu's largest city, and though the population had been evacuated in time (efficiency during emergencies was one of the benefits of universal psychic ability) power sources were disrupted for half a day, and a number of buildings whose protective fields had failed had been badly damaged. Thinking of it, she shuddered. This is the risk one takes, when one trusts a planet.

It was hard to admit, because she resented the Institute—resented it for making her live, and for controlling every aspect of her life since that time—but she was glad to be here. It was comfortable. She belonged.

Hasha, help me.

2

A bout of swordplay in one of the Institute's practice rooms: the lights were off and the sunlight, coming through frosted windows, was less than wholly adequate. Thus telepathy was more important than sight, an arrangement many psychics preferred.

You mustn't limit yourself to your own kind, Yumada had warned her. *Most of the galaxy lacks your gift, thus develops other skills. You must learn to compensate.*

The pleasure of rhythmic exchange—the linking of minds: trading plans, devouring secrets. The shadow of a movement before the movement was made, followed by action. The joy of telepathic competition.

You wish to do battle with physicals? Then you must practice against them, live with them, learn their ways. This the Institute can never offer you. It serves as a refuge from pain because it shelters you from the most difficult challenge of all. It comforts you, and because of that it limits you. Contentment is an enemy to your purpose.

Eight points to her, three to her opponent. Her technique had improved, it was obvious. Briefly, she wished for stronger light. Madness!

To defeat the Braxins, you must think like a Braxin.

"The true warrior eschews comfort"—Dialogues 3/124V.

"Strength is derived from adversity"—Dialogues 12/9H.

Mind intertwined with mind, gleaming strands of strategy interwoven with dizzying complexity; the body followed, expressing the mind's desire. It was an intimacy unequaled by anything save sexual concourse, and that she had denied herself in order to grasp at the future. A sword was in her hand, and the power was alive within her. Was there anything outside the Institute to equal that?

To do what is difficult is the most valuable training of all.

3

The station's observation ring overlooked the planet, and from it one could see the major features of Llornu drenched in morning sunlight. She looked at it, reached out to it with her mind, then withdrew. It was familiar—too familiar. As much as she hated many of the Institute's policies, she had to admit that Llornu was a telepath's oasis in a dry and empty galaxy.

Could she leave it forever? She had to. There was no room for weakness in her life, and this—her need for Llornu—was the greatest weakness of all.

"There you are."

She turned and found Director li Pazua approaching her. Bastion of telepathic etiquette, he had searched for her physically rather than interrupt her observations. "They said you might be saying your farewells."

"I was." She shrugged off the view with false nonchalance and began to walk with him, back toward the station.

"Probe zi Laure has finished his analysis of your progress." he told her.

She stiffened, imagining the psychefile. *Zeymophobia worsening. Obsessive nature more pronounced. Refusal to choose an adult name indicative of emotional instability.*

"It's no secret that your sensitivity has improved," he continued. "Dramatically. Your control is lagging a bit behind intensity of contact, but I've analyzed the situation and I find nothing amiss. It takes time to adjust to such a change. You're surprised?" he asked, noting her reaction.

"Not about that. Please go on."

He touched her with a questing thought, but she turned it aside in favor of mental privacy. "Disciplines: zi Laure says you've mastered five, the others are coming along. He anticipates full Functional ability within two to five years—excepting, perhaps, in the area of physical contact."

She shut her eyes. "That hasn't improved?"

"Did you think it had?"

"I didn't know. I've avoided coming in contact with people, you know that. If the tests say it hasn't gotten any better . . . I guess that's true." Her hands clenched in silent frustration. "I try and try, and no matter what I do, the Discipline continues to break down under stress. Why can't I hold onto it?"

"You'll learn to, in time. Zi Laure will help."

She finally found the courage to voice what bothered her. "And what if that doesn't work? What if I really can't master this one simple Discipline? What semipsychic status do I get—or do I stay a student forever?" *And thus remain in your control,* she added silently.

There was potential violence in her surface mind; the Director chose his words carefully. "If the time comes when you rate an FT status in all but that one Discipline, I'm willing to consider awarding it to you anyway. Theoretically, a Functional Telepath has a high degree of communicative ability and is master of all the Disciplines. Your skill promises to be so far beyond anything we've seen before that it would be a crime to refuse you your proper label. Master all Disciplines but that one and I'll see to it that you're properly corded. " He paused, and his thoughts were carefully guarded. "It would shame the Institute to do anything less."

That would never have bothered him before; she was suspicious but kept it to herself. "Thank you."

"Now, what's this about your schedule? Is there a problem with the Academy? I thought we had it all worked out."

Contact Discipline: it guaranteed her mental privacy, steadied her nerves. "Director . . . I'm not coming back."

There was silence for a long time. Finally he asked, "To Llornu?"

"Llornu, or the Institute."

"And your training?"

"I want to finish that. I *need* to finish it. But not here."

"You're not happy here?"

She stiffened. "Happiness isn't an issue. Fulfillment of my only goal is. I've decided that my purpose is better served by my staying outside of the Institute's domain."

"I don't agree."

Would he dare to forbid it? Would their animosity be out in the open, at last? She would almost welcome it. "You have Probes who can travel," she challenged. "Torzha can arrange for their lodging in the Academy's system." Again, as always, she sensed his resentment when her sponsor was mentioned. *She took me away from you,* she thought. *Freed me from your autocracy. Is that the source of your bitterness?* "You said you'd support me."

"In your fight against Braxi, yes. But this . . ."

"This is a step in that direction."

"I don't see how."

"I didn't expect you would." *I'm not sure I do myself.* "It has to do with war, Director, and preparing myself to fight. This place . . . weakens me. I can't afford it."

"You need the support of your own kind."

"I can't afford to have a need like that! There are no trained psychics in StarControl; the Empire distrusts your 'conditioning' programs and isn't about to let itself be overun by your agents. I'm going to spend my life among non-psychics, and I'm not going to learn how to do it if I have an easy escape waiting here for me. I have to crush that need, Director. Help me, and I can finish my training. Hinder me . . ." She paused, savoring the vision, "and we become enemies." *If we're not already,* she thought privately.

He was long in answering; perhaps he was considering his options. Surface mind carefully controlled, he said at last "All right. I'll send you a Probe. *Not* because you threaten me. I'm not afraid of you, Anzha. But I'll take a chance on trusting your judgment. We'll try it your way, though it mans the loss of a Probe in this system; we'll have to work round that. I did promise you support," he agreed, the barest hint of irritation in his voice. "You'll have it."

She smiled, careful not to broadcast her triumph. Whatever his secret plans were, they required her dependence upon his authority. Slowly she was working free of his control, and at must be bitter fruit.

Meanwhile the Academy was calling to her, promising adversity—and strength.

"Thank you," she said quietly. "I'll be leaving as soon as possible."

Harkur: If the Braxaná, or any other single tribe, were to try to rule Braxi for an extended length of time, they would have to set themselves apart from all other Braxins. They would have to create an image so alien to the rest of Braxin culture that no other group could aspire to it, and do it to such an extreme that the image itself becomes synonymous with power. Then and only then, no man would dare to question their rule.

TEN

The mass that was called Lamos entered the House.

It wasn't easy for him to climb the three flights of stairs leading to his private rooms. As usual, he paused for breath midway on each flight to curse the laws which prohibited tubes or lifts in Braxaná houses. Blessed sadistic move! Why should a man have to climb stairs all the time just because his blood was that of the Master Tribe? Then, when his overworked lungs had recovered from the immense effort of the most recent flight, he continued onward. On a particularly hard day, when the three flights of stairs required four rest stops, he used the extra one to deliver an active blessing on the Braxaná custom of assigning the Master's private chambers to the uppermost floor.

S'vethe, Mistress of his House, watched as usual from the topmost step. She had heard his complaints before and would doubtlessly do so again. She tried hard not to think that he had brought it on himself. Braxaná architectural tradition was as it was to discourage the sedentary and Lamos, to put it mildly, was just that.

The immense man finally attacked the very step she stood on and conquered it. As he stood there, gasping for breath, she handed him a print of the day's financial reports and personnel adjustments. He expected it, and received the reports from her hand every day with an air of authority. He never read them.

"A bath, my sweet little servant. With women. Nothing energetic, I venture—I'm tired today. Make them all well broken . . . yes, I'm tired of fighting with your sex." His immediate plans accounted for, he placed a plump hand on her shoulder. "My son, eh? He's well?"

"As he was when you left this morning."

"The little purebred! I'll have to nap after the bath, S'vethe, and then you'll bring him to me, yes?"

"As you command."

He yawned. "Yes, that'll be just fine. Send Ber'n to help undress me, will you?"

She nodded. Ber'n was a true alien, non-human intelligent, and passive. The Master had a taste for such creatures. S'vethe suspected that he sometimes vented his pleasure upon them, although few of them had anything akin to human sexuality and most were, to her taste, far from arousing.

As for Lamos, he waddled off to his chambers. To be fair, he really did need help disrobing, for to give his clothing a pseudo-traditional Braxaná fit over his bloated form he'd had to revise the construction quite a bit, and he simply couldn't reach some of the seams once they were fastened. His cloak, however, he removed immediately; the brooch which held it to his tunic cut deeply into the folds of his neck.

Ber'n arrived moments later, an interesting six-limbed creature whom Lamos found delightfully repulsive, and who was easily dominated. One more benefit of living on the outskirts of the Holding, he thought. No one here to demand his House consist only of humans.

He felt no more responsibility to that custom than to any of the others he had abandoned. True aliens were in common use throughout the Holding, but for some reason he had never quite understood, Braxaná Houses avoided them. Here on Vra-Nonn, however, who cared what type of servant he hired, or what kind of slave he bought? Ber'n's people made excellent menials, having been oppressed before Braxi's domination of their world by its other intelligent inhabitants. They were unable to imagine any other way of life. So different for humans! They could look at a hundred cultures and know that, with a little surgery and practice, they could pass themselves off as a native of anywhere. Yes, Lamos liked aliens in his House, and that justified—

Why am I excusing myself again? he thought, annoyed. *I've done nothing wrong. These Social Codes are optional things, don't we keep hearing that? They're not law. I can't be punished for ignoring them. So why do I keep making excuses for myself?*

Ber'n helped him to remove the restrictive gray clothing which he so hated. Here, surrounded only by his slaves and servants, he let the neuter-gendered creature strip him of the last Braxaná layer and adorn him in a robe of vivid scarlet. The damp touch of the creature's skin was pleasant against his own, soothing the irritation of a day's bondage in clothing designed to look—and be—uncomfortable. *Next life,* he thought, *I'll be born among some rich people who haven't even got a word for* gray—*much less* black!

His bath had been designed by a Meveshi artist, and accordingly it displayed an opulence which was uncommon in Braxaná Houses. Here, in a room where none except slaves and servants might enter, the wealth of Lamos was made evident. The circular pool, lined in gold, was set about the edge with a fortune in precious stones. The floor was tiled in harkesite. A commoner might spend a lifetime earning enough to purchase a single tile, yet here an entire floor endured the abuse of water and wine. It could be replaced easily enough, Lamos knew. The entire room could be replaced, if he wished it—such was the wealth of a Braxaná.

This is the way to live! Lamos thought. *Those Central Braxaná, what do they know of pleasure? Them and their foolish politics—this is what it means to be a member of the Ruling Race! Wealth, indulgence, and freedom . . . what more could a man ask for?*

Fountains sprinkled wine into the air; the mist fell upon Lamos' robe and stained it a darker crimson. He enjoyed the low entrance, the anticipation. A dozen human females adorned the pool, a fine assortment from as many different planets. They appeared frightened of him, which was good. S'vethe had come through again.

"My Lord?"

He turned back in annoyance. His Mistress stood in the doorway behind him, and it had better be important! Nothing was less sexually attractive to him than the kind of woman who could run a House, and he had made it clear to S'vethe that he didn't want her presence spoiling the atmosphere of his pleasure-rooms.

"What is it?" he snapped.

"The Kaim'era Zatar. He would like to speak to you, Lord."

"Well, arrange a time!" He waved her a dismissal and turned back to his gleaming pool.

"Lord Lamos . . ." She waited until he faced her again. "He's here now. He came in directly from the House of War, on some sort of state business. He says that he needs to return as soon as possible and therefore must see you now."

Demanding an audience—well, wasn't that rude! Lamos considered giving her a message for the intruder which would show him just how welcome he wasn't. But then, unhappily, he thought the better of it. It wasn't wise to antagonize the Kaim'eri; they had their hands on enough of the Holding's commerce that they could easily strangle his sources of income in retribution. And a man who came from the House of War was doubly dangerous, since he either intended to go planet-smashing at the head of a fleet or, as a strategist, ordered other men to do the same. Never antagonize the military, he told himself unhappily.

"I'll go to him," he decided aloud.

S'vethe sighed in relief. "I'll send you someone to help with the changing—"

"I'll go as I am!" He stroked the velvet robe lovingly. "If he's going to barge in on me like this he can take me as he finds me. Go announce me, little servant."

He followed her slowly to the topmost landing, giving her time to do her duty. Once there he paused to take stock of his visitor. The entrance hallway below opened up to reveal the entirety of the main staircase, and Lamas found that the intruder was assessing both the interior architecture and his own person when at last their eyes met.

Hatred uncoiled inside Lamos. This man—this *Kaim'era*—represented everything he despised about the Central Braxaná. He was tall and lean and perfect. (Weren't they all?) His clothing fit tightly and displayed the lack of color which no man with taste would have any part of. Worst of all was that incessant arrogance. It was an attractive characteristic, true, but not when one was at the receiving end.

"Zatar." He bowed very, very slightly. "You've made yourself welcome, I see." He mixed disdain and scorn in his language and was pleased by the result. "So sorry you've found me short of hospitality. But you see that I was hardly expecting you."

Zatar regarded the brightly clad Braxaná with obvious distaste, "I've come on business," he said coldly.

"Oh, I'll come down." He imagined that the other man felt uncomfortable; that amused him.

"No. I'll come up."

What vile manners, Lamos thought—to invite himself to the private chambers of a Braxaná Lord! Nevertheless it would save him from a repetition of that unpleasant climb, and so he disdainfully nodded his agreement and waited just beyond the topmost step.

Zatar climbed the stairs easily, and seemed about to speak when his eyes fell upon the other's ungloved hands. "By the gods who abandoned us, Lamos, have you gone mad?"

He drew himself up proudly. "In my House, Kaim'era, you will accord me respect or leave."

He ignored him. "I'm here on state business, so let's go somewhere where we can talk. In your private wing," he added scornfully. "Since that's what you're dressed for."

Lamos scowled his displeasure but nevertheless led Zatar to his personal rooms. Whatever amusement he had garnered from the other's discomfort regarding his appearance was rapidly fading in the face of his arrogance. When they arrived, Lamos made a great show of sealing the door and activating the soundproofing. The sarcasm went unnoticed.

"How may I serve you, Magnificent One?"

If Zatar was irritated by his use of the ironic mode, he didn't show it. "I volunteered to deliver this message because of all the Kaim'eri, I was closest to your planet at the time it was composed. I was with our tactical forces on Garran," he explained, and his voice mode—impatience—indicated that he was in a hurry to return, and would not tolerate pointless delay. "And quite frankly, I'm appalled. Is that suitable dress for the forehouse?"

"What, this?" Lamos stroked the velvet of his robe lovingly; the gesture was obscene and he knew it. It pleased him to annoy this man, who came to his House crowned with arrogance and obnoxious physical perfection and dared to criticize his lifestyle; for that was what the Kaim'era had come about, he was certain. "This? It's soft, and it's comfortable. And I like bright colors."

"We all do! That's the point: an image of personal sacrifice to support our power base." He gestured toward the other's garment impatiently. "What does it matter what we prefer? We have an image to maintain, Lamos. You can wear what you like in your own rooms, tradition permits that. But not out there, where aliens might see you."

Lamos folded his hands disdainfully in front of him. "Your traditions don't interest me."

"They support the structure of our society."

Lamos shrugged. "That's no concern of mine."

"Isn't it? You're happy enough to live at the expense of the state, Lord Lamos. What would happen if suddenly the government didn't support your indulgence? Would you be so smug then?" He pointed to the other's hands in frank incredulity. "This is beyond indulgence. This is beyond personal pleasure. We do *not* display our skin before commoners—"

"Ah." Lamos glanced at his hands as he stroked the palm of one with the forefinger of the other. "It bothers you that my hands are naked."

The dark eyes smoldered, but Zatar's voice was calm. "We've all seen men ungloved, if that's what you mean. You didn't invent sexual diversity, you know. Must you make this harder than it has to be?"

Again Lamos shrugged. He was beginning to enjoy himself. "I've done nothing."

"Exactly the problem."

"Kaim'era, there are no laws in question here—only some vague and outdated customs which I happen not to care for. I'm no commonblood, you know. You can't just . . . push me around because you don't like my style. Legally, you have nothing on me." There! It was said.

"This is true. And I haven't come to criticize you personally, although you certainly inspire it. The point is this: the Kaim'erate has given formal consideration to your right to live as you're doing, and we have decided that it's not within our power to pass official judgment on you—you, personally."

Smugly, Lamos waited.

"However, we have decided that assuring the image of future generations is within our jurisdiction. And so, on behalf of the Kaim'erate of the B'Saloan Holding under Braxi/Aldous, I am here to inform you that you will be required to turn over your son to a more traditional House, in order that he might receive the upbringing which is his birthright."

Lamos paled. "What?"

Zatar's expression was unreadable. "I think you heard me."

"You can't be serious. *They* can't be serious. Give up my son? It's unheard of!"

Zatar waited.

"I won't have it! I won't!"

The Kaim'era's voice was loaded with quiet threat. "Shall I tell the others that you mean to oppose our decision?"

"No . . . no, I didn't mean that."

"Then I should perhaps tell them you mean to oppose our right to make such a decision."

"Yes . . . I mean, no!" Lamos was alarmed. Nowhere in Braxin history was there a precedent for anyone successfully standing up to the Kaim'erate. The rulers of Braxi, notoriously suspicious regarding the motives of their own kind, never failed to ally when their power was threatened. For Lamos to oppose them would be folly, if not outright suicide.

"Kaim'era Zatar, you don't understand. . . ." He searched for the proper words, but at last had to settle for, "He's my *son.*"

It was Zatar's turn to smile.

Lamos was panicking. To lose a son . . . was there any way to capture that horror in mere words? One's lifesblood, the offspring of pleasure, a creature to mold and cherish, the hope of decades, of numberless fruitless attempts at conception! The filthiest peasant was still permitted to raise his own sons, or to seek such where they had been abandoned. The need to raise a child was as basic a human drive as . . . as . . . well, as any other which the Braxaná respected!

"Kaim'era Zatar . . . please tell me this is not true." The disdain dropped from his voice and he found that he had adopted a formal mode. "I cannot believe that the Kaim'erate would make such a decision."

"What you choose to believe is of no consequence. The fact remains. You may submit to our order, or file formal opposition."

"Surely there is *something* else I can do."

The Kaim'era's expression was cold, as was his voice. "I know of nothing."

The absolute mode which Zatar employed frightened Lamas even more than his words. "But surely something. . . ." He swallowed his pride. "I could . . . reform my image?"

"It's too late for that."

"Nonsense!" He exploded in anger—an acceptable display of emotion, he knew. (Ar, he was starting to think like them!) "That's the problem, isn't it? Well, it can be fixed."

He waited breathlessly for the Kaim'era to answer; Zatar was painfully slow in doing so. "They wouldn't believe you."

"I could demonstrate—"

"You can't demonstrate that type of commitment, Lord Lamos. Now, I'm on a tight schedule; it isn't Peacetime, you know. I'm supposed to bring the child to Braxi before I go back to Tactical. Can we cease arguing the merits of this decision and get on with it?"

Who was it said that to kill an only son was to emasculate the father? Was this not much the same thing, at least as far as Lamos was concerned? "Kaim'era . . ." The pleading tone of his voice horrified him, but he made no move to disguise it. Better to humiliate himself in front of this man now than have all the Kaim'eri laughing at him for the rest of his life.

"The decision was made," Zatar said sternly. "To oppose it now, even to modify it, would require an advocated case. That would mean someone putting his reputation on the line for you. I'm not willing to do it."

"But if I could prove my sincerity—"

"How? Be realistic, Lamos. How can you prove anything like that?"

"There must be some way. Lord—Kaim'era—I appeal to you as a Braxaná! As a man." As a *father*—he was about to say, but that was dangerous; he didn't know Zatar's reproductive status.

Zatar's expression changed slowly, from one of disinterest to a look of thoughtful consideration. "I can think of one way," he said finally, "although I can't guarantee the Kaim'eri's response to it."

"Of course not, of course not!"

"Much of the Braxaná image, you know, is based on physical attributes. It strikes me that if you enrolled in one of the military training programs on Garran, this would certainly be a powerful statement regarding your intentions."

Lamos' eyes widened in alarm. The Garranat House of War existed to turn men into soldiers, with little concern for their comfort. Located in one of the most desolate corners of the Holding, it was notorious for weeding out those who lacked the stamina for battle by breaking them in training. (*Better a commoner's death on Garran,* it was said, *than a weak sword in war.*) The fact that fully half of the system was devoted to military analysis and tactical command was of little comfort to Lamos, as was the fact that most of the Braxaná who entered the House of War breezed through the initial training with ease and dignity. Those were men who thrived on discomfort, and who were—he admitted sulkily—in better shape than himself. It was reasonable to assume that they could complete the training in a few zhents, and be no worse for wear. With him it might take years—and unpleasant ones, at that.

But his *son*!

"Is this really necessary?" he managed.

"Not at all. As a matter of fact, you'd have to convince them to accept the move at all, and that would require an advocated case. The alternative is much simpler. So if you'll bring out your son,

I'll take him with me and end the matter." He looked around. "Where is he?"

"I'll do it," he said hurriedly. "Ar knows, I'll regret it—but I'll do it. Great Kaim'era, say you'll advocate this for me, I beg of you."

"I've made a commitment to Tactical, at the House. This would require too much time on Braxi. I don't know, Lamos."

"I have a planet out by the Border." Lamos spoke quickly, lest the Kaim'era should make a negative decision before he could convince him to do otherwise. "A pretty little thing which was a colony of Fenda, before we wiped out Fenda. It's a nice little place for a vacation now and then . . . I would be honored if you would accept this, in return for this favor."

He held his breath as Zatar considered. It was a good bribe; all Braxaná had the means to purchase planets, but real estate by the War Border was rare and owning it imparted considerable status. And it was a blessed nice planet, too.

"Get the records."

With undignified haste Lamos summoned his Mistress and bade her fetch the proper documents. When she returned with the rings he pulled out a reader and quickly dropped them, one after the other, onto it.

Zatar observed the screen in silence. Surely the planet would please him! It was a lovely piece of property, a little low on the gravity scale perhaps, but the location was beyond reproach. "Agreed. I will attempt to convince the Kaim'erate to accept your proposal."

Lamos was breathless with relief. "I can't express my gratitude to you, Kaim'era."

"Transfer of ownership would be most eloquent."

"Of course!" He nodded to S'vethe, who opened a line to the local Central Computer relay, which admitted their voicecodes and gave them access to the proper records of ownership. Lamos dictated adjustments. The computer recorded and filed them, and sent out a copy of the transaction to the Central Computer itself. It was official.

"Very good." Zatar nodded his approval. "Now, if you'll excuse me, it's three days to Braxi, and then some to handle this business."

"I'm grateful for your time, Kaim'era." There was no doubt about it, Zatar had saved him from a bad situation. The future wasn't all that attractive, but at least he'd retain his offspring. That was what mattered, to a true Braxaná. "Your presence has done my House great honor. " He noticed S'vethe staring at him in amazement, but what matter? She was only a woman, and only half-Braxaná. This was between the Lords of Braxi. "See him out, my Mistress," he said in his most dignified tone.

Wordlessly, she obeyed. Nor did she glance at the Kaim'era as she led him out, Zatar noted, or speak to him as they descended the main staircase. The Kaim'era sensed that she was teeming with questions, all of which would have to go unanswered—unless Lamos was willing to satisfy her curiosity, which was unlikely. He wondered if she would ever learn enough of what had transpired to tell Lamos that the Kaim'erate didn't have the power to take his son away. Doubtful.

When the great doors shut behind him, before he entered his shuttle, he took a flatrendering from inside his tunic and opened it. Smiling slightly, he read.

To Kaimera Zatar, son of Vinir and K'siva:

These are your instructions regarding Lord Lamos, as confirmed after debate on this, the eighth day of the fifth zhent, '97 after the Coronation of Harkur.

It is the decision of this body that Lord Lamos must embark immediately upon a course of action designed to bring him more in line with the traditional Braxaná image, both physically and emotionally.

Since we have no laws which permit us to dictate such action, we ask that you employ more subtle means to achieve this end. You are free to use whatever threats, bribes, and/or coercion you deem necessary, in the certainty that the Kaim'erate will back you.

It would please us greatly to see Lord Lamos enrolled in some regular regimen of mental and physical discipline, such as that employed by the military training schools. Whatever action he does take, it is considered highly desirable for him to believe that he takes it of his own free will.

The Kaim'eri of the Holding under Braxi/Aldous
Present: 109
In affirmation: 91
In negation: 3
In abstention: 14
Absent: 18

Zatar laughed softly. Then, with the deed to his new planet nestled snugly on the index finger of his right hand, the Kaim'era boarded the shuttle which would take him back to Garran.

Harkur: We must assume that the thought-processes of human and non-human differ so greatly that without direct mental contact there can be no true understanding between the two.

ELEVEN

The ice-plains of Derleth were bleak and gray that morning, as they were every morning beneath the fog-laden canopy which comprised the atmosphere. Here and there the light of a tired sun fell on some ice-formation and a flash of brightness signaled a ray of hope; then a particle-cloud filled the gap and made the celestial grayness whole again. And the sun, if anything so ineffectual could truly be called a sun, was content once more to filter its light through the omni-present gray of Derleth and give its warmth, not to the planet's surface, but to the insulating cloud-cover.

It was a planet that truly deserved to be devoid of life. Yet life was there; not human life, it is true, but a form of being whose nature did not yearn for light or comfort. It is true that they were somewhat human in form, these natives, though protective fur covered their limbs and their extremities had evolved to meet the challenge of eternal ice. Yet they were clearly not human, for what creature of that designation would shrug at the sight of true sunlight and praise the return of the everpresent grayness, as these creatures did?

But all this was very subjective. Azea had discovered life on Derleth a mere Standard Year ago and had not yet investigated the nature of local anatomy. Bipedal life of human proportion had been known to develop independently, and perhaps Azea avoided close examination of the issue deliberately. It would be difficult to look at the natives of this bleak and terrible place and feel any kinship with them, or with their aspirations, no matter how human science made them appear. It was far, far preferable to believe that underneath the ice lay evidence of local evolution than to accept that human stock had been placed on Derleth, as elsewhere, to evolve in response to local conditions.

This morning the wind was calm, for which the lone traveler in the wastes was grateful.

The ice-plains were not on the equator; there, where the warmth of Derleth's weak sun was concentrated, the planet was almost habitable. Instead they stretched across the western hemisphere just south of that livable zone, bordered by impassable mountains on three sides. It took a native half a year and a tremendous amount of luck to cross the plains alone, alive. And it was assumed that no one but a native could manage the feat.

Of the twenty fersu who had departed from the mountain village with this traveler, ten remained. All that was necessary was for the woman herself to reach the far mountains; how many of her supportive team of native animals came with her was inconsequential.

The lone traveler—who was not a native—stopped to review her body temperature.

She had spent nearly half a year on the ice, cold and without human company. The latter didn't bother her as much as others had anticipated; she had never been a social creature and was just as content to be left alone with her thoughts for a while. But the all-pervading cold of the wasteland exhausted her, and the bleak grayness filled her days with an intolerable boredom which was as dangerous as the ice itself.

I must not only come out of this alive, she reminded herself, *I must come out of this sane.*

Azea had made overtures to the fur-clad natives of Derleth and had received the kind of response that gave ambassadors nightmares. Yes, Derleth would be happy to deal with Azea, happy even to swear loyalty to that foreign empire and offer their unpopulated lands as a base of operations for future imperial expansion. All these things would Derleth do and more, in celebration of the wonder of discovering that there was life beyond the omnipresent canopy. And as soon as Azea sent them a worthy representative to work out the details, they could get started.

To the natives of the ice-planet the issue, of course, was simple. Their own young, in order to earn the right to live on the ice-fields, first had to prove that they could master them. And so one by one they crossed the southern wasteland, and one by one found death or renown somewhere along the journey. This also must be done by these strangers from beyond the gray sky.

Since the Derlethans assumed that all societies functioned

along similar guidelines—as those on Derleth did—they did not understand the necessity of explaining their customs to the Azean visitors in their midst. Each ambassador in his turn was taken to the eastern mountains and shown the deadly expanse of ice, glimmering unevenly in the filtered sunlight. The Derlethans assumed that one of them would offer to make the crossing, and were confused when none did. The ambassadors, on the other hand, didn't understand what they had done—or not done—while standing on that mountain-peak to rate the designation "unworthy."

But Azea prided itself on its diplomatic skills and had the experience of a thousand populated planets to draw on. It soon became clear what the Derlethans expected, and just as clear that only a madman would go along with them.

The Empire searched, finally finding sportsmen who would take on the challenge. Derleth turned them away. This was not a game, the natives insisted; the one whom they accepted among them must be an individual trained for leadership, not exceptional endurance. Else how could they know that the Azean race was worthy of their attention?

The situation was aptly summed up by the last ambassador to leave Derleth, who noted that the stubbornness of primitive peoples regarding their absorption into the Empire was in direct relation to how much the Azeans made fools of themselves while establishing diplomatic relations.

And the Director of Diplomacy looked elsewhere.

Who would be willing to face cold tedium and alien carnivores in service to the Empire? Taking into account that such people had already joined the ranks of Azean diplomats, ver Ishte was not optimistic. But he kept up the search and at last found a volunteer, a young part-alien woman enrolled, against all tradition, in Azea's Academy of Martial Sciences.

She was willing to go; that was of course the most important thing. Though she appeared frail, her record bore witness to exceptional stamina and a fiercely competitive nature. She had been trained, as all persons in the command program were, to adapt to any planetary conditions and to function well in the most primitive of situations. Derleth would certainly require both skills, and in excess.

All she asked in return was temporary Diplomatic status, which carried with it Imperial sanction. Ver Ishte shrugged and made out the proper records. The Council of Justice lodged some kind of formal protest which the Director of Diplomacy promptly deposited in the permanent exit file. This was his department and the only person who could order him around was the Director of Star-Control herself, or, on rare occasion, the Emperor.

And so the young woman was titled Temporary Ambassador and received the coveted "Imperial" with which to prefix her name. She quickly won over the Derlethans despite the handicap of being a female amidst a patriarchal society, so much so that they held her back for thirty days while the worst of the weather passed over the plains.

She was given unlimited hersu; she chose twenty. She was offered unlimited provisions; she chose instead to fill her sled with the means of hunting native game, recognizing that any attempt to pack a half-year's provisions for her and the animals would be futile. She harnessed the animals as she had learned in the ice-lands of Luus Five, explaining to the Derlethans, when they asked, why this formation would prove most effective in the crossing. They neither agreed nor disagreed; the technique would prove its worth by getting her across the ice-plains before the winter's cold made even breathing deadly, or demonstrate its failure by her death.

And so she departed from the eastern heights. It was a comment upon her relationship with the Empire that as many people hoped to see her die in the alien cold as prayed for her success.

If Anzha lyu sought to master Derleth's wasteland, it was as she had mastered other terrains—by submitting to them. When she lacked food she hunted; when she was tired of traveling she erected a semi-permanent camp and waited until the motivation to continue returned. Neither pursuit was easy or pleasant; the game was rare, well-camouflaged, and dangerous, and to stop and rest for a day could be deadly in the cold which mimicked warmth as it lulled the unwary traveler to sleep the Long Sleep—as the natives labeled death. But it would be folly to hurtle forward and expect to keep up the pace for half a Derlethan year. Determination could substitute for endurance for a while, but in that long a stretch even determination would wear thin. She chose instead to take her time, moving quickly when she could and accepting delay when she had to. Her advisors at the Academy had approved of this approach once they came to understand that the greatest enemy along this route was not cold, but boredom.

Day after day wore on with hardly a break in the cloud-cover. Pale gray faded into dark gray and back again as the Derleth day-cycle continued. Sometimes she dreamed of death and it was warm and welcoming; on those nights she shook herself awake and saw to some menial but comforting task, such as maintenance of her weaponry or repair of her furs.

And she was alone with her thoughts, which she had not been for twenty years.

This is all that matters, she told herself. *That I've been given temporary Imperial status and that I will serve the Empire as no one else could have done. The precedent is all that matters. The people I'm serving will not forget—although the Council of Justice might like them to.*

In the long days of endless gray she did not ask herself if she was happy, or even satisfied, with her present lot in life. She had learned never to probe so deeply, lest she come in touch with the layer of pain which, after all these years, was still so near to the surface.

I am, she recited. *I strive to enter the military. That's the sum total of my existence. I won't look beyond it.*

Her dreams spoke otherwise, as though the featureless regularity of the gray-lit plains had become a canvas to her inner vision. Surrounded by the ice of her waking day, she lay entrapped by surrealistic images that stormed her dreaming mind with reminders of hungers too long suppressed, needs too powerful to lie peacefully submerged within her. They were human hungers but they were unacceptable ones, and they had been cruelly but necessarily denied satisfaction in the waiting game she had learned to play. Azea did not hunger for blood, therefore she would discipline her vengeance. Azea did not thirst for sensation, therefore she would channel her sexual energies elsewhere. *I am Azean,* she repeated, and she forced herself to fit that mold despite the price her dreaming mind exacted from her for it. The time would come she could do what she wished. But that time was not now, and so dreams were her only possible outlet in a world where moderation defined nationality.

Yet even those visions began to weaken, submitting at last to the everpresent gray which was the soul of Derleth. There came a day when she tried desperately to recollect the nightmarish images, to bring some variety, if not to her world, then to her thoughts. But the dreams, like all else, faded into the eternal gray, and their images were lost as the tedium of Derleth became more and more overpowering.

She suffered from frostbite, but not so excessively that it hindered her progress. Azea could regenerate what died in the cold, provided she survived to get back there to have it done. As for her hunting, telepathy made that as easy as it could ever be in this desolate wasteland. At times she seduced her prey to spearpoint, and at other times cast out mental tendrils over the ice in search of life; there was usually none. *At least,* she thought, *when there's nothing to hunt I don't have to waste time and energy trying to ferret something out.*

The days became shorter. Although she had kept count of them, that number was a theoretical thing; the winter-length day was more real in terms of her inner calendar. Soon the storm-winds would come and the blizzards of Derleth would slow traveling to a crawl. If she didn't reach the far mountains by then she probably wouldn't do so at all.

And then the kisunu came.

It is curious that in the face of danger the telepath dreamed of love. It was a foreign concept to her and not one she fully understood; whatever memories of human affection she retained from her youth had been blocked from conscious recall by that same process which dealt with her period of trauma. Certainly her recent life, filled with the scorn of her fellow students and the ever-present hatred of Azea's Council of Justice, was not the place to learn of such gentle emotions. But in her sleep she lay in another world, cradled in the arms of a man who was marked with her own alien stigma—the blood-red hair of an unknown heritage. "I know you face an unknown and possibly terrible future," he whispered, "I know you're more accustomed to hatred than respect, and have been raised to be ignorant of more gentle human interaction. But know now—and remember when the pain becomes too great—that one man cared deeply enough for you to call you *mitethe.* You know my language. You know what the word means."

And as she reached to embrace him she awoke suddenly to cold darkness, and to the scent of death.

Kisunu.

Her mind had touched a carnivorous instinct and applied the

proper Derlethan label. Kisunu—the ice-killers. Wolf-like predators who hunted in packs and who, needing little food to fuel them for long periods of running, were capable of hunting down and patiently driving to despair any creature unfortunate enough to come across them.

They were intelligent. Anzha classified them instantly with her telepathic sensitivity and was unnerved by her conclusion. They were chaotic in nature and lacked any physical structures to stand as monuments to their intelligence, but despite this they could not be classed with common animal life. They had a culture; Anzha sensed she would not understand it, but there was something in them which tasted of more than simple pack mentality.

And they were very, very hungry.

She built a fire; they backed away warily, but displayed none of the instinctive fear one might associate with such creatures. Two reasoning species on the same planet? It was rare, but not unheard of.

But why hadn't the Derlethans told her?

Perhaps they didn't know.

Impossible, she corrected herself. One couldn't evade these creatures without comprehending that they had more than animal intelligence.

Yes, the Derlethans knew. And those who understood survived the half-year journey through the heart of kisunu territory.

Again she reached out a tendril of thought; quickly she drew it back, burned by the touch of animal hunger and the promise of a mind so alien that no human could hope to understand it.

Very well, she thought. *I will speak the universal language.*

She chose a bow from among her possessions and lined up arrows, heads imbedded in the snow, before her. Yellow eyes regarded her with unblinking intensity and the creatures took one or two steps backward, alert and ready. It was clear they expected her to aim. It was fortunate she didn't have to. With one motion she lifted the bow and left fly a well-feathered shaft; it embedded itself in the torso of a surprised kisunu and evidently lodged itself in a vital organ. The creature howled shortly and fell; blue-black blood stained the snow in splotches and his death cry resonated in the gray emptiness.

She waited, tense, for a reaction.

And they studied her. They now knew how fast she could move, and if they were indeed capable of advanced reasoning they would know just how accessible those upright arrows were. I will take you with me, Anzha's action promised, not one or two but many. And who will be the first to come at me, in that case?

One by one they turned away from her, still wary but with their attention focused elsewhere. Each went up to his fallen fellow and laid his great teeth against that one's hide, then each ritually gave way to the next, and he to the one after, and so on until all members of the pack had performed the ritual action.

This confirmed Anzha's suspicions, for mere animals do not indulge in death-rites. And starving animals more often eat their dead than revere them. The gesture of the kisunu seemed almost designed to say, "Although I starve, I will not eat my kind. This sets me above the beasts of the ice." *Hasha,* she thought. *Predators with moral instincts.*

She set a circular fire about her camp and hoped they would be unwilling to cross it. The Derlethans had given her skins filled with flammable powder and now she understood the reason for it, for no fuel gathered from this desolate place would burn as brightly; the native branches which occasionally broke through the ice were good for heating dinner but would scarcely frighten a high-grade predator.

But morning would come and she would have to move on, and if the kisunu would not let her do so she would surely die. Not that day perhaps, but later, when food and fuel ran out and she was at their mercy. She would have to deal with them tonight—establish some kind of working relationship that would allow her to continue. The western mountains couldn't be far off now; surely if she could buy a few days' time she could reach them.

She walked over to where the frightened hersu were huddled. With a telepath's hand she calmed them, and then with surface analysis chose the two most paralyzed by fear. They would do her the least good in the days to come and should be the first to go. With a steady hand she removed their harnesses.

It seemed to her the kisunu were smiling.

She placed a mittened hand behind each of the animals and pressed against them, thinking *threat* as loudly and as primitively as she could. They bolted forward in blind terror and jumped the fireline; by the time they were free of her imposed fear they had fallen, and the hungry kisunu made short work of their gentle but muscular bodies.

I have made you an offering, she thought, *and I'll make more if I have to. And none of you need die for this.*

Is it enough?

Apparently it was, for as the kisunu finished eating (and she noticed they divided the animals evenly among them) they withdrew to a safe distance and stretched out on the snowy surface, to nap or to wait as each one desired.

It was the first of many long nights during which she would not sleep.

They did not leave her in the morning; she had hoped they would, but not really expected it. Again she sent out mental tendrils among them, and again drew them back quickly. The hunger evident in their surface minds was less demanding, but it remained. It was only a matter of time, then: a single woman and eight passive hersu could not hope to stand against an entire pack of carnivores, intelligent or no. There might have been some hope for her through her telepathic skills, but the kisune mind was evidently so alien that she would not be able to hold on to it long enough to establish control.

Because there was nothing better to do, Anzha repacked the sled and hitched the hersu up to it once more. To her surprise the kisunu parted before her, encouraging the progress of the sled by lack of interference. Not one to question small favors, she headed dutifully westward.

Previously she had napped while traveling. Now she dared not do so. The ice-fields were smooth and without crevasses, the armor-barked branches which breached its surface exceptions rather than the rule. It was a very different place than the cracked-glacier surface of Luus where she had done a terrain internship. This, in its way, was almost more dangerous, for on Derleth there was no need for the constant alertness that kept one's mind occupied and fought back the edge of madness. She allowed herself to smile. There was little risk, now, of seeing boredom drive her to insanity. A little more risk of being eaten, perhaps, but that was in many ways a preferable death to slow torture by unending gray tedium.

"Yes," she said aloud, surprised to find herself talking. "I should be grateful to you. You've spared me something very terrible, without even knowing it."

And for the first time in that half-year, human laughter resonated in the ice-laden wastelands.

"Such a polite enmity, my gentle escorts! The Braxins would like you." She was talking as much to herself as to them, discovering that any human voice—even her own—was welcome in the gray emptiness. "They make a ritual of enmity, and devise rules by which to control hostility and drag it out for the lengthiest possible enjoyment."

She looked over the pack, a good thirty strong if not more. She had no desire to count them. "A race, then. I think we understand each other. I will feed you for as long as I can and you'll play escort while I do. And the question is, which comes first—the western mountains or the last of the hersu?"

But long before that, she thought, *I'll be walking.*

Time enough for that when it comes.

She camped before nightfall and built a small fire, saving most of her flame-dust for when she might need it later, to drive back death. Then, acting as though nothing in the world had changed since yesterday, she slaughtered another of the sled-animals and spent an evening rendering it into its component parts. With the rich organ meats she fed herself and the remaining hersu, upon whose strength she was coming to depend more and more. The majority of the meat she flung to the waiting pack.

"Your share," she muttered, watching the ritual division.

It surprised her, in the days to come, just how strong the hersu were. Not until there were only four left did she need to start lightening the sled, a painful task, since everything in it was vital to survival. The kisunu could run long days on little food, and so were satisfied to lope along beside her in the rapidly shortening days. She fed them when she sensed their hunger, and she fed the hersu regularly, lest they be too weak to carry her forward; herself she fed only when she had to, and sometimes less often than that. Over and over she repeated, *Azean medicine can undo all of this.* So she bribed the predators to keep their distance and sacrificed her own strength for forward motion, in the desperate hope of getting home.

Sometimes she slept. She tried not to, but exhaustion would beat her down until she awoke suddenly, finding she had napped without knowing it. The days dragged on without end and hunger was a constant companion. She ceased to look for the mountains; they had become a dream of the past, something which stirred in her memory but which took too much effort to identify. An eternity had passed on the ice and the rhythm of it, chilling and regular, had finally conquered her.

Too soon only a pair of hersu remained, and they could not pull the sled without killing themselves in the process. Resigned, Anzha strapped those items of vital necessity to her back, improvising leashes for the frightened animals and continued, determined, on foot. The yellow eyes of her enemies seemed to be filled with derision. It had only been a matter of time all along, they taunted. In the still of the Derlethan night she heard the words as though they had been spoken, and in the voice that spoke them there was no inflection she recognized, nor any hint of a language she could relate to.

Each night when she camped she cast forth her thoughts in search of possible game; each night the ice-fields proved barren of any life outside of her own hostile gathering. If a snowsnake had moved in the distance she would have tried to hunt it, trusting to her guardians' sense of amusement to let her do so, but there was not even that. If the kisunu did not eat her they would not eat at all—and that left very little room for bargaining.

Soon the last of the hersu was gone.

"This is it, my friends." She had gotten used to the presence of the pack and talked to the kisunu with some regularity. Painfully, she looked out over the ice fields. Half a year . . . it was a much longer period of time than she had thought possible; when one lived it day by day without variation it became an eternity. "This is it. . . ."

Far to the west, the cloudcover broke. She had come to turn away from the brilliant flashes of sunlight, for their promises were empty and hope, in this wasteland, was only cause for torment. But as light danced over the ice-fields she stiffened, seeing something in the distance which had passed out of her imagining.

Then the clouds closed overhead and the mountains passed into grayness again.

She found she was trembling.

"Hasha . . ." she whispered, and in that nearly forgotten name was a link to a people she had lost all hope of ever seeing again. They would be waiting for her there, along with the natives, spread out in a band along the foothills to welcome her wherever she happened to arrive. It was within sight—and it was beyond hope. The kisunu would never let her get that far, and even without them she doubted she could walk the distance without sustenance.

Have you come all this way to give up now? she asked herself. *Remember that the issue is not your own life, which you never wanted, but the revenge you hope to earn. Remember that all that matters about Derleth is the Imperial sanction granted you and the influential people who will owe you favors. That's all this ever was.*

The kisunu were watching her.

Her people would be waiting at the mountains with food; that was the ultimate irony. A short journey westward and she could feed these predators until they burst. If only she could make them understand!

She reached out with her mind, and once more she touched something so alien that she could not endure the contact, but instinctively withdrew.

No.

She gritted her teeth and tried again. This time she touched a kisune soul and held onto it. Alien awareness flooded her being and she shook with the strain of maintaining the link. Then, with great suddenness, there was no contact at all.

"Damn!"

It was going to be harder than she had assumed. At the Institute they trained certain instinctive responses into the telepathic subconscious; one of them, Distinction Discipline, was automatically cutting off her access to the kisune minds. The Institute's intentions were good; the Discipline was meant to interfere any time a telepath became so engrossed in another personality that he began to lose his own, or when a telepath reached out to a mind so alien that any contact would be harmful.

"But a lot of good that does me now," she muttered.

She would have to override a Discipline—and that had never, to her knowledge, been done.

She closed her eyes and concentrated.

Anzha lyu was not a Probe; she did not have the ability to deal with abstract thought without the aid of visualization. Perhaps a Probe could have contacted the kisunu without damage, able to absorb kisune thought-patterns without the need for more familiar images. Anzha lyu could not. Nor could she anticipate the reaction of one of these creatures to a mental invasion such as she was about to launch, and if their minds were alien to her, hers was equally so to them.

But it is that or death, she reminded herself grimly.

Deliberately she opened herself, pulling down all her natural defenses and leaving nothing to stand between her and the subject of her telepathy. Then, tentatively, she reached out toward the kisune she had approached before.

Again there was a terrible feeling of foreboding, and like a sliding wall something in her mind started to break off the contact. She struggled against it. Its strength was tremendous, but her will was no small thing. Soon she had lost awareness of the kisune altogether, caught up in an internal struggle for conscious mastery of her telepathic potential. She held back a wall—she bound a struggling animal—she frayed a tightening noose. All these images and more, until she lay panting on the floor of her inner mind, secure in the knowledge that she was strong enough to do the one thing the Institute sought to make impossible—attempt telepathic suicide.

Again she reached out to the kisune.

This time there was no interference. She was astounded to realize how much of that had been due to her training, and how little was due to any personal unwillingness to mindshare with an alien. With her training stripped away, she faced the predator's mind as she would a new frontier, dangerous and seductive, deadly and fascinating—a challenge; no more, no less.

The kisune welcomed her.

She hunted on the ice-field as it glowed with qualities she could not name, radiating heat in minutely small bits which her yellow eyes interpreted. Through her paws she could analyze vibrations from a long day's running distance, and could tell through that wonderfully sensitive tactile ability what was in the distance, and how far. Through means of an organ whose function she did not understand she sensed the presence of life, and distinguished between edible and inedible, intelligent and unreasoning, as easily as an Azean would distinguish between red and green. She found no color sense as such; what was the point? On the ice-plains there was no color, only the varying intensity of infra-red radiation which laid out before her eyes a landscape of wondrous variety, a subtle and wonderful place where the ice glowed for having been trod upon and bodies darkened to white as they died.

She did not share her own senses with the kisune; she was embarrassed by their paucity. How could she have called this place tedious, a place so filled with wonders? Had the sky in truth been monotonous? Now it radiated distinctions of density and degrees of warmth, and was as rich to her kisune senses as a sunset would be to human eyes. Had the planet been uniformly cold? Sensory threads in the white-furred coat saw as well as felt minute variations in temperature so that there was warmth in the breeze, chill in the still air, waves of variety pouring forth from every warm-blooded thing which one ate, or accompanied, or mated with.

She knew the kisune hunger for what it was, remembering the feeding. How good it would be to feel that again, not only renewed strength but the ecstacy of absorbing living warmth and watching it radiate through her system—of having her own body transparent to her life-sight—of sharing the boundless pleasure of feeding with one's pack-mates. What stronger bond could there be in the universe, and what richer world to inhabit?

Motionless upon the ice, the fur-clad woman whom Azea had sent to Derleth sat quietly on the cold white plain, surrounded by kisunu. She had ceased to monitor her metabolism and it slowed to the rhythm of the kisune system. Her hands were limp by her sides and her eyes closed, as if nothing she could ever see or touch would again be of consequence. She was, in all things and in all ways, silent and still.

In the distance, sunlight kissed the planet. Such warmth, though momentary, was painful to the heat-sense of all the creatures of Derleth. Those who saw it strike turned away from it, grateful when it passed for the return of that quiet regularity which allowed them to enjoy the subtle beauty of their world.

At the western edge of the great ice-plain, within sight of the bordering mountains, a pack of thirty-five kisumi sat in silence. One by one they arose, and one by one turned westward. Then, as if it were one individual creature, the entire pack set off toward the mountains, under the rich cloud-canopy of Derleth. It would take them many days to get there. But the kisunu could run far on little food and had all the patience in the world; thus it was that day after day the pack drew closer to the foothills . . . where the aliens, presumably, were waiting.

In the distance, for a moment, the sun flashed silver on the ice-field.

It was only a brief annoyance.

* * *

Ivre ver Ishte was tired of waiting.

He had been on this dreary planet since the Academy's young student had taken on the burden of native tradition. That was . . . what? Half a local year ago? Nearly three Standard Years, at any rate.

The Derlethans would not permit him to send aircraft low over the ice-fields, as he otherwise would have done to keep track of the young woman's progress. Since Derleth was to be absorbed and not conquered, the natives' will was law; ver Ishte couldn't take life-readings through the particulate cloud-cover and therefore had no access to reliable information. "She would be this far" a Derlethan would say, indicating a point on the ice-map, "*if* she is still alive."

The unpleasant thing was, he had a feeling the Director of Star-Control would kill him if he were responsible for her young protégée's disappearance.

Periodically, meandering packs of local life wandered close to the western mountains. An alarm would ring inside ver Ishte's ear-clasp and he would hurry to the point of possible contact; then the local life would pass on its way south, or continue north, or turn back to the east, and ver Ishte would be left waiting. So on this night.

The alarm rang shrilly, awakening him from a restless sleep. "All right!" he muttered. "What is it?"

A voice came through the receiver. "Section five, Ambassador. Looks like a pack of kisunu. Major predators."

"And our agent would be among them?"

He could almost hear the other shrug. "You said to let you know any time a lifeform approached the mountains."

"Yes, I know." Already he was rising. "I'm coming."

Section five—halfway across the length of an unbelievably boring mountain range. When he had first come to the western mountains, he had thought them beautiful; pale white cliffs and ravines, matte here or glossy there as the snowfall dictated, but if you had seen one ice-mountain you had seen them all. And ver Ishte had been looking at them for nearly three years now.

He let the window of his transport fog over on the way to section five and didn't feel he was missing anything.

"Anything clearer?" he asked as he disembarked.

"Pack of kisunu, all right. Large ones—no young." The agent for this section handed him a copy of the readout. "And something that isn't a kisune."

Ver Ishte looked up sharply at the man; it was a question.

"Could be, sir," the other said softly. "And it's coming right this way."

Alive. If only she had made it across the ice-plain alive! Whatever damage had been done to her body, Azea could repair—whatever hurt her mind had suffered, psychic morale adjustment could handle. All she had to do was deliver herself to them. . . .

One of the Derlethan natives manning this post waved to him. "Over here," he called, in that monotonous collection of sounds that Derleth termed a language. "One can see them."

Ver Ishte climbed up to where the native stood, on the last high point before the flat plains began. Sure enough, something moved in the distance.

"If it's a pack of kisunu . . ." he began.

"They do not come into the mountains," the native assured him. "They remain on that which is flat."

Ver Ishte took the news with a goodly proportion of skepticism. If three years on Derleth had taught him nothing else, it had given him an appreciation of how much his native guides really knew about these predators—and weren't telling.

They came swiftly, white upon white. Their approach was without shadow and from certain angles, when the light was right, they were invisible on the shining plain.

"How many?" ver Ishte muttered.

"Thirty-six," the local agent told him. And then, after double-checking: "One of them's human."

Praise Hasha! the Ambassador thought fervently.

They were clearly visible now, and if he looked carefully ver Ishte could pick out individual animals. They were each as long as a man was tall, or more so, and carried a good deal of body weight on slender but well-muscled legs.

"Is this normal?" he asked in Derlethan. "Some kind of escort—?"

The natives did not answer him. They had fallen to their knees.

He could pick her out now, a tiny figure staggering to match the kisune pace. Her walk was uneven and spoke of pain—some injury, no doubt. His first instinct was to run forward to meet her. His second, that of self-preservation, kept him from doing so.

"Anzha lyu . . ." he whispered.

She had come to the foot of the first rise and laboriously began to climb. Now that he could see her face he discovered it was that of a stranger. Patches of dead white covered its surface, which had aged twenty years, it seemed, in three. Her eyes glowed with a cruel fervor which was at once more and less than human.

She felt her gaze upon him and raised her eyes to meet his. There was suffering evident in them such as he could only begin to guess at. Her cheeks were hollow with hunger and dark circles underscored her gaze; if he had imagined a manifestation of Death it could not have looked worse.

She seemed to struggle with her thoughts, as though fighting to recall the nature of human language. "Feed them," she whispered finally.

"Anzha lyu—"

"Feed them, damn you!"

He waved hurriedly to his own agents and they ran back to the shelter to get meat for the ice-killers.

"I . . . promised them." She seemed to be struggling for each word, as though it were an effort to think in human terms at all. She looked at the kneeling Derlethans. "As well you should . . ." she whispered.

The men came back with meat and threw it to the kisunu. The starving animals waited until it had all been set before them and then, as was their wont, divided it into thirty-six portions. The last they left behind as they exited, each with his own rightfully earned share, seeking the silence of the ice-field and the privacy of the pack presence in which to share the joy of eating.

The young woman did not stir until they were gone. Nor did she wish to be approached. Only when the kisunu had passed from sight did she take another step forward, weakly, as if she meant to join the human company but lacked the strength to make the climb. Ver Ishte went to her, half-running and half-sliding, and came to her as she fell.

As soon as he touched her he sensed what was so desperately wrong.

"By the Firstborn," he murmured, and rather than lifting her as he had meant to do, he sat by her side and cradled her in his arms. She resisted, as a wild animal will do, but only for a moment. Then with a low cry she buried her face in the fur of his coat and clutched at him in terror, and in need.

He held her for some time like that, sensing that this was something she needed more than food and warmth if he was to bring her home again. And she held him tightly until she could pull herself no closer, desperately absorbing the essence of humanity from him through the closeness, fighting to reestablish her connection to their mutual species. Slowly, gradually, the frightened whine which issued from her throat became a human sobbing; tears, which the kisunu do not shed, began to squeeze frozen from her eyes.

And the world was gray once more.

Harkur: Never underestimate man's ingenuity in masterminding his own destruction.

TWELVE

To Kaimera Lord Zatar, Zarvati, son of Vinir and K'siva
From the Elders of the Holding

The Elders respectfully remind you that it is required of each purebred Braxaná male that he sire four registered purebred children during his lifetime. While we recognize that you are still young in age, your involvement in the War forces us to consider the possibility that you may not enjoy the full life expectancy of the Braxaná. Therefore we urge you to deal with your reproductive responsibility as soon as possible. Attached you will find a list of purebred Braxaná women who have not yet borne their quota. We hope you will consider this request in light of your military interests and do your part in maintaining the number and thus the power of our Race.

* * *

The Braxaná estate on Karviki sprawled across acres of lush territory, richly purple in the fading red sunlight. The main house was an odd mixture of traditional Braxaná (or Neo-Barbaric, as some critics called it) and the local architectural styles.

Zatar regarded it for a long while before approaching. It disturbed him in a way he did not fully understand. Many Braxaná designed their homes to incorporate foreign elements (his own tended toward Aldousan) but the mark of the Master Race was always dominant. Not so here. The primary impression was one of glass: glittering, fragile, worked in patterns of rose and blue between gleaming stone arches. Not true glass, he knew, nor a modern substitute, but the aurastone native to this planet. Viewed from inside, it would shatter the sun's ruby light into a kaleidoscope of star-like fragments. Beautiful . . . but vulnerable. He had a warrior's distaste for any House guarded by such insubstantial walls, but was not surprised to see it. Given its owner, it was appropriate.

He glanced at the letters he had brought with him; one was a flatrendering of the Elders' message, which he had perused so often that the plastic was noticeably worn. The other was a message from Yiril, which he held in his hand a moment longer, rereading it in the dying sunlight.

> *Kaim'era Zatar—It means what you think it does.*
> *Make your choice with care.*
> *Kaim'era Yiril, Lord and Elder*

Tucking the letters back into his tunic, he walked from the landing platform to the main house. It gave him time to admire the native sunset and its attendant blood-colored shadows. Workmen fell to their knees as he passed and touched their heads to the ground in a Karviki gesture of reverence. *Yes,* he thought, *there are advantages to leaving Braxi proper.*

The door opened as he reached it; he smiled his appreciation of the timing, a subtle expression that received its acknowledgment in the groveling of the guard who admitted him.

"Kaim'era Zatar," he told him, "son of Vinir and K'siva. I would like to speak to Lady L'resh."

"The Lady is at home," the native responded in fairly good Braxin. "Please come in and be comfortable while I tell her you are here."

Zatar nodded and followed him into the House, through the forehall and into one of the visiting rooms. It was comfortably furnished in a Karviki/Braxaná manner, this time less ostensibly native. Thick cushions covered the floor, intricately covered in geometric examples of Karviki embroidery. There was a firepit, bounded on three sides by a lowtable of inlaid wood. A golden decanter sat ready upon its surface, flanked by twelve matching goblets, each with a spray of Rask bloodstones upon its lip. And of course there was the last of the sunlight, filtered through aurastone windows that were set in golden tracery, sprinkling the room with patterns of its own. He was pleased by the interplay of shadow and color even as he mused upon the rarity of such display in the Central System. There, this room would have been a conference chamber, hence without windows, and with a minimum of distraction.

Here, the decorating was much more attuned to pleasure than to politics. It was, he admitted, very much to his liking.

"Lord Zatar. You honor me."

The woman in the doorway was attractive—all Braxaná women are—but in a way that was alien to Braxi. Her smile was naturally welcoming, and if she meant him any insult by denying him his political title it was not evident in her expression. "May I offer you wine?" she asked, and when he nodded she came to the lowtable, knelt beside it, and poured some. Blue, he noticed, surprised; one could not take even the color of wine for granted. He sat down beside her as she offered him his choice of glasses, pleased to note that the cushions were as comfortable as they were attractive. Seeing her, he could imagine nothing else.

"You are welcome in my House," she said formally, and with a wave of her hand encouraged: *drink!* He bowed slightly and did so, with genuine pleasure. Her presence was even more pleasing than he had expected it to be, from her gentle appearance to the natural delicacy of her smallest movement. It wasn't an image he was accustomed to seeing.

"I'm surprised, of course, to find you here, but a visit from a Central Lord is always welcome and yours is no exception. Will you permit me to offer you further refreshment?"

"Please." He watched as she gestured to a servant in the hallway, issuing orders that were not commands only by virtue of linguistic technicality. *It would satisfy this man to have food brought. . . .* Briefly he wondered who served as Token Dominance, acting as Master of her House, and what the relationship was between them. Female-owned Houses were always a careful study in social balance.

She turned back to him, her face a thing of sunlight. "If you tell me it isn't some sort of business that brought you all the way out here, I'd be pleased. Of course, I wouldn't believe you for a moment."

At that moment the light entering the room must have fallen below some preset standard, for a golden beam from the ceiling ignited the firepit, which burst into matching flames. The fuel had apparently been scented; as it burned it released a gentle perfume into the room's cool air. "Lovely," he admired.

She lowered her eyes, acknowledging the compliment. How strange she was, how non-Braxaná! All the body language he had come to associate with his people was absent in her, and in its place was an uninhibited lightness which seemed entirely alien to his tradition. Yet what was there in the social codes that decreed excessive seriousness? Even her manner of dress, though technically Braxaná, displayed more individuality than Central tradition usually inspired. The hands which poured him more wine were clothed in dove-gray sueded leather, and the surface of her matching tunic had been brushed to a soft nap. The harsh line of the high Braxaná boots were missing from her; instead of tight breeches and black leather she wore soft leggings of the same gray, and the tips of her footwear barely peeked out, matching, from beneath the hem. The only black she wore was a sash—which drew attention to her small waist—and a collar, which set off by contrast the glowing white of her face. Over her shoulders black hair spilled richly, thick with curls, a pure and velvet black to be silhouetted against the firelight. To Zatar, who was accustomed to the harsher Central styles, she seemed delightfully exotic and strangely fragile.

"If somewhat alien," he added.

"But pleasing?"

"Oh, yes." He sipped the wine and found its surprising lightness not without attraction. "Very much so."

"The Karviki excel in many areas, food and decor being two of them. I think one of the greatest advantages of living far out in the Holding is an opportunity to taste the truly alien. Don't you?"

"One of them." He dared, "Is that what prompted you to leave Braxi?"

He had shifted into a more sexual speech mode and perhaps it was that which caused her to look away from him, as if something she saw in his eyes disturbed her. She forced a laugh; it lacked the spontaneous lightness of her previous expressions. "I wasn't Braxaná enough for Central life, if you must know. " She had begun the sentence in the Basic Mode but concluded in the Negative, as if to say that what lay beneath his words should not be discussed, was an unwelcome topic. "I found it nothing more than a progression of unwelcome political maneuverings, and the Central Braxaná no more than the slaves of their politics." She caught his eyes and her expression clearly said: *men such as yourself.* "I stayed as long as I had to and then sought out a better place." She leaned against the table, languid and comfortable. "Here I'm a goddess. The locals adore me. I feed their pride just by being here; would a purebred Braxaná make her home on Karviki if the planet wasn't in some way superior. And that's what our image is all about, I think—certainly a just reward for all the social nonsense we put up with. But it's different here. I don't have to spend every waking moment proving I'm more Braxaná than anyone else. These people take my racial superiority for granted. And they would do anything to please me—anything at all." She smiled. "I like that."

A servant entered, bowed, and presented a golden tray for their perusal. "Sihk-tail, broiled in sekwa-butter." It was clear from his demeanor that he was bound to her more by awe and devotion than by mere wages. "A Karviki delicacy, Lord."

Zatar accepted a long, slender fork and lifted one of the bits of spiced seafood to his lips. He tasted it, savored it, then nodded. As if that signaled the appropriateness of the offering, L'resh had the man put it on the table between them.

"Most unusual," he assessed, not unpleased.

"Most of Karviki is, to the Central mind." She leaned forward, then hesitated, as if she lacked the proper words to begin what she wanted to say.

"Please be free," he encouraged.

"All right, Lord Zatar. Why have you come here? I told you—" she spoke hurriedly "—I hate the social games of your planet. And I don't play them well. So please, if you would just come to the point and explain yourself. . . ."

He put down the fork and looked at her carefully. Whatever doubts he had entertained regarding this move had been banished by the light of her presence. "If I must," he said finally, then softly, as befit her person: "I've come to court you for Seclusion."

It was hard to say if astonishment, anger, or fear weighed more heavily in her expression; a moment later, however, all but the first had vanished. With careful control she told him "I've borne four living children."

"I know that."

"Do you also know what that entails? Do you have any concept of the pain involved?" Emotion poured into her voice—proud, angry, wounded. "Do you know what it's like to endure those zhents of waiting, to live with that hope, and never know if it's going to prove worthwhile in the end? A man knows *nothing* of such things, Zatar! I'm an Elder. I've had my four children for the sake of the Holding. What makes you think I would ever willingly go through that again?"

It was not in his best interest, he knew, but nonetheless he countered, "Perhaps I forget your earned title as easily as you forget mine."

"Very well, *Kaim'era,*" she snapped, and then, with an effort, calmed herself. "You're right, and I'm sorry. The fact that men of your position were a constant annoyance to me during my years on Braxi is no reason to deny you your right to stand among them. Nevertheless, another Seclusion is out of the question; there are no words you can say that will change that. Surely you knew that would be the answer. Why did you come all this way just to hear it?"

"My bloodline is Plague-prone, " he said quietly. He was using the Basic mode but added a sexual undertone, to indicate that his attraction to her was above and beyond his proposition. "A condition that was probably worsened by my parents' inbreeding. I think you can understand that if I'm going to be pulled away from the War to sire a child, I would like to create one that might stand some chance of survival."

"Is that the only reason?"

"Isn't it enough?" Her eyes chided him: *Have it all out in the open. No games.* Very well. "I need a Seclusion close to the War Border."

"So you came all the way out here? Wrong direction, Kaim'era."

"The women in the Central System can't afford to put that much distance between themselves and their Houses for any length of time. I sought a woman whose House could function in her absence—as yours can—and one who might bear a living child in a reasonably short period of time. I'm working among commoners, L'resh. If I desert my work at the Border to obsess myself with a woman, they won't understand it. Braxaná power can't survive ridicule—voiced or unvoiced. If I let this interfere with my Border activities, I may as well return to Braxi and give up on the War entirely."

"I wouldn't wish that on anyone," she said dryly. "But you're young. Why are you going through all this now, if it's such a problem?"

"The Elders 'suggested' it." The look of anger that passed over her face confirmed one of his guesses: Elder though she was, she hadn't been consulted. "The majority of them would probably like to see me safe on Braxi, where they could keep an eye on me."

"Other Braxaná have gone to war."

"And remained islands in the midst of battle. A brief call to glory, the sacking of a planet or two, and a triumphal return to the Mistress Planet. Never making contact with the men who serve them, or the planets that depend on them. The Central Elders are afraid for their image, L'resh, afraid of what might happen if one of their kind lives day in and day out among commoners. Also, the Braxaná who've gone to war have been young men seeking to make a name for themselves. Never someone who already wielded considerable power on his own. Never a Kaim'era—until now. They feel threatened. They're trying to pressure me back into civilian life, where they think I belong."

"So it's politics again. How dare they! Don't we have troubles enough fulfilling our quotas, without making reproduction a tool of politicians—a weapon?" She shook her head in amazement. "More than anything I've ever heard, your words make me glad I left Braxi when I did."

He smiled, clearly amused by some secret thought, and withdrew a slender vial from his sash. "In your anger you remind me, Lady. I brought you a gift."

"A bribe?"

"'The Braxaná collects bribes as just tribute; only a fool pays before he bargains.' He uncapped the vial and poured its contents—thick, golden, translucent—into one of the goblets. "I thought I would bring you some small taste of what the Central System does have to offer. I'd be pleased if you'd accept it."

She looked up at him; her long dark lashes were like bird's wings framing her eyes. It struck him that he had never seen a woman more attractive to him. "What is it?"

"A Central liqueur." He threw the vial into the fire, where it melted, crackling. "Both rare and expensive. A suitable offering?"

She sipped from the goblet, then stopped to savor what remained on her tongue. "Sweet," she said approvingly.

"Central taste."

He sat in silence while she finished the tiny portion; she was grateful that doing so spared her from having to speak. Once she looked up at him, startled, as though it had just occurred to her that he might drug her, but the thought was ludicrous; what could he gain in a single night that wouldn't cost him more when she brought him up on charges? When she had finished the liqueur, she set the goblet on the table and slowly pushed it way from her. "Zatar, I . . . I can't. I'm sorry you had to come all this way to hear that. But it's just not possible."

He touched the side of her face with a black-gloved finger and felt her tremble. "Your features would find beautiful inheritance in a son, L'resh."

"I can't, Kaim'era, please. . . ." She pushed his hand away, reluctantly, it seemed. "I fulfilled my duty early in life so that I could move away and enjoy my freedom."

"And you don't even realize the magnitude of what you're saying! L'resh, there are women who spend their lifetime trying to fulfill their quota. You're not fifty, and already you're done with it! Four living children in eight pregnancies—I want to breed that back into the Race."

"It's not my responsibility," she countered weakly. He was pleased to note that in response to his use of the sexual modes she had finally come to use one herself. Longing. . . .

He moved closer and when she did not move away he touched her, then drew her into his arms. She was warm and fragile, and she trembled as he kissed her.

"No," she whispered.

He reached for her again but she drew back suddenly. "*No.* I turn you down. That's my right as a purebred. I'm sorry. I refuse." Her eyes were wet and her voice was shaking. "Please let me go."

He made no further move but neither did he release her. His original guess, he realized, had been correct. "L'resh," he said softly, with as much sympathy as his language was capable of expressing. "How long since you've tasted a man?"

She shuddered in his arms, but made no additional attempt to draw away from him. "There are other pleasures," she said finally.

"You know what I mean."

She lowered her eyes. "You don't understand. I almost died, Zatar. What pleasure is worth death?"

"And without pleasure, what is life?" He began to take off his gloves, and although she knew the implications she said nothing. "Sometimes, in the Center of the Holding, one can obtain a liqueur whose taste is so sweet to women that they embrace pleasure as they never dared before."

She looked at him, alarmed. "What was that you gave me?"

He put his hand against the side of her face, gently, reveling in the touch of smoothness against his bare skin. "Contraception," he said softly.

Her eyes widened.

"You're going to tell me it's illegal, and I'm going to say I know it. Would you like to remind me of the death penalty? I've destroyed the only evidence."

She was still in shock from the revelation. "How . . ."

"There's nothing so illegal that no one supplies it—and nothing supplied that a Braxaná can't get hold of. Do you think that we on Braxi can afford to lose our mistresses to pointless labor, much less death in childbed? We're not that barbaric, although we play at it."

"But isn't there risk?" she breathed.

"There's risk." He kissed her, long and sweetly, reveling in her response. There was a decade's hunger in her, if his guesswork was good—not an unpleasant prospect. "Tell me no," he offered, "and I'll leave."

She clutched him tightly to her. There were no more words after that, or any need for them.

The rising sun woke him.

He got up slowly, careful not to jar the bed they had later retired to—or rather, the webbed whatever-it-was that passed for such on Karviki. The skin of his face was taut and dry, and it occurred to him that he had never removed the previous day's cosmetics. Quietly he searched the room for astringent, soaked it into a cloth lying beside its jeweled bottle, and cleansed the excess white from his face.

She stirred, and awoke. Her dark eyes wide, she watched him. "You're leaving?"

"I have to." He dampened the cloth again and brought it over to her. "I have the War to get back to."

She closed her eyes and let him wipe the paint from her skin. She seemed hardly paler for its absence. "I wish you wouldn't," she whispered.

He kissed her. "So do I," he said, and his regret was genuine.

Then she drew him down to her, and for a short, sweet time the War was irrelevant.

The red sun rose higher and its light first approached, then washed over the two of them. He lay back for a while, content with the moment, forestalling a reassessment of his purpose in visiting her. Then he caught her eyes. She was leaning on one side, watching him, and the look on her face said that she knew what he was thinking.

"It came to me one day how overwhelmingly stupid we've been," he said quietly. "Nature guarantees fertility. Fertile creatures reproduce. Infertile creatures don't. And then we, self-made gods that we are, defied that law."

She took his hand in hers; was there any contact more sensual than that? "Four children," he mused. "No fewer. And under no circumstances more than that. Their sense of responsibility satisfied, the women of our Race find alternatives to childbearing. Exactly four offspring per person, two and hopefully no more to die of the Plague, perhaps another in the War. If we had just let it *be*. . . ." He squeezed her hand. "It would have bred out."

She nodded, her eyes lowered. He was right, and it hurt to acknowledge it. "If you don't force those who have trouble with it to make the quota—"

"Then we'll surely die out. We don't have the numbers to support that strategy, now. It has to come from the other end." He stroked her face, her hair. "There's more at stake than my own contentment, here. I didn't want to say it, but there it is."

"Why didn't you want to say it?"

"Because we're a selfish people, and the good of the group isn't supposed to outweigh the pleasures of the individual."

"Ah," she said softly. "More Central custom."

"Braxaná custom, I'm afraid." He tipped up her face until she was looking at him. The corner of one eye was wet. "Give me a child, L'resh. I own a planet right by the War Border, more than suitable for human habitation. I'll build you a House to equal this one, and have artists from all over the Holding brought to you. I'll give you a thousand times more beauty and pleasure at the Border than any other place could ever offer you. Give me a living child, and I'll keep you supplied in contraception for the rest of your life."

There was the bribery. How long had she hungered, how desperately had she dreamed of finding a solution? Would she be willing to risk her life once more, in order to live the rest of it more fully?

She looked away from him, her thoughts elsewhere, and after a moment slowly nodded. "If you stay the afternoon," she whispered. There were tears in her voice.

Which was better invitation, he thought, than any speech mode could manage.

Harkur: If a man understands the priorities of his fellows, he can lead them. If he fails in this, all the good intentions in the world won't buy him loyalty.

THIRTEEN

The wind driving dust into her eyes, Anzha lyu Mitethe waited.

Her face was not the face of youth, although she was still young. Her eyes may have shone with strength and determination, but they never radiated warmth. The lines of her face bespoke bitterness and anger and, had she smiled, the resulting rounded creases would have been at odds with those already there.

She was not attractive. She was not unattractive. The aura of command was too strong about her for one to be able to isolate physical appearance for judgment. She had presence.

She also had control, and now she exercised it. Like all Braxaná she had learned to hide her emotions. If she trembled now, it was inside; no one observing her would think that she was afraid.

That was as it should be.

When the ramp was lowered, she took a deep breath of the local air before ascending to the transport. Being on a planet's surface wasn't pleasant for her; more and more the evidence of nature at work made her uncomfortable. Her phobia was growing stronger year by year, despite her efforts to overcome it. It was therefore with great pleasure that she would exchange the dusty, threatening air of this planet for the human-controlled atmosphere of a warship.

A warship? *The* warship!

Inside the transport they were courteous, and she refrained from explaining that no, she didn't require instructions in ground-star safety precautions. She smiled politely as they explained the workings of the stabilizer attached to her couch—granted, all warships generated their own gravity, but how ignorant did they think she was—and she even allowed the pilot to personally see that it was set correctly. Not until he left did she reset it.

There was no further waiting to endure; she was no sooner lying on the couch than the tiny transport lifted from the planet's surface. She closed her eyes and reveled in the multi-gee sensation as they pulled free from the planet, a feeling the couch lessened but no longer nullified. It made her feel as though she had truly left the planet's surface, and she could feel the phobia settle within her, ready for its next excuse to surface.

Now, at last, she had time to think. Perhaps it was the first time in two Standard Years she'd had time to do so; perhaps instead she hadn't dared. Now the memories came, and with them the anger. Images: Subcommander ti Vasha demanding reassignment. "I will not serve an alien in War!" he had cried, and that was that. There were other confrontations, not as dramatic but equally frustrating. She had commanded the *Destroyer* for two years and had never won over its crew. Did that matter? She tried to convince herself that only the actual combat was of any importance, but she failed. Battles were few and far between, and in the interim Anzha lyu Mitethe was a human being. The fact that she had grown accustomed to being alone did not ease the pain of hearing those half-whispered conversations, or of knowing that they were intended for her ears. She was an alien. That was that.

She could have lost herself in the joy of battle, but circumstances had been unobliging. She lacked seniority, hence she lacked tactical authority. She was bound to obey the orders of men and women who, though they had served far longer than she and wore more decorations on their sleeves, were decidedly her inferiors. They were so conservative in their strategy that the War she had longed to fight had practically passed her by.

Until now.

When the transport was outatmosphere, the generators kicked in and supplied a minimum of artificial gravity, for safety purposes. Anzha arose from the couch and took out the files Torzha had sent her. Here was detailed information on the nature of her new command, from the ship's specifications to its crew. She put the former aside. The *Conqueror* was not something that could be captured on paper; she knew it already from legend. It had no equal in the Azean fleet and it would have none among the Braxins until the Sentira was back in active service. From the day it was built it was capable of greater maneuverability, more extensive sensor range, and more precise firepower than had been thought possible for a warship, and since then it had been improved. It was a command assignment one dreamed of getting.

Why me? she asked for the thousandth time.

She questioned more than the advisability of putting someone of alien appearance on such a ship. At thirty she was a mere child; the officers of the *Conqueror* had been serving on their ship since the time of her birth, if not longer. And they had gone through commanding officers with a speed and regularity that was unnerving.

She pulled those files and reread them. Li Dashte had resigned his commission after one year. Ver Buell had filed charges against his prime subcommander for disobedience, then had left when the man was acquitted. Er Pirjare was in a rest home on Ikn. Five more commanders now served on other ships; one had resigned from the fleet entirely.

The problem was the crew. Insubordination or eccentricity, or both—from the brief reports it was hard to tell. StarControl had issued reprimands on numerous occasions, but it had no real power to correct the problem; the *Conqueror's* officers were apparently careful to obey rules to the letter, if not to the spirit. The ship's battle record was outstanding, which was amazing considering the discord in its command center. But the *Conqueror's* crew lacked one important thing: a Starcommander who could handle them. Was that why Torzha had assigned her to this ship?

One by one, Anzha reviewed the personnel files. The men and women who had served under her on the *Destroyer* had been professional soldiers: officers who had made war their avocation because they were good at it, fighters who had chosen military service because it was the most intense flight training they could obtain, technicians in search of the perfect resumé. The officers of the *Conqueror* were a different breed entirely. It wasn't obvious at first. One had to look long and hard to discover the connection, but when she realized what she had found Anzha nodded her understanding.

Every man and woman in a position of authority was a child of war, as she was. Raised by military officers, spoonfed armaments and tactics along with their more solid nourishment—as she was, for the first six years of her life. They lived and breathed war as no civilian could; it ran in their veins alongside the blood, sometimes perhaps supplanting it entirely. In addition, most of them had known loss as a direct result of the Great Conflict. Fathers, mothers, lovers, friends, colleagues . . . Braxi had robbed them of what they valued most, and they were seeking vengeance. Under those circumstances, she thought, their behavior made sense.

She read the records over again, and began to comprehend the pattern. Starcommanders had run into trouble every time they had tried to get between this crew and the enemy. Commanding officers bogged down in red tape, giving precedence to protocol . . . these were the men and women the crew of the *Conqueror* rejected outright. And they knew how to get rid of them. Not a move was accidental, not a single act was careless. They could drive a man insane if they had to, without even actually defying regulations. In one case they had actually done so.

A smile, the first in years, transformed her face into something a little less harsh, a bit less unyielding.

I understand, she thought.

In her half-jacket was a letter from Torzha. She didn't open it; she didn't have to. She knew its brief text by heart and could recite it from memory, especially the closing line: "Succeed, and I will ask no questions."

It was a promise she needed if she was to win these people over.

"Starcommander?"

She gathered her things and rose to follow the attendant. Her thoughtful demeanor seemed to inspire him to silence. Good. Otherwise he might have explained to her how the airlock of a transport functioned.

Outside, protective fields wavered and dispersed. The transport eased into dock and the *Conqueror's* field was reestablished, containing both ships. Anzha braced herself as the portal slid open and a ramp drew itself into place.

And then she stepped out.

In theory, the reception dock of the *Conqueror* was supposed to be kept free of debris, so that a visiting dignitary might be properly impressed by its gleaming emptiness. But her own transport was flanked by four fighters, ready and waiting to be sent off into battle. It was a flagrant violation of StarControl custom, but not of regulations. No, the rules said nothing about what might be kept here, only that the place must be spotless and impressive. And it certainly was that.

The presence of the fighters could be read as an insult: *you are not important enough to justify extra work for us.* But she thought it meant just the opposite; the crew had probably moved the fighters here just for her arrival. Was it a challenge? She smiled to herself. From what she understood of the nature of the officers here, that would be typical.

With a slight nod to indicate her approval of the gesture, she strode down the ramp to meet her crew.

One of the subcommanders, probably her prime, came up to greet her. "Welcome, Starcommander." Guarded, wary thoughts accompanied his ritual bow: *I think there's no danger of this one being like all the others,* "Zeine li Tenore, Prime Subcommander." This was her counterpart then, the man who would be responsible for fulfilling her duties when she was offshift or—Hasha forbid—incapacitated. A warship was a world in miniature, and the Starcommander was its governor. Other subcommanders might limit themselves to one or two aspects of war, but she and li Tenore were responsible for everything, from the deployment of troops in battle to the thousand and one little details of shipboard life that kept humans occupied when they weren't fighting. Dark, violent thoughts clouded his foremind, but his hostility was not directed at her. It was like a reflection of her own hatred, directed toward Braxi.

We share a purpose, she thought.

He took her down the line of officers and introduced each one. Subcommanders of Security, Armaments, Astrogation, Engineering . . . their thoughts were all the same. Dark people, violent in outlook, with dreams that tasted of death; they must have appalled her predecessors. Now she could understand why the other Starcommanders had clung to the rulebook. It promised control in a world they didn't understand, on a ship peopled by aliens. The Azean mind was even-tempered, rational, congenial. These men and women, cast in a different mold, were warriors in the Braxin sense. One by, one they had found their way to the *Conqueror,* had discovered others who shared their priorities, who were ruled by similar hatreds. No Starcommander would be allowed to threaten that.

At the end of the line a man stood apart, civilian in dress but for a band of rank-markings fastened about his arm: Tau en Shir, civilian medic. Torzha had rescued him from the soon-to-be-dead, when he planned to consummate his misery by opting for legal suicide. He had watched his bonded mate killed in a Braxin raid, not quickly and not pleasantly; the memory—and the hatred—was more than he could bear. But Torzha had talked him out of it. *This is my weapon,* she told him, indicating Anzha. *This woman will bring the enemy to its knees.* He was her private physician, whose only duty was to learn the alien intricacies of her body and mind and keep them sound, that she might attain her maximum potential. Those eyes met hers, and the emotion that poured forth was like a blow across the face. Grief intermingled with hope, and a strange new sensation: loyalty. She savored that a moment before greeting him; it was something she had never experienced before, and she was not entirely comfortable with it. "My pleasure to serve you," he told her quietly. And he meant it.

"Your orders, Starcommander?" The thoughts of her second-in-command reeked of challenge. *Shall we sit here for days of pointless ceremony, as custom would demand? Is that your will?*

"Let's get underway," she said brusquely. "We have a War to fight." Approval rose from the minds surrounding her. "There's time enough for ceremony on the way."

They were hers—or they would be, soon enough.

She had come home at last.

Harkur: War is the fire that tempers men's souls.

FOURTEEN

When the bulk of the fighting was done and the only vessels within sight were marked with the Holding's identicodes, First Sword Sezal allowed himself a moment in which to scan the surrounding Void directly. From his brain, in which the special implants rested, his senses rode outward—first to the band of contacts which nestled snugly about his head, then to the computer and its myriad scanners, and lastly, magnificently, into the Void itself.

He saw no stars; he was moving too fast, had left the tardionic universe with its finite visual display behind him. Yet the Void was not empty. Photons crossed the dark expanse, and though their patterns could not be interpreted by the human eye, the computer noted their existence and translated them into fleeting sensory images. Thus it was that he saw light where light could not exist, and tasted with his other senses all that the Void contained, rendered in familiar sensations. Gases and dusts, the residue of a swordship's passage . . . he tasted them, smelled them, reveled in their familiarity. Then he focused his attention on the composition of the residue and had his computer run an analysis. Yes, it was a trail—the trail he wanted, the one which he must follow to make his triumph complete.

He took a moment to transmit a victory message to the *Sentira. Enemy offensive neutralized,* he informed Commander Herek. *Ten Azean swordships destroyed, three remaining. Pursuing.* He brought the signal insync with the mothership's course vector and sent it off to the nearest relay. Now he needed to be well on his way before a response could reach him. Because Herek would respond, he knew that, and would order him back to the safety of the talon. Therefore they needed to be out of sync with the *Sentira's* contact network before Herek had time to transmit his orders.

One last glance at his pilots: impatient but disciplined, their attack formation steady, they knew the rules of the game as well as he did and were anxious to be underway. Sezal nodded approvingly as he called up his computer's speculative matrix and had it run an array of possible courses for the fleeing Azeans. There, that one . . . he set up an intercept course and locked it into his ship's computer. One, two, five pilots acknowledged locksync with him—they'd fly this one on automatic linkage—then the last of them and it was *GO* and they were accelerating—

—out of sync with the relay system; was that Herek's signal coming in?

Sorry, Commander, but I received no orders.

FREE.

He breathed a sigh of relief as the slender swordships passed through the *Sentira's* contact periphery, into the freedom of the superluminal night. Riding point on their formation, Sezal's ship gobbled up the residue of the enemy's passage, digested it for content. Speed, course, defense . . . the pattern of exfuel discharge became a wealth of information, and Sezal adjusted his flight vector accordingly.

It appeared that the Azeans were not expecting prolonged pursuit. That was good; it would make them easier to catch. To be sure, only a fool would commit himself to a chase like this when his prey was in full retreat. There was too much danger of running into the Azeans' contact net, of coming suddenly within the range of a mothership's fire. That was a nightmare which plagued the best of pilots, and a reality which all too often claimed the lives of the unwary; it was with good reason that the Azeans expected a safe ride home. But their very certainty made them vulnerable, and Sezal was not one to let such an opportunity slip by.

"Estimated time to scanner contact, three six oh and counting." That was *if* he had figured the intercept properly, *if* the Azeans had kept to their course, *if* they did not reach their home ship first—*don't think of that!*—a blessed lot of *ifs,* but Sezal was reasonably confident. The computer called time for him, relayed the countdown to his pilots. Acceleration, just so; a strain on his compensatory systems, but not too much to handle. Then slow, to the speed of the enemy ships (anticipated speed, he corrected) which should be in range *now*—

"Got them!" His pilots peeled out of formation with the competence born of endless practice; twelve against three should mean a quick clean-up, if luck didn't turn against them. *There is always that factor,* he reminded himself, as he locked onto the nearest target. Three Azeans had come within range of his scanners—no more. Sezal breathed a sigh of relief. No reinforcements yet, and if they moved quickly enough, none would come. The faster they worked, then, the safer they would be.

His men were dividing into assault teams, one for each of the Azean fugitives. Sezal took his position among the nearest swordships, making it five against one. Good odds. They began to lay down a pattern of random fire; computer-synchronized, it defied analysis, hence could not be anticipated. Since a swordship was vulnerable in the moment it fired, such randomness assured their safety. The first Azean must outrun its opponents or die—and it could not do the former, their containment formation saw to that.

With grim satisfaction Sezal watched as the other swordships in his group fired upon their prey, and he added his own energy to the barrage. The enemy's outer forcefield deflected what it could, began to absorb the rest . . . and exploded at last in a star of brilliance as its defense generator, overloaded, succumbed to the sheer force of the attack.

One down. No damages. Time elapsed . . . not good. Sezal tapped up his speculative matrix, assigned it to the problem of the enemy mothership. *Where is it likely to be—what is our chance of contact?* It answered with an array of probable courses, based on previous scout reports, fleshed out by mechanical reasoning, and a gross estimate of the odds of immediate interception.

Twelve percent.

Not good. Not good at all. Sezal considered turning back, decided against it. They hadn't come this far to give it up now . . . but a two-digit risk factor was bad news. Quickly, he reviewed his pilots' positions and was startled to find that the third group had lost control of its prey. Apparently the Azean's point ship had also proven more dangerous than anticipated; two of Sezal's swordships had been damaged and a third had withdrawn, its defense field disabled. But how—?

Then the warrior's answer: *it doesn't matter.* Anyone who dares an attack risks a moment's vulnerability; that was part of the game of war, whose rules they all understood. Good strategy would help make you safe, good timing was invaluable, but there was always luck—and the third Azean seemed to be turning theirs against them.

Fourteen percent. He tried not to think about it. Across past the second team—their victim was weakening, would not last much longer—on to the third group and its elusive prey. The Azean seemed to be turning back. Was that possible? Yes, to help its remaining companion. Hopeless!

Or was it? Sezal tapped up the Azean's course figures, frowned, tried again. This couldn't be right. Physics was physics; there were simple limits to how fast a swordship could decelerate, how tight a turn it could manage . . . and the Azean was defying them all.

With a growing chill in the pit of his stomach Sezal sent a warning to his second team. Too late; the Azean fired, hit one of his men even as the swordship's outer field dropped. Bless it! Clean shot across the fireports, disabling the pilot's offense. Sezal ordered him out of the way; too many swordships in that small an area was asking for trouble with crossfire. Ten against two was still good enough to guarantee Braxin victory—wasn't it?

He discovered he was no longer certain.

He locked himself onto the renegade's tail, made no attempt to analyze its movement, just followed it. Its movements were careful, precise . . . and patently impossible. Sezal's men could not seem to land a shot on it. They fired, but it was gone, had moved, had decelerated—*something*—and their carefully focused energy sped off into the Void, wasted. Sezal tailed it, watched it battle his swordships in a desperate attempt to reach its companion vessel, did nothing until he felt, with a warrior's certain instinct, that the moment for action was *now*

and he fired

and the heavens were immersed in white, the Void a field of incandescent splendor as his scanners fused, their housing struck dead on. For a moment he was blinded as the implants seared his inner vision—but then he had control again, of the ship and of himself, and by the time his senses cleared he had managed to put some distance between himself and the enemy.

Bless the luck! He quickly assessed his damages: all scanners out, internal systems at fifty percent efficiency . . . the com network was still functioning, though, and his defense fields were intact. *It could have been worse,* he told himself. With a few seconds' work he was able to lock into another swordship's field display, so that he might have the illusion of scanner efficiency. But it was not precise enough for him to rejoin the battle; the temporal distortion was too crippling.

How in Ar's name had the Azean managed to hit him like that?

Contact risk up to sixteen percent; they were running out of time. He watched as the third Azean dodged the best efforts of his men, even struck one of the Braxin swordships in the moment it opened fire. Bless it! They weren't going to get this one, that was clear, not without a detailed analysis of just what was going on inside that shipshell.

But as for the second Azean . . . that was a different matter. Already its defenses were weakening, and even as Sezal watched, the crucial shot was fired. Straight into the generator housing. The forcefield folded, imploded, and shattered its shipshell into a glorious shower of tachyonic atoms. Two down.

Now they could focus all their energies on the third ship.

But even as Sezal planned his attack, the last Azean puffed out of range, and with a burst of what must have been painful acceleration took off toward its starship. Nineteen percent chance of mothership contact if they followed, the computer said, and that would grow worse with each passing moment. *If* they could follow him at all; Sezal was beginning to have his doubts

When given the choice he preferred to fight—but only an idiot would commit himself to a chase like this without some knowledge of the enemy. This last Azean ship seemed to be functioning in defiance of Heyer's Ratio, and that was not a possibility that could be explored in the heat of battle. Sezal needed a complete analysis of the vessel's movement, a composite scannerlog and all the stats that went with it. And that could only be compiled back on the Sentira.

Regretfully—but not without haste—he ordered his pilots toward home.

Talon-Commander Herek was an impressive man, possessed of a restless energy that often overflowed the bounds of his discipline. In shape and coloring he was a curious admixture of human traits, as though each one of the Scattered Races, having the opportunity to add something to his genetic background, had chosen its single most evident trait to mark his appearance. Thus his height—typically Aldousan—was supported by the hard, clean lines of a Vrittan physique, and the narrow features of his part-Laissan countenance were streaked irregularly with tan and brown, in the manner of the Tukolt veldtlanders.

An impressive man, and a dangerous one. His pacing consumed

the length of the room in seven long strides, from the wall of monitor screens to the computer console which controlled both starmap, display and library access. He was silent, pensive (musing over Sezal's report, no doubt) and since his next words were likely to be those of condemnation, Sezal was not anxious to encourage him.

"You took out eleven, am I correct?" he said at last. "And their attack was neutralized. Excellent. Damage?"

Startled, Sezal offered, "Minimal." This wasn't like the Commander. Was he so preoccupied with other matters that he'd forgotten his usual opening—namely, criticism of Sezal's tendency to leave the Sentira's contact network? "Swordships One, Four, Seven, Twelve, and Twenty are undergoing systems review now; damage appears to be localized in all cases."

As he heard Sezal say *One,* Herek stopped his pacing. He looked at the First Sword, forked eyebrow raised in surprise. *Not like you to be hit,* he seemed to be saying. Sezal flushed.

"Tell me about the Azean," Herek urged.

Sezal described the third ship's unusual capacity—in acceleration, in maneuverability, and in aggressive timing. It was the last which disturbed him most, for although no machine could predict with any certainty when an enemy would be vulnerable, the Azean had seemed to *know* when such moments would come, in time to take advantage of them.

The Commander nodded as he listened, his expression dark. "Let's get a composite on it," he said at last. And he turned to the computer, which could combine the scannerlogs of the *Sentira's* fighters into a single image. With a practiced touch he brought its display to life.

Stars: invisible during battle, now added to the display by the *Sentira's* computer. They moved slowly, fluidly, as the viewer's point of reference sped between them. Now the fighter was taking form in the darkness, gaining solidity and definition as log after log was added to the composite file. At last it was whole, and Sezal had the opportunity to study it.

It *was* different. One could see that immediately. Changes had been made in the generator housing, and the structure of the fireports had clearly been altered. Other differences, less obvious to the human eye, were being outlined via statistics at the side of the display. Changes in shipshell structure, realignment of the primary drive . . . the list scrolled up before them, first the adjustments which were certain and then those which were merely probable, accompanied by speculative figures.

"Heyer gave us the optimum balance for high-speed Voidflight nearly ten thousand years ago," Herek said quietly. His thoughts echoed Sezal's own: if the famous Ratio could be improved upon, why had it taken this long to do so? "Over the years, we've pared our swordships down to mass-minimum. A pilot has only his ship-shell and weapons and the equipment necessary to move them. There's nothing on board that isn't absolutely essential, either for flight or survival. Nothing! So where have they made the adjustment? Or have they found a way around Heyer's Ratio altogether—discovered another variable, perhaps, which can be entered into the central equations? I don't like it. I don't like it at all."

Sezal nodded agreement. Better maneuverability required more gravitic compensation, which required in turn a larger generator, which added to a ship's basemass and thus limited maneuverability . . . the optimum balance for all those elements had been known for centuries. If there was any room for improvement in Heyer's equations, either Braxi or Azea would have discovered it long ago. Wouldn't they?

"I want a full analysis," Herek was saying. "Speculative as well as deductive. Run this swordship's behavior through an open matrix and see what the computer comes up with. Omit no possibility. We'll assume for the moment that the Ratio still stands," he added, "and that the Azeans have discarded some part of the internal package. Take a swordship apart piece by piece, if you have to, until you find some combination of items whose mass would account for the change we see here."

"Understood, Commander."

"Now: on to other matters." A pause; Sezal could feel the tension in him, noted the care with which he chose his words. "We're to have a visitor," he said at last. He caught Sezal's eyes and held them; as always, the alienness of Herek's features made his gaze twice as riveting. "A Lord Commander."

It took Sezal a moment to recall the title. "A Braxaná?"

"Purebred. With the right to enter the fleet at will, at the head of any talon. *My* talon, in this case. " His voice was bitter, controlled. "No accident, that assignment. It was by his own request. The *Sentira* will be his warship, and the talon it controls will belong to him. As will its swordships."

The thought of serving a Braxaná awakened emotions in Sezal in strange, unfamiliar combination. Resentment, foreboding, these he could understand—but fear was there also, accompanied by a terrible kind of awe. A Braxaná—here? "What does he want?"

"Who knows? Amusement, perhaps. Conquest. Authority. What do they ever want? The law which makes such things possible doesn't question a man's motives, only permits the act."

Sezal could hear the indignation in this Commander's voice, and he sympathized with it. According to tradition, a Braxaná purebred Lord was entitled to enter the fleet as one of its highest ranking officers. As Lord Commander, he could move onto any ship he chose and take command of it, as well as directing those warships which were assigned to the same talon. No more earned rank among the talon's commanders; race would dominate experience, the black hair of the Central Tribe commanding higher title than a lifetime of expertise.

Usually the Braxaná gravitated toward the lesser fronts—K'vai, the Bengesh stretch—in hopes of earning their glory with minimal risk and not much effort. Often they even chose other wars; battles of expansion and the conquest of new cultures offered far more gratification to the Braxaná mindset than the difficult and often unrewarding conflict with Azea. Never did they move into the center of the Active War Zone. Never did they place their inexperience at the head of a high-risk talon, or unseat a commander whose expertise was renowned throughout the Holding. Until now.

"He'll be taking your place?" Sezal asked. He was trying hard to control his emotions; it was dangerous to hate the Pale Ones. "For how long?"

"For as long as he wants." Herek's hands clenched, unclenched, silent witness to his anger. "And you understand, there must be no resistance. Not from you, not from your men. The Braxaná reward defiance with death. And this one's a Kaim'era," he added bitterly. "So on top of all the rest of it, we have Whim Death to contend with."

"I thought military officers were immune—"

"No one is immune!—how could they be? This is the scepter with which our Holding is ruled, Sezal, and don't you forget it. The right to put anyone to death, for any reason, at any time."

He sighed. "Tell your men. Make it clear. There'll be resentment in the ranks, I know; how can we help that? But any sign of it—spoken, unspoken, it doesn't matter—can cause us to lose a pilot. We can't afford that. *Make them understand.*"

If you can control your own anger, Sezal thought, *which must be considerable, we can do no less.* "As you command. When is this Braxaná due?"

"A fleet transport will bring him to Y'maste, where we'll meet him; ten days from now, if all goes well. Ar!" His eyes, naturally narrow, were slits of anger. "Only a Braxaná could order us away from the Border for that long." The tone of his voice was, unfamiliar to Sezal; was there few in it, perhaps? "At any rate, it could be worse. He's a tactician; never set foot on a warship, but at least he knows the rules. If any rules hold, for his kind."

"Who is he?"

"Public name of Zatar, son of Vinir. And K'siva," he added, remembering the matronym. "Lord, Kaim'era, and now Commander. And we will all be on our best behavior while he's here, *at all times.* The Braxaná have ways of knowing what goes on, even in private. As for your pilots, I myself have indulged their idiosyncracies, but to expect the same of him might be tantamount to suicide. They must understand that."

"I agree," Sezal said tightly.

"He'll leave us eventually. Then things will return to normal—if we survive the period of his command. *We can't afford mistakes.*"

Sezal wondered which of them the Talon-Commander was trying to convince. "Of course," he answered simply. "I understand."

He would do what he could, but would it do any good? Who could say why this Kaim'era was coming in the first place? Who could say what his intentions were, in invading their ordered domain? All guesses were futile, as always; when it came to motivations, the Braxaná were a mystery.

"I'll see that my men are prepared," he promised.

The day of Zatar's arrival was a bad one for Herek. Not just because it was the day of his deposition; he had grown accustomed to the fact, had forced himself to accept it. It was simply one of those days in which everything went wrong, in which even the smallest detail of life on board the warship could not proceed smoothly without his personal attention.

By the time they were due to make rendezvous with the Y'mastene transport, his patience and his nerves had been worn dangerously thin. If one more divisionmaster were to come to him for judgment in a matter that his subordinates should have been able to handle, the odds were good he would kill the man outright; he was that tired of incompetence.

He wondered how well this Zatar would do when saddled with the responsibilities of command. The Braxaná were nothing if not spoiled, and he suspected that this one had not given much thought to what went on behind the command chair he so coveted. Blessed groundling! He could take the ship and be welcome to it, and let the Holding see what happened when a self-indulgent noble ousted one of Braxi's most successful commanders.

But his conscience would not let him continue in that vein. *You know why he's coming,* an inner voice chided. *You caused it to happen.*

He refused to face that possibility. If it were the truth, he would know it soon enough. He was angry enough without adding such guilt to his burdens.

What about Klev? D'argash? Musrii?

Concentrate on particulars: the thousand and one details that must be taken care of before the Intruder arrives. Clear the reception dock of all its cargo, have every inch of it scrubbed (by hand, if necessary) until it was so immaculate that dirt would never think of settling there. The Braxaná were nothing if not showmen; very well, prepare the theater. A path of black carpet for the Pale One to tread, a thousand men to flank him on each side. That was a start. His officers would wear Border dress uniforms; it was an unusual choice, as Y'maste was in a stabilized zone, but it was among the Commander's options. The sharp contrast of black and gold would be a more suitable environment for the Braxaná than a field of charcoal and tan, the usual alternative.

And then see if that helps. See if showmanship alone is enough to settle the nagging fear that you *know* why he's here, and it has nothing to do with a Braxaná's vanity. It has to do with his Garranat involvement, and with the power that a Central Lord can wield above and beyond that of military discipline. And with Kley—D'argash—all the others. . . .

He shuddered.

Zeroday, zerotenth. Two thousand assembled, as nervous as he was but with less specific cause—and hiding it better, he suspected. It took all the self-control he could muster to keep his hands open, to let them fall naturally to his sides. The dock was perfectly prepared, the reception would be flawless, the tour of inspection would proceed without a hitch . . . and he was afraid. Afraid! He, who had faced the enemy numerous times—Talon-Commander Herek, scourge of the Border! The Braxaná had reduced him to this without even setting foot on his ship; how much worse would it be when this Garranat authority stood before him, cloaked in the invulnerability of his Race?

You don't know why he's come, he told himself sternly. *You're only guessing. You could be wrong.*

He would find out soon enough. The transport had completed its approach, passing through the *Sentira's* outer forcefield and then the inner one, until it rested on the gleaming, immaculate floor. A pause; it seemed to Herek that he could hear his heartbeat, and the rhythm was not reassuring. Then the portal dissolved and a ramp was extended—

And *he* emerged.

Magnificent: the description fell short of the truth, but it was the best Herek had. Here was the human form developed to the point of physical perfection, the warrior's essence expressed in flesh. He was the spirit of Taz'hein clad in mortal guise, with the mark of the god still evident. Herek had never seen a purebred Lord before, could not have imagined the power of that presence, or its effect upon his men. Or on himself. It was small wonder to him that on some worlds the Braxaná were regarded as demigods.

He is just a man, he reminded himself, irritated by the awe that the Braxaná inspired.

The Lord Commander came toward him, his authority evident in every step. It was there in the way he looked over Herek's men, in the way he held himself, the very way he walked . . . who could help but be affected? It took all of Herek's strength to resist the power of this man's presence, to stand before him proudly, as a Talon-Commander should.

He voiced the necessary lie.

"Lord and Kaim'era Zatar: you are welcome."

Almost a smile, not quite a nod; the black eyes were fixed on him, their depths unreadable.

"My commission," Zatar said, and he held up his left hand. A message-ring fit snugly over the index finger, the mark of Garran upon it.

The hated, hated ritual. "My ship is yours. My talon is yours."

And he bowed.

"Your officers?" said the Lord Commander.

He tried not to read hope into Zatar's choice of words, merely went through the motions which law and tradition demanded of him. Introductions: Garol, son of Hedrek, Master of Voidat Armaments. Huzal, son of Sezret, Master of Astrogation. Feval, son of Temak, Commander of Ground Forces. Name after name he presented them all, the men who ran the Sentira, the names that had made her great. And last of all, First Sword Sezal—who was taking it all in with guarded hostility and not a little unease. He was small and slender, as all pilots were, and it was much to his credit that he stood before the Braxaná as proudly as he did; the physical presence of the larger man came close to overwhelming him.

"*Your* officers," the Talon-Commander concluded.

Zatar nodded. "We will set course for the Border immediately. Huzal—you will see to it."

The astrogator bowed. "My Lord."

"Meanwhile, Commander"—he meant Herek—"I assume you have quarters set aside for my use. With a briefing chamber, as I requested. You will take me there now, and we will discuss the details of my commission."

"As you wish, Lord Commander."

"The rest of you will continue in your accustomed duties until such time as you are instructed otherwise." His dark gaze swept over them, taking their measure, as they acknowledged his orders. Then he turned and looked over the ranks upon ranks of soldiers, and in his eyes there was a look that might have been pleasure. *You are mine*, he seemed to be saying.

"Commander Herek?"

With a last sullen bow to his conqueror, Herek submitted to his authority. And led him into the ship—*his* ship—where the throne of his experience had just been shattered.

The briefing chamber which Herek had reserved for Lord Zatar was by far the finest the talon had to offer. Its domed ceiling was honeycombed with flatscreens and studded with outlets for a starmap display, so that one might experience visual data in limitless formats. Let stars sweep across the heavens, radiating out from one wall to cross the center of the room and disappear at the opposite side; let the galaxy fill the room with light while starcharts display the constellations along its rim. There was no image so complex that the room could not manage it, no guest so auspicious that the chamber could not do him justice. Until now.

The ancient Braxaná had rejected technology. Now, though they used it, it failed to impress them. The chamber was a tool, nothing more, and Zatar's manner made it clear that it would take more than a mere technoarchitectural wonder to impress him.

He looked at Herek—assessing him, it seemed—and then said simply, "You know why I'm here."

"I can guess," he said quietly.

"Tell me."

"The Kaim'era is no doubt familiar with my record." How could he describe the situation without condemning himself? "My talon was the first to breach the Suraan front, and we led the attack on Zerenk'ir and Fri. Our territorial gains in this sector have been numerous—" *Until recently,* he admonished himself, and stopped his recital suddenly, embarrassment clogging his throat. *You are like a schoolboy, listing your accomplishments in the hope of delaying punishment.* Or of earning sympathy? The thought was repulsive. "My recent record . . . has not been so impressive." Were there no better words? "I'm sure the Kaim'era knows the details."

"Losses—erratic, unexplained, inexcusable. Defeat under circumstances which should have guaranteed victory. Punctuated by triumphs every bit as brilliant as those we have come to expect of you. And that is the problem, Commander Herek. If this were simply the case of a warrior past his prime . . . well, there are ways to deal with that. But it doesn't seem to be the case. Yes, when we look for the fruits of your excellent reputation, we are often disappointed. But if we seek for evidence of the decline of a great mind, we are equally frustrated.

"Garran has sorted through every file connected with your progress, and all our computers have failed to come up with a pattern to explain your losses. So: I've come here to investigate, Talon-Commander. Both you, and your circumstances. To determine the cause of your recent defeats, and take whatever action is necessary to correct the problem. The House of War will abide by my decision. Any questions?"

If he had leveled a neural stun at Herek, he could not have left him more speechless. Was it possible that the Braxaná—so quick to punish, so blind to the concept of innocence—would work to save him and his reputation, rather than simply replacing him? It was incredible; he could not accept it. He had feared a confrontation such as this for so long that he no longer had any realistic concept of his value as a commander. He could only wonder why Zatar was bothering, and offer lamely, "How can I serve you?"

"I need access to your files—public, private, the things you sent to Garran and especially the things you didn't. I'm in willing to bet that somewhere on this ship is the information I need to establish a pattern; it isn't in the House of War's computer, hence it must have been edited out at this end. I'll want scannerlogs, composites, any and all material that pertains to the battles in question. And unlimited computer access, to run the analytic matrices. That's a start. I will want you to search your own memory, painful though that may be; I want to live those battles with you until I can see, through your eyes, just what happened. Somewhere there is a key element that Tactical has failed to isolate; we must find it if we are to understand how the enemy has managed to better you. Now: satisfy me as to your own endeavors. You've looked into the possibility of a single strategist masterminding the majority of your defeats?"

"I have, Lord Commander." That would have been the easiest course: identify the enemy, analyze his tactical preferences, and develop a plan to neutralize them. "The Azean system for determining tactical authority is somewhat chaotic, but I've managed to work out who was responsible for what in each of the battles in question. There is no common thread there, I regret to say."

Zatar nodded. "That agrees with Garran's research. What about spies? Informants? A leak in your communications network?"

Herek had investigated all that, to the point of issuing false orders in the hope of manipulating such a leak to his advantage. But the five fully prepared warships who met him off Yusudru made it clear that this was wasted effort. However they did it, the enemy seemed to know his plans. Just as the strange Azean had known when Sezal would fire upon him. . . .

He must have looked startled, for Zatar asked, "Commander?"

"A report from my First Sword . . . he came against a fighter who managed to evade him by anticipating his attack." Wasn't that what had happened in each one of those fateful battles—that the enemy had known, somehow, what Herek had planned to do?

"Please continue," Zatar urged him.

"That's all. It seemed unnatural to him—" *Just as those battles did.* He looked up at the Braxaná and offered, stunned, "There *is* a pattern. But how do we determine its source?"

"One thing at a time. Is this pilot's confrontation in your records?"

"Of course. Along with a composite analysis of the fighter in question."

"Compiled by—?"

"First Sword Sezal."

"Excellent. I'll want to see it—and him. You'll arrange it?"

He bowed. "Of course, my Lord." Muscles were relaxing now that had been knotted for days—since he'd learned of Zatar's assignment to the *Sentira.* The flood of tension from his body left calm in its wake, and with it hope. "I am the Commander's servant."

"Yes." The Braxaná nodded. "And a good one."

He gave the compliment a moment to sink in, then added, "I do not intend to lose you."

It was hard to keep the men in line.

At first they were merely sullen; hostility surfaced now and again, but on the whole things were quiet.

Then the storm began.

Who is this man, anyway? What right has he got to march in here and take over?

Questions Sezal himself had asked. How could he hope to answer them?

Just what in Ar's name is a Lord Commander? What's Herek going to do now—wait upon him hand and foot? Who's in charge when we're under attack, that's what I want to know!

Herek and Zatar were in constant conference—sharing notes, feeling their way around an awkward relationship. It was not yet necessary for the pilots to be briefed. When it was time to fight, they would be told who was doing what. Wouldn't they?

He's a groundling, a blessed useless aristocrat. Put him out there in the Void and he'll go crazy. What's he doing here?

They were his own thoughts, sometimes his own words. It was hard to silence men when they spoke the truth.

He's fine on flatscreen, but has he ever been on a warship before? What does he think will happen when we come up against the enemy? Does he expect everyone to wait while he consults his maps and his charts and whatever blessed else he's got going on in there?

He could only remind them that Zatar was Braxaná, he was their ruler, he had the right to kill them at will. It quieted them, but only briefly.

For they were afraid. Not of his power, but of the man himself. They saw him in the corridors and were stunned by his physical perfection. They came into the gym and saw him working out there, his woolen costume stretched tight against his flesh as he drove himself on and on without stop, managing feats of strength that Sezal's men could only dream of.

And there lay the crux of the matter. Zatar played upon their deepest insecurities, causing them to reevaluate who and what they were. They were used to being valued above all others; now someone new had been added to the top of the social ladder. They had lived in a world without class distinctions; now, inspired by the presence of a fullbred Lord, some of them recalled their lower-class origins and cursed the name that had awakened bad memories. They were strong men in their own right, but when they saw his strength they wondered at their own relative weakness; when they stood before him the very slightness of build which made them successful pilots seemed a badge of shame, a less than masculine framework.

Easier to curse him, then, to recite over and over the list of his limitations. *He has never fought. He wouldn't know how to fight. He is a rich and spoiled Lord who will take one look at the War and turn tail for home. You would certainly never catch him out there in the Void, with nothing but a forcefield between him and the enemy!*

It gave them some comfort, to put it in those terms. Sezal found that he could not silence them. He managed to confine he worst of such outbursts to small, enclosed areas. The pilot's quarters, mostly. And that should have made them safe.

But he remembered what Herek had said, and he was afraid. *The Braxaná have ways of knowing what goes on, even in private.* Were they being watched? Had Zatar in fact heard their outbursts? Was he biding his time until he could invoke the demon of Whim

Death to thin their ranks, or was he planning a more subtle vengeance?

Like all good Braxins, they feared for themselves.

He feared for Herek.

With a sign of exasperation, Zatar turned the starmap off. The pattern of losses defied analysis. Battle after battle had been reconstructed for his study, yet he was no closer to finding an answer than he had been on Garran.

And yet . . . the feeling that something was *wrong* here, that some unspoken rule had been broken, grew stronger with each passing shift. There was no reason for it that he could put his glove on, but the more he watched the interplay of swordship and fighter, the more he observed gunships laboriously dragging themselves into position and warships, the gods of interstellar battle, coming in behind them, the more he was certain that something was amiss.

Take Kley—or rather, take the battle which had preceded the loss of Kley. It was the custom of both sides to focus their attention on centers of civilian population: people could be conquered, empty space could not. Besides, in the vastness of the War Border it was almost impossible to locate the enemy, much less come in-sync with his frame of reference. Or so Garran had always believed.

The key word was *almost.*

He called up that battle again and watched it unfold, brow furrowed in thought. The enemy had come upon them unawares, striking at the talon's vulnerable flank. A long and bloody confrontation followed, in which numerous swordships and even a gunship were damaged; Herek and his men fought well, but they were hard pressed to correct their initial disadvantage. By the time the Azeans broke off their offensive, a good part of the talon's mobility had been damaged.

Swordships were vital to a planetary campaign: they alone could withstand the inferno of atmospheric friction, fighting natural gravity and dodging the best efforts of a land-based defense system to lay waste to choice targets, then fleeing too swiftly for outsync instruments to get a fix on them. Gunships were for space stations, blockades, the rare but deadly outsystem battles; it was on its *swordships* that a talon depended when a grounded target must be convinced to surrender.

Herek had been concerned about the risk of going ahead with

the Kleyan campaign—his log made that clear—but had decided to risk it. His swordship capacity had not been critically damaged. The Kleyan offensive had been coordinated with the efforts of two other talons, so that Azea's attention would be elsewhere when he struck. To delay his attack would lose him that advantage.

He made certain he had sufficient firepower to destroy a planet—he had, ten times over—and sent out scouts by the hundred to comb the nearby Void for shipsign. Nothing. Reports from the Lyrellan system indicated that the bulk of Azea's fleet was there, and he knew that Talon-Commanders Rejik and Kamur would keep them occupied. It was all arranged. Now there was only Kley itself. . . .

And disaster. Because the Azeans were waiting, five motherships and a horde of fighters, waiting to prey on the *Sentira's* weakened forces. A smaller number of ships could not have defeated Herek, and even these five could not have done so had they not known, with frightening accuracy, the speed and angle of the talon's approach. By the time the battle had begun, it was already over. It was the first of many nightmares, a harbinger of the zhents to come . . . and the beginning of the end for the Holding's greatest Commander.

So where in Ar's name was Azea getting its information?

He dismissed the starmap display, called up a composite image of Sezal's recent adversary. The First Sword's analysis of the fighter had been both thorough and disturbing. He had stripped the ship of its only nonvital mass, but still could not explain its alarming capacity. Nor was he content with that result. To cut the base-mass down to absolute minimum, he had removed both the emergency grounding gear and the fighter's small store of rations. A pilot's survival often depended upon his ability to land on a planet and wait for assistance; that Azea might have discarded these things seemed highly improbable. But then, everything about this fighter was.

For instance, the identicode. *CON.419FA12* it said. The *Conqueror.* Zatar had called up stats on that ship, had found nothing helpful. Its Starcommander was new to the Border, therefore low in seniority, with little authority . . . so what in Ar's name was the *Conqueror's* prize fighter doing in someone else's campaign?

Not for the first time he thought: *They're breaking the rules.*

In war, there are no rules.

Established fact: fighters traveled in units. Each unit was answerable to its mothership. Units might be allied in their action, but the lines of authority were always clear. Fighters from different motherships might do battle side by side, but they did not mix.

Had the *Conqueror* discarded that tradition?

It was while he was thinking along those lines that a strange feeling came over him. A whisper he could barely hear flitted across his awareness; he felt as though a pair of eyes had been fixed upon his back. He turned around, half-expecting to find that someone had entered the room. But the door was still closed—sealed, in fact—and except for him the room was empty.

Strange. And disturbing. He tried to ignore the sensation, focusing his attention on the display and its meaning. The *Conqueror* had sent a single fighter to accompany the Venture's pilots . . . why? Because the new ship was technologically superior, and would give Azea the advantage? Because it was still experimental, and needed to be tested in the context of a traditional battle?

The *Conqueror:* what role did it play in all this? He called up a list that Herek had compiled, an analysis of the enemy's hierarchy in each of the battles that had been lost. No pattern. Here the *Destroyer* had been in command, there it was the *Venture* . . . the *Conqueror* wasn't even listed in the command sequence. It was extremely active, though; he noted its presence in each of the crucial battles.

And stopped, chilled.

"Computer?" he asked softly.

He had programmed it to answer him aloud, in the manner of his House. RESPONSIVE.

"Speculate. Odds of a starcommander being given authority over those with higher rank and/or greater seniority. Current Star Empire, War Border."

There was a moment's pause as it chose its data.

.000012 +, it answered. UNLIKELY, BUT POSSIBLE.

"Data?"

PRECEDENT. ONE: PERIA LI UZUAN, ASSIGNED THE VENGEANCE 8194-8240 A.E. TWO: TAEN ER KALLEDAS, ASSIGNED THE GUARDIAN 9056-9099 A.E. THREE: TABYA

ZI OKROS (LATER EMPRESS), ASSIGNED THE DESTROYER-

"Enough. Other data?"

CURRENT DIRECTOR TORZHA ER LITZ NOTED FOR NONTRADITIONAL ORIENTATION REGARDING STARCONTROL POLICY. SOURCES: ANALYSES, PRECEDENT, STATEMENT OF POLICY. REQUEST SPECIFICS?

"No." The feeling that had bothered him was growing more intense, but it was not enough to distract him. What if a single mind *had* masterminded Herek's recent defeats? That made the problem finite, thus correctable. He was on to something. "Other data?"

SPONSORSHIP BINDING DIRECTOR ER LITZ AND STARCOMMANDER LYU MITETHE, ASSIGNED THE CONQUEROR. CLOSE PERSONAL INTEREST INCREASES ODDS OF FAVORITISM.

Sponsorship. It had no parallel in the Braxin system, so his understanding of it was limited. Unless one compared it to the Kaim'erate tradition of having an established member bring forth the name of an aspirant for consideration . . . yes, and in that case there was often favoritism. How much more so among the Azeans, who had no reason to fear a protégé's treachery?

So there could well be one mind behind it all. One single mind: eccentric, unpredictable, capable of second-guessing the Talon-Commander with rare acumen. And dangerous—very dangerous. There was a pattern in the very oddity of the engagements. In how often the enemy would initiate a confrontation in the open Void. In how this Starcommander seemed to know certain details of Herek's planning—details that should never have gotten out—and yet was unaware of others, as though a supreme effort of will might net him one or two secrets, but no more.

Here was a pattern that could be analyzed—an enemy that could be defeated. He had rendered the problem finite, and thus were his goals defined. To understand the enemy, so that he might neutralize and destroy him. To restore Herek's reputation by giving him the key to victory. And to set his own mark upon the Border fleet, so that the name of Zatar became synonomous with triumph. That was the most important goal, which had brought him to the Border in the first place.

Circumstances were playing right into his glove.

It was while they were astrogating the long, empty stretch between Irya and Zeliash that Herek's optimism began to return to him. Perhaps that was because the Lord Commander made such a show of confidence; genuine or feigned, it was reassuring. Perhaps the promise of battle was awakening the warrior in him, driving out his lethargy and the doubt that had accompanied it. Perhaps it was simply that the Braxaná's presence was a constant reminder that the Holding had chosen to support him. Whatever the reason, as he slipped the contact band over his head and prepared to launch his senses into the Void, it was with a more positive attitude than he had felt in many months.

Before he could lose himself in the talon's contact network the door slid open. It was Zatar. Herek tipped the contact band back on his head, out of its. proper alignment. And waited.

The Braxaná looked around the room, at the dozens of men who were carefully not watching him, and nodded. "How is our contact network?"

"Good; not without holes, as you see," he indicated the screen, "but it is extensive."

Zatar studied the display, nodding as he did so. A warship's scanners could only accomplish so much; in order to detect fine detail at great distances, it was necessary to send out a portable scanner bound in relay to the mothership. Thus a hundred scouts, perhaps more, were presently combing the Void for data, each of them forwarding their readings back to the Sentira for coordination and display. The trouble was that such a widefaring network as this one was, by definition, thin. There were areas of darkness which no scanner could reach—*holes in the net*, they called it—and these were dangerous weaknesses. The contact periphery, however, was solid, and extended far into the Void on all sides of the mothership. That was what Zatar wanted. That was what would keep them from being surprised again.

"The Dar'mat should be in position by now."

Herek nodded. "Hand in glove so far. Do you mind if I take a look?" He indicated the contact band.

Zatar motioned for him to proceed.

He settled the band back in place about his head, felt the click of its sensors as they locked into position over the implants within his skull. Now: he relaxed, letting the inner vision come. A normal man was limited to flatscreens and starmaps if he wanted to view the Void. The flatscreen, of course, was two-dimensional, therefore of limited value in battle. The starmap was better, but a man was still limited by the senses he used in viewing it. You could only be on one side of a starmap at a time—even if you stood in the middle of the display, you could only see in one direction without turning. Man had no eyes in the back of his head . . . until science created them.

It had taken him years to adapt to the band, long zhents of hypno-treatment designed to teach him an alternate mode of vision, while keeping it distinct from his regular sight. It gave him an advantage no unaugmented man could equal. Now, as he looked out into the darkness, he saw ships on all sides of him. He was their center, their focus, their guardian. There was nothing they could do that he would not see, no data coming in through their scanners that he would not share. Nor would there be a delay while he translated flatmaps into starfields in his mind; science and the strength of his will had made that unnecessary.

Carefully he looked over the network, dictating orders which would close up too large a hole here, extend the periphery there. Balance was crucial, as both Commanders knew. And this was more than mere exercise. Though their next objective was a day's flight in the distance, this was the time when their risk was the greatest—the time when the *Conqueror* usually chose to strike. If Zatar was right, they could expect action soon—if not an attack, at least a scoutship. For which reason the swordships were already out, ready to move at a moment's notice.

Almost in answer to his train of thought, a signal came speeding in over the network. AZEAN SCOUTSHIP, it said. IDENT CON419:FAI2. TRANSMITTING VECTOR COORDINATES.

"Lock onto it," he ordered.

The Master of Armaments determined its course, set up a firing sequence that would intercept it. And was ready to fire when the scoutship disappeared, swallowed up by a long stretch of scanner-darkness.

"Ar!" Herek's hand hit the console in frustration. "Proceed with attack," he instructed his men. "Determine all possible course adjustments, points of exit. Get them covered."

There was a hand on his shoulder.

"What?"

Zatar's eyes were fixed on the central display. "That isn't a scoutship," he muttered.

He understood at once. "Sezal's fighter. . . ."

"It has to be taken. We *have to have that ship.*"

He shook his head; taking a fighter alive was a next-to-impossible task, all the more so when it could easily outrun its attackers. "Not possible. We'll get it when it's back in range; that's the best I can do."

Zatar's hand on his shoulder tightened. "The secret of that ship is worth more than a single battle."

"We know the *Conqueror* is in this vicinity. Any attempt to run down one of its fighters would be a study in suicide, nothing more. Especially this one." He looked up at the Braxaná. "I can't risk my pilots against such odds."

The Lord Commander regarded him with what should have been anger. Instead his eyes were calm, his expression determined.

"Quite right," he agreed. "I'll go. Which swordship?"

He answered before the magnitude of the situation struck him. "Take Twelve, Dock Four. But you can't—"

He did. There was the swirl of his cloak and that crisp, determined stride, and then he was through the door and gone. Herek might have followed—what he was planning was insane!—but at that moment the Azean came back into live space and he had to focus all his attention on trying to keep it there.

It was too fast, too far away, too lucky. They missed it by inches, but inches were enough. The computers had not been prepared for such erratic flight, could not make the leap of imagination required to find the space the fighter would occupy. Mere seconds after it had emerged from the region of dead space it had broken through the periphery, and was out of range of all his scanners.

"Sezal!" he ordered. "Zatar's coming out in Twelve to run down our visitor. Go with him. Take five other fighters. See that he comes back in one piece—"

Or you might as well not come back at all, he thought grimly. Not with what the Braxaná would do to them.

Lord Commander Zatar . . . I hope you know what you're doing.

* * *

He refused to think about what he was doing. If he did, he was likely to stop. The job needed doing and no one else could handle it, so there was no question of turning back . . . but if he thought about the risk he might, and so it was that Zatar kept his mind on other things as he ran through the *Sentira's* halls, acting on a warrior's instinct.

That fighter was the key to everything. They had to have it, had to understand it, if they were to defeat a dangerous enemy. He kept repeating that to himself as he ran across the floor of the central dock, shedding weight as he did so. First the sword, its scabbard loosed from his belt, fell clattering to the floor. Then his medallion, the heavy cloak, his sash and sword belt, all stripped from him as he ran. Once he was in the swordship, every extra ounce he carried would cost him dearly. Would that there was time to strip off the heavy Braxaná costume, to slip into a featherweight, formfitting pilot's uniform! But he settled for removing his gloves and then vaulting over the swordship's low side, giving no thought to his manual nakedness. In the face of what he was doing, concern over sartorial tradition seemed ludicrous.

Into the formchair, pull the ends of the forcefield harness forward—so!—and lock them across the chest. Personal field, recycler, it was all ready for him, and even as the Sentira drew his swordship into launch position, he was pulling on the gauntlets and halfhelm that would allow him sensory access to the outside world. A glance at the control panel, verifying that all was well. Yes; he was ready. A whispered command, voiced before doubt could take hold of him, and the *Sentira's* launching mechanism had control of his ship, and—

Voidflight.

He let out a sigh of relief, stretched his hands in their heavy gloves, and let his fingers wander over the controls. The gauntlets magnified sensation so that microscopic differences in pressure supplied volumes of information; he tried to remember his training, assigning meaning to each of the two dozen priority controls resting beneath his fingertips. These were for velocity, and these for computer access, and these for communication . . . he depressed a series of shallow buttons, saw the contact display fill his flatscreens with data.

"Fighter twelve, this is Sezal in One. Acknowledge."

He spoke softly, counting on the helmset to magnify and transmit his voice. "Zatar in Twelve, coming into line now. Do you have verified trail?"

"Seventy-one percent certain, Commander. That's not bad," he added, probably for the benefit of Zatar's inexperience. The Braxani smiled grimly. He would chance single-digit certainty at this point, if he had to; they needed that fighter too badly to let mechanical speculation scare them off. "Transmitting now."

He watched as the data filled his screen, the curve of the fighter's known path combined with its likely course and probable velocity . . . he looked at the figures and shuddered. It was going to be a bad trip. "Locking in now."

"Swordships One, Two, Eight, Ten, and Fifteen will follow. Locksync established—unity automatic. Acknowledge."

He did so. "Wide field, maximum scanner sensitivity. We need to confirm that trail."

"Acknowledged." They spread out around him, maximizing the distance between them. It was bad for defense, not good for offense, but it gave them the greatest chance of picking up the Azean's trail. "Your lead, Commander."

With no hesitation he set his course and committed his ship to full acceleration. His compensation factor was good but not unlimited; in that he was carrying extra bulk, it would probably not be sufficient. He tried not to think about that, focusing on his screens instead. Stars: the computer suppied them, placing them in appropriate formations in an illusionary Void. He was tempted to banish the display, to witness the superluminal night in all its unnatural glory, but common sense got the better of him and he moved his finger away from that control. It was a wholly unnatural region, a world that man was never meant to see, that the magic of technology had finally disclosed. The sight of it had turned men toward gods—or away from them—and it could drive even the strongest of warriors insane. Zatar did not understand the phenomenon; no man could, who had not opened himself to the superluminal night. But now was not a time to risk madness, and so he let the display remain.

"Shipsign!" Sezal announced. Sure enough, their outermost ship had picked up the residue of a fighter's passage. From that almost nonexistent trail, course and speed could be determined. Zatar waited, breathless, as the computer did its work. At last the long-awaited data filled his screens, and he quickly worked out an intercept course.

When he transmitted it to his companion ships there was a moment's silence, then Sezal protested, "This exceeds your parameters, Lord Commander. Remember that your personal mass—"

"I'm aware of the mathematics," he said dryly. "The choice is mine to make, is it not?" As the one most likely to suffer, he would be the first one to give up the chase. Or so they thought. "We can't overtake this fighter if we don't push for it, Sezal. I understand the risk. Course acknowledged?"

The answer came: affirmative.

And then the chase began.

Fools! he thought. *When your ancestors first gathered themselves in cities, building walls to protect themselves from the violence of nature, my people were hunters and warriors in the northern steppes. While your people developed civilization, we developed Man. When you made it possible for the weak and the crippled to endure, encouraging them to reproduce, we killed any child who showed sign of weakness in body or mind, lest they taint future generations with their incapacity. We are superior, in strength and endurance, to any people your tribes have ever produced. We are the children of Taz'hein, the warrior-god—and the strength of his bloodline will persevere, in the darkness of Void-flight as well as on the plains of Kurat.*

The G-count rose steadily, but he had yet to feel its effects. The same gravitic control which had made interstellar flight possible protected man from the worst of its effects; within the limits of his compensatory system, he could travel without discomfort. Unfortunately, he needed more than that system allowed for. With steady fingers he set new accelerative parameters, and any fear he might have had was banished by Braxaná stubbornness. There was no other way to have what he wanted; therefore he must endure.

"Speculate," he ordered the ship. "Time to interception. Odds of mothership, contact."

5.4 STANDARD UNITS TO VECTOR INTERSECTION, informed him. CURRENT CONTACT RISK 05%. And it added, CURRENT POSITION OF DESTROYER AND MESSENGER 95% CERTAIN. RISK FACTOR MAY RISE ABRUPTLY.

He could feel the pressure now, the first gentle promise of pain. He looked at the G-scale—MAX +.255, it said—and then turned it off. What good would it do to know the figures? If he passed out, the ship would stabilize velocity, allowing him to recover. What did numbers matter?

"Status report," he transmitted.

Three of the swordships were hitting their limits, as he was; two of them had yet to do so. Sezal was well within his safety zone. None of them were running figures as high as his, which was understandable. His basemass exceeded theirs by a considerable amount.

The pressure was greater now, a weight upon his chest that pressed against him when he tried to breathe. He concentrated on taking deep breaths, slow breaths, on building up the strength of the muscles that he needed to expand his ribcage. But each breath was harder to take, and he found himself hoping that the enemy would come into range before the forced gravity proved too much for him.

5.0 STANDARD UNITS TO VECTOR INTERSECTION, the computer informed him. He refused to look at the risk factor. What number would be enough to turn him back—ten percent? Twenty percent? Only a fool, it was said, would push two digits. He had a feeling that by the time this chase was over, they would have come close to pushing three.

And he *was* pushing himself, perhaps too hard. Breathing was a fight against unbelievable pressure, each breath coming harder than the last. His heartbeat echoed within his ears, labored and irregular. He toyed with the idea of adopting a gentler pursuit, then forced his hand away from the controls. It was clear, now, why the key controls were situated in the arms of the pilot's chair, beneath his fingertips. Struggling against the pressure of unnatural acceleration, he could not have managed any adjustment that required him to move his arm.

There were spots before his eyes as he looked at the computer display—4.6 units left. And that was to *probable* interception; nothing was guaranteed. What if it took longer? He tried not to think about it.

What were the others suffering? He checked his screens, noted with some surprise that their numbers had been diminished by one. Swordship Fifteen was gone. Its pilot must have lost consciousness, cueing the program for pilot safety. It would return to the *Sentira* on automatic, at a pace that would do no further damage.

It had not occurred to him before that by the time he caught up with his prey, the others might not be able to help him. If he made it himself, that was. He could no longer fill his lungs, could only gasp for shallow breaths as the pressure squeezed him with crueler and crueler power, forcing his flesh back from his face, turning every wrinkle of clothing into an instrument of torture. 3.4 units left. Should he level off now, adopt a less painful course? *Your ancestors never feared pain,* he reminded himself. And answered: *My ancestors never had to face anything like this.*

"Lord Commander Zatar, please acknowledge."

Sezal. His voice was strained, his own endurance pushed to the limit. "Acknowledged," Zatar managed. Ever the slave of image, he managed to sound stronger than he was.

"We've lost Two, Eight, and Fifteen. Estimate .25 before Ten is forced to drop back. Recommend course adjustment now, while there are still three of us."

He did not mention his own situation; that was clear in his voice. He was suffering terribly but he would endure. He was stronger than the others, and his swordship was the best. His compensatory system would be the most effective, and his basemass was nowhere near Zatar's. He would keep up, Zatar knew—if it killed him.

"Maintain present course," the Braxaná managed. He tried to look at the computer display, saw only spots and flashes of light. Or perhaps a number, dimly lit: 2.5. At took all his effort just to live now, and all the strength he had to forget such possibilities as heart failure, asphyxiation, the collapse of his ribcage. If Sezal could make it, he could do no less; the fact that the pilot had an easier ride than he did was barely compensation for Zatar's physical advantages. The Braxaná were known for their stamina.

Swordship Ten was gone. Had he heard Sezal announcing it, or had he caught sight of some display, picked out a number from between the swimming lights that blinded him? He could not tell, and it did not matter. There was only raw endurance now, the darkness of pain and an eternity of waiting, which was measured in breaths and heartbeats and accompanied by the roaring of his blood in his ears, louder than any other sound in his universe. And darkness creeping in, around the corner of his vision—

—got to hold on!

the spinning of lights, the pounding of blood in his veins, his heart all but bursting—

I am Braxaná!

and then sudden release, a ringing in his ears, the display screen flashing VECTOR STABILIZATION—and Sezal was still with him. He allowed himself a second in which to recover—no more—then checked the countdown. .05.

"Prepare for enemy contact," he managed.

.03. .01. —And there it was, right where the computer had said it would be.

The enemy.

Stronger than his ship, faster, and desperate for time; as soon as it saw them it shot forward into the darkness, leaving them behind. They adjusted their own speed and followed. The Azean was outnumbered, was close to home, would avoid a confrontation; they were at risk every moment they followed it, must force it to face their fire or accept certain destruction at the hands of the Conqueror.

Against his better judgment, Zatar checked the risk factor.

Thirty-two percent.

He turned off the display.

The pressure was building again, but this time he was prepared for it. The pain had taken out four of Sezal's best men without conquering him; how well would the Azean fare when put to the test? True, his compensatory system was better than most—but he was Azean, and that race had been designed to resemble Zatar's in all but coloring. The enemy would be tall, solidly built, lacking in a warrior's heritage. His mass would work to negate his advantage, making it a contest of endurance. And in that arena, if no other, Zatar knew himself unequaled.

Turn and fight, he thought to the alien ship, but instead it tried to outrun him. A bad sign. It should have taken advantage of its heightened maneuverability; they would have been hard put to follow it through a series of sharp course adjustments. That it was continuing straight onward implied that it was close to home, and that meant—

But he had turned the matrix off for a reason, and now he forced himself to consider other things. Such as whether they dared open fire, when the enemy had proven that it could anticipate such action. They needed a better position first, but they would not have that until the Azean relented. . . .

The pain did not bother him as much, this time; the heat of battle dispelled the discomfort, the act of breathing was as natural as the thrust of a sword. He was distanced from his own agony, was aware of the suffering of his body but was disconnected from it, as though his corporeal form was no more than a burden he had to drag with him, only partially connected to his person. A warrior's strength, or the harbinger of dissolution? He never had to decide. The empty flesh that sat in his ship shivered in pain for a long, long time and then suddenly it was over. The enemy had stabilized and his own ship, locked insync, had followed suit. He had survived.

He took a moment to catch his breath, then dared, “Sezal?”

The First Sword took a moment to answer. “It’s a trap, I think.”

He didn’t agree—but that was instinct, not reason. How did he know that the enemy had succumbed to the pain of the chase? How was he so sure that the Azean’s consciousness had flickered slowly out, encased in a body that could not stand the pressure? There was no time to wonder; every minute wasted ran the risk count even higher.

“Let’s take out its field,” he told Sezal.

There was silence. Then: “That takes time.”

“I’m aware of that.”

“What do you mean to do?”

He smiled, but did not answer. *You’ll see.*

He opened fire upon the enemy, testing it for opposition. There was none. Given that the Azean fighter had proven itself capable of taking out a swordship in the moment that it fired, its inactivity was reasonable proof that its pilot was no longer in control. Excellent.

The field absorbed his fire, glowed briefly, then dispersed the energy. Dismantling it would require extreme precision. Too weak an offense, and the forcefield would simply disperse it. Too sustained, and it would overload. They needed that perfect balance: enough to damage the generator, not enough to make it self-destruct.

The pilot, of course, could awaken at any time.

And then there was the mothership. . . .

“Go,” Zatar said, transmitting an attack sequence.

Carefully, carefully: fire just so, this strength, this rhythm, a little bit more than the forcefield can handle and then ease up, ease up quickly! and feed ever so little energy in for the final blow—

EXTERIOR FORCEFIELD DISPELLED, the computer informed him.

“Well done,” he whispered.

“What now, Commander?”

He noted that Sezal’s voice was unsteady; either he had been badly damaged by their flight, or he had looked at the rising risk factor. It could have been pain or fear in his voice; the result was the same.

"Now we take him," Zatar said lightly.

Silence. No comment was necessary. He knew the pilot's thoughts as well as if they were his own. *He must be crazy. He can't mean what he said.*

But he did. They had to have that ship in order to know what they were fighting, and therefore it had to be boarded. While in Voidflight. At a risk factor so great than any sane man would have turned back long ago, under circumstances that would render the boarder defenseless.

He hesitated only a moment, then shut down his outer field.

No response.

With steady hands he checked the controls of his personal forcefield. In theory, it would protect him from the Void; in practice, it paid to make certain. But everything appeared to be in order, He reached across to his shipseal and unfastened it, letting the air bleed out. A tingling on his skin: that was the forcefield, using his body's conductivity as a template for activity, stabilizing itself against the pull of vacuum. The recycler clicked into Voidmode; now it would not only supply fresh air for him to breathe and maintain his body temperature, but it would monitor his infield pressure as well.

He thought of all the things that a nonpermeable forcefield might accomplish, and wondered that man had ever braved the Void without one. To face the Void with nothing but a layer of matter between one's self and the killing vacuum—that was a terrifying thought. He checked the controls one last time, then cracked the cockpit open—

And chaos, black and malignant, assaulted his eyes and mind.

The superluminal Void. A secret world which nature had not meant man to see, it was a reality no human mind could grasp. An infinity of darkness in which reason defied observation—an emptiness so absolute that the mind fought to deny its existence. Where movement was lacking, the unconscious mind created it. Darkness crawled, writhed, twisted across the eyes and pierced the unwilling brain, driving back rational thought in favor of sensory chaos. There was noise, but it defied description—noise that blinded, noise that choked, a black, hollow sound that filled the universe with its emptiness. The senses mixed and merged, each seeking in the other some genuine stimulus to serve as an anchor in the eternal Nothing—and failing. The mind floundered, lost in chaos . . .

and welcomed fear as a concrete thing, a familiar sensation in a universe gone mad.

"Commander?"

Zatar closed his eyes, tried to focus on the sound coming from his halfhelm.

"*Commander.* Do you require assistance?"

He managed to find his voice. "No," he murmured. No one must see him like this. "I'm all right." *I must be.* "Cover me: I'm going."

By feel alone he found the safety line; he hooked it to the harness of his forcefield as the computer brought him closer to the enemy. LOCKSYNC, it informed him at last. The Azean ship was an arm's length away, and appeared to be hanging motionless beside his own. He tried not to look at the chaos which surrounded it as he set his own ship for thrust compensation. It would do what it had to in order to maintain its position relative to the Azean vessel; if luck was with him—and if the enemy pilot did not recover too soon—he would be able to board the enemy ship and lock its computer insync with his own. That was the theory, anyway. How few times had it been done?

Focusing his vision upon the enemy's hull, he eased himself out of the swordship. He had Voidwalked before, but never at such speeds; the theory was the same, but the risk was much greater. He was careful not to look into the Void as he worked his way over to the enemy ship, ran a support line over one of the fireports, and anchored himself to it. *If the pilot comes to now . . . not a pretty picture,* he thought. He searched for the shipshell release, panicked for a moment when it wasn't where he had expected to find it. Wasn't Azean technology supposed to be the mirror image of his own? Then he remembered the reverse principle, shifted to the far side of the hull, and searched there. After a moment he had it. Application of pressure, just so, released the safety catch . . . it was similar to the ships he had trained on. There was a moment's delay, then the fighter split open. And he had access.

The pilot was slumped against the far side of the ship, blood staining his face around the eyes, ears and mouth. The bioscan indicated recent death. Zatar looked closer, realized that *he* was in fact a *she*—and then saw something which made his blood freeze in his veins, which did more to unnerve him than all the powers of the Void combined.

With a trembling hand he touched the cord which was wound around her helmet. Since the forcefield ended at the helmet's surface, he was able to lift it without difficulty.

Red and silver. He looked at it for a moment, then tucked it into his harness. Then, trembling, he turned his attention to the computer. The implications of what he had seen were sunshattering in magnitude; it took effort to push them aside for the moment, to fix his attention on what he was supposed to be doing.

He knew computers—he was fluent in Azean—he had trained for such a moment and was as prepared as a man could be. Still, it took long minutes for him to convince the fighter's guiding brain to accept locksync with his own ship, mostly because he did not know the pilot's security code. But eventually he had it. The fighter accepted his guidance—or rather, Sezal's—and even as he worked his way back to the welcome security of his own tiny vessel, they began to turn away from the enemy, lowering the risk factor considerably.

When he was safely ensconced in his swordship once more, Zatar broadcast an ALL'S WELL to Sezal. And put his hand to his forcefield harness, where the cord was safely hidden, and wondered if he hadn't lied.

The First Sword's voice was strange; he seemed stunned by what had happened. "Prepared to intercept the Sentira, Lord Commander. I have a course vector ready for you."

He reviewed it—and flinched. Yes, they would have to endure considerable deceleration. Not as bad as the trip out, to be sure, but no pleasure cruise.

"Acknowledged," he told him. "Initiate."

This time he had much to think about.

First there was pain. Then light: shadows against a brilliant background, slowly resolving into color and form. Gradually his sense of self returned to him, and with it the omnipresent Braxaná concern.

"Where am I . . . who is with me?" His throat was raw, and pain consumed his speech; the most he could manage was a whisper. Red-hot needles were piercing every limb, fires raging in every joint. He had thought, in his last conscious moments, that he could not possibly suffer more. He had been wrong.

"Fevak, son of Seras, chief medic of the *Sentira*." The voice was low and even, with just a tremor of nervousness. Didn't the

Braxaná kill those who witnessed their weakness? "You're in Surgical, in a private chamber. Can you see?"

He took a deep breath before answering, and forced his voice to be strong despite the pain. "Yes."

"Good, There was some superficial damage to the eyes; I believe we corrected it."

He recalled bursts of random light that had almost restored him to consciousness, and nodded. It hurt to move. "Anything else?"

"Minor internal damage. It's all been taken care of. Your eyes were the last, and the hardest. I'd like to test you for sensory reception as soon as you feel up to it."

It was acceptable for a Braxaná to be wounded in battle, and there was no shame attached to medical treatment, but the battle was over now, and it was *not* acceptable to indulge in convalescence. Gathering his strength and his courage, Zatar forced himself to sit up; the agony was such that a return to darkness would have been welcome. But he could make out the medic's face, and was pleased to note the look of astonishment his movement had inspired. "What's my present condition?" he asked.

"Frankly, incredible. You shouldn't even be alive, much less conscious." There was awe in his voice. *Good,* Zatar thought; from here it would spread through the ship. "Your body is a mass of bruises, inside and out. I think we fixed up the worst of it, but you're going to be uncomfortable for a good long while."

"I am a warrior," he answered. Let him make of that what he wished.

He could see the room now, hastily rearranged for his comfort. His clothes had been cleaned and were laid out beside him. Behind them, on a hook, was a loose black robe of some soft-surfaced fabric.

"Your clothing took its toll," the medic explained. "There's a reason that pilots dress as they do. Under pressure such as you experienced, every fold of cloth is hyperabrasive. I recommend some more moderate attire until you're done healing."

Now that his vision was finally in focus, he could see the damage the medic was talking about. Dark purple stripes scored his legs, arms, and torso, and bloody lines—now bandaged with clearflesh—marked the places where folds of thick woolen cloth had been driven into his skin. He would have to spend some time undergoing forced regeneration if he wanted to recover without scars.

Drawing a deep breath for strength, he forced himself to his feet. Alone, he would certainly have fallen; in the presence of another man, he could not afford to do that. It took all his strength to maintain his balance while the room swirled around him at dizzying speed. "How is Sezal?" he asked.

"In bad shape, but he'll live. He was dressed for the ride, and we got to him in time. Some damage, but nothing we can't correct. I restricted him to bed for the time being. In your case," he said dryly, "I lack that option."

He focused on reaching for his clothing—hands burning, room swaying, but image was the ultimate master. Then he had it, and somehow managed to get himself into the tight gray garments without help. It would have hurt a lot less to wear the robe, but that wasn't an acceptable option. "How long since the battle?"

"You've been out for two days," the medic said quietly. "Some of that because of sedation. Herek's been asking after you at regular intervals. He'll want to see you as soon as you're up to it."

"Of course."

There was a glass jar by the side of the bed. The medic picked it up and opened it. "I thought you might need this."

Skinwhite. Opaque—that was good. He normally used more translucent cosmetics, but this would hide the discoloration. A glance in the mirror told him just how bad his condition was, and he applied the thick white cream as much for his own peace of mind as for anyone else's benefit. Perfect: between that and his clothing, he appeared remarkably undamaged. "You'll tell Herek I'm ready to see him."

"Here?"

"In my quarters."

"But the healing—" Zatar's glare cut him short. "Of course, my Lord. May I recommend that you schedule some time for regeneration? The damage is not yet fully corrected."

"Your advice is noted," he told him. "For now, have Herek meet me in my quarters. And inform Sezal that he is welcome, as well."

"He's in very bad shape," the medic protested. "He needs rest."

"All the more reason to invite him. The choice must be his. You understand me?"

"Of course, Lord Commander." The look in his eyes spoke volumes. *You should not be walking. You should not even be moving.*

There is a strength in you beyond what is rightfully human. "As you wish."

Two days of constant worry had taken their toll on Herek. The color of his face had yellowed, giving his markings an even more animal cast. There were lines about his eyes and mouth that had not been there two days before, which spoke of sleepless nights and endless tension. Had he feared that Zatar would die? It would seem so, for his face as he entered the room was a mask of utter astonishment. "My Lord," he muttered, and he lowered himself to one knee, in ritual homage. "You are well?"

"It would seem so." He allowed a moment for that to sink in, then asked, "You've studied the fighter?"

Herek stood. "We have. It wasn't what we expected—or rather, it was, but more. It wasn't just the grounding equipment that had been removed."

"Communications," Zatar mused.

Herek was startled. "You know?"

"I guessed." *What need has that kind for a transmitter?* "Tell me details."

"The system was stripped of certain key facilities. Signal augmentation, relay input . . . they're working on a complete analysis now. Enough hardware missing to drop the fighter's basemass below its normal range. Although to accept such a handicap . . . I just can't understand it."

Zatar did, but said nothing to enlighten him. Now was not the time; there were political ramifications to what the *Conqueror* had done, and he wanted them firmly in hand before he revealed the truth.

This, too, would ultimately serve his purpose.

"It's not necessary to understand it," he counseled. "It's been done; it remains for us to respond effectively. And we mustn't assume that because the equipment is missing, the fighter was out of touch with its mothership." *Just the opposite.* "It's more than likely that they compensated elsewhere."

"They must have," he, agreed, but his expression said *How?*

"As for the rest of it: You've been fighting one enemy, Herek, though the truth has been obscured by your circumstances. The Starcommander of the *Conqueror* is your nemesis; analyze his strategy, and you will find the key to victory. And there'll be other benefits, as well. When we attributed the *Conqueror's* battles to other commanders, we were handicapped in analyzing their work as well. Garran certainly has its analytic work cut out for it," he mused.

"With all due respect to House of War," Herek dared, "I've begun such work myself. When you first mentioned your suspicions to me—"

"No need to excuse yourself, Talon-Commander. I commend your initiative, and your skill. I have no doubt that you will be able to adapt to this new information, and adjust your plans accordingly."

Trembling slightly, Herek bowed his head. "Of course, Lord Commander."

You are mine, Zatar thought. It was an excellent start. "I had hoped—"

YOU HAVE A VISITOR, the computer informed him. In confirmation, the portal chimed.

"Who is it?"

FIRST SWORD SEZAL.

"Let him in."

The door hissed open.

Sezal was a mass of bruises, even as Zatar was, but he bore his wounds with naked pride, having no cosmetics to disguise them. His eyes were rimmed in red but they were alert, and if his face tightened in pain as he forced himself across the room that was only to be expected. Unlike Zatar, he was merely human.

"My Lord," he whispered. There was awe in his voice, a depth of emotion as new to him as it was to Zatar. Perhaps it was the memory of what the Braxaná had done, and against what odds, that overwhelmed him; perhaps it was simply the unflawed visage which the Braxaná presented, bruises masked by makeup and a body that refused to acknowledge pain. Either way, the image had its desired effect.

Painfully lowering himself onto one knee, he extended his arms in the manner required by the rites of formal submission. "It is an honor to serve you," he said.

It was worth all the pain to receive such a gesture. Pain was but temporary; the loyalty of such men as these was priceless. Zatar approached Sezal, moving with a grace that belied his suffering, and set his hands about the pilot's wrists. "You don't know what you're offering," he warned him, "but that which you understand, I accept." He released his wrists without saying the ritual words: *I choose not to bind you.* Sezal didn't know that his gesture of submission, inspired by the passion of the moment, made him Zatar's property according to Braxaná tribal law. And there was no reason to tell him; that he was moved to do it in the first place was enough.

"You'll be going back to Garran?" Herek asked quietly. There was a hint of regret in his voice.

"Back to Braxi," Zatar corrected. He helped Sezal to his feet, though he barely had the strength to do so. "After sending a full report to Garran, of course. But I have things at home that require my attention. " Such as research. Politics. Planning.

What would you say if you knew that your enemy was psychic?

"Will you be returning to the Border?" Herek asked quietly.

He looked at the Talon-Commander, read his expression for what it was and smiled. *You are mine,* he thought. *You and the pilots—you and your crew.*

"I will," he promised them. "In my own ship. When the time is right."

The future was beckoning.

Viton: The relationship between hatred and desire is this: that they are born of the same passionate source; that, being observed, they are often confused; and that each one intensifies the other.

FIFTEEN

1

Sila opened the door noisily, that the Kaim'eri might be warned of her entrance.

"Ah, what timing! Zatar, your Mistress is unequaled in her choice of servants."

"I pick them out myself, you know that, Sechaveh—or you should. Have some wine."

The delicately built Duveix woman knelt before him, extending the jeweled tray with its three full glasses. Sechaveh removed one and nodded her toward Yiril. "The air of fragility appeals to me."

Zatar smiled. "I thought it would."

"Am I so predictable?"

His dark eyes were eloquent over the rim of his goblet as he sipped the wine. "Sometimes."

They took the moment to taste the vintage and comment in low voices upon its quality; not until the woman had left and the soundproofing was reset did they take up their conversation again.

"I'm with you," Sechaveh said. "For my own reasons, of course. And I don't necessarily approve of your methods. But I'll support you."

Zatar raised an eyebrow in Yiril's direction.

The Kaim'era shrugged. "Who am I to defy the great Zatar?"

"I want more than that, Yiril."

"What can I give you? You show me plans based on superstitious fears. You tell me how you'll manipulate fools. I have to ask if that's enough."

"The time is right." Zatar put his glass down and pushed it away from him, the motion underscoring his modal intensity. "Century after century the Kaim'eri have considered alternative structures for our government. If there's a change to be made, it must be made *soon.* Before our numbers are too few. Before we're so weakened that the Holding rises against us. Then it will be too late."

"All agreed—many, many times over. But Zatar, there still has to be a man willing to bring the issue up for a vote, and enough men willing to sacrifice their own power to avert a catastrophe that might not come in their lifetime. You tell me they can be manipulated psychologically. *I* tell *you* that they're selfish—and in any battle on Braxi I have utter faith that the latter quality will triumph."

"And I agree. Therefore they must believe that the restructuring is necessary for them personally. Now, not later."

"There are still a lot of Braxaná left," Sechaveh said dryly. "Even at an average loss of fifty percent per Plague season we have centuries to go before the Kaim'erate is depopulated."

"Just so." Zatar nodded his agreement. "But I contend that there are other dangers facing us besides racial extinction."

"Equally threatening?" Yiril asked sharply.

"In many ways more so. Now consider: a lone monarch such as Harkur has power that other men can never equal—and also more responsibility. That, I think, is the crucial point. So far we've been thinking of a Braxaná figurehead position as something only favorable for the person gaining that position, something any man would want. But I contend there's a reverse side to the issue, and that's the part I mean to play upon."

"The Braxaná aren't known for cowardice in the face of responsibility."

"But they're cowards when it comes to facing the truth—certain truths, at least. Watch this."

He reached over to the wall and flipped a panel open. "How long since we've received a complete military report in session?" he asked, fitting a chip into the input slot.

The other two, startled, looked at each other. Now until that moment had they realized that the standard mapped presentation had recently been abandoned, and that the messengers delivering military news had been, if more dramatic, also more vague.

"Right." He swung back into position. "Watch this."

The lighting in the room dimmed and a starmap took shape before them. Fully half the room was taken up by the three-dimensional display, with points of light proportionately placed in the darkness to represent stars and thin colored fog, red and blue respectively, to represent the territory held by Empire and Holding. "The War Border five zhents ago." He tapped the controls and the fog shifted slightly. "Four." Again. "Two." The red crept slowly forward like a living thing, engulfing the cooler space before it. "Last zhent." He let that sink in for a moment, then: "Our last report."

The two were speechless.

"Yiril?"

"I can see why this wasn't presented to us," he said quietly.

"Yes," Sechaveh agreed, "And I think a few messengers have much to answer for."

"Granted." Zatar regarded the starmap with a mixture of pride and affection. "But for the moment, ignore that problem. Because we've got one much more worthy of our attention. Kaim'eri, we are losing the War."

"Exchange of Border territory is old news," Sechaveh protested.

"Very true. But look at this." He walked into the map and indicated a peninsula of red extending well through the Border and approaching true Braxin space. "Kaim'eri, I ask you this: how will Braxi react when for the first time in ten thousand years our secure inner border is breached?"

Pensive silence; at last Yiril muttered, "Very badly."

"Let's be more specific. We've never lost a war. I contend we don't know *how* to lose a war."

Sechaveh smiled. "And it follows therefore that the Braxaná have a great emotional stake in keeping that from happening during their rule."

Viril was less convinced. "The loss of a minor star or two—that *is* Birsule, isn't it? I thought so—is not in and of itself the loss of the Great War."

"But they'll be afraid."

Sechaveh nodded. "Oh, it's a vile omen."

"And it won't hurt that it happened without most of them knowing about it."

"So you can add to it the feeling of being out of control. It's *still* not enough."

"All right." The map faded and the lights came on. "What if the enemy were female?"

There was a pause as that information was digested. Sechaveh darkened noticeably, ominously, but said nothing. Yiril broke the silence. "You mean that female Director of—"

"I don't. The lead ship among those due to break the Braxin border is commanded by a female, as is the whole move from start to finish. And there's more." He paused, savoring their tension. "She's a telepath. Fully Functional, to use the Empire's terminology. She's employed at least one psychic in the past, and may be planning to bring in even more. Kaim'eri, what we're facing here is a change in the very nature of the War! A change which will destroy us. I ask you, will that frighten them?"

"If it doesn't, I would question their sanity. But is it the truth, Zatar? Or convenient fabrication?"

"Unfortunately, it's the truth. I realize there have been psychics among the Azeans for centuries; why have they joined the fleet only now? I can't tell you that. But this I know: communication is the key to all transluminal warfare. We are limited only by the range of our instruments. What happens when the Azeans extend their range—to infinity? I say to you in all honesty, Kaim'eri, that this woman is the start of something which—if allowed to continue—will mean our defeat."

"At the hands of a woman," Sechaveh muttered.

"Combine the loss of all power with the threat of the shem'Ar. Draw them a picture of the Holding on its knees to a woman. Bowing down to a psychic—we, who have killed our own children to keep that mutation from ever dominating us! If they don't fear that, Kaim'eri, then they aren't Braxaná."

"It's a good scare," Yiril agreed. His voice was tense. "And it would seem that this woman knows it."

Pleased that he understood, Zatar nodded. "That's the irony of it. In actual trade of territory across the *length* of the Border we're in a stronger position than before. Did either of you notice that in the map? Did either of you think to ask? The concept of being defeated by a female—by a *psychic* female—is so disturbing that it overwhelms your reasoning. I believe she's counting on that. I believe she's fighting to break into Braxin space for just that reason: because the move will dishearten us, giving her the psychological advantage. Her psychic abilities give her a unique advantage in that arena." He paused; the tension in the room was palpable. "She means to win the War, Kaim'eri. And given her nature, she could possibly do it."

"Who is she?" Yiril asked quietly. "I gather you know."

"Her name is Anzha lyu Mitethe. Daughter of Darmel lyu Tukone and heir to his insight. Technically non-Azean; she had the misfortune to inherit a gene-grouping from some foreign ancestor, and the racial authorities raised enough of a fuss to have her denied citizenship. A living paradox—and a dangerous one. I propose getting rid of her. Now. While it's still possible."

"Very good," Sechaveh agreed. "How?"

"I don't believe she can be killed at the Border. They're having a hard enough time trying to contain her forces; I don't think they'll be able to destroy the *Conqueror* itself. But StarControl enforces periodic ground leave on a regular basis. Eventually, Anzha lyu Mitethe will leave her ship."

"You propose a raid?"

"An assassination. Slip one man into the Empire, where they least expect a Braxin to be."

"Security is tighter than it once was," Yiril pointed out. "Because of you."

"I did it once, and I believe it can be done again. The Azeans are blind to the concept of racial impersonation. They don't live with the variety of humankind that we do; they're not accustomed to looking at strangers and trying to determine their origin. Their racial instinct dictates that anything which looks Azean and acts Azean is, in fact, Azean. The only risk would come in the presence of Security personnel, but that's a very small part of the overall picture. A necessary risk."

"You would go yourself," Sechaveh said suddenly.

"Of course. Who else could manage it?"

Viril was clearly skeptical. "You were younger the last time. More adaptable. And you had less to lose."

"How long will it take?" Sechaveh asked.

"Two to three years, I estimate. That includes time to master the assimilation and an approach route that circles back around the Empire, to a lightly guarded border. Say three."

"Three years without an appearance at the Citadel," Sechaveh mused. "It would mean tremendous political loss."

"Kaim'eri—we're in this together, or not at all. Listen to what I propose: I'll go to the Empire and deal with this woman. You, in the meantime, have two to three years in which to work on the other Kaim'eri. Take control of the War advisory and its reports. Alter them if necessary! Play on your colleagues' fears. The threat's real enough, and falls in line perfectly with Braxaná mythology. Most of these men are more superstitious than they would ever admit; I believe they can be manipulated through that weakness.

"We all accept that the current division of power is self-defeating. Offer an alternative—a small body of men to deal with threats of this magnitude. Figurehead positions, at first. What we need is to establish the precedent."

"And you, playing Savior of the Holding—"

"They would never elevate me alone; the Braxaná mind doesn't think that way. There would have to be others to help me wield the power—the two of you—and an equal number of those opposed, to balance it. And one uncommitted Kaim'eri to give us a prime number. Seven in all. Does that sound reasonable?"

"A High Kaim'erate, in other words." Yiril was thoughtful. "We've considered it before, you know."

"Exactly. With you laying the groundwork and me supplying the catalyst, it could work."

"The threat is good," Sechaveh said. "The timing is certainly right. It would require the proper showmanship. . . ."

"Ah, yes." Zatar resumed his seat; his eyes were shining as he picked up his glass again. "The necessary melodrama. How would this be for a climax, Kaim'eri—the terrible Anzha lyu Mitethe dying the Black Death right before our very eyes, in a Truce Station, with her people unable to help her?"

Sechaveh smiled. "I'd say that might do it."

"Or nothing will," Yiril agreed. "If, as you say, the right ground were laid for it. . . ."

"That," the young Kaim'era told them, "is your job."

2

Dayshift was over.

Alone on the observation deck, Anzha lyu Mitethe regarded the star-studded blackness. On the level below, a room full of instruments measured the nature and extent of that empty vision. But they could not capture its majesty, she thought, more than this simple observation.

Breathing deeply, she let her senses reach out into the darkness. Far off and to the right the consciousness of a planet's population radiated psychic warmth and she identified it: Ikn. Farther still, almost farther than she could reach, focused hostility marked the War Border. There: the familiar touch of her colleagues, well-intentioned but mired in tradition. And there, beyond them: points of violence in the darkness, singing of blood and death and the ecstacy of violence, surrounded by minds that could never share their music. Braxins. When the *Conqueror* came closer, she would be able to pinpoint specific identities, and begin to chart their locations; for now, there was only the welcome caress of their hatred, spread out across the stars.

With a sigh, she limited her awareness to the ship. Ground leave was a necessity, but she would be glad to get back to the Border. Her stop on Adrish had done more harm than good. Hopefully, it had accomplished better things for her crew. She suspected that most of them felt the way she did, and would rather not leave the War at all. There was so much to do, and time was precious. . . .

A quick walk took her from the deck. The dayshift crew was settling into public rooms or private quarters, to eat or rest or amuse themselves as individual tastes would have it. She made her way through tubes and corridors to a door which beckoned "GYM II" and opened at her approach.

It was hers. Not in fact, for the great ship's gyms were open to all, but in atmosphere. Its close confines had been dominated by the barbaric decor she had added—racks of bladed weapons, modern and antique, sharp and blunted; scores of feather-tipped projectiles and bows to give them flight; staves and slings and even some weapons alien to the Empire, as well as from all cultures within it. The interest which Yumada had encouraged had become an obsession; there was something in the games of death that suited her nature as no other pastime could.

She chose a matched set of throwing daggers and the gym, obliging, supplied the proper target. They were from Rahn, the gift of a grateful people in return for her timely support. She smiled as she tested their balance. She had never publicized her hobby—she didn't have to. Merchants combed the galaxy for the bladed remnants of barbarism and sold the best of it, if not to her, to those who would seek to please her.

The fast dagger cut through the air and into the target, a hand's width from the center.

She frowned. Slipping. The second was closer, but the third, overcompensating, split the edge of the small target and lodged in the wall.

"Not your best day."

She turned to find her private medic leaning, smiling, against the portal. Reflexively she did a surface analysis—shallow good humor, underlying tension, something trying to communicate and not knowing how to start. Violence? Fear? No, that must be the weapon-associations, and her own frustration—not Tau.

"I've had better. Thought you had work to do?"

"I do. You're it. Can we talk?"

"Go ahead."

"Alone." That something inside him was looking for . . . an environment to inspire it. The gym wasn't right. What was, she couldn't read without violating telepathic etiquette.

"My rooms?"

"Fine."

She studied his surface emotions as they walked. Hesitation, apprehension. Why? In many ways that little was worse than knowing nothing at all.

Her personal seal on the door seemed redundant in light of the *Conqueror's* security and he had often remarked on it. Now he said nothing. Even his thought pattern projected an unnatural stillness; clouds, drawing together before the storm.

Setting people at their ease had never been her forte. She waited.

"It's about the medical probe on Adrish."

She said nothing. Her face, well trained, betrayed nothing more than politely concerned curiosity.

"As you know, the Adrishite Elders requested my counsel on an unusual autopsy. They thought my unique experience might be of value."

"So you said at the time."

"I didn't complete the procedure."

Her face darkened. "You should have told me this insystem. Stellar rank gives you the right—"

"I wasn't stopped, Starcommander. I *chose* not to continue. The studies they showed me were enough to confirm certain unpleasant suspicions I'd had for some time, suspicions I dared not put to the test for fear the Elders would come to draw similar conclusions. And I wanted us to get away before I talked to you. I was. . . ."

She voiced his thought. "Afraid."

"Yes." He hesitated, his mind working loudly to find the right approach. "I think it will be clearer if I describe the case."

"Then please do. " Overly polite? She would have to watch herself.

"The man was—had been—Sem Che-Li." He seemed to be watching her for a reaction, but she revealed nothing. "An outlaw whom they would have killed if they could have caught him. Ruthless, vicious—a cold-blooded killer with an explosive temper who prided himself on being wanted in every human system."

"I know the type." *Too well.* "Go on."

"He died five nights ago; the authorities found his body and arranged for an autopsy. What they discovered confused them. It was as though he had suffered a sudden injury to his brainstem; a number of functions necessary to maintain life had simultaneously—and mysteriously—ceased to work. Yet there was no damage to the brain. At least, no *physical* damage. They wanted to discuss with me the possibility that some psychological element was responsible. They wanted to know how that would be reflected in his physiology."

"They should have called the Institute for assistance."

"They did. It was the obvious course. And they were refused, or rather, delayed indefinitely. Which amounts to much the same thing. Your Institute isn't blind, Anzha. A man's mind doesn't burn itself out without good provocation. You tell me he died of fear, despair, even self-disgust, I'll show you signs of it in the chemical balance of his brain. Normal emotion doesn't kill without leaving any evidence. Telepathy, however, can."

"Accusation?" she snapped. Too fast, too defensive—she regretted it even as it was voiced.

"I've seen the records," he said quietly. "Leviren, Kei San, others. You killed them. I know."

She was deathly still. "You've drawn some rather hasty conclusions."

"No. You weren't as careful at first, which leads me to believe that at least then it wasn't premeditated. I saw you with Leviren myself. Easy enough to call up an obituary when you have Imperial status: sudden death, cause uncertain. The morning after we broke light for the Border. Then Arvaras—you had mentioned him to me, remember? After that one, you stopped talking. They got harder to trace, but never impossible. Once I had begun to connect such deaths with your ground leave, the restcame easily."

"There is no proof." Her voice was cold, belying the fire which those memories awakened. *Damn you!* she thought.

"I want to help."

"It's not your concern."

"I'm your assigned medic—it *is* my concern."

"There's nothing you can do!"

"Let me judge that for myself."

"Tau—"

"What do you want from me, Anzha? A triple-sealed affidavit attesting to my loyalty to you? I've been with you on this ship for five years now. I *know* what you're capable of. If you told me tomorrow that you had turned into some mythical creature that had to devour a human being a day to survive . . . Hasha knows, I'd probably help you hide the bodies. The good you've done is measured in *planets,* the people you've helped in *billions.* What are six individuals compared to that?"

Taken aback by his vehemence, she quickly reappraised him. "I never realized you were so cold-blooded."

"Single-minded. That's why they picked me for this job, you know—anyone less stubborn than that you would have turned into your doormat before you let him get a good look at that damned precious anatomy of yours, much less your mind."

Despite herself she smiled; he was right. "Well struck." She took a moment to settle the tightness in her stomach and partially succeeded. *Why do you want my confidence in this,* she wondered. *To help me—as if you really could? Or to learn my ways as they ordered you to do, so that Azea might have all my secrets?*

The last thought was unworthy of him and she knew it. Turning away to hide her discomfort, she offered quietly, "It wasn't meant to happen. It won't happen again. Let that be enough."

"And if charges are brought against you?"

She was scornful, "Who would accuse me of civilian murder?"

"The first member of the Council of Justice who thought he could pin the charge on you." He waited. "Well struck?"

He had sliced through her armor and emotion stirred in the wound. Longing, and frustration, and the need for human contact.

With whom, if not him? He offered support. His concern seemed genuine, Why couldn't she accept it?

"You don't know what you're asking for." She caught the promise of defeat in her own voice, foresaw the collapse of those barriers which had always protected her from the judgment—and scorn—of others.

"Try me," he challenged.

She studied him inside and out, deeper than she had ever done before. His offer gave her the freedom to reach inside him, to evaluate his confidence, and she used the opportunity to uncover those facets of him which telepathic etiquette had previously cloaked in privacy. He met her with openness, and with frank display of his motives. Concern. Curiosity. Friendship. She tasted the last with care, and despite its alien tone it struck a responsive chord within her. *I* need *to talk,* she thought, *and here at least is acceptance.* More than that she would not consider.

"What do you know," she asked hesitantly, "of telepathic contact within the pairbond?" She could be no clearer than that without speaking of the matter outright, and expected only his confusion. Yet he seemed to understand what she meant.

"It's said that in the course of sexual contact, telepaths experience an extreme degree of linkage—*with or without* pairbonding," he stressed. He would accept her; that was the undedying message. If she lacked the pairbonding instinct which was an Azean's birthright, she would of course seek her pleasure elsewhere. He took it for granted.

She had never anticipated that.

"You know the process?" she pressed, relieved that she might not have to explain everything.

He shrugged, but his eyes were focused upon her. "Hearsay."

"The Institute didn't prepare you?"

"Not regarding this."

"They should have. They should have expected—" She broke off, disturbed by the revelation. Why would they have neglected to explain such a crucial part of her background to him? Had they failed to anticipate that she would risk exposure in order to experiment. . . . No, that wasn't like them. They were too thorough. Yet they *should* have briefed him on everything.

Suddenly it all fell into place. They had wanted her bound to the Institute and this would have assured it. Unable to seek comfort among her crew, she would have had to turn to Llornu. Or bear the memories alone.

Damn you, she thought—*damn you all!*

She turned back to Tau; though her fists were clenched tightly in anger she forced her voice to be level, to make it clear that her rage was directed elsewhere. "Sit down," she said quietly. "I'll try to explain."

He took a seat by the side of her desk and she sat on its edge across from him, her fingers playing nervously on its surface. "Soon after I received this command, when we stopped at Sheva to assemble an escort for the Kol-Sua entourage—you remember?" He nodded. "I was . . . propositioned by Ambassador Leviren. Prior to that time I had been careful to avoid any sexual involvement for fear of the political consequences, but on Sheva . . ." she sighed. "I accepted. He wanted me; it's hard to turn someone down when you can feel it directly like that. I had earned it, I told myself. I had denied one part of myself all my life, but now that the most difficult time was done with I could let go just a little. I accepted.

"He had a house on the outskirts of Venesacha and we went there: a quiet, secluded place where we could expect to be undisturbed. I remember touching the intensity of his anticipation, and experiencing it—and everything within him—more acutely than I ever had with a non-psychic. Excitement of any kind stimulates telepathic contact, sexual arousal most of all. For a telepath, pleasure is a shared experience; the barriers come completely down, and each party tastes the pleasure of both . . . I imagine. That's how it's *supposed* to be. I never found out.

"Because he died, Tau. When he held me—when I responded to him—he died."

She watched him for a moment, waiting for his response; when there was none she touched his surface thoughts, expecting revulsion, or pity—or both. She found only concern. It surprised her.

"I tried to determine what could have caused it," she said quietly, soothed by his apparent sympathy. "All I could think of was that the violence within me, revealed mind-to-mind with all the intensity of direct contact, was more than he could deal with. He opted out of life—simply ceased to exist. I convinced myself that was what happened and that a more violent man might succeed where he had failed. I sought one."

"Arvaras."

"Kei San. Others. It never worked."

"Aren't there ways to block contact in such a case?"

"It's called Touch Discipline," she said dryly. "I can't do it. Don't ask me why—I have no idea—I was never able to master it.

My body is a conductor to thought, and the more tense I am the more it's true. My one failing. And a damned big one.

"I kept looking, though. I became convinced that the answer was to seek out the type of man whose own nature was so brutal that nothing I revealed would surprise him."

"Seru Che-Li."

"I spent a year researching the outerground to find the names of people who could track him down. When the time was right and we were due for ground leave I requested Adrish; I knew he was there," She shrugged, but the gesture was false in its lightness. "You know the rest."

"Same thing?" he asked gently.

She nodded. She was trying to prevent the memories from affecting her voice, but she was unaccustomed to such deception and knew that the anguish wasn't fully hidden. "He's dead. They're all dead. Something in me killed them, and that something is going to keep on killing any time I try to . . . any time I try."

"Maybe you can focus on it—"

She shook her head vigorously, no. "We're denied any insight into the telepathic process. It's guaranteed by our conditioning, supposedly to keep us sane. No, I'm stuck. And I'll tell you something, Tau. I didn't inherit my libido from my Azean parents. Accepting this has been one of the hardest things I've ever had to do." She looked away from him, wondering if he noticed her trembling. Probably. "But if not Che-Li, then no one. The violence in him was like home to me. I can't imagine a mind more suited to my own."

"So what now?" he asked quietly.

She stood, wrapping her arms around her. "I live. I serve the Empire. I go on." Her knuckles were white with the pressure of her self-embrace. "Reality, Tau. I have to live with what I am."

"And just let it hurt?"

"Is there an alternative?"

"Can you even ask that? Of course there is."

She looked at him a moment, considering it. "Yes," she said at last. "You could probably do it. But is it right to cure something that isn't unhealthy? To readjust sexual awareness just because it isn't immediately convenient? They would like that," she said suddenly. "They would like that very much. For which reason, if no other, I won't do it."

"You're certain?"

She looked down, pensive. The Council would applaud hormonic adjustment—and that alone was enough to decide her. "Yes," she told him. "Absolutely."

He could feel the tightness in her; he moved to where she stood and reached to offer her contact. Seeing it, she flinched. "That's not a good idea right now," she muttered.

He clasped a hand to her shoulder. A wave of pain and frustrated longing swept up the limb to his brain. Squeezing her shoulder, he thought supportive thoughts. She looked up at him. She wasn't crying; in the long years now behind her, she had forgotten how. But she was close to it.

She put a hand over his and smiled. "I'll take it all out on Braxi," she promised.

He nodded. "I'll hold you to it."

3

It appeared to be a merchant ship, but close inspection revealed it to be no such thing. First, it carried too much weaponry—and carried it in an obvious manner that seemed calculated to provoke hostility. Second, it carried no marks of licensing or point of origin. Last, it had not one but two exterior protective forcefields—which indicated that it expected to be shot at, and often.

Yiril and Sechaveh looked dubiously at each other but cleared it to land.

It seemed hesitant to enter the confines of the warship and came into the dock slowly, defensively. Not until it had to did it let the outer fields drop.

The guards of the *Sentira* stiffened as the ship's surface split and a ramp slid forth.

"Do you think we should have warned them?" Yiril whispered.

"Not at all."

A figure came to the top of the ramp and stood there, waiting for the inevitable inspection.

"Hold it right there—" an officer began, and then he looked at the Kaim'eri to see if his reaction was the correct one. He was startled to see the amusement with which they were regarding him and his hand, holding a stun, wavered.

Yiril walked forward. "Kaim'era Zatar, I assume."

"If not, your security is less than effective." He, too, looked amused by the confrontation. A makeshift headband secured his nearly-white hair to his forehead. His shirt was loose and flowing and open to the waist, but he had supplemented it with a wide scarf and a pair of Lugastine dressgloves, so no more of him showed than the crew of this ship should expect to see. He had even bought a cloak on the way back so that there was a cascade of fabric from his broad shoulders just as there ought to be—even if it was bright turquoise.

Perhaps it was his costume which was so startling. Perhaps. More likely it was the golden face which radiated Braxaná arrogance, a face free of facial hair but lightly scarred with the remnants of untreated burns.

"I trust all that is artificial." Sechaveh indicated the scars.

"Oh, quite." The false merchant ship had resealed and was waiting for clearance. "Let them go," Zatar ordered.

The officer in charge was confused; it took a repetition of the command by Sechaveh before he obeyed.

"Nothing personal," Yiril asked quietly, "but why are we not blasting him from the Void?"

"Because there's an explosive implant in my arm to which he has the trigger. Speaking of which, I need the ship's physician."

"Then why isn't he blasting you from the Void?" Sechaveh demanded.

"Because I didn't pay him in advance—really, Kaim'eri, this is hardly the welcome I anticipated."

They escorted him past the guards, flanking him on both sides. The men about them were clearly bewildered. "We're not pressing you for what happened, you'll notice. There are quarters set aside for you on this ship, and we have a few women from your House here—and wine, and a cosmetologist—"

"And someone to remove the implant."

"And that. So recover at your leisure. Afterward we'll expect a full account."

"Get me a physician and the cosmetologist and you can have it now." Yiril passed the request on to a guard and the man ran obediently off to find them. "Now tell me—what plans have you made?"

They stepped into the transport tube and it began to descend. "We offered a diplomatic truce on tenday this zhent—today is the fifth," he added "—to discuss the possibility of a conditional Peace around the K'vai peninsula. Azea is mining there and stands to lose a lot if it's declared part of the Active War Zone. We've implied that it might, otherwise."

"You haven't heard yet?"

"No. But the message just went out. Your plan didn't allow for much extra time, you know; it's taken us this long just to get here from Braxi."

The tube opened on a residential level which had been given over entirely to the needs of the Braxaná. Yiril and Sechaveh led their companion to the proper room.

"Ah." Zatar lowered himself to the floor and relaxed into the thick pillows which covered it. "One of the nice things about dealing with Azea-side outlaws is that they've adopted certain points of our decor. Skyve's miserable little cruiser was the first thing I've been comfortable in since leaving Braxi."

A man and a woman appeared in the doorway; he waved them in. Briefly they hesitated, but when he pulled up one sleeve to reveal the crude scar cutting across his arm the man came and knelt by him on that side, the woman on the other.

"You know the formulas I've been taking?"

She nodded. "Your Mistress gave them to me."

"Excellent. Mix me a counteragent, and in the meantime I'll need this cut and colored." He ran his free hand through the long white strands. "And curled again."

"And you'll want the skin bleached back?"

"Above the neck. I can wait on the rest."

He looked at the two expectant Kaim'eri, so careful not to ask questions, so obviously wanting information. But where to start? He had spent two years among peoples so alien that the sheltered Braxaná would have no real understanding of what it meant to pass for one of them, nor comprehend why choice of culture often caused him to detour from the path he had chosen. He told them briefly of his travels, and the difficulties involved; of swinging a wide arc around the War Border and entering the Empire in a region where Braxi was no threat, thus security was minimal. He told them of Tirrah and the planets like it, where he had first contacted the Empire's rejected scum and realized their worth as a tool. Where he had practiced his Azean mask. Where one man, guessing that he was from the Holding, tried to work extortion on him—and died, not realizing that a Braxaná thought nothing of killing a dozen people in a night to keep his secret safe. After that he spent money freely, and found that any further troublemakers were sold out to him long before they could take steps to safeguard the information.

When he felt he had the act down right, he had moved onward, into the Empire. The lack of starlines meant that one could travel practically unobserved. He found it foolish but to his advantage.

He didn't tell them of his stop on Llornu. If nothing else, the tension of that experience was such that he would rather not remember it. He had to have her medical records to mix a timed dosage of the poison, but there would be no chance of lifting that from the StarControl files, which held too many other things of value and were closely and carefully guarded. On Llornu, however, who anticipated theft? He counted on that as he forced his way into the Institute's file storage, and hoped it was enough as he searched for what he wanted. He had no illusions about the risk; any guard patrolling the grounds would be psychic and a moment's confrontation would bring the whole lot of them down on his head. His hands were shaking as he found what he wanted and beat a hasty retreat. The memory was still flavored with fear, and one he would rather not review at length.

In the long zhents that followed he had transmitted the information home by drone capsule, not wanting to trust either the time or vulnerability required for an augmented transmission. He sent a capsule and left immediately for a far planet, in case it had been observed. It never was. A runner from his House brought the formulas he needed and the chemicals he hadn't dared carry on him, and a smuggler, well-paid, got them to him.

He waited. He mixed the poison, whose formula was as distinct to its victim as her fingerprints were: given her metabolism and blood chemistry he could anticipate the time of her death down to the tenth, if not closer. He waited, and he watched the military frequencies with the special equipment he had brought, until at last the order came.

The *Conqueror* went to Adrish. He followed. His disguise was second nature to him by then, which it had to be if he was going to pass unnoticed by a prime telepath. He had heard that the thoughts of an assassin, focusing on a victim, were like a beacon of light to the mind trained to sensitivity; he hoped it was not true, or that he could find her distracted, or—by far the least likely—that he could manage the act without himself thinking of the consequences.

But he was lucky. He found her in a dingy gaming house in one of the lesser neighborhoods where she was busy making arrangements with one of the local scum. So intent was she on whatever she was doing that he had no problem emptying the small vial into a glass waiting to be brought to that table. He stayed around long enough to see her drink it. Then he quickly hurried out, lest the intensity of his thoughts act as an alarm and notify her of his presence.

His return to Tirrah, and thence to the Border, was unspectacular and he related it quickly, a bare sketch of necessary facts.

Then he flexed his arm in question; the physician looked up from his work. "Almost done, Kaim'era." The implant had been deeper than expected and the local sterile-field generator could only handle so much area; he was proceeding cautiously. Zatar nodded.

"Now tell me," he said, "what went on on Braxi?"

"As much as one could ask for," Sechaveh responded. "We worked on every front and we seem to have gotten results. War reports were reworked to inspire maximum tension, and the Kaim'eri seem genuinely afraid of this woman of yours. Telos' news service—which Yiril controls—put out a report estimating a maximum of two generations before the number of Braxaná is down to twelve thousand—which, given the fact that we always multiply the real figures times ten for the public, was quite a frightening prediction. The supposed author, by the way, was executed. They're getting very edgy about such things and it shows. We set off a Plague scare on the ninth moon of Dakra, which again set them to thinking. That little poet of yours threw in her sinias also. You should have heard the piece she did at the Sun Festival! We dredged up a few shem'Ari and rigged the trials for maximum effect. I would say that right now the Braxaná reaction to the image of a dominant female is about as vehemently negative as it can get. So psychologically, the groundwork's been laid."

Yiril continued. "We brought up the issue of reorganization and it was received very positively—particularly after the plague scare and the news scandal. There's a general feeling that once we can't maintain the Kaim'erate we're inviting widespread revolution, and a desire exists to restructure before that time comes. Telos' move made them aware that we don't actually have to fall under-number to be in danger, as long as the public thinks we have. I think a good fourth of the Kaim'eri are ours already."

"We need three quarters for something like this."

"We'll get it. Sechaveh and I singled out a few Kaim'eri for leadership positions alongside us and brought them here, as you requested."

"Good; they'll see it themselves. Have you told them anything?"

"Nothing specific. Three of them are an informal powertriad, as we are: Vinir, Lerex, and Saloz."

"My own father? Marvelous!"

"It was Sechaveh's idea. He felt the rivalry between you was so well known that the others would never imagine you allying. Lerex and Saloz also have private property right by the War Border, which means if they try anything risky they'll be the first to lose by it. That'll make them a safe bet for the others. Lastly Delak, for the tie-breaking vote."

"Does he also have relevant real estate?"

"Quite a bit of it."

"Excellent. A prime number of men who can never agree. That will appeal to the Kaim'erate."

"They'll all be at the negotiations. When she dies—" and he stressed *when* as if emphasizing that he had not said *if* "—they'll see the opportunity for what it is. We can talk then."

"I am pleased." He glanced at the physician, who had extracted a small chip from his arm and closed up the wound again. He looked puzzled. "What is it?"

"Writing, my Lord. In Braxin—a sort of primitive Basic Mode."

"Read it."

"It says—'Did you really think I would risk the indignation of the Braxaná by implanting an explosive in one of their number?'—Skyve"

Zatar laughed. "Ah, so instead he subjects me to unnecessary surgery. Much better."

"Less risk, however," Yiril pointed out.

"Is there? Even an outlaw and a killer can have a sense of humor. And the humor of Tirrah can be deadly." He looked at the surgeon. "Send that off the ship and far away. I expect, eventually, it will explode."

Eventually, on schedule, it did.

They made ready for conference.

4

"What I can't figure out is why they want this treaty, anyway. It's clear why it would be to *our* advantage, but what's in it for them?"

Her second-in-command asked, "Are you going to negotiate it, then?"

"I have little choice, Zeine. The Emperor wants peace. But once I've got enough authority at the Border I tell you it won't be this easy for them. It's a delaying tactic, that's all, and I'm tired of retiring from my offensives to—" Tau entered. "Hello." He was loudly in need of her attention. "What is it?"

"I need you to come to the medical level." His voice was tight. "Now."

She read his fear, touched his intensity, and nodded. "Take over for me," she said, sliding out of her seat. She followed the physician into the nearest tube. "What is it?"

He looked at her. He was trying so hard not to let his feelings overwhelm her that he was almost making it worse. "Not yet," he muttered. "In the lab. I'll tell you there."

She followed him down through the corridors of the medical section and to the door of his private laboratory, which opened as they approached—

—and the screams of something dying could be heard, but they were nothing compared to the waves of agony that beat against her, driving her back from the room. He had to take her arm and drag her forward, and in doing so he shared the pain himself.

"I thought you were being overcautious." There was sweat on his forehead as he tried to ignore the alien sensations he was picking up through her. "I really did. I'm sorry."

There was a clear tank in the corner of the laboratory in which a small animal was—or had been. Now there was only a mound of seething blackness with the last terrible whimpers of something that had once been alive, and the emanations of an agony more intense than a creature could know and survive.

The Black Death. Anzha felt faint. "How long?" she forced out.

"In you? At least two Standard Days, maybe three." He was leading her to a table and she let him guide her, helpless to shut out the animals pain because it came so close to having been her own. "I thought you were crazy," he told her, apologizing, "but I ran the samples through it anyway, any time you'd been off the ship. Its metabolism was faster than yours and its biochemistry such that the poison would act in it before it did in you."

She lay down on the surface he indicated and shut her eyes. "What are the odds?"

"If it's still in your blood, good." He hesitated. "If it's lodged in muscle, which it well might be by now . . . I don't know. It's never been done before. There's never been enough advance warning."

"Let's make it a first," she whispered tightly.

His assistants were bringing him instruments. He had designed them under her direction and the ship had made them, but he had never used them and had hoped he never would have to. How was he going to find the damn stuff without radiation, which could spark the terminal mutation? He was glad that her own fears kept her cut off from his.

His hands worked quickly and automatically to attach the experimental instruments. No anesthetic; they all speeded the fatal reaction, he knew that. At least the creature was finally dead, although the poison wasn't yet in its inert phase. She would have only her own pain to deal with from now on.

"Tau?"

"What is it?"

"Do you have a more specific estimate on when this was due to strike?"

"Why?"

"I have a suspicion. Tell me."

He nodded for his assistant to get the figure. "I wouldn't bet your life on it, Anzha."

"I don't intend to. Have it . . . have it translated into the Braxin calendrical system for me, would you?"

He did. "Tenday, eightzhent."

"Hasha. . . ."

"What is it?"

"That's when they called the truce for. It's all making a terrible kind of sense, now. Tau, get me through this. I don't know who did this to me, but I don't appreciate his timing or his sense of humor one bit. Keep me alive to have it out with him."

"I'll do my best," he promised, and attached the first of the filters.

She said something later, half-whispered, that he barely caught and didn't understand at all. For a moment he laid his hand on her forehead in the hope that she might project the thought, but apparently it wasn't meant for him—either that or she was past the point of telepathic subtlety. But the words stayed with him as he worked.

"That's two. . . ."

5

Truce Station IV was typical of its kind, a featureless creation set in orbit around an unclaimed sun somewhere in the dark expanse of the War Zone. Now, as ships from both sides appeared to make use of it, its facilities became more obvious: the protective field which required Azean and Braxin frequency-codes, transmitted simultaneously, to unlock it; the dual-culture design of the satellite itself, with equal halves dedicated to the service of each of the starfaring powers, in equal proportion throughout but of entirely distinct design. Of all the truce stations this was the largest, and it easily held the seven warships that each side supplied for this meeting.

"Blessed waste of firepower," Zatar muttered. "Six of these could be off taking a planet somewhere."

"And then what would we do if the treaty failed?"

He looked at Yiril in amazement. "Kaim'era, the treaty's not going to 'fail' unless we break it. But I know what you mean." He sighed, and turned back to the viewscreen. "Tradition is tradition."

The *Sentira* pulled into place on the Braxiside deck and affixed itself with an energy lock. Two dozen Braxins came forth from the great ship, among them the seven Kaim'eri. The other warships were there for image only and would supply no negotiators—and the same was true, Zatar assumed, among the Azean ships. Tradition again.

They walked through the forerooms of the Braxin half of the station, designed for the comfort of negotiation teams and the relaxation of their crews during long bouts of diplomacy. Until their arrival the place had been like a tomb; now, with a flurry of mechanical activity, it prepared itself for human occupancy. Dining halls furnished in the Braxaná style opened as they approached, responding to the computer's analysis of their racial makeup. Other rooms, more suited to the common taste, followed. Everything was opulent, from the polished pseudowood of the furniture, inlaid with wires of silver and Aldousan whitecrystal, to the tapestries and arras that obscured the windowless walls. Gold thread glittered in abundance, adding a sense of archaic luxury to the high-tech, computer-run station—a typically Braxaná touch.

Here there were rooms designed for pleasure: wide, plush couches, and baths filled with scented water offered a taste of luxury that few non-Braxaná officers were familiar with. Whatever needs a war-weary crew might have, the station was prepared to satisfy them. Peace, after all, was unpleasant; peace negotiation doubly so. Here, between bouts of verbal combat, a ship's crew might find some comfort in the physical pleasures which Braxaná culture encouraged.

A waste. Worse yet—an obscenity. Passing through the elaborate corridors, Zatar was angered. It was no secret that negotiations were often called into being because one side or the other wished to avail themselves of a truce station's offerings. And who could blame them? These were the best facilities for a prolonged ground leave that the galaxy had to offer, presuming that one didn't require natural surroundings. It was all part and parcel of a system that accepted the war, rather than striving to end it. An elaborate farce, Zatar thought. And the worst thing was, both sides *knew* it was a farce. But who had the courage to defy tradition and change it?

Five of the Kaim'eri had come in disguise, posing as military officers. As often as not such men were of part Braxaná blood and thus their racially distinct appearance would be credible. Yiril and Zatar had appeared in too many newsrenderings to go unrecognized; thus both Kaim'eri wore uniforms that designated their true rank. But to have seven men of such stature at a supposedly routine peace conference would arouse suspicion—and enough suspicion would cause the whole thing to be called off.

In the Braxin antechamber a computer-operated mobile unit collected their weapons. It was designed to find all of them and would doubtless do so; they had tried often enough in the past to work it otherwise. The Braxaná would be permitted to retain their Zhaori; the Azeans, likewise, their Peace Daggers. Zatar smiled a grim smile, thinking that for the first time in centuries of diplomacy one of those might actually be needed.

When they were done, and when, presumably, the Azeans were also disarmed, the doors which separated them from the conference room—and from each other—parted.

The room was like every other of its kind; circular in configuration, with a translator set mid-way between the two semicircular tables that filled most of its space. The Braxin custom of proceeding from the center to the left in rank seating admirably complimented the Azean custom which proceeded to the right. Hence, as they sat, each man supposedly faced his equal.

The central seat on the Azean side, however, was empty.

It was Zatar's first impulse to mention it; it was his second, and by far the superior one, not to. After a split-second of surprise he recognized it for the cut it was, and smiled appreciatively. Often enough Azea had been made to wait for them. If anything, it was surprising that it had taken this long for Braxi's enemies to turn the tables and adopt their traditional rudeness.

After what Zatar was certain was a carefully chosen period of time—not quite long enough to drive the Braxins out in a rage, but almost—Anzha lyu Mitethe made her entrance.

It was the first time he had gotten a good look at her. She was a small woman of wiry strength; her seemingly frail build, far from implying weakness, seemed to be imbued with a tireless energy, which flooded the room at her entrance and dominated its interior. His imagination, or her telepathy? He didn't want to know.

She nodded acknowledgment of their presence. "Kaim'eri." then she took a closer look, and surprise became evident in her voice. "*Seven* of you. I wasn't aware the K'ven mines were worth so much to you. I'm sure they're not worth that much to us."

The Azeans who understood Braxin, which she had spoken, were clearly stifling their amusement. Zatar knew Braxaná sensitivity all too well and admired the perfect aim of her scorn. And for that, he swore silently, if for nothing else, she would die.

The Starcommander sat, opposite and facing him. She had no notes nor recording apparatus, merely two hands which she folded in front of her. Leaning forward aggressively, she voiced her challenge. "Azea has given these talks to me, and I may proceed as I see fit. I do not desire peace. I do not see any advantage for Azea to pursue peace at this time, conditional or otherwise. Therefore, I leave it to you—*glorious* Kaim'eri—to supply me with some reasoning to justify our all having come here."

How careful, he admired, *how fine. Such scorn, and even insult—but not a word of command, even accidental, to actually drive us from the room.* He was always impressed by a command of language and more so now considering the source. A pity she had to die so soon. A pity.

"Braxi feels that the direct economic gain to both sides in the K'vai issue mandates an attempt at non-military settlement."

"Braxi has never placed economic welfare above militancy, in its entire history—short of some dishonest stories told at the diplomatic table, which we may discount. Kaim'era, I would rather fight you. You, I suspect, would rather fight us. Can't we cut through all the nonsense and get to the heart of whatever it is we're here for?"

He felt like smiling, and after a moment's thought allowed himself to do so. How could it hurt to let the woman know that the workings of her mind were a refreshing change from that of her fellow nationals—in many ways, from that of the Kaim'eri themselves? In all of his recent wheeling and dealing he had thought of her only as a pawn in a wargame, a mistake he had made, a receptacle for poison, an undesirable element that was due to be crushed, with time and place the only variables. The Braxaná mind tended to admire what could stand up to it; his was no exception. She pleased him. That, too, was a pity.

He had arranged a story to cover his offer, and now presented it. The nature of that presentation varied greatly from what he had anticipated, but that was necessitated by her openly hostile approach. Still, the man was a fool who could not adapt when necessity dictated. He improvised.

And while he spoke, he watched her. She was listening, not to his meaning alone, but to the two or three underlayers which occasionally enriched his language. He made very certain he had control of them, which was difficult, as his mind was wandering to other avenues of thought. He was beginning to regret her death—not its necessity, which was absolute, but the means he had employed to assure it. The Black Poison was undoubtedly the most terrible death that man had ever devised, in that it reduced its victim to the level of a pain-maddened animal—or less—in his last moments, and forced all but the most suicidal of supporters to stand aside and be helpless observers to its devastating progress. And the more he conversed with this woman, the more he was able to admit it to himself: she was admirable, by Braxaná standards. She deserved a cleaner death.

And it was too late.

Inside his ear a tiny computer-access whispered the time at regular intervals. He spoke to her with one half of his mind and listened to it with the other. He knew the danger in that; her mastery of his language was outstanding and it was possible, just possible, that without his full attention given over to the conversation he might allow something of his mood to be revealed to her. He smiled to himself: that was the price you paid for the most complex human language in the galaxy, and for finding someone who could do it justice. And she could. Taz'hein, where did they find a woman like this?

The time ticked off, the end drawing nearer. She countered his proposals with deft disdain. He had prepared enough material to last days, in case the poison was slow. But in refusing to grant him a single point, she ran through it all in less than a tenth.

Which was almost time enough. He allowed himself to be redundant; moments were all he needed. And she, answering him, permitted it.

And nothing happened.

He took stock of the possibilities, and inwardly flinched. It didn't show on the surface; nevertheless, she was a telepath; he was certain she picked it up.

Casually her speech mode changed, moving into the Triumphant Mode for two words out of twenty. The moment passed; he glanced at his companions, then realized that none of them had noticed its importance. None of them, not even his two associates, were aware of the exact time for which this deadly demonstration was set, and thus the vocal trick which depended upon timing for its meaning went right by them.

But what she was saying was clear: *I know. You failed. And for the moment, I'm willing to conceal it.*

Did she know the price he would pay if there were public revelation of the situation? The Braxaná tolerated many things but never, never humiliation. A Kaim'era who was humbled in front of the enemy would find his rank and title forfeit. The simple act of a public declaration on her part would be enough to strip him of what years of effort had created—a public image that suddenly was in jeopardy.

Yet she played with him, and he was forced to play along, not knowing whether the end result was betrayal, or something more subtle from which he could salvage some face. They argued, they fought, they piled metaphor on insult and ran through all the modes of speech in an exercise of verbal complexity and deception. And when it was over, Zatar's mind was as exhausted as his nerves.

But it was over. They broke off the truce in fury and each, appropriately, was then meant to storm off to his ship and clear the area within a tenth. The Azeans were satisfied—although they hadn't understood a word of the exchange, despite the translator—the Braxins, confused and dangerous. *I'm not looking forward to explanations,* Zatar realized. But he paused as he left, standing opposite her across the width of the two tables. He lowered his eyes slightly, as minimal a gesture as a bow of respect might be reduced to and still exist. She smiled with equal care.

When they had returned to the antechamber and the conference room doors had sealed shut behind them, the demands began.

"What was the point of this?"

"What happened in there, anyway?"

Only Yiril—whose strength of purpose Zatar was coming to admire more and more—managed action. "Vinir, all of you—get on board. This isn't a safe place to talk anymore." He waved short their protests. "Another tenth and they can blow up this station, and us with it. Shipboard will allow us conversation enough."

They obeyed him; his reasoning, all emotion to the contrary, was sound. Even Sechaveh went, doubtless afraid that in his current rage he would kill Zatar rather than get any useful information out of him.

There was silence. Then Yiril looked at the younger man.

"It could be worse."

"That's little comfort."

"It wasn't meant for your comfort. It was an assessment of fact."

"I know."

Another long silence.

"What happened?"

Zatar shook his head. "I don't know, Yiril."

"She took the poison."

"I watched her do so."

"Perhaps the formula was incorrect."

"Perhaps." His speech mode said: No.

Yiril sighed. "Well, that's what it was as far as the others are concerned. And perhaps Sechaveh, too—but I leave that in your hands. Getting a formula across two nations, and in secret—there's room enough for error there that I think we can save our project. For later, of course—much later."

And thus you also save me, Zatar thought. But it wouldn't do to thank him.

"Someday," Yiril said softly, "when it doesn't matter—if it ever doesn't matter—I would like to know what happened in there."

Zatar smiled faintly; he was relieved to see that amusement was still possible. "Someday," he promised in the Basic Mode.

"Are you coming back to the ship?"

He had hit a nerve. *You know me better than I know myself.* He looked back at the door. "Not yet."

"Half a tenth—no more. We'll need the rest to get out of range."

He nodded. "I know."

Then Yiril put a hand on his shoulder. "Shem'Ar," he warned, adorning the phrase with prefixes, suffixes, and variations in emphasis until it warned, admired, dominated, coerced and fretted—all at once. Zatar smiled. "Shem'Ar," he said in the Basic Mode: *I know.* The older Kaim'era left him.

Alone.

Why am I such a fool? Zatar wondered. He shook his head again, as if to clear it. Thought was thick within him, unfamiliar emotions clogging what was usually a structured cognitive process. He had made an enemy, a skilled one; the thought of leaving her free among the stars was bitter. He wanted at least to understand her, to comprehend her motivations for sparing him what would have been certain political death, when he lay within her power.

And he knew she was still there.

He turned back to the door. His weapons were still in the rack and he left them there; otherwise the doors wouldn't open.

He stepped forward.

The doors whisked to the side.

She was waiting.

He stepped into the room and heard the portal shut behind him. On her face was a mixture of triumph and pleasure, such as he would have expected to see on a Braxin countenance. In that moment, when all thought of the future faded before the power of her presence, he was glad that she would die any other kind of death than the one he had originally intended.

"Why?" he demanded. It had been clear from her behavior in the conference room that she detested pointless preamble.

She didn't have to ask what he meant; she had awaited his return to hear that question. "Because you're *mine*, Braxin. I'll let no other have you—not after what you've done. No politics are going to bind you to Braxi, out of my reach forever. Which is what would have happened if you'd been revealed as a failure. I spared you only in order to keep you accessible to my vengeance."

"Motivation worthy of a Braxaná."

"Spare me your insults."

"And what if I go home? What if I choose to make myself inaccessible?"

"I'd follow you, Braxin. With all my ships behind me. But you won't do that. You don't dare. I'm too much for your Border fleet to handle and you know it. They need your insight—they need you. Isn't that the case?"

He pictured the map again and the red fog within it, a glowing spear poised at the edge of the Holding, waiting for her hand to cast it at the Mistress Planet. *All for hate of me?* he wondered.

"Absolutely."

"Why?"

She laughed. "They fed me hate. It became my substance."

"Am I supposed to believe that? You're not a child, lyu Mitethe. In youth that kind of answer might suffice. Not now."

She seemed pleased by his understanding. "The man who murdered my father set in motion a fate that's entailed only suffering for me. I swore vengeance; I mean to have it. And you, Kaim-era, are Darmel lyu Tukone's murderer."

"Are you asking? Yes."

"There was no question in my mind. I thought there might be. I thought I might fail to recognize you in your native form. You were so different then . . . but the eyes are the same. And the arrogance. As soon as I saw you, I knew."

A picture was forming in his mind—had she put it there?—a memory from his first Azean journey. The enemy beguiled, his wife wholly charmed, and the child . . . for a moment there was terror in her eyes. Recognition? He should have killed her then, but there was no opportunity to do so. Her face had haunted him for years afterward, long after the rest of the assassination had faded from his memory.

". . . not two men in the Holding could have managed it," she was saying. "It had to be the same man, working twice. Congratulations, Kaim'era. Against impossible odds, you succeeded."

"I failed."

"No. You underestimated me, most certainly. But your assassination attempt was consummately managed. Slipping poison past a telepath isn't an easy thing to do."

She was going out of her way to express admiration for him, even as her manner dripped venom. Why? Was it pleasing for her to discover, after all these years, that her chosen nemesis was worthy of her? That was a sentiment he could well understand; he was experiencing it himself. Raised among the Braxaná, what a woman she would have been! What a warrior!

Startled, he examined his feelings toward her. Hatred, yes, but his admiration was just as intense. She was a worthy opponent in the traditional Braxaná sense. She would defeat the enemy by probing him for weaknesses and then turning them to her advantage. Her opponent would fall—or he would grow stronger. And she, likewise, must strip herself of all human weakness, lest she facilitate her own downfall. By doing battle, each opponent would force the other to improve, thus making war not only an act of destruction, but of creation as well. It was the ultimate Braxaná archetype, and one which no other people shared. The *K'airth-v'sa*—"mate of the private war"—was as attractive to the Braxaná warrior as he or she was deadly. And it could be a woman. Yes, though years of male dominance had buried that fact. And if any woman deserved the title, this one certainly did.

He would have to fight her; there was no other way. She had said it herself: she was too much for the Border fleet to handle. Only one who understood her could hope to defeat her, and the common Braxin would never be able to do that. Zatar could manage it, because he was not afraid of her. *If* he truly understood her. *If* he made no mistakes.

The ancient Braxaná would have valued such an enmity. They had created elaborate rituals to formalize the confrontation of equals, in order to increase its destructive/constructive power. Such rituals hadn't been used in centuries, perhaps millennia. No k'airth had existed since the Braxaná warriors left their native steppes and were absorbed by civilization; in the complexity of modern society, paired enmity had ceased to be valued.

Until now.

"I will kill you," he said softly, "by my own hands, in my own time." The words welled up from his subconscious, from that part of his soul which hungered for the sword and chafed at civilization's imposed restrictions. He hadn't even realized that he knew them. "In my own way." How would she take this? Would she even understand? He hardly did himself.

But she seemed to. Her eyes gleamed, and her body tensed. *This is what she wants,* he realized.

"I will kill you," she answered, "by my own hands. In my own time. In my own way. No other will have you," she added, smiling her pleasure at the anticipated triumph.

He tried to stop himself with the logic of his circumstances—this was madness, after all!—but reality intervened. Best right now to leave Braxi for a while, to find some other focus of activity while the Kaim'eri calmed down over what happened today. Best to simply be gone when they cried for explanations. This vendetta would serve his political ambition as well as his pleasure.

And it would certainly provide the latter. He looked into her eyes—gleaming, triumphant—and sensed the rare ecstacy there would be in orchestrating her death. *I could lose myself for a while in the killing of you,* he thought.

But one final barrier remained. And fear of that was so deeply ingrained in his Braxaná soul that it took all his courage to raise his sword-hand and offer it to her.

She was startled. "Do you know what you're asking for?"

"I would know my enemy."

"You won't survive it. Your people aren't made for such things!"

"You assume weakness in me where there's none."

"None at all? I doubt that." But she leaned against the table so that she might reach his hand, and then grasped it with her own. "You're a fool, Kaim'era. This battlefield is *mine.*"

For a moment there was nothing: falseness, a moment of ease before the storm. An instant later the fabric of the universe burst apart within his mind.

In the first few seconds it took all his strength not to go insane. *Easy to give in,* her voice came soundlessly, *abandon all the senses, embrace the fluid darkness.*

He fought the suggestions which seemed to plant themselves in his psyche. He struggled for a sense of self, and at last found it. He demanded understanding.

The sharp, intangible life which surrounded him yielded before the strength of his summons. He called forth all the power of primitive tradition and challenged her in the name of the k'airth: *it is my right to know the nature of my enemy.*

Sky, and earth, and air sweet by his face. He fell, startled. The grass moved under his glove and he pulled his hand away, quickly, only to notice that it didn't move at all. Fascinated, he stroked it. The life that was within the fragile blades sang to him with simple, primitive existence, a song of being without thought to complicate it. Something was overhead; he turned to face the sky and saw a formation of birds winging toward him. He touched them, knew their hunger, felt the drive which forced them onward with senses unknown to man and in their endless migration, tasted the call of their mating and the joy of melody as it rang through their souls.

And she was before him.

He stood. "What is this?" he whispered.

"What you demanded," she said, aloof. "An insight into my arsenal. Welcome to my world—or at least, to an image of it that our minds can share. Long enough for you to see the potential of what you face."

"You didn't expect this," he said, and he knew he had voiced her thought.

"Your will is very strong—your adaptability, atypical. Enjoy it for the moment you have it, Braxaná."

He reached into the earth and knew the hunger of the worms that burrowed there, saw the tunnels and caves and emptinesses of the planet's crust through the eyes and minds of the creatures that inhabited such places. He reached upward, outward, and felt the stars like a caress upon his mind. But not the stars themselves, no; the millions of living creatures who orbited those points of light, who formed with their cultural foci stars of emotion in the Void of thought.

"Marvelous!" he breathed.

She was amazed and he felt it. "You see nothing to fear?"

"I see nothing but wonder."

"Your people don't feel that way," she challenged.

"Then my people are fools." He looked at her with new understanding, underscored by jealousy. "To live like this—"

"To taste it is wonderful," she interrupted. "To live with it involves more pain than you can imagine, in ways the non-psychic mind can't begin to grasp."

He ignored that. "What are you?"

"My person? This body?" She indicated herself with a graceful motion that would have seemed out of place if done by her physical self. "This whole world is a thing out of our imagining, which the power I have sustains for your discovery."

"It isn't real."

"It isn't *material.* It's very real."

"But our bodies—"

"Are clasping hands across a conference table. How much time does a dream take? Thought takes less. This is real only to us, and only in the moment we live it."

He closed his eyes and drank in the sheer psychic richness of his surroundings. It was easier with his eyes closed, with that much less to distract him. The land, and the sky . . . and *her.* He could taste her hatred, flavored with just a touch of fear. She had expected him to break; well, he was not so simple a creature as to cringe from her power just because tradition would have it so. The potential of it was filling his mind with longing, and not just for the ability. For *her,* and everything she represented. For her hatred, which was an aphrodisiac to his kind. For the paradox of race that she was, and because she had bettered him. Most of all because she was a shem'Ar, and throughout history such females had driven the men of his tribe to their greatest hungers, and to their blindest passions.

"Take care," she warned him. A command; she was being careless. Did his digression make her uneasy? If so, it was his first—and so far his only—triumph.

Not willing to let the opportunity slip by, he approached her. Let her read his intent in his mind. She might be master of the psychic arts, but in the realm of human sexuality the Braxaná had no rivals. Physical indulgence was as natural to them as breathing, and more necessary. Whereas she, raised in Azean surroundings—

"You're making a mistake." She seemed shaken, unsure of her own objections. Did he sense a response in her, a calling of hunger to hunger that defied her rational purpose? Enmity and passion were a combination much valued by the Braxaná; the thought of tasting not only the pleasure of her body but the sharp bittersweet hatred of her mind stirred longing to new heights within him.

It was a dream, was it not? And a dream had no consequences.

He grasped her by the shoulders, and was stunned as a flood of sensory data overwhelmed him. He touched her—himself—their senses intertwined until he could barely tell one from the other. Yet their identities were distinct. He stroked her, feeling her flesh tremble beneath his touch as though it was his own. She was not unwilling, no, though clearly alarmed by his initiative. "You don't know what you're doing . . ." she whispered. Ah, but he did. He was tasting the pleasure of a woman while sharing his own, and that was an ecstacy undreamed of by his kind.

"Fool!" she told him, but she did not pull away. "You'll regret it. . . ." But there was hunger in her, and it rose to the surface, enveloping him in the rich conflict of her desire . . .

. . . and then there was a feeling of being disconnected, somehow, as if his senses were shutting down . . .

. . . and in fear he drew himself back from her . . .

. . . and in darkness, absolute, he foundered.

Where am I?

Restatement: *What am I?*

Thought without identity, being without focus. The time is endless. But the will is strong.

Zatar, he thinks, and he notes the act of thinking. *Zarvati:* the image of a bloodline, Plague-prone and beautiful. *Son of Vinir* (a tall and angry man, a proud leader) and *K'siva* (who can command men with a motion and never chooses to, a flower among barbarians, a thing too soft and too lovely to last).

He is.

Whatever was reality for him—and at that moment he doesn't recall—it is no longer. There is no darkness, for the concept of darkness implies the existence of light, and light is simply not a reality. He cannot wonder what this place is, for that implies the concept of location and the existence of somewhere else; neither of these things is a truth to him. Only by sheer force of will has he recalled the integrity of his personality and now it is at a loss to anchor itself to the non-world it occupies.

This is not acceptable.

He casts about himself for something, anything, to grasp as a basis for reality. He reaches out with his mind for his body. Surely the two are connected somehow! But there is only the eternal nonexistence of his prison. Fear demands his attention, calling for him to submit and have done with struggling, but he refuses. I AM ZATAR he repeats, clinging to the only shred of identity left to him.

A whisper of death passes through him and is gone. He is focused elsewhere, seeking the physical world that once he knew so well. But then a thought occurs to him and he stops to consider his purpose. In a reality where there is nothing but thought, then thought must be the key to any change. And pure thought is a thing of concepts, of abstract being, not crude reflections of material substance.

He lets himself drift in the nothingness, trying to detect any variation in the world he has come to occupy.

Again the thread of death touches him, and he grasps it, desperately locking himself to it. It has come from *somewhere,* and is going *elsewhere.* Suddenly there is distance, location, movement. He follows it to its destination, which, to his horror, is all to familiar. Yet he is still so distant from it that even as he feels the wave of destruction wash over his own body there is nothing he can do to halt its progress.

He is watching himself die.

No, he thinks sternly. *I refuse.*

The waves continue; that tenuous link which binds him to his material form is weakening, and behind him lies only the nothingness he has so recently escaped.

He becomes intention: he is the will to live and he forces himself down the same path his doom has chosen. *LIFE,* he commands, forcing the requirement into the threads of his being over and over again, until at last the sullen blackness retreats from its alien stronghold and withdraws to those places in the human mind where such things are stored.

He is exhausted and he rests, a thought anchoring him in the world of his body, another standing guard over his personal integrity.

An eternity passes, a moment too small to measure in human terms. He is aware of another mind besides his own, and remembers. Suddenly he is alert with excitement; if he means to know his enemy, then here, in a domain free from the bondage of wordly image, is the place to do so.

She is trying to pull back from him, and there is a material association . . . she is trying to withdraw her hand from his to break the contact. He wants to hold on to her; he wants to explore this thing which is so alien to him and yet is a part of himself. But his holding instinct does not affect the body from which he has detached himself. He forces himself into the limb in question: he becomes his hand, wrapping his will around the muscles and tendons and experiencing *handness* so thoroughly that as the impulse to grab hold of her possesses him he is aware of the extremity responding.

He maintains his grip.

Thought in the darkness; an awareness of Other. She debates whether to break the contact by Discipline, which she has the strength to do. One mental trigger and the wall will slam down between them. He can only struggle with her for as long as she is willing to let him, and she debates now just how long that is.

I will know my enemy, he demands again.

~ *Very well,* comes the thought, and a whisper of acid hatred with it. ~ *And as deeply as you probe, so shall I.*

He sees her mind. It boils with violence and engulfs him in its hungry substance. Here is the hatred, and here the bloodlust, and here the despair, perfect in their purity and not yet adulterated by being filtered through the body's imperfect biochemistry.

Like the winds of a storm her emotions batter at him and threaten to tear him loose from the mooring of his identity. Hatred—he welcomes it, embraces it as a familiar thing, passes through and beyond it unharmed. Fear of sexual inadequacy—he counters it with memories from his own youth, painful memories of genuine impotency, which he had hidden behind a mask of cynical humor and eventually genuinely forgotten. Frustration, in floods of painful intensity—but is it anything he is not himself familiar with?

The assault has an end but not a termination, as though he has come to the center of a storm. All about his awareness the seething emotions swirl, while before him is something no less intense, but in quality quite different.

He touches what no man of the Braxaná has ever known: the essence of female being, rich and warm against his complimentary touch. If he had doubted his own masculinity he might be swept away by it, lost to his former self and changed enough so that when mind rejoined body the parts would no longer mesh properly. But he observes, and appreciates, and is apart from it. This, then, is Anzha lyu Mitethe—this storm of emotion spiced with a death wish, this power of female life unable to find expression in the world of solid things.

She reaches for his Name.

He has no idea why the thought comes like that, only that it does. For the first time he knows a fear so great that it threatens to cut short his exploration. Is it unreasoning superstition, or is there reality to his fears in a world of symbols, where thought is reality and the Name of his soul might well be the key to his existence?

He remembers her words: *as deeply as you probe, so shall I.* Is he that close to the center of her, then, that if she had a Name he would hear it? He forgets his fear in the fascination of discovery, and casts about himself to learn even more. And in that moment, when the decision is absolute and cannot be unmade, when he surrenders that part of himself which previously has only conquered, he passes not through the eye of the storm and back into its turbulence, but deeper into it.

Here there is only mental silence, and the faint echo of his presence. *What is this place?* he wonders, and then he knows: this is the part of her mind sealed off from her introspection, which she herself has no power to see. The magnitude of it is awesome, and the quiet strangely unnerving. He wanders amazed through the secret avenues of her being. Here and there paths have been severed, reconnected elsewhere, forced to flow in a direction which was not their original intent. Potentials are cut short, others grafted to alien purpose, all by a human hand whose touch has left its mark in the woman's basic essence.

A mark he knows.

He cannot assign it an identity; it is too difficult for him, untutored as he is, to connect this abstract feeling with a human name. But as certainly as he knows what the man has done, he recognizes that their paths have crossed. The touch is familiar—and its work is monstrous.

He travels down paths of health and sees them cut short by a form of psychic surgery he can barely comprehend: he reads what has been done, and why, and is filled with an anger so terrible that it cannot be expressed in anything other than pure thought.

This is the dark side of the power, he thinks, *the agony that contradicts the life-song. This is the reason we have weeded out the psychic seed from our own inheritance. This . . . this foulness, which is a crime beyond words.*

As he witnesses the details of that crime, as he feels his anger growing, he realizes there are limits to his endurance. The horror and the ecstacy, intermingled, are becoming more than he can safely internalize.

How do I withdraw? he wonders.

And in that moment he has done so.

She stood against the opposite wall, gray eyes fixed upon him. Breathing heavily, as one might after a more pleasurable encounter, with the sweat and flush of sexual arousal still visible upon her face. As it was upon his own, he realized.

There was a pain in his left hand, across the palm. He looked down; the glove was torn and blood welled up in the resulting opening. Her nails, breaking free of him. But their contact hadn't been broken . . . he looked up at her and realized why there was just a touch of fear in her regard. She *had* pulled free. His will had provided the link that permitted them to continue.

He looked at her now with a mixture of feelings he could not have voiced had he wished to. Including sympathy: for what had been done to her was a crime against the very concept of humanity. They had linked death to her desire, he had seen that clearly. They meant her to be alone, and they meant her to suffer. They were counting on frustration to drive her to . . . what? That was not clear to him. But the work was repulsive to him, and to everything inside him that prided itself on being human.

If you knew what they did to you, and with what intent, then I would be the least of your concerns.

"Starcommander." He said it slowly; speech sounded strange and somehow limiting. Suddenly he longed for the contact they had had, the sure caress of hatred upon hatred . . . but that was gone forever. He had tasted something that was alien to his kind, and save for dreams he would never possess it again.

"You have quite a mind," she said. "I've never seen the like, outside of telepathic circles."

Did she have his Name? Curiously, it no longer mattered. And he had hers.

He looked down at his damaged hand, then slowly peeled the glove from it. The delicate leather was soaked with blood. He held it for a moment, then offered it to her.

She smiled faintly. *A trophy?* her expression said.

Of conquest, he thought. *Both ways.*

She took it from him, careful to put her hand beneath his and let it fall to her, careful not ever to touch. The gesture angered him for the proof it was of what had been done to her. After he was through with her, he would remember to hunt down the man responsible for such an atrocity. It would be a pleasure to destroy him.

"My enemy." The modes whispered meaning into his words without his intending it. Desire—for conquest, for power, for possession. "I will not forget."

He did not meet her eyes again for fear of being drawn into them, but turned and strode to the doors. They opened. For a moment he paused, tempted to turn back and look at her one last time. Though he was committed to seeking her death, the nature of stellar battle was such that they might never actually meet again. But then the impulse was gone and he had stepped forward, and the doors, closing behind him, sealed off that alternative forever.

In the conference chamber, alone, Anzha lyu Mitethe was still. Her hand closed slowly on the torn glove it held and a bit of Braxaná blood dripped down the length of one finger.

And then, quietly, she cried.

He had taught her how.

Harkur: The man who will not resort to violence must find his own ways to manipulate men.

SIXTEEN

HOUSE OF FERAN RINGRECORDING
MASTERCODE:PRIVATE

BAND ONE

They say that if you record your thoughts—if you witness them in the magnapatterns, review them at your leisure—that things will come together for you. In the absence of anyone to talk to (make that *confide in*) and the presence of a very disturbing problem, I'll try anything that might help. Here it goes:

There is a price to being Braxaná. I can't walk the streets without being noticed, I can't stop to observe something but it is immediately regarded as Something of Certain Value, and I can't make my leisurely way through some Braxaná retreat without being bothered by the brave and the curious.

There is one place, however, where even a Braxaná can go unnoticed, and that's the Museum of Erotic Art. Not because the place is obscure; on the contrary, it's the single most popular retreat in the Holding (and perhaps in the galaxy.) Its exhibits sprawl across—and over and under—acres and acres of prime real estate on the Capital Continent; its main building alone could house a modestly populated city and not be the worse for wear. Add to that the restaurants and hotels that crowd its periphery, and you have a world in miniature.

But not all of this world appeals to the general public. The bulk of the main building is a massive labyrinth whose twisting corridors (color-coded for entrance and egress) are a maze of erotic fantasy. Here, the pleasures of a thousand planets are made evident, grouped thematically and in ever-increasing intensity. One can wander through the drugdreams of the H'kekne, rendered in undulating fog by their greatest artists (and then buy, on the way out, a sample of the hallucinaphrodisiac that inspired them); one can share the ecstacies of the Floating Colonies and then move on to the dismemberment fantasies of the Qirdic neo-expressionists; one can view one's favorite fantasy rendered in primitive, solid materials, or displayed in the modern manner, surrounding the viewer. In short, every human taste is explored somewhere in these halls, and many that are truly alien are also presented, if not to inspire pleasure, then to satisfy curiosity.

But there are parts of the Museum that the general public doesn't find appealing, although the Braxaná frequent them. The Hall of Death, for instance—I don't think I've ever seen more than two commoners there at a time, and those looked pretty upset. The Braxaná mentality exults in strange and sometimes morbid images; the artwork that appeals to us doesn't often please the lower classes. Our sense of smell, also, is extraordinarily acute, and some of our exhibits combine odor with unconscious symbolism to support disturbing, often contradictory images. In short, the so-called Braxaná Wing can be a welcome refuge from the curiosity of the commonblooded.

I was in the Alien Pavilion (which combines images of non-human sexual practices with pheremonic projections designed to stimulate the equivalent human reaction), concentrating on a triple-layered hologram by Tonar Tz'Kuloz, when a well-dressed but decidedly middle-class man approached me. I was attempting to work up some enthusiasm for this piece of P'ladakanirk erotica, and was just beginning to draw some interesting parallels between human dualistic sexuality and the multiple-form omnimating habits of that curious species when a voice offered, "My Lord . . ." in that particular tone that indicates one wishes to be noticed and considers oneself worthy of the attention that it requires.

I admit, it was a welcome distraction. Turning, I found the source of the voice to be a man of medium height, unexceptional appearance, moderate class, unimpressive wealth . . . in short, a very average-looking person. I indicated by a slight ascension of the eyebrows that I was listening to him.

"My Lord, I am Supal of Ganos-Tagat. Do I have the honor of addressing Lord Feran, son of Sechavel and Kijannor, of the Braxaná?"

I never miss a chance to practice my arrogance. "You know you do," I said coldly.

He bowed and lowered his eyes for a moment, as was appropriate. "My Lord, I have an item which I believe would interest you." He spoke low, in a voice which indicated that what he had to say wasn't for public consumption. Because he used the Basic Mode (which many commoners do) I had no further insight into the matter. "May we speak in private?" he finally asked.

I considered that for a moment and then nodded gravely. "I was going to take a meal in the Restaurant. Will you join me?"

His hesitation indicated that he wasn't sure how much privacy could be had in such a public place, which in turn indicated that he wasn't familiar with the Museum, or with the customs of upper-class restaurants. Nevertheless he trusted me. A Braxaná is right until proven otherwise, and even then there is some question.

We passed from the Pavilion into the main portion of the Museum, and from there to the Restaurant. Here one might order food from anywhere in the Holding (or at least, so the advertising claimed). Because the Restaurant is situated at the exact center of the Museum, you have to pass through at least one set of exhibits to get to it; as a result many patrons hunger for privacy as much as for food. This is especially true of the Braxaná, who do not share their pleasure with onlookers.

I chose a lowtable with a privacy console, and lowered myself with Braxaná grace to the cushions before it. He sat down somewhat more stiffly, and was still struggling to make himself comfortable when our waitress appeared. Like all human servants in the Restaurant, she was dressed to stimulate our interest (but ironically, since she was working, she had Just Cause to refuse to consummate it). I myself have always been fond of the somatic variations of the Restaurant's women, who vie with each other for the patrons' attention (and thus financial favor) through manipulations of costume and form. This woman had a pseudotail that ended in a tuft of fur which matched the auburn on her head, and what little clothing she wore drew attention to it. My companion stared in open-mouthed amazement, and did not completely regain control of himself until our food arrived.

I set the console for soundproofing and began to eat. "I'm listening," I told him, and then added, "No one else can hear."

He looked dubious, but with a glance down at his plate (gafri bodies crisped on a bed of their colorful powdered wings) and a last nervous glance around to make sure no one was watching, he drew forth a small cloth-wrapped bundle.

"Maybe we'd better—" he began hesitantly.

I switched the opaque field on.

It took a moment for the forcewalls to stabilize in color, but they settled at last on a glowing blue speckled with gold. Not unpleasant. Now that he had his desired privacy, my companion was much more at ease. With considerable pride he unwrapped the small bundle, peeling back first the silken cloth and then a metallic mesh that was wrapped inside it. The mesh parted to reveal a crystal in its natural state, unpolished but showing much promise in its size and rainbow hue.

I was aesthetically impressed but failed to understand the importance of it. Unfortunately, Braxaná do not express ignorance; therefore I couldn't ask, "What is it?" as directly as I would have liked. After a moment I looked up at him, the elevation of one eyebrow indicating that I was intrigued enough to hear what he had come to say. I hoped that would include an explanation of the object's nature.

"It's a Uriese mindgem," he told me.

It stirred no memories. "Go on."

He offered it to me, and prompted, "Touch it."

I did so, noting that its surface was smooth and slightly warm. That was all. My look of irritation at this little charade caused him to glance down from my eyes to my hand, and he started at the sight of my glove. "I'm sorry, Lord, but it needs to come in contact with the skin."

"Your audacity borders on obscenity." I was rather proud of that one.

He paled but did not withdraw the stone. After a moment I took it from him and touched it carefully to the skin above one temple. I was startled, then, by a clear stream of thought that poured forth from it directly into my mind, and a shower of colors that filled my field of vision. For a moment I just watched, as visions of painful beauty danced before me. Then I removed the stone and the visions faded.

"It's contraband," he told me.

I had guessed that. "It's psychic. . . ." As soon as I spoke I regretted doing so—no one but a trained psychic would have recognized that intrusive thoughtstream for what it was. Fortunately for me, he seemed to attribute my understanding to Braxaná omniscience and thought nothing of it.

" Does it . . . interest the Lord?"

I fixed my gaze upon him, "You mean, do I wish to buy it?"

"I would not be so bold as to set a price upon such—"

"How much?"

". . . if my Lord would consider perhaps sparing some information?"

"What do you want to know?"

"It is said that Lord Feran has intimate knowledge of the ways of the Azeans, our enemy, having lived among them for many years."

I looked angry. I really was, too. "I am a Braxaná," I said in my coldest you-have-overstepped-your-bounds voice.

"I'm a writer, Lord. It's occurred to me that in your memories of Azea there might be material for an interesting cultural piece . . . the Sagdal news agency of Ganos-Tagat has indicated a strong interest in such work, and if you would but spare me a few of your memories of that people, I'm sure I could make something interesting out of it."

"And profitable."

"I would, of course, assign a portion of the profits to your House, although such income would be negligible in the face of your own riches."

It would, but tradition was tradition. "Half," I said. The idea of the project intrigued me. It would be dangerous, of course, to indulge at length in recall, since so much of my background dealt with my psychic history and would incriminate me if revealed. But after so many years on Braxi it would be pleasant to reflect upon my past and see what emotions it awoke in me, now that I was truly Braxaná. I would have been uneasy about undertaking such an indulgence alone, but being interviewed would impose a sort of structure upon the experience.

"Half," he agreed.

I thought that was a bit fast considering I had just demanded fifty percent of his income, but at the time I chalked it up to his deference toward my Race and his desire to ingratiate himself to me. (Little did I know!) He gave me the mindgem and I wrapped it up again; although I wanted to taste it once more I didn't know what emotions were evident upon my face when it played its psychic song in my mind. Alas, image is everything. I put it away without trying it a second time.

We made an appointment to meet at my House three days later. I went away feeling extremely pleased with myself, convinced that I had gotten the better of the deal on both counts. How little I understood! And how quickly I was to learn.

BAND TWO

It was no problem to get information on Uri, the mindgem, or Ganos-Tagat, and in the days between our first and second meetings I requisitioned all of it from the Central Computer. Uri is a small planet in the Braxiside War Border. It doesn't support humanform life, nor does it have any alien life of comparable intelligence. The only thing on Uri of any interest to non-natives (besides spectacular sunsets) is the life cycle of the so-called almonjeddei, one part of which is spent in a crystalline container formed from fluids which are extruded from the creature's mating end. This chrysalis protects the metamorphosing creature from the hazards of the outside world, and permits no contact except in one respect. Microscopic tubes in the crystal house filaments of nerve-fiber, which occasionally reach the surface and allow a human psychic to share the color-dreams of the sleeping creature. Apparently for non-psychics there is only a feeling of unfocused pleasure. (Reading this, I was very glad I hadn't said anything in the Restaurant regarding the exact nature of my vision.) As with all things psychic, importation of the almonjeddei in any of its forms was punishable by death.

It was unlikely, given the specifics of Braxi's atmosphere, that the creature would survive its awakening, but that wasn't due for at least ten local years anyway. The gem pleased me. It allowed me a peaceful psychic communion without any effort on my part, and there was next to no danger of exposure involved in using it. I was very grateful to Supal for bringing it to me and I was determined to supply him with useful information in return.

Ganos-Tagat was a paired city united across the Dipa River on the far side of the globe; as I had suspected, predominantly third class. So it didn't surprise me when my writer showed up in a rainbow assortment of colors that would have caused brain damage in any optically oversensitive species.

I welcomed him and offered him wine; he hesitated, then realized that the vintage in question was from a Tagattan winery, and accepted, smiling. I wondered what it was about Braxaná wine that disturbed him.

"I'm ready to answer your questions," I told him. I was feeling particularly amiable, and was anxious to make him feel at ease.

He took out styla and magnapad and then, with a last sip of the wine to stimulate his creativity, began a series of inquiries that were at best predictable and at worst extremely tedious. I was just beginning to wonder if this had been such a good idea after all when he finally came around to what I gathered was the main point of the interview.

"There's great interest in the question of Azean sexuality. Now, we know their propaganda—we know their ideals, and what they would like to believe about themselves. But how much of that is actually true?"

"What, specifically, would you like to know?"

"They are monogamous?"

"Entirely."

"I think you can understand that most Braxins find that incredible. Azeans have one mate only for their entire lives. Can you say with any certainty that they're never bored?"

I shrugged. "I imagine they are, sometimes."

"But they don't seek experiences outside the pairbound?"

"Not sexually, no." I thought I saw what he was driving at—but I also felt that something else was there, something he was leading up to for which this was mere introduction.

"Pardon, my Lord, but how can that be? We're members of the same species, aren't we? And no Braxin would be capable of tolerating such continual frustration."

I smiled. "They don't find it frustrating. You must remember that they redesigned their own race. The sex drive can easily be controlled through inwomb genetic manipulation. They really have no desire for sexual pleasure outside of the proper circumstances."

"But they must have some . . . special outlet within the context of the pairbond."

"I don't know exactly what you're asking." In truth, his questions had become rapidly more obscure as we delved deeper into this particular subject. Did my interviewer have a taste for Azeans—was that it?

"All human beings require variety," he offered.

"All human beings in their natural state," I agreed. "Azeans aren't the product of evolution, but of man's will."

He chewed that over for a few silent moments. "Nevertheless," he insisted, "sexual desire is a basic human drive, and man's hunger for variety is hardly something that can be excised in a laboratory."

I was amused by his insistence. Yes, I suppose to the native Braxin mind it's a very difficult thing to believe, but

I had known too many Azeans to doubt it. "What do you suppose they do about it, then?"

He was startled; clearly that was his question to ask. When he collected himself, he offered possibilities hesitantly, as if watching me for some cue that he was on the right track. "Isn't there some sort of . . . ritual? To help, ah, postpone desire?"

"Is there?" I asked innocently.

"You lived among them, Lord, not I."

"True. But I must tell you that I never heard of any such thing."

"Not any kind of . . ." he faltered. It was becoming clear what his true interest was in all this and I was trying not to smile too broadly. "Is pairbonded pleasure so intense then that it's worth waiting for? That everything else pales in comparison?"

I almost burst out laughing. The man evidently believed that the secret of Azean sexual moderation lay in some special pleasure that made the whole system worthwhile. The thought of two Azeans spending their spare time trying to perfect the sex act was almost more than I could take with a straight face. The fact that Azeans desired their mates in moderate doses and felt no longing for anyone else was hardly a mystery, but a simple combination of hormone cycles, olfactory impressions, and similar biochemical triggers which Azean science was perfectly capable of controlling. I did not, however, laugh out loud, but managed control as I said quietly, "I don't believe so, Supal."

He did not look disappointed; that was the frightening thing. He looked almost angry, as though he felt I was holding something back from him. "It's common knowledge that the Azeans consider their sexual experiences superior to ours."

"I've never heard that." Indeed, the only people I ever heard brag like that were the Braxaná.

Ar, but he was persistent! "The nature of a lasting exclusive relationship is inherently different than that which exists between two people drawn together only for pleasure, and only for the moment."

"I can't tell you," I said frankly. "I've never had a lasting exclusive relationship."

"But you have known those who have."

Telepaths? Hardly! "I was kept very isolated, Supal. I had little contact with the purebred Azean community. I'm sorry, but I really can't help you on this."

He seemed annoyed with me. I think that had I not been a Braxaná he might have freely accused me of lying to him and demanded either the information he wanted or the return of his bribe. I could not, however, give him the first, and I had no intention of giving him the second. To my mind I had complied with our bargain perfectly. And I was growing tired of him, besides.

Therefore I continued: "If you have no further questions for me, then I suggest we terminate this interview." But I felt sorry for him, so I added, "I really don't know where you're getting these rumors from, but I assure you there's no truth to them whatsoever."

He tried to resurrect his warm, respectful smile, but I could sense the irritation just beneath the surface. "I thank you for your time then, Lord Feran. You've been of immense help to me."

Smoothly lied, I thought. I returned the favor. "I'm sorry I couldn't answer all your questions more thoroughly, Supal. If you come up with anything else," (like a different subject matter, I thought) "you may come by."

The minute I said that I regretted it; this feeling was confirmed by the gleam in his eye as he contemplated annoying me again. Taz'Hein, I thought, I might never be rid of him! But then reason intervened: why should he return, when clearly I either could not or would not tell him what he wanted to know?

So I saw him out, and thought that was our final parting.

Ha!

BAND THREE

Sechaveh explained to me once about guilt—how it's a pointless, invalid emotion, one of the most crippling and useless things which man in his folly ever created. Brax-

aná are immune to it (and to its brethren, regret and sorrow). Or at least, they try to be.

When hand comes to glove, I'm afraid I'm less than purebred. The point is that I felt badly over what had happened that day. Whenever I touched the mindgem (not too frequently, for fear it would awaken my buried senses), I thought of him and of his determination to uncover this great Azean secret that he was so certain existed. He was a fool and an ignorant one, but I felt sorry for him. And since he gave me a thing of such value I regretted that I could not in turn satisfy his quest for knowledge.

There are times one is better off being a callous, mean son-of-a-slimemold, and this was one of them. Unfortunately, I didn't realize it at the time.

Supal returned to my House three days later and sought audience with me; having given him permission to come I did not feel it was proper to turn him away.

He had more information with which to stimulate my memory, and after quickly running through the demands etiquette imposed upon us got right down to business. "See, there is this book, Lord." He handed me a metallic plate barely larger than my palm, which I turned over and studied without determining its contents. I was so accustomed to the rings of the upper classes that I wasn't even certain my House had a reader for this. But I asked, and it did. It was sent. Meanwhile, he explained. "Bagar son of Kumust explains very clearly how the nature of Azean society mandates some form of sexual ritual to channel libidinous energies properly."

I said nothing. My guilt was rapidly evaporating and my irritation resurfacing. The book—I call it that lightly, although it had the form—was a never-ending compendium of pseudopsychological tripe intended to convince the reader that beneath the calm, serene surface of Azean sexuality lurked a world of dark ritual and alien indulgence. As a brief example the following will do:

> How is it that a people can so totally deceive not only their neighbors but, apparently, themselves as well? For it seems at first glance that the Azeans

> genuinely believe their protestations of "moderation," and are themselves convinced that their ancestors' science rid the race of its undesirable human traits—foremost among which was, of course, the constant human hunger for sexual stimulation.
>
> A close examination of the science of sexual mnemonics offers interesting insights into this seeming paradox. What if the indulgences practiced in Azean ritual release are genuinely forgotten between the times of their occurrence? Is it possible that complex subliminal symbology could be used to separate the daily (or "moderate") persona from that which is free to experience the full range of human excess?

I looked at him in frank disbelief. It said much for his fanaticism that he misread me entirely.

"You see, I know. I know, Lord Feran. And surely you must have seen it going on around you, all those years you spent in the Empire. Surely you must have known something of their ways!"

I said it very slowly and very carefully, to make certain I was understood. "What this book proposes is nonsense. Totally unfounded, absolute nonsense. I have never seen anything that would allow for such rituals existing and I firmly believe that never in the modern history of Azea has anything been practiced which would even remotely resemble the ritualized indulgences this book talks about. Do you understand me?"

"I hear your words," he said sullenly. Apparently he had been convinced that his knowledge of the Great Azean Secret would be enough to get me to open up to him. "And I see you still won't talk to me."

"We have nothing to say to each other," I told him firmly. "And having determined that, I will now ask that you leave here, and take this . . . *book* with you."

I flipped the plate disdainfully through the air and he caught it, angered by my stubborn denial of his convictions (not to mention my outright rejection of his pres-

ence). In fury he left me, and I thought I had seen the last of him. Certainly I hoped so.

It was not to be so easy.

Two days later I encountered him outside the Observatory in Kurat; it took just a moment to brush him aside, it's true, but the contact marred an otherwise bright day and I was moody for the rest of it. Soon his compatriots were appearing wherever I did and, far more annoying, insinuating themselves into the property adjoining mine, so that wherever I went and whenever I returned home I was treated to a brief summary of: 1) their sincerity, 2) their deserving natures, and 3) my own unfairness. Needless to say I was tempted to point out that "fairness" is not a particularly desirable trait among the Braxaná, but I was certain that any conversation would only encourage them, so I said nothing.

It finally reached the point where I couldn't stand it anymore. It wasn't only their presence, or their insistence on disturbing my peace (which I valued highly and worked to maintain), but the rank stupidity which they represented that I just couldn't stand witnessing over and over again. I asked them to leave. (They ignored me.) I threatened them. (They were frightened, true, but still didn't budge.) I was the One Possible Link between them and their imagined world of sexual mysticism, and they refused to leave me alone. Never talk to fanatics in the first place, or you may be stuck with them forever.

I even tried to find some legal loophole that would allow me to get rid of them, but to my surprise there was nothing useful. Finally, frustrated and angry (would that there were rituals to ease the strain of such emotions!) I turned to that bastion of Braxaná intolerance: my father.

Sechaveh has always welcomed me, more to irritate his purebred children, I think, than for any other reason. I'm never quite certain of his motives, therefore I'm usually wary when accepting advice from him. This matter was right in his glove, however, so I didn't hesitate to seek him out.

I explained my problem as well as I could. (No specifics on the mindgem, no mention of my own emotional trauma, minus the kinder words and plus quite a few harsher ones. Although as a son I shouldn't be turning to him for such things, he took a personal pride in keeping my Braxaná side dominant—perhaps because it proved the superiority of his genes over my mother's. Whatever the reason, I told him all the parts of this story that were acceptably Braxaná, and he assumed that was the whole of it.

When I was done he smiled, the expression of a man who is never without an appropriate answer. "Simple," he told me. "You kill them."

I wasn't quite sure whether he was answering me or trying to bait me; this is the usual state of our relationship. "Kill them?"

"You wear the sword," he pointed out.

"But how—"

"Draw and cut. Surely I don't have to explain killing to you, Feran."

I scowled. "I know how to kill."

Do you? his expression dared me. "Then do so."

"And the law?"

He laughed. "Law? *What* law? You're a member of the first class, Feran, fully halfbred and entitled to all the Braxaná prerogatives. They bother you? Dispatch them! They irritate you? Dispatch them slowly, and exact your revenge. Don't worry about the law. Nobody's going to prosecute you; if someone tries, the Kaim'eri will cut him down as quickly and efficiently as your sword will cut through these pseudoscientists of yours." He paused, then offered in a cloying tone, "I could take them out on Whim Death for you."

"No," I answered. "That's hardly appropriate." My father, invoke Whim Death on behalf of his offspring? Socially unacceptable, and I knew it. And he knew I knew. "No. I'll deal with it myself."

He smiled, and I realized I had been tested. Walking me to the door, he offered me encouragement and a few effective cuts and thrusts which would disable an opponent without killing him immediately. Teach these men a lesson, he prompted, and show them once and for all that none of their kind will be tolerated.

And learn a lesson myself? I thought. I thanked him

and left, committing myself to nothing. I should have anticipated that he would counsel me toward violence—but then, so would any other traditional Braxaná. So why did it bother me? Perhaps I resented his attempt to manipulate me because it implied I was no better than the mindless souls he usually practiced his influence upon. No, if Sechaveh was trying to force me to play a more violent role, then one thing was certain: I would search for an alternative.

BAND FOUR

I presented the matter to Lina. That's one of the first things you learn in Braxaná society; when you have run out of ideas yourself, consult a woman. More specifically, consult your Mistress.

I did so.

We've never cared much for politics, Lina and I, so I was quite surprised when she responded to my narrative with a straightforward, "We can look into his motives," and proceeded to outline a course of action which depended upon an involved network of informants in the news and publishing industries. I must have looked as surprised as I felt, for she smiled. "It shouldn't take very long."

It didn't. A mere tenth passed, during which time she must have waded through the whole of the Central Computer System, for the list of men she brought to me was connected to my tormentor by what seemed to me to be the most tenuous of ties. Nevertheless, she explained to me, one of these individuals was probably responsible for conning Supal into his recent course of action.

"Can we find out which one?"

Since I don't often play the political games—at least, not as viciously as my countrymen—Lina has never compiled the kind of records that would allow for that type of research. It requires a private spy network, for one thing, something that neither of us saw the need for. Until now.

"With help," she said at last.

"Whose?"

"Another Mistress."

I had a sudden vision of all the Mistresses of our

Houses collaborating in a giant network of domestic espionage. . . . No. Even women don't trust each other *that* much. But still, the thought that while we men were at each other's throats the women who were running our Houses were cooperating in such a way seemed . . . well, unwholesome. "Go on," I urged her.

"Who do you trust?"

"In Kurat?" I asked, using the Ironic Mode.

"Let me rephrase: Who can I turn to? Conversely, is there a particular House you don't want me to consult?"

It came to me immediately, and I could feel that old familiar coldness settle in my insides as I said the name. "Zatar. Under no circumstances do we admit vulnerability to anyone connected with that House. You understand?"

She did; she has lived with me long enough to know how nervous that man makes me, and offered a few other names for my consideration. A handful of one and a gloveful of the other, I told her. She could chose.

She chose Darak. The name meant nothing to me. But we must have help from some quarter and she thought that his Mistress would have the information she needs. Go, I told her. Do it.

We would have to chance the consequences.

BAND FIVE

The trail leads back to Sechaveh.

My own father!

Now that I consider it, it makes sense. That god-blessed motherloving . . . how could he? How *could* he?

Calm, Feran. Calm. You know the way he operates. You know he enjoys manipulating people. Look at the way he treats his pureson, Turak; why should you be any different?

Yes, but *why*. . . .

He set the whole thing up. The whole blessed thing! Why? To force me to kill? Would he really do that?

Sechaveh? Of course he would. If not for my benefit, then for his own amusement.

There's no question in my mind; I must deal with this matter without giving in to him. I didn't come to Braxi to be controlled by another man. I came here for freedom . . . and I will have it.

There must be a way, somehow, to solve this problem without pleasing him.

BAND SIX

I believe I have an answer.

I talked it over with Lina, and she agreed that it might work. She also added one thing: could it be that Supal's distaste for Braxaná wine was indicative of an aversion to the drugs normally present in it? She postulated that these Friends of Azea (as she called them) might not only venerate the heights of ecstacy which that people supposedly achieved, but their legendary self-control as well. Priceless woman! If she's correct, then there may indeed be a way out of this. And I think I have found it.

BAND SEVEN

I invited Supal over today.

He came promptly. His demeanor clearly indicated that he thought my invitation signaled a change of heart. And indeed—as far as he was to know—it did.

I welcomed him warmly.

He entered the room like a wary animal, made uncertain by my sudden amiability. Lying to a Braxaná is a serious offense; just how sure of himself was he? "You wanted to see me?"

I sat down opposite him in one of the comfortable chairs of my inner study. I had brought him this far into the House to indicate the sincerity of my good will, which obviously reassured him. I offered him wine, but he wouldn't drink. He wasn't that sure of me yet.

"I must say you're persistent." I modeled myself after Zatar, who plays the lordly game better than anyone else I know. "You know, of course, that what you're seeking is no small thing."

It hit him then: YES HE IS GOING TO TELL ME! was written in large letters across his face. I tried very hard not to smile. "I'm aware of that," he said, with an attempt at humility. Since he didn't feel it, it didn't come off too well. But I looked moved.

"The point of fact is, Supal, that there have been an lot of your people around lately—"

"I'll send them away. I'll get rid of them. Don't worry, Lord Feran, a tenth after I leave here they'll all be gone forever!"

Good, I thought.

"Do you . . . do you want some kind of assurance of secrecy?"

I laughed, striving for that knife-edged disdain that Zatar does so well. "Do not insult me, Braxin! What good are your vows, or anyone's, in such a matter as this? No, do what you will with them, but I will deal with you alone. Do you understand? Let me be more emphatic. If they ever bother me again, I will have you killed. Clear?"

His eyes wide with awe/anticipation/fear, he nodded.

"Good. Then we can begin immediately. I assume you have no objections?"

No, no, he shook his head adamantly, not at all.

"Excellent." I picked up a calendar which I had prepared for this meeting, an ornate thing embellished with Ikna astrological motifs and various arcane runes that I half-remembered and half-didn't. Meaningless though they were, they looked impressive.

I indicated that day with one finger. "We are here. The next appropriate day for a Great Union is . . . here." I indicated a date some zhents hence. I looked at him dubiously. "Do you really think you're up to this?" I asked, implying by my tone that I didn't.

He nodded.

"Fiveday, twelvezhent. Can you remember?"

"Certainly, Lord." Then he looked confused. "What am I remembering?"

"Why, to be celibate, of course. Surely you don't think you can manage an Azean-style Union after a steady diet of women?"

His eyes said clearly that he had, but manfully he swallowed his fears and agreed to that condition.

"Entirely celibate," I added. "Women, men, small boys, you name it."

"And, ah. . . ."

I guessed his concern and waved it into the realm of inconsequential trivia. "Yourself? It doesn't matter in the same way. Of course, if you really mean to go about this right. . . ."

He nodded, eyes wide. "Nothing. I understand."

I'll give him this, he really meant to try. I threw in other lines of semi-mystical nonsense, but the crux of the matter had already been presented. For good sex, no sex. And we'd see how long he lasted with that.

BAND EIGHT

I had hoped he would never come back.

He did.

"The others have left you alone, Lord?"

I nodded. He looked lean and haggard, as if I had ordered him off food and water as well as women. "You have done well, Supal. Would you like something to eat?"

To my surprise he accepted, but when the food came he merely picked at it.

"Have you been obedient to the rules I set forth?" I was certain he had but decided to rub it in.

He nodded. He still had a zhent to go but had asked to see me, to work out some of the details of his upcoming Union. I must admit I thought the celibacy itself would be enough to drive him away. Given Braxin society, that's a pretty heavy burden. But no, here he was.

A shapely woman came in carrying a tray of sweets. When I say shapely, perhaps I understate her; certainly her effect upon Supal was like a ton of bricks falling on him. His mouth gaped wide, and it took her (scented) fingers to stuff a candied fruit into it.

Poor man! He was in pretty bad shape already. I would feel sorry for him when the aphrodisiacs in the food hit home.

"So how are you doing?" I asked.

He was forced to swallow the fruit in order to speak. "Not well," he admitted. "The tension is just terrible . . . the frustration. . . .

I guessed that he had been denying himself any satisfaction at all, even that which he could manage alone. The slave popped another bit of fruit in his mouth. I was really enjoying myself.

"Do you think you can make it?" I asked gravely.

"Oh, yes, Lord!" His gaunt face animated with something akin to religious zeal. "And you will . . . that is to say. . . ." He was too embarrassed to finish.

"When the time comes," I soothed him, "I will direct things."

"With whom?" That was clearly his concern in coming. I smiled. I had foreseen that.

"My Mistress, of course." I paused for dramatic effect. "Who else do you think I would trust with this?"

His eyes wide, he nodded agreement. My slave popped another delicacy in his mouth, and lightly touched his neck as he ate it. I warned her off in a seeming fit of concern for my apprentice's welfare and she rose, pouting prettily, and stalked sinuously out.

Poor Supal. I looked in his eyes as they followed her exit and saw his hunger clearly revealed. And if not there, certainly elsewhere. It was a good try. But I doubted he'd make it through the night.

And if he did, I was ready.

BAND NINE

Sixday, Twelvezhent.

Last night he came.

He was a mere shadow of his former self, a lean and desperate man who sought to master his all-consuming eagerness as he bowed to me and we exchanged the ritual greetings of Braxaná life.

"We're all ready," I told him. "Come this way."

Lina had helped me prepare the ritual room. Indeed, it had almost been worth this whole affair just to do the decorating. Picture: A moon entangled in the rays of the Braxin sun splayed in mosaic across the ceiling. Arrases worked in impressively meaningless arcane symbols covering all the walls save where the one door was located. Dualistic symbolism painted in vivid lower-class colors on the polished black floor. A table, with swept-crystal candleware and a matching goblet, and a smaller goblet with a sweetly smelling dark-red substance that looked suspiciously like blood. (It was actually semi-evaporated palla juice—not because it couldn't have been blood, but I felt that once we had begun to plan such a deception we might as well go all the way.) All in all, dark, impressive, dramatic. Supal sighed. Was it what he had expected? More, his face said. Not for nothing had I spent the lastzhent reading all those ridiculous books!

Lina was waiting for us and she gave Supal the smaller goblet to drink from. Shivering, he looked to me for support; I nodded gravely. He drank the sweet stuff slowly (it's hard to get down in that concentration). Lina had mixed in an anaphrodisiac just in case our little game failed, so that he would have only himself to blame. I hoped it was a strong one.

Then, solemnly, she undressed and I bade him do the same. He was trembling now, and it obviously took great self-control for him to lie down on the floor beside her, some distance away as the arcane symbols indicated.

He waited, eyes shut in anticipation, on the cold black floor (I had refrigerated it) and I began the Ritual of Preparation.

"Know you who come here this day that there are two things which raise man above the level of animals, and they are these: his pleasure, and his discipline. For although animals mate they do not know a pleasure equal to man's, and they do not have the will or the strength to deny themselves consummation for the sheer pleasure of discipline. So, today, are these two Principles combined, when by an act of pleasure discipline is yielded up to consummation and the ecstacy of man will be complete."

Lina helped me write that. I thought it was a bit overdone, but no more than similar ceremonies in those ludicrous books. Supal seemed to take it all in all right. Anything, I suppose, to justify all that celibacy.

I brought over the largest goblet of wine and gave some to Lina, my body between hers and Supal's so that he couldn't see she wasn't really drinking. Then I had him finish off the rest.

"What was it?" he asked a moment later, as its effects began to be evident.

"Drugs. Shh. They are necessary."

He looked more nervous now, and rightly so. It was a mild hallucinogen, little stronger than that present in so many Braxaná wines. But Supal didn't drink such wine. And he didn't expose himself to hallucinogens. And he wasn't going to like it.

By now the suggestibility imposed by the drugs in the first goblet would have taken hold. I crouched by his side, a specter in gray and black, and tried to prepare him.

"You will feel as if you're floating for a while, and that's fine. Don't worry about your body. It won't hurt itself, whatever it does." His eyes opened wide at that one. Yes, Lina had guessed right; this was a man who would willingly taste any experience except lack of control.

If that was so, we had him.

I went on to describe the contortions that might overtake him, and how he would watch his body go through them as if from a distance, floating in the sexual aether and experiencing growing excitement. He was more and more nervous, a condition magnified by his altered blood chemistry. Nervous side glances told me that he was beginning to see things. Now is the time, I thought.

"Then," I told him, my voice quiet, low-pitched in the mystical room, "when the two of you have passed each other in the aether and have each taken on the other's form—"

"What!?"

He sat upright suddenly and grabbed me by the tunic front. "What do you mean?"

I feigned surprise. "I thought you knew. You said you knew."

"Knew what? Tell me, bless you!"

I knew then that the drugs had hold of him, for he would never have spoken that way to me otherwise.

"Why, that you will experience this Union as a woman." Before he could respond to that outrageous concept, I added another. "There shouldn't be too many physical ramifications in your case, so I wouldn't worry about that. . . ."

"What? What ramifications? Worry about what?"

"Well," I said with seeming reluctance, "It *is* true that among the Azeans the sexes gradually come to resemble each other. But that's after many years of practicing the ritual," I added hurriedly, "and it rarely affects the primary sexual—"

He had heard enough. He was trying to stand.

"—characteristics." I acted concerned. "This isn't proper behavior."

"A god to your 'proper behavior'!" The drugs we had fed him were adding image to my words, making him feel as if the change were actually taking place, as if he were exchanging height, organ, shape, and all details of sex with my Mistress.

"But to experience a woman's pleasure!" I cried, seemingly dumbfounded. "Isn't that what you want? I thought you understood!"

With an effort of will he reintegrated himself; that is to say, he ceased to have the illusion that he was "blending" into my Mistress. "I thought I did, too, Lord Feran . . . I. . . ."

He shook his head and stumbled out of the room, grabbing his clothes as an afterthought, desperate to get away from my House before he was impressed with the persona of a woman. I could imagine the nightmarish images his drugged mind was supplying as he found his way to the door and out, naked, into the street.

I waited for the computer to acknowledge his exit before I collapsed, laughing, on the floor. Lina joined me there, and we vented our energy in a fine display of Braxin sexuality. Not that experiencing pleasure from a woman's point of view is such a terrible thing; in my telepathic days, I did it often. But Braxins will be Braxins, I suppose. I doubt he'll be back.

Only one thing bothers me. I go over these recordings, and everything makes sense—all except one detail. How did Supal get that mindgem in the first place? The Braxaná Black Market is the only source for such a thing, and those people would never risk their lives for a lower-class patron.

I looked up the planet's location. Maybe I shouldn't have. Maybe I should have left well enough alone.

Too late now, though.

Uri's in the Active War Border. In a sector that Zatar controls. Which either means that some smugglers got through his defense network—unlikely—or that he's somehow involved in all this.

I'm going to try very hard not to think about that.

Viton: Between natural enemies there is never peace.

SEVENTEEN

Anzha strode quickly from her shuttle to the Institute. She was in no mood for delay—not for savoring the planet's aura, admiring the magnificent scenery, or reconsidering her actions. She was angry, and barely contained herself. Woe betide the man who set that torrent loose!

Familiar steps and familiar halls; life went on, but the Institute never changed. She sent a brief thought ahead to warn him of her coming—a token courtesy—and then arrived only moments after it had faded from his mind.

"Admission," she told the door. "Anzha lyu Mitethe."

There was a pause; the Director gathering his thoughts, no doubt. Finally the door *pinged* clearance and slid open, admitting her to the inner sanctum of the so-called monarch of telepathy, Nabu li Pazua.

She neither smiled nor bowed. "Director."

"You honor me, Starcommander." A surface thought chided her for her unexpected arrival. "What business brings you this far from the War Border?"

In answer she removed a thin packet of documents from her half-jacket, opened it, and spilled its contents onto his desk. "I think you know."

He looked at the papers and shrugged; his surface thoughts were running a lightyear a minute but she couldn't catch any of them. He was too guarded for that. "Ah. Your request?"

"Just so. It was refused. I want to know why."

He indicated one of the documents. "You have my reasons right here."

"I have a standard rejection form. That's not enough."

"You're assuming complexity of motive where there's none."

"And you're stalling. I requested the services of an omnicultural Communicant. I went through the proper channels. You turned me down. I want to know why."

He tapped a stence briefly against the top of his desk, a parody of non-telepathic thoughtfulness. "The Institute isn't required to supply you with personnel. And I'm not required to give you reasons."

He could feel her trying to control herself, not quietly and not well. "This is true." Her voice and mind were rich with threat but she said nothing more, waiting.

"All right." The confrontation must be, so let it. "It was our decision that since as a Functional Telepath you're fully capable of transcultural communication, it was pointless to expend another mind merely to satisfy your desire for redundancy. There's nothing that Siara ti can do that you can't, and better."

"I'm only one person," she pointed out. "There's a limit to how many jobs I can handle."

"Then recruit physicals. We're not a supply house for Star-Control personnel, you know."

"There isn't a physical in the galaxy who can do what Siara ti can," she said coldly. "Having the skill myself, I understand that."

"Your relative isolation from telepathic kind has given you a strange view of our relationship to the physical world. There are perhaps ten thousand of us in an Empire with millions of times that many people—and I'm sure I need hardly remind you that there are no true telepaths native to areas outside the Empire. Most of them stay with the Institute and serve its cause, hoping someday to change those numbers. You chose to leave; very well, that was your option. But now you seem to think you can recruit psychics regardless of *our* needs, *our* purposes. Well, you're wrong."

"Isn't the War important? Isn't that cause enough to spare a few people?"

"I *have* spared a few people. I've given you five psychic-receptives—against my better judgment, I might add. But they wanted to go, so I let them. Now two of them are dead."

"I regret that. But such things happen in a war."

"War isn't my concern! Psychogenetics *is*. I have a responsibility to breed, protect and train as many human psychics as I can. I defy my own purpose when I send them out to die. You've wasted your time in coming here, Anzha lyu. The answer is no."

She tried to explain. "Director, the War is changing. We've gotten closer than ever before to the Braxiside Border as a direct result of having these psychics. With them, I can send scouts and fighters far beyond the Conqueror's scanner-range. With a Communicant, I could manage even more."

"You told me this when you were first assigned to the *Conqueror.* And again, when you applied for each psychic. Once I could see the truth of it. But your progress has slowed, Starcommander; how do you explain that?"

She darkened. "The enemy's changed. Zatar—"

She stopped suddenly, unwilling to let him share her emotions. The anger. The hunger. He would misinterpret that, reading it as weakness. When in fact it was just the opposite. Her determination to bring Zatar down was her strength, her emotional refuge, the passion that fueled her very existence. The fact that li Pazua would stand between her and her victory was incomprehensible. Inexcusable. *Unacceptable.*

"He knows what I'm doing," she said softly. There was awe in her foremind, and rightly so; what other Braxin could have managed to second-guess a psychic? "He understands. He's learning to work around my telepathy. He makes plans that have no meaning, takes action designed to confuse a psychic. All with the intensity of purpose that usually indicates sincerity. I need another mind that can read him. One that isn't bound by my . . ." *passions?* ". . . limitations."

"And your enemy won't simply adjust for the new personnel?"

She shut her eyes, hating him. "Probably. But it would take time."

"It seems to me that while you're busy designing a new kind of war, you're also creating a new kind of enemy. Isn't that self-defeating?"

It was so close to the philosophy of the k'airth that she was startled to hear it from him. How much had she been broadcasting during their argument? "Director, this War's a race. Little by little we're pushing closer to the Holding; when we get there, all the rules will change. Every new element, be it psychic or strategic, buys us that much more time, advances us that much further. He isn't psychic himself; there *must* be a limit to how much he can second-guess us!"

"Your own subsidiary images cause me to wonder if that's true. But regardless, I'm afraid I still have to refuse this request. I have many responsibilities, some of which outweigh this one. And one of them is to protect the psychic community."

"Am I a threat to it, then?"

"Two psychics have died in your service. That's fact. I'm not willing to lose any more."

"*Is* it your choice to make?"

"In Siara ti's case, yes. He's young; I'm sure the War sounds very exciting to him. I doubt he comprehends the reality of what you're asking him to do. Or the risk. Two deaths is *enough,* Anzha lyu. Be satisfied with what you have."

She touched his surface mind, smiled at what she found there. "Are you really upset over those deaths, Director? Or does it bother you more that the ones who still live might transfer their allegiance from the Institute to me?"

She had hit a nerve; he was quick to conceal it, but not quick enough. *You are the start of a dangerous trend!* his surface mind told her. Then his control was back. "You imagine yourself to be more important than you are. You offer the excitement of war; I offer training. Here at the Institute a psychic can reach his or her maximum potential. In the long run—"

"Do you really believe that?" she interrupted. "Can you look at me and still think it? Out there, that's where the power comes from! From having to deal with humans whose minds are closed to you. From being alone in the Void until your mind screams for contact—from skimming whole planets with your thoughts, hungering for the touch of a familiar soul. Not here, in this spoon-fed environment where you try to nurture strength by fulfilling our needs. Power like mine doesn't grow unless it has to—and mine has had to. The very existence of your Institute inhibits the talent you're after."

She let that sink in, then told him, "I offer you the War, the ultimate testing-ground. Send Siara ti to me and he'll become stronger than you ever dreamed possible. I guarantee it."

"Very dramatic," he said dryly. "And I don't doubt that you've discovered your own fulfillment in combat. *And* found new ways to focus your talent. But your limitations are still the same, here or elsewhere."

"Are they?" Her eyes gleamed, and anger was evident in her foremind. "Are they really? Let me demonstrate, Director, just what sort of talent we're arguing about."

She launched an assault on his mind slowly, so that he might have warning and find no recourse in the excuse of surprise. Even as he withdrew to cut himself off from her, he felt his eyes, alien things, widening in astonishment. This was in violation of the most basic tenets of Telepathic Etiquette!

She pushed the release forms toward him, a remarkable display of motor control; it was hard to do anything with one's body while exerting that much power. "Sign them, Director."

~ *I will not!*

He tried to build walls for himself while staring her down, but could not. One by one his physical senses shut down, allowing him to concentrate on the deadly battle within him.

~ *Have I overestimated myself, Director?*

She was trying to move his body as though it were her own and he was fighting to stop her. And losing. Mental claws tore at the walls he erected even as they were begun, until he battled merely to lay down a foundation for the struggle. Distinction Discipline, he begged his memory. The key patterns snapped into place and he began to withdraw into the dark isolation of self-only. Then she followed him there—followed him *there!*—and destroyed the flowing pattern which had promised salvation.

~ *You can't hide from me, Director. I'm too strong. I'm stronger than you ever meant me to be, and perhaps stronger than you thought any of us could become.*

He was seeing again, but only as a spectator to the vision she had activated within his eyes. She saw through her own eyes and controlled him. Not possible!

"Yes." She wanted him to hear her so she heard for him, letting him share the sensation. Inside he was still struggling, but his will, overpowered and afraid, was succumbing at last to her battering strength. "So much of what you taught us was wrong. Abandon the physical senses to concentrate on the mind. Nonsense! Integrate the two and both are strengthened. You learn that when you have no alternative."

His hands clenched, then unclenched—her doing. He couldn't stop it, slow it, lessen it. His body was hers to command. This wasn't possible!

"Why not?" she demanded. "If my body were strong enough, I could force you physically. I might manipulate your intellect through reasoning if my debating skills were outstanding. Why is this so unexpected? There isn't a man or woman who could stand up to me if I were determined enough—receptive, telepathic, or otherwise. Not if you can't."

She pushed the request toward him. "Sign it, Director."

~ *under duress*—

"Your own propaganda will be your undoing. One telepath can't control another, remember?—*Sign it.*"

He fought as his hand reclaimed the stence, fought as he pulled the forms toward him. Fought desperately as she squeezed the signature out of him, calling his own mind into collusion with hers to make the mark perfectly his. He fought, and he lost.

"Thank you, Director. I knew you'd see reason."

Like a fist holding a rag from which water had been wrung she relaxed and released him, and like a damp rag he fell to the desk before her, emptied.

She refolded the documents and tucked them back inside her half-jacket. "I'll expect Siara ti Lann at Base Twelve in ten Standard Days."

"And if he's not there?"

"You've released him already. If you interfere with StarControl now, I'll have you up on trial for treason. And you know as well as I do how many people in the Empire want you there. Including myself; it would give me access to your private psychefiles, and the notes on my conditioning. So don't tempt me." Again her thoughts grew dark. "And if I ever have reason to suspect that my conditioning—or that of my psychics—is interfering with my work, I assure you I will burn this Institute to the ground and its precious records with it. Do you understand me?"

It was all he could do to nod; his body felt numb, and was slow in responding.

"That's all, Director. Once more, I thank you."

She left his office as she had entered it: a whirlwind of mad, half-disciplined energy. Exhausted, Nabu nursed his injured mind. They had always been impressed by her potential, but this exceeded their wildest dreams. If only it were under control!

What about her conditioning? he asked himself. *Is that still functioning?* It was hard to judge. They had taken in an outcast child and had raised her to hunger for the stars. They wanted something, and had wagered that she could find it. If things had gone according to plan she would be traveling now, supported by the Institute, wandering from planet to planet until she found the information that would satisfy them. They had instilled zeymophobia in her for that reason, so that she might never be comfortable enough on any surface to settle down and abandon her quest.

Who could have foreseen that she would join the military? By sending her to the Border fleet, StarControl had destroyed the environment required for her conditioning to function properly; who could say what would happen to it under the present circumstances? The first break had already been made: by treating Nabu as she had, Anzha had made it clear that her conditioned dependence upon the Institute was no longer operative. How much else had been similarly annihilated?

His confidence badly shaken, the Director of the Institute forced himself to face an unpleasant truth.

We've lost control of her.

Harkur: The Braxaná are wrong if they think that they will never be intolerant toward human indulgences. They simply have not yet encountered one that offends them.

EIGHTEEN

My name is Venari. It's a meaningless thing, a collection of syllables whose combination has been applied to me. When it's called, I come; when others speak it, visions of me are called to mind. But it has in itself no meaning. I have in myself no meaning. I exist. I live. I serve. Venari.

My memory extends back nearly a year.

I'm told that I was in a terrible accident once, and that my mind has blocked that part of my memory, to keep me from reliving the pain. Perhaps I malfunctioned. In any case, I've lost not only the memory of that terrible day but of all days before it. My life is fifteen zhents old; of my soul, who can say? I speak seven languages but have no memory of having learned them. I have skills no one taught me and every day I am aware of memories nearly coming to mind that were supposedly lost forever.

I have dreams.

This is my most common dream: I am in a small starship speeding through the Void. The image comes of a knife slicing the substance of that darkness, of myself plunging through the wound. There are instruments all about me, upon which my life depends. An image comes of gold hands over a control board, dancing. There is a weight over me, and also an exhilarating sense of joy, of coming triumph. I laugh, wildly. Then fire burns about me suddenly—fear envelops me. I have a glimpse of a golden egg, to match the hands, freefloating in the Void. I strive to reach it.

And I awake, screaming.

I'm learning not to scream. When that half-state comes where I am still in the dream but no longer entirely so, I stifle my cries with the terror of my days and the memory of what's done to me when this dream is made public. That's usually enough. The memory is a strong one.

Identity: the mirror, conjured, reveals a human woman with the mark of the foreign-born strong upon her. Prehensile toes, nails that are better called talons, a broad face splayed out in horizontal features that make a mockery of the cleanly chiseled details of the Braxaná, by whom I am surrounded. I am tall—too tall—spare in the chest and hips, and so dark that I could slip unseen from shadow to shadow. When I'm cut, the interior of my flesh is pink-white, like theirs, as if my color were makeup and could be easily removed. Sadly, I observe this often.

Which brings me to the next point of identification: I am a slave in the House of Sechaveh.

Some primitive peoples believe in a variety of afterlives; my Mistress has told me of these things. They're based upon the concept that some god—or goddess—has taken the time and trouble to remain in the human sphere of affairs and oversee the eternity of the immortal soul. I imagine this would be terribly boring, for a being that was truly omnipotent. So, for the sake of variety, said deity devises a series of distinct and memorably atmospheric subafterlives. One of these, though it's called by many names, is recognized by all believing peoples as a place of eternal suffering. What that suffering is, no one is quite sure. What they *are* certain of is that this place has a Master, whose pleasure it is to concoct new varieties of human anguish for the diversion of the creator-god in charge. I have met this man. In fact, I serve him.

They say that Sechaveh's character was formed in his childhood, when he was ruled by women and made to suffer for his parents' arrogance. I don't believe this. The mind freely imagines many terrible things, and none of them, not even in their most fearsome intensity, could turn out the sort of being that Sekav, son of Lurat and M'nisa, became.

Of course, I'm prejudiced. I am a woman. I don't know what men think of him and I imagine I will never find out. I wonder sometimes if the Braxaná could really approve of him, they who speak of the right to pleasure and revere their own women above the men of all other races. Sechaveh's not like that. He's different, and knows it, and as a sign of that difference he bears a different name, the one the aliens gave him. But the Braxaná use it, and perhaps they really do consider him one of them. To me they are very different. But then, I am his.

I've become disturbed recently over my identity. The formula of it is cut and dried, nothing to question, every bit of it in its proper place. Yet there's a piece missing. I have never thought of my life as a puzzle, but more and more I wonder about those missing years. What sort of person would I be now if I remembered my entire past? Such memory doesn't seem to be a positive thing. Whenever my words or actions lead my Master or Mistress to believe that a fragment of memory has surfaced I'm punished soundly and then made to undergo such treatment as will erase it entirely. But that never completely works. I don't tell them that; after undergoing such pain as Sechaveh's fertile imagination supplies and then spending days in drugged hypnotreatment, I'm in little mood to inform them that the whole process failed. But fail it does, more and more as I'm subjected to it. It's as if I'm building up an immunity to the process, or perhaps my memories are finding ways to circumvent Sechaveh's surveillance, and only gradually succeeding.

This is why I try not to wake up screaming.

Despite all this speculation, it was more than likely that I would go to my dissolution without ever unveiling the mystery of my past. But then He came . . . ah, I shudder to think of it! . . . and the world changed in an instant.

He had come back from the War for a time. Who can say why? There are as many Conditional Peaces as there are stars in the Braxin sky; perhaps one of them encompassed his region, his command, or his ships. Maybe concern for his House brought him back to his native moon, or repairs on his vessel made it possible for him to leave the front for a vacation. Who can say? I had been sent forth on some errands that day, and was running behind schedule. As I hurried down a lunar thoroughfare, anxious to reach my House at the appointed time, my thoughts were not upon the road. And so it was I ran into him, and the impact sent me sprawling.

My first reaction was fear. Almost all the residents of Zhene were high-born. What would my punishment be, for daring to inconvenience a Braxaná? But then I looked up, and saw Him, and the fear gave way to wonder.

It is not enough to say that he was beautiful, for beauty is common among the Braxaná, and I had long ago become accustomed to it; judging between the Lords of Braxi would be like judging between the gods themselves. But I was used to my Master's features, harsh and unyielding, twisted by years of anger. Had a slave inconvenienced him as I had just done to this stranger, rage would have quickly deformed his features into a hideous mask. This man showed no anger, sought no vengeance. He even seemed—could it be?—amused by the encounter.

"On your feet, woman." I struggled to obey, feeling the heat rise to my cheeks. Praise the gods for my alien skin, which hid my blushes in its darkness! His presence unnerved me in a way I didn't understand, yet which was not unpleasant. He stepped closer as he looked me over, and touched a gloved finger to my face tilting it upward until I looked directly into his eyes. His delicate nostrils flared, and I was as uncomfortable as always with the awareness that the Braxaná sense of smell, animal-acute, can pick out a thousand chemical messages which other humans cannot consciously detect.

Whatever he saw in me pleased him, for he smiled.

"Whose are you?" he asked me.

A voice out of memory—it startled me, made the words slow in coming. "S . . . Sechaveh's, Lord." I saw his medallion, corrected myself. "Kaim'era."

"And your name?" His voice was rich, melodic . . . and familiar. An island of memory in the wasteland of my past. Stunned, I choked out an answer. "Venari, Kaim'era."

He looked me over, and I trembled. With heat? With fear? Yes, and with a thousand other reactions that had no place in my present life. "Forgive me . . ." I began.

"Does he take pleasure with you?"

My face burned in shame. "No, Kaim'era."

"Ah. Predictable, given Sechaveh. But a waste," His fingers caressed my face, brushed my neck and breast, left fire in their wake. "I'll borrow you for the night, if he agrees. Would that please you?"

I could feel my legs shaking, and wondered how long they would support me. "I . . . as you wish, Kaim'era."

"Tell him, then. I'll come to him tonight, to make a formal request. To taste what he doesn't have the sense to desire."

A moment more, I knew, and I would surely collapse. "Your name, Kaim'era? Who shall I say—"

"Zatar."

The name was familiar, a fragment from my missing past. Stunned, I nodded, bowed, backed carefully away from him. My only hope was that my legs would support me long enough for me to get away safely.

He wanted me! I exulted, as I broke into a run for home. And beneath that a growing certainty: *I knew him before.*

I was punished when I returned home; my Mistress saw to it personally. Sechaveh demands perfection from his women, a curious thing from a man who considers women by their very nature incapable of perfection. That day it suited his whim that the more primitive physical tortures be applied, and so I was whipped soundly, and rather than recover soon after, as more modern punishments allow, I was forced to take my bleeding flesh to bed with me and learn to live with the pain. I did not speak to him of Zatar; I would not mix such pleasure—or promise of pleasure—with the torment of Sechaveh's service. And I was afraid that his name, like all other fragments of memory that had returned to me, would be cause for further "treatment."

But I dreamed of him. How I dreamed! That marvelous face drew close in illusion, and, free of my pain in a world of my own devising, I reached for him. They mystery of Man was to be revealed to me, a mystery that concerned me even more than that of my identity. But even as my hands reached for him, I awoke with a suddenness that told me I had not done so by accident.

There were voices in the distance, coming from the forehall. Loud voices, and hostile. I crept from my mat and looked out into the hallway adjoining my sleeping quarters; no one was about. With care I crept toward the central House. The closer I came, the more I could hear of what was transpiring.

It was him; the timber of his voice had awakened me. Again I was struck with its familiarity. I held my breath as I listened.

". . . and done with this nonsense," he was saying.

"This 'nonsense,' as you put it, is my own affair. According to the bargain we made—"

"Informal."

"But binding! She is *my* slave, Zatar—and for the million I've paid out, she'd better remain so. I don't want her tasted."

"That is the most senseless—"

"I don't have to explain myself to you. We made a bargain. It cost me enough that it should be kept. The woman is my property and I don't want her tasted. That is *my* pleasure, and like it or not it has precedence over yours. I've listened to your request. I've heard your arguments. The answer is *no*."

My heart was pounding. A millon? Had he paid a million sinias for me, or spent them doing . . . what?

Their anger spent, they were too quiet for me to hear them. I stayed where I was until the footsteps sounded on the wooden flooring, until the door shut and locked behind him. Alone. I was alone again, as always.

I will not have her tasted.

He had *wanted* me.

I leaned against the wall, ignoring the pain from my whipscored back, eyes shut tightly against the flow of tears that I felt was imminent. The nights I had lain awake tormented by doubt—the days I had wasted on futile questions! No man had wanted me. No man had *ever* wanted me. Suddenly that was revealed to be, no, not the natural state of things, but the result of countless bribes and maneuverings. Why, Kaim'era Sechaveh—*why?*

I forced myself to return to my room, to close myself away in that space that was my only refuge. I managed to choke forth a single word; if two had been required, I don't think I could have managed them.

"Mirror."

The appropriate space glossed over with reflected light. I stood before it. With trembling hands I let my shift fall over my shoulders and drop from my body. How many times had I looked myself over, wondering what was so wrong with me hat I had never inspired a man's desire, or even received one's anonymous lust? Now it was with a different eye that I saw myself.

Was this body so displeasing? I ran my hands over it and had to answer: no. There was nothing wrong with me that wasn't also wrong with other women. That is to say, before the Braxaná, what alien or commoner can be beautiful? We are all flawed when compared to them. But as alien humans went, I was well-proportioned—if not generously, nevertheless sufficiently for a man's interest. Yet in the fifteen zhents of my current identity no man had wanted me, demanded me, or, as happens so often in the ranks of slaves, simply taken me.

And now I knew this was no coincidence. To be sure, I had suspected it. Chastity is alien to Braxin society, but still one is hesitant to imagine a conspiracy of such an immense scale as was active here. Had he bribed every man on this moon to leave me alone—and was that why I had always been kept on Zhene, never taken to surface? I was chilled by the truth as the pieces fell into place. On the moon there would be a limited number of men, all of them settled in Braxaná Houses or themselves of the Master Race. Such could be bribed, and clearly had been so. Oh, toward what end had he designed this misery!

I sobbed myself to sleep.

And dreamt.

Golden hands dancing over controls labeled in an unseen tongue. The glory of the Void without obstruction, the perfection of planned action becoming realilty.

A hand on my shoulder.

I turn about suddenly—who could be here with me, sharing my dream and my death and my loneliness?

Zatar.

Not right, not right. Something about him doesn't belong here, and I shield the controls with my body as if he would harm them. He tries to draw me to him; I am torn between my sworn duty and the fire which suddenly burns to life in the private recesses of my body. Sparks begin to play across the control board. I scream: "No! Not yet!" The end is too early, too early! I try to break free of him, to smother the growing flames, but his grip is firm and his caress undeniable. The fire grows about us, in me. I am screaming, and cannot say just what is the cause of it.

I awoke. By my side sat a figure dressed in sleeping-robe and nightgloves. It took me a moment to recover my bearings, and to identify the figure as Sil'ne, Sechaveh's Mistress. My heart still beating wildly, my face flushed with the heat of my dream, I tried to pull myself together.

"I heard you cry out," she said quietly. "The dream?"

I nodded, then shook my head no. "A dream. Not that one." I shivered with the force of unaccustomed falsehood; a day ago I would not have dared lie to her.

"Tell me."

I feigned embarrassment; it was close enough to the truth. "I dreamed of Zatar," I whispered.

"Ah." She stood. "They're allies, you know. Things may change. . . ." She looked closely at me, no doubt noting the signs of frustrated longing which were written all over me. "Do you need to be drugged?" she asked.

"No," I said meekly. "I'll be all right."

"Sechaveh wouldn't like to be awakened."

I shuddered. That had happened once, and I had barely survived his wrath in the morning. "I know, Mistress. I'll be careful."

She watched me for a moment as though analyzing my own reaction to those words. I had lied but evidently lied well; with a nod at last she left me, and the darkness—and the longing—closed in again.

In the morning I was summoned before my Master.

I trembled as I approached the door to his library, where I had been instructed to meet him. "Venari," I whispered. The computer digested that and then parted the door.

I entered, eyes lowered, and abased myself. He watched in silence, then rose from his seat behind the library console and walked over to me.

In size and power he towered over me. "Kaim'era Zatar has requested you."

I looked up hopefully. It was the first deception I had ever practiced upon my Master; he must never know that I had overheard their confrontation.

He smiled, an expression not without cruelty. "My answer was no."

Realizing that he had called me here so he could relish my disappointment, I let the anguish of the night before wash over me again. The misery, the fear, the uncertainty—it was all mine once more. My expression, reflecting that inner turmoil, pleased him immensely. He waited a short while longer in silence, making it clear to both of us that I did not dare defy him.

At last he turned from me. "Go back to your work."

I did so.

I dreamed the new dream often after that, but I learned not to cry out in my longing as I had once learned not to cry out in fear. Both could be fatal in this House and I had no wish to die. Sil'ne questioned me occasionally but seemed satisfied that I hadn't dreamt of the golden egg again, which seemed to comprise the sum total of her concern. At night I tried to sleep long enough to know the consummation of Zatar's embrace, to have that satisfaction, if nowhere else, at least in my dream-state—but the anguish and memory associated with my desire never failed to awaken me, and my last thought was never of him, but of the golden egg whose very meaninglessness was painful to me.

So my life passed for many, many days.

It was Sil'ne's custom to change our duties periodically, so that from time to time we would be working different parts of the House and its grounds. I think she did this partly to save us from Sechaveh, for he never knew quite where to find us when wrath overtook him; by the time she had fetched us he had usually calmed down somewhat. He hated her for it, but he hated her for everything: she was a woman, and therefore an enemy. If he could have done without her services he would have; Braxaná custom being what it was, however, he didn't have that option. The balance between them was extraordinarily tense: she, determined to maintain an acceptably traditional House, he, determined to vent his whims upon that entity regardless of consequences. I would rather have died than be in her gloves.

Some time after Zatar's visit—but no more than tenths later as far as my soul was concerned, for I dreamed of him nightly—I was assigned to the forehouse. There, while picking up after an emotional and somewhat messy business meeting, I heard a bit of conversation from the outer hallway that burned itself immediately into my awareness.

". . . your Azean doing?"

"As I planned. Did you anticipate otherwise? I have no doubts—"

A door hissed shut as they entered a conference chamber, and the House's automatic soundproofing concealed the rest of their conversation. I listened for a while longer, in case they should emerge again, but eventually I was forced to return to my work, and ponder their words in silence.

An Azean in Sechaveh's House? I could not imagine it. Why would one be here? Where would he be kept? What use would be made of him in this private place, that could not be accomplished better elsewhere? Even Sechaveh's penchant for torture seemed too trivial a use to make of one of the enemy. A captured Azean would have useful military inforation, wouldn't he? Why would he be sold—or given—to one individual?

The question distracted me from my work, and in the days that followed I realized I was going to have to do something about finding an answer. Surely the matter was simple enough; had only to ask the House computer for whatever information it had on the matter, and work deductively from that point. I waited until one day's work took me into the library, bided my time until all others had left the room, and approached the console.

Sechaveh's House, I instructed it. *Population statistics, by race.* Such information should be available even to a slave.

After a moment it answered me.

POPULATION OF THE HOUSE OF SECHAVEH
FREE/HIRED/ENSLAVED
CATEGORIZED BY (DOMINANT) RACE OF ORIGIN
(HUMANS ONLY)

BRAXANÁ, PUREBRED	1
BRAXANÁ, OTHER	14
BRAXIN, COMMON/MIXED	397
ALDOUSAN	54
R'LEGAN	3
DAKKAR	2
V'NASHT	61
ARANAKE	12
OTHER: WITHOUT CLEAR RACIAL DEFINITION/ SPECIAL CASES	23
SEE RECORDS BY INDIVIDUAL	

There was no Azean in the House of Sechaveh.

I looked at the list again. Had I made an error in interpreng it? No, Azeans did not intermate, therefore no Azean would be "without clear racial definition." That left only special cases—

I turned the console off.

For a long time I sat still, trying not to think. Perhaps if my last treatment had been successful, I would simply have shrugged off this problem as none of my business and returned to my work; as it was, the underpinnings of my amnesia, already weakened by half-memories of Zatar and the desire he inspired within me, were beginning to give way. I could *almost* remember . . . what? Had I known this Azean? Had he played some part in my accident, and thus become linked to my amnesia?

For as long as I remained awake that night, these questions haunted me. When at last I slept, there was still no peace—for I dreamt.

. . . tears which drench my face and the memory of a beautiful man with sun-gold skin and rich white hair, and a goal we shared that meant the galaxy to us, that took him away from me one terrible, bloody nightshift.

I want to die. I want to be with him!

Zatar holds me, smiling his pleasure, and those flawless black eyes catch and command mine. "An experiment," he whispers, and though his breath warms me I am also repelled. "To take a woman with a heritage of moderation and see if environment alone can force her to join the truly living. To see if a sex drive can be awakened where scientists have designed it to be absent. And to torment her with the cruelest blow of all—to awaken this hunger by frustrating it into existence—a special agony she was designed to be immune to. Sechaveh versus the best of Azean science. Observe!"

He commands and I turn. Gripping my shoulders, he forces me forward. "Mirror!" he commands, and it is before me. I hold my hands before my face . . .

. . . golden hands over the controls . . .

and he bids it to reflect. It does.

I, I am the Azean.

Liel!

I am awake, my body drenched in cold sweat. My mind is suddenly free of its drug-induced bonds, my memory struggling to be active again after its long sleep. It has all come back to me now—oh, the pain of it! Liel dying, and I with nothing to live for. I would give my life for Azea, I would splatter in glory across the stars and take with me the very center of Braxin knowledge and communication, and join my loved one forever.

And Zatar . . . yes, I knew him! I sat opposite him at the diplomatic table, when he dueled with words in that complex tongue of his and a half-dozen translators, myself among them, watched his every move, analyzed his slightest change of expression, in the hope of adding some insight to Starcommander lyu Mithethe's observations. I sat by her side, watching him—captivated by those eyes, which held such power and promised such violence that one had to fight not to cringe before them, hating him and admiring him as I fought to curb his advantage.

The memories return now, faster and faster, and my mind is flooded with a cacophony of information. Liel, my precious Liel, leaving with the fighters and dying in a burst of pyrotechnic glory—my own hunger to die, for I could not live alone—the hatred of Braxi, which runs too hot in my blood for me to give up life without a last blow at the enemy. Nightshift after nightshift I studied, going over details of the Citadel, the B'Saloan guard station,

Braxaná mentality—everything I could get my hands on. The Star-commander encouraged me. Though she could not share a love so strong that to be separated from one's adored was worse than death, she could sense the determination within me, and she helped me channel it where it belonged—into vengeance.

I studied what little information we had on the B'Saloan station again and again, probing for weaknesses. And I found them. Approached at this velocity, from this angle, under these conditions . . . see? The forcefield will overload, there will be weakness in this part of the field for just so long, and a specially built ship might manage to get through . . . it was all there. I proved it to her with numbers, and she agreed to let me go.

And so I designed my ship—a suicide vessel, designed to do one job and one job only. Even if I had wanted to return, it would not have been possible; the alterations required to allow me to breach Braxi's forcefield and that of the Citadel (my ultimate target) did not allow for self-preservation

The Citadel. Home of the Kaim'erate, a golden satellite which contained not only the Hall of the Kaim'eri but also the main storage banks and operating center of the Braxin Central Computer System (that vast network of mechanical semi-intelligence that stored all information and regulated all commerce within the borders of the Holding). So immense an undertaking had its building been, and so effective the result, that some civilizations willingly took on the yoke of the Braxaná in order to have access to the System.

If the Citadel were destroyed—or even damaged—it would be catastrophic for the Holding.

I intended to destroy it.

There was one more thing I had to go through before I could leave, and she called in a Probe to manage it. The nightmares I experienced while the fabric of my memory was analyzed, dismembered and reformed, are things I would rather not repeat; the result was that whatever military secrets I had shared as an officer of the Conqueror were buried beyond recall, their mnemonic associations permanently severed, so that neither conscious will nor drugged inquisition might ever force me to betray my people.

Ready at last, I departed.

A tiny ship, designed just so, can slip between the Braxin star-lines without being noticed. So it was that I pierced the enemy's domain, gathering speed as I went. Nothing could detect me quickly enough to prompt useful action, and so I went unhindered. I reached the proximity of the B'Saloan system, planned my approach, and struck. The sheer force of my entry would overload the static defense field that guarded the system, I was certain of that.

But we had all underestimated the Braxins. These are people for whom war is not an isolated event, but a state of being. They do not assume, as the Azeans do, that there are things man will not try. They expect warriors to attempt the irrational, and design their defenses accordingly.

Who can say what I struck, beyond the twelfth planet of B'Salos? It was not the static field I had anticipated. It was something that *gave* with me, and therefore did not overload; I missed Braxi by a hairsbreadth and hurtled out into the enemy Void. They tracked me down, eventually; no hard task, since my life-support was down and I carried no defense machinery. And they brought me back to Braxi—and to this. This body, this reality—and this one man who, through his vain insistence upon his own sadistic pleasure, broke the bonds of my memory and gave me back myself again.

I call up the mirror. My body is strange to me, a creation of foreign surgery that has no relation to the form I once wore. But the hatred inside me is unchanged, and so I am the same woman after all.

It will be no hard thing for me to leave the House. Escape is an irrelevant concept; on Braxi's moon, where is there for a runaway slave to go? There is no point in locking anyone inside their House, and Sechaveh hasn't bothered to do so. I thank Hasha he chose to bring me here. On Braxi, or elsewhere, the problem would have been quite different.

In the place of my sleepwear I put on a sturdy shift which can stand the chill air of Zhene's dark tenths. I regret that I have no weapons, but only a fool would approach the House arsenal without proper clearance. I'll make do without.

Indecisive wisps of plans are forming and unforming within me, but one thing is certain: I must act before morning. I can't pretend to be an alien slave, now that I know the truth about myself; Sechaveh would see through such a pretense in an instant. I must act, and quickly.

I enter one of the guest rooms as silently as possible, and lift such small objects as I can reasonably carry. The storerooms are sealed and the kitchen likewise; I have no access to tools save where my ingenuity makes them available. I hope that these things will do. And I thank the Academy for insisting that we learn to function without advanced tools and weapons (although it's true, I cursed them at the time).

With a look of *I belong here* firmly fastened on my face, I leave the House of my bondage. The guard at the door nods to me and makes a note of my exit; by the time the Kaim'era rises I must be far gone from here, for he will read the threat inherent in my departure and set out in immediate search. And I don't doubt that he can find me. He is a monster, damn him, but efficient, and he knows human psychology better than I would like to give him credit for.

In the meantime, I must trust that self-assurance is a universal language. I do not sneak stealthily down the broad Zhene streets, but make my way with a firm stride that speaks of my right to be there. Of those few who are about, no one notices me. I am a slave going about my business; the only thing that can give me away is my own unease, and that is something I refuse to exhibit.

Tense, planning, I make my way to the nearest port. The Kaim'eri are in the habit of commuting—and entertaining guests—via private landing fields adjacent to their Houses. Nevertheless there are other vehicles that must come to Zhene, and these are stored directly beneath the moon's circular gravlocks. It's no hard task to find one, although the walk is long. The silver circle ahead of me beckons, promising freedom. I refuse to believe that an intelligent, careful woman can't get off this pile of glorified rock alive—particularly someone with as strong a background in stellar technology as I have. I will find a way, of that I am certain.

I only wish I had some inkling of what that might be.

There are perhaps a dozen ships in the port; with care and in silence I approach them. I see no guards. Again, what need for them? What need have the Braxaná to steal, and what freedom have their leash-bound slaves to do so?

Suddenly cold, I put my hand to my neck and feel the slender ring there, my neuroleash. Hasha, I had forgotten. If I step outside my assigned area the damned thing will flood my body with enough pain to incapacitate me, and a signal will go off to alert

Sechaveh to my whereabouts. I'll have to get it off soon, or else neutralize it somehow. But first things first.

Hidden in a convenient shadow, pressed against a cargo ramp, I observe the ships before me. Seven will not serve my purpose; they are too large, or too foreign, or too likely to be guarded efficiently. I need something small, not terribly valuable, a ship whose owner wouldn't anticipate theft—and one I can figure out how to fly.

I choose my craft, step forward . . . and then stop.

Once before I underestimated them and paid the price for it. Am I so certain now that there is no trap here, if not for me then simply for any slave attempting escape from the moon's confines? It would be very much like them, I realize, to leave a ship here for just that purpose, carefully designed to appeal to someone with a specific set of needs.

Regretfully, I step back and reconsider.

There are a handful of starcraft left to choose from, no one of them any better or worse than the others for what I intend. I decide to choose one at random (I am, after all, adaptable) and thus thwart any plans they might have made based upon anticipation of my needs. At least chance will be with me.

I choose. Checking one last time to see that the port is truly deserted, I approach my choice and study it.

I'll have to circumvent the security system entirely—the damned handplates that the Braxins use are too complex for me to falsify an ID. Somewhere on this vessel, as on all starcraft, there must be an exterior access, a means to override the security system in case of emergency. It takes me some time to find it; the ship's design is alien to me and access plates are meant to remain hidden from anyone except an engineer. Fortunately for me, that was once my occupation.

Footsteps; I hide behind the bulk of my vessel and pray that those approaching have another craft in mind. Guards—two of them—look over the field and then, satisfied by the relative quiet, leave. I suppose it's a sufficient enough review, given the likelihood of crime on Zhene. Won't that change, though!

I locate the hidden pressure-points on the access plate and depress all four with my fingers, simultaneously. A thin sheet of pseudometal drops into my hand. Behind it is a small opening in the ship's hull, in which racks of macrosized circuitplates are stacked in all directions. I break the fasteners open and pull a plate-

landing mechanism. No good. I pull a few more and, reading meaning into their intricate patterns, get an impression of the order they're stored in. Which should put the security system—I pull a plate—here.

Well, it sort of looks like one.

My hands are shaking. All right, so I have no idea what the plate for a Braxin lock should look like. Nevertheless, negative thinking will get me nowhere. There's a logic to stellar design which I was trained to interpret; also, it's a known fact that Braxin and Azean technology are identical in all but the most trivial details. I break open the plate and study it. The circuit in question should be (at the last minute I allow for the Braxin tendency toward lefthandedness and reverse my mental image) *there.* I pull out one of the items I brought with me from the House and carefully, very carefully, scrape off a minute bit of metal, then blow off my scraps and reseal the plate.

I put it back in place, reset the fasteners that lock it into the ship's override computer, and seal the access plate back over it. If I've made a mistake in judgment, I'll find out soon enough.

The entrance to the vessel is on the other side and a black plate, hand-sized, sits ominously beside it. With only a slight hesitation I press my hand against it. Now, if I disconnected the proper circuit. . . .

The door slides open.

Breathing a sigh of relief, I enter. The door closes behind me, the lights automatically coming on as I enter each section. The control panel is foreign but not undecipherable.

However, that's not my immediate concern.

"Computer?" I ask tentatively.

RESPONSIVE.

Get this miserable collar off me. "I need . . . a personal forcefield, microtools. . . ." I list anything and everything I can think of that might prove helpful. It instructs me where on the ship all this can be found.

I believe that with the parts in the personal field I can neutralize the neuroleash . . . Hasha help me if I'm wrong. The damned thing is hard to take apart but eventually—there. I lay the pieces out before me.

Right.

I put some of the pieces back together, not necessarily in the order I found them. The field itself is close in theory to what I want. What I come up with is a strange-looking gadget indeed, and it's with more than a little doubt that I fasten it onto the thin band around my neck and activate it.

Nothing apparent happens—which is as it should be, but still isn't very reassuring.

With a muttered prayer I slip the forceshears about the band and turn on the blades. The collar is severed easily and falls from my throat, inactive. I shudder, only now considering that if I had failed to deactivate it the very act of removing it would have killed me.

I take my seat before the control panel. Logic dictates the power source would be here, the field control *there* . . . I study the dials and reassess a few first impressions. Within a few minutes I believe I have grasped the thing enough to risk flight. I do so.

The small ship lifts easily from the moon's surface and maneuvers with commendable grace to the lock above us. Nice design, I decide.

DO YOU WANT AUTOMATIC DRIVE?

I start, unaccustomed to computers that initiate conversation. "No. Manual only, please."

DO YOU WISH ME TO REQUEST A STARLINE ASSIGNMENT?

Oh, Zephra, that's right! "Do we have to have one?"

We are entering the lock, and my stomach does flip-flops as internal and external gravities rebalance themselves about me. IF YOU WANT TO GO SOMEWHERE, the computer answers me, the epitome of mechanical logic.

I'm thinking. . . . "Yes, request a starline. To Kurat, on Braxi." Getting that should be easy enough, from here.

The computer turns its attention away from me and toward, ironically enough, the Citadel. It gives me a moment to think. The starline assignment will get me past the lock; after that I can use manual override and go wherever I want to.

WE ARE CLEARED, it tells me.

I edge the craft forward and exit through the outer lock. Free, I am free! Oh, space has never looked so good!

I notice the main continent of Braxi passing beneath us, and I stiffen. Kurat, the capital of my tormentors. Momentarily, I wish that I carried some weapon of note with me, that I might drop it.

The logic that it would actually land somewhere in the Taklith Sea is little comfort.

I put the astrogator on automatic and set it to move toward an orbit out past Aldous; I need time to think, and I badly need rest. The forceshears cut easily through my heavy bracelets and I send the last vestige of my slavery into the autotrash.

The screen seems wrong, somehow.

I check our course; it isn't what it should be.

"How do I make this thing accept my course coordinates?" I ask.

I CANNOT ACCEPT YOUR COURSE COORDINATES.

"I put the controls on manual."

THE ENTIRE SHIP IS ON AUTOMATIC.

I ignore the tight, cold feeling that's beginning to grow in the pit of my stomach.

"Explain yourself."

I HAVE BEEN PREPROGRAMMED FOR YOU.

Hasha. I take a moment just to sit, my eyes closed, calming my nerves enough to talk. "By whom?" I ask it, dreading my Master's name.

I AM NOT AT LIBERTY TO SAY.

Exasperated, I demand, "What difference can it possibly make if I know?"

YOU CAN EXIT THE SHIP. YOU CAN ADJUST ITS CIRCUITRY. YOU CAN MAKE CONTACT WITH OFFICIALS OF THE HOLDING, OR ATTEMPT A MESSAGE TO YOUR OWN PEOPLE. WE CAN BE STOPPED IN FLIGHT—

"I get the picture." Now I'm angry. All this effort, just to be made captive again! "So just where are you supposed to take me?"

TO THE CITADEL.

I wasn't expecting that; it takes a moment to digest. "Why?"

I don't really expect it to answer but it surprises me by doing so. TO COMPLETE YOUR MISSION.

"What mission?"

THE DESTRUCTION OF THE CITADEL . . . HAVE YOU FORGOTTEN? I AM SUPPLIED WITH DRUGS TO STIMULATE RECALL IF—

"No." I can't believe this. Part of me observes the ship pulling into an orbit that must parallel Zhene's; the other part wonders if I'm dreaming. What would any Braxaná stand to gain from this?

"Your programmer would let me destroy the Citadel?" I ask, incredulous.

THE HALL OF THE KAIM'ERI, it responds, NOT THE CENTRAL COMPUTER SYSTEM. THE CITADEL ROTATES, AND YOU WILL STRIKE WHEN THE HALL IS BEFORE YOU, SO THAT THE COMPUTER FACILITIES WILL REMAIN UNDAMAGED. HOWEVER, AS YOU COULD NOT POSSIBLY HAVE HAD INFORMATION REGARDING THE CITADEL'S PERIOD OF ROTATION, INVESTIGATORS WILL CONCLUDE THAT MERE CHANCE FAVORED THE CENTRAL SYSTEM.

I am astounded. "What's the point?"

IT WILL BE DEMONSTRATED THAT YOU ARE, AND ALWAYS WERE, A DANGER TO THE HOLDING. THAT BECAUSE YOU WERE PERMITTED TO REMAIN UNBOUND ON ZHENE, THE HOLDING WAS PLACED IN PERIL. THE MAN RESPONSIBLE FOR YOUR CONTINUED EXISTENCE WILL BEAR THE WEIGHT OF THAT JUDGMENT, AND WILL COME UNDER SEVERE POLITICAL CENSURE.

"Sechaveh," I breathe, understanding.

THE KAIM'ERI RECOMMENDED THAT YOU BE DISPOSED OF AFTER YOUR INTERROGATION. SECHAVEH CONVINCED THEM TO LET YOU LIVE, IN ORDER THAT HE MIGHT INDULGE HIS MISOGYNY UNDER THE GUISE OF EXPERIMENTAL RESEARCH. HE GUARANTEED THAT YOU WOULD REMAIN HARMLESS.

I began to smile. "And when I strike at the Citadel—"

HIS JUDGMENT WILL BE QUESTIONED, AS WILL HIS PRIORITIES. IMMEDIATE RESULTS: POLITICAL EMBARRASSMENT AND LOSS OF UPPER-CLASS SUPPORT. A FORMAL HEARING REGARDING A MAN WHOSE SELF-INDULGENCE THREATENED THE SAFETY OF THE HOLDING. A CHANGE IN POLICY REGARDING PLEASURES SUCH AS HE PRACTICES. EVENTUAL RESULTS: A CHANGE IN CULTURAL FOCUS, SUBTLE BUT—MY PROGRAMMER BELIEVES—NECESSARY.

Now the golden Citadel is visible beyond the gleaming planet's edge. We are coming closer, and gaining speed rapidly. "The forcefields will stop us," I challenge tensely.

I HAVE BEEN GIVEN AN APPROACH CODE FOR DOCKING, USED BY THE HOUSE OF SECHAVEH. AFTER OUR

DESTRUCTION IT WILL BE ASSUMED YOU DISCOVERED THE CODE YOURSELF.

Hasha, it could work!

The satellite rises higher and higher above the planet's edge, visible to us now as we approach it. It is egg-shaped, the narrow end pointing downward, with a docking ring about its center. It's not quite like the Citadel of my dreams, but it's similar enough.

And this time I will not fail.

We're accelerating now and I fall backward as the force of it slams into my chest. Starcraft such as this have minimal capacity for compensation. Nevertheless I accept the pain, even welcome it, as a sign of my victory. No, I will not do what I came to do . . . but I will strike back at the man whom I've come to hate more than anything. It is a Braxin death.

"How did your programmer know I would choose this ship?" I demand.

THERE ARE TREMENDOUS DIFFERENCES BETWEEN THE BRAXIN AND AZEAN AESTHETIC SENSES, AND ALSO BETWEEN MILITARY AND CIVILIAN. SUBTLE ELEMENTS IN SHIPSHELL DESIGN GUARANTEED THAT THIS VESSEL WOULD BE YOUR CHOICE, ALTHOUGH YOU WOULD NOT BE CONSCIOUSLY AWARE OF THE REASONING BEHIND IT.

"I did indeed underestimate someone," I whisper.

The Citadel looms larger and larger before us. I can see tiny ships now, dancing around its outer ring. My blood is pounding in my veins, whether from the force of our forward thrust or my own exhiliration, I cannot say. Images rush before me—snatches of my life, so soon to be ended. And Zatar. I try not to think of him in that Braxin way which makes my blood run even faster, try to limit myself to enmity . . . but it is impossible. Apparently I have lived among the Braxins long enough to become tainted by their abominable culture. Yet I cannot regret having such feelings, for were they not the first step toward my mnemonic recovery? Fortunate coincidence, that I ran headlong into the only Braxaná who was part of my former life, and that he displayed an interest in me which forced me to question my present circumstances—

Coincidence?

Faster than my vision can take it in, the golden satellite fills the screen, rotating so that the Hall will face us when we strike. A glow envelops us and then lets us pass through; the computer has gained access to the great Braxin seat of power. We are past the ring now, and past the spokes that connect it to the Citadel proper. Alarm lights spurt across the golden surface, but they're too late! In triumph I lean forward, into our progress—the world is turning gold before me—

"Who programmed you?" I demand. I know what the answer will be.

THE HOUSE OF ZATAR.

Impact.

Viton: Nothing frustrates the true warrior more than political necessity.

NINETEEN

"Director, the Quezyan Councillor is here."

Torzha pushed aside her starcharts. "Send him in, please." With a touch to her desk's heat-sensitive surface she banished her starmaps, and their colorful displays faded from the air before her. A few quick movements sufficed to straighten up those items which remained, leaving the center of the desk uncluttered. By the time the Quezyan entered, the room was neat and the Director was standing.

"Welcome, Councillor." She performed an approximation of the Quezyan greeting-gesture and indicated the cushions which she had laid out at the far end of the room. The Heir Designate of the House of Non-Humans bent his serpentine body in graceful greeting and then warbled the trill which was his people's greeting call. He understood Azean, which was good; her understanding of Quezyan was less than perfect. She had been studying it since the Heir-Designate's appointment, but that had only been a short time ago, and the Councillor's native tongue was distressingly complicated. Since the Quezyan palate was incompatible with human language and vice versa, they would each speak their own language. Mechanical translation, among diplomats, was a last unpleasant resort.

"Will you be comfortable?" she asked him. One end of her office was a well-appointed conference chamber, whose, furnishings had been hurriedly adapted to suit the Quezyan's needs. Spreading his gliding wings in acceptance, the Councillor chose an acceptable cushion and curled himself upon its center, until a length of neck lifted his golden head to the height of a seated man. When he was clearly content, Torzha took, a chair and sat opposite him. A touch to a nearby console brought up forcewalls of a soothing beige, guaranteeing them privacy.

"May I offer you thrrr?" she asked.

The Quezyan stretched his gliding wings. "I would be pleased to accept."

She took up a ceramic bowl from a nearby table and placed it before him. Its aromatic contents, called the Water of Welcoming, quickly filled the room with scent.

He breathed in its vapors and then asked, "May I share this with you?"

She brought the bowl up to her face and inhaled the sweet, spicy odor. Quezyan tradition claimed that this particular combination of scents would imbue a creature with the Spirit of Reason. Although it did not affect Torzha as it did the Councillor, the mutual offering was an important part of Quezyan diplomacy. Setting the bowl aside—hoping that she hadn't neglected some fine point of Quezyan etiquette—Torzha assumed a human approximation of the Welcoming Posture and asked him, "How can I serve you?"

"May I speak?"

"Your counsel is welcome."

"I address you in military capacity, and as a Councillor of the House of Humans."

She frowned. "The latter title's honorary. If you want to speak to that body, you would be better off addressing its Crown directly."

"The time for that may yet come. I ask, are we private?"

"I had intended to record, Councillor. If you object. . . ."

"Forgive me. I rephrase: Are we *confidential?*"

She nodded solemnly. "Of course. I guarantee it."

He lifted a line of feathers, indicating satisfaction. "I recall the High-Councillor's illness."

"Yes; I mourn her suffering. Is she recovering well?"

"The T-san is far aged; even recovery won't bring youth again. She has decided to retire, and will set me on her throne in life. You perceive? In confidence, Director."

"I perceive," she answered. Indeed she did; the Heir-Designate's assumption of Crown duties would mean a drastic change in non-human policy, a change Torzha hadn't expected to have to deal with for years to come. The Quezyan was a notorious Pacifist, and rumor had it the House would follow his lead. The thought of having one fifth of the government pitted against the War was something that had already provided the Director with many nightmares. But she managed admirable control as she responded, "In confidence. I thank you for telling me. Is this what brings you here?"

"Concern is what brings me here. Concern for us, for you and me and the humans who rule; concern for the Empire. May I speak openly?"

She nodded. "I welcome your honesty."

"We in the House of Non-Humans are disturbed by what we perceive to be a new attitude regarding the Braxin-Azean conflict, the so-called Great War. Much debate has been devoted to this issue inside the House, and a few of the human Councillors have been approached—informally—on the matter. Concern grows, and the High Councillor cautions patience, but now her term ends and I am made acting Crown. It is my judgment to approach you in confidence and speak to you of these things. Is this acceptable? We can wait until the debate is made public, if you prefer, and go through the proper channels at that time—but I fear the damage that might be done to our sense of unity in the meantime. I desire that we cooperate. You perceive?"

She did, barely. The Quezyan language was hard to follow, but she was recording the meeting in order to review it later; the fine points of his speech could be studied at that time. "Your visit is welcome," she assured him. "I would rather address such problems now than let them build to weaken the Empire. Speak openly, I encourage you. I listen." And she adopted (as well as she could) the Quezyan Receptive Posture.

"Our concern is this. We perceive the Empire to be an entity of peaceful intent. Is this not plainly stated in the Articles of Founding, in the Declaration of Purpose? Is not the very structure of Imperial government based upon the assumption that peace is the ideal state?"

Standard Pacifist argument; Torzha had heard it before. She countered it with her standard response. "Unhappily, circumstances dictate our action."

"Do they? We wonder, Director."

She had studied his background, and so was not surprised by his sentiments. Quezaii was a peaceful world, located in a part of the Empire that rarely knew trouble. To the Heir-designate, and to most of his non-human colleagues, the War with Braxi was an abstract thing that lacked the power to inspire either fear or respect. A *human* affair, which had been prolonged indefinitely due to human obstinacy. "Azea is more than willing to pursue peace,

Councillor. The problem is that our enemy neither values peace nor keeps to its agreeents. Treaty after treaty is broken, and each time innocent men and women are made to suffer."

"Innocent *humans,* Director. Who choose to live in the shadow of war, and should be prepared to suffer the consequences. *We* do not settle in the War Border; therefore *we* do not require your protection. I contend that humanity thrives on conflict. Insofar as this concerns your own species, it's no interest of mine. But insofar as it affects the balance of our government, I must demand redress."

"There are over a thousand habitable planets inside the Border," Torzha answered, keeping her voice carefully even. "Rich planets, with resources that cry out for attention. Some of these haven't been in the line of battle for generations. Why shouldn't humans settle there? They know the risk; they take their chances. No one *wants* war, Councillor."

"Indeed? Then why was Braxi's last offer of peace refused?"

How could she hope to explain the Braxins to a non-human, when their nearest evolutionary kin could barely comprehend them? "One must consider Braxin motives," she explained, choosing her words with care. "In this case, it was the judgment of my senior negotiator that Braxi needed preparation time to counter our H'rett offensive, and so offered us a Peace—which we were *supposed* to accept with gratitude. To have done so would have negated our advantage in that sector, a high price for a year or two of non-aggression. The War will go on until one side triumphs, Councillor . . . that's the unhappy truth of it. In order to achieve *true* peace, we must pursue victory."

"Peace through war? I reject that concept, Director, and so do many of my colleagues."

I'm sorry, she wanted to say, *but that's the way it is.* "Experience has taught us that the Braxins have no desire for peace—"

"And so it will always be, do you say that? I answer that the war *can't* be won. The sides are too balanced, the resources virtually unlimited. Azea knows this. Someday Braxi will come to realize it, too, and will seek an end to this pointless conflict. And will you be open to them, at that time? We fear that the answer is no. Under current StarControl policy, an opportunity for peace would be lost in a fever of Azean conquest. Your primary duty-as set forth in the Edict of 3467—is to *end* the War, not to prolong it."

"Our primary duty is to defend the Empire," Torzha answered dryly. "Article five, Subsections one through twelve. StarControl policy defines Braxi as a major threat to the nation; we're bound by the Edict to attempt to eradicate that threat. It can't be neutralized by treaty; time has taught us that. For as long as Braxi exists, the Empire is in danger of attack.

"There is no doubt; the Braxins are as stubborn as the Empire's humans, we comprehend this. But you defend your position with external reasoning, and avoid the question of internal balance. If the Great War is ended by treaty, who will then rule the Empire? For centuries my Council has also refused to consider this. Now *I* do so. And I perceive that the Great War serves Azea in one very special way: it guarantees the supremacy of humans, and therefore Azeans, over the nations of the Empire. Consider that our five Crowns were once three: the Emperor, the House of Humans, and our own House. StarControl was an arm of the government, nothing more; not until 'temporary' martial law was declared in 3467 was the Director of the military anything greater than a servant of the state. And not until the War Border became a longstanding problem, with its complex loyalties and periodic reproductive violence, did the Council of Justice command any more respect or power than a collection of social philosophers deserved.

"If the Great War ended tomorrow, wouldn't the purpose of the Edict be fulfilled? StarControl would come under the Emperor again, and Diplomacy would be given back to the Combined Council of Nations—where it belongs, I believe. The Council of Justice would continue to reign until the home race was stable once more, and then after that . . . who would need them? *Three* Crowns, Director: that was the Founders' plan. One human, one non-human, and an Azean figurehead. We accepted that, my people, when we joined this Empire. We'll endure two additional Azean Crowns for as long as we nave to. But we wonder now: if we're given an opportunity for peace, will the military *allow* us to give up this war? Power is addictive, Director. Can you say this situation has no effect upon your policy?"

"It has no effect upon my policy," she said coldly. "I have a goal to accomplish. Everything I do, I do toward that end."

"A lasting settlement with the Braxin Holding?"

The destruction of Braxi, and everything it stands for! "The end of the War, Councillor. However that can be accomplished."

"I perceive that words are easy, Director. As they've always been. What the non-humans require now is *action*, to demonstrate StarControl's sincerity."

She stifled her anger. *I invited him to speak openly,* she reminded herself, *I should have remembered that the Quezyans aren't known for their subtlety.* "And what would you suggest?"

"Simply a demonstration of faith. As an example, your senior Border negotiator favors war; perhaps that can be changed? Or another can take the post. A gesture, you perceive?"

She did indeed. The Quezyan imagined calumny between herself and Anzha, designed to prolong the War and keep Torzha in power. Not unreasonable, had the two been Braxin; totally unreasonable, given who they were.

Fools! she thought. *Do you* know *how the Braxins treat nonhumans? Don't you realize what would happen to your precious Council if the empire were overrun?*

"The senior negotiator acts upon my orders," she told the Councillor, "and I'm pleased with her service. But I will consider what you've said."

The Quezyan smoothed a violet feather. "The time for words is past," he warned her. "There *will* be action—if not yours, then mine. I tell you now, in confidence, to give you time to consider. I would far rather work out this problem in private, between two individuals, than allow it to divide our government."

How much time do I have? she wondered. She could postpone the Quezyan's coronation by demanding a review of his background, but that would only work for so long—and in the long run, it would make matters even worse between them. She could work on the Human Councillors—find out just how widespread this philosophy was, see how much influence the Pacifists commanded in the human House. There were things she could do; they all required time. She was no innocent when it came to internal politics, although she rarely indulged her skills. But if a radical Pacifist were going to be crowned . . . she needed time. *To clip his wings,* she thought darkly. *To make sure that he can't interfere with my work.*

"I'm grateful to you for coming," she assured him, and she assumed a soothing Posture. "I, too, would far rather work this out privately, than let it upset both the Crowns and the populace. I'll see what can be done to demonstrate StarControl's true intent. In the meantime, I welcome your counsel. Please forward my best wishes to the High Councillor, when you speak to her.

He opened his wings, an acknowledgment of leavetaking. "I am grateful to you, Director, for having heard me out on this matter. I believe I speak for the High Councillor when I say that the unity of the Empire is our primary concern."

"As it is mine," she assured him, and she passed him the bowl of thrrr.

Not until he was gone did she give vent to her anger.

"Damn!" She threw the thrrr into a waste receptacle, bowl and all. Why did the next High Councillor have to be a Pacifist? Why did he have to come into power now, when they were so close!

So close. . . .

I need time. She went back to her desk, turned on the starmap, and studied the Border. *Time.*

She needed to make some kind of gesture; that would quiet them, for a while. After that, the way the War was going, things would take care of themselves. Day after day, the Empire's position strengthened; Zatar was a problem, but not enough of one to keep them from eventual victory. Anzha would win the War for them yet!—if political necessity didn't get in her way.

Political necessity . . . there were a thousand and one responsibilities binding Torzha, and while military victory was the most important, it was not the most immediate. As one of the Crowns of Azea, she had a duty to preserve the unity of that state. And she had sworn a personal fealty to the Emperor; in theory, she served his will.

What would Pezh il say to her? *The War has raged for ten thousand years; it will not be ended tomorrow. We have a responsibility to maintain lines of communication between human and non-human, for those are the ties which will bind us when the War is over and done with. The Empire was Founded to unify, not to destroy; that must be our overriding priority.*

Damn.

She considered all her options, a wide range of conciliatory gestures that she might make. All noxious.

Peace. . . .

What had happened to the warrior she had once been? At what point along the line had she sacrificed the simplicity of her youth? She had never wanted power, would gladly relinquish it when the time came. *But in victory,* she promised herself. *I will turn in my Crown amidst the smoking ruins of the Citadel.*

One more Peace: an investment in purpose? Let the Council of Nations see for themselves the negative consequences. She would publicize each disaster, using her position to make sure the point was driven home. One more Peace, and—if she played it carefully—that could be the last. Forever.

Anzha, forgive me. I know it will be hard. In the end, we will benefit.

She began to compose a letter.

Harkur: You can remove undesirable emotions from society's repertoire by careful manipulation of cultural trends. You can revise your language so that a man has no means of expressing that which is forbidden; lacking a familiar label, he will eventually lose his grasp of the concept itself. You cannot, however, wholly excise emotions from a man's character and still expect him to be a complete human being.

TWENTY

Her finger is long and graceful and the nail at its end is perfectly manicured. A slender silver ring has been fitted so that it rests above the middle joint. Inscribed upon it in magnapatterns is a challenge once issued by a rival; the rival is no longer and the ring is but a memento. The finger hesitates, then pushes upward on the noiseless switch. The lights of the ship are extinguished and through the portals the stars shine brightly. B'Salos is behind them now, rapidly dwindling in the distance as they move faster and faster away from it. Their destination has no star to mark it and is a bleak, uncomforting prospect. But there is no other choice.

His breathing from the sleeping alcove is labored and erratic, but at least, it appears, he is sleeping. Perhaps, in the dark quiet of uninterrupted travel, there will be some peace for her at last. . . .

* * *

My Lord and Master—wrote Ni'en, Mistress of the House of Zatar—hard news has come to Braxi. I wish I could pretend to understand it; I can only hope that, hearing the details, you will make sense of it.

The tsank'ar has broken out here. The symptoms are extreme for the virus: unusually high fever and bronchial congestion are the worst of it, and there are a variety of lesser symptoms that aren't dangerous in themselves but that complicate recovery. Nevertheless, how serious a threat can the tsank'ar be? I've had this strain myself; it passes in a few days, or at the worst in half a zhent, and barring complications caused by attendant illnesses causes no lasting harm. So I thought. But now there are reports coming out of Montesekua's Virology Center that this is due to be an epidemic of new proportions; the tsank'ar virus, they say, hasn't undergone such a major mutation in centuries.

And the Braxaná are dying of it. First there was Sadar, of our House, and then Kaim'era Bamir fell ill and died, leaving his own House in unexpected chaos. The Braxaná are locking themselves away, in some cases fleeing the planet entirely. The Kaim'eri met one last time and have disbanded until the trouble passes. I knew of the Plague in so many words, Zatar, but this? I see fear in faces where I have never seen a sign of weakness before. Tell me what this is, my Lord, in order that I may serve you. For I realize now that I am from a different world entirely, and that frightens me. What is this thing?

* * *

Many days have passed now, punctuated by short snatches of fitful sleep and detours to dodge Braxin guardships. *They must never know,* she has thought, *that a woman commands his movement. They would execute even a Braxaná for such effrontery.*

Now he twists and turns in the agony of Plague-fever. She has tasted it herself and can sympathize; she also know there is nothing she can do to ease the delirium that grips his soul. When he's awake she smooths his black hair back without tenderness, carefully and always without tenderness, and feeds him a bit more of the potion that keeps him oblivious to his surroundings.

Why are you doing this? she asks herself. *Why are you risking so much for this man?*

She does not answer. She dares not.

* * *

My Mistress—wrote Zatar—It's good that you wrote when you did. There was a particularly fierce battle in the Ornar'n sector which left both our forces limping home and, certain that even the great Iyu Mitethe would take some time to recover, not to mention my being without a viable attack force until lengthy repairs could be made, I had thought of leaving Selov in command

and coming home for a time. Now that the Plague has come, however, such action is impossible, and will remain so for a long, long while.

What can I say to you, regarding such a time as this? We live with this fear from our birthtime and know it all our lives. You know the virus; once a year it may briefly discomfort you, but it is on the whole nothing for commoners to fear. Not so with us. We watch it mutate every year of our lives and live in perpetual fear of the results; we turn to science, quarantine, *anything,* but remain helpless before the inevitable epidemic. And now this.

We have no immunity to the tsank'ar, Ni'en. We bred that in when we bred other weaknesses out, and because only one particular strain in a thousand is capable of laying us low, it took us a millennium to realize what we had done. And by then it was too late. This is the price we must pay for the Shlesor, that misguided indulgence in "eugenics" which guaranteed our strength and beauty—and no, if the Plague is loose on Braxi I will not come home.

Now listen to me carefully; I have planned for this, and though its arrival is unusually early, still it is useful to me. I place you in command of my House, without reservation; my seal on this ring will be your proof of that. You will have to act, and you will have to give orders directly, and do all this without hesitation if the House is to be saved. The ravages of the Plague are seconded only by Plague-politics, of which you will soon enough have a taste. You must be ready to act without consulting, me; the distance between us puts too long a delay on communication. Remember: I count on you, and will support you in everything.

Bring my purebred children into the House and watch over them yourself; if you've truly had the Plague, as you say, then you're no danger to them now. Quarantine any member of my House who shows the least sign of sickness. Let their only contact be with those few who have survived it. *There can be no exceptions.*

Soon after this reaches you, I expect that Braxi and Zhene will both come under strict quarantine, as well as any other planets where the sickness is prevalent. This wreaks havoc with commerce and we must do the best we can to compensate; do what you can with our trade contacts to keep them solvent during this disaster. Spend what money you must in bribery to keep the alien merchants happy; only remember, no matter who threatens what, all Houses on Braxi are in the same position, and all are equally incapable of getting trade cargo out of the B'Saloan system. You will find a list of merchants and officials filed under "Plague" in my private files, with notes on pressure tactics to be applied in time of emergency. I have put them there for just such a time; do not hesitate to use them.

Watch especially closely my rival Houses, those of Yiril, Delak, Lerex, and Saloz. These men are my most skilled rivals in politics and finance, and it is from them that we can anticipate interference. Also, be wary of Sechaveh. After that Venari fiasco he's no great political threat, but there's a lot of hostility between us and I don't doubt he'd strike at me for the sheer pleasure of doing so. It is a Braxaná custom, during Plague-time, to cut at the roots of a rival's house.

Send Feran to me. We must have peace, alas, or the Holding will crumble from both ends inward, and we must have it before the Azeans realize why we want it. In the old days there would have been no questions—they were so anxious for a treaty—but now, with the Starcommander acting as senior negotiator for the entire Border, and with the Plague biting at our heels, we dare not risk delay. Feran knows them; more important, he knows *her*. Together we can manipulate the enemy, and buy time for our people. In addition, she and Feran will be forced to deal with each other directly, and I have suspicions regarding the two of them . . . but no, not until I'm certain will I speak of that.

Keep well, and wield this power to my ends. I rely upon you.

* * *

He cries out incoherently in the grips of his delirium. She has not slept in many days, and has eaten very little. The sound of his suffering pierces through any wall of sleep, causing nightmares that shatter her rest. There are moments when she regrets, and must remind herself again that mere doctors could do nothing for him. There are moments when she fears and must remind herself again that he must live, he must live, he must live at any cost. And she must never question why.

Once, the sounds become words, and the words a cry of anguish. He opens his swollen eyes and seems to recognize her. "My children—" he whispers. She lowers her eyes. "Dead," she says. Their relationship has always been one of simple honesty; she wishes now she knew how to lie to him. "My House—" he asks, his voice thick with fever. "Gone," she answers. "Abandoned. What's left must be rebuilt from scratch."

He winces as if in pain, although the sharp pains ended days ago. "Then I've lost everything," he whispers, in a voice as cold as death. "Everything! My children, My House, my power . . . what is left to me? All is gone, gone. . . ."

She turns away. It's right for him to cry, for he is dying a horrible death and has lost the only proof of his fertility. It's not right for her. Yet she feels the tears coming, alien things to Braxaná eyes, and fights them so that she need not answer the question they force upon her.

He has lost everything. Everything?

* * *

My Lord and Master—wrote Ni'en—if I've taken a long time to contact you, it's because I've devoted every waking moment up to this one to dealing with your orders. Feran has left and should arrive soon at the military base orbiting Akkar—and just in time, for quarantine was announced immediately after he departed. It will be hard to communicate with you without great delay after this; I can't send the rings directly, but must transmit the text to a neighboring system and have it sent from there. How much should I trust to discretion this way? And should I fight for time on augmented transmission or send it underlight to the guard station outside B'Salos Twelve, and have it forwarded in hardcopy from there? In short, which do you trust more, and how much?

Y'sila is here, and two of your other daughters on Braxi

are due to arrive within tenths. Terak, sick, is fuming at your imposed quarantine, but is ill disposed to face you later if he disobeys; therefore he is compliant.

The Kaim'era Saloz is dead of the Plague, and his Mistress also. Most of his holdings were absorbed by Delak and Korov, but I was able to get a good share of his interest in the mines of Kest and I'm not so certain that some of Delak's new property can't be loosened from his grasp before his ownership is finalized. Lerex fled Braxi to parts unknown, just before quarantine was established; I am attempting to track him down. Sechaveh is under self-imposed quarantine. His House, obviously expecting you to pry while he is weak, is well guarded against my efforts. I will continue to try.

Regarding Yiril . . . this disturbs me greatly. His Mistress D'vra took ill and recovered—her line is strong in that manner, I understand—and resumed the running of his House. Then the Kaim'era caught the Plague. His bloodline, I understand, is particularly weak in this regard. I assumed (we all did) that D'vra would nurse him through it, being one of the few purebred Mistresses who could manage such a feat. Instead she has abandoned him and his House. My contacts inform me that over half the population of his estates are dead or dying, for most of his household had a goodly proportion of Braxaná blood in them. The House is falling to ruins, and although her hand could have saved it she has apparently broken quarantine and fled the system. I don't pretend to understand it—but then, did I ever really understand your people?

* * *

She steers through the rubble, her hands trembling. They should never have tried to stop her. They should have left communication to their computers, sexless machines that disguise their pilots' identities with mechanical monotones. What could she do but destroy them?

"Taz'hein,"she whispers, her voice shaking, "what have I done? I've killed men, I've killed Braxins, all to bring him to shame. . . .

* * *

My Mistress—wrote Zatar—you've done well, and I am pleased.

I'm sorry to hear about Yiril. It surprises me to feel this way, for we were rivals, but my respect for him ran very deep and I would have wished him a cleaner death. As for D'vra? There has never been anything between her and Yiril other than their House to my knowledge, and I knew him well. Even their sexual tastes differed so drastically that they never shared pleasure, outside of one Seclusion. Yiril had an extensive and powerful House and D'vra was a proud, capable woman. Still, that was all, and it's not much in the face of a Plague, my Mistress.

But the ramifications of what she's done, if she has indeed abandoned his Household and if he survives, are very grave. I don't need to tell you how much we depend upon the Mistresses of our Houses; you know it better than I could ever express, We have no contracts, no binding agreements, it's true—even so, she's set a dangerous precedent. If he should manage to live through this (and without a House to return to, I don't know if I'd wish that on him), she would be well advised not to return to Braxi, or any planet in the Central Region, for a long time to come.

Regarding Lerex, I would not be surprised if the matter were not already out of our hands. He has many rivals and his enemies are fanatic; I would not be surprised to hear of his "unexpected" demise. Forbidden things can become suddenly possible, under cover of Plague-time.

We are working toward a Peace; I am keeping a diary of our conferences, in order to go over them in detail later. The Azeans suspect something—*she* suspects something—but ten millennia of Plagues have taught us the value of secrecy, and no certain news has reached her. It is to our advantage also that the Plague has come so early this time; in another ten years, when it was due, she might have refused us any conference at all.

Feran has been invaluable. He knows them well and

has more patience than I at playing their word-games; in addition, the fact that he and I both speak Azean is not without its benefits when they wish to argue among themselves.

Oh, but to see her again, to be so close and unable to act! My blood rages within me at the sight of her, and surely she can feel it; but what can we do, bound by the chains of necessity? I long to fling the blessed treaty in their faces, to call for the death we both hunger for . . . but the Plague ties my hands and I force myself to act for the good of my people.

There is hatred between her and Feran, Ni'en. I can feel it at the conference table, as thick and as cold as though ice had grown between them. And there is also something else, which I had not expected. *Fear.* A terror that hides inside her, almost invisible beneath her facade of unfeeling competence; a trembling within him, so poorly concealed that I can feel its substance within myself, undermining my confidence along with his own. Are these things apparent to me because I know her so well, or because proximity reawakens that link which was once between us, allowing me to share her psychic vision? Or is it really that obvious? At any rate, there is more between them than I had anticipated. And I must understand it, if I am to use them both.

Be wary of Sechaveh; in his mind we were lone rivals until Venari struck at the Citadel, and he will always hate me for it. His House is the most deadly because he doesn't need to strike for power, merely for vengeance —and thus is dangerously adaptable. Take a look at Korov's holdings on Suzeran. I seem to recall he had some problem there. Do not only be cautious, but take advantage of the Plague for all it's worth. It's not only death to the Braxaná, but a call to Central politics that can make or break a household. I think you're beginning to see that.

Go for the augmented transmission if you can; I trust our relay in the military far more than the secretaries who man the B'Saloan guard station. But either way, be circumspect. Once our business goes through the hands of strangers we must be careful to speak little and avoid details. Any man can be bought, and prices are paid quickly in Plague-time.

* * *

She sits still for a minute, gathering her courage. She smoothes her gloves for the twentieth time, checks the position of her scabbard for the tenth. The mirror reveals an image which is thin and alien to her, but which should overwhelm any man unaccustomed to Braxaná splendor. She is tired, uncertain. She sways in coming to her feet and longs to relax. But the time for that is far distant; as she hears the footsteps approaching her lock from the station she has docked at, she stiffens automatically into the image of perfect arrogance. For once, it is false.

The outer doors, then the inner, slide open. And he enters. "Lady D'vra?"

He speaks her language poorly; his Azean tongue is ill-suited for it. Nevertheless, that was one of the conditions of the bargain. A Braxaná does not study in order to communicate with lessers.

Haughtily, she steps aside. A minimal gesture indicates the man in the alcove.

The medic steps into the ship and approaches the body. "Alive?" he asks.

"If not, I wouldn't be here."

He seems startled by the icy coldness of her voice; *what a pity,* she thinks, *he should have known to expect it.* He leans over the body. In that moment she hates him and all his kind with such a mindless fury that she almost draws the sword at her side and ends the charade then and there. But she dares not. She forces her hands to obedient stillness and promises herself: *later.* For now she must pretend. It does not come naturally, this kind of pretense—but she will have to learn.

He signals with a control box and a stretcher wheels itself into the ship's small confines. She moves forward to help him but he doesn't require it, and quickly he transfers the feverish body from one resting place to the other. He looks up at her and smiles; doubtless he is tying to be reassuring. "It's not too late," he promises.

"How fortunate," she says dryly. And she thinks: *For both of you.*

Walking behind the suffering Kaim'era, she follows them into the station.

* * *

My Lord and Master—wrote Ni'en—I have tried to carry out your orders well. The zhents are endless and each day the deathlist grows longer and longer. All three ports on the moon have been closed to incoming and outgoing traffic, and both Braxi and Aldous are effectively quaranfined.

By now you must know of the revolutions on Erengarr and Tziri. I have heard that Tziri will be destroyed as a gesture, being the least valuable of the two. The Kaim'eri believe that a reminder of Braxi's willingness to destroy an inhabited planet at a moment's notice will suffice to abort other potential problems.

What I do not understand, my Lord, is why this weakness hasn't destroyed itself? Those who have it the worst die of it; why haven't the centuries bred stronger survivors?

News has come that Lerex suffered Plague delirium on Astargall and plunged to his death from an airborne platform. Given what you told me and what my research has turned up regarding his House, I'm not surprised—and no one else seems to be, either. But what proof is there for prosecution? And more important, in Plague-time who cares enough to bother?

I've managed to waylay some funds going from the House of Sechaveh to certain black marketeers. They're bitter, evidently, being denied their regular market, and he meant to bribe them into complacency; instead I will bring them under your wing, when the time is right. At the moment Sechaveh knows nothing, and if he should check into it he'll find out exactly what has been done—by the House of Lerex.

Lenar, of your House, has managed to get himself assigned to the Station and is acting as our go-between. I assume this is satisfactory?

Oh, and also—there have been three attempts to break your monopoly on the Darkon silk market, by Korov,

Saran, and Memek. All have failed. You should have told me this was going to happen, my Lord. I could have made more ambitious plans.

* * *

She looks up. As soon as she sees him enter she ceases to wring her hands, letting them fall with a false ease to her lap.

"You're done quickly," she ventures. It is a question.

"The process is complicated—"

She interrupts the coming explanation; she wants none of it. "But you *can* succeed."

He is startled, unaccustomed to such abruptness. "Yes, Lady. I believe I can."

"And you'll do nothing but what we agreed."

He looks puzzled by that. "Of course, Lady, if that's what you want. But once I have a carrier prepared and the body is ready to receive it, it's little enough trouble to add a bit more encoded information—"

She stands; she is trembling with rage. "His person is not to be toyed with, *Azean*. Bad enough I have to subject him to your meddling in the first place! Do you realize that he would kill himself rather than submit to your science willingly? And I would agree with his reasons."

"I don't pretend to understand. . . ."

"I don't *ask* you to understand. I don't *care* if you understand." She points toward the treatment room, where Yiril's Body is being irradiated. "You touch one codon more than I've bargained for and you're a dead man. Understand that?"

There has never been a man she couldn't intimidate, and this one is no exception. Unnerved by her vehemence—and the obvious sincerity of her threat—he nods. "And when the time comes for your end of the bargain, you'll be equally cooperative?" His voice is uncertain but hopeful.

She nods curtly, hating him and his science and everything that's caused her to come here. Submit to his tests? Before that she would die, and take Yiril with her. And the man is a fool who thinks otherwise!

The Azean accepts her reassurance.

* * *

My Mistress—wrote Zatar—we have our Peace, for the duration. I think she knows the truth. Who can say what was in her mind as she signed? If she pressed forward in War to defeat our nation she might have cost me my House, and that wouldn't be a clean death. In the end our k'airth may have saved Braxi. Yet that alone does not seem as if it would be enough. Unfortunately, that very Peace which I longed to win keeps us apart from each other; the treaty is binding to her Azean soul and while it's in effect we can't meet in personal combat, as I think we both long to do.

Feran was invaluable and I tried to convince him to stay here with me, but he insisted upon returning to B'Salos, or at least its environs. I think, being foreign to our background, he underestimates the horror that his home has become. But the man is free and can do as he chooses. It would be a pity, though, to lose him now.

Can you even *ask* how this happened? Can you, who have lived among us for so long, doubt for a moment our ingenuity in engineering our own destruction? At this very moment the Zarvati, myself included, are cowering in the far corners of the Holding, waiting for the storm to pass. It will eventually, and we will return. Simultaneously, those bloodlines more likely to survive contact with the Plague are still on Braxi, fighting to maintain their household power and contracting the tsank'ar in the bargain. A good number of them will die of it. So you see, Ni'en, interstellar travel and the nature of our society combine to breed the weakness in, not out. And in truth, could anything but our own stupidity have brought our numbers down from the hundreds of thousands it once was to a mere—but no, I will not commit that to print.

I heartily commend all your actions. Dare I say, in the midst of this tragedy, that you seem to be enjoying yourself? Little did I know when I took you out of Sulos that time would mature you into such a worthy adversary! When I installed you as my Mistress I did so for reasons that had nothing to do with politics, but your growing acumen is commendable and the reports I have of your business dealings are impressive. For a man who cannot come home during the Plague, everything is in the hands of his Mistress. I consider myself very fortunate in you. We will conquer Braxi yet.

* * *

Blood—rivers of vengeful crimson flowing free on the sterile white floor, the stuff of life spewing forth from its owner; the smell and color of Death.

D'vra steps back from the body. Her Zhaor dripping spots of red about her feet, she surveys her work. Except for the human blood pouring from him, her victim looks like a badly gutted fish—a long gash cleaving him from above one ear through the face, throat and chest, across the stomach and, halfway through a thigh. After a moment she takes a bit of his cleaner sleeve and wipes her sword blade with two swift motions, then sheathes the weapon. The killing required no effort, merely a moment's release of that deadly hatred which had focused on him ever since her arrival. Was he psychic; did he see it coming? Or did he find it hard to distinguish between the desire to kill and the act of doing so, when there was only the barest thread of self-control separating the two?

She stands still for a moment, exulting in the simple animal pleasure of the kill. She hungers for a man, too, to finish it; somehow the action is less than complete without a man inside her to drive her raging blood to climax and fulfillment. It is unfortunate that the circumstances are unobliging.

The interior of the mobile station is still; only she and Yiril breathing and the slowing burble of Azean blood break the Void-bound silence. She steps over the warm body and notes that the face—what remains of it—looks surprised. Well. He *was* stupid, after all.

The flush of the Plague-fever is fading from the Kaim'era's brow. For a moment she is overcome with wonder, and placing a gloved finger to his temple she thinks: *they have changed him; they have altered his essence; they have made him something he was not meant to be*. If the True Name reflects the soul and the soul is altered, must the Name also be changed? She lets her finger drop away, then her hand. *You were meant to die,* she tells him wordlessly. *And I changed you. Grateful as man is for life, could you do anything other than hate me for this?*

She lifts Yiril—if it *is* still Yiril, of which she is philosophically uncertain—and carries him with little difficulty, as the station's gravity is minimal. With care she lays him out in her ship's alcove, folding his strong hands over his chest. Already he is breathing more easily. She hears the Azean's voice again in her mind, his last words. "It's done—he'll live."

Once more the rage of indignation comes over her. Did they really think she would contribute her Braxaná genes to their hated science, and undergo—what was it?—psychic testing? Enraged even by the memory, she stiffens with anger. But no, the promise had bought her Yiril's life. And if they wanted a purebred Braxaná badly enough for their tests and experiments, well, it would do them good to keep trying. The warrior is strengthened by repeated efforts, and no one suffers from practice.

She refuels the transport from the station's storage and then puts dark space between her and the site of her kill. After a moment's consideration she fires at the other vessel, again and again until its forcefields collapse and it succumbs at last to the purging vacuum of space. A final shot disperses even the remains, so that nothing is left but minute debris to bear witness that there ever was a meeting here—and nothing at all to tell of its nature.

Only then does she set a course for home. Home? She laughs bitterly. No longer for her. She knows her kind and she knows the Plague, and since she can never tell Yiril what she did in those days of her absence she can never expect anything but the most vehement enmity from him. That is as it should be, but no less painful for it.

She sinks to the floor beside him. Only after these many days does the exhaustion come to claim her, and she lets it . . . and the tears come, and she gives in to them. It will be a long flight home for him—and a much, much longer one for her.

* * *

My Lord and Master—wrote Ni'en—they say the worst has passed now, and to tell the truth I'll be glad to see it ended. On the whole your House has gained, in all but population; in the latter, I'm afraid, all Houses suffered greatly. Nevertheless, I think you will be pleased by what has been done in your absence, and—every bit as important—by what was not done.

Have you heard of the disaster on Klune? The planet, you may recall, was only recently brought into the Holding, its first extrastellar contact. Unfortunately this tsank'ar proved more than they could handle; such a proportion of the population has died that there are serious doubts about whether the local culture will survive. But then I think of the Braxaná, and I realize that a culture doesn't die for lack of numbers, only for lack of strength.

The official toll of Braxaná life brings the number of purebred to slightly under nine thousand. I'm sure that when you return you can get more detailed statistics than I can; for all that I'm a Mistress on Braxi, I'm still of the common blood, and—let us not forget it—a branded traitor.

I hear that some newsmonger on Tey declared that the true number of Braxaná is much smaller, perhaps even half of the publicized total, and that carefully prepared propaganda keeps the Holding from knowing how few of its rulers are really left. He was executed, I believe, and there may have been repercussions against his city of origin; I'm afraid I haven't kept up with it. On the whole, only three civilizations rose up during the time of trouble and had to be obliterated. I'm told this isn't too bad for a Plague; however, by what standard is that judgment made?

I fear for you, and although I want you here I would rather you be gone forever than risk the death I have seen. I'm glad, Kaim'era, that I'm old enough not to expect to see this again. I am glad to do you service, and more than a little pleased to better those men who have despised me from my first days on Zhene, but the constant death and the almost tangible sense of fear have worn me down. I am very, very tired, and will be glad when it's all over. Please come home when you can.

* * *

Two ships outside the forceweb of B'Salos; one small, a transport meant for shorter diftances and unfortunately pushed to make the longer ones, bristling with weapons that were obviously not included in the original design. The other larger and more comfortable, a staryacht such as the Braxaná use, capable of supporting life in comfort on long journeys between the stars.

They meet; their locks join and are sealed together.

With a single touch to her hair, hopelessly insufficient to settle the unruly mass it has become, D'vra leaves her ship and enters his.

He is waiting. *What is it,* she thinks, *that draws me to him?* He's not purebred, only moderately attractive, barely passionate by her standards. Then he comes forward and embraces her, and she remembers. The peace. The outward flowing of tension, as though some sort of psychic sponge had soaked it up and squeezed it out somewhere far, far away. After so many days the relaxation comes, and the stillness inside. She remembers.

"Yiril?" Feran's voice is quiet, as so much about him is. In other men she has despised it.

"Alive. He'll be well." She draws back and looks at him. She doesn't want to say it. It shouldn't be important, "I killed him."

He doesn't ask who, or how, or why. He nods, knowing. "I thought you would."

"But you promised him—"

He smiles. "As did you."

She, too, smiles, amazed that she can recall the expression. "You *are* Braxaná, after all."

"I thank you." He nods toward the transport. "He's in there?"

"Yes." Despair comes rising up from the depths. *Not yet,* she tells it, *not now, not in front of someone.* "There's an alcove off the control area."

"I'll take that ship back to Braxi," he tells her. "Quarantine's over. You wait here, in this one."

She sighs. "I would have liked to see Braxi again."

He looks at her, puts a hand to her face, and soaks up the sorrow. "I wouldn't be welcome," she says finally. "Maybe not even safe."

"I think you're wrong."

She is irritated, but only mildly. All her negative emotions are mild in his presence. "You don't understand our ways."

"You don't understand the Plague," he says softly. "It was bad, this one. Pandemic even for the common blood. They say there's been nothing like it since the disaster of 5287, and that one made even the Azean histories."

"Blessed well should," she says bitterly. "They gave us the thing in the first place."

He nods; what can one say to the truth? "You're a healthy woman, D'vra, and a purebred Braxaná. They can't afford to drive you out."

She glares at him. "Don't lie to me." Then she softens; "Don't lie to yourself," she whispers.

He kisses her once, but the fire of death is gone from her and there is only the quiet pleasure of human contact. "Seclusion?" she asks finally.

"On Vikarre. Is that all right?"-

She nods, dully. Fine.

Then she warns him, "I can't promise results—"

"I understand. All I ask is an attempt."

She looks at him and, perhaps for the first time, realizes just how Braxaná he has become. The dream has possessed him, the driving obsession of the halfbreed male which only the pure can fulfill. To have a son of his own status he must give it a purebred mother. That simple. How many of his kind die without knowing fulfillment? But Feran bought his with Yiril's life, using the last of his tenuous Azean contacts to bring a geneticist from some psychic Institute to the War Border, for a trade of favors. Fair enough. D'vra sighs; she'll try. Maybe it will work. Probably it won't. But where else has she to go?

"I'll be back soon," he promises.

* * *

My Mistress—wrote Zatar—the news from Montesekua is good at last: the Plague, as the Braxaná know it, is over. The virus still holds sway on a few backVoid planets but simple quarantine will hold it there until it comes to its natural end.

Your numbers cause me great dismay, but I would rather not commit my reason to ring. Soon enough we can discuss them directly.

I am coming home.

* * *

The house of Yiril is empty; one can feel it from the approachway, and even though physically nothing has changed, the aura of death is strong about the ancient stonework.

Zatar pauses to notice details: the lawn has been kept under control, the landing platform is empty of starships, there is a noticeable lack of people about. Then he steps up to the door and places his hand beside it.

It opens. There is a guard stationed behind it, although not one that Zatar remembers. "Kaim'era." He bows. "Please enter."

The Kaim'era holds up his forefinger, displaying the message-ring nestled over his glove. The gesture is a question.

"Your curiosity will be satisfied," the guard promises. "Please follow me."

He does so. He is puzzled by the message he wears. *Please come to the House of Yiril at your earliest convenience.* No explanation, no signature, only the address of the mansion in question and that one simple sentence.

The guard pauses before a pair of doors; his distance and his position far to the side of them indicate that they will open automatically if approached. Zatar is too curious to have misgivings, and steps forward confidently.

The doors part. The interior of a dimly lit room is revealed, and—

"Yiril!"

He steps quickly forward and the doors slide shut behind him, sealing them off in privacy. The older Kaim'era is gaunt and tired, with deep circles under his eyes that the best of cosmetics cannot disguise. But still. . . . Zatar walks to where he sits and clasps a hand to the other man's shoulder. Not till now has he ever expressed the closeness between them—perhaps because not till now has he admitted its existence to himself.

Fully in the mode of sincerity he says, "I'm glad to see you alive, Kaim'era."

"Surprised, though."

"I heard you were dead."

"Rumors." The older man smiles but it is a weak expression and, like all his gestures, speaks of the terrible illness and its toll on his health. "Wine? Food?"

"If you're up to it," he says cautiously.

Yiril looks vaguely amused. "The *House* is up to it." He summons the computer's attention and orders refreshment. Somehow that bit of mundane business makes him seem more alive to both of them. "And yours?"

He answers carefully. "Satisfactory."

Yiril looks at him curiously. "An understatement, as I understand things. She's done you proud, that little bit of 'gutter-slime'—your father's words, not mine. How he hated her! How he hated *you*—all very Braxaná, of course. It hasn't exactly set you behind to have a commoner running things when the Plague hit. More than one commoner, as I understand your House. How they all laughed at you, until now!" He studies the younger man, and his look is strangely paternal. "You surprised them."

"But not you."

Again the faint smile. "No. Not me."

A servant enters, humbly, with a tray of wine and delicacies. Although he lacks the grace common in forehouse staff his attitude is commendable. When he leaves Zatar raises a glass in toast. "To our emnity. New staff?"

"Nearly all of it. You seem no worse for the experience."

"Traditional Zarvati cowardice. The Plague never reached me. But you—Yiril, the last I heard—"

"I was in a coma," he says quietly, putting his goblet down. "Apparently for a long time. I remember only bits and pieces of things, and none of them makes any sense. Dreams, maybe. Most of the staff that cared for me then is dead, and those few who remain won't answer my questions."

He has to ask it. "D'vra?"

He sighs. "Off on Vikarre. Seclusion with Feran, believe it or not. Better for the moment that way."

"For the moment?"

Yiril looks at him, considering something—perhaps the extent of his confidence. "For the moment," he repeats. "How bad was it this time? I haven't been up and about long enough to request the real statistics."

Zatar hesitates. "Very bad," he admits, his speech mode that of doom and finality.

"The public figures range about nine thousand."

Zatar puts his drink aside and inhales deeply. "Would you like it all at once?"

"Please."

"There are five hundred and forty-one of us left."

Yiril is visibly shaken. "Men?"

"Men, women, children, and social misfits. Five hundred and forty-one purebred Braxaná, period. And, just to put things in their proper perspective, we have also lost a noteworthy portion of the common population. It's been bad for all the human worlds, but for us, it was devastating."

"What about the Kaim'erate?"

"Fifty-one at present—I'm sorry, fifty-two—including new members. We'll be hard put to fill out the roll at all, much less do so with the quality we need."

"So you'll need to move quickly."

Zatar freezes. "Kaim'era?"

"What if the Council were full—what then? We'd go on another eighty, ninety years just as we've been doing and then the next Plague would come and *that* would be the end. The *real* end, Zatar, because these political infants, these flounderers who weren't fit for the Kaim'erate until we had to have them, aren't going to become leaders just because they're the only ones left. The Holding will consolidate or fall in *this* generation; it has no other options. And you will be at the forefront of that change." He coughs, dryly. "Am I wrong? How I misjudged you?"

Zatar's dark eyes flicker momentarily, in response to his thoughts. "Perhaps."

The elder Kaim'era reaches out and clasps his arm with surprising strength. "Take the throne, Zatar. Now. While the Kaim'erate's in chaos."

"There is no throne," he says evenly. Basic Mode: *I reveal nothing.*

"There has to be. I will create it myself, if I must—out of my own flesh and bone, if that's what it takes!"

"The Kaim'era will never allow it."

"Then force them!" He coughs again, phlegm loosened by his vehemence. "Are you telling me you can't?"

Zatar watches him, cautious, silent.

"Very well." Yiril nods. "I bow to tradition. Were the universe to end tomorrow, we would still not trust each other; perhaps that's the only way." He hesitates. "I will put myself in your power, Zatar. Will that bring you out? If you know for certain that in no way can I possibly prove a threat to you?"

"Perhaps," he answers.

Yiril settles back in his chair. His features, although noticeably strained by the illness, have regained something of their customary animation. He is clearly as amused by his coming confession as he is disturbed to be making it.

He says it simply, and in the Basic Mode. "I'm taking D'vra back."

"You're doing—"

"*If* she'll come back. Of course, she'd be a fool not to, the way things stand right now."

"She betrayed your House!"

"She abandoned it—and me—for dead. Although I do concede the point: that is, technically speaking, betrayal."

Zatar is clearly astounded. "But why?"

He laughs softly. "Hard to say in our language, isn't it? We've been together since I was first made Kaim'era, over a century ago. I know it's foolish to say the whole thing can't be as simple as it seems, but I believe that. I know D'vra. Whatever she did, it was not simple treachery."

"The fact remains."

"No. The *image* remains. And that's what concerns you. She'll be off with Feran for a few years at least, and I'll work on pulling together what's left to me. When that's done, when I tender her an invitation to return to Braxi, I will forfeit my influence among the upper classes. Whatever you're thinking right now, Zatar, others will think a thousandfold. What would my chances be then of leading them?"

"Nonexistent," he says softly.

"So you see? A threat to you no longer. " He shakes his head, smiling sadly. "I never was, you know. I told you once that to be the second most powerful man in the Holding would satisfy me. You never believed it. You and Sechaveh, competing for the galaxy's record on political paranoia."

"Why, then?"

"You? Vinir? Because I governed Braxi, and I was trying to do it well. And I saw in you something that most of us lack—an ability to reach out and grasp hold of the popular imagination. We can't rule if our subjects won't be ruled by us. That's where Vinir failed. He was of overwhelming influence in the Council, but outside of it he was nothing. That was enough a thousand years ago. When there are only fifty-odd Kaim'eri, it isn't enough any more. Now tell me: if you needed a revolution tomorrow, could you start one?"

For a long while Zatar sits as still as ice, considering. Then, very slowly, very slightly, he smiles. "I don't know about a revolution. Maybe a little trouble out on the Yerren front—a planet or two, here and there—and of course, six or seven talons out at the War Border."

"Is that all?"

"Not quite."

Yiril nods his approval. "Somehow I didn't think you were wasting all those years in combat. Civilian?"

"Possibly. But a civilian revolution is meaningless. It's the military that always breaks it up, destroys planets of instigation . . . you know."

"Sound reasoning." He waits. "Well? Could you do it?"

"By tomorrow?"

"A zhent?"

"Make it three."

Yiril nods his appreciation of the fact; he had guessed it, but the magnitude of it is still impressive. "You lied to us all."

"Didn't you expect that?"

"All that nonsense about a revolution from within!"

"They believed it. *Sechaveh* believed it. They're all so tied up in their little world of power-plays and internal pecking order that they forget we're outnumbered centillions to one. All that ever assured our power was the strength and loyalty of the military, and its willingness to act without hesitation. They never even considered what would happen if the fleets turned against them."

"And the fleets will?"

"When the time is right."

He hesitates. Yiril looks closely at him, then asks, "Is it her? Is that what's holding you back?"

"Nonsense!" he says quickly. "I have plans—"

"Did your plans allow for a Plague this early? Or one this devastating? No, I thought not. Whatever timetable you had before needs to be scrapped in favor of immediate action. As for the k'airth, I understand how—"

"It's not that," he interrupts.

"No?" He studies Zatar, then asks softly, "What is it, Zatar? The woman? Or the power she represents?"

"They are one and the same." He looks away, not sure of his control over his own feelings. Why does it hurt so much? There should be frustration, yes, the loss of a hunter who has seen his prey go free . . . but not this pain, that tears at the very center of him. Not sorrow. "I've known all along that I would have to leave the fleet when the time was right. I'm more than ready, I assure you."

"That's fortunate, because the time *is* right. Not for you alone. Braxaná law is a problem, since it forbids you from initiating any legislation involving yourself. You would have had to work around it, and I don't doubt that you were planning to. But with the help of another . . . you can move now, and do so within the law. The damage to our system will be minimal; the benefit to yourself is obvious. I'm offering.

"You're asking for trust," he says quietly.

"*You're* asking for change. Let it start with you."

It is a valid request, but the very concept of trusting another man goes against his Braxaná grain. "I thought you were the great traditional Braxaná."

"Yes. Does that fit in with my taking D'vra back? Does it allow for a future for our people? Have you ever really *believed* that nonsense? We have a very short time to settle our power structure before word of our actual losses gets out, and then even if we keep control of the Holding, a century at the most, to learn to. . . ." He hesitates.

"Rework the foundation of the Braxaná culture. And come to terms with applied genetics."

"You said it, not I. At any rate, closed-minded conservativism is something we can't afford. I didn't always feel this way, mind you. But I do now. And I'm ready to act in support of that conviction."

"What changed your mind?"

Thoughtfully, giving his hands something to do in order that he might not have to speak for a moment, Yiril pours more wine into their glasses. Already the strong drink has given him a semblance of color. "When I looked up one day and saw that where there had once been an angry, impetuous youth there was instead a fit ruler for Braxi."

He gives Zatar's glass back to him and takes up his own again. For a long while the two men look at each other in silence, dark eyes meeting in careful curiosity, each trying to read the thoughts that serve the other as motivation. Finally, very cautiously, Zatar nods.

Yiril smiles, and raises his glass.

"To revolution, then?"

"With your help," he answers, accepting the offer. "To revolution."

Harkur: He who controls the soldiers, controls the throne.

TWENTY-ONE

The Most High and Illustrious Patriarch of the planet Keyegga-under-Braxi shook his head with fine determination. "We're willing to discuss these things, yes," he said. "With *you,* no."

The Braxaná facing him was angered, not so much by the man's obstinacy as by his obvious belief that his behavior was entirely reasonable. "Look: I am the agent the Kaim'eri sent to you in order to settle these problems. I am the official envoy of the Holding."

"You are the official envoy of the *Kaim'eri,*" the Patriarch corrected him. "You are not, however, an envoy of the Holding's ruler."

Exasperated, the Braxaná told him once more "There *is* no single ruler."

The Patriarch steepled his fingers thoughtfully. "You understand that I want very much to cooperate with you in this matter. Keyegga recognizes the absolute sovereignty of Braxi over her lands and people. But regarding the tariffs in question, I must speak to someone who is truly in charge, or else his chosen representative."

Forcing his voice to remain even, the Braxaná tried again. "The Holding is ruled by a body of men whose consensus opinion is law. When the problem with Keyegga arose, the Kaim'eri discussed the issues involved and chose to send someone to help work out the difficulties. That someone is me. I represent," he said slowly, in the manner of persons who, not being understood, assume their listeners to be either simpleminded or hard of hearing, "the ruling majority vote of that body of men."

"A *vote* is not a creature; a *vote* is not a man. A *vote,* most respected Lord, is subject to change tomorrow as chance and circumstance dictate. Can you answer for the Kaim'eri's state of mind when they decided this thing? Can you tell me they won't change their minds tomorrow—and again the day after that, if they so desire? With the laws that govern voting as complicated as they are, can you say with any certainty that Keyegga's supporters will always be present when this situation is discussed? You can't. No one can. Is it unreasonable of us to demand a little more security than that?"

Frustrated and angry, the envoy told him, "Subject planets don't 'demand' things of the Holding."

"They do when they've been designated avoke'ur class—wholly voluntary submission, no lack of cooperation noted at any point, successful and immediate absorption into the Holding—I quote conquest law. Would you like a paragraph reference?"

"It won't be necessary," he snapped. "I understand the rating, and I know you've got it. Is that your final word, then?"

Unshakably calm, the Patriarch nodded. "Tell the Kaim'eri that we of Keyegga-under-Braxi welcome the envoy of their leader and intend to work out this trouble regarding the tariffs in a manner acceptable to him, as befits a planet of our class."

The Braxaná scowled acknowledgment, then turned and quickly left the room. Only then, alone, did the Patriarch seem less formidable, and perhaps less certain of himself. Slowly he walked to the side of the airborne audience chamber in the hovering palace reserved for Keyeggan royalty; through the window he looked down at his world, and his people.

"Have I done the right thing?" he wondered aloud. He remembered the impetuous young Braxaná who, years ago, had sought him out. "Braxi is coming," he had warned the Patriarch, "and soon its might will be turned against your independence. There's no way the limited technology of Keyegga can stand up to that. If you try to defy us, there'll be great destruction and perhaps even the enslavement of your people. But if you choose to submit, and you do it in this one particular way, you can spare your people that suffering and even retain some degree of autonomy."

The Patriarch had considered it, long and hard. The young man had showed him maps and battle plans and at last the absolute monarch of the proud planet agreed that, yes, they stood little chance of turning back the coming Braxin invasion, and the cost if they tried would be terrible. At last he had agreed to the submission. The young Lord—Zatar, his name had been—had counseled him through all the intricate maneuvers of diplomacy and had gotten him past the grasping claws of greedy Kaim'eri and Commanders who would rather see Keyegga subjugated and stripped of wealth than more peaceably absorbed.

His people—had they prospered? More so, he had no doubt, than if Braxi had entered their system treading a carpet of blood, as they would have done otherwise. Yes, Keyegga owed much to this Zatar, and the Patriarch had promised to repay the favor if ever there were the means of doing so. And now, apparently, the time had come. *Stand up to the Kaim'eri,* he had said, *and be steadfast in demanding your rights. You will not be overrun. Trust me.*

Trust a Braxaná? The Patriarch sighed; well, this one was better than most, so perhaps there was a chance.

But he trembled as he heard the envoy's shuttle take off from the palace landing field.

* * *

("I want to break the Peace."

Silence.

"The Plague has weakened them, Torzha, If we move now, when they least expect it, and we can take them!"

Silence. Then, quietly: "This has occurred to me, Anzha.")

* * *

At last all the commanding officers of the War Border were gathered together. At the head of the table sat Herek, flanked by his subordinate Commanders and the captain of his fighters. The others had brought a similar array of companions and so the conference room, despite its size, was hard pressed to accommodate them all. They were five deep about the table, with additional men seated on or leaning against any other reasonable surface the room had to offer.

Herek stood. "Commanders of the Great War: first, let me thank you for coming. My talon has received an assignment which concerns you all, in that it asks us to move into a peaceful system and take action against one of the Holding's own planets. Not to put down a rebellion in the making," he clarified, "nor to avenge any wrong committed against our rulers, our race, or our fleet." All of these were legitimate causes for action and he didn't want them confused with the truth. "Keyegga-under-Braxi is an avoke'ur of the Holding; a voluntary subject who is to be protected from military and political abuse. In a recent altercation with those who would poison their economy, the Keyeggans demanded to speak to a Braxin authority. Specifically, to the master of the Holding—or his representative."

There were snickers at that, quickly stifled. "But there isn't such a master," one of the Commanders pointed out.

"Exactly. So the Keyeggans have refused to negotiate a settlement, and we've been ordered to move in. Commanders . . ." He drew a deep breath, for courage. "I have no intention of moving against Keyegga."

A chaos of protests, of disbelief, of fear. Nevertheless, when Herek studied the men staring at him, he found that more than one was calm and pensive. They weren't surprised by this, any more than he had been. Discontent had been growing among the Border officers for a long time. *Now,* he thought, *how much can be made of that?* "Listen to me, my comrades-in-arms. Fortune has granted us an opportunity which may never come again. Keyegga has made a demand which is wholly within its avoke'ur rights; Braxi must crush the planet or satisfy it. If we move as ordered, what will happen? Keyegga will fall, the other avoke'uri will tremble, and life will go on as it has. We'll continue to serve a body of men who can't unify behind any single purpose, and the War will suffer accordingly. The men who give us orders would never dare to come out here themselves—no, their Braxaná skin is too precious to face the fire—but they will debate us into corners and bury us under administrative details while they argue amongst themselves over who deserves the most profit from our work."

He leaned toward them, eyes gleaming. "*We have a chance to change all that.* Think: If we don't move on Keyegga as ordered, what will happen? The strength of the Holding has always been based on its power to destroy anything that stood in its path. What happens when that power is compromised? Braxi must meet the demands of the Keyeggans or face the consequences! And just what are those demands? That a single man act as figurehead of the Holding—something that most of us have wished for at least once, I'm sure."

He had hit a nerve there. The current system, designed to encourage competition among the Braxaná, was not without its toll upon the military. And for the most part these were men of common blood. *Their* culture didn't venerate a nomadic oligarchy that had preferred primitive steel to civilization, but an absolute monarch who had unified Braxi and then conquered the stars. There was not a man in the room who hadn't dreamed of that time, when a leader's Name might be worn into battle like armor for the soul. Herek saw it in them now; he knew it was his to manipulate.

"Commanders, there is no risk. If we act together in this, simply refuse to move into the Keyegga system, we can't be hurt! The same law which protects the rights of an avoke'ur planet forbids us from moving in unless there's some direct threat to the Holding. And there isn't. Even the Kaim'eri must realize that. We will be blameless."

"There's Whim Death," someone muttered.

Herek smiled. "No, there isn't."

Commander Darov stirred. "A Kaim'era of the Holding has the right to commit to death any individual, for any reason, providing said person or alien is not of the Braxin upper class. Meaning Braxaná." He looked around the room. "An awful lot of us haven't got enough of that blood to save us."

There was commotion following that; Herek shouted it down. "Commanders! Listen to what I have to say. *The law you quote no longer exists.* Or rather, it still exists, but it no longer involves us."

That quieted them—stunned them, in fact. "Since when?" a man demanded, and another asked, "What do you mean?"

"Simply this: A short while ago, the Kaim'era Zatar introduced legislation to render Commanders of the War Border immune to such a threat. After much debate, the Kaim'erate passed it. I have a copy here—" He held up a flatrendering of the edict and then offered it to the man nearest him. "Have a look at it, all of you. There's one man in the Holding who *does* know what war means. He's been out here among us, risking his neck with the rest of us. He knows what we need in order to triumph. Ever since he left the Border he's been working to free us from the policies that stifle our efficiency. This commanders, is proof of it. How much more could he accomplish if the system were . . . say, *simplified?*"

He let the plastic make its rounds. He knew the shock they were feeling; he had experienced it himself, when the news was first made known to him. There was no logic behind such a reaction; no Commander of the Border fleet had ever been executed without good cause. But the threat still existed. It had made it clear to all of them that they were worth no more in the eyes of the Braxaná than the scum who populated a thousand planets. This move of Zatar's gave them independence of spirit, something most of them had never tasted. It confirmed them in their sense of their own importance. And it showed them that *one* man—one Kaim'era—valued the War more than he valued his own fleeting pleasure.

That was a startling concept.

"You see," Herek said at last. "Fortune has dropped the perfect tool into our laps. By simple non-action we force the Holding's hand, at no risk to ourselves. The Kaim'eri will consolidate their power in a single man, and we will know war as *Harkur's* troops knew it."

"They'll move in another fleet," came the protest. "Pull in the yerren talons, or those working rimside. Any of which could deal with a single planet."

Herek smiled; if they were arguing details, the main point was won. "The yerren fleet won't move. The rimside fleet is too far away to make a difference; by the time it reached Keyegga, the Holding would be much too unstable."

"You know for a fact that the fleet won't budge? That front isn't known for heroes," a Commander remarked.

"The fleet will not budge," Herek assured them. "I have it on excellent authority."

What could they say? They were offered a dream—independence, respect. They were offered a status that no commonblooded man had attained since the Braxaná first took over. All this, for the simplest non-action. What could they say but yes?

"It would be Zatar?" one man challenged. Zatar alone was acceptable; *he* had fought the War. Stories of his exploits had won him respect from these men, even awe. And *he* had been the one to grant them their freedom. " No one else?"

"It will be Zatar." Herek grinned, "I guarantee it."

* * *

(". . . but it's not our way, to break a treaty."

"It's not our tradition—does it have to become a fieldclad rule? Torzha, they're weak. They're confused. There's some trouble inside the Holding and the Border fleet is refusing to take orders. You were a Starcommander. You know the implications of that! If the chain of command isn't functioning properly—"

"I know. But we can't do it, Anzha."

"It would be completely unexpected."

"Yes."

"It could give us the edge, Torzha!"

"I don't doubt it. But there are things we simply can't do. And this, I regret, is one of them."

"Because it would be too much like them?"

"Because it would be too much like what we've tried so hard to escape. Think of the Founding, Anzha. Think of what it meant. A chance for a clean start—a chance to do things right, to set meaningful standards for ourselves. Our national honor is one of those standards. We can't give it up just because the moment doesn't favor it.")

* * *

The Prince looked out over his domain. Golden sky silhouetted the great city in the plains below, streaked with the orange of the setting sun. From up on the mountain peak he could see as far as Oru-Hani in the west, and far down the dividing line of the mountain range to the north and south. All along the plains the Tsamaka grew, its leafy vines turning the land a deep orange and the sweet fragrance of its slowly drying fruit rising even as far as the milk-white castle which ruled over the fertile plains. Soon the fruit would be ready, its concentrated juices fermented and mixed with resins and drugs until the Holding's headiest wine—and its finest vintage—came forth.

Yet where there should have been pleasure in him, there was instead darkness. A new parasite had attacked his fields this spring and he had called to Braxi for help. That such a thing should happen was not unexpected; with millions of humans planet-hopping on a regular basis, and a large number of them coming to taste of the richness of Sedanka-Muraam, it was only logical to expect foreign insects and illnesses to invade the fertile vineyards.

But help had been too slow in coming. Half the crops had been lost by the time specialists had arrived—an inexcusable delay, to the Prince's way of thinking. Only recently had he heard rumors of the cause, and although they were merely rumors, they were exceedingly disturbing. Could the Kaim'erie's private economic wars really be so terrible that they would be willing to sabotage the finest Tsamaka in the Holding? Could there be a man who would deliberately tie up the xenobotanists in red tape long enough for Braxi to lose its favorite vintage? Kaim'era Janir had invested in the Prince's crops, and Kisil in Prince Otoma's. Could it be true that disagreements between these men were enough to cause them to make Sedanka-Muraam barren?

Righteous anger filled the Prince, and indignation moved him. Above him in the growing night the star of Keyegga was newly visible, and he regarded it. That planet had demanded its rights. And though the Kaim'eri had threatened it, the military had refused to move in. Unheard of. But if such things were becoming possible . . . perhaps an alliance of the Princes might accomplish something. And if there *were* a true ruler of the Holding, then there might be someone to turn to for justice, someone not under the thumb of his fellow Kaim'eri.

Yes, he thought darkly. *The time has come for Sedanka-Muraam to make itself heard. I will speak to the others.*

* * *

("The planets are rising up, one by one, in protest of the seeming anarchy. A few, no doubt, genuinely desire 'the best for the Holding.' For the rest of them it's a matter of economics, politics, custom . . . a stable monarchy would benefit every planet and colony now suffering the whims of the current regime, and they know it. And the Border fleet won't get involved. It's only a matter of time before the Kaim'eri's hand is forced. A more efficient government, Torzha, means a more efficient War. We have to move—we have to stop it—"

"But we have to do so within the system, Anzha. Or we can't do so at all.")

* * *

Ground Commander Lamos came to the address given him. Soon after his arrival the door opened again, and a figure he remembered from his past entered the darkened building.

"You're looking well," Zatar told him, his speech mode one of mild amusement.

He was indeed. Life on Garran had not only stripped the excess meat from his frame, it had given him a taste for pleasures that only existed where there was new territory to be conquered. Lamos was a changed man—a man no longer exclusively interested in excesses of the flesh. The ancient Braxaná blood, running true in his veins despite a bad beginning, had sated itself at last in combat. Not the star-and-Void stuff, where a man was so wrapped up in machinery that he made no contact with his work, but *real* combat. *Ground* combat. Somewhere in between the blood and the dirt, the violence and the rapine, Lamos had found himself at last.

"I said I owed you one," he told Zatar. "I'm ready to make good on it."

"Tell me about your influence among the officers of your fleet."

"That depends on what you want. The Commanders like having a Braxaná among them—provided he doesn't threaten their precious pecking order. I've done my bit to make life easier for them now and again and they'll do theirs when the time comes. Be sure of it. What is it you want?"

"You know about the business with Keyegga."

"Does this mean you were behind it?"

The years might have taught Lamos to look and act like a Braxaná, but it would take centuries to begin to teach him subtlety. "Your fleet will be called in next. Disciplinary action against Keyegga, perhaps against a few other planets as well."

"Ah," he said. Then, smiling a bit, he asked, "Where does Kurgh fit into this?"

"Kurgh."

"My fleet's current objective. A high-tech planet with five colonies, staunchly independent . . . surely you've heard of it?" He looked amazed when Zatar shook his head, an expression too extreme to be genuine. "Kaim'era, with all due respect, my fleet has better things to do with its time than play interstellar police in territory they're not even assigned to. We've been planning this Kurgh thing for zhents now. I can't imagine anyone giving that up to go slap some hands halfway across the Holding. We're not the Border fleet, you know."

"You guarantee this?" Zatar asked quietly.

"Of course." His eyes sparkling, he added, "For a price."

The Kaim'era raised up one hand to display a ring snugly nestled about his index finger. "A planet," he said, removing the piece of jewelry. He offered it to Lamos. "A pretty little piece of real estate right by the War Border. You might be familiar with it. I've made some improvements," he added.

"I've left that part of the Holding for good," Lamos pointed out. Then he took the ring. "But no doubt this has commercial value."

And he bowed. "I will see that the fleet stays put."

* * *

(The honor of the nation is the pride of the nation. Let us never do as the tormentors of our ancestors did, speak words only to bury them with actions. Let us meet the future with our national honor held sacred, so that no matter what the temptation, no matter what the cost, we will never resemble our tormentors and our society will never come to resemble theirs in any way.)

* * *

"We have no choice," Yiril said formally. "More important, we have no time. Kaim'eri, we've argued for days now—and every day the Holding grows weaker, both in power and in image. There's only one course of action open to us and very few variations of detail to chose from. Therefore, for the good of B'Salos I am going to force the issue, here and now. Vote for our destruction if you want, but recognize that that's what you're doing.

"Kaim'eri, by my right as Kaim'era of the B'Saloan Holding under Braxi/Aldous, I present the following for debate and decision: that the Kaim'erate choose from among its number one man to act as nominal ruler of the Holding, and that he be given sufficient real power to make him effective in this capacity. That we do this immediately, bearing in mind the present need for such a person. For that position I present the name of Zatar, son of Vinir and K'siva, who I contend is the only one among us capable of settling the unrest in the Holding immediately and in an acceptable manner.

There was a moment of silence, and at last Zatar rose, as custom demanded, and left the Hall. Following which there was much debate, all of it heated.

But there was no real question of the outcome.

* * *

Alone in the observation dome, Anzha reached out with the force of her frustration and touched the stars. *I've lost him!* She brushed a planet and passed it by, snaked her thoughts past a half-dozen scoutships, then insinuated herself into the thoughtwinds of a colony. Like sought like: the wounded warrior hungered for balm in the form of others' misery. *We were so close to victory. We could have won this damned war!* And the ultimate pain: *I'll never reach him now. They'll bind him to Braxi. . . .* She swam through a multitude of minds, tasting the surface thoughts of one and then passing on to another. The impressions were vague at such a distance but the exercise was soothing, as though reminding her that others suffered, others knew loss, others tasted the bitterness of frustration. Instinctively she gravitated toward the most familiar minds, those humans whose present mental state was most similar to her own. She touched their awareness—and was alarmed.

. . . lost to me forever, my adored one, would that I could bring you back from the dead!

. . . emptiness, and hurt, and longing . . . I still hunger, but only for you . . .

. . . when the pairbond is severed, what is left that's worth living for?

Shaken, she withdrew her thoughts from that foreign arena and limited them to the confines of her body. She was afraid to try again. What did it mean, that the thoughts which drew her were not those of ambition thwarted, but of pairbonding shattered? She had lived with her obsession for so long that she had ceased to analyze it. Azeans paired for life; was it possible that she had done that? Had that one Azean instinct bred true in her after all? Hasha, if that were the case. . . .

"I thought you might be up here."

She turned. "Tau! You startled me." The wetness of a tear was running down one cheek; quickly she wiped it away. Her hands were trembling badly. "I was trying to convince myself there had been no way of stopping it. I failed." The anger came back, and with it indignation. "Who do they think they are, anyway! My whole lifetime spent serving them, and then they tie my hands at the very threshold of victory! Them and their damned honor—I could have *ended* it!"

"They're your people," he said quietly.

"I *have* no people," she answered bitterly. "A few individuals here, and maybe Torzha. Maybe Torzha. But Azea?" All her pain was pouring out, all the years that had suddenly become futile. "We could have won it." She laughed bitterly. "His new title is Pri'tiera. Do you know what that means? It's from prizhe, 'that-which-has-waited,' and tiera, 'that-which-rules,' From the same prime root as the name of the Waiting Poison . . . suitable, don't you think?"

"There are still ways to fight," he told her.

"I've thought of that. I've gone over all my alternatives, and each one amounts to treason. Tau, I'm loyal to very few people. Torzha er Litz is one of them. She believed in me when no one else did, and risked her own reputation to get me to the Border. I can't betray her, no matter how much I'd like to. Besides, most of the crew wouldn't go. They believe in my cause only second to serving Azea; they'll push regulations, but they won't break them outright. And I couldn't do it alone."

"You wouldn't necessarily be alone." He was exuding tension of his own, more than a match for hers. "You're right about most of the crew, and therefore the ship itself. And you're certainly right about Azea. The Peace will last until Braxi consolidates its power; by then it may be too late to act. The War no longer serves your purpose," he told her quietly. "Possibly other things would."

She was stunned. "I never expected to hear from you—"

"You forget where I came from! You forget that before I was assigned to you I had given up on life. I agreed to serve you because I believed you would *break* the Holding. I *still* believe that. And there are a few others, I know, who feel the same way. Your psychics have no loyalty to the Empire—only to you. Choose a course of action, Anzha, and there are those who'll follow you.

"This has been discussed," she challenged him.

"Often."

"Never in my presence!"

"The price of telepathy, I suppose. People assume you know." A convenient lie. The truth was that if she had ever heard such things, she would have considered them treasonous. Until now.

She looked out toward the stars. Was there a way? Not to reach Zatar; that was no longer a realistic dream, and if she clung to it, it would destroy her. Every plan she'd made up to this point had been focused on him, as was the pain of her loss. But Braxi might still be crushed. Not by the hands of StarControl; Azea had forfeited that option when they forced her to sign the last treaty. But maybe by her.

"Give me time," she murmured. She had taken it for granted that Braxi would fall to the Conqueror; now she had to discard that assumption, along with many others. What might she do to break the Holding—what might a handful of people do to bring down the greatest warrior-nation the galaxy had yet known?

It's enough, Zatar, if I destroy that nation. You have your people, and live to rule them. I have no people. And except for the destruction of Braxi, I have no purpose. Only you. . . .

She shook her head, trying to banish the thought. That hunger was one she was going to have to live with.

I'll focus on Braxi, she promised herself. *There must be a way. . . .*

Hakur: A man's greatest enemy is his own fear.

TWENTY-TWO

Feran passed quickly through the halls of erotica. Not that the exhibits didn't interest him; he had seen them before, many times, and would willingly relish them again. New additions arrived every day, from all corners of the Holding, so that even a walk down familiar corridors would reveal unfamiliar treasures at every turn. But this time . . . no, he would let nothing distract him. This was one appointment he dared not be late for, and he needed his thoughts in order when he arrived.

Ostensibly, there was nothing amiss. Zatar had asked him to share a meal with him in the Restaurant, a simple enough request. They had met before under similar circumstances; in the tight-knit Kurattan society, social contact was unavoidable. At one time Feran had even prided himself on having the courage to entertain the Kaim'era at his House, and had genuinely enjoyed doing so. But that was before the Plague—before he had placed Feran opposite *her* and then watched them interact, dark eyes probing for secrets. All the fears had come back, that day, from that first terrible vision which he had shared with a catatonic child to his early paranoia as he struggled to assimilate into the Braxin culture.

He forced himself to be rational, and tried to analyze the source of his nervousness. Why would Zatar bother with him? The Kaim'era was now a Pri'tiera—*the* Pri'tiera—and his time was precious. Why spare any part of it to socialize with a man who could neither aid nor effectively threaten him? And why here, of all places? The only reason which Feran could think of was that the Pri'tiera might desire neutral ground, and therefore could not meet him in either of their Houses. That, of course, was itself disturbing. Lastly, why had he asked to meet Feran where he had, in an obscure corner of the Braxaná section? What *was* this wing, anyway, where they were supposed to meet? Following the instructions he'd been given, Feran found himself in totally unfamiliar territory. He glanced at his instructions, turned another corner, and—

Stopped.

Stared.

Shem'Ari, the inscription read. Of course. Feran realized he had been here once before—when he had first arrived on Braxi. It was a wing dedicated to the most forbidden pleasure of all—an image so threatening, a taboo so absolute, that it must have its own place in this collection of human indulgence. Out of the way, where a man could study these women—and his own desire—in private; away from the center of things, so that the conservative (and the ignorant) need never admit to themselves that these women, damned by all Braxin tradition, possessed a sexual fascination that some men could not resist.

There was a new statue by the entranceway, a simple thing of carved obsidian that might have been created in another, pretechnical age. Simple . . . but effective. Feran took a step toward it; drawn by its aesthetic power, fascinated despite himself.

It was she, Anzha Lyu Mitethe, rendered in volcanic glass as he had known her in life. The same imperious lift to her head, a hand upraised in command as she might have held it aboard the *Conqueror* . . . the statue was a work of genius, capturing the essence of the woman, the strength of her, as though the glass itself had come to life. A strength that was compromised only by the golden bracelet that adorned her uplifted arm, proclaiming her slavery.

"Do you like it?"

He stiffened at the sound of Zatar's voice, but could not take his eyes from the statue. She must have submitted voluntarily, the bracelet was too rich to mean anything else. Yet she was still in command. What man could have possessed her without crushing her spirit, would have dared to own her, and then would have the boldness to let her exercise her power again? "It's remarkable," he breathed.

"Thank you," Zatar smiled as he came to Feran's side; he was obviously amused by his reaction to the work. "I commissioned it. Shall we go?"

He was gesturing toward the exhibit itself. After a moment, somewhat hesitantly, Feran entered. Having been raised among a people where women often ruled men, it was hard for him to understand the obsession such women inspired here. But it was also hard not to be moved by the power of these artists' visions. On all sides of him, shem'Ari reigned—and fought, and fell, enticing the viewer against his will, in images that were both arresting and repellent. Many of the artists' subjects were Azean, which unnerved Feran; some were Azeans he had known. All were conquered, in some way, for the spirit of the shem'Ar must ultimately be sacrificed upon the altar of the Pale Ones, who might desire them but must never, except in unliving art, indulge that desire—lest they compromise themselves in doing so.

Feran was grateful when at last they reached the Restaurant, and sat down as soon as he was able to. The Pri'tiera lowered himself with considerably more grace, and sat opposite him. Before either of them could speak a waitress appeared, and their attention turned to food. As soon as she had left them, Zatar turned on the soundproofing.

"I'd like to mix politics with pleasure," he said to Feran. "If you don't mind—"

"Of course not," he answered, wondering what this was all about.

"My new position demands certain things of me; it also makes options available that weren't before. I need some information, Feran, and I believe you have it. I want to review some facets of our traditional relationship with Azea. I was hoping that you, with your special background, could help me."

In truth he dreaded such an inquiry because he dreaded revealing himself, but there was no way out of it. "I am the Pri'tiera's servant," he answered. True enough. "Just let me know what I can do to help you." He forced a laugh. "It would be nice to make some constructive use of all those wasted years."

Zatar raised an eyebrow curiously, but at that instant a flashing light indicated human proximity; a moment later their waitress stepped through the sound barrier and delivered their food.

When she was gone, he said, "Then perhaps we can both benefit from this, Lord Feran. I must say, I'm very grateful to have you here." With a wry smile: "Fortunate for us that Azea sent you."

Feran forced himself to pick up his wine and taste it before speaking. "I somehow doubt that this was what they intended."

"I will speak plainly. What I need is this: an unbiased account of psychic activity in the Empire."

He was so startled he almost spilled his wine. "What makes you think I would know about such things?"

"I've always suspected that the kind of secrecy we imagine surrounds the psychic world is our own invention, and that the Azeans in general are much more familiar with telepathic lore than we've been led to believe. After all, the power was proven to exist over a millennia ago. Wouldn't there be some common knowledge of it by now?"

Feran nodded slowly, carefully. "They speak of it openly," he chanced.

"As I suspected. Feran, you know them. No matter how much you might have been isolated from the common public, you still lived among the enemy for a good part of your life." He sighed. "Circumstances are soon going to force me to make decisions that no Braxin monarch has ever had to consider, and I need facts to work with. We can't simply ignore the psychic problem any longer. Telepathic contact is instantaneous, requires no relay stations or artificial augmentation to work . . . and its effectiveness in war is something Starcommander lyu Mitethe has made painfully clear. To hide behind a facade of primitive superstition and ignore the ramifications of doing so would be foolish—possibly suicidal. I need your help."

He was confused. "You're considering tolerating psychic activity in the Holding?"

"I'm considering *using* it; there's a difference. There's no question that we can't do what our enemies have done; but can we afford to ignore the weakness which results from such a policy?" He sipped his wine, thoughtful. "To use it, we need to *control* it—and that requires understanding. That's where I want you to help me."

He didn't know quite how to respond, and was certain that the Kaim'era had noticed his confusion. "Whatever I can do," he managed. "I know very little."

"Whatever you do know will be welcome." He was speaking in the Triumphant Mode—why? "For a start, I'm interested in the class divisions imposed by the Institute. Specifically, what is the difference between a telepath and a Probe?"

He tried not to stare. He tried not to sound frightened. He thought; *he knows!* "I . . . that isn't something I really understand, Pri'tiera."

"Try." His dark eyes demanded obedience, as did his voice. "Tell me what you've heard."

He buried his attention in his food for a moment, trying to collect himself. How much would a non-psychic know? How much would a Braxin/Azean non-psychic remember after all these years? At last he offered hesitantly, "It seems to me that the difference had something to do with the capacity for . . . abstract reasoning."

He stropped; Zatar waited. Unhappily, he continued. "Because people don't develop any psychic awareness until long after their other senses have started functioning, there is a tendency to translate psychic input into some other format." Was that too much? No, that was common knowledge; he might reasonably know such things. "Probes . . ." he faltered, "don't have to do that."

"Is the abstract ability limited to psychics?"

"No. To the degree that Probes require it, it's somewhat rare, but it occurs in society at large. It's just that when chance combines the two abilities . . . you get a Probe."

"How does the format translation take place?"

"I'm not sure, Pri'tiera."

"Share your uncertainty."

"Well, as I understood it, if I were to . . . if a person were to send a thought to another person, the latter would, say, hear a voice, or see a picture; in general experiencing the sending in some familiar sensory format. Likewise the first person would use such imagery to send the thought in the first place."

"Probes are immune to this need?"

"I don't know, Pri'tiera. I'm sorry. It seems to me that that was the difference, but I'm not sure. It's been a long time."

"I'm sure it has," Zatar answered, and there was something in his voice that Feran didn't like the sound of. "My major concern is with the threat of violating mental privacy. Or more specifically, with conditioning such as the Institute employs."

"It takes complete mastery of the power to read a man's unwilling thoughts." This came easily; it was Institute propaganda. "And telepathy gives no man the ability to 'control' another. As for conditioning. . . ." He tried to struggle for the memory as he would have had to had he truly been a non-psychic in the Empire. "I believe that can only be done by a Probe."

"Why?"

Why do you assume I know so much? he wondered bitterly. He wished he dared not answer, but he knew that if he lied about his ignorance the perceptive Braxaná would notice the deception. And that would be dangerous. "This is my understanding of it—and it may be incorrect, Pri'tiera. I never studied these things. If a thought-image were inserted into your mind it would have a certain result, but there would also be side effects. What would that particular image mean to you? What other things might it mean to the telepath probing? All of that would be added to the transmission, a sort of mental undercurrent, and would affect the conditioning."

"So because a Probe can work without supportive images—in pure thought, let us say—he can work safely within a stranger's mind and change the patterns of thinking."

How did you come to know so much of this? he wondered. But he was also relieved to hear it; if a traditional Braxaná understood that much of the psychic world, perhaps it was reasonable that he, too, might have some knowledge of it. He calmed down somewhat. "That's how I understand it."

They ate for a while in silence; the Pri'tiera was lost in thought, and Feran was not anxious to renew the conversation. After a long time Zatar spoke again. "It would seem to me," he said, "that limited psychic power is not in of itself a terrible thing."

Feran tried not to betray his tension. "I can see that point of view."

Zatar looked up sharply. "I'm glad to hear that." Again Feran sensed an unpleasant undercurrent. For a moment he wished his talent was functioning, that he might read its source, then, horrified, he shoved that thought into the back of his mind and left it there. "True telepathy, of course, is something we could never tolerate, and from what you tell me of the Probes they are dangerous creatures, and I support tradition on that point. But there may be a few things I can work with. . . ."

He stood. "Well, I thank you. You've been most helpful to me in this, Feran, and I appreciate it. Would you do me the pleasure of being my guest this fourthday coming? I'm having a few people over in the evening and I would be pleased if you joined us."

"How can I refuse?" he asked lightly. *How, indeed?* "I would be honored."

"Excellent. Ni'en will let you know the exact time. I look forward to it, Feran."

I wish I did, the ex-Probe thought sullenly.

* * *

He knows.

It came in the middle of the night and awoke him, the dreadful certainty that the secret relied upon for survival was a secret no longer. How? Why? And what on Braxi could he do to save himself?

* * *

The most upsetting part of the fourthday gathering came after dinner. Though he was ill at ease among the powerful Kaim'eri who comprised the rest of the company, Feran slowly came to believe that the invitation had been one of genuine good will and was unconnected to whatever suspicions the Pri'tiera might entertain regarding his role in Azean life. Or so he thought until the entertainment began.

"My poet," Zatar introduced simply. "I believe you're all familiar with her work?"

They all were, although Feran had not heard her perform in many years. Lanst'va was a plain woman of common blood, but the love of art that she radiated made her almost beautiful while performing. She waited for their attention and then began.

What thoughts are these, that I dare call my own?
What privacy this, that I defend its sanctuary?
How dare I cloak my intent in rituals of silence
And inspire the invasion that I will not abide?

The combination of modes she used was beyond Feran's conscious understanding, for they changed too quickly and their purpose was more picturesque than precise. But something in her language disturbed him, beyond the fluid chant of words and the dark flavor of her poetry. Something directed at *him,* specifically.

This is the bastion of my soul, which I have fortified
    with spears
Against an enemy whose very form is fire.
I hold forth my arm and my sword in defiance
While the enemy's power seeps into my very blood.

I don't like this, Feran thought.

What thoughts are mine, and which another's fear?
The fortress of my hope is laid low, the barriers de-
    serted.

My arm is caught in winds of motion foreign to my soul
The enemy sweeps by, is gone, remains . . .

Feran forced his mind away from the entrapment of her words. *It means something else,* he told himself. *When you know all the modes, as I do not, the story is different. It must be!*

He forced himself to think of other things. (If he paid no attention to her, would her words affect him anyway?) Like the statue of Anzha lyu that stood in the Museum. Like the single darkest secret of his life, the need to share it, the fear that he would do so. The guilt, and the suffering.

Something made him look toward Zatar. The Pri'tiera was watching him.

Why are you doing this to me? he thought. The words lacked the power to span the space between them. Once, they didn't. Once he could have lifted the answer delicately from the Pri'tiera's surface mind without Zatar ever being aware of it. Now he was limited to words, and to all the vulnerability which that implied.

And I am so vulnerable, he thought. He plastered a look of attentiveness on his face and turned to face the poet, but inside, he was trying to block out her words and master his unease.

And Zatar kept watching him. Alarmingly, Feran *knew* it—as certainly as if he were looking back at him, meeting his gaze, hearing his challenge.

The power is coming back, he thought, chilled.

* * *

Nightmares: Anzha lyu Mitethe screaming in the darkness, tearing him apart to bloody bits and pieces while his hands, bound in heavy bracelets, were helpless to stop her.

He awoke in a cold sweat. Lina was beside him, curled against his arm. She too was awake.

"I just had the most terrible dream," she whispered. His throat tightened; he knew what was coming. "I was being dismembered alive. . . ."

He was frightened.

* * *

The Pri'tiera summoned him again.

"Don't look so anxious." He seemed amused. "You act as if I mean to incriminate you merely for having knowledge of a thing you've never experienced." (Surface impression: You *have* never experienced it . . . *have* you?)

Feran fought down the awareness, forced shut the door to unnatural feeling. "The subject makes me uncomfortable, Pri'tiera." That was true enough.

Zatar shrugged. "Then you must come to terms with it."

I did! Feran thought. *And what right have you, with your prying, to drag it forth from me? To unnerve me so that I lose hold of the self-discipline that has been my only armor against the possibility of Braxin wrath?*

Ar, he was shaking. Better stop that, lest Zatar notice. "What do you want to know?"

"Tell me about Telepathic Etiquette."

"Just custom, as I understand it. The mind gives off . . . surface thoughts, a sort of running commentary on things of immediate concern . . . those are up for grabs, being broadcast. One isn't supposed to reach for anything else without deliberate encouragement."

"So there *is* concern over the possibility of invasion of privacy, after all. Encouraging. This 'reaching—as you call it—what does it consist of?"

He forced the lie to his lips. "I don't know, Pri'tiera."

"Nothing? Not even hearsay?"

He wouldn't accept the excuse; this was dangerous ground. How much would a non-psychic really know of such things? "I can tell you only what I've heard." He forced a laugh; the sound seemed hollow even to him. "You can hardly expect me to know the details of such things."

Can't I, the thought came, a whisper entering his mind without his reaching for it.

No!

"Of course not," the Pri'tiera said quietly. "But you've been of tremendous service to me, Feran. Even the little you recall is far more than any another available source has to offer. You'll have a large part to play in whatever decision I finally make."

"What do you think that will be?"

Zatar was amused. "I can hardly say at this point. There's still much to consider. But I will tell you this: I believe the traditional

Braxin fear of telepathy is well-founded where there is the power to alter a man's mind. As I said, psychics we may be able to tolerate—but the elite, the telepaths and the Probes, we cannot."

The words echoed in his surface thoughts; if Zatar were psychic he would see them reflected in the halfbreed's mind. "Interesting," Feran managed. "But what likelihood is there that the psychic strain has survived all these years of bloodshed?"

"You told me yourself that the power comes late in life. Isn't it possible that the only psychics we've been killing are the ones weak enough to be discovered?"

"The power can be evident from birth," he blurted out.

"The Institute doesn't believe so."

He met the Pri'tiera's eyes and forced his voice to be steady. "I've heard rumors," he said quietly.

Just rumors. . . .

* * *

The hell of an uncontrolled planet, heaving torments of geological strata and streams of molten rock forcing their way through the tortured ground to spurt loose on the surface, steaming, flooding, bloody ice crashing down into a sea filled with dark creatures, screaming and crying, shreds of torn flesh caught in the suction of the tidal wave battering the shores and earth breaking loose before the hurricane—

"My Lord!"

Lina was shaking him. He clutched at her, shuddering as the vision faded.

"What is it?" she asked, frightened by his need for her.

Slowly the trembling subsided. "Nightmare." His chest was tight in the aftermath of fear. Concern bled into him through her fingertips; he jerked violently away. "An attack of . . . fear . . . nothing . . . I'll be all right."

"Just that?" She didn't want to pry but she did want to help.

"Just that," he forced out. "Sleep. I'll be all right. Don't worry."

Darkness. Awareness of a self next to him, a female presence pressing against his side. Emptiness and fear—not his own.

I am sorry—I am sorry—I am sorry! Leave me alone!

The visions resumed.

* * *

Walking in the streets of Kurat: a woman passing, restless at some delay, another whose sexuality lay rich beneath the surface, pleading for attention. A man, annoyed over some business deal, another planning vengeance, a third anticipating dinner. A pregnant woman, as yet unaware of her condition. (Oh, B'Salos! Not *that* much, please!) Lust. Hunger. Hurry. Exhaustion. Anticipation. Concern.

The House of Zatar.

He put his hand to the plate and the doors parted. "Lord Feran," he announced.

The guard nodded. "You are expected, Lord. In the—"

"—study, yes, I know." Alarmed by his own carelessness, he hastily added, "He already told me."

The guard thought a shrug.

Ar, I'm acting like an amateur! Even children can divorce thought from physicality better than this. Listen to the voice, internalize nothing else. . . .

Zatar welcomed him but offered no wine. In that alcohol dulled the edge of telepathic sensitivity, Feran would have appreciated some. "I'm so glad you could come, Lord Feran."

He knows, he knows, he knows. . . .

"I'm glad to be of service." *Leave me alone!*

They sat. Zatar pulled and turned on a ringrecorder. "Tell me what you know of the Disciplines."

Nothing! Nothing! What would a non-psychic know of such things? "I . . . really don't know, Pri'tiera."

"Nothing at all?" (I don't believe you.) "Not even the names of some of them?"

"There is . . . Touch Discipline, I think." (*Why* that *one? Why do I torment myself?*) "And . . . something affecting recall. . . ."

"Memory Discipline," he prompted.

"If you know, why ask me?" Feran's tone was blatantly miserable.

Ever calm, ever in control, Zatar smiled. "Don't be upset, Feran. I want some things that are buried deep in your memory, obscured by years of Braxin life. I'm trying to push you to reach for those things. Since you're not a psychic you can't have complete knowledge of the telepathic world—I realize that—but you may have heard enough here and there to be useful, if I can unearth it. Don't worry, Lord Feran." There was amusement in his voice. "I don't bear you any malice for what you remember."

You would if you understood. "I . . . don't feel well, Pri'tiera. I think that's the problem. Do you think we could continue this some other time?"

The dark eyes fixed on him, exploring his soul. For a moment Feran was lost in the memory of a child's terror, staring into the eyes of a predator and knowing, *This one is deadly. This one hungers for the kill.* Then it was gone, and the present returned.

"Very well," Zatar said finally. "If you think it will help."

Nothing will help but confession, but oh, I dare not! Why do you drive me like this, Zatar—why not just kill me and be done with it!"

"Thank you," he managed. "Thank you."

"Tomorrow?"

The velvet eyes, the hate, the hunger. . . . "Tomorrow will be fine."

"Take care, Lord Feran." A hunter's smile, a hunter's aura. "I hope you feel better."

I hope I do, too.

* * *

He whimpered in the night, and there was no one to hear him. He dared not sleep with a woman lest he share the terrible dreams and so reveal himself.

Anzha lyu beckons to him, a bloodstained child with empty orbital fossi and a third eye branded into her forehead. "I've been waiting, Feran. Come join me. . . .

Wake me up, wake me up!

The earth shakes, the sky thunders. Pieces of rock fall down all around him, and hailstones the size of fists plummet from the heavens, only to barely miss his head. He runs, terrified, and a chasm splits beneath his feet, releasing a gasp of hot air and sulfurous fumes that send him choking into the volcanic depths, falling, screaming. . . .

* * *

In the morning he walked the streets, shaken, preferring the surface thoughts of strangers to the unpleasant tangle of foreboding that his House had become. How many had shared his dream? At least five, probably more. It was the talk of the morning.

His powers were coming back, but his control wasn't: that was the painful, unavoidable reality of his situation. He was as helpless in the grip of his power as he had been those many years ago, when puberty and full telepathy fought for dominance of his attention and both were broadcast to all hearing minds in the Institute and even further. Those had been terrible years; he had barely survived them, crying night after night in fearful hysteria and practicing the Disciplines until his mind was numb, trying to turn it *off* . . . why wouldn't those same Disciplines work now?

It's been too long, he admitted. *I'm out of practice. There's no magic to it—simply a skill which once learned can be forgotten. I forgot it.*

He knew the solution, but it frightened him. He would have to learn control all over again, drill the alien patterns into his inner mind until the needed protection snapped easily into place with a simple memorized stimulus.

But once I begin that process, he thought, *I'm utterly committed. All the sensitivity will come back to me, all the power I worked so hard to bury, I'll be a telepath again. And worse . . . I'll have the memories.*

On the far side of Kurat he found an appealing woman whose surface mind was amenable to more intimate contact than the streets allowed. Calmer, he invited her to his House; she accepted, gladly. Arousal glowed about her like a beacon, and for a moment he was almost glad for his reawakening.

But when he touched her she trembled, and when he attempted to lose his fears in the warmth of her flesh she drew away from him, frightened.

Touch Discipline, he begged. The barely-remembered pattern flooded his mind. He touched her again, feeling the softness of her skin beneath his hand and the warmth of fingers on his female shoulder, resonating dual pleasure. . . .

She screamed and she fainted, and when she came to, she cried. He killed her. He had to. He would have to kill from now on, if he meant to have pleasure.

B'Salos! he thought, trembling uncontrollably. *What am I going to do?*

* * *

Fearful but determined, Feran raised his hand to the doorplate.

"Welcome, Lord Feran. " The guard was his usual amenable self. "The Pri'tiera is waiting for you in his study."

He walked the distance slowly. *Do I look like a doomed man?* he wondered.

He would throw himself on Zatar's mercy. Or rather, he would confess his power and ask for asylum. The Braxaná had no equivalent of mercy and scorned compassion in all its manifestations, but Zatar would understand the usefulness of having a telepathic ally and would spare his life. Perhaps. But if he were to discover the secret himself, Feran knew, then the Probe's life would be forefeit. *A choice between death and destruction,* he thought grimly. *But still my choice.*

With a pounding heart he rapped once to announce his arrival.

A slave opened the door and bowed as he entered, then passed by him in exit. Lounging comfortably, the Pri'tiera nodded. "Feeling better?"

He drew a deep breath, albeit a shaky one. *Wait through the preliminary social repartee? Bring the matter up right at the beginning?* Suddenly he found he lacked courage.

"Have a seat, Feran. You don't look well at all." Again that faint taste of triumph to make the words biting. *He knows,* Feran assured himself. *No man would act like this who didn't.*

He sat, and at least there was the comfort of letting his legs relinquish the weight of his body to a more solid support. "I have a question, Pri'tiera, regarding the things we've been discussing."

He nodded pleasantly. "I'm listening."

"You said once—or implied—that there might be psychics living among the Braxins all along, who had never been discovered because they learned to hide their secret before anyone noticed their abnormality." *Courage!* "What would you do with such people?"

"Again, you rush me. The particulars of this issue are complicated, and Braxin society is, hardly ready to tolerate such men, regardless of my will. Yes, ruler though I am, I need to be careful—too strong a defiance of tradition can unsettle my throne yet. But, in general, let me say this: mild psychic power, I believe, could be safely channeled—no, let me say instead *must* be safely channeled. If our enemies have this power, Feran, then we can't afford to ignore it. The lesser psychics could be tolerated, if our society were properly prepared to receive them. I see no hope, however, of controlling the greater talents. Everything I read, every word you speak, convinces me they must die if the fabric of our culture is to be maintained. That's my current thinking. Does it answer your question?"

All too well. "Yes." *There is no hope.* "Thank you."

"Telepaths only, you understand. And Probes. The rest might be spared, for their limitations make them vulnerable, and thus they can be controlled."

But where does that leave me? "I understand, Pri'tiera."

"Now, to the business of the day." He sat upright, running his questions through his mind and assigning them an order. "I would like to return to Touch Discipline. What can you tell me?"

Everything. Nothing. To his horror, Feran discovered he had forgotten what he had already told Zatar regarding his knowledge of that Discipline. All he needed now was to contradict himself! But he was shaken by the disruption of his plans and could hardly bring himself to speak, much less think. "I . . . don't remember, Pri'tiera." He didn't dare reveal himself, he knew that now. But everything was in chaos.

"Then let's start with something simpler." He looked concerned, but his surface thoughts sent a different message entirely, *You are mine!* "You don't look well at all, Feran. Can I get you anything?"

"Some wine," he murmured. "Foreign." He couldn't handle the trace hallucinogens which were present in the Central vintages. "Please."

Zatar called for a servant and passed on the order; a few minutes later the wine came. The Pri'tiera poured, in silence.

"Try this," he offered.

Feran took the goblet and raised it to his lips. Half of his mind begged for physical control, for the delicacy of the upper class, the gracefulness that would disguise his inner turmoil. But the desperate half of him needed the alcohol in his system to help shut out the other man's thoughts, and he downed it quickly.

Minds dulled—his, and that which he was reading. "I'm ready," he said at last.

"Are you sure?" Zatar asked him.

The room was swimming. Too much wine, on too little sleep. How many days since he had gotten rest?

"Pri'tiera, I—"

This was wrong. This wasn't the alcohol, it was something else—but something in the drink, certainly. Yes. Was this a vintage he had never tried, whose hallucinogens were not acceptable to his system? Or . . . would Zatar drug him? . . . why?

He tried to speak. Instead, he fell.

Blackness.

* * *

A planet is a hideous thing, a mass of seething malignance bound together by wild and unstable gravity. It boils, it slides, it buries life in its fathomless depths and suffocates it with miles of dirt and ash. The rocks grind and the mountains tremble and lightning rains down from the heavens to eradicate man, who has dared to sully its surface and threaten all with his dreams of a controlled environment. A planet abides that life which accepts its whims, but man it rejects, man it seeks to obliterate, pitting the monumental force of its instability against that pitiful life form, driving man forth to seek the stars or die. See! The flowing hot rock of the volcano's fury, the destructive trembling of the earthquake, the awesome motion of the seas and the rhythm of the icy regions with their capture and release of water—all beyond the hand of man, all determined to humble his arrogance in a display of absolute devastation. The mountains revolt at last and move to crush you, and winds to drive the seeds of illness into your skin and eyes. Below you the earth is seething with dark intent, waiting for the perfect moment to claim you for its vengeance. Don't stand still a moment longer than you have to! Visit no land twice, lest it know you too well, learning your weaknesses, plotting your demise! Flee, daughter of the stars, child of the dark and empty regions, before this hot realm rejects you entirely and crushes your soul in its killing embrace! There, in the darkness between the stars, there is peace, there is safety. Run to it child, run . . . !

* * *

He awoke in a strange room.

Hasha.

He had dreamed it again, just like in the old days. A nightmare rising from the depths of his guilt: images he had placed in a young girl's mind, returned to haunt him. Anzha lyu's conditioning.

And then the most terrible knowledge of all:

I shared it.

His heart was still pounding and only slowly did it resume its normal rhythm. His face was cold and wet, and his clothing adhered to his skin.

Where am I?

As soon as he asked it, he knew—*the House of Zatar.*

And he remembered.

A tendril of thought searched the room for contact, found none. He was alone. The tears came then, and the shaking, so violent that he terrified himself with the outpouring of emotion. *Keep it contained,* he begged himself, *don't broadcast it to the others!* But he knew he had lost all control, and that last night he had had none whatsoever, and that he had dreamed his dream for the whole House to see. If they realized it. . . .

I am doomed.

He rose. His joints were stiff and the wool clung to his trembling limbs. His legs would barely support him. *I look a mess,* he thought—Braxaná reflex. Then he laughed, mirthlessly.

What does it matter?

A sudden vertigo of helplessness almost brought him to his knees. What would he do? Where would he go? How would he live, and how hide his power, when it had become so strong?

Fool! he answered bitterly. *The whole House knows by now, which means that he surely does.*

Why has he let me live this long?

It was just a glimmer of hope, but he grasped at it.

If the power was controlled, Zatar would tolerate it. If he himself controlled it, surely he could trust it!

His legs grew slowly steady; his chest stopped heaving and air came more easily to him. Hope? Did he dare?

It was that or die. *And bless you all,* he thought, *I want to live!*

When he had at least partial control over his body he wiped the wetness from his face and braved the door that led into the light.

A servant bowed, appearing not to notice his disheveled state. "My Lord."

"Where is Zatar?" His voice was uneven, his throat tight.

"In his library, Lord. Do you wish to be taken to him?"

Yes. "Yes." Speaking did not come easily to him. Nor did walking, as he realized while following the servant. His body was preparing for death, gathering itself together in anticipation of the final condemnation.

The servant slipped into the library and announced him. A moment later he was ushered inside.

"My Lord . . ."

He lost nerve.

"Yes?"

He was drowning in a sea of the other man's power and could not get hold of his intent.

Zatar watched him for a moment and then called for his Mistress. She must have been nearby for she appeared but a moment later, from a room at the rear of the library.

The Pri'tiera pointed to Feran. "Get the Probe a drink."

The walls of fear closed in and he was crying, crying, voice and soul pouring out anguish and fear and pleading, not wanting to die, not knowing how to live. . . .

A goblet was touched to his lips. He looked up and visions swam before his eyes: a tall and dangerous man, a kneeling, supportive woman. He sipped the wine. Central. Strong. His vision cleared.

"Leave us," Zatar ordered.

His Mistress left them alone together.

"Pri'tiera," he gasped. "Take the power! Use it! I will serve you in everything! Please. . . ."

Zatar waited.

Slowly, understanding, Feran looked up at him. Trembling, he extended his arms before him, his hands turned palm down. Despite the shame of the act there was a comfort to it, as though he had finally made a commitment so total that now his fate was out of his own hands entirely. And it was. He waited.

"A gesture," the Pri'tiera said at last. "And perhaps, on the surface, sincere. But beneath that?"

Horrified, Feran drew back. It had never occurred to him that he might be rejected. "What do you want? What must I do?"

"Prove your commitment. Tell me what I want to know."

"Anything!"

"You were a Probe for the Institute."

The shame . . . "Yes."

"You worked the conditioning on Anzha lyu Mitethe."

He tried to hold back the answer but it came, obedient to the other man's overpowering will. "Yes."

"And designed it."

He nodded, miserable.

"What was it? All of it, Feran!"

The words rushed out, a tidal wave of guilt and memory. "They wanted to know her racial background. He was choking on his own voice, but somehow continued. "They were certain that studying it would help them find at least one of the genetic sequences they wanted."

"What did you do?"

"I . . . made sure she would keep moving. I cut her off from human contact. I cut short capacity for Touch Discipline. I instilled a long range Dominant Tendency."

"Which is what?"

"A goal. An intent. It colors everything, so that you serve it without knowing. You want other things, other goals—but only because when you have them it will bring you closer to That."

"The conditioned purpose?"

He nodded helplessly.

"And in her case—what?"

"To keep moving, to be restless, to want . . . to find her people. To discover the alien source of her genetic background. In support I instilled progressive zeymophobia, fear of being planet-bound. We didn't know she'd wind up in the fleet! We wanted to make certain she would travel—"

The Pri'tiera reached down and pulled him to his feet, a hand in his collar. The power of his revulsion was so intense that it was painful to receive, and Feran cringed before the onslaught. "You! You don't deserve life, Azean! You are the darkness we try to avoid—you! You are everything we feared in the infancy of our tradition, so terribly that we were willing to sacrifice our own children to see that you never came among us." His face darkened. "And what about your children, Probe?"

Not that! "What about them?"

"You killed them."

Tears came to his eyes as he nodded. "Two."

"Psychic?"

He nodded.

"And the others?"

No, no. . . . "There is only one other," he managed.

"Alive?"

"D'vra's child."

"*Alive?*"

"Yes." He choked on the admission.

"And psychic, I suppose. No, don't answer me—I see it in your face. So it enters our Race at last, despite all our efforts. Now tell me, *Azean:* what mercy do you, think you deserve? What weakness do you see in me that you think I would grant you life after all you've done?"

He released Feran suddenly and the Probe fell heavily to the floor, broken. There were tears in his eyes—of terror, of shame—and he wept as they flowed down his face, mourning the death of his Braxaná identity.

Zatar had planned this from the beginning. Now that Feran was forced to face the truth, he could see that. First there had been the incident with the almonjeddei, followed by hints that he now recalled . . . how many traps had Zatar set for him, letting the tensions build until they were nearly intolerable, choosing that moment to break him?

Zatar looked down at him as he wept. Finally, in a voice as cold as death itself, he demanded: "What was your purpose in coming here?"

"I was sent to spy on you." The Probe's voice was hollow, automatic, "They knew I would come to be of value to you, and that you would involve me in Border negotiations. I was to broadcast your plans. . . ." He shook his head, his expression pained. "But it didn't even work," he whispered. "They put me against her. How could I permit any contact? She would kill me—"

"What else?"

He was struggling with himself now, trying to stop the flow of self-damnation, incapable of exerting any conscious control over the terrible outpouring. "I was to procure a purebred Braxaná for them, so they could obtain a psychogenetic profile. That was my Dominant Tendency—" He stopped suddenly and his eyes widened in fearful understanding as seemingly unrelated motives fit themselves into a large pattern.

"D'vra," he whispered, horrified.

Even his most Braxaná hungers had not been his own; they had been instilled in him for a purpose, for *the* purpose, and his natural desires had developed to fit that mold. Was any thought his? Had he ever done anything that did not have, somewhere, the mark of the Institute upon it?

He was speechless. Drained. He knew suddenly why such care was taken to see that a telepath never learned the full extent of his conditioning. To do so removed all pretense of free will—and a creature without free will was not a man, only a tool made of flesh and blood, with no more initiative than a House computer and considerably less freedom. Desolated, he bowed his head in shame. There was no hope left, not even fear, only an emptiness of purpose that left him shivering before the force of the man who had stripped him of his humanity.

The Pri'tiera seemed satisfied. "Understand this:" His voice was emotionless, not compassionate by any means but no longer overtly threatening. "I had to break you; there was no other way. It was clear you were sent here to fulfill the Institute's purpose; I had to find out what that was, and there was only one way to do it. I've known about you for years, Feran, ever since I found your name in the Institute's files. As for your relationship with the Starcommander, that was only hinted at in the files themselves—li Pazua was careful to see that no one could learn the details of their conditioning—but when I watched the two of you interact at the conference table, I knew. You are a resource I need to tap, Feran, and in order to do that I must own you. If you submit to me, I will use you. But the choice is your own—which I daresay is more freedom than the Institute ever gave you." His voice was quiet, but his command was absolute. "Decide."

He wanted freedom, and he wanted his pleasure, but he knew now that those things were tainted for him. Looking up, he raised his arms—though the weight of his training pressed downward upon them, screaming blasphemies at his betrayal of The Cause—and extended his hands toward Zatar, palms open. And he spoke his Name, softly—not the one li Pazua had given him, but the one he had chosen for himself years later, the one which was his True Name in a way that no sounds of Azea could ever be. It was the ultimate submission a man could make.

Slowly Zatar's hands came down and clasped his wrists tightly, in the ritual of acceptance. It was like a warm blanket that came down over Feran and soothed his hurt, until the guilt receded and the pain was less and he was at last able to meet the man's eyes again. A terrible weight was gone from him which had been worse than any slavery, for self-hate is more merciless than any human master.

"I choose not to mark you," Zatar told him. "Go back to your House and work on controlling your power. You're free of the past, now; I've broken that bond. And I'll send you women who won't talk, until you're in control again."

Feran bowed his head. “I am yours,” he whispered. And then, from the depths of his being, came words he had never expected to say—but they were the truth, and he let them come.

Softly: “Thank you.”

Harkur: In order to make the most of the future, we must first comprehend the past.

TWENTY-THREE

The messenger was trembling as he put his hand to the doorplate. "You're sure he isn't busy?" he stalled.

"I'm sure he's busy," the guard said irritably. "But he'll see you. Go ahead."

He pressed his hand against the warm black surface and tried to gather his courage. Inside the room his presence was being announced to the great Pri'tiera, as well as details of his identity. After a moment the door opened, signaling Zatar's acceptance of his visit. Still shaking, he entered.

"Great Pri'tiera—" he began.

"I received your message," Zatar interrupted. His voice was cold and unwelcoming; clearly he had been doing something important and was annoyed by the intrusion. "Well? What is it?"

"The administrators of the prime excavation of Berros beg that you join them at the site of their work. They want you to . . ." He lost all the carefully prepared words, retained only their meager substance. ". . . to see something. They ask that you come immediately."

"I don't like mysteries," the Pritiera said coldly, "and I haven't time for them. What's the problem?"

"Please, Magnificent One. I wasn't released to tell you. Only to bid you come, and—"

"But you know what's going on?"

Miserable, he nodded.

"And you feel it merits this much drama?"

He whispered it. "Yes, Lord."

Zatar sighed, nodded, and stood. The messenger could feel his stomach unknot as he did so. "All right. It isn't that far—and the site director knows better than to bother me for trivial matters. I'll assume it's important enough to merit my attention—for the moment. You have a transport waiting?"

"On your platform, Great One."

"It will be a short while before I can leave; wait for me there."

The messenger had never been so grateful for dismissal.

Berros was a planet-subservient—more accurately, a large moon orbiting the gas giant which was fifth in the B'Saloan system. Almost as large as Braxi, nearly as comfortable, the natural satellite had been explored in the ninth decade before the Coronation, had served as a base of operations for Project Skysearch in the fifth, and had been planetformed by Harkur himself in the years immediately following his ascension to the Braxin throne. It was he who had colonized it. He had made it beautiful. He had moved the seat of Braxin government to its rusty earth and red-hued skies in order to settle any question of which country the first Braxin monarch was going to rule from. Braxi was united, and, until the planetforming of Zhene could be completed, Berros was its capital.

Then the Braxaná came to power, sun-reverent barbarians who clung to their native soil with superstitious fervor; the glory of Berros waned and died. There were only memories now, dry plants blowing in a dry wind, and lifeforms that had strayed so far from their immigrant origins that their original species could only be guessed at. And ruins. The glory of Harkur's first court had been reduced to these few feeble monuments, which sand and iron dust had worn to near shapelessness. No one cared about Berros, or what memories it might contain. No one had bothered with it for centuries, preferring the glory of the present to the uncertain rewards of investigating the past.

No one—until now.

The site director was a lean man whom Zatar had never liked. It was with ill patience that the Pri'tiera endured his lengthy non-explanation, listening to him say nothing in a multitude of ways until at last he could stand it no longer. "Just take me to it," he commanded, in a tone that would brook no disobedience. "Whatever it is."

A brief nervous twitch distorted the other man's face, saying volumes for his discomfort. He himself could not go, of course, he had . . . ah, *business* with the main palace that had to be *reviewed*. . . .

Making a mental note to have the man's contract investigated,

Zatar permitted the evasion. The messenger who had brought him to Berros was assigned to be his guide. He was clearly upset about it, but said nothing.

What could be here, Zatar wondered, *that these people found so unnerving?* Harkur had emptied the planet of all its treasures, save only in those few buildings which he maintained for his pleasure after making the move to Zhene. His successors had ignored the place. What could have survived that many millennia of neglect, that would inspire such fear?

They took an aircar to the site of the mystery, a hunting palace which Harkur had frequented until his death in '57. Zatar had no real interest in it, or in its ruined environs; politics alone had moved him to begin his excavations, and politics were his only concern. He was his planet's first Braxaná monarch, and he needed to fortify his image as such until the two disparate concepts—Braxaná and autocrat—became indivisible in the public mind. What better way to do that then to draw a parallel between himself and the greatest of all Braxin autocrats, the incomparable Harkur? And what better way to accomplish *that* goal than to become identified with the last remains of Harkur's greatness?

He would have given his Name for a woman of that descent, for the Braxin mind would readily accept their sexual union as a link between the two bloodlines. But such could not be found. Harkur was of a common bloodline; the Braxaná considered such men to be of inferior stock (Harkur's very success was as embarrassing as it was gratifying to them) and it was unlikely that any records of that lineage had survived the centuries of their rule. Still, it was Zatar's seeming respect for common-blood concerns which had given him control of the Holding. And thus: the ruins of Berros, with himself as renovator.

The aircar slowed to a stop, hovering some two feet above a field of rubble. In the distance was the northern palace—or all that was left of it, which wasn't much. He looked at the messenger curiously; the frightened man nodded, indicating the ground ahead. Too rough for the aircar.

"A portion of the hunting palace," he explained hurriedly, "buried intact. We thought you should see it . . . as it is."

Briefly—because it was Braxaná reflex, as natural to him as breathing—Zatar considered the possibility of a trap. But the field was empty, and there were no weapons about—he had checked—not even human life, save that of himself and this wretched excuse for a courier. Besides, he was prepared. Turning his personal forcefield on, he stepped over the side of the car and set foot on the broken, dried-out ground.

"Which way?"

The messenger indicated an opening some short distance from where the aircar waited, a dark hole leading to a narrow passage. It was clear from the nature of the rubble that this had once been part of the original building; apparently the lower floors, sealed off by the collapse of the upper stories and the accumulated dirt of centuries, had endured.

"Precede me," he commanded.

The messenger took a light from his pocket and led the way through a twisted, winding passage. Force-supports held back debris where the walls themselves had failed to do so; in the deeper recesses of the building, less and less aid was necessary. Finally they came to an inlaid staircase; lightly strewn with dirt and gravel, it was a finely-worked symbol of the opulence that had once existed here. And of the preservation which the dry Berros'n air had encouraged.

The staircase led to a room, high-ceilinged, which the messenger entered. "A dining hall," he said. His voice was shaking badly. What could be here, in this well-preserved place, that would so frighten the man?

Then Zatar entered.

And saw.

Part of the Braxaná system was anticipation. *Expect the worst of man,* tradition said, *and you will never be surprised. Expect the worst of the world and you will never be disappointed.* That was part and parcel of the game they played, the elaborate mental exercise called *image,* which allowed them to go through life without ever revealing their true selves to another human being.

In this case, the system failed.

Slowly, incredulously, Zatar the Magnificent walked toward the painting which hung at the end of the dining hall. Acids inherent in the medium had eaten away a good deal of its surface, but not so much that its subject matter was obscured.

Amazed, he stared at it.

The inscription in the gold frame was also clear, and he brushed the dust from it and read what he simply couldn't believe.

"Impossible," he murmured. He turned off his forcefield and touched its surface; a chip of paint adhered to his glovetip and came off when he removed his hand. No, it couldn't even be moved until a supportive field had been worked into it, and that would take time. "How many people know?" he wondered aloud.

"The site director, the archeologists concerned, myself . . . all sworn to secrecy, my Lord."

Yes, he thought, *the only problem with that is that only one small group in the history of man has ever managed to keep secrets, and that is the Braxaná.*

He looked at the man. His image had collapsed and he knew it; it felt strangely naked to be merely human, a creature rendered helpless by surprise like everyone else. True, it took something on this scale to break the image down—but it had been broken, and that had been witnessed.

"I have to kill you," he said, almost apologetically.

The man was clearly terrified, but he nodded and slowly dropped to his knees. He had expected this—they all had. There was no way this discovery could have elicited any other reaction, and no way the Pri'tiera could allow a commoner to live who had seen him so taken aback, so vulnerable, even for an instant. This assignment had been his death sentence.

He waited.

"You could have run," Zatar said quietly. "Or protested."

"I know the custom." The man's voice was barely a whisper. "Should I defy the Master of the Holding?"

He had strange feelings, new feelings, feelings that were not wholly welcome. "You have family?"

"Three sons, my Lord. One of them is my own offspring."

"The site director can reach them?"

He nodded, confused.

Without looking Zatar drew his sword. The man's eyes were locked on his, also refusing to look at the deadly steel.

"Your family," Zatar said quietly, "will be taken into my House."

Startled, he managed, "Thank you. My Lord—may I ask. . . ."

"Anything. Right now, you're the only man in the Holding who can hear the answers."

"What will you do?" he whispered.

Zatar shut his eyes. *Isn't that the question?* "I don't know."

"But something?"

"Preserve the painting. Make it generally available. It will take some time before we can remove it safely, more to restore it to its original condition . . . it belongs to the Holding.

"That isn't what I meant," the man ventured.

"I know. And I can't answer you." He looked back at the painting, and shook his head in wonder. "I don't know myself, right now."

The man bowed his head.

—And the sword was a crescent of light through his neck, cleanly separating head from shoulder and leaving both halves to drop to the dusty floor.

Without resheathing the blade, Zatar turned back to the painting.

"Hasha . . ." he whispered softly.

It was a long while before he left.

Harkur: A man does not truly understand his limitations until he has tested them.

TWENTY-FOUR

In the velvet black of space the station was like a jewel, its sunward side gleaming with the mirrored surfaces of luminal collectors and a thousand needle-fine starships radiating out from its protective center like sparks of light glinting off its surface. In the darkness around it a protective field glowed softly, and its amber warmth added luster to the star-like display.

The thousand ships turned slowly about their watchful center, streamlined lengths of polished pseudometal with the barest hint of dormant energy fields woven into their hulls. They were children, waiting to be set loose in the world—Starbirds, close by their silver nest, longing for freedom. Their wings lay folded against their sides, fitted carefully into the smooth, slim length that could cut an atmosphere without effort, and fully half of their bulk was filled with the generators of travel: shipshell field, strong and resilient; gravitic compensation and interlocked accelerator; three fully operational defense fields whose combined deflective power could turn aside the wrath of a warship. They were creatures of speed, strength, and beauty, and they needed only the hand of man to send them into flight.

Inside the global station, guards were quiet but watchful. Only a fool would seek to breach that amber glow but fools there were in plenty, and so they watched.

"Ship coming out of Lurien orbit." The report was made in the calm voice of one who never expects trouble.

The station captain glanced briefly at the scanner display to see that everything was in order. Lurien was densely populated and it was not unusual for interstellar traffic to pass their way. "Too close," he commented. "Clearance?"

"Military. StarControl priority one—warship in for repairs, from the Active Zone. This is its shuttle."

The captain nodded. Lurien was the capital of the Empire's

technical expertise, and those same qualities which had assured the Luriens of contracting the construction of the Starbirds also meant that from time to time military ships came by for repairs and updating. He checked the broadcast codes; everything seemed proper. "Slow," he commented.

"Deliberate minimal velocity until clearing this station, they explained."

"All right." He stared at the screens a moment longer, looking for trouble. There was none. "Let it pass."

He was somewhat psychic and, as a security officer, painstakingly thorough. For a moment he stilled his body and reached out with his special sensitivity, searching the sphere in his keeping. Nothing greeted his touch which spoke of life or sentience, and no intent from farther away speared his searching mind with focused malevolence.

"Feels good," he told them. "But keep on standard surveillance."

The small ship drew near to them; he double-checked its ID and found it appropriate. From the *Conqueror,* eh? It had been many years since *that* ship had last been to Lurien.—Come to think of it, wasn't there a repair station closer to its sector?

"Watch it anyway," he muttered. Charts displayed its speed—constant, and its course—close but nonintersecting, as it slowly passed them by. Not until it was out of scanner range did the captain fully relax. "All right," he said. "Wish they wouldn't come so damned close, though."

* * *

In the darkness of space, a single figure floated. Immersed in an ancient and bulky vacuum suit it gave no hint of form or sex, and the supportive field woven into its suitshell was so minimal as to barely register on the station's screens.

It tensed as a thought came questing in its direction, then turned the inquiry aside. *Nothing is out here,* the intruder thought aloud. And it inserted that thought into the station captain's mind with a skill that few could manage.

The figure waited, floating.

When all inquiry had passed it by, it reached one bloated arm in an insulated glove to a control panel built into the suit's chest region. The control panel and its forecefield had been added; the long umbilical tubes of primitive space travel had been removed. Tanks supplied air by strictly mechanical means and the insulation was sufficient to support human life for a short period of time without a heat generator or dehumidifier.

It was an artificial skin, and in it a man might face the stars unprotected by the focused energy of human science. For ten thousand years no man had chosen to do so; when a human might swim naked in the darkness with only a special forcefield for cover and a minimal generator to support the living functions, why immerse one's body in this monstrosity of early technology? But it was clear that one person, at least, had the motivation necessary, for the hand pressed down against the heavy switch and turned the suit's generators off.

Then there was silence; not the hum of a recycler, nor the steady vibration of a forcefield generator. For the first time in millennia a human being faced the cold of space with nothing but matter for protection, and it was only with difficulty that this pioneer restrained her enthusiasm to the tight proximity of her own padded body.

Now, she thought.

A touch to one panel brought the portable accelerators briefly into play, and for an instant there was the forward thrust of their action. Afterward she floated, again lost in the silence of nonpower. In all her plans there was only that one weakness, that the station might pick up her minimal output and deduce her intent. But from the guardians of the Starbirds there was nothing, neither probing fields nor pangs of mental concern. The computers attributed her motion to the residue of her shuttle, which had left a faint trail in its wake. Such power as they detected was not sufficient to support life, fire a weapon, maintain a computer or even fix a navigational probe; hence it was meaningless, and mechanical reasoning assigned it to the most logical nearby source.

Slowly the figure approached the amber forcefield, which shone like glass in the starlight. Much like a diver, propelled by a momentary burst of minimal force, the figure breached station security and passed through the amber wall. Slowly, like a meteor might; lifeless, because life requires generators to exist in the Void. It was not aimed at a ship and could not be a threat; the computers let it pass, consigning it to the realm of insignificant data. The captain didn't notice it; the others never would.

Still guarding against involuntary thought-broadcasting, the stardiver chose an objective and turned, with one tiny burst of power, to approach it. Then she checked: she was unnoticed, at least as far as the minds in the station were concerned. Good. She could easily blanket the station in a cloud of non-awareness, but she doubted she could hold so many minds against the distractions and alarms of their security equipment. Besides, there was a psychic present, trained to recognize the same techniques she had mastered, and that meant still another variable.

So she strove for silence, both mechanical and mental, as she approached her chosen starship and slowed, coming to its surface.

Nearly motionless, she touched the silver shipshell. She worked swiftly; the station hadn't detected her yet, but that didn't mean there wasn't a power-sweep operating which would catch her when she split the Starbird's field. With certain fingers she sought out the access panel and cracked it open; the emergency override switch, hidden so well that no one could find it who hadn't studied the ship's carefully guarded plans, locked easily in the desired position. Slowly the shipshell field drew back from the vessel's portal, and a moment later the seamless silver surface divided, permitting entrance.

Agile despite the hindrance of her primitive spacesuit, the trespasser entered the lock quickly and sealed shut door and field behind her. Responding automatically to her presence, both ship and lock filled swiftly with air and the lights of the interior came on. A few minutes after she had entered, the inner door slid open.

She went inside.

It was not hard to find the control panels, nor to decipher their meaning; she had served as a consultant during their design. Three motions sufficed to prepare the generators for action, one to check on life-support and a last to lock in the gravitic compensation.

Now there was only one thing left to do, and then she would be free. Letting her mind reach forth from its bonds, leaning on the nearest panel for physical support, she sent out a bolt of mind-force to the station, focused on the most receptive man within. In an instant she tapped his vision and knew where he was, and where she wanted him to be. The attack was so sudden that by the time he had ascertained its existence he was entirely overwhelmed by it; a mental convulsion so powerful that it blotted out his consciousness and threw him violently against the far wall, jamming his arm into a line of controls—one control in particular—prepared for emergency use. Blood dribbled from his head and from the corner of his mouth and he fell. Yet still his body twitched, caught in the grip of something far stronger than he had ever been prepared to fight. Assistants ran to his side and his feet, checked where he had been standing, discussed the possibility of power leakage, and in general sought to analyze the unknown force that had struck him down. In that momentary chaos (which she deftly encouraged, even while urging the Starbird forward) no one thought that perhaps he had been thrown against one switch in particular. And by the time they did notice, it was too late.

"The field's down!"

They brought it up again, quickly, but by then they knew their loss. One of the silver needles was gone, thrust magnificently forward by man's finest accelerative achievement and lost forever in the darkness beyond Lurien. They reported the theft, but they knew that nothing could be done. The Starbirds had been designed to outrun anything; no one doubted that this one could do so now.

In the depths of space, freed at last from the bonds of law and servitude, the figure unfastened its bulky helmet and pulled the globe free from its moorings. Rich red hair, bloodblack and magenta, poured down her back as she laughed her triumph, and she set her course with eager fingers.

One last rendezvous with the *Conqueror,* to collect those who shared her dream. *I'm sorry, Torzha.* She turned toward the warship—no longer hers, no longer important. *The true warrior will not be disarmed.*

One last stop, and then freedom.

* * *

Feran tried to still his nervousness as he approached the House of Zatar. Thus his hand was almost steady as he put it to the door's black plate, and his stride, as he passed the portal guard and walked the length of the forehall, was almost confident. But it was a sham, and the Pri'tiera would be quick to see through it. Zatar had a skill that was almost psychic—and perhaps in Feran's case, where continued psychic contact was part of their relationship, the power might indeed be developing.

Was that possible? Might the Probe be acting as catalyst for a latent, as-yet-undiscovered talent? Feran shivered. The thought of Zatar with all the options of telepathic mastery allied to the force of his personality was a terrifying one. But even if the Pri'tiera *did* have the proper genetic prerequisites—which Feran half-believed, despite evidence to the contrary—it would take more than a handful of surface-mind exercises to bring them into play. It would take . . . what? A Probe's talent, he decided, and a Probe's willingness to rework the very foundations of thought. If it could be done at all.

B'Salos willing, no one would ever try.

As he approached Zatar's private chambers, the feeling that had been nagging at him since he left his home became even stronger. Something was different this time. Zatar hadn't called him here for a discussion of psychic privilege, nor to explore the limitations of that special skill. Today his concern was something else, something . . . frightening. Feran had felt it all the way from his own House, halfway across Kurat, and he tensed as he tapped on the heavy wooden door, announcing his arrival.

"Enter."

He took his place before the Pri'tiera and knelt, as befit his station. There was a strange comfort in it.

"I have a job for you." Zatar's voice was cold and his surface thoughts made it clear: *You won't like this.*

"I am the Pri'tiera's servant."

"Of course." He waited a moment, letting the fact of their relationship sink in. "Come with me," he said at last. "I have something to show you."

Feran rose and followed him, into a section of the House given over to workrooms. Here was Zatar's armory, and a room devoted to the upkeep of the building's mechanical intelligence. Here there was a whole room full of books, real fabric-and-paper books, awaiting restoration, and fragments of primitive artwork, painstakingly preserved. Everywhere workmen labored, most of them were busy with archeological finds. Zatar's interest in Berros was clearly paying off.

"In here." The Pri'tiera indicated a pair of metal-and-wood doors, which slid open at their approach. Inside three men were laboring over something—a painting, perhaps?—but the natural gloss of the item's surface, combined with the angle of the lighting, prevented Feran from making out what it was.

"Go," Zatar told the men; they obeyed him without word, leaving the two Braxaná alone.

He closed the doors and locked them, then set the soundproofing. "This was found in the dining hall of a hunting palace, on what was once Harkur's estate. The preservation is remarkable, given the painting's age; we can thank the dryness of the Berros'n air for that. I'm having a molecular restoration done to save it." He looked at the painting, then at Feran. Tension radiated from his body but his voice, as always, was steady. "Look at it, Feran."

He approached it slowly, wondering at Zatar's behavior. In all the time he had known him, he had never tasted tension in him as strongly as now. It was even evident in his body language, if one knew how to look—and that was unheard of. Walking along the side of the worktable, Feran sought a position that would allow him to view the glossy surface without interference from the lighting. He found it at last, by the side of the portrait, and gazed down upon a work of art which the centuries had buried.

And he trembled.

"You see," the Pri'tiera said.

"Hasha. . . ." Feran reached out a finger to touch the ancient paint, on the section which the workmen had finished. It was real. If it was the *truth*. . . . "Forgery?" he managed.

"I checked. The age is right, the molecular composition of the materials, the condition of the sealed room I found it in, everything. What you see was actually created over ten millennia ago—although it was in considerably worse condition when my men first found it than it is now." He paused. "My guess was correct, then; the alien figure in the painting is Azean."

It took him a moment to find his voice again. "Many millennia ago, before the race was Standardized, this was what they looked like. With great variation in pigmentation, of course; that was the point of Standardization." He looked at the figure's warm brown skin, guessed at the secrets it had housed, and shuddered. "The structure of the face gives it away. But what I don't understand is how this happened. There *couldn't* have been contact that early. Azea had no superluminal travel before Standardization; Braxi never expanded past Lugast—"

"History is an inexact science at best. What we understood of the past was evidently inaccurate. Certainly both our peoples have reason enough to pretend that there was no peaceful contact between them."

"This is collaborated by other sources?"

"No. There are gaps in early Braxin history; this is one of them. Harkur the Great kept notes on every alien race he encountered, but many of those were lost when the Braxaná took over. Lost on

Berros when the government relocated to Braxi. Another reason to study the place." He laughed, a bitter sound. "I seem to have gotten more than I bargained for."

Feran read the inscription in the frame, felt himself shiver. "If the writing is accurate—"

"I'm certain it is."

"—then *she* . . ." He couldn't finish.

"Anzha lyu Mitethe is Braxin. More accurately, the mutation responsible for her odd coloring appeared among our own people in Harkur's day, at a point when there was contact between our home planets. A contact which involved her ancestry."

"Have you told her?"

"No."

"But will you—"

"It's no longer that simple, Feran." He hesitated, and the turmoil of his mind was a moving backdrop to his words. "Anzha lyu Mitethe has deserted."

He heard the words, but could not accept their meaning. "Deserted?"

"Left the Empire. Without a word of explanation, I gather, to anyone. Even StarControl seems stunned by her actions. That could be an act, of course, but—"

"Impossible. That she would desert—no. I can't believe it."

"Believe it or not, it's happened." And he told Feran the story as his spies had told it to him. The Conqueror had made a repair run to Lurien, and shortly afterward the Starcommander and five members of her crew had disappeared. Along with some sort of new diplomatic runner the military was working on, meant for transportation inside the Active War Zone. The connection was obvious; the list of charges soon to be leveled against her began with theft and ended with treason.

"It's not like her," Feran muttered, while a voice inside him argued, *Yes. Very much so.*

"An enemy is most dangerous when he is unpredictable."

"But she *lived* for the War—"

"And politics forced her into a Peace she didn't want. Come, Feran, surely you realized that! You were sitting there beside me—didn't you pick it up? If she were left to her own devices, we would never have had this last Peace. And she could have worked untold damage during the Plague and afterward, had they not stopped her. How could any warrior not resent such limitations?

Every day we kept our part of the treaty must have been a thorn in her palm. Until she broke. And went—where? I must know that, Feran. She's too dangerous, loose in the galaxy. Too unpredictable. *I must locate her.*"

Like a worm gnawing at his insides, knowledge of Zatar's intentions grew within him. "Pri'tiera, there's no way—"

"You'll find her for me."

"It's not possible!"

"Your Institute's theory says it is. Distance is no barrier to telepathy—"

"—but focus is, Pri'tiera! With the whole of the galaxy to search—"

"We can narrow the field better than that, Feran. Quite a bit better. Starships move quickly, but their speed is still finite. That gives you a limited range to search."

Fear—the old fear—overwhelmed him. "She would kill me!"

"A chance we'll have to take. Surely you're not afraid, Feran. Probes have tricks that mere telepaths can't master. Or so you've told me. Can't you use any of those to safeguard your own life?"

Maybe. An abstract touch, divorced from material identity, might go unnoticed. *If* he could find her. "Nothing like this has ever been done—"

"Then you'll be the first." There was anger growing within him; Feran could feel it. "Let me make this very clear. You belong to me, or you die. You will serve me—successfully—or I will kill you."

Feran's colorless face went even whiter. "Pri'tiera—"

"She is a threat, I must find her, you are my only available tool. Choose!"

He could feel the weight of bracelets on his arms, where imagination had affixed them. "I'll try," he managed. "But I don't know that such a thing is possible—"

"If you're incapable of serving me, the result is the same as if you had refused. It's that simple, Probe." He opened the doors, cutting off any response Feran might have made by terminating their privacy. The workmen reentered, dutifully uncurious.

"Report to me in the morning," the Pri'tiera ordered. "With results."

Feran stood on the roof of the Zarvati mansion, muscles knotted in fear, trying to work up the courage to begin. Which was the worse fate, he wondered. Failing, and facing Zatar's wrath? Or succeeding, and facing hers? He shivered at the thought of it. But of the two, Zatar was the more immediate threat, and so he settled himself against the observatory wall and let his mind roam free of its corporeal bonds, to search the stars for life.

. . . touching violence and mining hunger, images of faceted brilliance and shining gold wealth . . . a cultural fix, nothing more. He was so unaccustomed to this type of work that it was hard for him to focus on what he was supposed to be doing. There, a mind or two standing out bright against the darkness . . . (he strained) . . . a governor, avaricious and cancer-ridden, incurable because of some cruel medical law he himself had introduced, never expecting it would backfire on him . . . a woman reaching for the stars so strongly that her need vibrated across the Void and brought tears of emptiness to the Probe's eyes . . . a thousand others, equally outstanding; equally normal, waves in the fluid of the Voidmind that rose, submerged, and rose again elsewhere, elsewhen . . . and none of them *her,* in power or purpose.

He withdrew, exhausted. His hands were shaking and his mind was weak from the unaccustomed exertion. Where was she? What was she doing? How did one even begin such a search? He could explore the galaxy planet by planet and die of old age before he'd searched a fraction—while she, flitting from port to port, might find refuge on planets he had already searched. Should he look for hatred, vendetta-violence, frustration, or what? What aspect of her personality-signature would be most likely to stand out among the myriad semipsychic minds that filled the Void with thought?

There was a presence beside him. He touched it: *Zatar.* Without turning, in a voice full of bitterness, he said, "I haven't found her yet."

"So I gather."

The Pri'tiera remained. Feran tried to send his questing senses out into the Void again, but years of habit kept him from doing so in front of another man. He picked up his reflection in Zatar's mind and noticed the tears glinting like starlight on his face—the tears of an unknown woman, far off in the Void and now lost to him. He did nothing to wipe them away, or to indicate that they weren't his; they might as well be. "I've gone over one of the Border territories as well as I can. Maybe I missed her. If I didn't, I couldn't even tell you what planets I looked over, only what direction they were in and what their cultural signatures were."

"Your abilities seem insufficient for the task."

He bit his lip in silence a moment before answering, "Then they'll have to improve, won't they?"

A stiff plastic sheet touched his shoulder. He took it. "What's this?"

"Culture-patterns for key planets in the holding, by sector. Computer-generated; I make no claims for their quality."

Feran looked at the information in amazement. For each planet there was a listing that included its exact position, its visual position relative to the B'Saloan heavens, and a count of how many centers of human population there were between it and Braxi—vital landmarks for telepathic work. Psychological generalities were noted: "Colony on unpleasantly hot lowgravity planet with severe water shortage, slow diurnal cycle. Local religion revolving around water—and sun-symbolism, death fixation common, hostility ritualized about winter solstice . . ." It was the telepathic equivalent of a starmap.

He looked at Zatar, surprised and relieved. "These will help—"

But the Pri'tiera was already gone.

He studied the chart for a while, familiarizing himself with its key points, then steeled himself and reached out again.

. . . a forest of minds tangled between the stars, bright points here and there . . . counting one, two, three outward through the constellation of the Warrior Exultant, *there,* focus tightly . . .

He grasped the planet Talmir and turned it in his mind, caressed its surface with his questing thoughts and noted here, and here again, a mind bristling at the unaccustomed contact. Latent psychics, carrying the genes for power but not the patterns for operancy. He touched them with only a moment of longing, born of the pain his power had brought him. *Why couldn't I be like that?* Then he sifted through the planet-mind in general, finding nothing that would lead him where he needed to go.

I don't want to die! Fear poured out from him in all directions, until the currents of the Voidmind had touched all planets in the Holding with his desperation. That was dangerous. If she sensed him before he sensed her, she might strike at him while he was wide open. He withdrew his mind from Talmir, and focused back on his material circumstances. His body, responding to his fear, had crumpled to the floor of the observatory and was tightly balled in dread, hands clutched over stomach, trembling.

Must break through . . . must!

A bolt of sheer need cut through the Void and seared the mental fringe of some unknown planet. *I'm losing control!* he thought helplessly. He imagined the patterns of Distinction Discipline, ran them through his mind once, twice, three times before they took at last and closed him off from the world. It's my years here, he told himself. *The training's slipping.* But he was pleased that he had made it work.

After a time the Discipline relaxed and he worked a careful tendril outward again. Then he withdrew to think.

I won't survive this, he admitted, if I go blindly from sector to sector—even if I don't have to do them all. There has to be a better way. I have to find it. . . .

He let his thoughts sink into the pool of his innermind and waited to see what impressions surfaced.

I'm a Probe, not a telepath. Yet I'm going about this in a way that any telepath could attempt, and have no greater chance of success. Is there an approach that would allow me to use all my power, even the abstract specialties, in a way no mere telepath could manage? There would stand my greatest chance of success.

It was a hunch and nothing more, but the Institute taught that hunches were valid cognitive experiences, and he trusted this one.

I've been thinking of her in concrete terms. Telepath. Renegade. K'airth-v'sa. These are the crutches that a telepath needs, that limit power to the realm of sensory imagination. I know her mental signature. (Ar, do I know it!) I need to think in pureform.

He wondered at the very nature of his search. If one had to find an object in a large house, he reasoned, one wouldn't necessarily begin by a thorough study of each detail of architecture. One would look over the entire property quickly to see if the object was in open view, or was in such a position that it readily caught the eye.

Why not the stars?

Tense, afraid, he readied himself. Fighting off all self-imposed barriers, he mustered the full extent of his power and stripped it of every binding thought and image, until his entire being was a mass of pure telepathic sensitivity. Then he opened himself to the cosmos.

Thought and emotion without label, familiar and unfamiliar, stable and unstable, lasting and fleeting . . . a sea of the stuff of thought without thought to guide it . . . concentrations here, there (don't think "planets," he begged himself) and there again . . . this one of such a tenor . . . that one filed with disruption . . .

It seemed an eternity that he swam the thoughtwinds; he had forgotten what pleasure there was in the act. In order that he might focus his attention upon the mindsea between the stars he left control of his body to a few parts of the brain that could manage it automatically, and floated free of all material concerns in the pure joy of sensitivity. Worlds turned about him and with them the thoughts of millions revolved in their private cycles, sleep-silent to waking-alert, reflections of light and dark and season in a slow progression about his mindfocus, pinpoints of mental radiance to dance the emptiness before him . . .

Anzha.

He touched her carefully, oh-so-carefully, ridding his mind of any personal identity, allowing only the briefest whisper of *other* to touch her sensitivity with warning. She was too preoccupied to notice, or perhaps (it occurred to him only now) she couldn't recognize a truly abstract sending. He withdrew, and gently stroked her environment. Five minds, four of them psychic, focused on the future . . . it was safer to read their minds than hers, so he did so. Darkness, lightyears and light-years of it, and time passing without action . . . a mass of obscurity, defying detection . . . an investment in purpose, intentions of triumph . . . *patience,* above all else. Always the image of darkness; it would mean something to Zatar, he was certain. He touched the nearest planets and drank in their cultural essence: luxury growths/seasonal sexual festivities at harvest/mild, unthreatening environment; colonial tensions/excess male population/mining in the colder regions . . . he tasted what he could of the planets she was passing, memorizing the culture-fixes that might give some clue as to her location, straining to continue despite the growing exhaustion—

—burning pain in the centers of thought, it is too much, too *much,* the mind strained, the body falling, *desert of my enemy I am drowning! Return, return* (Reintegration Discipline) *return . . .*

He opened his eyes.

For a moment, nothing.

Eyes. He touched them. Sensation. Cloudy vision, clarifying . . . the sun, burning, baking . . . with a low moan he turned away from it.

"Lord Feran," a voice said softly.

He looked up, surprised to find the Pri'tiera capable of such gentle inflection.

Zatar crouched by his side and two women also knelt there, flanking him. One of them handed him a cup of water, the sight of which brought waves of thirst and physical need to his awareness. He spilled half of it, his bodily control still far from perfect, but his parched membranes greedily drank in the rest.

"I *reached* her," he croaked, his voice dry but exultant.

Zatar waited.

He burst forth with the details of his vision, and with the culture-fixes he had picked up. Zatar fed it all into the computer; hopefully the massive brain that guarded the House would be able to make some sense of his rambling, and relate it to a location and a purpose.

"I found her . . ." Feran whispered. His eyes fell shut, the sunlight burning his vision even through the layers of skin. *I touched her . . . who ever thought one man could know such power?*

A woman bathed his forehead with cool, fresh water. The touch of her hand pained him more than it should, even with his heightened sensitivity. He reached out to her mind for the proper label: sunburn. Then his senses recoiled violently, rejecting the effort, and his psychic/physical reaction was so strong that he vomited helplessly on the tiled floor.

A woman's hand stroked him gently along the neck, soothing his discomfort. He lacked the strength to move, but lay there where he had emptied himself. After a moment other hands cleaned him, and then the floor, of his misery.

"You did well." It was the Pri'tiera's voice, somehow disassociated from the body looming over him. "She's headed away from the Holding, toward the Barren Zone off our yerren border. We won't be able to track her inside the nebula itself, and it's a year's travel or more to cross it but at least we have something to work with. It looks a lot like she's fleeing the War," he commented.

"I don't believe that."

"Neither do I. We'll get a better directional focus from the computer, then I'll send out scouts. We'll find her."

"Pri'tiera—" He coughed, then tried again. "If you tell the scouts what they're looking for . . . they'll focus their attention on her. She'll pick it up. Physical distance means little to us; mental focus is everything. Be careful. . . ." He gasped for air; his throat was raw and breathing was painful. "I'm sorry it—took so long. . . ." What a ludicrous thing to say! "Missed the morning. . . ."

Zatar was amused. "Missed it by three days, Feran. But that's all right." A strong hand clasped his shoulder. "It was worth the waiting."

He slept.

Viton: It is when a man's House seems the most secure that he is most vulnerable to attack.

TWENTY-FIVE

Darkly, like a shadow, Sechaveh strode the length of the poorly lit corridor. The walls about him were of stone, as was the staircase that led to this place, as were the chambers whose doors lined its walls. Cold stone, rough and gray and damp with the moisture of underground humidity. Fungus gathered here and there on the irregular slabs, and ate at the mortar between them; the odor of decay drifted thickly between narrow doorways, hinting at tortures which had been, and—dramatically—of torments yet to come.

He was tense; he had always been tense. But now his tension wound like a cord around his heart, strangling his very soul. Anger poured from him in torrents and reverberated between the mock-ancient walls, drowning him in a cacophony of rage.

He had lost! No, he had *not* lost. That was important: *He could not lose.* The others, with their pitifully compassionate natures, trusting women and underestimating their enemies, their own colleagues . . . *they* might lose, and see their plans die the eternal death. Not him. Only for the moment was life's aspect bleak, only for the single, temporary moment . . . he squelched his anger as well as he could, forcing himself to promise himself. *Tomorrow. Tomorrow I will have my vengeance.*

But there were no more tomorrows, and he knew it. He had hungered to control Braxi since the day he had first set foot on it, a cynical youth still bearing the scars of his alien humiliation. Every moment since had been spent either working to achieve that goal or dreaming of the moment when it would at last become reality. He had allied with Yiril because that man commanded respect among the Kaim'eri, had offered the ruthlessness of his youth in exchange for the older man's guiding hand. It was Yiril who calmed him, Yiril who taught him the ways of Central intrigue, Yiril who later used him for his savagery and was used in return. They had allied with Vinir because it was a sound political move at the time they did it; three men acting in unity could wield much power in a government where it was assumed that no man would support another. Then Zatar . . . he cursed as the name came to his lips, spat it out as though he were regurgitating some vile poison. *Zatar.* He had made a throne possible and then claimed it himself, while Sechaveh, struck impotent by a single careless incident, was forced to sit back and watch, and do nothing. Zatar! Sechaveh had meant to unseat him at the last possible moment, to drive the Holding into chaos and then restore it himself. He had used Zatar in his youth and was fully prepared to counter his growing strength; he had spent the years planning for that moment, had dreamed of it, and considered himself ready.

And then there was Venari.

And the Plague.

And impotence.

With a snarl he slapped the handplate of a steel-barred door, which lifted itself into the ceiling to admit him. He signaled it to close again behind him and it did so, sealing him in the tiny stone cell with the stink of mold, and death—and fear.

Zatar, I will destroy you!

He studied his surroundings, drinking in their dismal atmosphere with relish. This cell was one of his smallest; he had designed it to mimic the dark confines of the Illean catacombs. Dank, odiferous, and above all else stiflingly close, it was a claustrophobe's nightmare. The walls pressed tightly about their victim, and the low ceiling was cunningly paved with stones and boulders so that it appeared to be only loosely fixed in place. Might it fall, crushing the room's helpless occupant? For one who did not know the details of its construction, the answer that came could only be *yes.* The walls, similarly misleading, leaned inward at the top, and beneath their irregular stonework one could easily feel the weight of the earth overhead, the thousands of tons of rock which pressed down upon the tiny and primitive chamber.

He had broken many men in this room, and had not had to do much work in the breaking; the room itself had power enough, applied to a people long accustomed to wide open spaces and the infinite reaches of the Void. Now it held a single prisoner: a woman, feverish, chained to the uneven wall. He came to stand before her, touching a gloved finger to the side of her face. She was shivering with fear, and a fine sheen of sweat was her only garment. In the dim, unwholesome light her golden skin seemed gray and withered; her fine white hair, straggling down about her shoulders, was streaked with mud much as the hair of an Azean diplomat might be frosted with golden powders. Subcommander, fighter captain, lead scout . . . he could no longer remember her exact rank, and it did not matter. They had brought her to Braxi and he had broken her, squeezing military information out of her pain-wracked body like one worked the juice from a sarafruit. Now the empty rind had been cast to him for his pleasure, and he explored its flaws with relish.

She looked at him—or past him, or through him—with eyes that had long since lost their luster, and her breath stank of fear. His mere proximity was salt to her wounds and he knew it; he moved even closer, pinning her against the wall with his bulk, and smiled as a tortured moan squeezed up from the heart of her. She was a latent claustrophobe; it had not taken him long to discover it. Now, knowing, he possessed the key to her soul—her Name, as it were, if Azeans might be said to have Names. Her fear had been mild to start with, a commonplace discomfort, and she had dealt with it simply, by avoiding situations that would inflame her phobia to life. But in doing so, she had not entered Sechaveh into her calculations.

Looking into her eyes, he saw the effects of his work: the finely drawn line between horror and madness upon which this woman balanced, longing for the latter but suffering, at his hands, the former. If kept carefully she might survive for decades; what peaks of intensity might her phobia reach if he had a lifetime to work on it? The thought excited him, set his blood to stirring as nothing else could. At one time the flesh of women might have pleased him, the contraction of their bodies as they screamed, or pleaded, or died . . . but now his pleasure was in pain and pain alone, his hunger a burning hostility that had its own special demands, and its own satisfaction.

He touched a finger to the woman's eyes, noting her reflexive response. Was it not amazing how the body sought to protect itself from harm, long after the soul had abandoned hope? He would tear her eyes out soon, and see how the darkness of the blind compared with the blackness of his dungeon in the heart of her phobia. Would there be a qualitative difference? Would the imagination of the newly blind make her unseen prison seem more confining, or would it lessen the effect of a blackness that no light would ever enter? The question made his blood stir, hotly.

She cried out suddenly, her eyes wide with terror.

As for Zatar . . . he cursed the name, the House, and most of all his own stupidity. But he would have his revenge. Law or no, his would be the ultimate triumph. Because of the man's own weaknesses Zatar would wither and perish; Sechaveh had not spent his life in a study of human suffering for the mere fleeting pleasure of it. He knew how to hurt Zatar, if not how to bring him from power; he could make the man's soul bleed until the throne of Braxi held only emptiness for him—until he tasted, himself, the very sort of impotent fury that Sechaveh was destined to endure.

He had planned it all out, and it soon would begin. Ni'en would be the first blow: struck down bloodily, painfully, perhaps even openly. She had no Braxaná blood in her and the law, therefore, did not protect her from Whim Death. How like Zatar that he had taken her safety for granted all these years! What grief would the great Pri'tiera know, who had removed his gloves before a woman? Only so much as he deserved, Sechaveh assured himself.

The woman cried again, sharply; her face was pale with fear and she writhed against the wall, pulling desperately at the chains that bound her. *This* was an interesting development! He grasped her chin in his leather-bound hand and forced her to stare at him. Blood dribbled from her screaming mouth, staining his glove. Internal damage, or cuts to the mouth's interior? What convulsions of fear had his presence inspired? Elated, curious, he stared at her, studied her, and stepped back quickly as the cause of her suffering became apparent.

"No!" He hissed it, backing up as far as the tiny room would permit. Black froth sizzled over her lip and ate its way down her chin, following the trail that her blood had already blazed. The pit of her stomach was churning as well, and spots of blackness began to appear here and there on the taut, sweat-soaked skin.

The Black Death.

The initial shock passed quickly and his reason returned to him. He was safe for the moment, for her torso was bound, but if her arms and legs flailed as they were eaten away, he might be in grave danger. He moved swiftly to the door and placed his hand upon the plate that controlled it.

Nothing happened.

Again.

The door did not move.

Sweat broke out across his brow; he found that his hands were trembling. Again and again he tried to coax the portal's controls to action. Finally he leaned down to the door's lower edge and sought to raise it by brute force—but there was no handhold, none at all, and friction alone would not suffice to raise the slick, heavy stone.

He was afraid.

The screams were deafening now, and in another place and time they would have pierced his soul with pleasure; now his blood ran cold, his hands and heart were like ice. He backed away from her, as far as he could get, and drew his cape before him. One more layer between him and man's ultimate torment; could it even help—would it be enough? To scream for aid would be pointless; who would pick his voice out from the woman's squalling? And would they help, if they heard? *Someone* had sealed the door behind him; such things did not happen by accident. Someone with access to House security, who might also have sabotaged the computer. . . .

"Call Sil'ne!" he commanded. A bit of living rot landed right by his face, and it barely missed his shoulder as it slid, seething, to the foot of the wall. It humiliated him to call for a woman's help, but the facts were simple: Sil'ne was the only one in the House who could not afford to let him die. Bereft of his support she would be Houseless, homeless; a woman who had failed her Master in this way would not find upper-class patronage again. She *dared* not fail him . . . and therefore he trusted her. "Sil'ne!" A line of blackness was eating its way through one of the woman's legs, and as she twitched in her death-throes it scattered the seeds of torment to all sides of him. A bit caught on his cloak and he discarded it quickly. "Inform her—bring her to me!" he cried, desperate. His cloak was being consumed; he watched in horror as it writhed, alive in its dying, and shuddered at the thought that the same might happen to him.

"Computer! Call—"

Airborne, a piece of the putrid substance was flung against him, and it quickly took root in the wool of his tunic sleeve. Were he dressed in a foreign manner he might have had one moment to brush the stuff away—with his Zhaor, even the scabbard, anything made of metal or synthetics—but the threads that had been spun for his clothing were of animal origin, rich in protein content, and were as much food for the dreaded Death as the flesh that lay beneath it. He moaned as the poison bit into his arm, attempting to voice a last cry for help, but he managed only a wordless scream as the poison ate his nerves, hungry for suffering as well as flesh.

Mindlessly he moved to brush at his arm, stopping only a hair's breath from the boiling surface before he remembered: to touch it was to spread it. How then could he save himself.? He forced his body to be still, to endure the hot knives of pain which pierced through his arm and upward toward his shoulder, and which ate at his fingers until black sludge dripped from their stumps. *There must be a way to survive this!* he thought feverishly. The Azeans were poisoned often, and didn't always die of it; what technique did they employ?

As a nova of agony burst to life in his upper arm, he remembered.

He gritted his teeth and prepared himself for courage. Now there was hope . . . and a morbid fascination, which he would never have admitted to, in watching himself master the death that had overwhelmed so many. *Pain and I are old companions*. . . . He reached his right hand to his Zhaor, carefully, and applied his thumb to the lock. It was programmed for any Sutrakarre hand and opened in response to his touch—and he sighed in relief as it did so, though tears of pain poured from his eyes even as he drew the blade free. Amputation: that was the secret. To sever the host-limb before the poison could spread. He maneuvered the Zhaor as well as he could right-handed, and brought it down on his better arm before he could start to question his actions. It had to be done quickly. Before the malignancy spread to his torso. And before agony overpowered sentience.

The sword—which could have severed real metal and *should* have sliced through his flesh like butter—bounced off his arm—bounced!—and fell to the stone floor, far out of reach. He stared at it aghast and then screamed—for the poison had invaded his torso. Mindless sound, sightless agony, pain beyond human endurance. . . . The Death touched his cheek and took root there, so that when he gasped for breath it choked him; then, with sadistic humor, it ate through his windpipe so he might still have air. He fell, but that was a minor injury; he was being eaten from the inside out, as though the poison had a living mind and intended to cause him maximum suffering. In that, it was succeeding.

And then—the ultimate mockery—the poison stopped short of his heart. Bits of it hardened and crumbled, consumed at first by that which followed, later joined by it. The seething subsided; the blackness grayed. Raw nerves sang of their torment while the heartbeat labored on, struggling to preserve a life that was already worse than death itself. But the battle had long since been lost. The blood, pumped outward, did not return. The brain, lacking its supply of oxygen, clung to the pain for as long as it could, then slipped slowly, unwillingly, into darkness.

Lord Elder and Kaim'era Sechaveh, son of Lurat and M'nisa, was dead.

Sil'ne waited in the library, using Sechaveh's Central Computer link to toy with the structure of his financial holding. Already the carrion-birds were gathering, Mistresses of the Braxaná picking apart the remnants of Sechaveh's power, seeking a bit of carnage to add to their own estates. Through the network of the Central Computer she fenced with them, buying and selling shares of her ex-Master's interests with the expertise born of a century's practice. Let the House of Marax hunger after the Ayyaran mines, now masterless; she was there to foil it, and the Houses that followed it, tossing away scraps to feed the greedy as she saved, by her skill, the bulk of a now ownerless estate.

It was for amusement, nothing more. She hated waiting. Sechaveh's House would be assigned to a stranger—some Lord of the Sutrakarren bloodline—and then she would be outcast. No Mistress who failed her Lord might ride the crests of the Braxaná social system. Very well; she would go. But they would remember her. Remember that Sechaveh's economic holding was one *she* had built and maintained—remember that the power others had hungered to ally with was as much her doing as his, and that the ruthless efficiency which made him such a dangerous enemy was based upon decades of her labor, and depended upon her loyalty.

She called up the estate's T'sarakene contracts and remoded relevant clauses so that an immediate transfer of ownership would be next to impossible. T'sarak's Computer found the new phrases synonymous with the old and accepted them; no non-B'saloan system was programmed for use of all forty-two Braxaná speech modes, and therefore one could sneak legal changes past their otherwise careful vigilance. Leaning back, she regarded her work on the flatscreen. Yes, that was good . . . it would keep the vinefarms out of Kaim'era Lasir's grasping hands for a good while. Long enough for the estate to be divided. . . .

She started as the door before her split open.

"Lord Turak!" She stood, deftly touching the console to darkness as she did so. Sechaveh's son entered and the door resealed behind him. The library, as they both knew, was soundproofed. "Have they finished?"

"*We* have finished." He paused, drinking in her discomfort. How like his father he was, in that! "It seems that an unfortunate accident has befallen the Master of this House."

"An accident," she breathed. "Then—"

"The residue's been analyzed, the remains studied, and all evidence points to the same conclusion: Sechaveh meant to witness the Black Death in a woman, and to that end poisoned her with a timed dose of the Waiting Poison. Protected by a personal forcefield, he entered her chamber to observe her unpleasant demise. Unfortunately—for him—the unit malfunctioned, offering no protection. The poison reached him late in its vital phase and managed to eat its way through several organs and arteries before going inert. So say the investigators, and who am I to argue? He bled to death."

"Slowly," she murmured.

He grinned. "How like Sechaveh's woman to notice that point! Slowly, yes, compared to what would have happened if the poison had remained vital a bit longer. I imagine he suffered. Does that please you?"

Her voice was rich with derision. "I think you confuse me with my ex-Master, Lord Turak."

"How easily the title comes to her lips! *Ex*-Master, indeed! How will you live, without him? Did you hate him, Sil'ne? Enough to kill him, perhaps? No worry on that score, now that the investigation's cleared you! Was it hard to govern your pride all these years, in order to get the power you wanted—or did you share his interests? No one seems to know."

"I don't imagine it need concern you."

He crossed the room and came to where she stood, behind her, his voice a whisper over her left shoulder as he searched the console screen for insight. "They even checked the field belt for poison contact, and found the leather encasement eaten away, just as it should be. Imagine that! I would think such a man would test his forcefield, before committing himself to such dangerous circumstances."

"Maybe he was preoccupied."

"Maybe." He placed hands on her shoulders; strong hands, eager hands. "His Zhaor sheath was of finely worked brass. I had always thought my father was more fond of leather and silken adornments—but then, I might be wrong. Surely such things would have been damaged by contact with the poison." He forced her to face him. "That wasn't the sword he was wearing, was it?"

She pulled away from him, stood, and walked far enough that he could no longer touch her. And turned to him, stonefaced. "Apparently Sechaveh's blood bred true," she assessed.

"His blood and his training—and yours." He closed the distance slowly, appraising her as he did so. "Gentle, *innocent* ex-Mistress. " She flinched at the insult. "I want the sword you took from his body," he demanded.

"Why? So you can reveal me to the Kaim'eri? No thank you, Turak."

He came to her swiftly and gabbed her by the shoulders; she twisted in his grasp, but could not free herself. "The sword, Sil'ne. It's my right!"

She glared at him. "It's the only evidence of what really happened. Do you think I kept it intact?"

A faint smile mitigated his anger. "I know you. You did."

"There was never the Braxaná that could resist a trophy, is that your reasoning? Am I no better than the rest of them?"

He shook her, more violently this time. "I gave you the poison. *Give me the sword!*"

She broke free of him and glared—and then laughed, a sound rich with scorn. "As you wish, Lord. If you'll follow me?"

He did so in silence, to a room which was much the same as many others—except for the narrow space hidden behind one of the walls, which she opened with a touch. "It was part of our arrangement that Sechaveh would never come in here. Here." She withdrew a Zhaor, its rich, silk-covered sheath half eaten away, a crusty black ash falling from its damaged edges.

She handed it to him, and he unsheathed the blade.

"Fully blunt." He placed a finger against the deadly edge, withdrew it uninjured. His eyes glowed. "The forcefield; did you—"

"I neglected nothing, Lord Turak. I'm no more anxious than you to die for this. The malfunction will seem reasonable, the House's records will all bear witness to the supposed truth . . . I was very, very careful."

"You always have been."

"Thank you." Then she dared: "And the estate? Have they divided it yet?"

"Part of it. The main House is to be mine." Sliding the blade back into its sheath, he set the Zhaor aside. "And its staff."

"So I . . . ?"

"The choice is mine."

He watched her for a moment, enjoying her discomfort. "What shall I do with a woman who betrayed her Master?"

"I was loyal!" she snapped. "I was always loyal—until he threatened my people. When I found out that he was plotting against the Pri'tiera—! What could I do? What *should* I have done?"

"Exactly what you did. I have no argument with that. But a woman who let her Master die . . ." he let the words fade into meaningful silence as he stepped toward her, touched his hand to her skin. "You have fulfilled my most fervent dream. Could I do anything but reward you? Stay, if you want, and keep this estate going. You'll be under my own Mistress, but no other. The power will be little less than you enjoyed before—and the company, I think, will be more pleasurable." He kissed her, hungry for ownership. "Say yes."

She whispered it: "Yes."

He embraced her, and aroused her, and possessed her; how could he do otherwise? Each thrust of his killing passion sent his father that much further into the grave, and by possessing her he made his triumph total. And she—inspired by the kill, hungry for normal sensation—she was a match for him, a proper companion for the night of his ascendancy. The power of women had always excited him, and violence was an aphrodisiac. How could his father have failed to respond to her? How could he have been so . . . inhuman?

"The sword," he whispered, deep within the night.

"What of it?"

"The tip was also blunted; why?"

She smiled, and he saw the fire rise in her eyes. "I was afraid he might kill himself."

"Before it had ended. . . ."

"Didn't you guess?"

"No." He laughed. "I should have."

"We were not so very different," she said softly.

"You and my father? Or me and—"

"All of us." She breathed it into his skin, and it stirred his blood anew. "All the Braxaná. Do you deny it?"

He let his body answer.

Harkur: Nothing, not even pleasure, can bind two humans as close as a long-enduring vendetta, for it forces upon each a constant awareness of the strengths and vulnerabilities of the other, and commits them to a common purpose which colors all other activities.

TWENTY-SIX

Most Magnificent Lord and Glorious Sovereign of all which is ruled by the might of Braxi: I, Aldar Na-Trev, independent scout in service to the Holding, beg you to receive these words and heed the warning which they contain. I realize that it's customary for a freelance scout to give his report in person, but the nature of my news is such that every tenth is crucial. A drone can reach Braxi much faster than I can, and so I'm sending this on ahead of my ship, in the hopes it will get to you quickly. Ar alone knows what may come between me and the Holding in the next few zhents, but I believe that if I'm careful I can see that this gets to you. Even the days matter now, which is ironic in light of a plan meant to affect the centuries. Listen:

I own one of five ships which left the Holding nearly three years ago at your command, in service to your House. You gave us the task of charting specific regions beyond the Barren Zone, and of recording what manner of intelligent life we should find there. (I remind you because it was a long time ago and I know you have other more important things to concern you, Magnificent One, so please bear with me.)

It took us well over two and a half years to cross the Barren Zone. I don't know what we expected to find once we got across, we were just so glad to see the stars again and to have something to do besides argue amongst ourselves that we pounced upon the first opportunity to scan for life. And what we found!

I'm sorry, Magnificent One, I know this all must seem chaotic, but I don't know where to start and I haven't got much time to organize my thoughts. I never expected anything like this. You see, there's a human-populated planet out here all right, we found it, right in line with the Schedule of Progress that Sukar worked out so many millennia ago—that is, just getting into early technology, not yet aware of what's going on in the galaxy. Or they weren't. They are now. They've made it to their moons, Magnificent One, and they're going to be taking to the stars soon enough, because SOMEONE'S BRINGING THEM UP TO DATE. That is, someone from a Base World has been forcefeeding them technology, teaching them all about gravitic control and compound acceleration and you give it a True Name, we found them playing around with it.

I checked the Plan of Expansion and found out that Braxi isn't due to hit this region for a good two centuries or more—and I don't have to tell you, in two hundred years these people can become prepared enough to put up a blessed good fight. Because there's something else, too. This isn't just some troublemaker out to make all the Base Worlds miserable. The planet's been told all about Braxi and it's already making plans. And in two hundred years, in a part of the galaxy where no one's going to get in its way, these people are going to go far, and fast.

Now here's the worst of it. Nyser said we should come right back with the news, but I said no, we needed to explore first and find out just where all this was coming from. What good would it do to tell you about the problem without knowing if it was an isolated instance, or if it was just the edge of some widespread campaign? So we tapped into the local transmissions—they had just started using artificial satellites, which made it easier—gave them a rough translation, and when we realized what was happening, we just couldn't believe it. You remember that Azean Starcommander, the one who ran off with a diplomatic runner some years ago and was never heard from again? Well, she's out here. And she's bringing these people up to Base World standard and pointing them toward Braxi all the while. There's going to be one mess of a battle when Braxi does hit this region, if things keep on going the way they are, and I for one am glad I won't be around when it happens.

The other scouts and I felt it was imperative that you be told all of this immediately so that you could act on it, so I'm rushing off this message (along with travel coordinates, etc). and we're all coming home, and hopefully one of us will get to you. Because I think they spotted us out here. And if rumor is truth, she's got hold of a ship that can make us all look like we're standing still, and peel the forcefields off us like the skin off a fruit. So take care of Braxi, Lord. And do something, I beg you! For our children's sake, if not our own. What would the Holding be in a universe without conquest?

Zatar's face was flushed with anger, but his voice was still under some vestige of control as he said, "So that's her game. I knew she wouldn't simply run away. I knew she was planning something. But *this!*"

Then the control broke down and he slammed the flatrendering to the desk in front of him, with enough force that the swept-crystal structure trembled. "Go ahead, read it." He waved Ni'en toward the message, turned away in rage. "How *dare* she! How dare she play with the very technological balance of the galaxy like it was another starchart, or maybe a fighter, just some tool of War to be plugged into the computers along with everything else. . . ."

Numbed by the letter's contents, Ni'en let it slide from her hand to the floor.

"She's right, of course," he muttered. "That's all it is."

She whispered it: "What will you do?"

He laughed, bitterly. "A complicated question, my Mistress. B'Salos! I thought of *everything* she might do, where she might go, how she might still be a threat to me . . . but I didn't anticipate this. How could I? The scope of it is so far beyond anything that's been tried before! Who else could have conceived of such a plan, much less carried it out with such callous efficiency?"

He turned back to her; the flush was fading from his brow, but his eyes were dark with rage. And fear? "The Barren Zone is a lifeless realm of dust and gases that no ships have bothered to penetrate, prior to this. There are no stars in it for light-decades, nothing but microscopic debris and scanner static. One travels by faith and one's starcharts; taking reliable readings through the stuff, provided one s traveling at augmented speeds, is impossible.

"Without going into great detail, suffice it to say I can't simply send a fleet to deal with this. It would take preparation—zhents, perhaps years—we would have to establish supply facilities along the way, some kind of beacon that could function in such a place . . . and we'd be traveling blind, which is a real danger in any case but more so if she knows we're coming. That's one problem. Then, too, there's the question of tactical preparation. Even if I gave immediate orders to withdraw certain ships from their current assignments and send them out to get her, there would be unavoidable delays: planning and building in order to bridge the Barren Zone, strategic sessions, diplomatic preparations to keep the newly unguarded regions from rebellion while the fleets are elsewhere. And the time! Two years minimum, to get there, Ar alone knows how long to conquer, another two to return—at least! No communication with them while they're out there, no hope of reinforcements. Any word sent to Braxi from that far out would be outdated long before it got here. And even if we—*when* we conquer this miserable upstart world, we'll never get hold of *her*."

"If she leads them into battle—"

"She won't. Not if she really means to destroy the Holding. She'll disappear as soon as the tide turns against her, with all of the unclaimed galaxy for her hiding-place, until she can find some suitable planet and start all over again. And how could we stop her? Ar!" He struck one hand with the other, a gesture obscene with violence. "She's trying to get someone to do to us what we did to Lugast—and I won't allow it!"

Quietly, the perfect complement to his rage, she asked "What can I do, Lord?"

He shut his eyes for a moment, letting the rage settle, trying to think. "We have to act. I have to do something—*soon*. Call in the fleet commanders: Benex, Sirin, Tuvir . . . and Herek. We've got a Peace, thank Azea for that; one bit of luck in our favor. It can last a few zhents more, while we work out some plan of action. As for her. . . ."

He smiled to himself. "I forget, sometimes, the full extent of my arsenal. For the war, we will summon warships. As for the warrior . . . we will summon her maker.

"Call Feran to me."

When Feran answered his Master's summons, he was disturbed to find Zatar aloof and restrained; and when the Probe tried to read his surface mind for cause of it, he found his query turned aside with a skill that was alarming.

How could a man who had never lived with psychic awareness manage so perfect a shield? Was mere strength of will enough? He had been teaching the Pri'tiera the basics of telepathic discipline, but that was mere theory, meaningless to the non-sensitive; he had never expected Zatar to internalize it.

If you were psychic, he thought, *in addition to everything you already are, no man could stand against you.*

"Welcome," the Pri'tiera said, but there was no welcome in his voice—only tension, finely tuned and carefully controlled. "I have some news that I think will interest you." *Some news that I know you fear,* his surface thoughts added.

"I am the Pri'tiera's servant."

Of course. The dark eyes were watching him, ready to assess his reaction to news that was clearly disturbing.

"I have located Anzha lyu Mitethe," he said simply.

The skies swirled about Feran in maddening chaos—and were still, and he managed a small measure of control. "Where? Doing what?"

"Plotting the downfall of Braxi." He gave that a moment to sink in, then withdrew the scout's missive from his tunic. And read it.

Then silence.

At last Feran spoke, his voice an unsteady whisper. "What will you do?"

"What I must. The planet will die; there's no other way. Even now my fleets are being prepared for the effort; we'll find a way to cross the Barren Zone, and then we'll crush this world and its fledgling colonies. Not a single native will survive, I assure you. Which takes care of the immediate threat to our security." He looked at Feran, his gaze so intense that the Probe had to turn away. "But it doesn't address the real problem."

"Anzha lyu."

"As long as she's free to roam the galaxy at will, Braxi is in danger." He saw panic stirring in Feran, and nodded his approval.

There was only one solution; the Probe wasn't likely to welcome it. "As for what to do about her, the portrait has changed all that. Her bloodline is as precious to Braxi as my own. If I kill her now, knowing that, I may undo all my work. Braxi would turn against me; the common people are not yet so loyal to me that they would allow me to desecrate their history; even the military might have second thoughts after I cut short their proudest bloodline. No, I can't kill her—but I *can* and *must* neutralize her. She must cease to be a threat, and that's where you come in."

"What do you want me to do?" he stammered, fearing the answer.

"I have no illusions that my fleet will be able to find her, much less capture her. Only a mind attuned to her own could second-guess her intent as finely as would be required, or call to her across the vast distances involved. Only a mind that shares her background could pry her loose from her dream of conquest, and bring her back to Braxi.

"She would kill me," Feran said quickly. His voice was thick with fear. "Have you taken that into account? Her hatred of me is only second to that which she reserves for you. She would kill me in an instant if she had the chance, and you're giving her the perfect opportunity! How can I serve you if I'm dead?"

"You fear death," he observed.

"Don't you?"

"Not in the same way. I fear defeat more. Which is why I must take certain risks, in order to negate her advantage."

He paced for a moment, thoughtful, then addressed Feran anew. "How will she react, do you suppose, when she learns the truth of her heredity?"

It pained him to answer, to remember. "The child I . . . adjusted . . . could not come to terms with such a thing. I know that."

"And now?"

"Who can say? You can't design a person, Pri'tiera. You can only design his tendencies, then let him follow his own course. If your foresight was good, if your planning was adaptable, if the environment is amenable to your intentions, you may get something like what you wanted."

"And in her case?"

He chose his words carefully. "I see, in her actions, the results of what we did. I also see many choices open to her that we didn't anticipate. She's much stronger than she was, stronger than we ever thought she could be. Not just in power. In stability. Li Pazua thought she would go insane," he confided. The memory was rank within him. "That suited his purposes, so we made our plans accordingly. As she reached adulthood, the programming would take effect. Denied human contact, national identity, even the limited comfort of a planetary home, she would be driven forth in a desperate search for something to give her ties to the rest of humanity. That was the plan. What actually happened was something else again."

"You never foresaw her fleet service."

"I foresaw a frightened child, fleeing some inner darkness that she couldn't comprehend—which I had put there," he said defiantly, as though daring the Pri'tiera to pass judgment on him. "Li Pazua envisioned a woman wholly dependent on him, whom he would support financially and otherwise as she searched throughout the galaxy for the information he wanted so badly—the information you now control. You must understand, he believed in racial memory. If somewhere in her psyche the key to her past was in hiding, it stood to reason that emotional duress might unearth it. Desperation does strange things to the mind."

"And you?" The dark eyes studied him for reaction. "What did you think of that?"

"I obeyed orders," he snapped. "That was programmed into *me*. What I believed then is irrelevant; the point is, we failed. She didn't suffer quietly. She didn't fall apart. Most important, she didn't turn to li Pazua for support. She made her own destiny, in ways none of us would have anticipated. So you ask me, what will happen when she finds out that the Race she hates is her own? My answer is that she *should* fall apart, unable to cope—or she *should* go running back to the Institute, so Li Pazua can have his answer. But she won't. She doesn't need him any more. She doesn't need any of us."

"What does she need?" he demanded.

He hesitated; even now, years later, the memory of that child's mind was overwhelming. "Consummation of a self-hatred so intense that all the Probes in the Institute couldn't alter it. It took me years just to redirect it, and you see the result. That's why I say, she has no way to deal with news like this. None." He shuddered. "I suspect there's a good chance that when a link is demonstrated between herself and her enemies she may well identify with them—

and in that case, everything we did to save her from herself may be undone, and quickly."

"She would die?" he pressed.

Feran looked away. After a long and painful silence he ventured, "That would be the most merciful end."

"And what if the hatred were consummated?"

He looked back, startled. "But that would take the destruction of Braxi—of you—of *herself,* once she learns the truth."

"What if it were redirected?" he asked evenly.

Suddenly Feran understood—and feared. "Not at this point. She would crush me if I tried, do you understand that? Programming the mind of a child is one thing. Inserting suggestions into the mind of a Functional Telepath is suicide!"

"And your commitment to serve me?"

"Pri'tiera, there are things that have passed between Anzha lyu and me which you simply can't understand, things that make it impossible for her to accept any kind of probic contact."

"Don't underestimate me," Zatar warned him. "I know the full extent of your work, including the details you never told me. Yes, even what you did to her sexuality. I don't doubt that she'd jump at the chance to kill you—I would myself, under the same circumstances. For now, just answer my question. What would happen if her destructive tendencies were channeled elsewhere?"

"Toward whom? I see why you would want to do it, but I don't see how it could be done."

The Pri'tiera's voice was low and even, a sharp contrast to the intensity that poured forth from his surface mind. "What if she understood that you weren't responsible for what you did? What if she placed the blame where it really belonged—on those who gave you your orders, taught you your techniques, manipulated your emotions? What if the Institute became her enemy?"

It took him a long time to remember what it meant to be innocent of motive; it was a concept alien to the Braxaná mind, which punished doer and planner alike. "I might, then, be spared." He spoke softly. "Is that what you want? Turn her against the Institute so she'll go back there to fight them—start her all over again in some new vendetta? I don't know if I can do that."

"But if you did," he persisted, "there would be an end for *you,* at least. You've learned to live with the memory of what you did to her, but you've never really come to terms with it."

"I would be doing it all over again," he said bitterly. "Taking away her certain victory and giving her an empty dream in its place."

"*Listen to me.*" Stepping forward, the Pri'tiera grasped him firmly by the shoulders; emotion, strong and unbridled, flowed through the contact. "I am sending you out there. I have no other way to reach her. All other things aside, I must get control of her—or Braxi is doomed, Feran, do you understand that?"

"She'll never submit to you. The kairth—"

"Is ended! Haven't you realized that? She abandoned the endless battle for one that promised victory, and I say, put it in those terms again. Promise her vengeance. Promise her consummation of that hatred which has ruled her life. I give you that power."

"What do you mean?"

"*I* will destroy the Institute. I've intended to for years, for military reasons, but I'll do it now, in her name."

He was stunned. "But how—"

"My means are my own secret. It will be blamed on her, never fear; the Peace will remain intact until I choose to break it." Emotion poured forth from him in torrents—hatred, determination, hunger. "I can't leave her out there; she'll destroy Braxi if I do. I must reel her in, and for that the Institute will be my bait. As for the rest. . . ." He released him, suddenly shielded. "She's no longer simply an enemy. Knowing her bloodline changes everything."

Feran caught the undertone to his words and whispered, "You *want* her."

"How could any man not want her? She's the woman my ancestors sought, when they chose their mates to strengthen the Tribe. Braxaná have fought for her kind, died trying to possess her, waged war and moved nations—how could I fail to feel desire for such a woman, when she embodies everything my people value?"

The mental block, slowly slipping, was suddenly reestablished. "But that's beside the point," he said coldly. "I must have her, and only you can bring her to me. As for what happens once she gets here, that's my concern, not yours."

"*If* I can stop her," Feran said quietly, "and if she lives—if *I* live—do you really think she'll come to you? After everything?"

"*Because* of everything. Yes, Feran. She'll come. I can't say what will happen after that, but when I tender her an invitation sealed with the Institute's lifeblood, I have no doubt that she'll accept. And after that. . . ."

His words faded into silence, rich with conflicting emotions.

"She has my Name," he said at last. Then his mind focused back toward the workroom, and the painting it contained. He let Feran share the image, and all the thoughts which it inspired.

"As I have hers," he whispered.

Harkur: Above all else, never underestimate the enemy.

TWENTY-SEVEN

He walks to the terrace, looks out into the early dawn. There, at that angle, the star of Llornu is rising. Not visible to the naked eye, not this morning, not from Braxi. He calls for a magnification field and waits while the proper forces align themselves in response to his summons. There . . . yes, he can see it now.

"How much longer?" he asks.

The House responds: .21 TENTH.

"Tell me when it happens."

UNDERSTOOD.

He considers what he has done, and what is about to happen, and what the ramifications of it will be. He indulges his imagination at length, knowing the supposed danger of it.

Sense my thoughts, he dares the telepaths, taste my intentions, read my purpose. And stop me—if you can.

But the distance is too far and he knows it; no one can hear him, despite his powerful intent-focus.

The House of Zatar speaks:

IT IS TIME.

He smiles.

* * *

Nabu li Pazua awoke suddenly, convinced that something was wrong.

He surveyed his immediate surroundings with a master's telepathic touch, hoping to discover the source of his alarm. In this small room, in the adjoining chambers outside, in this whole section of the building, there was nothing that might have disturbed his sleep. Perhaps his own stream of consciousness? He reviewed the dream which was only now fading from memory, and found in its content nothing to arouse suspicion. No, whatever had disturbed him was clearly external to his own person. And it was *wrong*.

He scanned the mental horizon for the source of his discomfort, found it in a stranger's thoughts. There—a tendril of concentration so faint that it almost evaded his perception. He touched it with all his skill, seeking its source and purpose. Something to do with the Border, it seemed. No; he tested that possibility, discarded it. Someone connected with the Border, then.

Anzha? Could she be planning her revenge at last? In theory, her conditioning made such action impossible, but she had broken so many rules already—why not that one as well?

He opened himself to the foreign thoughtstream—so weak, so indecipherable—and overlaid it with Anzha's own mental signature. To his relief, the two failed to match.

Feran? He tested that thought as well, though he seriously doubted that the Probe could span Holding and Empire without relay, and again the answer was negative.

That left no one—at least, no one li Pazua had ever heard of. From that direction, once could almost imagine a Braxin source. Except of course that there *were* no Braxin psychics.

Or were there?

He took what he knew of the Braxin mindset—and he knew a lot, having trained Ferian del Kanar for his defection—and he compared it to the alien thought. To his horror, he found that the two images were very similar.

All right, he told himself, be calm, think it out. A Braxin source (the distance alone made it incredible!) focused upon the Institute, or upon Llornu, or li Pazua himself. With what purpose? The contact was too weak for him to read that clearly, but one thing was painfully clear: it was hostility that had strengthened the signal, making it strong enough to reach across Holding and Empire and awaken him in the night.

Some kind of imminent attack? he ventured.

Yes.

It could be anything, provided it touched upon his person (or his cause, they were the same thing), and provided that culmination of the Braxin's plan was in the immediate future. Only such a combination was capable of channeling surface thoughts to him with such intensity, perhaps without the sender's approval.

Attack! They had prepared defenses, had never expected to need them. Li Pazua tried to calm himself enough to manage a cool, rational sending. To the first rung of Llornu's special defense network: relay.

Five psychics were on guard, quickly roused from lethargy when he filled their minds with his warning. They would warn the others, spreading word in an instant with flawless precision, setting various plans in motion with far more efficiency than nonsentient technology could ever hope to equal.

He trembled, waiting.

~ *Director?* It was his relay captain, a skilled Communicant.

~ *All stations alerted.* That meant machines were scanning the heavens for activity, telepaths were searching the boundaries of thought for threat, computers were analyzing the psychefiles of Llornu's current population. Would it be enough? Li Pazua wished he had some idea what kind of threat they were dealing with; it would narrow the search considerably. How much time did they have?

~ *What is it we're looking for?* the relay team group-queried.

~ *I don't know!* He paused, trying to give a name to that feeling which had crept with icy claws into the heart of him. Dread? Terror? ~ *Hostile focus, manifestation expected shortly. Maintain full alert, telepathic and mechanical.*

It could be an assassin, plotting li Pazua's demise, which had worked its way into his awareness. Or a saboteur, preparing weapons of destruction. Even a political enemy, negotiating Llornu's doom—any source that combined hostility with a Llornuan intent, focusing upon this moment in time . . . too many possibilities, too little information. Li Pazu a fumed at his own impotence.

He reached out for contact with the psychics in the defense center, the ones in charge of Llornu's limited martial capacity. A Communicant was waiting to relay his consciousness to the operations center; he tapped into the man's senses even as the head psychic announced his presence. So far, the system was working well.

Briefly, Nabu regretted his decision to ban StarControl from the system. They could have used Security's help at a time like this. But that would have set a dangerous precedent, compromising Llornu's autonomy. And once the veil of secrecy had been lifted, StarControl would hardly allow him to restore it. No, when Director ni Kahv had offered to fortify the Institute, Nabu had made the only choice possible. Who had ever thought that Llornu would come under attack?

~ *What's going on?* he asked.

~ *There are fifteen objects inatmosphere. Thirty-two insystem. We're identifying them now.*

He nodded, but the gesture didn't affect the body he was now sharing. Normally, computers controlled all of Llornu's traffic, from the movement of passenger transports to manned and unmanned cargo freighters. Llornu had a large population, psychic and non-psychic, and supported a good deal of trade. But computers could err, and certainly they could be misinformed; it was important to have humans verifying identification at a time like this. ~ *Let me know when you have something.*

He shifted his awareness to the guards of the aether.

Harr'yd, a gifted psychic-receptive, shared consciousness with him. Not all the telepaths assigned to this duty were in the same room, but a network of thought bound them together as certainly as if they were.

~ *Dyri and Calsua verified the signal,* Harr'yd told him. ~ *Source: apparently Braxin.* A note of wonder accompanied that information. ~ *Spatial focus is general rather than specific. Dyri feels that the ultimate target will be conceptual as opposed to material. Although that may involve a material assault.*

A sinking sensation filled the pit of li Pazua's stomach as he realized what all that implied. ~ *The Institute?*

~ *Possibly. Temporal focus seems to be in the immediate future—*

Yes, he knew all that. And more was becoming clear to him, parcels of alien thought which he had previously been unable to identify. Waiting—that was what he had perceived, the sense of someone *waiting,* anticipating the destruction of everything they had worked for.

He returned to that defense center. ~ *Progress?*

He was given a glimpse of the main flatscreen, with the paths of six objects etched across the heavens. ~ *These are still unidentified,* a Communicant reported; there was a tinge of fear in his surface mind.

Those were it, then. ~ *Find out what they are. Our defense fields?*

~ *Already established, Director.*

But are they adequate? li Pazua wondered.

Llornu was not equipped for war. They had never expected to fight. The Institute's last Director had put in basic defense fields in response to StarControl's advice. In li Pazua's lifetime, Ebre ni Kahv had urged him to accept that Llornu might well become a military target. But the Institute was above such petty concerns as war and conquest; it served Knowledge, which was the domain of all humankind. Who would want to destroy that?

~ *!!!Objects entering lower atmosphere!*

It was Anzha lyu who had brought them to this pass. She had turned telepathy into a weapon, negating the Institute's treasured neutrality. Damn her! What had Braxi ever cared about Llornu, before she came along?

~ *We have an identification,* one of the guards projected; his thoughts were thick with death. ~ *Battle drones, from Tirrah. Should we—*

~ *Fire!* he answered quickly.

War had come to Llornu.

* * *

Zatar reviews his planning, is pleased. He has seen to it that Llornu will not be warned of the coming attack, by a complicated network of misinformation which has resulted in no one but himself knowing the details of the assault. The outlaws on Tirrah who constructed his battle-drones did so without asking questions; the astrogator who programmed their course thought he was programming for cargo transports. Bits and pieces of fact, peppered with strategic untruths, served up to carefully chosen men . . . there is no way that any of them will focus their thoughts upon Llornu today, giving him away. Zatar has seen to it.

As for himself, he is too far away for it to matter; so Feran assured him. Thus he revels in his plans, projecting his triumph out to the stars and daring Llornu to anticipate him. In moments the attack will be underway; there is nothing they can do to stop it. The glory of Llornu will be leveled at last, which serves both Braxi and his own ambition. And it is because he is not psychic, because he is parted from them by the breadth of two great nations, but most of all because his planning has been perfect, that he can laugh his triumph to the Void, unnoticed—while the Institute meets its destiny.

* * *

The bombs fell like rain, dropping to Llornu's surface, at seemingly random intervals, powdering the landscape with hot white flashes. Li Pazua's men tried to pick them off as they fell, but there were too many, and there was no pattern to their descent. They seemed to be coming from two of the drones, and so li Pazua concentrated his firepower upon those mechanisms; but while he did so hundreds died, screaming their fear and their pain into the thoughtwinds of the psychic community.

So much loss—and for what purpose? He could understand an attack upon the capital complex. That was where the Institute's files were housed, where the most damage might be done. But so far, not a single drone had addressed itself to that target. Instead they fired at random upon the planet, striking terror into psychic and non-psychic alike as they blasted the outlying communities with white-hot death. Why?

A flare in the night, blossoming into molten fragments of destruction. "One down," Karallen muttered. It was safer to speak, to trust to the limited power of words, than to brave the hell of psychic sensitivity. The planetmind had become a sea of desperation and fear; if one opened up to it, even for a instant, there was no telling what might happen.

And there it was: what the strange attack had accomplished. By making enough psychics suffer, by causing the thoughtwinds to be filled with their pain and their fear, the enemy had severed mind from mind—had negated Llornu's single great advantage. Now the psychics were no more than human; even less—they, who were now limited to physical communication, were the least practiced in using it. The outlook was dismal indeed.

Li Pazua pulled out of his host-body just as a tide of rising insanity threatened to engulf him. Cursing, he returned his awareness to his own body and bolted from his room, heading toward the nearest exit. A quick sprint across Capital Park brought him to the Institute's main building, where the defense center was located; he tried not to look up as he ran, knowing that nothing but a shell of balanced energies stood between him and the enemy. Five halls, two staircases—the lift was too far away—he planned the journey in his mind as he raced from one building to the next, cursing the circumstances that made physical travel necessary. When he came to the defense center, he had to stand by the door for a minute, leaning against its frame and trying to catch his breath.

The outlook was not good. The five remaining drones had

turned their attention to the main array of buildings. They seemed adept at dodging the Institute's fire, or perhaps li Pazua's people were simply too inexperienced to hit them. Again he wished for StarControl. *Too late, too late. You made your choice!* "Be careful," he muttered, using the warning to announce his presence. It was all that he could do.

Suddenly, one of the battle-drones dove for the main building. It was all that li Pazua could do to keep breathing; his hands clasped so tightly that blood was drawn, he watched as the fledgling warriors sought to cut the drone down in mid-flight. And they hit it—but it absorbed the energy of their attack, dispersed it, and threw itself against the building's forcedome in one final, blazing explosion.

For a moment all screens went white, as Llornu's forcefields absorbed the strength of the assault. Li Pazua found himself praying. *God of our Founding, Father of the Firstborn, do not let all our work be destroyed, I beg of you. . . .* He looked up in time to see the night sky displayed anew.

"Forcefields intact," Karallen announced. There was an audible sigh of relief from all the room's occupants.

"Damn!" Susha's voice was shaking; the strain of keeping her mind safely closed was telling on her. "Here comes another one."

It came, and like its predecessor it concentrated all its power in one suicidal plunge. They tried to stop it, but the most they could manage was to burn off its outer forcefield. Then it struck, and the screens blazed white-hot as their own fields fought to protect them.

This time the display took much longer to clear. *How much of this can we take?* li Pazua wondered.

"Choose one," he instructed the defense crew. "Focus all your fire on it, regardless of what the others do. We can't take them out once they're diving. Maybe this will work." *And if they come two at once. . . .* Then the Llornuans would die, Ii Pazua realized, along with all their work. The thought of it filled him with rage, which in turn increased his sensitivity. He had to fight to tune out the cries of the dying while his psychic warriors chose a drone, and focused their fire upon it.

"Number five is diving!" Susha warned.

"Keep going!" They had to destroy these things, or sheer numbers would defeat them. Li Pazua held his breath as the third suicide-drone fell toward them, as they kept the outer forcefield down in order to fire upon its companion—a hit, there, and then another; they were getting it!—and then the field was brought back up, just in time.

Drone number five was stronger than the others, or else the defense-fields were getting weaker. It took long minutes for the screens to clear, and when they did so they were not fully functional.

"We got one," Susha announced. Her hair, sweat-soaked, was plastered to her face. "That means one more to go. Hasha . . ."

"We can do it." Li Pazua glanced at the generator readings. Bad, very bad . . . one more dive like the others and they'd be stardust. They had to get this one before it got them.

But as they focused their aim upon it, it began to drift away.

"What the—"

"It doesn't matter," li Pazua said hurriedly. "Destroy it!"

Malfunction? Change in plans? Whatever the cause, it was moving away from them as the last of their aggressive power was vented upon its forcefield. After a moment, the drone began to glow. And an instant later—an eternity, to those watching—the drone itself imploded, scattering the enemy's remains in a burst of pyrotechnics across the wounded landscape.

For a moment there was silence, psychic and physical.

"We got it," Susha whispered.

"Is that the last?"

"Find out," li Pazua ordered. "Full scan of the system."

"And damage reports?" Karallen asked softly.

Oh, Hasha—the dead, the dying, the suffering . . . "Yes. As soon as you can. Use the equipment," he added, and the message was clear: *don't open yourselves to what's out there.*

There were hundreds of psychics living on Llornu, and thousands of people who lacked the talent but preferred that society. Lovers who had tasted telepathic union and now could enjoy nothing less; scholars of the genetic arts who reveled in the Institute's research facilities; sociologists and morale adjusters who struggled to reduce the bizarre Llornuan culture to a collection of finite statistics: innocents, all of them, psychic and physical alike. He could understand why Braxi would strike at the central grounds, where the Institute's records were stored, but why the murder of so many innocent souls?

"I'm going to check the Archives," he murmured. There were physicians who could handle the wounded far better than he could;

he needed to see that their records were safe, to reassure himself that although lives had been lost, their purpose endured. Contact with the Archives would be his shield against insanity when the chaos of the thoughtwinds began to break down his barriers, when the newborn terror of his world engulfed him.

If not for that warning, we might all be dead. Thank the Founding that our enemy forgot our strength: that the thoughts of an assassin mark his purpose like a beacon. We owe our lives to our enemy's lack of mental control.

The Archives were buried deep beneath the surface of the planet, in a series of vaults fortified against man and nature. Originally they had relied upon the tons of earth which surrounded them for their protection; then, after the quakes of '234, they were rebuilt to withstand any disaster. The result was a strange admixture of primitive tunnels and gleaming catwalks, of natural caverns buttressed with a spiderweb of forcefield relays, of pseudometal cabinets filled with hardcopy backups and a glistening array of the Empire's finest computerware. Though the myriad halls and winding tunnels were contained in a perfect sphere, it was impossible to see at any one point how many rooms there were, or what form they might take, or where this twisting path—now a stone-paved walkway, afterward a catwalk that spanned the breadth of a massive cavern—might lead next. The only real evidence of the Archives' structure lay in the generator situated at its central point. From there a thousand silver threads shot out to the sphere's circumference, the struts of a forcefield assembly so powerful that were Llornu itself destroyed, the Archival Sphere—and the Institute's records—would endure.

Here was the lifeblood of the Institute, the culmination of all their work. Here the precious records were stored, complex genetic scans and their associated psychefiles, biohistories of all known psychics (as well as projected histories for those who had died before the Institute was founded), and millions upon millions of comparative analyses that crosschecked the patterns of amino acids against the measures of psychic talent, hoping to discover a relationship between them. Here there were rooms equipped for the analysis of DNA, and chambers filled with sample strands, held in stasis. Here, li Pazua thought, was the Institute; all the rest existed so that *this* might endure.

He walked across paths that spanned the irregular chambers, touching the surfaces of sleeping machines as if to assure himself that they did, indeed, exist. Not that there was ever any doubt. No enemy fire, no act of nature, and (most important of all) no despoiling radiation could reach this place, where the Institute's hopes were housed. The Archives were unscathed.

With pride he walked through the underground chambers, drawing strength from the hope that this place represented. He stopped only when he noticed that the flatscreen of one computer was not wholly blank. Walking up to it, he frowned. A malfunction, no doubt; well, it happened. Or perhaps someone working down here had forgotten to clear the board when he left. That was possible.

Then he read the display, and the world spun maddeningly about him as he tried to absorb its message.

TRIGGER SEQUENCE AFFIRMED.

DETONATION SEQUENCE STAGE ONE.

He struck the control marked PROGRAM IDENTIFICATION. A file number appeared; it could mean anything. He tried to call up the program, but for some reason the computer wouldn't respond.

At last, in desperation, he asked it for the so-called trigger sequence. That, apparently, was not protected.

THREE SURGES IN MAINBASE DEFENSE FIELD, it told him. It proceeded to list specifics: how long between surges (just how long had it taken for each drone to dive at them?), strength of each surge (it was right, it was right . . .), to be followed by a period of inactivity.

That was why the last drone had pulled back . . . Hasha help them all, the attack was merely an attempt to focus their attention elsewhere, while this, the true assault, was triggered by their own defenses!

He tried to call for help—and the wall of pain was so intense that it sent him gasping back to his own body, unable to bear the torment of Llornu's thoughtstreams. Who was there to hear him, anyway? They were all trying their best to close themselves off, to shut off those senses which even now could save them.

He tried to stop the program from running.

DETONATION SEQUENCE STAGE TWO it responded, oblivious to his efforts.

There was a noise from the other end of the Archives; he searched for the source, but could see nothing out of the ordinary, Somewhere between the banks of computers, squeezed beneath the walkways, buried in rock, perhaps in the files themselves!

someone had planted something—and he, li Pazua, had caused it to go off.

"Hasha forgive me," he whispered, as the display altered one last time.

DETONATION SEQUENCE STAGE THREE, the computer warned.

FISSION.

* * *

"Is it done yet?" Zatar asks.

97% PROBABILITY. The House isn't anxious to commit itself, but the figure it gives is promising. He'll have to wait until news of it reaches Braxi to be certain, but that shouldn't take long now. Something like this can't be kept secret.

It's a good thing I planted that trap when I did, *he tells himself.*

Which is a part of his journey to Azea that he's shared with no one, not even Ni'en. Now he is glad, very glad, that he took the risk, and glad that he kept it a secret. The Institute is gone, the psychic community ruptured, and Anzha lyu Mitethe will be blamed for the destruction. He'll see to that.

His vengeance and her purpose, combined: the neatness of it pleases him.

I am ready for you, my vendetta-mate.

Viton: The true k'airth is a complex and dangerous sport, in that it forces one's enemy to continually improve his skills. The most successful participant is he who can manipulate this factor. To cause the enemy to overextend himself, or to channel his energies down paths that will ultimately destroy him, is often the subtlest and most pleasing of all strategies.

TWENTY-EIGHT

The planetary governor of Do Kul was a portly man, red-faced and swollen-eyed and clearly fond of luxury. He walked the halls in robes of irridescent watersilk, hems sweeping the floor in regal waste, and the clatter of precious stones against crystalline tiles spoke volumes for his wealth, his willingness to spend it, and his desire to have it noticed.

"I've had your things brought to the Master Suite," he told Zatar, plump hands clasped before him. "I think you'll be more than pleased with it,

The Pri'tiera was too distracted to respond, which was just as well; it was doubtful the governor was listening for his answer.

The fleets were due. Overdue, if one took for granted their success. For nearly four years now he had managed to push that situation to the back of his mind, telling himself over and over again, *There's nothing you can do. You sent them out—they're beyond all contact—you can only wait.* But now, finally, zero-day had passed. A messenger might return at any moment, bringing him news of his success. Or of his failure. How could he play the diplomat with that hanging over his head?

"A fine example of Do Kullad workmanship," the governor was saying, "unequaled anywhere in the galaxy—save perhaps on your own planet." Briefly Zatar wondered how the man had gotten appointed to such a post, and he longed for the days when a moment of anger was cause enough to execute such irritants. But he was Pri'tiera now, and if he wanted his throne to endure there were certain games he needed to play—for a while longer, at least.

"I'm sure they will be adequate," he answered.

They came to a door, silverstone and crystal set in gleaming white forceform. "Observe," said the governor, and with a flourish he dissipated the forcefield; the ornaments which remained, strung on fine silken lines at varying heights, swayed in the open doorframe.

He turned to Zatar, his face aglow, but saw something there which sobered him rapidly. "With your permission, Pri'tiera." He bowed, and there were no more expansive gestures. Holding aside the curtain of strung crystal, he waited until Zatar had entered, then followed him into the Master Guest Suite of Do Kul's Floating Palace.

"You see, we've used Aldousan flexicrystal, but in a manner uniquely our own." Beaming with pride, the governor indicated their surroundings. And yes, the antechamber was magnificent. Filaments of finely drawn flexicrystal stretched from ceiling to floor along three of the chamber's four walls so delicately, and so lightly bound in place, that any disturbance in the room's scented air set them to stirring in ripples and starts, much like the surface of water. Zatar observed their motion with a look that might pass for approval, nodded, and muttered a word or two of commendation. But his mind was elsewhere. "The fourth wall?"

"A display screen, Pri'tiera." With a touch he made it active—and stars set in blackness filled the wall's confines, with a hint of Do Kul's sun at the lower edge and Nabor, a natural satellite, rising. But that was not what arrested Zatar's attention. There, in the constellation the locals called the Dancer: black in the night, a streak of darkness that hid the stars behind it, the Dancer's Veil. Somewhere beyond that were his fleets, and a war. And his enemy.

"You approve?" the governor dared.

He nodded slowly, savoring the sight. So: his rooms in the palace faced the Barren Zone—all the better. He was obsessed with the region anyway, he might as well live with it in plain sight, "Excellent," he said softly. "This will do."

The governor's rapid movements were mirrored by crystalline undulations as the stout man saw to the lighting, adjusting the controls so that crystals embedded in the ceiling sparkled with rainbow fire. "The furniture is all forceform," he told Zatar, "and can be adjusted for temperature, texture, kinetic activity—"

"I'm familiar with the type." He wondered just how to get rid of this man, who had given him a grand tour of the palace and now seemed determined to stay with him. Whim Death was tempting, but it seemed a bit extreme. "I imagine the Museum is unloading about now." He used a speech mode which implied great personal concern: *to serve the Museum is to serve me.* "Many of the items in the Grand Exhibit belong to my House; I would be greatly reassured if someone of noteworthy station would oversee this operation."

It took the governor a moment to catch the hint, but when he did so he bowed deeply, imagining himself honored. "Say no more, Magnificent One." A wave of his hand was mirrored in silver shock-waves on the wall. "I will see to it myself. If you will but excuse me—"

"Of course." He watched with some amusement as the governor bowed extravagantly and left, leaving a wake on the surface of the walls that was some minutes long in fading. Only when the motion had stopped did Zatar feel truly alone.

Soon . . . it would be soon. It *had* to be. They would have sent a message to him as soon as triumph was certain. And triumph *was* certain—wasn't it? The best of the Braxin fleets against a single, quasiprimitive planet?

And *her*, he thought, with a cold twisting in his gut. She could defeat them. He had no doubt of that, though all logic was weighted against it. She was no longer wholly human in his eyes, but some demonic creature midway between woman and the essence of War; she embodied all the variables that he could not predict, all the tricks of fate that were wont to bring a warrior to his knees. She and she alone could reduce his offensive to chaos; he had no doubt of that. Only Feran could stop her. . . .

But could he? The Probe was weak, and even under Zatar's firm control he was likely to break under the strain of his current assignment. Zatar had no illusions about that. He had planned the best that he could, but now his strength depended upon the work of others—and the waiting was killing him, slowly but surely.

Turning away from the starscreen, he forced himself to pay attention to his surroundings. Walls that followed his motion—the ultimate in egocentricity—with a tinkling sound like that of some crystalline rain, and rainbow forceforms that might or might not be furniture. Elegant, yes, but not to his taste. He preferred a solid world, a Braxaná universe of earth and steel and women. *Armed* women, who could stand in battle with their men and bathe in the blood of the Pale Tribe's enemies, glorying in their destruction. Women like the Starcommander. . . .

Stop that.

Needing to distract himself, he passed through a large archway at the far end of the antechamber and found himself in what might be considered a conference chamber. The walls were the same as in the antechamber, the huge central table and twelve attendant chairs of the same forcefield construction, but here there was one thing different. Against the far wall, shielded in black plastic, there was a blot upon the ethereal substance of the crystalline surroundings. As tall as a Braxaná male, as wide as Zatar's arms could be spread: the portrait from Berros, awaiting exhibition.

It never left his possession; he valued it too much to entrust it to common hands, even those of the Central Museum's staff. Now he stroked its case, resenting the circumstances that had caused him to bring it here. He would much have preferred to keep its existence a secret, using it as the bait with which to lure his treasured quarry back to Braxi . . . but rumor had leaked out of Berros somehow, and he had had to adjust his plans accordingly. Rather than let common gossip shape her preconceptions, he had chosen to unveil his secret at the Central Museum, on Braxi. The public reaction was one of astonishment, more so when it was explained that the second figure in the portrait—the dark-skinned, round-eyed female, who differed from any race currently in existence—was *Azean.*

Now they were on Do Kul, jewel of the yerren frontier; in the morning the portrait would make its second appearance. And he would be beside it, presenting it, his name thus linked with that of the man who'd had it painted in the first place. *Harkur the Great.* They would travel through the Holding together, he and his treasure and the Museum's grand exhibit, *The Birth of Braxi.* But this was the closest they would ever come to the great nebula which masked his victory. The closest they would come to *her.*

Banishing that thought, he left the conference room for a connecting chamber.

—And stopped suddenly in the archway that joined the two rooms, stunned by what he saw.

The space beyond must have been meant as a bedroom, for a large rectangular slab of rainbow light hung suspended above the floor at such a height that it could serve as a mattress. In each corner of the room a cylinder rose from floor to ceiling, glowing with a faint white light that offered additional illumination. But neither these nor the ubiquitous flexicrystal wallfleece was what had stunned Zatar into immobility.

There was a person lying on the bedfield.

Loosening his Zhaor in its sheath, Zatar approached. It was

hard to tell, what with the glow of the forcefield mattress, but the body seemed to be bound in some sort of stasis field—which not only indicated that it was dead, but implied that it had been dead for quite some time. He leaned closer and swore, and his hand trembled where it touched the Zhaor, in a way it had never trembled before.

The body was Feran's.

He whipped around, his sword sliding free of its sheath even as he moved. Steel glinted in the dim, irregular lighting and he brought his own blade up, guarding his face from the coming thrust. Contact: a strong arm—an able enemy—and purpose like electricity flowing through his blade, through his hand, into his body.

He stepped back, managing to turn his attacker's blade aside as he did so. It whistled past his ear and swept into a graceful recovery

By her side.

She looked at him for a long, long time before speaking. She was thinner than he remembered her—or had his hunger for her added weight to her in his imagining, providing curves where there had been none, making her flesh reflect the sexual richness of her inner self? What did she see when she looked at him? An older man, with the weight of his unprecedented responsibility just starting to make itself evident. There was silver in his hair now, a few slender strands to adorn the black; did that surprise her? What changes had her own imagination wrought in the long, empty years of her absence?

She stepped back, eyes fixed upon him. "Any slower, Pri'tiera, and you'd have died."

He picked out the conflicting modes in her undertone and smiled. Who else could do his language such justice? "Any slower," he told her, equally scornful, "and I'd have deserved to die."

Against his better instincts, he sheathed his sword.

She had changed, true, but not in any way that mattered. Her hair was black and her eyes had been stained to match, but there was no mistaking that energy beneath. It was as if she had never left him—as if mere moments had passed since she had pulled free of his grasp, leaving his palm streaked with blood.

"You have the portrait?" she asked abruptly.

"Of course." With a nod that bade her follow him, he turned and led her to the conference room. His back was to her; it was a calculated risk. Feran had given him the formula for her defeat—after many days of argument, to be sure—and he knew that he could not afford to delay in applying it.

He brought her to the painting and stripped off its case. He had not dared to anticipate this moment. But her reaction was all he could have hoped for.

She stepped back as though she had been struck. "Hasha . . ." The color drained from her face for a moment, then was restored as her self-control was reestablished. He hungered to reach inside her as she had once done to him, to know the truth of her emotions and to share the violence of his.

"You believe it?" he challenged her.

"*You* do," she whispered. "That's enough."

She stared at it a while longer. "Hasha!" she repeated. "Braxin?" She must have known the truth for some time, but not until now had she believed it. She shook her head slowly, amazed. "Li Pazua would have given his life for this," she mused.

He smiled. "He did."

She fixed her eyes upon him, black with the essence of gray beneath—the gray of stone, the gray of steel. "I have seen men kill before, Zatar. Many times. But never to win my favor." She laughed softly, mirthlessly. "How Braxaná. And most effective—in ways I'm afraid poor Feran was not equipped to appreciate."

"You killed him," he said, in the speech mode of inquiry.

She darkened. "You did that. By sending him out there. By being what you are, and expecting him to come back to you. He chose death, Pri'tiera, rather than face you."

"Or you."

"Perhaps. But we made our peace, so I can't take full credit. He undid what he could of his early work within my mind, and gave me the key to deal with the rest; that freed him from the bulk of his guilt. You may therefore take credit for his suicide."

He undid what he could. . . . Was she free, then? Had the sexual traps been removed from her psyche, that a man might indulge in her pleasure without risk of death? A terrible jealousy possessed him, an unfamiliar emotion to his Braxaná soul. "And you? What next, for a Braxin warrior?"

"You've scattered my kind. Killed their teachers. My obvious course would be to help them."

He laughed. "Not likely."

"They're my people," she snapped.

He shook his head. "No. Your people are here."

"I mean the world of psychics."

"And *I* mean the Holding." He was pushing her, he knew, but he had to make the identity stick. "You're Braxin, and you know it. You've always known it. This find merely confirms the truth." Feran had given him key words to use and he did so. "What home will you make among Azeans? You're as alien to them as a non-human would be, and more threatening. Here, you're an enemy, but Braxi reveres its enemies. Here they'll *accept* you. Did Azea ever offer you that?"

It was a telling blow; he could see how shaken she was. "That isn't the point."

Quietly: "No?"

"I'm a telepath, Pri'tiera, that's all that matters. You and I may share a heritage, but those people are my *kind.* I understand them, I—" (she hesitated) "—share their pain."

He considered a long shot, decided to chance it. "What about your crew?"

The look she gave him was one of burning hatred, but the thoughts that accompanied it tasted strangely of guilt. "You killed my psychics when you killed that planet, Zatar. They couldn't absorb the death of five billion people and sustain their personal integrity."

"But you managed."

She would not voice it, but he heard the thought: *That's because I'm different.*

"Very true," he agreed. She seemed startled; was he picking up on thoughts she did not mean him to hear?

"They died in droves on Llornu," she said bitterly, "not only the ones you struck down yourself, but others who shared their pain. And for those that remain, death would be a kindness. They were innocents, most of them—more naive than you can imagine, when it came to things like war and politics. Content to live a dependent life, under li Pazua's wing. You killed their protector. You threatened them with death. You drove many of them into actual madness, and the rest have fled to far corners of the Empire, even beyond . . . they won't gather, and non-psychics won't take them in. They're afraid, Zatar. Of madness. Of killing. *My people*." she said, and her voice was filled with hate. "That's what you've done to them. They need my strength."

"But will they accept it?"

"Why shouldn't they?"

"You attacked them," he reminded her. "The assault on Llornu was your doing."

"They don't believe that!"

"Don't they? I think they will, given the 'evidence' I've left in the Empire."

She stiffened. "They won't believe it—not the ones who knew me."

"How many knew you?" he demanded. "How many were close to you? How many could taste the essence of your mind and not cringe before its violence? You're fully capable of doing what I did, and they know that. If it had served your purpose to destroy Llornu, you would have done so years ago, without a moment's hesitation. The true warrior isn't swayed by death, Anzha, his own or anyone else's."

"You know me well," she muttered, clearly shaken.

"You're Braxin. I know my people."

She shut her eyes, said nothing.

"Stay."

"I would kill you, first."

Now: to risk all in order to master her, using the key that Feran gave him—to play her against her conditioning. He drew his sword out, glanced at its blade, then cast it aside. Across the room, and out of reach.

"Then do so," he dared.

Her dark eyes narrowed, and the intensity of her loathing seared his foremind; he was relieved to feel it, for it meant his safety. "Would that I could!" she hissed. "But if you die, the Holding will fall—and it may just be that I can't be the cause of that."

"Why not?"

"Don't toy with me, Zatar! You know damned well—" She stopped herself. "Maybe you don't. Maybe Feran never explained. Maybe even he never understood what it was he was doing." There was scorn in her voice, but also pain. "I was programmed to search for the key to my heritage." She indicated the painting. "For this. But that's not all. No, not nearly enough humiliation to please li Pazua. There are subsidiary programs. Having found this race, I must now accept it as my own—exactly what you're trying to get me to do. That means accepting you as my ruler—an unlikely prospect, to say the least. One that I can resist. But to kill you, to defy my conditioning outright, that I can't do. The price is too high."

There was triumph in his foremind. "Then stay, and fulfill your programming."

"I have no place here!"

"Your bloodline is as precious to Braxi as my own. Even more so. You would be welcomed."

"Braxi would destroy me—or vice versa. As for you and me—"

She shut her eyes, and he thought he saw her tremble.

"I'm Azean, Zatar, enough to give that special meaning. Tau checked the codes, and they're all there. Any intimacy would bind me to you in ways you can't imagine, ways I can't accept. Already—"

She stopped herself, and he thought he saw the promise of tears. "There's an alternative," she said hesitantly. "I wasn't sure whether I would offer it, but it seems to suit both our purposes."

He was suspicious, and let her feel it. "What do you propose?"

"Are you willing to risk real contact with your people? I could give you insight into them, such as no man has ever had. I wonder if you'd dare to use it."

"I'm not afraid of your power."

"If so, it's because you don't understand it."

He thought of his sessions with Feran.

"That's nothing," she said to him. "Children's exercises, at best. So he showed you the Disciplines, shared some sensitivity. . . . Ask why he didn't come back, Zatar. Ask why he was afraid to face you again!"

"Tell me," he dared her.

"First understand, that Feran had a theory. He believed that environment, not genetics, supplied the trigger for telepathic awakening. That Llornu had a high rate of psychic development not because of its breeding programs, but because the children there were exposed to psychic activity every day of their lives, until during a time of physical and emotional trauma—such as puberty—their inherited shields broke down. The potential had to be there, of course, but potential is common. You of all people should know that," she added meaningfully.

He had the sudden sensation of being on the edge of a precipice, about to fall. "What do you mean?"

"After all that contact with Feran . . . didn't you notice a change? I can sense the difference in you, even without trying. Though if he hadn't warned me about it, I would have attributed it to my imagination."

He saw where she was leading, felt the bite of fear—and elation—in his soul. "There are no Braxin psychics," he said quietly.

"Because your people have always killed them. But only the ones they discovered. What happened those who learned to redirect their power, to channel it into what you call *image*, what we call *charisma*? Wouldn't they thrive? Wouldn't they reproduce? In your culture, which encourages a man to dominate others, wouldn't they rise to the top of the social hierarchy . . . just as you've done?"

He found he was afraid. It was not a feeling he relished, but he could not seem to master it. Worst of all, he knew that she was aware of everything that went on inside him, and was savoring his fear.

~ *I can give you immortality, Zatar—by guaranteeing the strength of your dynasty. By giving you such insight that you'll be able to negate Azea's psychic advantage. I can even give you the key to discovering whatever power remains among your own people—while showing you such pain that you'll regret this meeting for the rest of your life. I can make you a ruler, Zatar, such as no ruler has ever been!—and I can and will cause you such suffering that at last my hunger for vengeance will be satisfied.*

How her black eyes gleamed, how the emotion poured forth from her! Hatred upon his mind like a welcome caress, the touch of a familiar lover.

"Feran showed me how," she told him. "I'm not a Probe, so I can't do it cleanly; any contact we have will be tainted by my experience. But he set the patterns in my mind, and showed me how to work them. To give you power, Pri'tiera Zatar. To restore the balance between Empire and Holding once more. To fulfill my conditioning—which will give me my freedom." She whispered his Name then, a sound rich with pain and longing. "The choice is yours," she whispered.

He came to her across the silver carpet, in front of the ancient painting that declared their kinship. "It was made long ago."

She offered her hand to him; he took instead her arms, and her body, and held her as a lover might, with hatred and lust combined. "My enemy," he murmured, as the sharp, bittersweet essence of her enveloped him. "Do your worst."

Were there tears in her eyes? Perhaps in her mind . . . or in his.
"I will," she whispered.
Memory:

* * *

Glorying in freedom, and in thoughts of conquest; free in the Void, with a handful of chosen companions and a dream, *the* dream, for sustenance.

Taste the planet, stroke its surface: Ceylu, it is called, and its crust teems with five billion human lives, all devoted to your cause. Watch them, guide them, relish their existence, for they are the tools of your vengeance, and therefore more precious than any treasure.

Was *ever*, a planet so beautiful? True, the crowded streets are thick with smog, and the oceans choked with the refuse of these careless, stupid people. But clear skies and fertile earth have never appealed to you; this is true beauty, the colors of progress. Does the very air stink from man's abuse? It will soon be scented with triumph, which is the sweetest odor of all. Does the night sky glow with unwholesome light, when airborne debris reflects the illumination of cities? In two hundred years it will be the ultimate battlefield, washed clean by the blood of the enemy. Have patience and wait, for vengeance is yours; you have planted the seeds of death on Ceylu, and Braxi will reap your harvest.

Now, the Void: search it, caress it, reach out with your senses and revel in it, for it is your lover, your ally, the giver of time and the guardian of your secrecy. The Veil of the Dancer will be Braxi's undoing, for the Dancer is Death, and her music is of your making. Touch the darkness with your special senses and revel in its emptiness—

—which has been violated, you realize suddenly; while you were lost in an ecstacy of anticipation, the enemy has breached your fortress. Very well, it has been done before; there were scouts once, five of them, and you ran them down and dealt with them as they deserved, before they even left the system. So it shall be with these. Ascertain their numbers, then, and determine their strength—

Suddenly you fear, and your body is trembling. Can there really be that many? Would Braxi abandon its ongoing wars for this single effort, embracing peace on the home front to send its warriors

Veilward? You count the warships, and they are more than you have ever seen gathered in one place; you taste the minds of the men who run them, and are aware of a ruthlessness which exceeds anything you have known in the enemy. Can you hope to fight them, these hundred warships, with but a single Starbird and a handful of psychics?

You must withdraw and you do, into the shadow of a sheltering planet. Here you will not be noticed, with your Starbird lying low in the harsh methane winds. Here you cannot be hurt, but you are also helpless—and you must wait here, impotent, while they sow your fields with salt. There is no other way.

A hundred warships stabilize at subluminal velocity; two thousand fighters spew forth from their wardocks, coming into position about the doomed planet. Ten millennia ago the Lugastine scientists sought an understanding of Life, and though they could not determine a means of initiating it, their experiments did prove fruitful in one regard: they developed a process which drained and destroyed life, which they called the negation field, which Braxins labeled Zherat. Turned into a weapon, it is something only the Braxins will use—too terrible a tool for other nations to contemplate, but perfect for the needs of the Holding. And it is this which they plan to use now—die one tool which will strip this upstart plane of its life, wiping the slate clean for some more humble attempt at evolution.

Slowly the fighters take their positions. Computers have determined their placement, with the intentions of raising a balanced field. At all points surrounding the planet, the intensity of the Zherat must be the same. Only then will the dreaded negation field do its work.

As for Ceylu, it knows nothing. It does not see the enemy, for it lacks the equipment to do so. It does not watch in horror as two thousand fighters take their positions about the planet, nor cry out in fear when the lines of field support are first extended between the ships. Not until the sky is streaked with a network of burning blue lines does the planet fear—and then it is too late. The work has begun; the Zherat is established. There is only the waiting, now, and Ceylu will be a threat no longer.

Horrified, Anzha touches the thoughtwinds of Ceylu—and is captured by the planetmind, and forced to, share its dying. Five billion people; they do not die slowly, nor easily. The thoughtwinds are filled with desperate plans, with the slowly dying vestiges of hope, with the screaming last thoughts of those who would do battle with Death himself, if he would but make himself visible. Children are dying, and mothers weep; fathers are drained of their caring, and infants starve to death. The Zherat is merciless, and agonizingly slow. Six days are needed to suffocate Ceylu, so that no life remains on its surface. Six days during which people die, and fear—and six days during which Anzha shares their dying.

And they blame her. The hatred rises in torrents, blasting waves of accusation that send her mind reeling, seeking shelter from the onslaught—but there is none to be had, for the dying are everywhere. They have invaded her ship, her body, her soul; their fury is inescapable. For nearly six days they hold her prisoner, tormenting her with their suffering; when they are gone at last the silence is so deep, so absolute, that it is hard for her to regain her bearings, to return to the world of the living.

She struggles to regain consciousness. Her skin is parched, her mouth dry, her body nearly dead from lack of water. She manages to drag herself hand over hand to the outlet, and weakly prods it into activity. Water splashes over her face and hands, and she manages to swallow some; it hurts to drink, but already she can feel life returning to her. Now, to find her crew—

She does so, too late to help them. For a while she stands there, stunned, and tears would surely come to her eyes if her body had fluid to spare. As it is she leans against the cabin wall, shaking, despair near to overwhelming her at last.

Siara ti is dead; there are signs of dehydration about him, and perhaps that was what killed him. For Zefire li, death was less merciful. Caught up in a storm of accusation, he became no more than a tool of Ceylu's hate, turned against himself. Anzha looks at his bloody form, at the empty sockets where he gouged out his own eyes, and shivers. He destroyed himself, as they all might have done if they had been weaker. The death-throes of Ceylu were that powerful; even now they resonate within her.

Searching the Starbird, she finds her other two psychics. Both dead. It seems that one killed the other, then turned on herself as Zefire li had done—responding, no doubt, to the incessant hatred of Ceylu. And Tau? he had been on the planet's surface, she realized suddenly, sharing his medical skills with Ceyluans, hoping to win their trust. Did they rend him in their hatred, or did he live to feed his soul to the Zherat? The loss of his loyalty hurts worst than all the rest combined.

I have killed you, she thinks—and the thought is painfully familiar.

Ceylu: she must see it, must come to terms with what happened there. That entails great risk: she is hurt too badly to chance any psychic activity, must brave the Void without searching for enemies first. Perhaps it is her death-wish that drives her forward, into space which Braxi so recently occupied. But the system is empty. She alone is alive to see the devastation that remains, and as her Starbird spirals down to the planet's surface, she wonders if this loneliness is really any greater than that which she has always lived with.

Ceylu is dead. Even more: it is death incarnate, a monument to the concept of mortality. Everywhere the bodies of the dead lie unburied, human and animal alike. Corpses are strewn upon lifeless grass, under lifeless trees, felled by the Zherat wherever they stood when the last of their vital strength left them. There, is no rot, no decay; even the microbes are dead.

And Tau . . . his body is irrecoverable, lost somewhere among these five billion corpses. For some strange reason, that seems the cruelest blow of all.

She kneels on the gritty pavement, overcome by her sorrow. The deaths of five billion people could not truly move her; the death of one man who risked his life out of loyalty to her, and lost it, is suddenly overwhelming.

I failed you, she thinks. *I let you die.*

She lowers her head and weeps, and for a long, long time there is nothing but sorrow in her universe.

~ *Anzha. . . .*

With a start, she looks up. The mind that speaks to her is familiar, but she is too wounded to identify it. Who else would be out here?

She turns, and she sees him.

Feran.

Suddenly, all the hate that she has been directing at herself has an outward focus; she lashes out at him with all the force her mind can muster, and only when the pain of it leaves her gasping for breath does she accept the truth. Ceylu cost her too much strength; she lacks the power to kill him.

How did you get here? What do you want? . . . Have you come to gloat, Braxin?

He comes to her side and reaches out to her. She pulls away

from him, and in the violence of her action, falls. The ground is hard, and the impact sends her senses reeling; she can do no more than lie there, stunned, as the first tendrils of his thought begin to whisper their secrets into her brain.

~ *See, this is your heritage . . . not a thing to be ashamed of, but a bloodline rich with history. Witness the truth of it, observe how it will shape your future. As for Ceylu it is dead, there is no saving it, you must leave it behind. Let it go, Anzha.*

I am not Braxin, I am not Braxin, I am not Braxin!

He inserts probing thoughts deep into her mind; they feel like fragments of molten steel and she struggles to force them out, to strike at this man who dares to take advantage of her weakness.

~ *Relax, Anzha. I'm not here to hurt you—Ar knows I could never do that again, not even if he required it. But there is a way. Gently, my Starcommander; let me touch you one last time, and I promise you there will be an end to it.*

She does not want him inside her brain, but she is too weak to stop him; tears of frustration squeeze forth from her eyes as he touches his hand to her forehead, steeling himself for contact.

~ *The key is identity; master that, and you will control the rest. You can be free, Anzha. I will undo what I can of your conditioning, and then what remains can be dealt with. I have found a way.*

"Conditioning can't be undone," she gasps.

There is sadness in his mind. ~ *Institute propaganda. I can negate my original work; it will require the last of my strength, but it can be done. As for the rest, you must deal with that yourself. A lifetime of habit has reinforced the patterns I set into your mind. You must deal with that directly—satisfy the conditions of your programming, in other words, and then you will be free of it.*

"Submit to Braxi? Bear a child of that race for li Pazua to study? I refuse!"

He is not surprised to hear that she knows the exact nature of her conditioning; nothing she does can surprise him any more.

~ *Li Pazua is dead, Zatar killed him in your name. The Institute is gone and the psychics are scattered. Any part of your conditioning that depended upon him is now invalidated. You need fear no sudden surge of maternal instinct,* he assures her. ~ *As long as there is no Institute, that part of the conditioning will remain inoperative. As for the rest. . . .*

He hesitates, and she senses how much this will cost him.

"I have a plan," he tells her. "Listen."

Whispers of thought in her mind, affecting the secret paths of being; she can feel the work being done and she fears it, but there is nothing she can do to either help or hinder him. For a while she is a child again, and the emptiness of her youth comes back to her. Then his voice comes to her, softly, pouring truths into her mind. *His* truths.

~ *We are not the lords of creation, though we've convinced ourselves that we are. Sensitivity is a weakness, not a strength, and I'm convinced that nature abhors it. Think of the predator, stalking his prey. What good does it do him to be psychic, if the intensity of his hunger acts as a warning to his chosen victim? How does an animal manage to hide, when its very fear is a beacon leading to its presence? Only the emergence of an advanced intellect allows us to encourage such a weakness, and even so, we need all the tools we can muster to turn it from a handicap to an asset. The Disciplines. The carefully controlled community. Control, Anzha, that's the key, a control that the primitive mind lacks. For which reason primitive society fears the psychic, as much as it worships him. It proclaims him a seer, it clothes him in honor—but it binds him in rituals which set him apart, and more often than not sees to it that he dies without issue.*

The Braxaná are to be congratulated, for they are the only people honest enough to kill their psychics outright. They fear telepathy, with all the strength of primitive instinct, and will not endure the telepath in their midst. And that is the weakness which you will exploit, in order to regain your freedom. Listen: I will tell you what to do. . . .

* * *

Come to me, my enemy, my hated one—come to me and share the richness of my talent, which you have hungered after as avidly as you have ever hungered after woman. Let me open your mind to the touch of the cosmos, the song of thoughts and purposes that makes the Void vibrate with life. Come deep into me where the power lies, in that center of being where the thoughts of others are mastered. Come taste the power, Zatar, which other men dream of, and fear; come make it yours, if you dare, and it shall be yours in truth.

See: the life that is Braxi writhes, its consciousness like a body that is bound, struggling to be free. Shards of agony cut through its awareness at irregular intervals, causing the planetmind to quiver. Here is the sharp spear that is a woman's despair; there the honed edge of a man's tormented impotence. Touch the planet and it pierces you, spear after spear of tortured thought arising from the muddled surface, bits of pain, and stillborn dreams and a hope that is only birthed so that it may die. This is the homeworld, the Mistress Planet, the land that the traitor-god chose; this is Braxi, the planet that the Braxaná claimed, the throneworld of Zatar.

What can you do for it, my hated one? What can you do in a single lifetime that can alter the pattern of eons? Taste the thoughts of Braxi's women, rich with despair, dark with envy. Taste the pettiness of her men, the terrible isolation in which her people live. Build your dynasty if you will . . . but know that the foundation is rotten. The thoughtwinds of Braxi stink of desolation, and it would take more than one man to correct it. This is reality, Zatar, compared to which your throne is little more than illusion. Is it what you want? Does it satisfy you?

You were my catalyst, in the maelstrom of my youth. You with your velvet eyes, beautiful beyond imagining, pure in your warrior-essence. You drew me out of myself and left me open, like a wound scraped raw, ready for the trauma which would unleash my power. Now I will make the cycle complete, and apply my substance to your fledgling skill.

By your will, Pri'tiera, The choice was your own. Remember that.

The flavor of desire. The touch of consummation.

Fire. He falls into burning, clasped to the heart of her. All about him rages the storm of her being, emotions he tasted once, decades ago, and he drinks in their substance with relish. They are not different, but stronger. Refined by the k'airth, her hatred is a thing of beauty; he touches it with his own killing passion, and lets their thoughts mingle as he sinks deeper and deeper into the fire of her soul. There is pain, but a welcome pain; he knows it is the price of their union, therefore embraces it as a necessity. And thus he is laid bare, his latent skill stripped of all inhibition, until the richness and anarchy of cosmic thought invade the deepest recesses of his Braxaná soul, and exact their terrible price.

He clings to her, his only anchor in a universe gone mad. This is sensitivity as she once knew it, when the trauma of her father's death opened her mind to every passing thought; he gave her this terror, and now she is returning the favor. This is the torment that the awakening telepath knows, a chaos so terrible that the mind would rather repress its inborn talent than experience it even for an instant. It is the birth of the True Mind, the telepath's soul; it is his universe, and he fights to master it.

Order imposed upon anarchy: he focuses on his sense of self, separates it from the primal chaos which surrounds him, and builds walls which will keep the two distinct. *How like the gods,* he muses. The sea is quieting, the fire dying. The thoughts of the universe are a song, no more, a quiet ebb and flow of being that caresses his mind with wonder. This is what it means to be psychic; this is what it means to live.

Why have we denied this thing? Why have we feared it?

A whisper of thought, carried to him on a gentle breeze of the Voidmind:

You will see, she promises him.

Darkness parting, and the shimmer of a silver ocean. He raised his head, heard the wallfleece tinkle in response to his motion. It took him a moment to remember where he was. He looked for her, but she had left. He scanned the nearby region for her mental signature, received no response. Some time had passed, then, since the healing darkness had claimed him.

"Lord Zatar?"

He tried to sit upright, lacked the strength. Footsteps came from the suite's entrance, echoed in the tinkling of the rug. A woman's voice: L'resh? What was she doing here?

"My Lord?"

She came through the doorway and saw him, and in a moment was by his side. "What happened?" she asked breathlessly. "Are you all right?"

Her concern for him was too intense; he applied one of the many Disciplines that Feran had taught him, managed to lessen the sensation.

Think of the power! To have this special talent in *his* universe, which was not prepared to combat it. To be able to pick out the motives that prompted speech, to taste the plans of his enemies before they came to fruition. She had given him the ultimate tool and he, as a ruler, intended to use it. And if she thought that this would bring him suffering . . . well, she didn't know him as well as he'd thought.

He tried to rise again, managed to raise himself up on one elbow. L'resh reached to help him, placing a gloved hand beneath his shoulder—

—and fire burned him through the contact, noxious emotions in painful profusion.

He pulled away from her, startled.

"What is it?" There was fear in her voice, in her foremind. "What happened?"

I don't know. "Nothing. I'll be all right."

Will I?

He struggled to his feet. Something fell from his chest to the floor as he did so, but it took all his concentration just to stand, so he let it be for the moment.

Then he swayed, and she moved to help him, and she was pressed against his side

—and there was a female essence in her, but not like Anzha's: not something to savor, but an unwholesome, unclean sensation, tainted with dark and terrible emotions that threatened to contaminate him. Weakness, there was terrible weakness; her mind could not focus properly on 'self,' was more concerned with his welfare than her own. Madness! And what was this ugliness, this clinging darkness that had moved her to risk her own life time and time again, bearing him children? Not a hunger for pleasure, no, but something darker, something that reeked of bondage and destruction. Was this what the enemy called 'love'? He shuddered to discover it in one of his own kind—and he began to be truly afraid.

"My Lord, what—"

"How did you get here?" he interrupted. He pulled away from her. Better to keep her talking, to give him time to sort out his thoughts.

"You asked me to come. You sent for me—here, see?" She pulled a keyplate from her sash, set it on the table. Black on the mirrored surface: a cancer, like her emotions. "You invited me to join you, don't you remember? What's wrong, Zatar? I want to help."

What's wrong? I'm beginning to guess.

He held out his hand to her, bracing himself for the contact. Distinction Discipline, Integration Discipline, Touch Discipline:

he ran the patterns through his mind as she reached out for him, and clung to them as she grasped his hand.

—And the world exploded in a burst of emotion too alien to contemplate. He drew back from her. His hand was trembling, and his mind . . . that was in turmoil, consumed now by fear as the full extent of the Starcommander's vengeance became clear to him.

(. . . *any contact we have will be tainted by my experience* . . .)

Anzha!

"I'll be all right." A lie. He knew his fate for what it was, recognized the terrible isolation that awaited him. "Just give me a minute." He had surrounded himself with women who would bond themselves to him; there was not one he could touch now, if touching them meant psychic contact. They were like a different race, even a different species, filled with disturbing emotions that had no counterpart in his own identity. And he could not afford to give those emotions a chance to take root in his psyche.

He had taken it for granted that what he'd experienced with the Starcommander was typical of telepathic rapport; now he acknowledged, for the very first time, how wrong he had been. Now he knew that she was unique, and that he might search a lifetime for another soul so well suited to his own. If there was another—which he doubted.

Until then, he was alone. More alone than any man had ever been; more alone than any woman—save one—could have endured.

"I need air," he whispered. Outside, in the open spaces surrounding the palace, he could perhaps come to terms with this; in the confines of this room, any room, the tangle of emotions seemed too overwhelming.

What would it do to Braxi, to have an involuntary psychic for a ruler? What would it mean to that nation of hedonists that their figurehead denied himself sexual contact? And what would happen to his House, whose very structure was founded upon sexual intimacy?

Ni'en . . . he thought, but she was lost to him. They all were lost to him.

Your choice, Pri'tiera.

"Zatar?"

He forced himself back to the present. L'resh was radiating fear and compassion, and the mirror of her emotions showed him just how strangely he'd been acting.

He calmed himself. Feigned composure. Glanced down at the floor where a small, black item lay, and picked it up. His hand, he was pleased to note, was steady.

"What is it?" L'resh asked him.

He turned the crusted object over in his hand. It was a glove, torn across the palm and stiffened with blood: his blood, long since dried. He nodded, understanding.

"It's nothing," he said at last. He dropped it. "Nothing that matters."

You have destroyed me, my enemy.

"Come," he said softly. As he walked across the floor his foot fell upon the glove, crushing it.

He was careful not to touch her as they left the palace.

Viton: And then—say the Braxaná—Taz'hein turned on his Creator, and war came into being. The gods turned their men into warriors, pawn against pawn, brother against brother, and blood was spilled on the surface of the planet. Thus was man baptized by the treachery of the gods, to know the rich variety of conflict . And when Taz'hein was supreme in the Void he saw what men had become, and he withheld the hand of destruction which he had meant for them. "This is good," he said, "and since you have truly learned to live, I will not take that life from you. But if you must seek guidance, look to the Void—for it is as likely as I to answer, or to care."

EPILOGUE

(The following document was destroyed in Dyle's landing, Year 1.)

I shall describe it all chronologically, Beyl-my-brother, and perhaps the information may be of use to our people some day. As for the rest, that is for your eyes alone. You will see.

There is no need to describe to you the scene when civil authorities pulled me from church in the middle of services. I have always found it of some significance that at the time we were reciting the Litany of Blessed Abstinence, which I suppose I accepted as much as anyone. We were not the first people to venerate sexual abstinence, although I do think we were the first to be encouraged to venerate it by another people. But these are things I recognize now, after Harkur; then I accepted it without question, as most of us did. What more bloodless genocide?

You were there, when they pulled me forcibly from my prayers and dragged me from the sanctuary. You all feared for me, but who dared act? Were we not all slaves in fact, though some of us were not so yet in name? Frenell life is cheap to the Mristi. Once in utmost secrecy, when I was a child, a playmate whispered to me that there had been only one race on Zeymour to start with. I didn't believe it then. Just look at the differences—their pale skin and sharp features, the dusky brown of our coloring and our distinctly curvilinear faces—and all the cultural disparities, as well. But I believe it now. I have seen the beginning of a class system based on race, and I can now conceive of a planet where one race—or sub-race—gains such power that it becomes distinct from all other subraces on the planet. But never have I seen, among the stars and the men that rule there, such a deliberate attempt to eradicate one particular racial type.

I was terrified at the time. I was not a rebel, as you were. I was, I see now, well conditioned. You know I had nearly turned you in when you harbored pregnant Elise in our home, that she might bear her child to term. I had nightmares for months, fully believing that for indulging in the grosser instincts Elise was damned, and that for keeping her from punishment I would be, too. No, I never questioned that the Mristi could enjoy such things while we were damned for it. They were different.

How many generations, I wonder, did it take them to perfect this training, geared toward our annihilation? What had we ever done to deserve such hostility—how long ago in history had we been merely a lesser caste, with a church under our control, a doctrine that allowed for the continuance of the species? No matter. They threw me in a shieldcar and drove me to the Discipline Center, nearly hitting two hotspots on the way. My terror was not lessened by the fact that there was a quakeling as I was pulled from the 'car. You can tell me all you like that there are an average of three quakelings a day in the City; it was a sign from God or I had never seen one.

I wondered if they knew of the conspiracy. Not from me, certainly, who only knew because I was your sister and you were involved. . . . I have never seen men frightened as they were when the quakeling struck. It was almost as if they knew to the number how many there would be before the destruction of Zeymour came at last, and were counting down.

I was taken to the office of the President of Disciplinary Action, Frenell Division. I was terrified; they had to half-carry me most of the way, my legs were so weak with fright. How many of our people had entered these halls, never to emerge again? There was a distant rumbling and my captors set themselves for another quakeling, but there was none.

The President was a large man, overweight and foul-smelling. The Mristi say that is because he deals so closely with the Frenell, while we have it that it is because he is a Mristi agent. But he was both Mristi officer and High Priest, and I trembled as I prostrated myself before him.

"What have we here?" he said. His voice was foul, everything about him was foul. If he was indeed God's agent then I was sorry for the unkindness of the observation—but it came to me nonetheless, and stuck.

"Frenell crap," one of my captors said. The room was heavily guarded. "We have her name in connection with the child-43 conspiracy."

That was Elise's child, I realized with a sinking heart. But why had they taken me, and not you?

The President raised an eyebrow. "Yes? Well, that's over with, so there's no point in interrogation." Foul, foul, foul. He oozed it.

"What then for punishment, sir?"

The President went to a file and drew out a clipboard. It was of beaten gold and the clip was set with huge emeralds. He put the end of the garnet-tipped pen in his mouth and hemmed and hawed. "Awright," he muttered past the pen, without removing it. "We need a Frenell piece for this expedition. That'll settle the damnation, which'll make a good example. Publicize it."

My captor smiled his pleasure at the thought.

"Here are the papers." The President handed him a folder. "Have her disinfected and indoctrinated at the Space Center. I'm sure our astronauts will take care of the rest."

"Sterilized, sir?"

He laughed. It was an ugly sound.

"Naw. She wouldn't dare get pregnant."

They snickered as they pulled me from the room. I felt faint, not quite understanding the specifics of my fate but having a good grasp on the general idea. I was to serve my slaveterm on the *Explorer,* that experimental stellar ship about to be launched from Aringvil Hotspot. How ironic, I thought, that with you obsessed with the intra-stellar ships, I should be on the first inter-stellar ever launched. But it was with sinking heart that I knew it. For my fate was to endure rape by the astronauts waiting in the unknown dark of uncharted space, and through that to be damned beyond redemption forever.

I chanted the Litany of Abstention all night in my cell; it only depressed me more.

In the morning I was taken to the Space Center in Aringvil where I met the four astronauts. They stripped me and I had to stand motionless while the Mristini men subjected me to inspection. The shame of being naked was unbearable; the other shame, that of being touched, was something so alien that I could not even deal with it emotionally. God, forgive me, I had no way of stopping it. . . .

They approved of me and I was enrolled in a haphazard program designed to prepare me to survive the long months—years?—ahead. Often as I underwent tests and exercised I was aware of one of the four leering at me through the one-way visipanes which surrounded my quarters. I couldn't sleep. Whenever I dozed, hell rose up to meet me, reminding me in tones of demonic laughter that soon, very soon I would be committed to the radioactive flames for the rest of eternity. By the end of a half-month I was a wreck, physically and emotionally.

They strapped me into a small section right by the cargo and off we went. No one had prepared me for the pain, the gut-wrenching agony of the special drive that would theoretically allow us to get from star to star in less than a generation. I heard one of the men crying out, but he had friends to comfort him. I had no escape and no comfort. I never even saw the astronauts until the third day, when we had completed the first acceleration-series and one of them freed himself from his mechanical life-support system to use the facilities—me. I fought him, but it was hard. They had companionship and pain-killers, and I had only fear; I was not fully recovered yet from the trip out. Still I fought, fought not only him but the damnation of my soul. I lost. I would have died then if mere self-neglect could have killed me, but they left me strapped in with the wires and hoses and the coldly efficient machines that kept me alive, despite my prayers. If hell there was, then hell I saw. My dreams were full of it and my waking hours also, for the men not only used me, but reveled in my pain and shame in other ways as well, having little other source of amusement in the small and sterile starship.

But enough of this, my brother. You see the point.

We had spent more than a month like this, and five times we endured that pain which permitted us to conquer the reaches of space that once man only dreamed of. It was a long journey and a wearing one, and they were lost in drunken oblivion when it happened. Evidently the navigational instruments had gone out of alignment sometime during our journey, and pinned senseless under their drunken stupor they failed to notice the error until it was too late. We came back into normal, painless space, and for a few minutes I heard their cries of fear and I knew, as they did, of their helplessness. I struggled to be free, but my bonds were too strong; to that I owe my life. We had come back into instrumented space too close to a planet to ignore its gravitic demands, and as we cut through the atmosphere they tried desperately to kill the momentum, to save themselves. They failed. And I . . . I only survived because the section that I was in, filled with instruments of more worth to the Mristi than the men of their own race, broke free of the doomed ship and managed a violent but infinitely more successful landing.

We crashed. Whether on land or in water I do not know. There was a jarring pain and the sound of tearing metal, and fire filled the air and scorched my lungs from the inside out. At last death came to embrace me and I welcomed the darkness that closed my smoke-injured eyes. Lastly there was the sensation of being lifted, but I knew that for death-spawned delusion and gladly accepted the black nonexistence that had finally come to free me.

I awoke in a panic, struggling to free myself from my bondage. Kind hands held me down, and voices called in a strange and musical language very close to me. I opened my eyes and saw with bleary sight men and women who were like us, but not so. At first I thought I was home, for where else would one find human life? And then, as I watched them, as I noted the differences, I knew the truth.

They nursed me to health, Beyl-my-brother, kindly and

carefully. Although I saw more and more how alien they were in sound, form, and action, I never ceased to wonder at their perfectly human form.

They wore slick synthetic clothing which hid little of them, and the women dyed their hair bright blues and greens and purples, to match their garments. The hospital I was in was decorated in the same colors, and the men who tended to me wore heavy jewelry in complimentary hues. They tried to teach me their language, and I tried to learn it. I got the basic vocabulary down in a few weeks—they kept me in the hospital even after I had healed, studying me—but the concepts of their tongue were completely beyond me, filled with Starsymbolism that I couldn't begin to grasp. After much discussion among themselves they decided to try another language, one more suited to Zeymourian thought-patterns and my native phonetics. This one was called Braxin and I found it much easier, although objectively it was far more complicated.

The planet we had struck was called Lugast, and its inhabitants were good to me. They were an ancient people who had long been among the stars, for they were at the edge of a cluster so crowded that even their earliest spaceships were able to explore the stellar neighborhood and come home in less than a generation. Lugast was the capital planet of a multistellar Union of Planets. I learned a small bit of their culture and liked what I learned. They meant to unite the human-dominant galaxy, and from there reach out to more alien forms and establish cultural interchange.

Now—I will try to explain this, but I don't really under stand all of it, Beyl-my-brother, so you must bear with me if I'm unclear on some point. They told me that life is the rule rather than the exception, and that most solar systems with suitable planetary environments give birth to some kind of life-form. They explained a theory called parallel evolution, which says that similar environments tend to give rise to similar patterns of evolution, and ultimately similar life-forms. Does that explain our own likeness? I asked, still skeptical of the perfection of the imitation. No, they said, humans are different. They—and five other lifeforms—have been found in numerous systems where they clearly did not evolve, and even more mysteriously have been found dead on planets where man had failed to survive, a small buried indication that someone meant to test the possibility of their adapting to that place. The first explorers discovering this gave credit to the gods (the Lugastines recognize more than one) but current thought tends to accept that some ancient starfaring nation was experimenting with the adaptability and endurance of certain species. There is even a school of thought, I am told, to the effect that the great Experimenters were themselves human, and that they scattered their own aboriginal remnants among the stars to see how much of human nature was biologically determined, and how much would change in response to alien environmental stimuli. They call this the Seeding, and the resulting human types the Scattered Races, and support their theories with scientific deduction. (On many of these planets, for instance, there is no evolutionary branch that could possibly have given birth to the human form; even where there is a similar type evolving, the true human form often appears so suddenly that part of the story is missing, a link between similar but distinct forms that is never discovered; certain myths are common to mankind from the most primitive tribes—those whose environments kept them limited to a slow rate of progress and the most advanced interstellar nations: those of the Great Flood, for instance, and legends of shapechangers who take human form to drain true humans of strength.) The list of wondrous things goes on and on, Beyl-my-brother, but if I attempt to write it all I will never reach the end, and I don't know how much time I have left. So forgive me, please, if I hurry on from here—there is so much more to tell!

They were a peaceful people, the Lugastines, utterly devoted to the reunification of humankind and successful interaction with the non-humans who also filled the galaxy with life. They had few enemies, and only one of consequence. That was the planet Braxi, the source of the language they chose for me, a recent interstellar upstart who had entered the galactic community suddenly and with vehemently martial intent. Although Braxi was almost as primitive as Zeymour in terms of interstellar competence, it was far enough away from Lugastine space that it had managed to repulse Lugast's advances, military and diplomatic, and was carving out a block of unclaimed space for its own military domination.

When I was well, and when my surroundings were a little more familiar and I had learned to communicate, they showed me starmaps. It took me a long time to find our sun in those three-dimensional displays, for I had to search through section after section of two-dimensional renderings at all angles until constellations which were familiar began to appear. At last I found Zeymour—and oh, the pain of it, for when I realized the truth I dared not reveal it to my hosts! We were pitifully close to Lugast, and had that people not been guided by the clustering of stars in another direction we would long ago have been discovered and absorbed by them.

Wonderful, you say? Welcome them? We are slaves, my brother, and must remember that rulers side with rulers, and that the coming of the Lugastines to Zeymour, for all their good intentions, would have given such strength to the Mristi that we could never have dreamed of breaking free of them. And so I said nothing. I scanned the renderings day after day and said no, I saw no stars that were familiar, the heavens were an unknown code. At last they resigned themselves to that, and let me be.

I was content, now seeing before me some hope of living at peace in this fascinating civilization. But before my dreams could hint at becoming reality my circumstances were torn from me and Lugast was lost forever. It happened swiftly; I was walking on the hospital grounds at the time and nothing would have caused me to suspect that here, of all places, there could be danger. There was a moment, then, when I was grabbed, and I was dragged backward under cover of bushes, and a strongly-scented cloth was pressed against my face. I did not have time to struggle, so stunned was I by the action. The face above mine was terrifying, skin without color, features sharp and merciless, eyes and hair as black as shadow. That was my last observation, and then I fell into darkness.

I awoke bound, in the small confines of some vessel

which I quickly identified as a starship. Screens all about me displayed the alien heavens. There were three men sitting not far from me: my captor, cleanshaven and hard of countenance, and two men of softer coloring, one bearded, who seemed to be operating the ship. One of them saw me as I moved and nudged his black-haired companion.

"The prize awakens, Sokuz."

"And the Lugastine patrol?" he demanded.

"We've lost it," the other assured him.

My kidnapper came over to where I lay and with certain hands released me from my bonds. "Stay calm, and all will be well. Do you speak Braxin?"

I nodded, still struck dumb from astonishment and fear.

"So they said. Don't bother struggling, we're out of Lugastine space and it will get you nowhere. Just relax and enjoy the ride, and everything will be fine."

Again I nodded. I was trembling. These were Braxins—a people entirely without morals, loving warfare for its own sake, opposed to the very existence of the human society I had come to respect and—yes—love. But my terror could not keep me from eating when he offered me a bowl of food, for I was starving, and afterward, tired and weak, I drifted off to a more natural sleep.

They answered no questions, but otherwise they were passably kind to me. We talked much; the endless silence of space was as boring for them as it was becoming for me. They were very sexually oriented, which I knew from studying their language, and they asked me many questions regarding the customs of my home planet, which I answered as well as I could. Unlike the Lugastines they either assumed that I could not spot my planet for them or didn't care to have me try. I was given no starmaps.

Their leader had ordered my kidnapping. He had heard news of me and had decided that he would see me with his own eyes, and simply ordered me taken, right out from under Lugastine surveillance. His planet consisted of twenty-three nations divided roughly by tribal background, and a wide expanse of frosty steppes as yet unclaimed by civilization. The two astrogators, the gentler men of the group, were from tribes known as the Hirinari and the

Dambarre, and their nations had sworn loyalty to a man called Harkur the Great, who had come to unify the greatly diverse planet under one throne. Sokuz, the black-haired man with the eyes of death, was a Braxaná. A few of his tribe served the charismatic leader, but for the most part they were nomads on the Blood Steppes, a land mass they had successfully held secure against the encroachment of civilization for all of recent history. They were brutal, aggressive, and ruthless, and for this reason Harkur valued their service for errands such as this. Only a Braxaná, Sokuz assured me, could have stolen me out from right under the noses of my guards across half a hostile Union. I listened, and I watched, and I saw no cause to doubt him.

But of their ruler they would tell me nothing. I would meet him myself, then I would know. Sokuz even laughed when I asked, which did little to allay my fears.

And I feared. No less so when I awoke to hear a bit of conversation they had imagined secure from my notice.

". . . ripe for his amusement, don't you think?"

"I think the Kaim'era will be more than pleased with her."

Ripe for his amusement . . . was that my fate, then? To be rescued from one enslavement only to be granted another? I trembled, but I said nothing. They would tell me nothing, and I would rather keep my fears to myself. Time would show me the truth.

How can I describe to you, Beyl-my-Brother, the wonder of that palace set among the stars? We did not go to Braxi directly but to Berros, a small planet rescued from a barren fate by Harkur's determination to settle there. A ruler of the stars, he felt, should have for his home an entire globe, and though they planned to adapt their own moon for his usage that was a project that would take years. Until then, the tiny Berros would have to do.

The palace and the planet were one and I have no words which are sufficient to describe either. From all over the galaxy, from every corner of Braxi-controlled space, riches had been brought for the glory of Harkur, the warrior and statesman who had united a war-divided people and given them the stars. But these were not the garish riches of the Mristi, which hurt the eye and pleased only the sense of greed in a man; these were tasteful treasures whose colors delighted the eye and whose softness cushioned the step, and pleased the touch. Incense burned heavy and aromatic in room after room of the Kaim'era's domain and thick carpets of wool and skins of exotic animals quieted the step to silence. The wealth of the galaxy was in art and Harkur had gathered it together, making the planet a cathedral to the glory of human accomplishment.

I was presented, at last, to the man whose name struck such chord of fear in me. At the far end of a ceremonial chamber he waited, arrayed not like a statesman but like a warrior, before and not seated upon his throne, and by his side stood a Braxaná. Harkur was broad and barbaric in costume and countenance, his light skin tanned and coarsened from exposure to the elements. The only regal element about him was a narrow band of gold, not even a finger's width, lying across his forehead and confining his hair. And the hair! Its color was not even Braxin, but a deep blood red or wine color, and it shone as though it were metallic in the chamber's primitive lighting.

The man by his side was taller than he by a handswidth, and his white skin looked almost sickly beside the healthy exposure of his master. He was a man of dramatic features, though I would not say he was attractive. But the contrast of his face was arresting, and his frame and stance spoke of power, both in attitude and in body. I wondered fleetingly what price such a man would have brought among the Mristi, for he would have pleased them. He was dressed in raw black silks, rich but not ostentatious, drawing attention to the medallion of rank which shone golden from where it lay on his chest.

As instructed, I approached the pair and knelt. Harkur walked over to me, regality obvious in every step, his aide following. The Kaim'era's presence inspired such confidence that for a moment I forgot my supposed fate. The other man I feared, a gut reaction so intense it was hard to speak when I had to.

Harkur reached a callused hand under my chin and

gently drew my face upward. Never before had I known a man's touch in anything but cruelty; it was sweet, now.

"You are Dyle, the Zeymourian?"

I lowered my eyes. His voice was harsh, but strong and pleasing. I had never heard its like before. "I am, great Kaim'era."

He nodded, his eyes meeting Sokuz's. "I am very pleased. Were there losses?"

"Only theirs, Great One. A few."

The ruler of Braxi smiled, then regarded me again. "You've had a long confinement in the Void—I imagine you could do with some rest under proper gravity, and perhaps a bit of real food. My servants will show you to rooms, and supply you with all you need. I would be pleased to have your company at dinner this evening."

I was confused. What choice did I have? "As you wish," I managed. Why play this game of freedom when we both knew the truth?

He gestured toward the Braxaná beside him. "This is Viton, my personal aide and advisor. He's offered to make himself available to you while you settle in. Should you require something more, or should that which we supply be unsuitable for your race, you may speak to him."

I knew I would never have the courage for that, but I nodded.

Viton stepped forward and offered me his arm, to guide me. I tried not to tremble as I touched him—wouldn't that be amusing, the primitive alien terrified!

Sokuz stepped forward as Viton led me away, and I heard Harkur speaking words of praise. ". . . and I am pleased beyond expression. Now come, and tell me all you know . . ."

Viton led me to an exit behind the throne. We passed through many walkways, all richly and tastefully adorned, until we reached apartments consisting of some five rooms. There women waited to receive me, and Viton turned me over to them without a word. He bowed as he left, but there was a smile on his face that I found disturbing and I looked away quickly.

One of the women, alien in feature and with hair the color of the sun (our sun) brought me to the bedchamber, where all manner of gowns were laid out, ranging from diaphanous sheaths with light embroidery to rich, fur-lined robes-of-state. I chose one, and the rest were taken away. I bathed—marvelous, welcome luxury!—and slept in a heaven of softness. When the time came for me to awaken they saw to it, and they insisted on dressing me. The dress was soft and its lining done in velvets, so that where it touched me there was only pleasure in the contact; it was also modest to my eyes, although not as much as something I might have designed myself. They pulled my hair back tightly and bound it there, then made curls to hang down about my neck and shoulders, and added to them small tinkling ornaments that brushed unexpectedly against my skin when I moved. All was so tactile, and thus so alien! Our people touch so rarely, and theirs so naturally, that I knew more human contact in that dressing than I had before in all my life.

Viton arrived, he said to give me a tour of the palace, which was now available to me. How could I refuse, even though he terrified me? There was something about him which was animal, not human, even predatory, an urge to violence which seemed barely under control, a hunger for indulgence that was in his black eyes whenever I looked in them, so clearly that I trembled. And I realized that he, not Harkur, was the embodiment of the evil and violence that had been presented to me as the Braxin nature.

We passed libraries, terraces, chambers filled with art and music, halls rich in scent and lit primitively with torchlight—for Harkur had a taste for barbaric symbolism and found such things appropriate. Then he showed me the gardens, and oh! what beauty!

A fountain was central to this private place, its spray perfumed and its mist felt even by its enclosing walls. Plants grew about and between marbled pathways, and golden urns held ice and wine ready for the unexpected visitor. Benches covered with embroidered velvet cushions were half-hidden by the leaves and flowers, the pillows piled high and occasionally covered by bits of luxurious fur. All about were things of pleasure, touch, and intoxication . . . I am beyond describing them, Beyl-my-brother. But it was incomparably beautiful, and I gazed at it long before allowing him to lead me away.

I dined with Harkur, Viton and other respected advisors, and also their chosen women. We reclined on cushions and sipped drugged wine, and women danced for us, and the incense filled the air with a heady sweetness that was almost too much to bear. And that was all. I feared him, I feared what he would do to me, and I came to be ashamed. For he did nothing. After hours of pleasure had passed he sent me back to my rooms, saying that he sensed that to be my true desire. And for the first time I truly understood that I had the freedom to turn him down—and that frightened me, somehow, more than anything.

I spent the days alternating between my rooms and the wonderfully voluptuous gardens which had been made available to me. I even thought fleetingly that if Harkur meant to keep me like this I should like to serve his will in return. I think now that that is as close as I dared come to desire for the charismatic ruler.

For desire, though utterly repressed, was born in that place. I hope you will understand enough to not think me utterly evil for it! After all, I was damned already beyond redemption just by having been raped. The softness, the spray of the fountain, everywhere the tactile richness of my surroundings did to me what no words could. My body territory was violated by the women who attended me, again and again, until its border became less sensitive; everywhere there was softness and pleasure, things to touch and feel, velvet for my hands and satin against my cheek. Is it a wonder I changed, in such a place?

I spent an easy month in the palace (seventeen days reckoned by the Braxin calendar, as Berros was without a moon). In the beginning I was fearful, but even fear could not lessen the wonder of my new circumstances. I learned to lose myself in the pleasure of my surroundings, for therein lay forgetfulness. There were warm baths in marble halls, attended by females of many Scattered Races, which I enjoyed, although I was a bit distant when they gathered in small groups to discuss, laughing, the tastes of the Master of the House. There were pools for swimming and I used them often. There was wine and music and rich sensation all about me, and by the time Harkur desired my company again I was very different from what I had been when I arrived.

I knelt when I was brought to the dining hall, took his hand and kissed the ring of rank he wore. It was the first time I had ever touched a man of my own will. He drew me to my feet and fed me again the richness of Braxi, gave me wine in jewel-encrusted chalices, brought forth musicians and dancers and humorists to entertain me. By the end of the night my head was weak and I excused myself, humbling myself as I left as I had when I came.

I didn't make it to my apartments. I passed the gardens, saw the starlight shining through the skylight, and entered. I walked through the fountain's spray and let it tingle against my skin, deliciously cold against the warmth the wine had instilled within me. And then I threw myself upon a pile of cushions, and they sank beneath me. And as I drifted softly into sleep, I was aware of my hands slowly stroking the velvet and furs, with a life of their own.

I awoke a bit later, disoriented but happy. The starlight was gone but someone had lit candles, and the light caught on the flying water in the center of the room. As I slowly took in my surroundings I became aware that Harkur was there as well, sitting beside me, watching me, his vivid red hair falling over his shoulders, heavy ornaments wrapped about his waist and wide metal bracelets adorning his bare upper arms.

And do not condemn me, my brother, until you have been intoxicated by pleasure yourself and had a creature of such presence beside you. My hands ran of their own will to his shoulders, fingered his skin, the ornaments, the shining hair. I was hungry for the touch of him; I had only recently learned to feel with such perception and now I reveled in the combination of softness and metallic rigidity that he offered me. I wanted him, not for sex, that evil, but to touch him, to feel the mysteries of him, to have this sensation to add to all the others. I never made the connection between the damning indulgence and what I was feeling. Harkur had planned this moment and done it well, for even my conditioning could not defy the sensuality of my circumstances, and it died unheard in the back of my mind as I drew him slowly down to me and tasted the unbearable sweetness of a man's lips for the first time. Oh, Kaim'era, how could any woman be frightened in the face of such pleasure—and how could any mistake it for sin, my master, how?

I give you words, my brother, but I cannot give you my feelings. Nor can I help you to rationalize or understand what I have done, the sins I indulged in that were no sins at all except in the eyes and words of our oppressors.

Oh, Beyl, take this new world and help our people escape their suffocating heritage! Once I was against you, believing so strongly in what I was taught—or so terrified, perhaps—that I would have turned a pregnant woman over to the Mristi for the crime of having loved. I, now, have loved, and if that's a crime there's no sweeter one in the world. And I also—but that later, I will get to it in time. . . .

What can I say of my position in the palace on Berros that can help you understand it? Pleasure is so alien to our kind—can you conceive of my being draped in riches merely because the ruler of Braxi found pleasure in me? Other women were more intelligent, all were more knowledgeable—can you believe I was so treated simply because I asked nothing of him, had nothing to gain from his favors that I did not enjoy at that moment, never sought to use him and would hardly have known how had I tried? In his way, Harkur loved me. I gave him pleasure and I gave him myself, I amused him and could not hurt him . . . for a Braxin, that can be enough.

I was moved, though, when he had a portrait commissioned of us together, for he was self-conscious about the harmless mutation that had caused him to have hair of such an odd color and texture that he had allowed no picture to be taken of him, even frowned upon written description. This he hung in one of his hunting-palaces, in a dining hall, for it pleased him to look upon it when he vacationed there, away from the pressures of the Berren court.

I lived many zhents at the palace. He spoke to me sometimes of his work and his dreams, and of politics I barely understood. He told me that he meant for Viton to inherit the throne, and when I paled he declared, "I have no choice. My children, my advisors, my princes, they all talk of uniting Braxi, making treaties, birthing international organizations, bringing the tribes together. There is only one way to do that, and that is with blood! Give them war and they'll fight together, promise them power and they'll band together to grab at it. Viton will settle for no less than mastery of the galaxy, as much as he can grasp at in a lifetime, and the tribes will follow him to share in that glory. Nothing less than that will do, Dyle . . . but oh, I wish there were a better way."

He told me that the Braxaná are so suspicious even of their own kind that a Braxaná Kaim'era could never rule them all. "The entire nature of our government would have to change if they tried to hold the throne." And he didn't say what we both knew: once they had the throne, it would take nothing short of slaughter to dislodge them from it. One by one he was dragging them into his court and forcing them to learn the games and ways of civilization, hoping that by the time of his death they could take his place and keep the Braxins united—for or against them, it didn't matter to him. The planet had to act as one nation if it was to prosper. That was all that concerned him.

He spent long sessions in his private chambers with Viton, comparing their philosophies and seeking common ground for a unified Braxin tradition. Oh, but I fear to say it was only a dream at best, though they were both devoted to it! Even at his court the hostility between the members of different tribes was open and often violent; could he ever create out of that a Braxin whole that would outlast his lifetime?

On religion they disagreed. Harkur saw some value in it, Viton saw it only as a crutch of the weakminded. This was strange to me since Viton recognized a small pantheon of deities while Harkur was himself an atheist. An active god, the Braxaná explained, cripples man by limiting his potential. And can any rational mind accept that a being with unlimited horizons would really bind itself down to the care and feeding of man for all eternity? The

Braxaná see their gods as having abandoned man and do not expect them to return. But on this the two men agreed, and I also: that religion, properly controlled, is the single most powerful manipulative tool in the arsenal of man against his own kind. I have seen that, looking back on Zeymour and my past, and I shudder to think of the other uses such faith might be turned to.

At night I awoke often, shivering, a nightmare all but gone from my mind. When I was with him he held me. He never asked me of their nature or wondered aloud at their cause, even when I awoke crying out or with tears blinding my eyes. For my part I never remembered the content of the dreams, or what they meant to me that they terrified me so. But I could guess.

I was wrong.

One day, many months after I had first arrived and long after my place with him had become established, he bade me follow him into a section of the palace that previously had not been open to me. Perplexed and curious, I obeyed.

What he took me to was a closed dock, although I didn't realize it until we had passed through the last code-sealed door. There was—oh, there are tears in my eyes to remember it!—a starship, yes, but not only a starship—a vessel that captured the line of the long-lost *Explorer*. Oh, it was Braxin to be sure, and there was no mistaking the gravitic generator for anything else, or the fact that the very machinery which had caused me such agony on the way out was missing from this model, but still its purpose was clear . . . I wept. Long and hard and fearfully, my brother, until I was empty of tears and could cry no more. "How did you know?" I whispered.

He stroked my head and answered softly, "You talk in your sleep, my little one. Now tell me." He pushed me back from him, enough to look in my eyes. "Do you really believe they have a chance? I won't let you go back there just to commit a grand gesture of racial suicide."

I thought, and I answered as I believed. "The odds are very bad," I admitted. "But my brother said there was hope, and I have faith in him."

"And you want to go back?"

I lowered my eyes. "I have to go back. What they're doing, even if they succeed, will mean such suffering . . . they need the hope of knowing what's out there. The universe is filled with life, if only they can manage to reach it! They need to know it's worth fighting for. I need to tell them."

He nodded, and I thought he looked very sad. "Come," he said quietly: "I'll show you how it works."

He was long in teaching me how to fly the starship, perhaps because he feared my ignorance and perhaps . . . but no, that is private and I will leave it so. Suffice it to say that one night he took me in his arms and said to me that he knew what I might be returning to, and that I might well be hated, and that he wanted me always to remember that once, here, a man had called me *mitethe.* He whispered the word, an endearment from a language so descriptively rich that it spoke of tenderness as no word from any other language could. I held him again, and that was the last time. For in the morning I left him, and Braxi.

I skirted his empire ("That-Which-Is-Held-By-B'Salos," he called it) and cut through a lesser portion of Lugastine space. I prayed that they wouldn't detect me, but as Harkur had said, space is so vast that the odds of single starship being noticed if its arrival is not anticipated are astronomically small. Just so, for they didn't notice me, and I passed through and beyond that well-meaning nation and I turned . . . toward home.

Home?

Sunward are the asteroids. They weren't there when I left, at least not in that form. Some of them glow, with a dull blueness that I can see when the angle is right. A large group of them are traveling together, and how many bodies, how many shreds of man's glory in between them? This, Lord, was Zeymour, and you may spare it Your judgment because it managed to create its own.

The fourth planet: I circle it, far out. It has no moon, little atmosphere, nothing to welcome man but its convenient proximity at the time of disaster. At the edge of one continent I imagine I see light, perhaps searchbeams from a spaceship, perhaps imagination, perhaps nothing.

Beyl, I lack the courage! I sit here in orbit and want to believe, with all my heart, that at the last moment you rebelled and took the ships and are below me, waiting—but I know the odds are against it, and the thought of facing the Mristi now is almost more than I can bear. I am pregnant, my brother, and I have waited as long as I can. I have supplies for many zhents more, but the child will not wait. Even now the first pains come . . . oh, I should have been careful, but what do I know of such things besides Mristi-warped legends, and what do rulers care? Harkur would have welcomed our child Into his court, and I would have learned to care for it. Now?

I've waited as long as I can. I'll follow the light and hope that it indicates people, and pray as I land that the people are my own. If not . . . it's been a long trip, my brother, but at least I'm home. There's something in that, isn't there?

* * *

Notes in the journal of Beyl vi Dakros, YE 1

Third Zeymour-month after the Exodus, third day.

Dyle is dead.

We did all we could for her, but still we failed. It seems years ago that we pulled her free from the wreckage of her ship in the mountains. I wonder if she was aware enough to see her child born, forced from her prematurely but safely adapting to the air here. The atmosphere was too thin for Dyle, or perhaps the deathwinds swept by while she waited for us to find her. Either way she's gone, lost to us a second time.

We lost five more today, bringing the total to half our number. The winter is coming quickly now and we struggle to have the shelters raised in time. We were shoulder to shoulder during the journey from Zeymour; even with our numbers reduced by half, we can't hope to survive this planet's long winter packed into the ships that brought us here.

Sometimes I despair. Then I remind myself of our original goals—and if only a pair of us makes it through to the spring, that will be enough.

We salvaged nothing of the Lyu. It ignited even as we pulled Dyle out of it; we barely had time to cover ourselves before the whole of it blew. The child, thank God, survived. We could not have saved her mother.

We are calling the infant Hasha, which means Firstborn. She is a symbol of hope to us in this barren place, the first new life in a world of death. Nevertheless, there are some who would have her killed. She appears to be part Mristi, and the only logical cause of her existence would have it so. They would put her to death for that reason. But isn't that just what was done to us? What we sought to escape by coming here?

Fragments of a community are beginning to form at last. Perhaps predictably, they are centering around the ships that brought us here and the settlements which were organized accordingly. We've taken the ship's numbers as secondary names, a grim reminder for future generations of what man can do when he has to—and of what man's stupidity can make necessary. I wonder if that's enough.

Today we broke the seal on the Zi's innermost laboratory. Already our would-be scientists have begun to study this new cache of treasures, and they have high hopes that we will soon find the texts and equipment for that most crucial science: genetics. We must unlock the secrets of human inheritance before this planet destroys us all. Unhappily—ironically—we are dependent upon the foresight of our oppressors for hope. Did they have time to store the information we need? We can only pray. . . .

The Mristi. Like ghosts they hover around us, banished only by the promise of a world so different from their own that they would truly have no place there. For we will take this planet and build a new life for ourselves, setting standards we can be proud of. We will never do as our tormentors did, speak words only to bury them with actions. We will meet the future with our honor held sacred so that no matter what the temptation, no matter what the cost, we will never resemble our tormentors and our society will never come to resemble theirs in any way. Thus will the

Mristi be laid to rest at last, and the people of the Firstborn be sustained.

Dyle, this I swear to you: your child will be treasured and remembered, the first human born on this hostile soil. We will conquer Azea and make it ours—all in her name, my sister, and yours. Be sure of it.

GLOSSARY

Absent Gods: The **Braxaná** believe that whatever gods might have been responsible for the creation of the universe no longer have interest in it and are not actively involved in its maintenance. They regard this as a positive development, noting that creatures with eternal life and nearly unlimited power are not likely to share humankind's priorities or care much about the welfare of a single life form. In the words of one theologian, "There is nothing more dangerous than a jaded god." The Braxaná creation saga as recorded by Davros in the third century is an excellent illustration of this principle, with its chilling images of **Taz'hein** and **Avra-Nim** driving human armies to bloodshed simply for their own amusement.

The Braxaná regard with scorn any culture that maintains a belief in active beneficial deities, both for emotional dependency and philosophical shortsightedness, and the phrase "Bless him with an active deity" is regarded as one of the most condescending insults in the Braxaná lexicon.

A.C.: After the Coronation of **Harkur**. The Harkurian calendar was adopted seventy-six years after Harkur's death to honor the man who unified Braxi and brought it to interstellar prominence. Historians note that it was a **Braxaná** government that chose to institute the new calendar, and may have done so to placate disparate tribal factions in an era when its own power was less than certain.

Ada: The traditional weapon of Dari's **Hyarke** combat, the ada consists of a staff with blades at both ends. Although the shape of the blades can vary, it is required of all true ada that one blade be designed for thrusting and that other be a curved blade designed for slashing.

Of late some combatants have chosen to resurrect the ancient Hiyu style, in which the thrusting blade is armed with tooth-like barbs. Used properly, the hiyu-ada can eviscerate an opponent in seconds; however, there is also the danger of it becoming caught on bone and being unable to withdraw. Hiyu combat has its own unique strategy and several fan associations have arisen that focus upon this variety of the sport.

Aldous: Sister planet to Braxi, closer to their shared sun, Aldous is made habitable by dense atmospheric components that block out a portion of the sun's radiation, making a human-compatible environment possible surrounding both geographic poles. Believed to have been seeded with human stock in the first wave of transplantation (see **Scattered Races**), Aldous became home to a civilization which was advanced in technology and yet wholly planetbound. Scientists postulate this was the result of cultural evolution in an environment in which neither stars, moon, nor open space was visible, causing human imagination to focus upon more local elements. Those who study the Scattered Races regard Aldous as one of the clearest examples of targeted experimentation, and use it to bolster arguments that the purpose of the Seeding was to study the effects of planetary environment upon social evolution.

Braxi made contact with the human inhabitants of Aldous in the third century before Harkur's reign and quickly established dominance. The inclusion of the lesser planet's name in the full title of the **Holding** represents its symbolic importance as a satellite of B'Salos, rather than any political or military significance.

Ar: Now regarded as the goddess of Chaos Incarnate, Ar is believed by some scholars to have once been an active member of the **Braxaná** pantheon, and the deity responsible for the yearly cycle of death and rebirth witnessed throughout nature. Historians trace the change in her aspect to the period following the reign of **Viton the Ruthless,** a result of the deliberate politicization of Braxaná mythology by Viton's successors.

The Braxaná claim that in any situation where a woman commands men the spirit of Ar will be manifest. This is used as the justification for the exclusion of women from all facets of Braxin government, as well as the harshest of the **Social Codes** regarding women's behavior. As with most of the Social Codes this restriction is of least concern to the Braxaná themselves, who admit to admiring strong women, and who long ago developed customs and language to allow their own females to wield considerable power, albeit indirectly.

Avra-Nim: God of creation and sunlight in most Braxin pantheons, Avra-Nim was the pre-eminent deity prior to the rise of the **Braxaná**. Some historians postulate that he was originally the dominant figure in Braxaná mythology as well, and point to the solar nomenclature of the **Holding** as evidence of this. Others theorize that this was a purely political move meant to facilitate the absorption of other tribes into a greater Braxaná whole.

A failed god whose human creations have long been dominated by his brother's get, Avra-Nim has not been accorded worship in many centuries.

Azean Star Empire: See **Star Empire.**

B.C: Before the Coronation of **Harkur**.

Betrayer: see **Taz'hein.**

Bi'ti: The essence or spirit of the warrior, which is considered the core of the **Braxaná** identity. It is believed that both men and women possess the bi'ti, and acts of violence that would have been considered unsuitable for women in other tribes are accepted among the **Pale Ones** as a natural expression of this fierce inner spirit.

Early Braxaná believed that a strong bi'ti could be inherited, for which reason triumphant warriors were permitted to mate at will with fertile members of the tribe. It was believed that such sexual union would strengthen the woman and all her offspring, lending even to the child of another man the fierce spirit of the warrior. It is this tradition which was later written into law as the Code of Sexual Access, though critics note that in its current form it has little to do with the custom's original form or purpose.

Black Death: Literally translated from the Braxin as "Waiting Death" or "Ravenous Death", the Black Death is one of the most deadly and feared organisms in the human worlds. Derived from a life-form originally found on Ekkos IV, the poison has an inert phase, during which it invades its host and lodges in internal tissue, and an active phase, during which it rapidly consumes its host for energy, growing so rapidly that witnesses may mistake its advance for locomotion.

In its natural form the Black Death was responsible for the decimation of several human colonies, and its home world was subject to biological cleansing by **Zherat** in 1,972 A.C in order to keep it from invading the **Holding** at large. The controlled strains have been bred to be dependent upon human science for reproduction, and fertile samples are carefully guarded.

The most common strain becomes active ten to forty days after invading its host, usually at a single point of catalysm. Less common is the so-called "timed dose", which is developed to suit the individual organic template of its host, allowing for refined control of its activation schedule. The Black Death has no known cure or treatment, and is 100% fatal to organic hosts. The only hope of survival for a victim is to remove the affected limb before the activated Death can spread. (See **Peace Dagger**) It is considered a capital offense for anyone but a **Braxaná** to possess the poison, and research facilities adapting the strains for military use are under tight government control. Nevertheless it is rumored that the Black Market has occasionally seen trade in the Death, and the use of weakened strains by non-Braxaná is occasionally rumored.

Bloodletters: Gladiators in the **Hyarke** bloodsport of Dari, Bloodletters get their name not from the bloodshed of the match itself, but from the custom of drinking their opponent's blood after the kill has been made. This custom has an active spiritual element and is believed to go back to the military sacrifices of the Duara era, in which the bravest warriors of a conquered nation were sacrificed and consumed by the victors.

Braxaná: Originally a nomadic tribe inhabiting the Blood Steppes of northern Braxi, the Braxaná were noteworthy for their rejection of modern culture and its social compromises, believing that such things weakened the sacred essence of the warrior spirit (**bi'ti**). Attempts to conquer, absorb, or even negotiate with this fierce barbarian tribe all proved futile, and in the 5th century B.C. the Council of Eastern Tribes officially (and grudgingly) ceded them the Blood Steppes in perpetuity, acknowledging that the only means by which "civilization" was going to encroach upon Braxaná territory was by inciting more bloodshed than the land was worth.

It was **Harkur the Great** who first realized the full potential of the Braxaná spirit, and he sought out members of the tribe to serve in his court. The most famous of these was **Viton the Ruthless**, who succeeded him in 86 A.C. Though Harkur never openly proposed Braxaná rule, historians believe that he saw in the so-called **Pale Ones** a possible tool for unifying the other tribes, and his discussions with Viton provided the foundation for subsequent Braxaná domination of global affairs.

Braxaná Dialect: Because early Braxaná culture relied upon oral rather than written records, little is known about roots of the so-called

Braxaná dialect. Most linguists are in agreement that its forty-seven speech modes were derived from a language once common on the Blood Steppes, which had ceased to exist as an independent tongue by the time of **Harkur the Great.**

Linguists agree that in complexity of form and in raw communicative potential the Braxaná dialect surpasses all other human languages. Gaten son of Vralos characterized it as "The one human language which no outsider can ever truly master." Forty-seven speech modes allow for fine communication of social and emotive context, and secondary and even tertiary messages can be imbedded in many simple statements. It is said that a master of the Braxaná tongue can hold several different conversations at once, and true mastery of the language is so highly regarded that Braxaná poets are among the most celebrated of artists. While non-Braxaná rarely use the more obscure forms, most are familiar with the major contextual modes, and the ability to use them fluently in one's language is regarded as a sign of intelligence and social refinement among the upper classes.

The Braxaná dialect contains a mode which is entirely neutral, and which has been adopted throughout the **Holding** as the "common Braxin" tongue. Speech in this Basic Mode is said to be acceptable in all social situations, though Braxins of the upper classes may look with disdain upon those who are too poorly educated to make their language more interesting.

Braxaná Rage: A state in which the Braxaná abandons all social inhibitions to give vent to his anger, usually through acts of violence. The experience is believed to be a cleansing experience for the **bi'ti**, kin to the battle frenzy of early Braxaná warriors, and as such is regarded as a valid emotional display by the Braxaná. Other Braxins are not quite so appreciative, and fear of the Rage being unleashed has caused many potential opponents to give ground.

The lives and property lost during a Rage are considered by the Braxaná to be the responsibility of whoever triggered it, and it is not unheard-of for a man who antagonized a Braxaná into a Rage to later be held responsible for murders the **Pale One** committed in that state.

B'Salos: The yellow sun of Braxi and **Aldous,** B'Salos was the focus of worship for much of early Braxin culture, and an assortment of sun-related deities peopled the pantheons of most early tribes. Theologians note this is typical of planets orbiting the outer portion of the **Galanj**

Region, where even a small variance in solar radiation can have catastrophic effects upon the ecosystem.

Central Computer System (CSS): The centralized data storage and processing system of the **Holding,** among the most complex of its type ever to have been created. The CCS functions as a central clearing house for all information in the Holding, both static and dynamic, and contains subsidiary indexing systems fine-tuned to the needs of a variety of species. Every citizen of the Holding is guaranteed free access to the system, and it is said that some nations have accepted the yoke of the Holding just to become part of it. There is no denying that the efficiency of the CCS has been a major factor in Braxi's ability to absorb alien cultures quickly and administrate them effectively, and it is rumored that the backup facilities of the system are so well planned that if the data-handling facilities of the CCS were damaged, it would only be a matter of hours before 95% of the system was back online, with full recovery to follow not soon after. Communication specialists in the **Star Empire** do note that this may be no more than propaganda, and that the failure of such a system for even a day could provide valuable openings to both political and military enemies.

Citadel of the Kaim'eri: A man-made satellite orbiting Braxi, which houses both the great meeting hall of the **Kaim'erate** and the main processors and storage banks for the **Central Computer System.**

Communicant: Second highest category of psychic functioning, indicating one who is capable of receiving the thoughts of nonpsychics and transmitting his own to them in turn, with near-perfect comprehension and reliability. As with the rank of Telepath there are various grades leading up to that of full Communicant, which reflect varying degrees of power and control. A true Communicant is capable of linking together several minds, as well as subsuming the power of (willing) colleagues to increase his range and sensitivity.

Communicants are rarely capable of complex communication with non-humans, although those who are gifted in abstract visualization have a natural advantage in this arena.

Comprehensive Peace: A peace treaty in the classic sense, in which both sides of a conflict are expected to refrain from hostile actions along all common borders. The **Holding's** scorn for such treaties is widely known, and its habit of breaking them repeatedly has caused most nations other than Azea to regard such treaties with Braxi as a wasted effort.

Although Azea's Articles of Founding require that the **Star Empire** pursue peace whenever possible, it has long been understood by diplomats that a comprehensive treaty with Braxi provides little more than an interlude in war's greater symphony. Although Azea insists that it remains optimistic a permanent Peace is still possible, **Star-Control** is known to maintain a department whose sole purpose is to anticipate the possible "breaking points" of each treaty. The resulting practice of Braxi seeking unanticipated (and sometimes barely credible) excuses for war has provided fertile ground for satirical commentary on both sides of the War Border.

The mean average for a Comprehensive Peace in the Great War is ten Standard Years.

Conditional Peace: A temporary ceasefire between Azea and Braxi, with clearly defined spatial and temporal boundaries. A Conditional Peace is most often invoked to evacuate colonies that lie in the path of the expanding War, or to rescue valuable resources that are about to be claimed by the enemy. Since both sides must agree to a Conditional Peace, it occurs most often when new territory comes into the line of fire and both sides have people or facilities they wish to salvage.

The fact that a Conditional Peace has as its core condition a concrete set of goals from which both sides will benefit makes it one of the few forms of peace treaty Braxi is likely to honor. Hence in some regions it has become the preferred form of negotiation, leading detractors (mostly non-human) to comment scornfully upon the practice of "buying peace."

Council of Justice: Created in 3,571 Y.E. to oversee matters of racial definition and loyalty among those of Azean heritage. The establishment of the Council followed nearly a century of bitter debate over whether Azeans should have yet another Crown that answered solely to them, and was only established when the defection of Zan er Tylosa cost the Empire several populated planets and more than a million lives.

Supporters argued that as it was the artificial genetic design of the Azean temperament which justified that race's domination of military affairs, it was advisable to have a panel of officers who were specialists not only in the behavior of that race, but in its genetic underpinnings. The Council consists of a dozen members, of whom a third are usually genetic scientists. It has the authority to mandate or proscribe any genetic alteration which affects the stability of the Azean people as a whole, and rules over the rare cases where mixed offspring exist.

Dialogues: A series of conversations which took place between **Harkur the Great** and **Viton the Ruthless** between 17 and 49 A.C., which were recorded by both parties for private reference and transcribed centuries later for publication. *Dialogues* covers a wealth of topics, both social and political, and is best known for laying out the formula by which the **Braxaná** would later establish and maintain their rule.

Of special interest to historians is the fact that although the two sets of recordings are theoretically of the same conversations, they are not identical. Volumes have been written upon the significance of these discrepancies, of which perhaps the best treatment can be found in Satar's *Between the Lines: Agenda and Intent in an Ancient Disparity.*

Disciplines: Mental rituals designed by the Institute for the Accelertion of Psychic Evolution, used to control psychic ability. The majority of Disciplines are defensive in nature, designed to protect the integrity of the psychic's mind when dealing with potentially destabilizing influences. Some are voluntary, requiring that the psychic activate a mental trigger to bring them into play, while others are conditioned into the psychic's mind as a last ditch defensive measure, to be triggered automatically when the boundaries of identity and/or sanity are threatened.

It was the development of such Disciplines which enabled the Institute to establish a viable psychic community, and to bring what was then a rogue power under enough control to be established as a measurable science. The full range of Disciplines is never discussed outside the Institute, and it is rumored that some have been developed which allow for the focusing of aggressive energies against a target. The Institute denies any such allegations, insisting that the Disciplines exist solely to safeguard the psychic mind against the hazards of uncontrolled sensitivity, but thus far it has refused to provide a comprehensive list of Disciplines for any outside agency to review.

Exodus: The emigration from **Zeymour** to Azea. It is estimated that nearly 100,000 began the journey, which took half a Standard Year.

First Class: The most prestigious of six formal social class divisions within Braxin society, the First Class includes all purebred and halfbreed **Braxaná,** as well as the children of halfbred Braxaná who serve in Braxaná households. The latter are defined by matrilineal descent only (though several political attempts have been made to institute a DNA-based standard which would allow for the inclusion of patrilineal issue).

Founding: The settling of Azea by human stock from **Zeymour.** Modern historians estimate the mortality rate of the first generation to have been as high as 92%, necessitating artificial manipulation of the remaining gene pool in order to establish a viable population.

Functional Telepath: The highest of fifteen ratings developed by the Institute for the Acceleration of Psychic Evolution, FT status is granted only to those who can send and receive thoughts at will, and with consistent accuracy. The Functional Telepath is required to have mastered all **Disciplines** and to be able to facilitate the mental communication of non-psychic minds as well. It is to be noted that many psychics may achieve telepathic-level communication without fulfilling all of the criteria perfectly or consistently, and the Institute also recognizes three lesser ranks of Telepathy.

It has been stated that the long-term goal of the Institute is to isolate the genetic codes required to make Functional Telepathy available to all humans. However, a series of studies done in '87 suggests that several of the factors involved are not linked to psychic coding, but to personality traits which are part of the Seling Complex, and which cannot be altered without putting greater patterns of mental processing at risk. Former Director Kalu er Tashenin stated at the time of the study that so-called Conditional Telepathy might still be possible for all humans, but less optimistic scientists cite **Communicant** status as the best that can be offered to the human race as a whole.

Galanj Region: The region surrounding a star in which orbiting planets may have the temperature range and chemical availability necessary for sustaining human life. The Galanj Region typically contains a single planet, though several systems are known in which special environmental factors have allowed two planets to qualify. The most famous of these is the B'saloan system, with **Aldous** occupying the inner edge of an unusually wide Galanj Region due to atmospheric factors. Although there are several known examples of such dual

Galanj throughout human-explored space, the B'saloan system remains the only place where both planets were Seeded with human life. (see **Scattered Races**). That fact, combined with the early foray of Braxi into interstellar space, has led to speculation that the true roots of the humankind may yet be discovered in the B'Saloan system.

Harkur the Great: The single greatest ruler of Braxi, Harkur the Great is credited with uniting the one hundred seventeen Major Tribes under one international government, and with establishing the Holding as a major interstellar power.

Hirinari by birth, Harkur supplemented his formal education with travels to the far reaches of Braxi, including tribal territories normally closed to outsiders. Though records of his travels are incomplete, modern scholars believe he may have visited the Blood Steppes and some believe that he witnessed **Braxaná** customs normally kept hidden from the eyes of outsiders.

Harkur's dream was a Braxi truly united in purpose, a far cry from the conglomeration of warring tribes whose throne he claimed in his fortieth year. Within zhents of his Coronation he had begun what would become the central campaign of his lifetime, focusing Braxin aggressive energies outwards, towards the stars. A rapid series of dramatic raids into Lugastine space won him support from the Braxin media, and the benefits to be reaped from cooperative efforts in interstellar warfare soon won even the most warlike tribes to his cause.

Harkur's manipulation of the Braxaná was either his greatest accomplishment or greatest offense, depending upon one's perspective. Without a doubt he paved the way for Braxaná domination of the **Holding,** believing it to be the one formula sure to keep Braxi united. Whether that unity has been a good thing in the long run, or whether the social cost of Braxaná rule was something no political goal can justify, is a subject matter hotly debated in scholarly journals outside the Holding.

Hasha: The first human born on Azean soil, Hasha's origins have long been shrouded in mystery. Early records hint that her mother was not among those present at the **Founding,** but give no explanation for her appearance afterwards. While historians search for some indication of an unnamed ship taking part in the **Exodus,** theologians prefer to postulate that the vast life-energies of a dying planet, focused by the desperate hopes of the survivors, gave birth to an actual miracle, and that the child that owes its life as much to the planet Azea itself as to any human forbears.

Whatever her origin, Hasha's birth was regarded in its time as a sign of divine approval of the Exodus and Founding, and a necessary symbol of hope to a people about to colonize a biologically hostile planet. Myths have arisen surrounding her birth which grant her nearly divine status in her own right, and references to "the Firstborn" appear throughout Azean literature as appeals to a supernatural patroness, much in the manner that lesser gods and prophets are called upon by other peoples.

Hasha's firstborn child was given the subname "lyu," a custom which has been maintained down through the ages to memorialize the significance of Azea's first birth. The name is believed to mean "birth" in the language spoken by the Founders.

Holding: The proper name of the territory ruled by Braxi, in its complete form the *B'Saloan Holding under Braxi/Aldous.* Some historians feel that the name is a holdover from the sun-worship of the early tribes, and trace the name of B'Salos back to Be-Nesaal, a sun god prominent in the northern hemisphere.

It is said that by naming the interstellar empire after a sun shared by two planets—and perhaps a god shared by many—**Harkur the Great** hoped to stress the unity of the Holding, rather than encourage competition between the various tribes and factions it contained.

Human: Full-sentient beings believed to be descended from the human stock of the **Source World**, being no more than 18% divergent from the mean genetic template, and capable of interbreeding with other humans to produce fertile offspring. The term is also used in a more colloquial sense to indicate those who belong to the "human community", and is rejected by some races which might qualify in a purely technical sense.

Because the governments of both the **Star Empire** and the **Holding** distinguish between human and non-human species for bureaucratic purposes, the issue of human status is subject to continual debate and revision. The requirement that Source World origin be proven beyond reasonable doubt was officially abandoned in '897 Y.E., when it was demonstrated that several human worlds had deliberately falsified their archaeological records to distance themselves from the existing human political structure.

Hyarke: A form of gladiatorial sport native to Dari, the Hyarke involves a death match between two individuals, using a bladed weapon developed specifically for ritual combat. (see **ada.**) The Hyarke has an active spiritual element, with victors drinking the blood of the fallen as a vehicle for absorbing their life-energy. This spiritual consumption is given as the reason for excluding other **Scattered Races** from participation, as outsiders are considered unworthy of absorbing the Darian essence.

Hyarke is the global sport of Dari, with a fan base numbering in the billions. While normally this would quality it for the PanStellar Games, the Human Sports Council has repeatedly chosen to exclude it from its gladiatorial venue, citing the element of guaranteed mortality as being counter to the Games' philosophy. This move is regarded as racist by many Darian fan associations and has been used as a platform for anti-Azean campaigning in numerous political contests. The Council's offer to include the Hyarke if participants would adopt the Kraulan Gladiatorial Standard—giving the victor the option of sparing the life of a particularly worthy opponent—has met with derision in both professional circles and among fans, and the phrase "bright as the Sports Council" has worked its way into the Darian language as an indicator of one who persists in making offers that have no chance of being accepted.

Inheritance: The **Braxaná** rite of passage, after which a young man may own property and establish a House in his own name. Requirements for Inheritance, established by the youth's father, originally entailed such warrior-specific feats as the capture or killing of an enemy, theft of valued artifacts from neighboring tribes, or kidnapping of leadership figures (preferably well guarded) from other nations.

The rite is still required for males, who by Braxaná law may not own property in their own name until satisfying their fathers that they are worthy. In these modern days the testing is more often political than martial, and may involve the manipulation of household accounts or the leverage of political pressures for some subtle and often secretive goal that only father and son are aware of. When public military feats are required, youths may elect to serve a tour of duty with the **Holding's** fleet, where their rank entitles them to a command position.

Braxaná women of the tribal period could choose to undergo similar testing, although it was never required of them, and the triumphant return of a warrior female with the appropriate prisoners or tokens of conquest was cause for tribal celebration. As ownership of property by women was always a more complicated issue than with men (see **Token Dominance**) it was never linked directly to the testing, but women who had thus proven their mettle on the battlefield were assured the most desirable mates and tribal support for all their children.

Just Cause: Reasons which are accepted as justification for a woman refusing sexual access to a man. Most are derived from **Braxaná** tribal practices and focus upon the female reproductive cycle: menstruation, pregnancy, and both pre- and post-menarche life stages are considered Just Cause for refusal. Health issues are also considered—the list of conditions which qualify being specifically detailed—and any occupational responsibility which would be compromised by lost time may qualify.

One category of Just Cause which was not derived from tribal practice is that of Ownership. Braxin law states that any woman who has surrendered her sexual independence to one man owes nothing to others. This in fact contradicts the underlying tribal tradition, in which it was considered desirable for warriors to impregnate all the women in the tribe, thus strengthening the women's own **bi'ti** and the children they would bear for their mates in the future. It is postulated that the original intent of the "ownership clause" was to encourage the establishment of long-term partnerships between men and women. If so, the adoption of such laws at a time when gender relationships were in turmoil did not bring about the intended results. Most Braxin men and women lead isolated lives, and the partnerships which qualify as Ownership among the lower classes are generally temporary conveniences. Among the upper classes, whose extended households may easily claim Ownership of those who belong, the question is not quite so pressing, and women who come to serve a great House sometimes bargain for Ownership as part of their contract.

Kaim'era: Originally the title of Braxi's ruler, in later periods one member of the planet's ruling oligarchy. From the roots *kaimras* (leadership) and *tiera* (attributes focused upon an individual).

K'airth: Ritual vendetta of the **Braxaná.** The name comes from *ko* (private or personal) and *sairth* (war), and identifies a personal vendetta which has been allowed to dominate the lives of both parties.

The Braxaná revere the arts of warfare and regard the true k'airth as a military campaign in miniature. Just as troops must prepare themselves to face the enemy, the *k'airth-v'sa,* or "honored mate of the private war", must focus his entire being upon gaining the skills and knowledge necessary to defeat his opponent. The more one devotes oneself to the contest, the more worthy one will be of eventual triumph. Since it is assumed that one's opponent is undergoing the same process, the k'airth is as much about the perfection of two opposing warriors as it is about the question of who wins what.

K'airthi figured heavily in the folklore of the early Braxaná and in the literature of later generations. Although it has been centuries since a true k'airth has been declared, the image of a man driven to perfect himself by the all-consuming hunger to defeat an enemy is a popular one in Braxin entertainment. The sustained passion of the unconsummated k'airth has inspired many works of art, often with strongly sexual overtones; the poet Beltas wrote in 1,243 A.C. that "when the hunger for combat is conjoined with sexual desire, it becomes the ultimate expression of human passion."

Llornu: Home planet of the Institute for the Acceleration of Psychic Evolution. The name is sometimes used as shorthand for the Institute itself.

Lugast: Believed by many to be the original **Source World** for humankind, Lugast was the first of the human-controlled worlds to achieve interstellar flight. Situated in the heart of the Belratis Cluster, Lugast's proximity to other human-populated worlds enabled it to quickly establish what would be the first of the great interstellar nations, the Union of Planets. Lugast's expansion went unchallenged until the rise of Braxi. Though war was never officially declared between the two nations, a series of raids and border skirmishes initiated by the **Holding** forced the Union to halt its expansion in that region. The rise of Azea soon after forced Lugast to face the possibility of waging war on two fronts, one against an enemy who derided all diplomatic attempts to seek peace, and one against an energetic young empire whose homeworld was located within striking distance of Lugast's most secure inner space.

In 1,031 Y.E. Lugast signed a treaty with Azea which provided for joint military efforts along the nesser frontier. By 1,187 it was clear that such measures would not be enough to hold Braxin expansion at bay, and the two nations joined together under the banner of the **Star Empire** in order to consolidate their efforts.

Lugast remains a prominent political player in the Star Empire and frequently controls the House of Humans, if not in title, then in influence.

Pairbond: An artificial human instinct, pairbonding was introduced into the Azean gene pool in the third century after the **Founding.** Based upon the precedent of various species that mate for life, pairbonding was meant to assure stable and lasting heterosexual relationships between Azean adults. As it was not possible to guarantee that all such pairings would be perfectly compatible, much effort took place in the centuries following to fine-tune the Azean sexual instinct so that it supported rather than stressed the pairbond. While critics claim that the result was unnatural inhibition of the human sexual experience, Azeans contend that the unique stability of their pairings makes for an environment of trust which more than compensates for lack of outside stimulation.

Pale Ones: A common term for the **Braxaná,** which refers to the distinctive coloration of that tribe. Although other melanin-deficient **Scattered Races** are known, the black hair and eyes of the Braxaná make their complexion seem uniquely colorless by contrast, and the habit in post-Shlesor generations of adding white cosmetics to the skin makes the nomenclature reflective not only of tribal appearance but custom as well.

Peace Dagger: An instrument designed for quick amputation of human limbs, the Peace Dagger is carried by all Azean military officers, as well as other notables of the **Star Empire** who are at risk for assassination. The blade is a micro-edged forcefield which cauterizes as it slices, allowing for quick removal of any limb infected with the **Black Death.**

The name of the Peace Dagger comes from the protocols which have arisen surrounding its use. The weapon is never drawn for any purpose save that for which it was intended, and is never used as a "normal" blade. These restrictions allow military personnel to carry Peace Daggers into diplomatic meetings where "normal" weapons would be banned. Several attempted assassinations have thus been foiled, and though some non-human species are not pleased that their Azeans counterparts can remain armed when they cannot, they recognize that the need is a real one and thus far have not officially protested the custom.

Plague: See **Tsank'ar.**

Probe: Technically a sub-category of **Functional Telepathy,** Probe status is wrongfully believed by many to be a "higher" level of psychic functioning. In fact the Probe designation merely indicates the concurrence of Functional Telepathy with specific patterns of cognition that are present in the population as a whole, and does not reflect upon either the strength or reliability of telepathic powers.

Because Probes have advanced powers of abstract visualization they are capable of sending and receiving thoughts in their "pure" form, without need for a verbal or metaphorical framework. This ability makes them particularly well suited to analysis of deep-brain emanations, as well as communication with non-human species. It is rumored the Institute uses Probes for its conditioning programs, whereby controlling patterns are woven into the fabric of a psychic's mind, along with short- and long-term triggers. It is their reputation for such work which makes Probes particularly mistrusted by the public at large, and although telepaths and psychics are often hired by outside agencies for specific tasks, Probes are generally regarded as suspect and are unwelcome outside of the Institute's domain.

As with other top Institute ratings, Probe status is only granted to those whose performance meets strict criteria of reliability and control, and several lesser grades exist which encompass the same set of cognitive abilities.

Psychic: In Institute parlance, any sentient being who is capable of receiving the thoughts or emotions of another, or transmit his own to another subject, without need for material vehicle. Psychic ability ranges from simple empathy (most common) to the full panoply of powers mastered by the **Functional Telepath.**

While general sensitivity is not uncommon among humans, most find that the power can neither be predicted nor controlled. The Institute has devoted centuries to perfecting techniques which can bring psychic sensitivity under conscious control, and among their own ranks the title of "Psychic" is only granted to one who has attained measurable control over their power.

Most Psychics fall into four general categories. *Psychic-Empathetics* are responsive to strong emotions in others. *Psychic-Receptives* can receive and interpret more complex thought patterns. *Psychic-Conferatives* can transmit their own thoughts and/or emotions to others. *Psychic-Connectives* are capable of initiating a two-way exchange, though not with the accuracy and control required of a full **Communicant.**

It is rumored there are other categories that deal with more aggressive powers, but thus far the Institute has denied all such allegations.

Public Name: Among **Braxaná,** the name by which one is commonly known, chosen by the same-gender parent. It is customary for the awarding of a child's Public Name to be accompanied by sizable celebration and/or political memorial. (For possible origins of this custom, see **True Name.**)

Rings: A recording medium common among the **Braxaná,** sometimes worn as jewelry over or under gloves. When worn for adornment they are traditionally undecorated, and derive their aesthetic appeal as jewelry from the text which their owner knows to be inscribed upon them. When worn beneath gloves such rings are considered the ultimate in "secret" apparel, and slender rings with erotic poetry inscribed within are among the most intimate gifts that can pass between man and woman.

Scattered Races: Human populations believed to be derived from a single genetic source, spread throughout known space in a past incident known as the **Seeding.** Humankind is by far the most successful species of those that were Seeded, and is believed to have survived on 78% of the planets to which it was transported.

Scattered Species: Species which were transplanted to other worlds during the **Seeding,** and which survived the transition to establish themselves as competitors to native life forms. Of the five known Seeded species, humankind alone has developed interstellar technology. By contrast, the cetacean transplant species has developed complex null-technology civilizations on several dozen planets, and two land-based sub-species are known to exist. Other transplanted species have not distinguished themselves, save by the fact of their survival. Scientists postulate that they may have originally been chosen for promising intelligence, but that they were not adaptable enough to rise above transplantation trauma in time to dominate local competitors.

It is possible that more than five species were transplanted during the Seeding, but the remainder may never be identified. Populations which failed to establish themselves would have left behind little or no evidence of their arrival, and would quickly have been subsumed into the native archaeological record.

Schedule of Expansion: It is rumored that the infamous Braxin blueprint for galactic conquest had its roots in **Harkur's** own writings. If so, it did not appear in its final form until centuries later, when the **Holding** was firmly established as a major interstellar player and the Lugastine Union of Planets had already been absorbed by the young and aggressive **Star Empire.**

Based upon Sukar's **Schedule of Progress** (below), the Schedule of Expansion was an exhaustive study of known human space, which sought to predict the rise of new interstellar powers both within and without human-charted regions. The Schedule set forth a plan for military expansion which took into account the need to crush such powers in their infancy, as well as a blueprint for manipulating the tides of human progress to weaken and ultimately destroy Braxi's great rival, Azea.

Although Azea was aware of the existence of the Schedule it did not have access to the document itself until 2,234 Y.E., when a copy was leaked to Imperial authorities. Historians have described this as a "wake-up call" to the Empire, who had apparently not anticipated the full scope of Braxin ambition. Only later would non-human critics suggest that it was the Empire's response to the Schedule which guaranteed Azean sovereignty over other races within the Empire, and that perhaps the contents of the document, if not its very existence, should be questioned accordingly.

Schedule of Progress: In 117 A.C., Sukar of Braxi postulated that the rate of technological development of a planet's human population was directly linked to the adaptation trauma it suffered during transplantation. (see **Seeding**). His argument was that human populations which were seeded onto hostile or unstable worlds must waste valuable energies adapting themselves to their new environment, delaying the onset of technological development. Based upon this pattern, Sukar claimed that the **Source World** for humankind could best be recognized by its early entrance into the interstellar arena, as it alone would have been spared any adaptational delay.

While scientists acknowledge the obvious political bias of Sukar's work (in his time, the only known candidates for Source World status would have been **Lugast** and Braxi), further study has indeed confirmed his basic hypothesis, that a measurable relationship exists between the environmental conditions of a particular Seeding and the pace of technological development which followed it. Later theoreticians expanded upon Sukar's work, providing a schedule by which one might estimate the time it would take for a transplanted population to achieve the technology necessary for starflight, and a statistical means of predicting how many technologically advanced worlds would arise in a given time and place. The latter study provided the basis for the infamous Schedule of Conquest, which predicted that military operations would become more difficult over time, as target planets became more and more likely to have advanced armaments of their own.

Seclusion: The practice by which purebred **Braxaná** guarantee the paternity of their offspring, by isolating the woman from all other sources of human sperm until implantation is confirmed. Seclusion was a practice unknown to the early Braxaná, and became common only after the **Shlesor,** when issues of genetic inheritance and tribal fertility took center stage. Although modern technology is capable of confirming paternity, such practices are considered unacceptable by the Braxaná, who have shown a lasting unwillingness to subject any part of the reproductive process to scientific "interference."

Seeding: The common name for the a past interstellar event in which human stock and that of several other species were transported to a wide variety of planets, and allowed to establish themselves without subsequent aid or interference. It is estimated that the Seeding took place over the course of 50,000 years, though scientists acknowledge that this figure is an estimate derived from studies in local space, and that future exploration may expand the figure considerably. The exact purpose of the Seeding is not known, nor is there any clear evidence of what species was responsible for it.

Lugastine scientists first suggested the possibility of such an event as early as 178 U.P., when studies first showed that humans from various planets within the Union were similar enough in DNA structure to be able to produce fertile offspring. These results were contrasted with studies of other species, wherein it was shown that even when parallel evolution produced species that were indistinguishable in appearance and/or behavior, disparity in DNA was still marked enough to make them incapable of interbreeding.

Five species are known to have been transplanted in this manner, although scientists acknowledge that more may remain undiscovered.

Of those, only humankind is known to have mastered the technology necessary for starflight. (See **Schedule of Progress; Scattered Races; Scattered Species**). Many human scientists regard the preponderance of human transplantations as proof that the architects of the Seeding were themselves human-derived, and theorize that they wished to study the effects of diverse environments upon the evolution of their own species. If so, then the true Source World for humankind may yet be undiscovered, and the most ancient human civilizations in known space may be no more than the first stage in a vast experiment, whose end has yet to be realized. (See **Schedule of Progress**)

Shem'Ar: Literally "Servant of Ar", the word is used for any woman who invites **Ar's** attention by dominating the actions of men. Tradition states that when this happens Chaos will begin to erode the rational underpinnings of the universe.

The Shem'Ar is the ultimate taboo in Braxin society, rejected by common culture long before it was proscribed by law. The effect of this taboo is most evident in language, where the circumlocutions required for women to communicate without ever giving men so much as a casual order has resulted in what has been called "the female dialect". (This is notably a lower-class phenomenon, as the upper class Speech Modes offer the means to temper any statement with modifiers that indicate "I mean this only as a suggestion.") While the lower classes abhor the Shem'Ar in all her manifestations, among the upper classes it is not unknown for a perverse sexual attraction to exist. **Braxaná** claim that this is the vestigial remnant of their warrior tradition, which rewarded women for military domination of men of other tribes, but psychologists outside the **Holding** suggest that the real reason has more to do with the absolute power of the **Pale Ones,** and the perverse appeal of "forbidden" indulgences.

Shlesor: A program of selective breeding among the **Braxaná,** believed to have lasted several centuries. The Shlesor was but one facet of a greater effort on the part of the Braxaná to set themselves apart from other tribes, in accordance with the counsel of **Harkur the Great:**

> *If the Braxaná, or any other single tribe, were to try to rule Braxi for an extended length of time, they would have to set themselves apart from all other Braxins. They would have to create an image so alien to the rest of Braxin culture that no other group could as-*

pire to it, and do it to such an extreme that the image itself becomes synonymous with power. Then and only then, no man would dare to question their rule.

The exact details of the Shlesor are not known, save that the Braxaná disdained to utilize genetic technology in their efforts, preferring instead the more primitive practice of infanticide to cull undesirables out of their gene pool. By the third century A.C. a change in the appearance and demeanor of the tribe had already been noted, and the writings of Janos in the seventh century made clear reference to the unusual strength, endurance, and beauty which had become characteristic of the Braxaná in his time. Geneticists note that the tribe was uniquely well prepared for such an exercise. Their breeding customs already allowed for giving preference to the seed of successful warriors, and those who were limited in their progeny rights might still take pride in passing down their **bi'ti** to the next generation. The reliance upon primitive methods had its cost, however, and by the sixth century there were rumors that repeated inbreeding had weakened the tribe in ways that were not immediately apparent. By the ninth century it had been noted that the Braxaná population was falling in numbers, and it is believed that the Shlesor was officially abandoned by the turn of the millennium. Repeated efforts by geneticists to gain the cooperation of the Braxaná in analyzing such changes have resulted in a tribal hostility towards genetic science which remains strong to this day.

Social Codes: Customs derived from the tribal practices of the **Braxaná,** some of which have since entered the body of Braxin law. The Social Codes were originally a warrior ethic designed to bolster personal strength and obliterate weakness, both in the individual and in the tribe as a whole.

The Braxaná Social Codes are best known for relegating women to a subservient position in Braxin society, and for mandating their sexual availability in many situations. (See **Just Cause**). Curiously, this infamous custom was not originally gender-specific. Among the ancient Braxaná it was not uncommon for females to take up arms, and those who fought beside their men were equally entitled to *H'kanit Sar,* or the Fruits of War. Those returning from battle, male and female alike, were entitled to take from among the tribe whatever mates they chose, for the needs of the warrior were considered more important than any other social restriction or contract. This not only guaranteed the free flow of sexual energy—which the Braxaná believed was necessary for the health of the **bi'ti** —but gave the warriors an opportunity to spread their seed throughout the tribe, thus guaranteeing the strength and fierceness of the Braxaná people as a whole.

Many historians believe that when the Braxaná adapted this practice to greater Braxin society and made it the law of the land, it was meant as a "bribe" to the males of the **Holding,** in order to win their support. Others are quick to point out that the Braxaná relationship between male and female was unique, and that the law became oppressive only when removed from its proper cultural context. The Braxaná philosopher Durat wrote at length about the custom in 897 A.C., deriding the fact that a law which should have encouraged men and women to establish stable households together had instead become an excuse for isolationism.

Source World: A planet on which human life evolved independently, rather than having been placed there during the **Seeding.** While no Source World has been confirmed as such, several are considered candidates by virtue of their archaeological record and/or placement in the **Schedule of Progress.**

Speech Modes: See **Braxaná Dialect.**

Standard: Terminology associated with the planet **Zeymour.** Measures of time such as the Standard Year were adopted by the **Star Empire** in 837Y.E., in order to provide a calendrical system which would not favor any existing planet. Though non-human cultures within the Empire periodically protest the "human bias" of the system, the Standard system of time measurement functions throughout the Empire as a neutral foundation for inter-species communication.

Star Empire: Officially founded in 1,187 Y.E. (the date of the absorption of **Lugast's** Union of Planets), the **Star Empire** is both aggressive and exploratory, and today comprises the largest unified territory in known human space.

Although Azea has always had titular control of the Star Empire—the Emperor or Empress is required to be of that race—the actual governance of planets was once equally divided between the House of Humans and House of Non-Humans. The Lugastine faction was particularly strong in human politics in the early years, and there was some speculation that Lugast would come to dominate the Star Empire in fact, if not in name.

In 2,234 Y.E. the discovery of **Braxi's Schedule of Expansion** and ensuing military escalation moved the focus of the Empire to martial affairs, and Azea's genetic advantage in that forum gave them added advantage in political circles as well. By 2,479 it was clear that the **Holding** did not intend to break off hostilities until the Star Empire was completely destroyed, and a new arm of government was instituted to focus on this tenacious and determined enemy. In 2,581 **StarControl** was given mandate to function as a ruling body of the Empire, thus beginning the so-called "Azean period" of Imperial governance. Despite periodic protests by the non-human membership of the Holding that this move upset the balance of the Empire in humanity's favor, StarControl remains an equal partner in the Imperial government, and is accorded precedence in any situation or region where Braxi is an active threat.

The genetic strength and conditioned loyalty of the Azean people have long been recognized to give that race a natural advantage in military affairs, for which reason the so-called Border Fleet has traditionally been dominated by Azean personnel. In later years it became the custom to restrict service in the Great War with Braxi to those of Azean heritage, and in 3,571 the **Council of Justice** was established to rule upon issues of racial heritage and loyalty among that people. While technically an equal partner in the Imperial government, the Council limits its scope to matters concerning the Azean people in particular, and is grudgingly accepted as a nominal fifth Crown in what has become a human-dominated Empire. Detractors are quick to point out that should the war with Braxi terminate, the need for both StarControl and the Council of Justice would cease to be of Imperial concern, and the balance of government might return to the Empire's original design.

Star-: A prefix used in the **Star Empire** to indicate any species, organization or event which is associated with interstellar culture rather than a particular planetary base.

StarControl: Technically the branch of the Azean Imperial government responsible for all military affairs, StarControl has as its special mandate management of the Braxin-Azean conflict, in peacetime as well as during active hostilities. As a Crown of the Empire the Director of StarControl answers to no one save the Emperor himself, and in matters concerning the Great War is traditionally granted complete independence.

While membership in StarControl is not technically restricted to Azeans, in practice it is rare to find humans of another race in any position of authority within the organization. Azeans cite the unique stability of their race as justification for this, while detractors are quick to point out that the establishment of yet another Azean-dominated Crown has political ramifications beyond the range of military affairs. Non-humans as a rule do not serve in StarControl, believing the obsession with Braxi to be a purely human affair; non-human negotiators have been known to refer to the conflict as "not our war."

Subname: The second name taken by Azeans, inherited through patrilinear or matrilinear descent according to the child's gender. Originally the numbers of **Zeymourian** ships used during the **Exodus,** subnames were adopted soon after the **Founding** to memorialize the planetary migration. They are used today in combination with the chosen name as a form of polite address, the Azean equivalent of "Mr." or "Ms." The subname "lyu" is reserved for the firstborn descendants of the line of Hasha.

Taz'hein: The "traitor god" of the Braxin pantheon, Taz'hein was recognized by neighboring tribes under a variety of other names, usually as a lesser god or demon. His destruction of the Creator served as a convenient explanation for why more benevolent gods did not involve themselves in human affairs, and historians note that much of Taz'hein's "worship" was not meant to draw favorable notice from the treacherous deity, but rather to encourage him to keep his distance.

It is not known exactly when the **Braxaná** first claimed a line of descent separate from that of other Braxins, with Taz'hein as their creator, but the myth was aggressively promulgated by **Viton the Ruthless** as part of a greater political agenda to set the Braxaná apart from other tribes. Under Braxaná influence Taz'hein would eventually come to dominate the lesser pantheons of other tribes, with the Creator relegated to a well-meaning but ultimately failed role in human history.

Transculturalist: (Azea) A translator who specializes in being able to express the underlying philosophical concepts of one culture in the language of another. Such communication often entails concepts that have no direct translation, and is complicated by subtle connotations of language and custom that simple translation programs cannot provide.

The best transculturalists are those who are raised in dual cultures, and such people are in great demand throughout the Empire for both diplomatic and commercial negotiations. Rare specializations include cultures which do not usually interact, whose philosophies are based upon incompatible values, and—most rarely—human/non-human combinations. Psychics are acknowledged to have a natural advantage in transculturalism, though only in "live" forums where members of both subject cultures are present.

Token Dominance: Among the **Braxaná,** a man who serves as personal assistant to the mistress of a female-owned House, representing it in legal situations where she cannot. As Braxin law does not permit a woman to give direct orders to men, token male dominance is required in any situation where men must be commanded, or where gender-sensitive negotiations must take place.

True Name: The first given name of a **Braxaná,** kept secret throughout his life. The custom derives from the primitive belief that to speak a man's name is to have power over his soul, and therefore the only safety lies in using a false name among enemies. Though the Braxaná no longer believe in human shamans who might use a man's Name against them, they retain the custom as a tribal tradition and regard the True Name as an affirmation of Braxaná identity.

Some historians regard Braxaná naming customs as proof that the tribe once practiced a more active spirituality, citing the elaborate formal announcement of a child's "public name" as an attempt to convince demons, wraiths, and other supernatural entities that the false name is a true one. Human enemies would not require such a display, it is argued, because they were already aware of the custom and knew the public name for what it was. Such theories are not well regarded by contemporary Braxaná, and most of the scholarly work on the subject has been of necessity published outside of the **Holding.**

Because of the power inherent in the True Name it is rarely shared with anyone, and when it is it serves as a powerful bonding mechanism between two individuals. Suzath's epic *Tales of War,* scripted in the 6th century B.C., makes reference to an exchange of True Names taking place between warriors who had faced death together, or in circumstances where one had saved the other's life. In the civilized calm of modern Braxaná society such situations rarely arise, but the True

Name remains an active dynamic in male-female relationships, and the giving of Names between man and woman is regarded as an exchange of power with almost religious significance.

Tsank'ar: A virus native to Braxi, which has spread through the interstellar community to every known human planet. Though the effects of the tsank'ar are usually mild, the virus is subject to episodes of mutation which occasionally produce more virulent and damaging strains. Attempts to monitor the virus and provide preventative treatments have proven successful among the human population at large, and lesser mutations of the tsank'ar have been rated by Montesekua's Virology Center as a class IV, and are rarely lethal.

Major mutations of the tsank'ar are cause for greater concern, and Montesekua keeps close watch upon potentially threatening strains. These mutations appear approximately once a century and are known to be particularly damaging to the **Braxaná,** many of whom will isolate themselves during epidemics. The disruption of normal political processes during such a so-called Plague provides a rare opportunity for Azean military aggression, and it is said that virologists within the **Star Empire** watch the tsank'ar as closely as do their counterparts in the **Holding,** seeking to anticipate the next period of Braxin vulnerability

Viton the Ruthless: Braxaná servitor to **Harkur the Great,** and the first **Braxaná Kaim'era** of the B'Saloan **Holding.**

Little is known of Viton's early life save that he was raised in the Braxaná tribal reaches, isolated from greater Braxin culture and technology. In his youth he made several forays into "civilized" territory, and while numerous romanticized tales have been written of his adventures there, the only acts that can be ascribed to him with certainty are the theft of the Zaldovi tribal relics in 4 B.C. and the assassination of a Brentasi prince in 2 A.C. Viton came to the attention of Harkur's agents in 5 A.C. and was invited to the new international capital to meet him. His ruthless Braxaná spirit impressed the monarch and he served Harkur as companion and advisor through the duration of his reign. Their discussions of political and social philosophy were recorded by both parties, and have served as inspiration for warriors and politicians ever since. (See ***Dialogues***)

Viton claimed the throne after Harkur's death in 86 A.C. Harkur's belief that the planet would take issue with Braxaná rule proved prophetic, and at least fifteen separate assassination attempts were known to take place during Viton's lifetime. He remained Kaim'era for nearly five decades despite such opposition, during which time he established the Braxaná so solidly as the power behind the Braxin throne that no man could hope to dislodge them.

Void: Braxin term for "outer space," more specifically the space between star systems. The Void refers not to lack of matter or energy but lack of consciousness, and hearkens back to the belief of many tribes that the universe was originally a vast pool of awareness. Each god born during the Creation drew his life from that pool, until at last there was nothing left but unfeeling darkness.

Periodically cults arise in the **Holding** which purport to have located or even "spoken to" some surviving fragment of the original Awareness. Although the **Braxaná** are loathe to act against any such movement for fear of creating martyrs, it is known they keep a close eye upon such groups, and will act if necessary to keep such religious cults from gaining a foothold in Braxin society.

Whim Death: The right of a **Kaim'era** to kill any commoner at any time, without the need to provide a reason. The definition of "commoner" is somewhat hazy, and several unpleasant political incidents have been caused by the use of Whim Death to remove a rival's servants or lower-class contacts. Though there are no laws outlawing such a political application, it is generally accepted that this could incite whole bloodlines to a death-feud, for which reason most Kaim'eri restrict their killings to commoners who offend them personally.

Wilding: An aggressive mating custom of the early **Braxaná,** common in their isolationist period, in which a male or female of fertile age would leave the tribe's territory to seek a mate from among surrounding peoples. While exogamy was common among Braxin tribes in order to sustain the genetic health of small populations, the Braxaná practice of mate-abduction, and the fact that they recognized no legal or cultural restrictions upon whom they might claim, made them less than popular with their immediate neighbors.

The practice was supposedly abandoned in the third century B.C, when the developing technology of surrounding nations forced the Braxaná to become more circumspect, but some historians believe that the custom was simply practiced more discretely after that point, and Braxaná females were known to aggressively seek impregnation by outsiders as late as the reign of **Harkur the Great.** The **Shlesor** put an end to all such customs, and is credited with turning Braxaná mating practices from an inclusive to an exclusive focus.

Y.E.: Year of the Exodus. The current Azean calendrical system begins its year count with the **Founding** of Azea.

Zeymour: Formerly the third planet in the Azean star system, it is estimated Zeymour is the source for 87% of the material in the Daylish asteroid belt. While Azean tradition blames the planet's inhabitants for its destruction, scientists now believe that the passage of an alien body through the system was responsible for the planet's breakup, either by direct impact or by combination with local gravitic stressors.

Zeymour is regarded as a possible **Source World** for humankind, mostly due to Azea's advanced placement in the **Schedule of Progress.** Given the current state of Zeymour's archaeological record it is unlikely that sufficient evidence will be uncovered to either prove or disprove this theory.

Zeymophobia: A syndrome unique to starfaring cultures, zeymophobia encompasses several disorders associated with fear of being planetbound. First noted among interstellar scouts on extended missions, Type I zeymophobia most often manifests as a fear of being unable to leave a planet's surface at will; in the most extreme cases this will produce crippling anxiety at the failure of any transportation device or system. Type II zeymophobia entails fear of natural ecosystems, and by extension all environments which are not strictly controlled by human technology. Though the symptoms of both types can be treated, the underlying causes are not fully understood, and sufferers are encouraged to develop a lifestyle independent of planetary habitation.

It has been long noted that zeymophobia is a purely human phenomenon, and several non-human scientists have speculated that this is the natural result of the human species "spreading itself too thin" among the stars. Other theorists postulate that it is a vestigial memory of species trauma from the time of the **Seeding,** and that if the other **Scattered Species** were of sufficiently advanced sentience similar symptoms would be observed in their populations.

Zhaor: The traditional weapon of the **Braxaná,** worn by members of the first class as a sign of rank, used in dueling challenges between them. The Zhaor blade has a triangular cross-section for two thirds of its length, with the final third being sharpened along both edges. Many styles of guard and quillons exist, the most common being a variety of openwork fashionable in the time of **Viton the Ruthless.** Early Zhaori were quite opulent, and while later models were fashioned to suit the understated image of the Braxaná, surviving relics from earlier eras still surface at high dress occasions among the older bloodlines, strangely at odds with the stark, colorless clothing that is their backdrop.

The Edict of 1,916 forbade the carrying of any bladed weapon by Braxins of "lesser blood", making the wearing of Zhaor one of the most visible and recognizable signs of a Braxaná inheritance. Although Braxaná women of fertile age are forbidden to duel they are permitted to wear the Zhaor, as a reminder to all that in ancient times they served as warriors beside their men, and were revered for their fierceness as well as their fertility.

Zhene: The single moon of Braxi, orbiting its mother planet in seventeen-plus Braxin days, and keeping one face towards the planet at all times. Zhene was explored in the second century B.C. and a government base was established there soon after, to be used for scientific experimentation and galactic observation. With the refinement of gravitic science it became possible to colonize the satellite on a greater scale, and in 474 A.C. Zhene was claimed by the Braxaná as a haven for their Race. Zhene is now restricted to members of the first class and their households, and shines in the night sky of Braxi as a visible reminder of the separatist policies of the **Pale Ones.**

Zhent: The passage of Braxi's moon through all its phases, or seventeen-plus Braxin days.

Zherat: Derived from forcefield technology, the Kudomi field was discovered by the **Lugastines** to disrupt the life processes of carbon-based species. While the full destructive capacity of the field was something the Lugastine government would not employ in warfare, Kudomi-derived science promised benefit to human medicine, and so experimentation continued under strict government supervision for several centuries

The defection of a Lugastine agent to the **Holding** in 1,172 A.C. brought Kudomi technology into Braxin hands, where it has since been developed into the most feared weapon of mass destruction currently in existence. The so-called Zherat field is more rightly named the Zherat Process, as it entails a rapid succession of assaults designed to disrupt surface-to-space communications, incapacitate planetary defense systems, and finally destroy all life upon a chosen planet.

Despite its certain destructive power, the Zherat is rarely used. Some historians would argue that even Braxin ruthlessness is thus shown to have its limits, but most agree that the motivation is more practical. Braxi would rather make sure its secret weapon remains secret, than risk it in frequent public display. Certainly the threat of the Zherat has been a tool of Braxin dominance for millennia, both as a real threat of planetary destruction and as a greater symbol of the Holding's willingness to destroy anyone and anything that stands in its way.

While it is believed that Lugast still has records of Kudomi technology, and most assume that Azea has obtained them as well, the ethical foundation of those nations does not permit its use or dissemination of its technology, and so it remains a weapon associated with Braxi, and is used by many detractors as the ultimate example of the Holding's inhumanity.

Read on for a preview of

The Wilding,

C.S. Friedman's

exciting sequel to

In Conquest Born

Coming soon in hardcover from

DAW Books

The Citadel chamber was large and sterile, and they put him right in the middle of it. Like a bug pinned down for inspection. About him sat nearly a hundred men, all of them Braxaná. The ones nearest him wore the medallion of the Kaim'eri, while those seated behind them wore similar seals as clasps on shortcloaks, tunics, scabbards. It had meant real power once, that sign, when the Kaim'eri had ruled the Holding in a political free-for-all. Now things were different. Now the true power lay elsewhere.

Tathas pushed the filthy hair out of his face and faced them, trying to imbue his posture with a confidence he did not truly feel. It was hard to stand before these men and not be unnerved, for their mere physicality set them apart from everything that was normal and human. . . . On the whole they looked more like mannequins than men, and the fact that there was so little variation between them in facial structure or even expression added an especially eerie note to the illusion. That was the result of inbreeding, of course. Tathas had heard of it, but he had never before seen so many of the Pale Ones in one place together that he could observe it for himself.

No wonder they needed fresh genetic material. Their gene pool was clearly in its last gasps. No wonder they'd had to come up with some warped and complicated ritual to get that material . . . since the Master Race could hardly be expected to let the blood of commoners mix with its own, could it?

Gods, how he hated them! More in that instant than ever before. And it must have showed in his face, because one of them narrowed his gaze somewhat, and it seemed to Tathas that a spark of answering hatred gleamed in those black, inscrutable eyes. Strangely refreshing.

Then one man who wore the medallion of the Kaim'erate stood, and he used the voice mode of disdain as he said, "Tathas, son of

Zheret. You stand before this Council accused of high treason against the Holding. Of encouraging tribal factionalism. Of participating in proscribed tribal rituals. Of illegal possession of arms and use of those arms in proscribed activities. Of intent to destabilize the united Braxin government." For a moment he paused, and the dark eyes seemed to drill through Tathas. Cold eyes, cold hate; he could taste it. "Do you accept the charges or deny them?"

For a brief, mad instant he actually considered answering the question. After all, the worst of the charges—and the one most likely to lead to a death sentence—could hardly be proven. For a moment he even entertained the fantasy that evidence might matter here, and that justice might be brought to bear in this case.

Ah, that must have been his battered brain crying out for help, to think something like that. The Braxaná might be accused of many things, but "justice" had never been one of them.

With pride he drew himself up, muscles aching at the unaccustomed strain. He could see himself reflected in a hundred eyes, sweat-stained and battered, and knew with sudden certainty that they believed him beaten. Three zhents of neural torture would break anyone, wouldn't it?

Anyone but a Kesseret. Anyone but the Viak'im . . . prince of the Kesseret tribe.

The knowledge put strength in his voice, and for the first time since his awakening the words came out clearly and easily. "I invoke the Wilding."

For a moment there was only silence. His heart pounded inside his chest as he waited, deafeningly loud in the emptiness. Though their expressions were carefully controlled, it seemed to him that shadows of emotions flickered across them. Surprise, of course. Dismay? Anger? It seemed to him one or two were mildly amused, but it was hard to be sure of that. And Braxaná amusement wasn't necessarily a good thing.

At last one of the Kaim'eri said, "That law is for the *Braxaná.*"

"The law doesn't specify a tribe."

Whispers flitted about the room. He kept his gaze focused on the first man, but from the corners of his eyes he could see the Pale Ones stirring. His words had not pleased them.

They can kill you if they want. Any one of them, on a whim, That's one power they didn't give up when the Pri'tiera took over.

"A minor omission," said a man in the last row. Tathas wasn't sure of the voice mode he used—that damned Braxaná dialect was so complicated it was hard to make out sometimes—but he was pretty sure it was part of the condemnation complex. Not a good sign.

"A *legal* omission," he challenged.

He saw heads leaning towards one another, heard echoes of whispered conferences. There was a strange intensity in the room now, and not all of it was focused on him. Braxaná politics. A council chamber full of men with agendas of their own, public ones and secret ones, each one assessing how this moment played into his own private plans. He felt a sudden fury at these men who could play with human lives in such a trivial way, not even pretending that *justice* or *legality* had any meaning to them. What on Braxi were they doing running the Holding? It was time another tribe took over.

Don't think that. Not here, not now. Too dangerous.

At last one man, an older man with streaks of silver in his beard, offered, "It is an interesting concept."

"It is an offense to our Race," another retorted.

"Did our ancestors use strangers to find mates for them?"

"They would have if it got them results," one said curtly.

"It's a dangerous precedent."

"Yes, shall we have all the common folk crying 'wilding' to shrug off their debts?"

"Enough of our own blood are doing it now," one of the older Kaim'eri muttered.

It seemed to him there was amusement at that. Grim and cold amusement, that barely cracked the porcelain masks. Whatever passed for emotion in this crowd, it was a different beast than he was used to.

The man who stood before him seemed about to speak again, and from his expression Tathas guessed it was not going to be good—but a sudden hush fell over the chamber, and one by one all of the Kaim'eri and their guests turned toward the chamber's single entrance. Tathas followed suit. Even before he saw the man who stood there, even before the details of his black and gray formal costume sank in, he could *feel* his presence in the room. A tingling along his neck. A cold, clammy crawling sensation up his spine. As if something had entered besides a man, and that *something* had its hands all over him.

"Pri'tiera." The Kaim'era before Tathas bowed to the newcomer. The others stood, that they might do the same.

He was young, if such a creature might ever be said to be truly young. His face was a perfect mask of powder and paint, and when he was still he looked more like a statue than a human being. Yet there was about him such an aura of power, such an absolute presence, that as he came towards Tathas, his long gray robes sweeping the floor behind him, the proud Viak'im had to fight the sudden desire to go down on one knee and offer him obeisance.

He had heard legends of such power, of course. The Pri'tiera's line was rumored to be many things, most of them related to tribal demons or vindictive spirits. He had always imagined that a strong enough man might cling to pride even in such a presence. But it was impossible. The essence of the man enveloped him, invaded him, and seeped into his very brain. He had to lock his legs in place to keep them from folding. It was as if a vast hand was pressing him downwards, exerting pressure upon each and every cell in his body, and he bit his lip so hard in his struggle to resist its power that blood began to trickle down his chin.

"Strong," the Pri'tiera murmured. He was young, so young! Barely past the start of manhood, and yet he wore the Pri'tiera's robes. How could such a youth gain power among the Braxaná, much less wield it effectively? The concept of a hereditary title was so alien to Tathas that even this close to the man, enveloped by his presence, he could not quite fathom it.

Then the Pri'tiera touched him—one gloved finger to the side of his face—and his legs folded utterly. It was as if his body answered to the youth rather than its owner. The sensation was terrifying, and it did not abate until he knelt, head bowed, before him. His hands balled into fists by his side, Tathas trembled with rage . . . and with fear as well.

For an eternity, it seemed, the Pri'tiera gazed down at him in silence. Tathas concentrated on the taste of blood in his mouth, refusing to acknowledge the submission that had been forced upon him. Again a cold and alien presence seemed to pick at the edges of his brain. He felt like vomiting.

"Let him go."

He looked up. The dark eyes met his own. The strange grip on his soul eased up a bit, but he stayed on his knees, knowing now that if he tried to rise up, if he defied him in any way, it would only grab hold more tightly the next time.

"The Wilding," the Pri'tiera said. "Let him go." He looked up at the Kaim'eri, scanning the chamber slowly, meeting the eyes of each in turn. "It is my will."

With a sweeping movement he turned his back on Tathas, and the strange force which had driven the Viak'im to his knees was gone. The suddenness of it made him head reel, and as he tried to rise up to his feet again it took all his strength not to stumble.

The Kaim'eri waited until their leader was gone, then turned their attention back to Tathas. His vision was blurred and it was hard to see their faces, but he was willing to guess they weren't pleased.

Braxaná never do anything without a reason. Without a hundred reasons, sometimes conflicting. What does he want of me?

"Get him clothes." It was the first Kaim'era who had spoken to him, who seemed to hold some rank among them. "And a ticket out of here. The nearest border. And see that he gets a copy of the Law as well, so that he knows exactly what he has taken upon himself. And how foolish it is for any *commoner* to choose such a path."

Slowly the Kaim'era walked to where Tathas stood. But though his presence might have driven a lesser man to his knees, it lacked the preternatural power of the Pri'tiera's own, and Tathas stood his ground.

"Your life here is ended," the older man pronounced. "Come back when you think you have the price to reclaim it."

It was clear from his tone what he thought of that possibility.

Then guards came forward once again and took Tathas roughly by the arms. He heard the Kaim'era declaring the session closed as they dragged him forth from the chamber. He heard Braxaná voices murmur comments upon the proceedings, too low for him to make out words. He heard the heavy door shut behind him, marking the end of one whole portion of his life. And the beginning of Ar knew what.

I'll be back, he swore.